THE ̵̵̵̵̵

SUSAN CURRAN ̵̵̵̵
read English at ̵̵̵̵
worked in ins̵̵̵
beginning her w̵̵̵̵̵
the author/co-author of sixteen books on
computers and new technology, including *The
Penguin Computing Book*. Her first novel was
The Mouse God, the story of the Siege of
Trojan Ilios. She now lives in Norfolk and has
two sons.

SUSAN CURRAN

THE HERON'S CATCH

FONTANA/Collins

First published by William Collins Sons & Co. Ltd 1989
First published in Fontana Paperbacks 1989

Copyright © 1989 Susan Curran

Printed and bound in Great Britain by
William Collins Sons & Co. Ltd, Glasgow

For my mother and father

Payes selonc vostre desserte
Puissés vous estre, faulz trompeurs!
Au derrenier dez cabuseurs
Sera la malice deserte.

D'entre deus meurez une verte
Vous fault servir, pour voz labeurs.
Payes selonc vostre desserte
Puissés vous estre, faulz trompeurs!

Vostre besogne est trop ouverte,
Ce n'est pas jeu d'entrejetteurs;
Aux esches s'estes bons joueurs,
Gardes l'eschec a déscouverte:
Payes selonc vostre desserte.

CHARLES DUKE OF ORLEANS
(1394–1465)

[May you be paid according to your deserts,
False deceivers!
In the end, the wickedness of the deceivers
Will be destroyed.

Between two blackberries, you must
Content yourself with a green one, for your efforts.
May you be paid according to your deserts,
False deceivers!

Your effort is too transparent
This is no game for dice-throwers;
At chess, if you are a good player,
Beware of the discovered check:*
Pay according to your deserts.]

---

*discovered check: this situation occurs when one piece is moved,
putting the king in check, deliberately or by chance, by another piece.

Major Characters in the Story

All of these characters have historical counterparts, though in some cases only the bare fact of their existence is known to posterity.

The English

Henry of Lancaster: King Henry VI of England, also crowned as King Henry II of France
Humphrey, Duke of Gloucester, the King's uncle and Protector in England
Eleanor, née Cobham, Humphrey's second Duchess
Henry Beaufort, Cardinal and Bishop of Winchester, great-uncle to the King

John Mowbray, 2nd Duke of Norfolk
Katharine (Kitty) Mowbray, née Neville; Duchess of Norfolk

William de la Pole, Earl of Suffolk
Alice Montagu, née Chaucer, Countess of Salisbury; later Countess of Suffolk
Thomas Chaucer, Alice's father: Oxfordshire landowner, merchant and politician

William Paston, a Norfolk landowner and lawyer; subsequently a Judge in the Court of Common Pleas
Agnes Paston, his wife
John Paston, their eldest son
Edmund Paston, their second son
Elizabeth Paston, their daughter

William (Will) Calthorp, a Norfolk esquire; servant variously of the Duke of Norfolk and the Earl of Suffolk

Elizabeth (Bess) Calthorp, née Grey, his wife

Miles Stapleton, a Norfolk esquire, and subsequently soldier fighting in France

William Yelverton, a Norfolk landowner and lawyer

John Heydon, a Norfolk landowner and lawyer; sometime servant of the Earl of Suffolk

Sir Thomas Tuddenham, a Norfolk landowner; sometime servant of the Earl of Suffolk

Thomas Wetherby, merchant and Alderman of Norwich

Sir John Fastolf, a Norfolk knight fighting mainly in France

John Welles, Norfolk-born Alderman of London, grocer and merchant, Fastolf's agent

Peter Basset, soldier fighting under Fastolf in France

Christopher Hanson, soldier fighting under Fastolf in France

Matthew Gough (subsequently Sir Matthew Gough), soldier fighting in France

The Burgundians

Hugues de Lannoy, Seigneur de Santes, servant and ambassador to the Duke of Burgundy

Jean Lefèvre, Seigneur de Saint Rémy, King of Arms to the Duke of Burgundy; subsequently Toison d'Or (Golden Fleece) King of Arms; chronicler of Burgun-dian history

Jean de Waurin, soldier fighting for the Duke of Burgundy, at one stage seconded to serve under Fastolf; chronicler of English history

The Bretons

Arthur, Count of Richemont, younger brother to the
  Duke of Brittany, soldier fighting in France; sometime
  Constable of France to the Dauphin Charles VII
Laurence de Fougères (Secret), Sir John Fastolf's
  poursuivant

The House of Orleans

Charles, Duke of Orleans, captive in England
Jean, Bastard of Orleans, half-brother to the Duke

1

FRANCE

Summer, 1424

Laurence de Fougères was sitting under an oak tree.

The tree was at the edge of the forest of Piseux. A few paces away the road from Damville began its dip into the plain surrounding the town of Verneuil. Laurence could see the road, yellowish and dusty, snaking its way towards the town walls. He could see the walls – it was a clear day – and the high redbrick tower that men called, for some inexplicable reason, the Tour Gris. Here and there he could make out the crops planted in irregular plots on the plain, wheat and cabbages and onions, and the stakes where cows and goats could be tethered to graze on the rough grass.

There were no cows or goats grazing that day. Instead, between Laurence's tree and the walls of Verneuil there were two armies.

The armies were set across the road in formation. There were row upon row of men at arms, dismounted, bolted into their plate armour, with their swords and axes at their sides; rank after rank of archers, in thick leather tunics with here and there a glint of silver, with bows and quivers full of sharpened arrows and long, heavy stakes with pointed, iron-tipped ends; division on division of cavalry, mounted for action, armed with swords and lances. They were all ready, all poised for the battle to begin.

They had been there for a long time, as had Laurence himself. He did not know how much longer they would wait; he did not know what they were waiting for. He knew the formal rules of jousts and tournaments, but this bizarre rule of warfare, this waiting, he had never heard tell of before.

This is a dead time, he thought, and gave a silent laugh, because it was so ironic a name. For many of the men down on the plain, this would be the last of their living time. And to spend it in such a way: standing in rows, sweltering in their armour!

He thought: I shall not die. Not today. He weighed that thought in his mind, and realised that he was glad. It was a realisation that surprised him, because it was not so many days since he would have welcomed death. But the time for that was past; and the time for fighting too, as far as he was concerned. He had lost the murderous rage that would have sent him out into battle with any stick or knife he could lay his hands on, just so long as he might have a chance to kill the Duke of Alençon. His desire for revenge was strong still, but he knew now that he would be able to contain that desire until he could find an opportunity to take his vengeance without signing his own death warrant at the same time.

Perhaps there would be no such opportunity; perhaps he was mistaken in his certainty, and he would die that afternoon even though he did not intend to fight. This was a place of danger, and he had no horse with which to escape. He had never witnessed a battle before. He did not know if his legs would work if the time came for him to run. He did not know if his hand would hold his dagger straight and firm if the time came for him to thrust with it. He wore no armour; he had not even the protection of a herald's tabard. Any man might kill him, for the hunk of dry bread in the leather purse fixed to his belt; for his dagger, short but well honed; even for no reason at all, save that this was a time and a place for killing.

It was best not to think of that: best to think of this not as a time for ends, but as one for beginnings. Laurence de Fougères might die that day, but if all went well a different man would leave the scene of the battle alive: a poursuivant whom men called by a name that the Duke of Alençon would not recognise, nor any other man at Fougères either.

If all went well, the Duke of Alençon himself might die, even though Laurence de Fougères was in no position to attack him. Think of that, Laurence told himself. Think of Alençon's shining armour crusted with blood and dust; of Alençon's pretty face locked in a grimace of agony; of Alençon's corpse, a useless hull discarded on the bloody ground.

He thought of all this, and fixed his eyes on Alençon's standard, that his thoughts might focus more intently. It was easy for him to make out Alençon's standard: in the time of waiting he had told over many times in his head the position of each captain in the two armies. He could read the scene like the first page of an open book, not by word but by banner and pennon. Closer to him, the Duke of Bedford and the Earl of Salisbury and the Earl of Suffolk; further away, Alençon and the Count of Aumale. The Scottish nobles, Stewarts and Douglases and Murrays – he had asked Suffolk Herald to tell him their names, but still they mingled in his head – and the Lombards under Visconti.

So familiar, Alençon's standard. But his hatred somehow would not centre on it as he intended: nothing stirred in his soul at the sight of the little square of cloth. He scanned the iron-plated figures beneath the standard, but he was too far distant to be able to tell which of them was the Duke.

His attention strayed. To Bedford's standard: a royal standard, emblazoned with the lilies and leopards of the Dual Monarchy claimed by the Lancastrian child King, whose Regent in France Bedford was. He thought of Bedford. Bedford was Anjou's master, and a fine man, for all that his King of Arms was an arrogant bastard. The Regent was tall and well built, though his face fell away strangely from his jutting nose. He was a quiet man, and a devout one. The Lancastrian army had

15

paused in its march at Evreux, so that Bedford might spend the feast of the Assumption in prayer at the Cathedral. Perhaps Bedford was praying then, Laurence thought. Perhaps Alençon was praying too, and the rest of them. Perhaps he should be praying himself. He did not feel like praying.

Anjou had scarcely been praying, he thought, when he had boasted loudly that the Lancastrian army could beat one ten times its size. Anjou had believed it, too: Laurence knew that because he had watched the King of Arms' face in the moment when they had emerged from the shade of the forest and seen the Valois troops for the first time. There had been no terror in it, no despairing panic. 'Fifteen, sixteen thousand, I'd reckon', Anjou had said in his cool professional voice. Against eight thousand of Bedford's men? A mere exercise, its outcome beyond question for the victors of Agincourt.

Anjou had been at Agincourt. Laurence had not. The Lancastrians told such stories of that battle: he could not make himself believe half of them. But still, he thought, it was no bad thing that he himself should be dependent on this battle turning into a Lancastrian victory. He would have had more to fear if things had gone otherwise with him: if he had been Alençon's man still, and down there on the plain in the midst of the Valois army.

This was no bad place from which to witness a battle. The proof of that was plain: Anjou had chosen it for himself. The King of Arms was barely a dozen paces away from his own oak tree. Anjou had not chosen this place for Laurence, admittedly. He had told Laurence to stay within the baggage enclosure, with the priests, the surgeons, the keepers of the tents and pavilions, Bedford's guides, valets and clerks, the cooks and bakers, carpenters, fletchers and bowyers; with the horses tethered in pairs, the collar piece of one tied to the tail of the next; with the pages and valets who sat on the horses. Laurence had eyed the horses, but decided that his chances of appropriating one in an emergency were nil; he had eyed the tightly aligned baggage wagons, and decided that the enclosure would feel like a trap. It was not that he believed Anjou had meant to trap him: he reckoned the King of Arms to be quite indifferent to his fate. But the edge of the forest was more open, and he liked the idea that from there he might be able to run.

He liked the idea, too, of staying close to Anjou and the other officers of arms. Anjou glanced his way sometimes: with a look of sleek contempt, admittedly, but he glanced nevertheless. As long as Laurence was within sight Anjou would not forget him. When, later, there was work to be done, Anjou would cast around for somebody to do it; and he would see Laurence, and perhaps choose him.

Maybe he should move closer to Anjou, he thought to himself. Maybe he should join the loose circle of men arrayed under the clump of beeches just to his left. True, he was not yet a poursuivant himself, but nor were all those men officers of arms. There were various pages among them, a couple of esquires, and three or four men at arms. Most likely, these had been sent by their commanders to Anjou with messages; and they lingered after they had been delivered, to exchange news perhaps; to ease the tension of this dead time; even to delay the moment when they would have to return to the plain and join battle like the rest.

Anjou would not object, Laurence thought, if he came closer. The King of Arms might raise his brows, but he would say nothing. Indeed he was quite possibly adding to Anjou's dislike of him by staying this short distance apart. Oh yes, Anjou disliked him: he had no illusions about that. Each small service, over the previous few weeks, had been accepted grudgingly; each look had told him that Anjou was appraising him, and coming to an unfavourable conclusion.

Laurence thought this quite objectively: it caused him neither distress nor concern. He understood what Anjou disliked in him. He had all the scruffiness of a runaway with no change of clothes – and he had never, even when he was in Alençon's service, cared two sous about his own appearance. He had a manner that Alençon's steward had once (long before the incidents that had led to his dismissal) described as impertinent. He had not been impertinent to Anjou, Laurence reckoned, but he had come across perhaps as overly self-contained, and insufficiently respectful. Many people found cause for displeasure, too, in his face, which was mobile, almost clown-like: an impression accentuated by the lank mane of yellow hair that was hacked in a straight line across his forehead, just above his brows.

Anjou would never be his friend; but then, Laurence had no wish to make a friend of the King of Arms. He wished merely to be recommended by him to a post. Anjou might dislike his appearance and manner, he thought, but he had nevertheless weighed his qualifications and found them adequate. If he had not, he would not have accepted the small services even grudgingly, because now he was in Laurence's debt, and he knew it. Anjou was the epitome of honour: this little debt would weigh awkwardly upon him until he discharged it.

Still, Laurence did not move closer.

He waited for many more minutes. It was hot, even in the shade of the oak tree. He was thirsty and hungry. He unfastened his purse, took out the hunk of bread and chewed on it. It was poor food, but he savoured it. When it was gone, he would have no more food; no money either. What should he do, he wondered, if he survived the battle and its aftermath and Anjou did not find him a master? Perhaps he would manage to steal a cabbage from the plain after nightfall. Even raw, it would fill his belly. He uncorked his flask and took a draught of the water he had filled it with at Damville. It was warm and tasted brackish.

He had a vague expectation that these actions would cause the battle to begin. They did not. He sat in silence for more minutes. He glanced over to the heralds again.

Are they nervous underneath? he asked himself. Do they think to themselves that soon they may confront frantic armed men who will care nothing for the sanctity of their tabards? Do they finger their daggers when they sense that nobody is watching them? Or is it real, their insouciance? Huntingdon Herald, asleep from the look of him; Dorset Herald and Bellêsme Poursuivant, playing at dice; is this truly no more to them than a lazy, sun-drenched afternoon?

At least Anjou was not relaxed. He was arguing. At times his voice rose loud enough for Laurence to hear the words. 'The Burgundians', he heard, and 'Nelle'. He thought: I know that tale. Every man knew that tale, for it had been the talk of the army over the previous two days that Bedford should have sent his division of Burgundians back to Picardy to resume the siege of Nelle, instead of keeping them to take part in the battle that every man had known was imminent. He had done this, knowing for certain that his army would be outnumbered by the Valois.

Now his King of Arms argued about that remarkable decision: and with other Burgundians at that. At Anjou's side was Saint Rémy, the Duke of Burgundy's King of Arms: Laurence knew his face, and his colours too. Standing above them, armed, in a pose that suggested that but for his armour he too would have been lounging on the short grass, was another familiar figure: Jean de Waurin, a man at arms whom Laurence had often seen in Saint Rémy's company, but who fought with the Earl of Salisbury. Suffolk Herald was with them, and as Laurence watched and listened, Salisbury's second poursuivant Eagle Vert came across to join in, along with one or two of the others.

Laurence watched and listened for a moment more, then he wrapped his legs under him, and in a tight, contained movement he rose to his feet. He stalked a step closer, then another; then to the edge of the group. He crouched on his haunches. He saw no need to make a secret of his interest, but neither did he wish to make any move that would draw Anjou's attention to him.

'Bedford cannot hold any of France without Burgundy's help,' Suffolk Herald was saying. He was a slight man, with thinning, brown hair, a lean face and a countryman's manner. 'And he knows it.'

'Perhaps he knows too,' Saint Rémy suggested, 'that Burgundy cannot hold any of France without Bedford's help.'

Anjou snorted like a high-bred stallion. 'If you wish to play Devil's Advocate, Saint Rémy, you must do it more subtly. Not a man here will believe you truly think that. You say it only because it has a nice symmetry.'

'Not only for that.' Saint Rémy gave a slow smile. 'I do not think Bedford a stupid man.'

'Neither do I,' Suffolk retorted, 'but I am damned if I know why he is choosing to risk the alliance now.'

'Perhaps he thinks the Duke of Burgundy too cocksure,' Eagle Vert offered. 'He wishes to point out that the Burgundians can sometimes be dispensed with.'

'Perhaps he wishes to appease my Lord of Salisbury,' suggested Anjou.

Laurence thought: that is an old story. It had been told even in Fougères, the tale of how the Duke of Burgundy had made advances to the pretty new Countess of Salisbury in Paris. He had heard in the tavern by the Porte de Chêne that Lady Salisbury had slapped Burgundy in the face in front of a crowd of onlookers. Later, much later, he had heard another version of the same story from Eagle Vert. In the poursuivant's version there had been no slap, but Lady Salisbury had made a witty retort that had brought spots of red to Burgundy's cheeks. The sense was the same, though: that although the incident had been silly and trivial, Philip of Burgundy had been made to appear ridiculous, and neither he nor Salisbury had forgotten it since.

'His Lordship was not offended. He merely learned that his Lady is well capable of looking after herself.'

'That she is not, Suffolk,' said de Waurin. 'Lady Alice over-reacted. She may have enjoyed the notoriety it brought her, but she was undiplomatic. Salisbury surely saw it so, and Bedford, no doubt, when the tale reached him.'

'I blame you, Eagle Vert,' Anjou said, glancing at the poursuivant. 'Had you warned the lady about Burgundy's army of bastards, she might have taken his proposition more lightly.'

Eagle Vert shrugged. 'But that is the province of the Burgundy heralds.'

'Not so, sir,' Saint Rémy retorted cheerfully. 'I warned Lady Alice of the jokes and traps she would encounter at Hesdin. To tell her more, it would not have been diplomatic.'

Anjou raised his brows. 'To tell her so much was hardly diplomatic. I do believe you have a tendre for her.'

Saint Rémy grinned. 'She is no fool, Lady Alice. She will submit to the trick fountain to satisfy the Duke; but she will do it wearing her oldest gown.'

'She plans to build a trick fountain herself in Paris,' Eagle Vert said.

'To trap the Duke?'

'Why, nothing so obvious. To trap Lady Anne.'

'Now that,' Anjou said, 'might well prove to be a master stroke.'

'Even Lady Anne will laugh. She has a good temper, that one.'

'She alone, I do believe, could hold the alliance together.'

'Indeed, she already does.'

'Perhaps not, Suffolk,' de Waurin said. 'Bedford overrates his Duchess's influence with the Duke of Burgundy. She may be his favourite sister, but she is not his only sister.'

'Ah, the secret of Burgundy's power. They say he hopes to have a sister married to every prince in France.'

'For now, Bedford and Richemont are sufficient. That is one alliance to tie the English to his side, and one to tie the Bretons. More would be tedious. Burgundy enjoys his enmities.'

'Even the lady enemies?'

'There too he is fortunate. Gloucester is no general, for all he is brother to Bedford and old King Henry.'

Lady enemies? Gloucester? What did all this mean? Laurence had no idea. He had heard of Gloucester, the King's uncle, but he did not know any tales of ladies associated with him.

More to learn, he thought: always more to learn. He had been used to thinking of himself as quick-witted and observant, well informed about politics and the war, but it had taken him only a few days in the company of Anjou to realise that compared to the best officers of arms he had been lamentably blind and ignorant. He was working on making it instinct to absorb every piece of information that came his way, but still it seemed to him that he was muffled, blundering in a fog.

Should he ask someone? he wondered. No; no, he would not. To ask was to proclaim that one did not know, and that demeaned any man. Nor was this matter obscure: that was clear from the way in which de Waurin had spoken. It was perhaps necessary for him to learn about it, but if he asked a direct question – even of someone whom he trusted a little, such as Suffolk Herald – then it might get back to Anjou, he thought to himself. That would give Anjou new occasion for contempt, and at the very worst of times.

'Ah, but Gloucester is –'

He was never to know what Saint Rémy thought of Gloucester, for the rest of the sentence was drowned in a trumpet call. The officers of arms abruptly fell silent, and the lone notes echoed, one by one, in the hot air. Then a second trumpeter joined in, and a third, until the air was filled with a cacophony of chivalrous calls to arms.

22

Laurence turned; they all turned, towards the source of the calls. It had been Bedford's trumpeter who had sounded first, Laurence saw almost immediately: Bedford's choice, presumably, to bring the dead hour to a close. Excitement seemed to radiate out from the little circle of men under the royal standard. In their midst was a tiny clear space; and in that, the armoured figure of Bedford himself, just rising from the ground. The Regent lifted his huge battle axe high above his head. There were cries, presumably, but these did not carry to the forest. In a rippling motion the Lancastrian troops fell to their knees to kiss the dry, iron-hard soil, and then stood to present arms.

'Avaunt, banners!' He was not sure if he heard the cry, or if it merely echoed inside his head. The motion was clear, at least, as the standard bearers moved a pace forwards. Then the greater cry came, startlingly loud. 'Saint George and Bedford!' And overlaying it in faint harmony, the Valois cries, 'Mountjoie!' and 'Saint Denis!' The opposing army lowered their lances and both lines began to march slowly forwards.

'You know Bedford's tactics?'

Laurence started, and swung round to see who had spoken. He was on his feet, he realised, though he had no recollection of having stood up. And there, at his shoulder, was the soldier de Waurin.

Nobody had spoken to him all day; he had spoken to no one himself. It was alarming to be addressed now. He knew that Anjou had noticed him, but it had not occurred to him that anybody else might have taken, or might ever wish to take, even a casual interest in him.

He did not think to reply: he simply stared at the Burgundian. He had seen de Waurin many times, in the company of Saint Rémy and Anjou, but they had never spoken before. The Burgundian looked back at him. He did not speak at random, Laurence thought: he chose to address me. Nor did he give me an order. I might almost take it for a gesture of friendship. But this man is

23

encased in armour, and I am exposed. We are no equals, not on this hill overlooking a battlefield.

His silence did not appear to disconcert de Waurin, who went on, 'He will advance the archers first. To longbow range, or a little less. Then the back ranks will hand forward their stakes, see, for the front rank to hammer into the ground. Those are the tactics of Agincourt: even now the Valois have no real answer to them. So simple, so easy, but it deadens the impact of even the best cavalry.'

And the Lombards are just that, thought Laurence. It was a rational thought, almost cool: it reassured him. He turned his back on the Burgundian, and looked towards the archers. In fact he had already known about the stakes: they had roused his curiosity long before, and he had asked a page why the archers all carried such heavy iron-tipped poles. He did not say this to de Waurin. Instead, he said, as if he were thinking out loud, 'Hard, the ground today.'

He sensed the other man moving a pace forwards, to his side; he felt a curious glance. Did my words surprise him, he wondered, or my accent?

'True,' the Burgundian agreed. 'And Aumale cannot have been taken by surprise: he has had hours to weigh the situation. So he will order an immediate charge.'

Bedford too has had hours to appraise the situation, Laurence thought; and Jean de Waurin. And I, too; but I did not think of it in this manner before.

'Bedford can scarcely welcome that prospect.'

'No; but if he advances his main force rapidly, and sets cavalry to cover their flank, they will perhaps be able to withstand it.'

Perhaps. Only perhaps. Eight thousand men, against fifteen thousand. Anjou had been so confident, Laurence thought; and he himself had barely let the idea of a Lancastrian defeat flit through his mind. But there was nothing certain, he now sensed, about the way in which events would unfold before them. He could think of no reply, and the other man let him watch in silence.

It was a shallow hill: their view of the battle was far from perfect. But by concentrating, Laurence could make it out: he could see, slowly, inexorably, both armies moving exactly as they had anticipated. The Lancastrian stockade began to take shape; but before it was steady the French cavalry swept round the flank of the main Valois army. An attack. The action seemed to speed alarmingly, as Laurence's attention shifted from the slow trudge of the foot soldiers to the flashing urgency of the horsemen.

He saw immediately that the archers had no hope of withstanding the charge. Their line seemed to bend and then crumble; and then it was gone, and men were fleeing across the cabbage patches.

This was only a fraction of the action, though; for in the centre, Bedford's men at arms were pushing steadily forward against Aumale's opposing forces. On the Valois right flank the Scots moved forward more rapidly than the French, and more raggedly, until they were within clashing distance of Salisbury's men. The sounds of the battle were loud now, even from the edge of the forest. The air seemed hot and heavy. Laurence felt as if the cloud of dust had reached him: it seemed to clog his breathing and block his senses.

'Your first battle?' de Waurin asked.

He managed a nod.

'It will be a good one to watch. The site is open; the light is good. A tactical battle, this one. It will never be set down as a great battle, naturally, since no king is fighting; but it will enhance the English fortunes. And whatever Suffolk Herald pretends, Burgundy will not desert the English while they are winning.'

While they are winning. How was any man to tell, from the confusion of bodies on the plain below, which side was winning? The banners and pennons dipped and wavered; the men shifted and clumped, as thick on the ground as ants devouring a carcase. It was bizarre, obscene; it made no sense, any of it.

They watched, in silence, for what seemed like a long

time. Occasionally Laurence glanced at the other man. Everything else around him was full of terror, but he felt an odd sense of safety in the presence of the Burgundian. He was tall, de Waurin: a good head taller than Laurence, straight and slim. To Laurence he seemed neither young nor old: perhaps he was thirty years old, perhaps thirty-five. He had a tanned face and dark, close-cut hair. On his surcoat was a crusader's cross; on his face, an expression of calm interest.

Strange, that attitude, Laurence thought. Not strange for a herald, but for a man at arms . . . Whatever reason de Waurin might have had for coming to talk with Saint Rémy, his proper place now was with Salisbury down on the battlefield. Did he think that himself? Did it fill his mind, the thought that he should be making his way down the slope and on to the plain, that he ought to be drawing his sword and wielding his axe like the rest? Did it bring him terror? Did he linger out of fear, or merely out of a desire to get a wider view of the battle? His saturnine face gave Laurence no clue.

It crossed his mind that he should despise de Waurin for not joining the battle; but there was something about the Burgundian that made such an attitude unthinkable. Instead, he envied him. He envied de Waurin's armour, which was plain enough by noble standards, but powerful protection nonetheless; he envied de Waurin's sword; most of all he envied that impression he conveyed of understanding, of making sense of the action.

Laurence could make no sense of it any more. There was now no trace of the fixed rows in which the soldiers had waited for so long; no neat demarcation between archers, horsemen and men at arms. He could make out an occasional loud scream, a trumpet blast, but even the noise of the battle was almost all confusion: a dull rumble made up of the thud of men's feet, the jittery prancing of the horses, the clash of the swords and axes, the singing whine of the massed arrow flights.

Only at the edges could he distinguish actions clearly. There were the archers who had been scattered by the first attack, regrouping at the edge of the plain. There were their trumpeters, raising their instruments; there was the high blare, there the charge. Further to his right, a few stray knights were drawing back from the rear of the Lancastrian lines. He saw one small division break ranks and run, clumsily, hampered by their weapons and armour, towards the nearer fringes of the forest; towards him.

Run. His own whirling movement was instinctive. He was animal: he sensed danger. But he had barely taken a step before his upper arm was caught in a firm, gauntleted grip.

'Hold fast. We are safe still.'

He had barely moved, but he was panting as hard as if he had in truth been running. Slowly, his breath subsided to its normal rhythm, and he brought his eyes up to meet the Burgundian's face.

'Some soldiers always retreat. It is easy, at close quarters, to misread the battle. They fear the worst, and they look to save themselves. But they are mistaken. See, Aumale is down; his line is beginning to break. Bedford will have his men on the run before long. True, Salisbury is harder pressed, but watch carefully: the signs are all there, the Scots are on the verge of failing. They are too impatient, the Scots: they throw everything into a first attack. They looked to break through immediately, but Salisbury held them; now they have no reserves of strength.'

De Waurin did not meet Laurence's eyes, nor show in any other way that he had noticed his sudden panic. He gazed at the battlefield, and pointed to first one spot on it, then another as he talked.

He communicated no sense of danger: in his manner there was nothing to be read but calm interest. It was infectious, almost as contagious as the terror of the flying soldiers. Laurence's eyes moved from the Burgundian, to follow his pointing arm. The banners, he thought: look for the banners. He began to see it then. He made out Aumale's banner, saw the crush of men beneath it, and understood that they were gathered around their fallen captain. He saw Salisbury's banner, waving high in the hands of a mounted man at arms, surrounded by a band of others with crests flying and swords outstretched. This is what victory looks like, he thought; that is defeat.

It is not so different, he thought suddenly, from a game of chess. I have no practice, I barely understand the rules: I see little but chaos on the board. But this man knows about these things, and for him the weak and strong points leap out to the eye. Events focus upon them, inexorably. Their influence radiates outwards. From Salisbury's sword or Bedford's battle axe spread lines of power that can shape this entire battle. Thousands of men fight on this plain; but I can believe now that one single undefended position, one strong commander, might determine everything.

De Waurin was still speaking, his voice steady and insistent, pointing out other focal points of the action, other small victories and defeats. Laurence listened intently. This is how I shall learn it all, he thought: this is the man I should follow.

Then the commentary stopped, abruptly. Laurence swung round, alarmed, to see what had interrupted the other man. It was Saint Rémy. He touched de Waurin on the arm, then drew him a pace or two away, ignoring Laurence. The two of them talked intently for a short while, in voices too low for Laurence to follow the words. Then the Burgundian turned to his squire and reached for his bassinet. He glanced back at Laurence and gave him a brief nod. He set the bassinet on his head, lowered the visor, and set off down the hill in the direction of Salisbury's troops.

Laurence watched him. He continued to watch until the distant figure was lost in the confusion of the battlefield. Then he watched the battle itself, trying to make himself see it through de Waurin's eyes; but it was no use, he lacked the experience, and the clarity of vision that he had sensed earlier was gone from him completely.

He turned, and looked around him. The officers at arms were still only paces away. He went to stand by Suffolk Herald. He had no urge now to be alone.

Nor was he afraid now: even without de Waurin by his side, it seemed to him that there was nothing to fear. Though he did not understand how and why the victory was coming, it was increasingly obvious that it was no longer in doubt. The officers of arms were jubilant already.

Laurence saw the Lombard horsemen repulsed by Bedford's reserve archers; he saw them gallop away towards the walls of Verneuil. He saw Aumale's troops follow the Lombards, and the Lancastrians chase after both divisions. A straggle of figures faded into the distance, spilling across the space between the battlefield and the town defences.

The pattern thinned, the dust began to settle. The noise of the battle faded. It was done, or nearly so. The plain belonged to the Lancastrians.

Eagle Vert took the arm of Bellêsme Poursuivant, and the two of them began to move down the slope, towards the baggage enclosure. Laurence watched them, then let his eyes move faster along the path they were travelling. By the baggage enclosure he could see a few knots of men. They looked to him to be Valois prisoners, and Lancastrian valets holding them at pike-point.

He should follow, he thought; he should find something to do, some way of impressing Anjou. He took a step towards the plain.

'Wait,' Suffolk Herald said, catching his sleeve.

'But there is nothing to see now.'

Nothing, that was, but desolation. There was a litter of bodies across the road and the fields. A smattering of soldiers were still roaming around, but it seemed to Laurence that they were moving almost at random: fighting in units no longer, but looking for stray adversaries or for plunder.

'True, but it is dangerous: you do not wear a tabard. Wait until Bedford and Salisbury have restored some order. There is no urgency.'

That made sense. Laurence waited, and Suffolk with him. He watched the bright tabards of Eagle Vert and Bellêsme, criss-crossing the road and the wheatfields; he watched a half-dozen other officers of arms following them. He thought of the walls of Verneuil. He thought of the men running up to that sheer stone barrier, up to the gates that the townsmen dared not open for them. He thought of the moat. It was deep, men said, at Verneuil.

'Suffolk!' Anjou King of Arms called sharply, somewhere behind his back. 'And you, de Fougères. We go down now, to make a tally of the prisoners. Then back here, when you see my sign; and afterwards we return to count the bodies.'

Laurence stopped when he reached the first bodies. He looked up at the sun. It was still high above the treetops, still bright and hot and indifferent. The birds were still singing in the forest. The battle had seemed to him to last for an eternity, but he reckoned it up now, and realised that it had in reality taken less time than a sung mass.

There were many men dead, more than he had expected. Blood clotted the crushed wheatstalks and pooled on the ground between the cabbages. An English soldier shouldered him out of the way, pike angled downwards, and prodded at a body huddled on the ground. The body groaned; the soldier thrust with his pike; there was a strange bubbling sound, a sudden, scarlet pool of blood, and the soldier moved on.

Laurence stared at the corpse. How red the blood seemed. Somebody else jostled him from behind, and he came to his senses, blinked and looked around him. He saw that the same casual slaughter of the injured was happening all over the plain.

No quarter. He had known that those were the terms that Anjou had negotiated with the Valois heralds, but there had been no picture in his mind to give meaning to the cold, precise words. This was what it meant, he thought with a kind of despairing wonder. The English would tend their own injured, but not the French and Scots. They would kill them, kill them all, unless they were noble and able to pay a ransom.

And what was that to him? War was a business: every man knew as much. Compassion was for women. Men who learned what life was really like did not show pity. They could not afford to, any of them; and he himself could afford it least of all. What did it matter to him that these cold-blooded killers were Englishmen? It made no real difference. If the positions had been reversed the Valois would have done the same.

'Here, boy.'

He wheeled round, and saw that the voice was Anjou's: the King of Arms stood just behind him.

'Sir?'

'Check those for blazons.'

Anjou waved, marking with the cursory gesture the patch of ground upon which Laurence was to work. Then he stalked off, leaving Laurence to stare at it.

There were maybe a couple of dozen corpses. Some of them were still lying where they had fallen across the cabbages, some had been dumped together in a rough heap. Their weapons had been taken, but a few were still in their plate armour.

Numbly, he crossed to the heap. He reached out to the topmost body, and pulled at the sleeve of its coarse, quilted jacket. Nothing happened. He pulled again, harder; and the body rolled over in a strange, loose motion and fell to the ground. He jumped back. For a moment, he had had the sensation that the corpse's hand was reaching out to touch him.

No pity. Anjou had given him orders: he must obey them. He bent down and rubbed some of the dust off the soldier's surcoat. The markings were faint, and it took him some time to make out the outline of a Saint Andrew's cross, crudely stencilled on the unbleached linen. A Scot, then: a pikeman from the look of him. A common man, of no interest to Anjou, or to anyone else. Laurence moved on. The next was a man at arms. He wore a device that Laurence did not recognise. And the next . . .

It was not a task he would have chosen, but he found it oddly calming. He did not look at the faces, only at the surcoats. Most of them were torn, all of them matted with dust and blood, but when he had brushed down and smoothed them it was generally possible to make out the devices. One or two he recognised, the rest he tried to memorise. His mind steadily filled with patterns in argent and or, vert and azure, gules and sable; quarters and chevrons, frets and bends.

It was heavy work turning the corpses, and once his initial apprehension had faded he grew rough with them. As he dragged at one of the bodies with no armour, a shivering heap of intestines slithered from it and across his feet before he could move them. The bile rose to his throat.

'You speak Breton?'

He turned from the voice and vomited on the grass, annoyed both at himself and at the unknown man who was watching him. He spat into the little puddle of vomit, swallowed air and swung back to confront the watcher.

'That is so.'

'Anjou told me you would do. Come and talk to my prisoner. I'll be damned if I can follow a word he says.'

Laurence went. The prisoner proved to be Italian, and as soon as he had proved himself useless as an interpreter he was turned off. Not knowing what else to do, he made his way back to the heap of corpses.

A group of archers had taken his place. He stopped a few paces off and watched them. They were scavenging, squabbling over the second-rate trophies that earlier looters had missed, shouting and shoving at each other with boisterous confidence.

Anjou, Laurence thought: I should find Anjou. He

stepped back a few more paces and looked around him to see if he could make out the King of Arms.

A trumpet sounded. He knew that signal, from his days of marching with the army: it was the call for a muster.

He was no soldier, so he did not think of it as a call for him. He stood there, an outsider, watching as the pattern of the muster took shape. The standard bearers lined up at the edge of the field and raised their flags high. Slowly, the troops began to regroup under their colours.

Order to chaos, thought Laurence; chaos to order. The English do this well; that is why they win their battles. They see the pattern. No, they do not only see it: they create it, they shape it to fit their requirements.

'Why are you standing there? Come! You should be with Anjou!'

Should I? The earlier thought had been driven from Laurence's head and he squinted at Suffolk Herald blindly, confused by the other man's urgency. This is an army of Englishmen, he thought: I have no place in it. But Suffolk caught at his sleeve and pulled him, and he followed the other man without protesting.

Suffolk Herald led him not to a standard, but to an even brighter signal: Anjou's tabard, staked out by its owner near the centre of the battlefield. They joined the edge of a rapidly forming crowd of tabarded figures.

So many heralds, Laurence thought to himself. So many poursuivants. There are many tasks for them to do, but there are many men also to do those tasks. Will Anjou really find a post for me? They had not looked so many, under the clump of beeches. The soldiers were fewer now, but not the heralds: none of them had turned to corpses. But still, he thought, it was strange that he had not noticed that blue and red tabard earlier, or that one . . .

It came to him suddenly. Those lilies belonged to Mountjoie King of Arms; that silver tabard, to Buchan

Herald. These were not only the Lancastrian officers of arms. The Valois had come to meet with them.

How strange. The thought pleased him in its oddness. On a field littered with Valois corpses, he thought, the Dauphin's King of Arms treads safely. He greets Henry of Lancaster's King of Arms – with sorrow, doubtless, for he is a man and many men he knew are now dead, but in friendship nonetheless. They talk calmly together, in the midst of this blood-spattered plain; they swap information, for it is important to them that they should know everything.

He stood with them, but in spite of Suffolk Herald's gesture in dragging him across to join the rest, in spite of the presence of the other Frenchmen, he did not feel himself a part of them. He felt no warmth towards them. He felt: empty. Detached. Everything that he saw, everything that he had seen during that long, strange afternoon had interested him, but that was all it was: not passion, not caring, just interest.

He looked, in a flat, indifferent way, at Anjou. He saw the King of Arms' smooth face, the sleek, brown hair that clung to his shapely skull, his gay tabard, and he thought quite suddenly: Anjou has it too, this detachment. They all have it, every one of them. They do not speak of the battle they have just witnessed with horror or compassion or pain: they speak only with interest.

He held that thought in his mind, fascinated, for some minutes. Anjou and Saint Rémy and Mountjoie were arguing over the number of French and Scots casualties: the Lancastrians estimated there to be seven or even eight thousand, while Mountjoie protested that there were surely no more than three. Laurence heard their argument, but it seemed to him then a matter of no real importance. He heard the litany of the dead: the Earl of Douglas, Sir James Douglas, the Earl of Buchan and the Earl of Murray; the Counts of Aumale, Narbonne, Ventadour and Tonnerre. The names, half-familiar, washed over his consciousness.

'So you will inform me, please, who has the Duke of Alençon?' Mountjoie demanded.

That name made a tiny pinprick in the shell of his mind.

'Alençon?' Anjou echoed.

'The Duke, and the Bastard too. We saw them both taken.'

Alençon! But this cool interest, this herald's attitude, should not be his! He was the enemy of Alençon. This was a matter of vital importance to him. Through a haze of weariness, he struggled to focus his concentration on what Anjou, Mountjoie and the rest were saying.

'Certainly,' said Eagle Vert, in a confident voice, 'it was Fastolf.'

'As always.'

Mountjoie frowned. 'Fastolf has them both?'

'So it seems.'

'And you think he will keep the Duke?'

Anjou shrugged. 'Who is to say? He'll keep some of the ransom, no doubt. Oh, and he needs a messenger. De Fougères.' He glanced across at Laurence, indifferently. 'Go to Fastolf, and tell him I sent you. I did not see that any English knights were taken prisoner . . . ?'

So the Duke of Alençon was not dead. He was a prisoner, the prisoner of Fastolf. And he, Laurence de Fougères, was to seek out Fastolf, on Anjou's orders; to seek out the man who was holding Alençon. These sparse facts chased each other around Laurence's head, removing all space for thought, for emotion.

He walked until he was out of sight of the heralds, and then stopped, disoriented. The sun was lower in the sky now, but it was still blazing mercilessly on the ruination around him. The air was motionless, and through it rose up a rich stench of clotting blood, of sweat and shit and crushed grass and onions. The sickness rose thinly in his throat this time: his stomach was hollow, there was nothing but bile to bring up.

He must find Fastolf. A thousand reasons swirled in his head, and all of them told him that he must find Fastolf. In the end, though, he needed only one reason: the fact that it was Anjou's order.

Anjou had given him work. And it was for this that he had schemed and waited and served the King of Arms: because he needed work. He needed food to eat. He needed a place to sleep. He needed to be given a new life to live.

From somewhere within him, the need for these things, for supper, a bed, a purpose, pushed him towards rational thought. Find Fastolf. Sir John, that was his name: Sir John Fastolf. Laurence could remember Suffolk Herald speaking the name to him, and pointing out its owner, a sturdy knight sitting at Bedford's left hand.

The picture of Fastolf was clear in his mind. The knight was a big, beefy man, well into middle age, with large movements and a narrow, calculating look to his eyes. Laurence would recognise him again. But how to find him? Laurence looked around once more. The soldiers were spreading out across the plain in loose files like unravelling ribbons. The musters must be over. They had been given new orders. Scout for fugitives; guard the captives; cook the suppers; raise the tents.

That was where the camp would be: on that slope just outside the town, an arrow-shot from the edge of the main battlefield. Already most of the wagons had been trundled there, and some were being unloaded. As Laurence watched, he saw men unfurling the gay canvas of Bedford's pavilion.

Think, Laurence, he told himself. Fastolf sat at Bedford's left hand, he has a position in Bedford's household. Now he has a prisoner, a very high-ranking prisoner. He will take that prisoner to his tent. I should find that tent. His banner will mark it out, and his device.

His banner. His arms. I know Fastolf's arms, he thought to himself. Quartered, they are: or and azure on a bend gules, with three cross crosslets argent.

36

Fortified by this piece of random information, he caught at a passing page and asked where he might find Sir John Fastolf's quarters. The page shrugged. Laurence hailed another man, and asked him. He did not know either. He asked another, and another; asked pages and valets and archers, asked the keepers of the pavilions, asked chaplains and grooms and men at arms. At last, a small and scruffy page piped up with the directions he needed. It was that tent: that large one over there, no more than twenty paces from the Regent's pavilion.

Laurence walked across, and stood looking at the tent. It was of red cloth, rather faded: in the usual circular pattern, with its roof rising high around the central post. Fastolf's banner was there, precisely as Laurence remembered it, its pole driven into the hard ground just beside the tent-flap. The banner was faded too, and its leading edge was frayed. It was his pennon once, Laurence thought. When he was promoted to knight banneret he did not trouble with a new flag: he just ripped off the point to transform it.

There was no sign of a guard. Was Alençon inside? Or the Bastard? Laurence stood and watched the tent for several minutes. A couple of soldiers entered it, another one left, but that told him nothing. He reached to his belt and fingered the hilt of his dagger. Then he moved forward: first one pace, then another, then the rest of the distance. He lifted the flap and deftly, silently, slipped into the tent.

He stopped there, his back to the canvas, his body shrinking into itself. The tent was crowded: that was the first thing he saw. That was good. He edged to his right, moving away from the entrance where men might notice him.

There was Sir John Fastolf, standing in the middle of the tent. He wore a green doublet and hose, both of which had a damp, compressed look to them, as if he had only just removed his armour, and the sweat was pouring freely down his red face. He was talking

– shouting almost – though Laurence could not immediately see who he was talking to.

He took all this in at a glance, and his eyes moved on. They found the Duke of Alençon; and stopped.

Alençon was only three or four paces away from Laurence, but he was not looking in his direction. He was staring upwards, at the shadows around the top of the tent-pole. Nobody seemed to be paying him any particular attention: he looked bored and disdainful.

So pretty, Alençon. Handsome, the women had said at Fougères, when he rode through the town on his black stallion; but that seemed to Laurence less apt a word to describe his slight figure, his very fair hair with its bouncing curls, his neat features, his petulant mouth. His doublet was yellow, figured in blue. It was immaculate.

Laurence stared. He had thought he knew every detail of Alençon's appearance – which seemed quite unaffected by the events of the battle and its aftermath – but it was three months or more since he had seen the Duke, and he saw him now with the detachment that only time can provide. He saw him almost as Marianne might have seen him; though even now, he could not understand how she could have let it happen.

He tried to recall Alençon's snarl, as he raised his whip ready to flick it outwards. He tried to recall his sneer, as he ordered the Chamberlain to throw Laurence out of the castle. But now he was neither snarling nor sneering; he was simply a pretty lad in a yellow doublet.

Laurence's hand went to the hilt of his dagger.

'You had a message?'

Strangely, the interruption did not surprise him, or even disappoint him particularly. He had not thought the action through in his mind, he had no clear idea what he had intended to happen next. He let his hand fall, in as casual a gesture as he could manage, turned to the man who had spoken – a common soldier – and said softly, 'No. I came to receive one. To carry a letter, I think. On the orders of Anjou King of Arms.'

'You came quickly. He's not finished it yet. You'd best wait here.'

The soldier turned away. Laurence blinked, to reorient himself. He did not think to move towards Alençon again, though it did occur to him that he should move out of the Duke's sight. Maybe Alençon would not recognise him: there had been many similar incidents at Fougères, and perhaps he had forgotten that one already. But then, maybe Alençon would. Laurence's face was distinctive. It was not his style to make himself conspicuous, but he knew from experience that few men ever forgot it.

It was not difficult to put several men between himself and Alençon, since the tent was so full. There were half a dozen English men at arms in various states of undress, their pages and esquires, a couple of less prepossessing prisoners, a poursuivant in Bedford's colours who was, Laurence assumed, waiting to press his master's claim to much, if not all, of the ransom for Alençon, and a man in the close cap and belted leather jacket of a Welsh archer. This last was kneeling by a campaign chest which he was using as a makeshift table, and busily writing. Laurence realised a moment later that he was taking down what Fastolf was saying.

Laurence moved closer to the archer, so that he could listen. It did not seem to him that the letter could be particularly private, since Fastolf's voice was so loud. The knight was grumbling, mainly.

'More money . . . useless scoundrel . . . that fool Tuddenham . . .' Laurence concentrated, trying to make out the drift of it, but it was difficult, since half a page had already been written, and none of the names Fastolf spoke was familiar to him. It was certainly not military business: it seemed to be addressed to some kind of a business agent. The grumbles struck him as trivial, but he did his best to remember what he heard. Maybe it would be important to him one day, he thought.

He did not think of Alençon.

Finally Fastolf's lengthy harangue came to an end without ever reaching a climax of exasperation. The archer's quill scratched to a halt a few moments afterwards. He turned the sheet of paper towards the knight, and Fastolf bent to sign his name, laboriously, at the foot of it. Then he looked up, and at Laurence.

He pretends that he has only just noticed me, Laurence thought; but that is not so. He has been glancing at me ever since I entered the tent. Did he see my hand touch my dagger? I do not know. But he will not mention it, I think.

Fastolf moved closer to Laurence, stopping only a pace from him. He was not a very tall man, but he was two, or perhaps three, inches taller than Laurence.

'Name?' he rapped out.

I do not have a name, Laurence thought to himself; not until you give me a new one. I left my old name behind when I left Fougères. The Duke of Alençon stole it from me.

That seemed to him no more or less than the truth, but in practice he had been forced sometimes to use it since: not least, to Anjou. There seemed no choice but to tell it to Fastolf, too. So he said, in a voice that he tried to pitch so that it would not carry across the tent, 'Laurence de Fougères, sir.'

'A Frenchy, eh?'

Many responses would have been worse, but still, this one annoyed him. Years the English had spent in France, and still most of them knew no better. 'A Norman–Breton, sir,' he retorted, in a voice that was considerably less respectful than it should have been.

Fastolf appeared not to notice his annoyance. 'Anjou sent you? Then I suppose you will have to do. You can deliver this letter for me. Hanson will give you the direction. Bedford's man will write you a safe conduct.' He turned away.

Laurence gazed at his fast-retreating back in astonishment.

'Sir . . .'

40

Fastolf wheeled back round with surprising agility. 'What is it now?'

'I imagine the man is hoping to be paid, sir,' the archer said in a mild voice.

'He hopes for too much. I shall pay you when you return. You have a horse?'

'No, sir.'

'Ask my grooms for a mount. Stable it with Graunger in Calais. I shall expect you back within three weeks.' This time Fastolf's departure was unassailable. He promptly embarked on a heated argument with one of the other soldiers.

But he should make me his poursuivant, Laurence thought. He should give me a name; there should be some kind of ceremony, surely. Clearly none of that was going to happen. Perhaps it is as well, he told himself, thinking suddenly of Alençon. He glanced again at the Duke and saw that he had barely moved, though his head was lowered now and his eyes were fixed on the floor. He seemed lost in a stupor.

Laurence turned his attention to the archer. 'You are Hanson?'

'Christopher Hanson. That was my name the last time I was told it.' Hanson was fumbling in the campaign chest.

'You are to give me my directions.'

'I am?'

Hanson emerged with a stick of sealing wax, a taper and a tinder box. He proceeded to seal the letter. When this process was complete he looked up and said abruptly, 'You know London?'

'A little,' said Laurence, who had never been to England in his life.

'The letter is for John Welles. You can try his house; I'll write the address for you. If he is not there you may find him at Sir John's house in Southwark, or at the Tabard. It is never hard to find Welles. Ask in any of those places and the men you find there will direct you to him.'

Southwark. The Tabard. Laurence did not reply. He repeated the names in his head. The other things he had heard he might forget, but this, he knew, he must remember.

'On second thoughts, it's maybe best,' Hanson continued, 'if you go first to Fastolf Place. Southwark High Street. You'll find John Payn there: he'll tell you anything else you need to know. While Welles, now, will tell you plenty that you do not.' He rose to his feet. He was a tall man, very tall: Laurence had to crane upwards to meet his eyes. He glanced across at Fastolf, who was some distance away, then looked back down at Laurence, and lowered his voice. 'Oh, and Welles will pay you if you ask him.'

'That at least is good to know.'

Hanson gave a crooked grin. 'Fastolf has talked for months of getting a poursuivant. But he'll test you before he takes you on; don't take it amiss.'

'That is prudent of him.'

'He is a prudent man,' Hanson said consideringly. 'Secret: that's the name he's been thinking of. Matthew suggested it to him. But there's a chance still that he'll settle for his motto, Me faut faire.'

Laurence considered these revelations. Secret, he thought. That is a strange name. But all poursuivants have strange names. Who is Matthew? He did not like to ask. 'Secret will suffice.'

'Don't tell him so, or he'll change it. Come, I'll help you to find the grooms. You should move quickly, and find some other men travelling towards Calais. It's too dangerous to ride alone. And you should eat here, before you ride.'

Hanson moved as he said this, pushing his way across the tent towards the entrance. Laurence followed him, without giving a backward glance to the men he left behind.

It had taken him a long time, he realised once they were outside, to find Fastolf and collect the letter. The sun was well behind the trees: soon it would set. The

42

plain of Verneuil looked desolate. Crows cawed over the corpses. The English camp alone was full of life and activity. Hanson set off, striking what seemed to be a random path through the maze of men, tents and cooking fires.

Laurence hurried after him. He had to run, almost, as Hanson's legs were so long. When eventually he caught up with the archer, he said, 'Tell me about Sir John.'

Hanson glanced down, as if he were considering whether to reply to this, or what to say.

'Let me see. He's a banneret, you'll know that. He is master of four score men at arms and two hundred and forty archers. He acts as Bedford's Chief Steward. He is sharper than he looks; and his wife is uglier than you would think possible. His estates are mainly in Norfolk, and the war is making him rich. And he will never pay you a penny if he can avoid it.'

Another sideways glance accompanied this last remark. He sees my tattered tunic, Laurence thought, and my bloody sandals. There is more than a hint of pity in his look. I do not like to be pitied. But at least it is not contempt.

'I have a letter for Payn,' Hanson said abruptly. 'I'll give you a salut for delivering it.'

'Could you pay me in advance?'

'If you wish. And I'll ask the others: they may have some commissions too.'

Hanson strode on for a dozen more paces, then stopped by a fire. Laurence realised that his progress had been less erratic than it had seemed. He greeted all the men around the fire by name. He himself paused a pace or two away, but Hanson motioned to him to approach, and introduced two of the men to him. One he called Peter: Peter Basset, a short English archer with a tense, furrowed face. The other he named as Matthew Gough. It was apparent from his tone that this was the Matthew he had mentioned earlier. Gough was a bearded man at arms, with sharp, grey eyes and a wide, thin mouth. He spoke with a Gascon accent.

To Laurence's surprise, Hanson had heard, and remembered his own name. He repeated it to the men.

'Fougères?' Basset repeated. 'So you are Alençon's man?'

Laurence's eyes narrowed. He had told his name to only a few men since he had left Fougères, and none of the others had questioned him further about his association with the town and its overlord – but for Anjou, and even his questions had been cursory. He had realised very soon that most Englishmen, and many Frenchmen too, had no idea who was the lord of Fougères. The town was on the Breton border, and sometimes men assumed that it was a Breton town, the property of the Duke of Brittany. He thought of contradicting Basset, telling him this. But where he would have let a mistaken impression pass uncorrected, he hesitated to tell a direct lie. It seemed to him that this would be a poor way to start on a new phase in his life.

'Now, I think,' he said carefully, 'I am Sir John Fastolf's man.'

There was a momentary silence.

'Then you shall be our friend,' Matthew Gough said. He clapped Laurence on the shoulder. It was a big, bluff gesture of the kind that Laurence generally detested. But he did not flinch on this occasion: it spoke to him of camaraderie, and that gave him an obscure pleasure.

'Fastolf cares nothing for the company of French Dukes,' Gough continued, 'only for their money. By the time you return, Alençon will be in Bedford's custody.'

Was that what he wanted? He did not know what he wanted. He could not have told these men that, though. He did not want to say anything to them, but he knew that he had to find some kind of reply that would show that he welcomed their friendliness.

'I think that will be no bad thing for me.'

'You'll eat with us?', Basset asked.

'If I may.'

One of the men already had a ladle to the cooking pot

44

and was doling out its contents on to rough trenchers. It proved to hold a stew of field cabbage and dried beef.

Laurence ate ravenously, tearing at his bread. A salut for delivering Hanson's letter, he thought. And with that he must get to England, to this place called Southwark, of which he knew nothing. He would do it somehow. He must. Only a salut, though: if he spent it on food he would have no money for his passage across the Channel. Perhaps he should take a cabbage after all, in the dark, or see if he might steal a loaf from the cooks' wagons.

A long shadow suddenly fell over him. He jerked to his feet, spilling a long streak of gravy down his tunic.

It was de Waurin. 'Anjou tells me you ride for London.'

Laurence swallowed a hunk of bread and said, as soon as he could speak, 'Tonight, perhaps.'

'Then you will carry a message for me? It will mean only a short detour on your way to Calais. I had intended Saint Rémy to carry it, but he has left already.'

'Of course.' He tried to say it casually, but there was nothing casual about the feelings which de Waurin's sudden appearance, and his request, had stirred in him. It would mean more money, he thought with an inner leap of excitement and relief: perhaps another salut. With that he could buy two loaves of bread, or maybe even a dinner of fish when he reached the coast.

De Waurin reached into the folds of his doublet. He withdrew a coin, and a letter. That surprised Laurence. He had expected a spoken message.

He took the letter, and stared at it. It was addressed to the Seigneur de Santes, a Burgundian lord. Unlike Fastolf's, this one would hold news of the battle, surely. That meant that somehow, in the short space of time that had passed since the victory, de Waurin too had managed to find paper and ink, and to have a message set down and sealed. But this man was no Sir John Fastolf with a tent of his own: he was a common man at arms.

This is a formidable man, Laurence thought, his eyes moving from the letter to the face of him who had given it. He is a man who knows much, but more than that, he is a man who finds ways to do all that he wishes to do.

'Fastolf has arranged a mount for you?' de Waurin asked.

'He offered. I must go now to ask his grooms.'

'Nicolas will show you the way.' De Waurin gestured to his squire, then he turned and spoke to the soldier Gough. 'Matthew, may I eat with you?'

It was a dismissal: not rude, but positive. Laurence waited all the same for another word, but it soon became clear to him that no more would be forthcoming. Still, it was something; it was much. He hastily finished his supper, then nodded to Nicolas.

Nicolas led the way; he followed. He did not look back until he was perhaps fifty paces from the fire, but then the temptation was too strong and he paused and turned around.

The sun had gone by then, but in the half-light of early evening he could see the Burgundian leaning forward to the cooking pot. His dark features were strongly outlined against the glow of the embers. Hanson and his friends were more distant, behind de Waurin from where Laurence stood, in the shadow. He could only make out their dark shapes, sitting together in a tight group on the rough ground. As he watched he heard Basset say something, though he could not make out the words. Christopher Hanson laughed out loud. The sound reached clearly to where he stood.

It was like a little dagger in his ribs, that sound and that sight.

But why do you sigh, Laurence de Fougères, he asked himself sharply. You too have had a warm supper. You have met a man who has said he will be your friend, and others who have shown you kindness. This morning you had nothing. Tonight you have a mission. You have a master. You even know what your name is to be.

It was more than he had dared to hope for. He was a fool, he knew, to ache for more. The plain of Verneuil is not really so very dark and treacherous and lonely, he told himself: it only seems so, because for that moment you sat in the glow of the fire. But that warmth is not for you, not any more. This is your path. Follow it.

Southwark High Street was lined with inns. The Boar's Head, the Crowned Keys, the Tabard and a dozen other hostelries provided shelter for pilgrims bound for Canterbury, merchants bound for Dover, foreigners coming from Sandwich and Southampton, and quiet men in dark, anonymous gowns who preferred not to discuss either their origin or their destination.

Behind these inns, buried in the private recesses of the borough, was an array of great houses: the Bishop of Winchester's town house, the Bishop of Rochester's, the Abbot of Hyde's, the Abbot of Waverley's, and half a dozen more. The innkeeper of the Crowned Keys told Laurence de Fougères something of these venerable and discreet old buildings, and something of their owners too. He also gave him directions to Fastolf Place, which was not difficult, since Sir John Fastolf's Southwark house adjoined his inn.

Laurence thanked him, left the inn – without buying any food or drink, since his two saluts had been exhausted long since – and walked out into the High Street. He looked up and down. There was the door of the Crowned Keys from which he had just emerged. There was the door of the Boar's Head. Between them he could see no sign of any entrance to the kind of impressive town house of which the innkeeper had just been speaking. There was only a flat expanse of wall punctuated by a row of high windows, all firmly shuttered, and a narrow gate that was shut fast. It could have been the entrance to another inn, except that there was no sign outside, and unlike the inns, which were all open and inviting, this building appeared to reject the world. Could this conceivably be Fastolf's mansion? Laurence thought it doubtful, but he could see no other candidates for that honour, so he took a deep breath and knocked on the gate.

No reply. He knocked again, and then decided that either he or the innkeeper must have been mistaken. He walked on, down the High Street. In the next mile he saw no building that announced itself as Fastolf Place. He asked again, a passer-by this time, and was directed one mile back.

Sighing, he retraced his steps, positioned himself once more outside the narrow gate, and knocked once more: this time considerably harder.

There was a long silence. Then, just as Laurence was about to give up and go and make enquiries in the Boar's Head, he heard footsteps.

The footsteps sounded oddly uneven, a fact that was explained when, with much groaning of rusty bolts, the gate was opened to reveal an old soldier with a wooden leg. He peered uncertainly at Laurence, demanded to know who he was, insisted on seeing his papers, and finally stood aside, grumbling, to let him enter.

Laurence stepped through into a squarish, cobbled yard. An assortment of buildings stretched around and behind it. There were storerooms, with huge padlocks on their doors. Stables, straw-strewn and almost deserted. Laurence had no horse with him: he had travelled by carrier's wagon and foot from Dover. There was a row of assorted huts that housed, he reckoned, the domestic offices and servants' quarters. In one corner was a heavy oak door with a cresset in a holder by its side: unlit, since it was still afternoon. Through this the old soldier disappeared. He made no sign to Laurence, but he left the door ajar.

Laurence waited for some time. A couple of mangy cats stalked in procession from the stable and disappeared round the side of one of the huts. He weighed the accumulation of stray leaves and decided it was a week or more since the yard had been swept. He considered whether the old soldier was likely to return and decided that he was not. He went through the oak door.

It gave on to a long, narrow corridor. Laurence walked down it. His feet in their thin leather shoes, the bloodstains almost hidden now with dust, made no sound on the earthen floor. He thought of calling out, but decided against it.

At the end of the corridor was another door, also heavy, also not quite shut. He pushed it open and found himself stepping into the great hall.

This room was wide and rather short, almost as square as the yard. It was plainly furnished with wooden trestles and forms. There was no sign of cloth on the seats or the walls, which were painted with a selection of faded coats of arms and hung with pikes and halberds. On Laurence's left was the wall that backed on to the High Street: he recognised the row of high windows. A few splinters of sunlight sneaked their way through the shutters; there was no other source of light in the room. In the wall facing him was a large empty fireplace. To his right was a low dais. The dais was empty. But behind the trestle that was set along the left-hand wall below the windows, a man was sitting.

Laurence could not have been expected, and it was only a short while since the old soldier had entered the room, but he had a sudden strange feeling of anticipation, as if the room and the man behind the trestle had been waiting for him. Then he moved forward, and the presentiment faded. He saw that the trestle was strewn with papers, and that the man was not alone. The old soldier stood behind him in the shadows, and there was another man, a clerk perhaps, sitting at the end of the trestle.

The man at the centre of the trestle watched him approach. He waited until Laurence had crossed half the floor, and then rose to his feet.

'You are a Frenchman?' His voice was loud in the silence of the room.

Laurence bowed. 'I am a Breton, sir.' It was a simplification he had chosen deliberately: he had decided that he would not introduce himself again as Laurence from Fougères.

'Fastolf entrusted papers to a Breton? Holy Mary, I'd never have believed it.'

'I was recommended to him, sir.'

'Let me see the papers.'

Laurence hesitated, and the man added, 'Harry cannot read. He saw only the seal.'

'Are you John Payn, sir?'

'Are your letters for Payn?'

'I was told I would find John Payn here.'

'Another day perhaps you would.' The man paused, frowning slightly. Then his expression changed and he grinned at Laurence. 'Saints, how many private messages do you carry? Do you work for Hanson and Gough and Basset already? At least you know how to guard your tongue. I am John Welles, sir. You need show me only the letters addressed to me.'

'Assuredly I shall do so.'

Laurence moved forward, and reached under the folds of his tunic to extract the precious package of letters. He could feel Welles' gaze checking him over as he fumbled for it.

'When did you last eat?' Welles asked abruptly.

'Yesterday morning, sir.'

'By Saint Winifred's elbow! Did Fastolf not pay you? Of course, the private commissions – I see it now. The stupid old fool. Harry, go and ask Meg to – no, on second thoughts, go to the Crowned Keys, and find the man a piece of mutton or the like. Set it to my account. And bring us both a pot of ale. Giles, you may go too.'

Harry gave a low mutter and stumped off to the doorway. The clerk Giles rose to his feet, a pale wraith, and drifted after him. John Welles sat down again and began to break the seals of his letter. Laurence did not sit, but he spread his feet a little, easing his weight. He watched Welles.

Welles' clothes all spoke of money. His houppelande was old-fashioned in its loose, generous cut, but it was not old: the wool was thick and creamy, and the red embroidery at the cuffs and hem had a bright newness about it. The shirt that showed at his neck and wrists was of fine, thin linen, and his fingers were weighted down with rings. On the trestle, a couple of small peacock feathers nodded in his hat. He had a round belly and red cheeks, a wispy mat of dark hair, and very bushy, black eyebrows. He breathed in and out noisily, puffing almost, as he turned over the closely written sheets of Fastolf's letter.

'You know how to read?' he asked, suddenly looking up.

'N–' Laurence began a lie, and then decided against it. 'Yes,' he amended, 'but these letters were sealed when I received them.'

'Latin?'

'I can follow the mass, sir, but I have no lawyers' Latin.'

'What do you know of the wool trade?'

'Why, nothing, sir.'

'What brought you to Fastolf?'

'Hunger, sir.'

Welles dropped the sheet of paper he had been looking at and met Laurence's eyes.

'And before?'

'I served a French lord, sir. I tried to attack him after I learned he had seduced my sister.'

'And he turned you off.'

Welles said this thoughtfully, as if he were weighing Laurence's story: there was no condemnation evident in his tone. Laurence wondered for a moment why he had given this information to a man he had only just met. He had told nobody else of it since he had left Fougères. He could find no answer that satisfied him; but still, he felt no regret either that he should have made such an unconsidered admission.

'That is so, sir,' he replied.

51

'Which Lord?'

'The Duke of Alençon, sir.'

'That I can believe.' Welles pursed his lips, as if he were thinking hard. 'You will take my replies to Fastolf?'

'I have my passage back arranged, sir. For this Friday.'

'And after that?'

'I hope for further work. As Sir John's poursuivant, if all goes well.'

There was a short silence.

'He plans,' Laurence added, 'to call me Secret.'

Welles threw back his head and laughed. It was a generous-sounding laugh: there seemed to be no malice in it. It was not the response that Laurence had expected, and he felt no inclination to join in, but neither did he take any offence.

A shuffle and tap along the corridor announced Harry's impending return. Welles stopped his laughter. The two men waited in silence while the old soldier deposited a small loaf, a hunk of mutton, a pot of ale and two cups on the trestle. Harry did not speak, but gave a slow nod and hobbled out of the room.

Welles watched him go, signed to him to shut the door, then turned back to Laurence, who was eyeing the food hungrily.

'You know,' he said, 'that I am Sir John's business agent. I deal with his bankers and lawyers, I keep an eye on his estates, I buy land for him.'

'So I understand, sir.'

'So you shall become Fastolf's poursuivant: but you shall serve me also.'

'If you wish it, sir.'

'I do,' Welles said. He held Laurence's eye for a moment longer, then he dropped his gaze to the pot of ale. He reached out and poured himself a brimming cupful. He raised it to his lips and toasted Laurence.

'Why are you waiting?' he asked. 'Eat.'

2

ENGLAND
Autumn, 1428

The fine, the fine. However he tried to turn his thoughts, they always came back to the fine.

He knew it was a small matter when set against the weighty cases he handled every day; but it had taken him three years to have Walter Aslake found guilty of trespass, and now another year's efforts had not seen his fine paid.

He was used to pursuing cases through to their conclusion, however bitter, but it was a different matter acting for himself rather than for a client. Acting for himself he had to count the cost, and it had already been heavy. He had even thought of abandoning the matter; but no, that would not do. It was not merely a question of a hundred and twenty pounds: it was a question of law, and of reputation too. Men in Norfolk knew that Serjeant William Paston had put his backbone into seeing Walter Aslake fined. If he failed to enforce the judgement they would see it as a defeat for him, and worse still, as a victory for Aslake and all his damned influential friends, from Sir Thomas Erpingham to the Duke of Norfolk himself.

There had to be something else he could do. There had to be a way of winning an audience with Gloucester, even if Agnes' limp-wristed cousin had failed to arrange it for him. Gloucester had his weaknesses, more so than most men. The thing was to settle on one of them and worry away at it.

Women: they were undoubtedly a weakness. But it

was not his style, William thought ruefully, to cajole and flatter the Duchess Eleanor into pleading for him, or to dangle another scheming beauty in front of the Duke. Power, reputation: that was more his own territory.

That was Thomas Chaucer's territory too. It was unfortunate that Chaucer was no intimate of Gloucester.

But Chaucer was a relative of Cardinal Beaufort.

Of course: he saw it now. Beaufort was Gloucester's great rival in the King's Council. There would be no need to plead to Gloucester, if he could persuade Chaucer to find him an audience with Beaufort instead.

Was it possible? Certainly Chaucer had direct access to the Cardinal: their mothers had been sisters, and it was common knowledge that they were as close as two puppies from the same litter. And though he himself was no friend of Thomas Chaucer's, he had the best of opportunities for stating his case, since he was standing at that moment in Chaucer's parlour.

Thomas Chaucer was not in his parlour, but William was expecting him to appear at any minute. There were the formalities of the Gresham deal to attend to, but afterwards they would surely talk, and drink wine perhaps – Chaucer was said to be a great man for wine – and he might slide the conversation round to the injustice he had suffered, and his need for a powerful patron to help right it.

He glanced around Chaucer's parlour, with the half-idea that it might show him how to achieve this. It was a very fine parlour. Chaucer's Westminster house was unprepossessing on the outside, just one of the little row of inns and houses that leaned over the churchyard of Henry the Third's Lady Chapel, but inside it was luxurious. The room was lined with linenfold panelling; the large window that looked out to the Abbey grounds was well glazed; on the window seat were strewn embroidered cushions, and on the walls were hung heavy tapestries thick with gold and silver thread.

It is true what they say, William thought: Thomas Chaucer is rich. Like Beaufort himself he has a hefty fortune, though nobody seems to know how he came by it. Not by inheritance, that is certain: old Geoffrey Chaucer had plenty of fine friends, but never two pennies to rub together. Did he earn it at trade? He dealt in wine, and successfully by all accounts, but not on so tremendous a scale. Fees for court appointments? Scarcely. Old King Henry never showed even his favourites more than moderate generosity, and Chaucer barely rated as one of those. Chief Butler, that was his post. He resigned it years ago.

But he has money still; and he spends it still. His candles are of beeswax. His bookshelf is full to overflowing, and many of the bindings have the pale shine of newness. The servant who showed me up here wore fancy livery, and that too was not far off new. Even this is only the half of it. His house in Oxfordshire is so large and grand that men speak of it even in Norfolk.

There is clever dealing behind this little establishment, William went on to himself. A middle-man, a fixer: that is Thomas Chaucer. He uses Parliament for his own ends, and does it well. He has sat in the Speaker's chair more times than I can remember, and there is no better position for a man to accept bribes and further causes, promote or mislay petitions, bring men to public notice or punish them by ignoring them. Stapleton mentioned dealings in France: Stapleton called Chaucer a spy. A spy for the King; a spy for Cardinal Beaufort.

And yet he allows a stranger to be shown into his parlour and left there alone, even though at the far side of the parlour there is a table thickly strewn with papers. Men call Thomas Chaucer crafty, but he can be none too young now. Is he perhaps growing careless in his old age?

William edged closer to the table. It was a mess: there were letters rolled up, letters flattened, letters with their seals still unbroken, broken quills, inkstains and bound manuscripts left open in the most slovenly manner. Never, never, would he have treated his own papers in such a way. His were all kept in a locked strongbox.

He stopped a good two paces from the table: there was no telling how much warning he would have of Chaucer's entrance. From that distance he could read only the headings on the documents, but those were enough to instill in him a rapid sense of disappointment. No state secrets; no important deeds. Routine stuff, all of it; lawyers' letters about minor wrangles, reports from France on the progress of the war, a few bills – and a few poems.

Poems? Not so strange, mind: his father had been a poet. Were these Geoffrey Chaucer's poems? He edged a pace closer and picked up one of the sheets. He read:

> Command me what you will in every wise
> To me that am your silly poor servant
> And ever more unto you obeisant.
> With mine whole heart, with power and service
> I ready am in what that in me lies,
> Out spying this or that, I dare avaunt.
>> Command me what you will in every wise
>> To me that am your silly poor servant.
> Cast all conceit away that doth you grise.
> Assay me where that I be suffisaunt
> To do for you as I have made you grant.
> And if I fail take never of me price.
>> Command me what you will in every wise
>> To me that am your silly poor servant.

No, that was not Geoffrey Chaucer's verse. Nor was it John Lydgate's verse, or indeed any verse that he recognised. Was it Chaucer's own, perhaps? It seemed to him a very peculiar poem: hardly the kind of effort a man would send to a casual acquaintance.

A thud, somewhere not far away. He started and hastily dropped the paper back on the table. He just had time to edge away before the door swung open and Thomas Chaucer stepped into the room.

In his left hand, Chaucer carried another sheaf of papers. Behind him trailed a small boy bearing a tray that held two handsome Venetian glasses and a pitcher of wine.

'Serjeant Paston, Serjeant Paston. So sorry to keep you waiting.'

A fussy man, William thought, as Chaucer went through his greetings and supervised the boy as he poured the wine. Slight, dapper even: there is something formal and old-fashioned about him. A tidy man, I would have thought, if I had not seen his table.

'And now this matter of Gresham . . .'

The papers Chaucer held were the deeds to the manor of Gresham in Norfolk. William recognised them, for he had called on Chaucer's lawyer months before to inspect them. Chaucer shuffled them in his hands, glancing at the occasional sheet, though without evident purpose.

'There seems to be a manor house opposite the church,' he murmured.

'Not so,' William said brusquely. 'The manor house is down in the valley. That's our Norfolk style: we build the churches on the high ground where there is any. There is a house opposite the church, but that's the bailiff's house. It's old, though it's in passable repair. The manor house is more of a castle: square, moated. Draughty, I reckon, but defensible.'

'You have been there?'

'Naturally I looked it over. I understood the bailiff had instructions to let me . . .'

Chaucer shrugged as if he had forgotten. 'Handy, a fortified manor, if there is any real trouble in the country.'

'Not that I expect there to be,' William said. 'Of course if the Burgundian alliance were to falter we might see a rather different situation.'

'Bedford will never let that happen.'

'We must certainly hope not; but men said the same of the Bretons once.'

This was all commonplace stuff: Chaucer doubtless knew all about the Breton change of loyalty. That damn Richemont was to blame, the Duke's brother. Seemed to think Bedford had failed to grant him sufficient honours, so he had carried his troops off to fight for the Dauphin, and promptly been appointed Constable of France. He and Bedford were brothers-in-law, as were Bedford and Burgundy, but that had made not a scrap of difference.

So William reckoned. He thought Chaucer might disagree. Then they could spar pleasantly over the war before settling into cosy agreement over the vices of Gloucester and the virtues of Beaufort. But no: the other man was not to be drawn into a political argument on the strength of a casual comment he might have found hard to substantiate. Instead he said, 'You are satisfied with the deeds? It apears to me that the title is as good as any lawyer could wish.'

'This lawyer is satisfied. Never take any man's word, that's my motto, when property is at stake. Why, it must be two years and more since I began to look into the situation at Gresham. A tangled mess it is, too.'

'Not beyond your ability to unravel, I'd wager, Serjeant.'

'I trust not. I'd not pay good money unless I were confident that the title is valid.'

Chaucer picked up his wineglass. He gazed into it for a moment, took several large sips and said, 'Mind, you will never need to prove it at law. There are no other claimants, and I doubt if there ever will be.'

'I hope not. You know as well as I that these days it sometimes takes more than a good title to win a lawsuit.'

He meant this too as a lead-in to the difficulties of lawkeeping in Norfolk; but Chaucer once more failed to play his game. He did not respond immediately. He drank some more wine, then he said slowly, 'You are Norfolk's man, of course.'

By which he meant, under the Duke's protection. William frowned: not only because he was temporarily thrown off balance by this remark, but because it still pained him to be reminded how very far that was from being true.

'I was for many years. I acted as steward to his estates in Norfolk while he was in France.' I did it well, he added silently to himself; and I was careful to let the unpaid bills mount up.

'But no more? Why, was there some kind of a dispute?'

That was quick, so quick that Chaucer might almost have known in advance what he was going to say. William glanced sharply at the other man's face. The expression on the neat features was perfectly bland: there was no sign of malice. This was the opening he had been looking for, but even so, he was suddenly not sure if it would be wise to take it.

Chaucer noticed his hesitation and said calmly, 'My damnable curiosity, that is all.'

Was it all? Perhaps it was. And even if it was not, the facts of the case were widely known; Chaucer could easily discover them from any of Norfolk's men.

'Perhaps you recall the matter. There was an incident at the Parliament of Bats, a petition against me from a man named Aslake. He threatened me years ago over a lawsuit that went against him, and has pricked and pinched at me ever since. He slandered me to Norfolk, and Norfolk was fool enough to believe him, and then to support him when I was forced to take measures to have him hold his tongue.'

'And you expected support from a Mowbray?'

Expected support? True, the Mowbrays had often been as unreliable as they were unfortunate, but all the same, the Duke of Norfolk was the premier lord of East Anglia. Of course his retainers expected support from him, even if they did not always get it. And though William's feelings towards the Duke were not of the warmest at that moment, Chaucer's remark annoyed him. He might grumble himself about Norfolk's behaviour, but that did not mean it pleased him to hear criticisms of his patron from a near stranger.

'I had certain expectations,' he said coldly.

Chaucer did not respond to the coldness: perhaps he had not noticed it. He turned away to hand his glass to the boy, who refilled it from the pitcher. He received it back and drank from it before saying, unhurriedly, 'Norfolk has no power, of course, when it comes to national issues. His influence with Gloucester is limited; with the Cardinal he has none at all.'

'Limited!' William echoed this with uncharacteristic vehemence. But he knew, even as he spoke, that this was a poor tactic: he was rising like a fish to the first bait dangled in front of him.

Or was it a bait? The more he thought, the less sense it made. Chaucer's remark was painfully accurate, but it fitted poorly with the drift of their conversation as he understood, or at least intended, it.

It seemed to him that his next response would matter intensely; but he could afford to delay it no longer. He said carefully, 'There is much truth in that. It appears to me that Gloucester listens to few men, and to those few only when they give advice that pleases him. He cares little, and acts less, over matters such as this Aslake affair. I think sometimes that I should do better to petition Cardinal Beaufort, but my difficulty is in the lack of intermediaries.'

'Intermediaries', Chaucer repeated. He seemed to slur the word slightly. William glanced at his wineglass. The second glassful, and that now almost empty. Chaucer's face looked quite normal: he was not flushed, his eyes were not bloodshot. No, he could not be drunk.

'Just so. I cannot now approach either Gloucester or Beaufort through Norfolk; but who else might I use? There is no other powerful noble in the county. All the men who would normally check the Duke's power, the men to whom men such as I would turn if Norfolk saw us ill, are in France.'

Chaucer did not reply. He drained the last of his glass of wine.

'You must miss the Earl of Suffolk greatly,' he said quite suddenly.

Miss Suffolk? But it was years since he had even thought of the Earl of Suffolk! Chaucer might be close on sober still, but he was certainly not listening. William felt his temper begin to fray and did not trouble to bind it. He said brusquely, 'To tell the truth, Chaucer, I'd not know Suffolk if I passed him in the street. Why, I doubt he's been in England once these past ten years; he has certainly not set foot in Norwich.'

'But things would be different if he had.'

'No doubt. Things would be very different if the county could boast a strong Earl of Suffolk. I wish it were so. I wish Fastolf was back, and Scales, and Oldhall. The county misses them all.'

'It does, I know it well. It is much the same in Oxfordshire. But you should also see the matter from the other side. With those men gone there is room for men like you to rise in the county: to extend your lands, and to let your influence grow with them.'

To extend your lands. Is that it? William wondered. Does he have second thoughts about the Gresham deal? Damn him if he does: I'll not go back on it now, not even to win a measure of influence with Beaufort.

'There is some truth in that, I admit. I have no cause for complaint: I've risen higher, and gained more, than my father ever dreamed I might. But a man can rise only so far, Chaucer; why, you must know that yourself. Men such as you and I cannot deal on equal terms with Gloucester and his like. Behind our backs men mutter what our fathers were. There is a greater gulf in this country than either of us can fill.'

'So there must be, with a child king and a foreign war to fight for him. But still, you have sons, do you not?'

Sons? William stared in astonishment. He had spelled

it out clearly enough by now, surely. Was Chaucer trying to indicate his reluctance to help, or was his mind so dulled by the wine that he still had not understood?

'True, I do,' he said, 'but that is no advantage in a difficulty such as this. It will be twenty years before my sons are in a position to intercede for me.'

Chaucer gave a little frown. He understands me now, William thought: he cannot fail to. He will be openly discourteous now if he does not offer to intercede for me.

'That is unfortunate. More wine, Serjeant?'

The disappointment swilled into his mouth: he could taste it, thick and acrid. He swallowed.

'Perhaps I will.'

Chaucer gestured to the boy, who crossed to take his glass and fill it. He refilled Chaucer's own glass too.

'I get my wine from Nevers,' Chaucer said conversationally. 'It has a finer taste, I think, than the wine of Gascony.'

'Excellent, indeed.' William sipped. He knew the wine was genuinely good, but the vinegary taste in his mouth drowned it. 'So you have contacts in Burgundy?'

'In the wine trade, yes; and in the army, too.'

'But not a son.' He recognised his own maliciousness, and it pleased him: the little cruelty helped to blunt the sharp edge of his disappointment.

And Chaucer recognised it too. Paston saw a thin shadow veil the other man's eyes. Then Chaucer blinked and smiled a smile of gentle triumph. 'There is no need for sons, Serjeant, when you have a daughter such as mine.'

The sun had almost set by the time William finally shook Thomas Chaucer by the hand and followed the servant boy down to the stableyard. Late, too late: he had meant to be back at Serjeant's Inn before dark. And all that time had been wasted. He had made a couple of further attempts to steer the conversation towards Beaufort, but in vain: once settled into the subject of Alice Montagu, née Chaucer, Countess of Salisbury, her father could not be prised away from it again.

He pulled his cloak more tightly around his shoulders, since the September evening was cool, and peered around ill-temperedly for Harry. Damn the groom, where was he? He stamped his feet a couple of times, ostensibly to warm them but in truth more to signal his impatience to Harry, and at last the groom emerged from the stables. In one hand he held Blazon's reins, and in the other the reins of the nag he was to ride himself.

'You have them, sir?' he asked.

'Have what?' William took Blazon's reins and patted his flank absently.

'Why, the deeds, sir. That was why you came, was it not, to collect the deeds for Gresham Manor?'

The deeds. That *was* why he had come, an age before. He glanced down at the sheaf of papers in his hand as if it surprised him to see them there.

'You'd best put those in your saddlebag, sir,' Harry prompted.

'So I had.'

He stowed them away and Harry helped him to mount. Soon afterwards they had skirted Charing Cross and were riding side by side along the Strand.

A heavy mist was beginning to rise from the Thames. It would be a cold night. But a fire would be burning in the hall of Serjeants' Inn, and the cooks had promised roast beef and stewed chicken for supper.

Perhaps it had not been so bad an afternoon after all, William thought to himself. He did have the deeds, and that was no small thing. It was not every day that he had the chance to buy a sizeable estate, let alone one less than a morning's ride from Paston village. A dozen men would have been glad to pay Chaucer a good price for it, but it was to him that it had come.

Money was well enough, but land was better. It took time to translate money into land: men knew that and weighed landowners accordingly. Perhaps bastards like Sir Thomas Tuddenham did whisper behind William's back that his father had once held his Paston estates in bond from the Manor of Gimmingham, but in twenty years' time nobody would whisper the same of John.

It was for John that he had bought Gresham. These days he did most of what he did for John. He had told the truth when he had told Thomas Chaucer that he himself could hope now to rise very little higher than he had already risen. At fifty he was a serjeant at law: perhaps within five years he would be appointed Judge in the Court of Common Pleas, but he could never aspire to the King's Bench. John could, though. Set him up with a dozen estates as good as Gresham and there would be no holding John.

Look at Alice Chaucer, he thought: daughter to a merchant, and today she is wife to the Earl of Salisbury. Chaucer has his cause for pride, true, but when all is said and done he has only a daughter. His bravado does not fool me: any man would rather have a son. Like mine. John is a fine boy, and little Edmund too. Agnes may have a tongue like a rusty knife, but she has done me well when it comes to bearing sons. When I go back to Norfolk I shall carry with me the deeds to Gresham, and I shall call John to me, and set him on my knee, and tell them over to him. Son, I shall say to him, this land shall be yours. The name of Paston is set down here in the finest of black inks: the deepest in hue and the slowest to fade. You can be proud of that name, son. And before you are finished, you and Edmund, you shall see that it is known and respected not only in Norfolk, but throughout England. Yes, and in King Henry's France too.

It still seemed to him a pity that he had made no progress with the Aslake business. But nevertheless, he thought to himself, it had been a tolerably good afternoon.

It was only when he was back at Serjeant's Inn, and the maid was setting his leg of chicken before him, that there came to mind the other matter he had forgotten to ask Thomas Chaucer. The poem: he had wanted to know what man had written that poem. A moment's thought, though, told him that he could never have asked Chaucer that. To admit that he had been struck by the poem would be to admit that he had looked over Chaucer's papers, and that would never have done.

Mind, it had been an odd poem, he thought, as he picked up the chicken and began to eat. Thomas Chaucer was a strange man, with some strange friends. A devious man, too; a stubborn man, William suspected. Perhaps it would be as well not to share any more pitchers of wine with him. There had to be some other way of gaining access to Beaufort, or to Gloucester.

Temple Stairs looked dark and slippery in the dull light of late afternoon. William shivered in his boots. He had already been waiting long enough for the cold to start to seep into his bones. A barge would come soon, surely.

He should have set out earlier, he thought with mild annoyance; or done the journey on horseback, perhaps. Quite a ride, that would be: from Serjeants' Inn across the width of the City to London Bridge, across the clattering timbers of the bridge and down along Southwark High Street. But it had been quite a walk to the river, through muddy and rutted streets, and there would be another longish walk after he alighted from the barge, from Saint Olave's landing to Fastolf Place.

A perversion, that was what it was, for Fastolf to favour Southwark over London. What could it be that led a Norfolk man to concentrate his purchases south of the Thames? Common sense would surely have made Bishopsgate or Aldgate his best bet. There was easy access from there to the Newmarket or Ipswich roads; while Southwark was no better than a den of thieves and whores, deliberately keeping itself free from the restricting rule of the City fathers.

Did the old soldier frequent the stews? William's lips twitched at the thought. Did he thieve? Surely not. Fastolf had always been tight as a Scot, but there was never a suggestion of anything underhand in his dealings. Yet he seemed to feel at home, the old fraud, among the disreputable shower of horse dealers and shipowners who congregated on Southwark's filthy street corners. No wonder. If Fastolf's gains from the wars continued to pour back home at the same rate, he would own the whole of Southwark High Street within ten years.

Ah; a barge was coming. He turned to nudge Harry, but the groom had seen it already and was slithering down the steps to hail the boatman. The passengers alighted, with much shoving and shouting, and made their way up and past the place where William stood. William craned forward. Was that four fingers Harry was holding up, or five? Too much, too much. Still, it was not outrageous, he supposed; he was too cold to wait for another barge. He nodded and made his way down the steps. Harry steadied the boat while he gathered his long, grey gown and stepped into the bows.

The journey was familiar. They slid on past the great bulks of Whitefriars, Bridewell Place and Baynards Castle; the tumbled wharves and frenzied activity downstream from Queenhythe; the barges and rowing boats that plied the river above London Bridge. Then they were through the narrow arches of the bridge and within sight of the great sailing ships, and the mass of the White Tower looming forbiddingly on the north bank against the streaked red and grey sky.

The faint smile that played around William's mouth was not in response to these sights, for he barely noticed them. His mind was full instead of his interview with the Duke of Gloucester earlier that day. It had been the second in less than two weeks; and so easy to arrange, too, once he had hit on the right line of approach. The Duchess of Norfolk had set it up for him. Gloucester was evidently susceptible to her, as he was to almost all women. She was no particular friend of William's, but she was a woman to whom it seemed to come naturally to act against her husband's wishes, and she had, as far as William had been able to tell, a positive distaste for Walter Aslake.

Gloucester was a weak and corrupt man, he thought, but all the same the Duke was easy to like. He was even easier to manipulate, unless you gave him cause to be stubborn; and William had been very careful not to do that. He had been equally careful not to appear too anxious, not to press too hard; and to ensure that he offered the Duke something in return for his undertaking to enforce judgement against Aslake.

A hint, that was all it had taken, that it might be useful to the Duke if he could depend upon a Judge in the Court of Common Pleas to oblige him from time to time. To do that would cause no difficulties in Norfolk: Gloucester had no land there, and no particular interest in the county. Nor was the Duke vindictive in his dealings generally, so it was not likely to create too many enemies for William in other quarters.

It would certainly cause no problems with his Fastolf connections. Fastolf was Bedford's man, and as such effectively neutral in the quarrel between Gloucester and Beaufort. Welles might have plenty of influence in the city, but he had none at court and was unlikely to care what William did there. He would be impressed, at least mildly, by William's elevation to the Bench. And naturally it might suit him, too, to have access to an obliging judge . . . William smiled to himself again as he began to imagine some of the favours he might perform, the rewards he might reap, when his appointment was confirmed.

He was still smiling when he reached Fastolf Place. He was smiling as he dismissed Harry and watched him head for the servants' quarters; as he walked down the dark corridor; as he made his way into the hall. The smoke from the fire caught at his eyes and throat as he entered, and the smile dissolved into a choking cough.

When his eyes cleared, he saw that the room was crowded. It reeked of ale and smelled like a cookshop.

He pushed his way to the dais, expecting to find Welles there. He was. William's eyes moved around the trestle, taking in the men who were with him.

John Payn was there as always, scowling as usual: he was Fastolf's Southwark bailiff, and responsible for maintaining Fastolf Place and his other landholdings south of the Thames. John Kirtling, dark and elegant, was Fastolf's banker, and William took the brace of men in rich Lombard-style costume who sat at either side of him to be other bankers. There was young Will Calthorp, a Norfolk man like so many of Welles' and Fastolf's cronies, a ward and servant of the Duke. A handsome lad, Calthorp, lithe and fit, full of charm and laughter, but a lightweight who had never given William any indication that his head was capable of holding a serious thought. In that he was as dissimilar as could be from his neighbour, Secret Poursuivant, who did not laugh, and who looked often as if he thought hard and carefully, though he kept those thoughts strictly within his own head.

William's eyes moved on past Secret, to stop at another familiar figure who sat at Welles' left hand. The last remnants of his smile evaporated.

'Why, Serjeant Paston,' said Thomas Wetherby, Lord Mayor of Norwich, rising to his feet and holding out his hand.

William extended his own hand, reluctantly. He withdrew it as soon as he decently could and turned to frown at Welles. Damn the grocer!

Welles met his eyes and smiled disarmingly.

'I thought you would come tonight, Serjeant. There's room next to Calthorp. Sit. We'll be eating soon.'

Calthorp, hearing his name, interrupted his conversation to glance across at Welles, and in response to the grocer's gesture he dutifully shuffled along the bench. William stared at the blank expanse of board for a moment, then he gathered up his gown, lifted his feet one by one across the bench, and claimed his place.

So Welles had thought he would come. In fact – why beat the air when the pheasant was in the grass? – Welles had damn well planned to have him and Wetherby there on the same evening. And Welles had surely known how he would take that, because it was only a fortnight since they had argued over Wetherby's slimy crony Sir Thomas Tuddenham.

William had encountered Tuddenham at Fastolf Place three times in less than a month. That had been three times too many, and he had told Welles so in plain, hard words. Doubtless Tuddenham did favours for Welles, but that was no more than any man – William included – would do when the carrot of Fastolf's fortune was dangled in front of him. Even if Tuddenham was (as his reputation made him out to be) a competent land agent, William could have named a dozen others just as capable. He had never been able to see why either of those factors should have outweighed the evident disadvantages of dealing with Tuddenham and his nasty associates, particularly when one of the disadvantages was his, Serjeant William Paston's, loudly expressed displeasure.

At this, John Welles had laughed. He had even repeated the tale Tuddenham had told him of Clement Paston serving as bondsman to the Manor of Gimmingham, and in a tone which had made it impossible for William to tell whether or not he believed it. And when William had stormed to the door and slammed it behind him, Welles had not even come running after him: because he had known, curse him, that William would have to come back. Now that he had lost Norfolk's favour, and Norfolk's business, he could not possibly afford to antagonise the man who was his only contact with Sir John Fastolf.

He had, at that, waited until he knew Tuddenham had ridden for Norwich before returning to Fastolf Place. And this was Welles' response: to invite Thomas Wetherby there to meet him instead.

It was – no, in fairness he had to admit that it was most likely not a deliberate attempt to alienate him. Welles did not work in that way. It had been done as the smile had implied: not because of him, but merely regardless of his opinion. I know what you think, that

69

smile had said, but I am not prepared to admit that I agree with you. Thomas Wetherby is useful to me, as are all these men. I shall continue to use him for as long as it pleases me to do so.

He could not let it pass, even so. He would have to speak to Welles again; but he could not do so in front of Thomas Wetherby. Nor would he demean himself by sulking, or give Welles cause to accuse him of bigotry by refusing to speak to the Mayor. So he turned to Wetherby and said in a cool voice, 'It's rarely that we see you down in London on business, sir.'

Wetherby settled back on the bench. He was a plain-featured man, slim and middling in height, brown-haired, who took on presence only when he spoke. His voice was deep, loud and confident, with a Norfolk accent that seemed more pronounced when set against London speech.

'In truth, I came – oh, mainly for business.' He turned to Welles and smiled conspiratorially, as if the two of them shared some secret knowledge of his real reasons for coming to London. 'I fear the Serjeant will never support me in that line, John. He suspects me of turning the city ordinances in favour of the county wool merchants.'

I do not suspect it, William thought to himself; I am certain of it, and you know that all too well. I suspect you rather of shady dealing at the customs in Lynn and Yarmouth. I am all but sure you have had a hand in the dealings of the Nowell gang, too, and I'd not be surprised to learn that you are hand in glove with Aslake. That is not merely a matter of twisting arms in Council meetings: it links you to thefts, extortions, even a murder or two. And you know that as well as I, John Welles, because I have told it to you many times, in considerable detail.

'You deny it?' he asked Wetherby curtly.

'I argue that we have no choice. Norwich will never thrive unless it continues to handle the bulk of the county's wool exports. We must oblige the merchants or they will take their trade to London, or direct to Yarmouth.'

Welles gave a little snort and broke into the conversation before the animosity between the two men came any closer to the surface. 'This is no night for business. War, now, that's a subject for any man. I reckon this business at Orleans will prove the undoing of Bedford's army.'

The news had reached London two days before that the Earl of Salisbury had finally decided to besiege Orleans: a decision that had once been considered unthinkable, for the Duke of Orleans was a captive in England and it was contrary to every accepted law of chivalry to attack his home city while he was not free to defend it. Men had spoken of little else ever since. Whether it should have been done; whether it had been Bedford or Salisbury who had made the final decision; whether it could be done successfully, and what the outcome might be: on every issue there was scope for violent disagreement.

John Welles knows that, William thought to himself, with a sudden rush of annoyance. He pretends that he is steering us to safe waters, but that is not so: he is simply casting about for a subject upon which we can be relied to argue without fouling his own yard in the process. He means it to form his evening's entertainment. Damn him to hell and back: I shall not take his bait, not this time.

'Maybe so,' he said offhandedly. 'You spoke of food, John? And there's ale to be had, I'll bet?' As he said this he glimpsed Meg, the cook's girl, pushing her way through the door from the corridor, and he turned to wave a hand at her, leaving Wetherby to take up Welles' challenge.

Which he promptly did. 'Not so, John,' he said firmly. 'True, the siege should have been started sooner; but better now than never. We need decisive actions that will extend our territory. I've always distrusted Bedford's caution. If the last King Henry were still alive he would have taken the whole country long before this.'

John Welles shook his head. 'That's not a fair argument, Thomas. Henry would have commanded a stronger army, and one with a good French contingent.

71

Even then, remember the sieges of his day, Harfleur, Rouen and the rest. Months they took, and wore the army to a scarecrow. That is no easy way to wage war.'

William heard this; and frowned. There was a surprising ring of conviction behind Welles' words. It seemed to him that the grocer was not just striking a pose for the sake of sparring with Wetherby, but expressing a deeply held view. And such a view: William would never have dreamed of attributing those opinions to him.

Curiosity made him change his mind and join in the argument. And on Wetherby's side at that, he thought, grimly amused at himself.

'But John, this policy has Fastolf's favour, does it not? From what I hear, the land's as bare as a corpse when the worms have done their work. The army must look for rewards; and they must come from the city.'

Welles grunted and shook his head.

'If you heard such words put into Fastolf's mouth, then you heard them from a man who does not know him. He's been set against the siege from the very start. Ask Secret.'

'I find that hard to credit.'

'Then you shall hear it for yourself.'

Welles promptly reached down the table and plucked at the poursuivant's sleeve. William opened his mouth to tell him not to trouble, but it was too late: a moment later half a dozen men had shifted along the bench, and Secret had slipped into the newly vacated space next to Welles.

'So Fastolf and Salisbury are at crossed swords over this business of Orleans,' Wetherby said.

The poursuivant fixed a thoughtful look on the Mayor. 'Sir John crosses swords only with his enemies.'

'Then let us phrase it differently,' William said curtly. He understood Secret's caution, but at the same time it annoyed him: almost everything the poursuivant did annoyed him. A sly man, Secret, he thought: his mind is as messy as that filthy tabard he wears. 'Sir John has opinions of his own on the siege of Orleans,' he continued.

'Sir John has opinions on many subjects,' replied Secret.

'And he voices them?'

'From time to time.'

'Then it is your role, is it not, to tell them to us?'

Secret opened his eyes wide and returned William's look, not guilelessly, but with transparent forethought.

'Sir,' he said, 'I deal not in opinions, but in facts.'

Welles cuffed him amiably. 'Come on, you son of a sheepdog, tell the Serjeant about Fastolf's report.'

'Ah, the report.' The poursuivant turned his eyes briefly to Welles, then back to Wetherby, then finally to William. 'That is a fact, the report.'

'A report to whom?'

'To the King's Council.'

Secret set his elbows on the trestle and began to outline the contents of Fastolf's report. The knight argued, he explained, that the Lancastrian army in France should act as a home army defending its territory rather than as an English invading force. Fastolf claimed that only by winning the consent of the French to King Henry's rule could peace ever come. He condemned siege warfare as an invaders' tactic, one that caused great hardship to both sides and thus strengthened the opposition of ordinary men and women. It could not bring about a lasting conquest, which would have to come by winning over the barons and landowners, or replacing them with Englishmen who could reconcile their tenants to the regime.

There was a short silence when the poursuivant finished speaking, then Thomas Wetherby gave a harsh laugh. 'So says Sir John Fastolf, Baron of Silly Guillem,' he said in a mocking voice.

Secret stared back, straight faced. 'Sir John takes his new title seriously. He buys land in Normandy as well as farms in Norfolk and tenements in Southwark.'

William shook his head. 'That's as may be. But Fastolf

73

is in the war for gain, and he will make no easy gains from such a scorched-earth policy.'

'Nor would he at Orleans,' Welles said. 'That's no treasure-house of a fortress: it's a city full of starving men and women, hard in the taking and poor in the winning, I'd guess. Do you imagine Fastolf covets a ransom for the Bastard of Orleans? That would be no prize by his standards. It's to dukes that Sir John looks to fill his coffers, but the Duke of Orleans is a captive already.'

'There are other commanders in the Valois army. Richemont would be a fat prize. Or perhaps Alençon will bring his men to the city's relief; perhaps Fastolf will take him again, as he did at Verneuil.'

'Perhaps Alençon will take Fastolf,' Welles said with a grin.

'No, John, I'll not credit that argument. It may be no easy task they've set themselves, but Salisbury's men are still unbeatable.'

Into William's mind, quite suddenly, came the picture of Thomas Chaucer's face, and the complacent satisfaction it had shown when he had spoken of his son-in-law's record as commander of Bedford's army. Chaucer, now: he is a good judge of men, he thought; he married his daughter well, even if he is too fond of showing that he knows it. Salisbury is a great soldier, and Talbot; and Fastolf too, although many men take him for no more than an old moneybags. Only fools speak in this defeatist way: Wetherby was right when he claimed that caution has all but killed our French campaign.

'It's trust in our army that we need,' he went on, with growing conviction. 'A willingness to risk all, as we did at Agincourt and Verneuil, in the knowledge that our men will not let us down. Salisbury's judgement has proved itself often enough to satisfy any sane man. He'd not take on the task of besieging Orleans unless he thought the city winnable.'

'Winnable perhaps,' Welles agreed. 'But at what cost?'

Wetherby slapped his hand on the trestle and threw back his head with a laugh. 'You grumble about cost, John, when you see Fastolf's profits from the wars? When we watch merchants like yourself growing fat on the soldiers' backs? We've not bled France dry yet.'

'If the wars go on at this rate we shall, before the King is of age.'

'Not with Bedford behind the campaigns,' William persisted. 'The Regent is no slapdash conqueror. No man doubts that he is an able steward for the King.'

John Welles shook his head and slid his hands together, twisting them so that their burden of rings winked in the candlelight. 'Even so, there are men who say that he is risking too much in this venture,' he said soberly. 'And there are others who say that Bedford opposed it from the first, and that Salisbury is undertaking the siege as a direct challenge to his authority.'

Some men had said that in London, true; but none of them had been men whom William would have believed. He had not thought that men would say it in France. Was Welles telling him that he had this information direct from Fastolf? If so, it would have to be accepted.

Mind, he thought, nothing comes direct to England from Fastolf. All Welles' information, and all mine too, comes through Secret Poursuivant. He glanced at Secret, with half an idea that the poursuivant's face would confirm or deny this story. The poursuivant was not looking at him. Secret was not looking at Welles, either: he appeared to be listening to John Payn, on his other side.

What Secret said earlier, at least, is true, William thought to himself. He deals in facts. Ostensibly he never expresses an opinion, and he relates other men's opinions only when he must. But every tale changes in the telling; and every time he tells a tale he chooses for himself which facts to pass on, and which to keep to himself. I wish sometimes – and never more than now –that we had another messenger from France, that we might also hear these tales in a different version.

He thought of asking the poursuivant outright whether he had it from Fastolf that Bedford was opposed to the siege. Secret would have answered him honestly, he reckoned: he had never caught the poursuivant in a direct lie, it was in more subtle ways that he was not to be trusted. But at the same time he was conscious of Thomas Wetherby eyeing him from across the trestle, and he knew that he could afford to do or say nothing that might strengthen the Mayor's position within Welles' circle, and weaken his own.

'Men say many things,' he said at last. 'At least, they do so at the start of a venture. At its finish their tales tend to change. We should wait until the end of the siege, John, and then we shall know which of them have spoken sense.'

'There's sense in what you all say,' John Welles returned easily. 'Though I prefer my own sense to yours, nevertheless.' He raised his voice a fraction. 'Will, we've not heard your opinion yet. Are you for the siege, or against it?'

Calthorp, like Secret, had been talking with Payn, but he swung round in response to Welles' question. His bright, facile smile shone indiscriminately on the group of older men. 'You asked me what, John?'

'The siege of Orleans. Do you have an opinion about it?'

'To tell the truth, I've none at all.' He grinned again. 'I'll be glad if it proves a victory, mind; and sad if it leads to defeat.'

'That's sane enough,' Wetherby murmured.

'I'm not claiming it to be profound.'

'I doubt any of us reckon our opinions to be that,' Welles said. He smiled at Calthorp as he spoke. William smiled too: it came automatically to him, as if the triviality of Calthorp's response were a relief after the intensity of his discussion with Wetherby and Welles. But still, he thought to himself, the boy did himself no favours: he reckoned to use his charm where he would have been wiser to employ his intelligence. He showed every sign of possessing some, and he would need it when he came into his estates. To fall into the habit of playing the fool was dangerous: once adopted, it was none so easy to break.

'Here's Meg,' said Wetherby.

The cook's girl had just appeared, with a platter piled high with chickens. The arrival of the food would have blighted the discussion even if they had been anxious to pursue it, but it seemed that none of them were: the conversation trailed to a halt as the joints of chicken, and the bread trenchers that followed, were passed down the trestle.

A moment later Fastolf's pipers emerged from the servants' hall, stationed themselves underneath the high windows, and began to play their jigs. To William, this had always been the least pleasurable aspect of the evenings he spent at Fastolf Place: he had no taste for music, and a positive distaste for this relentlessly jolly stuff that had briefly enchanted Fastolf during his period in Ireland, and then rapidly exasperated him after he had brought the pipers back to England with him.

Does Welles really enjoy it? he wondered. Welles always made the pipers play whenever he entertained at Fastolf Place in its master's name, but it was never clear to William whether this was out of pleasure in the music, a crude form of policy – discussions around the trestle often grew overheated, and the music invariably worked to kill them off – or an even more crude conviction that since the pipers could not be paid off without Fastolf's orders (which had either not been solicited, or not been forthcoming) they ought to be made to earn their keep.

He ate. The chicken was very hot and very fresh. Fastolf had always been a tight-fisted man, and Welles himself was never known to entertain in his own right, but at that time the food at Fastolf Place was always excellent. The drink was plentiful too and William drank several mugs full of strong ale. The pipers made their bows and retreated. The evening mellowed.

Calthorp and Payn and Kirtling took turns to tell long, crude jokes. Wetherby laughed uproariously. The Italian bankers smiled politely. Secret sat quietly, drinking steadily, turning sometimes to Payn or Wetherby and asking them questions in a low voice.

William watched all of this. He could feel the ale blurring the edges of his mind, but there was still a sharp point of watchfulness at the centre, focussed on Wetherby and Secret. Occasionally he glanced at Welles, and Welles eventually intercepted one of these glances and said in a cheerful voice, 'So you had a letter yesterday from Agnes.'

'So I did,' William murmured; and then his thoughts sharpened and he asked himself how Welles could have known that. Who had delivered the letter? He had not seen the man, he remembered: Harry had been handed the letter at the gate of Serjeants' Inn and had brought it in to him.

It had been one of the carriers, most likely: two or three of them travelled regularly between London and Norwich. Presumably whoever it was had brought letters from Norwich to Welles, too. In that case there would be nothing in his own, bar the domestic gossip, that Welles did not already know.

'You'll know about Erpingham, then,' Welles said, confirming the accuracy of this thought-trail.

'Erpingham? No; what should I know? Mind, Agnes is at Paston, not in the city: hers is family gossip, no more.'

'Why, that he is dead.'

'Dead!' William echoed. The news surprised him, not because Erpingham had been young and fit and unlikely to die – on the contrary, he had been an elderly man – but in the general way in which any death not presaged through illness comes as a shock to the survivors.

'Four days since.'

'No, I did not know.' He said this dispassionately, but in his heart there was a sudden strong outpouring of glee. Erpingham dead! That would hammer the final nails into the coffin of Aslake's crusade against him, for Erpingham had been Aslake's intermediary with the Duke of Norfolk.

The feeling was no sooner acknowledged in his mind than regretted: it was mean-spirited of him to rejoice at the death of an old acquaintance, and he knew it. Hastily he mouthed a few phrases of sorrow that would soften the coldness of his initial reaction.

Wetherby said, 'The Guild bury him next Monday in the Cathedral. Will you return to Norwich for it, Serjeant?'

I ought to, William thought. His business in London was virtually complete: there was nothing that his clerks could not finish for him. It would not do for anyone to imagine that he still bore a grudge against Erpingham; and nor did he need to bear one now, for he had gained the upper hand over Aslake even before this news reached him. And it was a ruling of the Guild of Saint George that every member should attend the funeral of every other member, or face a heavy fine.

Wetherby was a member too. Following this thought through, William said, 'So you plan to travel up yourself?'

'That I will. I had intended in any event to leave London tomorrow. You should join us: the roads are dangerous these days. There was a robbery near Thetford only last week, two men killed. It makes sense to travel in a large party.'

'Where do you ride from?'

'We'll be meeting at Bishopsgate. You know the inn just outside the gate, at the corner of Houndsditch?'

'I'll see you there, an hour after dawn.'

'He can't complain, old Erpingham,' Welles said cheerfully. 'Not every soldier dies in his bed. And he was what, seventy? Seventy-two? It's hard to remember that he fought at Agincourt. Things were different then. I'll tell you what, I'll give you a shilling to buy a candle for me.'

*

William found there to be nearly thirty men in Wetherby's party. Most of them were merchants but there were also a couple of soldiers returning from France and a gaggle of Blackfriars bound for the Norwich house. It was too large a party to fear trouble, but all the laymen carried swords, and even the friars had knives at their belts.

He knew a few of the men by sight, but none well. He tried to keep clear of the slight, brown-cloaked figure of Thomas Wetherby, but the Mayor brought his horse across before they were out of sight of Bishopsgate, and he could see no option but to accept the company he was being offered.

Wetherby was not alone. With him was John Heydon, a young lawyer, fair-haired, with eager eyes and a chubby face. William had heard reports of Heydon — some of them questionable reports — but he had never before spoken to the man.

'You're not a member of the Guild?' he asked.

'You'll not have known me for one, Serjeant, not yet. But that I am: Thomas persuaded me to join this summer.'

Persuaded? Nobody needed persuading to join the Guild of Saint George, not when every powerful man in the county was a member. It was his fellow guildsmen that Wetherby would have needed to persuade to accept this insignificant young lawyer. Presumably he had had his reasons. 'I'll look to know you better in the future, in that case,' William said.

'Doubtless you will. I hear we are to be neighbours.'

'Neighbours?'

'You've bought Gresham from Thomas Chaucer, have you not? My manor is at Baconsthorpe, not three miles hence.'

'Is it now,' William said drily.

The three men talked of North Norfolk, innocuously enough, as they rode over Lea marshes and up the Lea valley, following the straight line of the Roman road that led to Waltham and Ware. William soon discovered that John Heydon was no farmer: he evidently left his lands to the bailiff's care and spent most of his time in the city. In Wetherby's company, much of it. He mentioned other names too, all of which caused William to set him down as Wetherby's puppet. Presumably he was being groomed to take on a civic appointment such as Recorder or City Sheriff that would bolster the Mayor's position in the city.

The conversation seemed to be heading inexorably towards city politics. William tried to divert it: he had no wish to argue with Wetherby at the start of their journey. But both Wetherby and Heydon appeared quite content with the direction the talk was taking, and it was Wetherby who eventually raised the sensitive subject of the disputes between Norwich Council and the Church. There were nearly a dozen issues in contention, all of which had kept Norfolk lawyers in business for twenty years and more.

'You sat on a commission yourself, did you not, the last time they tried to resolve this quarrel over the fishing rights at Trowse?' he asked William.

'Some years ago.'

'The word is now that there is to be a new commission next year.'

'Tempers are running high over that,' Heydon said, with a braying laugh. 'The Prior will never forgive Norwich men for their little expedition this summer.'

The laugh annoyed William. He had always supported the Prior over the fishing rights.

'The Prior is hardly to be blamed,' he retorted. 'That damned gang of ruffians took twelve pounds' worth of fish from the river and millpond in an afternoon. They dragged it with nets. It will be years before the stock recovers.'

'So it is true, what I heard: that you will support the Prior?' Wetherby asked.

William gave him a cold look. 'Like any lawyer,' he said, 'I shall remain neutral until the arguments have been made. Further, I doubt if I shall even sit on that commission.'

'You underestimate your reputation, Serjeant Paston. I have no doubt you will be appointed.'

'It is not a question of reputation. On issues such as this it is necessary to select different commissioners each time, or they will be seen to divide into parties.'

'Men know you, surely, as a friend of the Prior?'

'I hope not; not in the sense that they know you as a friend of the city.'

Wetherby gave him a sudden smile. 'You follow Norwich affairs less closely than you think, Serjeant Paston. I am known to support the Prior's cause myself.'

That was a surprise, too much of one for William to succeed in hiding the fact. He turned his amazement into a considering look, then said slowly, 'That will win you no friends among the Aldermen.'

'On the contrary. There is a substantial party now which claims that the city is pressing the Church too hard. On most of the issues at stake, I suspect the Church will be proven to be right. My argument is that we should resolve the questions now instead of pursuing these disputes for years to come.'

'There are some issues for which there is no resolution that will satisfy both parties.'

'Then one party must be dissatisfied,' Wetherby said bluntly. 'I have obliged the city on many issues; but I prefer to work for its long-term benefit, not for short-term gain. On this, I intend to press hard for the Prior's cause.' He paused. 'Publicly,' he continued, 'you are right to appear even-handed. But privately, I would be glad to be assured of your support.'

'I can hardly give it in such circumstances.'

Wetherby stared at him, as if he were hoping to read more from William's face than was apparent from his words. William turned from him deliberately. He began to question John Heydon about the bailiffs at Gresham.

Wetherby rode alongside him for a few moments more, then he spurred his horse and rode up to join the soldiers who were a few paces ahead. William made a quick gesture to Harry, and the groom, never slow to catch his meaning, moved to take the Mayor's place. Thomas Wetherby did not speak to him again that day.

They spent the night at Newmarket, and at supper William and Harry sat among the friars. They ate in silence and William had leisure to think over Wetherby's words.

It was not personal, his dislike of Thomas Wetherby. The man could be pleasant company, he had seen as much that morning. Nor was it based on Wetherby's policies as Mayor. Of those he actually knew only a little: too little, he thought ruefully, or he would not have misjudged the merchant's position over the Prior. He had never had the time or the inclination to trouble himself with the squabbles on the City Council: his political concern was centred on Parliament and the King's Council, and he learned of the city dealings only when the issues came to court and he found himself professionally involved in judging them.

No, it was Wetherby's aggressive behaviour and his questionable associates that had drawn William's venom down upon him. That was why it disturbed him to realise that on the issue of the Prior and the Council, as in the argument at Fastolf Place the night before, he and Wetherby found themselves on the same side.

He could not change his own position. Legally, he believed the Prior of Norwich, the Prioress of Carrow Abbey and the other church people who antagonised the city to be in the right on almost every point; therefore it was his duty to find for them. He only hoped that if and when he did so, he would not also be taken to have supported Thomas Wetherby.

It is the supreme irony of a justice's lot, he thought to himself, that he must show himself to be neutral, and yet he must perpetually make decisions which favour one of two opposing parties. He did not want two opposing parties to take shape on the City Council. But if that were to happen, he could not help feeling that he would much prefer to support the party to which Thomas Wetherby did not belong.

It would be still better, however, to remain neutral; and he had spoken the truth in saying that he did not expect to be appointed to the new commission. With reason: commissioners were appointed by the King's Council, and he had been working on his contacts in the Council to ensure that this time he would not be one of them.

That went some way to allaying his unease; but some of it remained. Till then, William thought to himself, whatever Thomas Wetherby had done to the good or the bad he had done almost exclusively within Norwich. Wetherby was not a poor man, but he was no great landowner: he had no standing in the county. He had had few dealings, to William's knowledge, with the class of men who became County Sheriffs and Shire Knights, the men who sat on legal commissions. But now he had made an attempt – an open attempt, in the hearing of John Heydon – to ensure himself of William's support.

Was there, might there be, any deeper significance to that move? Was it conceivable that Thomas Wetherby might now be aiming higher? Was there any possibility that he might try to create a party division, not only on the City Council, but in the county at large?

It was the scantiest of evidence. But it tied in with other evidence, not least with Thomas Wetherby's presence at John Welles' table. And that was disturbing, because it was in his own interests, William was quite certain, to try to ensure that this did not happen.

The whole matter annoyed him intensely. For weeks, he thought to himself, every throw of the dice had fallen in his favour. The deal over Gresham: fair to Chaucer, mind, but more than fair to him. The promise of Gloucester's favour, a seat on the Bench and a chance to nail down Aslake. Even Erpingham's death, a final confirmation of the fall in Aslake's fortunes. And now he stumbled over this, this sticky pot which Thomas

Wetherby was threatening to stir and stir until the mess at the bottom began to burn. He could not clean it out; all he could do was try to damp the flames over which it cooked.

With that aim in mind he returned to Wetherby's side for short periods on the remaining two days of their journey and forced himself to talk civilly to the merchant. Wetherby's caution had evidently been aroused by his earlier stand and the Mayor made no further mention of politics.

Their roads parted five miles south of the city. Wetherby was making direct for his home in the outlying village of Intwood; William for Princes Inn, his town house off Elm Hill, only a few yards from the Cathedral where Erpingham's funeral would be held.

The party had ridden fast, but it was growing dark before its remnants crossed the Yare Bridge at Cringleford and set off up the last shallow hill that hid Norwich from their view. As they breasted it the city lay beneath them, wrapped in its grey flint walls, the castle dominant on its green motte at the core and the slim spire of the Cathedral soaring skywards amid a forest of church towers. Slicing through the circuit of the city, the narrow ribbon of the River Wensum, dull as pewter in the evening light, came round to join the Yare as it curved round from Cringleford to the east of the city, and slid off, limpid, towards the coast.

Candlelight shone already from within a few of the larger houses and brightened the coloured glass in the church windows. The riders spurred their weary horses so as to reach Berstrete Gate before the watch closed it for the night.

Once inside the city William loosed his hands on the reins and let Blazon amble down the familiar, darkening streets. The road was wide and straight as far as the Castle. He, Harry and the friars skirted to the left of the mound and cut down through the narrow alleys of the lawyers' quarter that divided the Castle from the massive bulk of the Blackfriars.

Princes Inn served both as home for the Pastons and as workplace for William and his clerks – more than a dozen of them, for his legal business was fast expanding. The main hall lay with its long side along the street. A narrow alley led past the heavy oak door in the gable end and through to a cobbled courtyard across which were the stables and the low room where the clerks worked. The hall was darkened – there had been no time to call Agnes or the servants back from Paston – but a light shone from the clerks' room. William made for this, leaving Harry to see to the horses.

He pushed open the door and saw that the light came from a fire, burning low in the hearth at the end of the room. At the high desk closest to the fire a man stood hunched over a sheet of parchment, quill in hand. A small boy stood by his side, holding a single candle so that its sphere of light shone on the sheet and on the sparse strands of red hair arrayed across the smooth dome of the man's head.

The man looked up at the noise of William shutting the door behind him and knocking the mud from his boots. It was William Yelverton, a lawyer who had once been William's pupil and was still his regular collaborator, though he had recently started a law business of his own.

He promptly downed his quill and moved forwards, hands outstretched. 'William. I'd thought you might come tonight, but it grew so late I feared you would have missed the gates.'

'Wetherby invited me to Intwood for the night, but I reckoned we would safely beat the watch.'

'Wetherby?' Yelverton glanced cautiously round at the boy, as if to see if that comment had drawn any reaction from him, then turned back to William. 'You'll not stay here? The hall's cold, and it's late to start a fire there. Come with me. I shall finish my draft in the morning. Jane can find supper and a bed for both you and Harry.'

William shook his head impatiently. He unfastened

his heavy cloak, threw it over a desk and moved towards the fire. 'Miles,' he said to the boy, 'run down to the Maid's Head and bring us three pots of ale. No, William, there are papers I must look over, and it will be best to do it tonight. I'll send Harry to the inn for supper. We can set our pallets down in here and build the fire higher. It'll be but for a night or two, before I ride for Paston.'

The boy Miles had gone, but Yelverton still lowered his voice as he said, 'So you rode with Wetherby?'

'And a large party. It was an illuminating journey. Tell me, William – what do you know of John Heydon?'

'Heydon? Less than I might. He's had work from Lord Scales, I heard, but he is Sir Thomas Tuddenham's man.'

'Tuddenham's man? Is he, now? I found him in Wetherby's company, as close as a duckling to its mother.'

'That's none so surprising. He's young, and struggling still: he'll doubtless take work anywhere he can find it. And there is plenty of work to be done for the Mayor and Aldermen, no doubt.'

'No doubt.' William stared into the fire, then picked up a poker and began to stir the ashes. 'He is a member of the Guild, Heydon.'

'You ask me that, or tell me?'

'I tell you.'

'Then you can look them out tomorrow, at the funeral: Tuddenham, and Heydon, and Wetherby.'

William withdrew the poker and gazed for a moment at the end of it, glowing red. 'So I can,' he said.

3

ENGLAND

Down the Thames from London, set in rolling hills and
ensconced in a green park, was a small palace showing
the signs of recent and continuing renovations. Once
the favourite home of Henry the Fourth, King of
England, it had now passed into the hands of his son
Humphrey, Duke of Gloucester, who called it his
Pleasance, or Bella Court.

Since there was little that was beautiful about the
court of the child King, Gloucester had chosen to make
his own elegant court at Greenwich. There the Thames
made a deep bend to the south, bringing a swift channel
of water close to the bank; into it had been built out
wooden wharves tipped with painted and carved poles,
to which were tied the canopied pleasure barges that
ferried the Duke's companions to and from London and
Westminster. Set before the house, which fronted on to
the river, was a parterre of low hedges and high rose
bushes; hidden more privately among the rambling
wings of the mansion could be found courtyards with
sanded paths and beds of clary and gillyflowers, hyssop
and sorrel, marjoram and feverfew. It pleased Gloucester to dabble in medicine; it pleased his Duchess to
invite wise women who knew the uses of the least
familiar plants, taught her to mix simples and
(whispered her enemies) prepared her love potions.

Italian musicians played in the galleries of the Pleasance; Flemish tapestries enlivened its walls, and French
and Venetian manuscripts filled its library, for Duke

Humphrey was – by English standards – a cultured man. Gloucester's companions, when he was at liberty to select them for himself, were urbane and civilised, capable of cruel wit and complex acrostics. When affairs of state forced him to, however, he condescended to invite to his Pleasance the powerful nobles who helped him to maintain his tenuous position at the head of his nephew's Great Council in England.

It was a cool day in early October, and the barges rocked restlessly on a slate-grey river; but a shaft of late sunlight lit the roses in the gardens, and the occasional high laugh brightened the air of the winter hall. A fire blazed in the hearth, for Gloucester despised economies and disliked the cold; and the owner of the Pleasance, his elbow on the carved wooden mantle, was discoursing to a little group who stood around him.

'A tedious man, Serjeant Paston.' Gloucester's drawl was casual, adding no depth to the weak insult. John Mowbray, Duke of Norfolk, turned unhurriedly from the conversation about hounds he had been pursuing with Arthur, Gloucester's young bastard son.

'Unutterably so,' he agreed in a careful imitation of Gloucester's tone.

Will Calthorp could see a suggestion of laughter in the curve of Gloucester's mouth; a hint of mischief in the limpid, pale grey eyes. Norfolk had not noticed these telltale signs, he reckoned. Gloucester was preparing a trap for Norfolk, and now he would bait it.

No; Gloucester had not sufficient patience to dig it deep. 'But an entertaining business,' he went on, 'this affair with Aslake.'

'Do tell us, Humphrey,' Katharine, Duchess of Norfolk, said, with a conspiratorial smile at Gloucester, as if they were sharing their amusement at seeing Norfolk caught out of step.

'A murder.'

Lady Katharine's face fell in mock disappointment, as if she had expected something more exotic. Gloucester went on, 'On New Year's Eve. Spilling the wassail bowl.'

'So the tedious Serjeant Paston was murdered?' asked the Duchess of Gloucester.

'Eleanor, my dear,' her husband retorted, 'you are sometimes less perceptive than you are beautiful. We saw Serjeant Paston yesterday, and today is not New Year's Eve. No, this is old news, years old, though it has its diverting touches. The victim was another Norfolk man, with his family and servants. Aslake and his gang dragged them from the house and up to the gallows.'

'A dull old hanging?' Lady Katharine teased.

'Nothing so workaday: a dismembering. Quite disgusting, I was assured.'

'No details?'

'Disappointed? That shall be your task, Norfolk: to extract them from the assassin for our delectation.'

'Why were they taken to the gallows,' Lady Eleanor asked, 'if they were not hanged?'

'Because the murderers forgot . . .' – Gloucester paused theatrically, with evident relish – '. . . that they had no rope.'

He, Arthur and the ladies exploded with laughter. Will gave a polite smile, as was appropriate to his place just outside their circle, and watched to see how long it would take Norfolk to join in. It was a full minute before he managed a splutter. Then he clearly thought again, and fell silent. As the hilarity died down he said quietly, 'There really is no proof that it was Aslake.'

There was contempt in the look Duke Humphrey turned on him. Will sympathised with Gloucester's exasperation: he often felt the same himself. John Mowbray was a scrawny, weak-chinned man, with a yellowed skin and shifting eyes. At thirty-five he could have been taken for a man in his fifties; and he seemed to think like an old man too, slowly and haltingly, frequently losing the thread of his argument. Tedious. Serjeant Paston, grey in dress and grey in manner, was indeed tedious, a fact of which Will had been reminded only the evening before; but he reckoned the Duke of

Norfolk to be infinitely more so, particularly to those condemned to spend long hours in his company.

But the Duke of Norfolk's favour was valuable; indeed to Will, who was still uncertain where his future might lie, it was all but indispensable. Gloucester had frequently spoken and acted as if he considered nobody's favour indispensable to one in his high position, but on this occasion he, too, seemed to take account of the need to keep on the right side of open insult. He swallowed the sarcastic retort that his expression promised and instead said in a mild tone, 'Perhaps so. But there is proof that Aslake threatened Paston with the same fate.'

Norfolk slowly moved his head from side to side. 'Not so; it was his man who wrote the bills that were posted up in Norwich, not Aslake himself.'

'And Aslake had nothing to do with it?'

There was a dangerous innocence in Gloucester's voice. Norfolk could not handle that tone: he had no weapons that he could use against this subtle baiting. His agitation was clear in his blinking eyes, and in the stammer with which he replied. 'N-nothing, my Lord. I have been assured of that. He is perfectly innocent, and yet Paston had him clapped in jail. He bribed the jurors so he would win the case.'

'Clapped him in jail! Bribed the jurors!' Gloucester repeated gleefully. 'What a resourceful gentleman Serjeant Paston is. What will, what determination, to be undaunted by a little difficulty such as the lack of any proof! I reckon he deserves a reward. I shall make him a judge.'

The laughter round his mouth faded and in its place there appeared an unremitting look that held Norfolk fast. Norfolk made no response.

'Or did you have different ideas?' Gloucester asked softly.

Norfolk's mouth worked nervously into something resembling a smile. 'N-not at all, my Lord. He would make an excellent judge.'

'He will; I am sure of that. He has all the necessary attributes. He is dull, but efficient. A great believer in the legal processes. Influential in Norfolk.' Gloucester's gaze raked John Mowbray from feet to crown, and then held the man's eyes. 'He *is* influential in Norfolk?'

'Undoubtedly, my Lord.'

'Like yourself.' Lady Eleanor relapsed into more giggles, but this time Lady Katharine did not join her. The look Gloucester turned on her was notably cold and she stifled her laughter hurriedly.

Her husband took pity on her. 'And now,' he announced portentously, 'I shall divert you all by relating to you, in execrable rhyme, Master Walter Aslake's man's threats to disembowel Serjeant William Paston. Et cetera.'

* * *

> Serjeant Paston you beware
> As Grice was killed, so shall you fare
> For finding against honest men
> We'll get your clerks and murder them.

The grisly opening of Walter Aslake's man's catalogue of threats to Serjeant Paston had stuck in Will's head; he found himself chanting it under his breath over and over again. Each time he got to 'murder them' he stopped for a moment, thinking that the next line might come into his mind; but it was no use, he had forgotten all the rest of it.

He started to recite the rhyme yet again, tapping his heel on the flagstones of the corridor in time with the words. He was waiting for the Duchess of Norfolk. He had spent many hours since they had arrived at the Pleasance standing in a corridor, waiting for the Duchess.

Walter Aslake's man. Or rather, Walter Aslake himself; for Will knew what the Duke of Norfolk did not, that it had been Aslake in person who had chewed the end of his quill over those unimaginatively expressed threats. It had been rash of him to set his intentions

92

down in black and white, but then Walter was not only a villain, he was a stupid and boastful villain. It had evidently not occurred to him that he might pay heavily for his pleasure in seeing Paston squirm, by being convicted of both the threats to the Serjeant, and the more than threats to Grice.

Mind, he was guilty of both. Margaret had told Will that. She had not written down what she knew, being considerably less rash and stupid than her husband, but when the chance had come she had whispered it to Will in her garden, apparently with some idea that he might make use of the information.

But how? He could scarcely pass it on without giving some indication of how he had come across it, and that struck him as dangerous: he did not want to see his sister suffer even more than she was suffering already. He would not have trusted Norfolk to use the information well; he would not even have trusted the Duke to believe him, now that his mind was set on Aslake's innocence. Telling Serjeant Paston would have been less risky, but he could see no point in telling Serjeant Paston. He had no proof to offer, only information, and Paston was already possessed of that information.

The real time for action had been earlier, he thought sadly: when Margaret's marriage had first been arranged, and she had written that agonised letter to him, begging him somehow to stop it. But he had not seen that at the time. Until he had met Aslake he had thought she was dramatising, and when he had met the man, and hated him on sight, it had been too late. Though even earlier, there was little or nothing he could have done. Orphaned minors were so damned powerless. It had been up to the Duke of Norfolk to pick a husband for Margaret, and Norfolk's decision would not have been swayed by the impassioned pleas of a sixteen-year-old esquire.

Norfolk was a fool, that was the real trouble. His foolishness corrupted everything in his household: there was no scope for a wise man to serve the Duke of Norfolk.

There was no disguising the fact: Will hated the Duke of Norfolk.

He did not hate the Duchess. That was the one good thing, in Will's mind, about serving the Mowbrays: he was coming to rather like Lady Katharine. He liked her energy. She did not droop and murmur like so many women: she showed enthusiasm for just about everything, bar her husband. She was a Neville by birth, one of a vast North Country family. Will knew that because he had met her brother Richard – now married to the Earl of Salisbury's daughter – at Westminster, and he had met her sister Anne, Countess of Stafford, at the Pleasance. They, like her, were boisterous people: it seemed to be a family trait. He admired it. So many people in East Anglia, even in London, seemed only half awake, but Lady Katharine and her sister appeared never to tire. The Duchess noticed everything, and responded to everything. And everyone, Will included. Orders from the Duke consisted of no more than a 'Hey, boy!' but the Duchess called him 'Calthorp', and smiled.

Lady Katharine smiled a lot. Sometimes she would meet Will's eyes when she smiled at him. Hers were dark brown, large, very slightly protuberant, and her lips were curvaceous and very red. At times the smile she gave him was almost conspiratorial, like the smile she had shared with Gloucester. He thought of the time when the Duke had slipped in the mud at the Pleasance's landing stage. Will had taken his arm and helped him to stand again, and the smile Lady Katharine had given him had seemed to say: he is a fool, my husband, but a powerful fool. We must indulge him, you and I.

Life as an esquire to a Duke, Will thought to himself, was not at all as he had imagined it. He had taken it for granted that he would admire his master, but he knew now that nobody admired the Duke of Norfolk. Admiration was not necessary. It was only necessary to be polite, and to obey orders.

There was a loud creaking of new hinges, and Will, who had been leaning against the wall of the corridor, hastily straightened up. The door to Lady Katharine's room swung open. Out stepped Jeanne, the Duchess's maid. She peered round the open door and met Will's look.

'Ah, M'sieu Calthorp,' Jeanne murmured.

'Ah, Jeanne,' Will said, with a grin.

Jeanne took another step into the corridor and almost shut the door behind her.

'The Duchess and Lady Anne are to call on Lady Warwick. You will order the barge for them, please.'

Will glanced at the not-quite-shut door and lowered the pitch of his voice. 'And you are to go with them?'

'Yes, but we return tonight.'

'Same place? Just after dark?'

'If I can get away.'

'Of course you can.' He smiled reassuringly and moved forward. Swiftly he set his hands on her shoulders and pulled her to him so that he could deposit a light kiss on her mouth. 'Ma petite poule,' he whispered.

A pink flush spread across Jeanne's freckled face, starting at her cheekbones and ending at the upturned tip of her sharp little nose. She gave Will a coquettish smile, then twisted free and disappeared back into the Duchess's quarters.

Will went down to the river to tell the bargemen to get ready. Then he returned to the Duchess's quarters. He knocked this time and a few moments later the Duchess emerged. Lady Anne was at her side, Jeanne was in attendance and behind them trailed a brace of other ladies-in-waiting.

'Ah, Calthorp,' said the Duchess. 'You may escort me to the landing stage.'

She held out an arm and bestowed on him a very gracious smile. He dutifully put his arm under hers. The Duchess turned her head almost imperceptibly and glanced at Jeanne.

Will saw that glance; he reckoned the Duchess intended him to see it. She knows, he thought suddenly; and it amuses her. He sensed that there was something else in the look, too, but he had no time to consider what it might be.

He walked arm-in-arm with the Duchess, with the other ladies following them, down the long corridors of the Pleasance, across the sanded paths of the parterre, and to the landing stage. The boatmen were waiting and the side-awnings were in place – it was a damp, windy afternoon. He held the side of the boat as the Duchess stepped in. She had to bend forwards to duck under the awnings and her cloak caught on one of the supports, pulling away from her. Will saw just a glimpse of the blue velvet of her gown. It was cut very low at the front, and above the blue velvet there was a generous expanse of white skin showing.

Dutifully he disentangled the cloak and the Duchess reached out her hand to draw it back round her. Her fingers just brushed against his. For a split second her eyes met his too.

'Thank you, Calthorp,' she said.

Will bowed. He handed in the other ladies, Jeanne last of all. He tried to catch Jeanne's eye, but she seemed to be sulking and she would not meet his look.

He watched the oarsmen pull away from the landing stage and stood there, still watching, as the barge, low in the water, its striped canopy flapping a little in the wind, made its way upriver. Then turned and set off for the lawns. He had missed his practice with the bow that morning; it was time he made up for it.

Just how old was the Duchess of Norfolk? Will considered this question as he checked the contents of his quiver. Her son was thirteen, so she would be thirty, perhaps; maybe a year or two younger. She had only the one child. Her figure was still good, and her skin was very smooth. Did she have a lover? Quite possibly she did, he thought. A lot of people at the Pleasance seemed to have lovers. At the Pleasance nobody seemed to disapprove of such goings-on. Take the Duchess's reaction to his dalliance with Jeanne. Other mistresses, in other places, might have been (doubtless would have been) horrified. But not Lady Katharine, not at the Pleasance.

Of course Gloucester would hardly invite stern moralists to stay at his palace, not after the scandal of his marriage to Eleanor Cobham. It had been a shocking affair, throwing over Jacqueline of Hainault as soon as he found he had not the resources to fight the Duke of Burgundy successfully for her lands, and promptly bringing her lady-in-waiting back to England with him. Maybe Gloucester had managed to persuade one of the rival Popes to annul his marriage to Jacqueline so that he could make Eleanor his Duchess, but that had not killed the gossip, only sent it deeper into the bushes. Lots of noble ladies refused even after the marriage to have any dealings with Eleanor. Katharine of Norfolk was evidently not one of them.

'Are you game for a contest?'

The voice disconcerted him; he had thought he was alone in the archers' hut. He looked up swiftly, his eyes passing over short legs, heavy shoulders, and finally settling on the plain, pleasant face of John Itteringham, one of the Duke's other esquires.

'I'd reckoned on a practice,' he said with automatic defensiveness. John was perpetually begging his colleagues to wager with him, and as perpetually failing, since everyone knew that he always won.

'Oh. Then I'll practise with you, if I may.' There was a falling note in John's voice, and hearing it, Will immediately regretted his refusal. John's family were poor, and unlike Will he never seemed to have a shilling to spare.

'Tell you what. A dozen shots to get my eye in, and then I'll wager you six pence on the next dozen.'

His reward came immediately. John's face lifted, like a steam pudding rising over the fire.

'That's good of you, Will.'

Will rose to his feet with a cheerful smile and picked up his bow. 'Didn't you know? I'm a good man.'

'The Duchess has been sulking today.'

Will watched Jeanne's face as he said this. They were lying side by side on a pile of old sacks in a gardeners' shack at the back of the palace. It was late in the evening and very dark outside, but he had brought the stump of a candle with him and lodged it on a high shelf, and he could see the maid's jaunty profile clearly outlined against the wavering glow.

Her nose wrinkled into a little scowl. That did not surprise him. He had guessed that the Duchess would be a sensitive subject, and he knew Jeanne was not an easy-going girl: the tiniest comment could tip her into moodiness. Usually he made an effort to keep her sweet, but this was a time when he was prepared to test her temper. He had nothing to lose, he reckoned; he had already tumbled her, and in a few minutes she would be lacing up her kirtle and creeping back to the Duchess's quarters.

'So?'

'So I am curious. I want to know why.'

Jeanne's shoulders lifted in an eloquent shrug.

'And you must have some idea,' he persisted.

'They had an argument.'

'She and the Duke? What about?'

Jeanne shrugged again and sat up, twisting her body so that she was facing away from him. 'How am I to know?'

'You are always with her. You must hear what they say to each other.'

'Not always.'

Jeanne reached for her shift. Will reached out too, and wrapped his fingers gently round her wrist. He pulled her back down towards him.

'True, not quite always,' he whispered.

Jeanne's face was hidden in the shadow; he could not

98

see her expression. But he drew her closer and his mouth sought out hers. She kissed him back for a moment, lingeringly, then her teeth closed on his lower lip and nipped it, stinging him, before she pulled sharply away.

This time he let her pull her shift over her head. She groped in the dark for her kirtle.

Will smiled to himself. 'Over here,' he said.

'You have it? Then give it to me.'

'When you've told me.'

'But there is nothing to tell.'

'You know they quarrelled, you must have heard something.'

'The shouts, I hear the shouts. But you know, the walls are thick here. I do not make out the words.'

You are lying, Jeanne, he thought. But he knew that he could not press her any further without kindling real annoyance, and he was not prepared to do that. He sat up himself, handed over the crumpled kirtle and began to lace up his points.

'In the winter hall yesterday,' he said thoughtfully, 'Gloucester and Norfolk argued about the war. Gloucester worries him: you've seen that, like a dog baiting a cow? Norfolk nearly lost his temper. And Lady Katharine laughed out loud.'

'She is a bitch, the Duchess.'

'In a way.' It cost him nothing to agree: this was Jeanne's constant complaint. Even so, it was not that, he thought; they argued about something else.

'And I should get back before she misses me.'

'So you should. Can you come tomorrow?'

'No, it is my turn to get her bed ready. Friday I can come.'

'Till Friday, then.'

Her farewell kiss was swift, but then it often was: Jeanne was not given to sentimentality. Will blew out the candle. He watched Jeanne's shadowy figure run across the herb garden. When she had disappeared through a side door he bolted the gardeners' hut and began to saunter back himself.

It was something else, he thought. What? Perhaps she does have a lover, and he caught them at it. Perhaps it is he who has a lover. He is ugly, but then, he is a Duke. Perhaps he made a pass at Jeanne. That would annoy her. It would annoy Jeanne too, but she can take care of herself.

By midday the following day, Will had still not discovered what the quarrel had been about. But he was sure of one thing: the Duchess had lost it. If she had won, he reckoned, she would revel in it; but instead she was sulking even more than Jeanne, and it was the Duke who seemed quietly exultant.

He spent a dull day: the Duchess kept to her rooms, and he was pinned once more to the corridor. She gave him no orders until after dinner. Then Jeanne emerged to say that the Duchess and their ladies were packing their bags, and that he was to call the barge for them.

'To take you where?' he asked.

'To Norfolk Inn, of course.'

A long time later the Duchess herself appeared. She was leaving in style. She wore her best cloak trimmed with sable, a headdress as wide as the doorway and a gown of yellow satin. Her face was painted. Will looked closely, but he saw no marks of distress under the paint. She is angry, he thought, but she has not been crying.

They proceeded to the winter hall, where Lady Katharine made many long and effusive apologies to Eleanor of Gloucester. And then to the landing stage, where the Duchess, all her ladies, and her grumpy young son, embarked on their journey upriver to the Mowbrays' city residence, Norfolk Inn. Will saw them off, but he did not travel with them: he was the Duke's man, and none of the Duke's men went to Norfolk Inn. They remained with their master at the Pleasance.

The Duke did not seem worried by his wife's grand gesture, or penitent, or angry. He seemed excited, in a rather furtive way. That interested Will. It was rare for the Duke to show such animation. He sensed that something else was about to happen, and he was curious to know what it would be. He missed the Duchess and Jeanne, but on the whole he was glad that he had been obliged to stay with the Duke: his head was full of questions, and he wanted them answered.

A few days later Gloucester made his excuses to his guests and set off for Westminster. Norfolk barely waited until the Duke's barge had disappeared upriver. Then he gathered together a large retinue, Will included, and called his own barge. They were to go, he announced, to Southwark.

Southwark. This was the answer, but what was the question? Since nobody was talking of their precise destination, Will spent the journey mentally running through the names of all the possible dignitaries whom Norfolk might be planning to visit. Before they were in sight of the Tower he had come up with the right, the only possible, answer. The Duke of Norfolk intended to call on Cardinal Beaufort.

The little group of men gathered at the top end of the very long great hall at Winchester Inn had been in earnest conversation for hours. Dinner had been served to them, and cleared away; the winejars had been replenished several times. The warm light that flooded through the high rose window had reddened and then faded until the window was no more than a sketch in the candlelit shadows of the hall.

Will glanced up at the window. It would be dark already on the river, he thought; and Norfolk had surely planned to return to the Pleasance by barge. Or did he intend to stay the night at Winchester Inn? It seemed unlikely. Even if Gloucester himself did not return to Greenwich that night, his servants would tell him that Norfolk had stayed elsewhere. Then Gloucester would doubtless wish to know precisely where Norfolk had been, and the resources at his disposal would make it easy for him to discover not only where, but also why.

Norfolk certainly would not wish him to know that, since he had spent most of the day negotiating a deal with Cardinal Beaufort that would effectively set the two of them in alliance in the King's Council, and in opposition to Gloucester. The details had bored Will, but the fact of the negotiation fascinated him, as did his realisation that it was over this that Norfolk and his Duchess had quarrelled.

Had Norfolk thought about the journey back? Will knew, as soon as he had asked himself this, that he had not. It was the kind of thing the Duchess usually thought of for him, but she was not at Winchester Inn. Norfolk's brother-in-law Sir Robert Howard might have done the job if he had not been as drunk as Norfolk himself. Everard Digby was drunk too, as were most of the others in Norfolk's retinue. Will was not drunk. He had been dead drunk only once in his life, and he had liked neither the sensation nor its aftermath, so he had never done it again. He wondered if he himself should remind Norfolk that it was growing very late. But it did not seem to him that he had any obligation to do so: after all, he was only an esquire. Anyway it would please the Duchess, he thought, if this little jaunt landed the Duke in hot water.

Clearly it would please the Duchess if the Duke did not, after all, desert Gloucester for Beaufort. It was not the Duchess who suffered Humphrey's ragging: she was on good terms with him.

Will was on no terms at all with Gloucester, but he had a liking of sorts for the Duke, and he had enjoyed his time at the Pleasance. He took another look at Cardinal Beaufort, and considered what he thought of Gloucester's rival. Henry Beaufort had a heavy face, with flat jowls that thrust into prominence his full, rather petulant mouth. His eyes were a pale blue. He had talked insistently, in a voice that was warm in tone but cool in manner. He had not spared any glances for William Calthorp, esquire.

Will considered what else he had heard about the

Cardinal. Men often spoke of him as a calculating man, a careful negotiator. They spoke of his money. He was supposed to have pots of it. They did not speak of women in his life, or of men either. They did not even speak of intense religious passion. In moral terms it was to the Cardinal's credit, Will knew, that he had an even temperament and no known vices, but in Will's eyes that made him seem less than fully human.

Unlike the Duke of Norfolk, Cardinal Beaufort was not drunk.

Will decided that he rather disliked Cardinal Beaufort. It would suit him very well, he concluded, if Norfolk were trapped at Winchester Inn overnight, so that Gloucester was given early warning of his plans, and both he and the Duchess of Norfolk had every opportunity to try and thwart them.

He shuffled on the hard bench, trying to ease the ache in his backside, and prepared himself for a further long wait. John Itteringham, seeing his shuffle, glanced at him, and Will gave a wry grin in response.

He was disappointed in his expectations, though, because it was only a few minutes before the Cardinal abruptly stood up. Norfolk followed him to his feet, moving slowly and unsteadily as if his befuddled mind were not in full control of his body.

Beaufort was a very tall man, and he was made to seem still taller by his flowing red robes and Cardinal's hat. He towered over Norfolk. 'You'll consider what I have said?'

Norfolk nodded. 'Consider it, yes. I must consider it.'

'And give me your decision.'

'That I must.'

'And soon, I trust. In any event I should know before All Saints': that will give me time to arrange the appointments before the Council meeting.'

The appointments, Will thought. He had been paying enough attention to the negotiations to follow Beaufort's meaning: this was the bribe that the Cardinal had held out to Norfolk and his retinue. Together they would be in a position to push whatever measures they chose through the King's Council, and their first move would be to appoint their own men to lucrative court positions. The timing was perfect, for King Henry's nurses had been dismissed that summer, and his court was fast taking shape. Howard and Digby and the rest would become Treasurer, Chamberlain and heaven knew what else in the King's Household, and would collect fat salaries in reward for their thin services.

He himself was doing his part to deprive them of this pleasure, Will thought. He did not regret it. It seemed to him a sordid business to bargain allegiance in return for hard cash.

'It's late; Your Grace, your conversation has absorbed me for longer than we had intended.' The Cardinal looked up at the window. You old flatterer, Will thought; you old fake. You have never lost track of the time, you have always intended . . . His path of thought squelched to a halt; he was caught by the uneasy suspicion that he had miscalculated somewhere.

'What's more, there was a storm brewing earlier,' Beaufort continued. 'If you listen you can hear the winds even in here. It would not be wise, I think, for you to return to Greenwich tonight. But no matter; my servants can make beds up for you here.'

Will saw it suddenly, with cold clarity. Beaufort had never intended to give Norfolk until All Saints' to think over his offer. He meant to trap him into an immediate commitment, and how better to do it than to keep him overnight at Winchester Inn, and ensure in the morning that Gloucester came to hear of it? Norfolk would panic when he realised what he had done, and Beaufort would be on hand to explain to him how best to extricate himself from his sticky situation.

'I thought to . . .' Norfolk murmured.

'The bargemen are waiting,' Howard said with drunken impatience.

He could not let it happen. It would be the worst possible outcome, it would give Gloucester no chance, it would give the Duchess . . . That was it. They should go, all of them, to Norfolk Inn. Then that drunken fool of a duke would surely give in to the temptation to tell his wife what a wonderful deal he had squeezed out of old Beaufort, and the Duchess would have a chance to talk some sense into him, and to send immediate word to Gloucester so that he could make his own efforts to back her up.

'Your Grace,' he said, in an obsequious tone that the Cardinal himself could not have bettered, 'I fear you have forgotten, but you had planned to ride from here to Norfolk Inn. You intended to give the message about Sir Thomas Erpingham's funeral to the Duchess in person.'

Norfolk turned, slowly, until he was facing him. Surprise was the first expression on the Duke's face. Then it dissolved, like an ice-sculpture melting, into an interesting mixture of gratitude and annoyance.

He knows there is a trap somewhere, Will thought; but he is too drunk to decide whether I am laying it, or offering him a way out of it.

'I am sure this young man could take the message for you,' the Cardinal said. 'I will call my clerk to write it; and I can easily provide a mount.'

'Oh, young Calthorp can write it himself if your man brings paper and ink.' Norfolk's face now showed a satisfied conviction that he had chosen sensibly and had put his importunate servant back into his proper lowly place.

'And I will have beds made up for Your Grace and your companions.'

Norfolk's expression changed again. Curse him, Will thought; his mind is working as I hoped, but too slowly. Now he sees what I meant him to see, but it is too late.

'B-but,' the Duke stuttered, 'we must get back to Greenwich.'

The Cardinal leaned towards him as if to protest; then drew back and shrugged. 'I still think it unwise,' he said in a frosty voice, 'but I shall not detain you, naturally, if you insist.'

Norfolk had to go through the charade of dictating a letter to his Duchess, full of information she already possessed about Erpingham's funeral and undecipherable hints about the brilliant deal he had stitched together; the Cardinal took his time over his farewells; his servants slowly fetched their cloaks and hats. It was black night by the time the men left Winchester Inn. There was a bare sliver of moon, it was raining heavily and a wolf of a wind howled misery and plucked at the folds of their cloaks. Will stood dutifully on the riverbank and watched the Duke's barge set off downstream, then he mounted the nag the Cardinal had provided and rode alone towards London Bridge.

He was soaked and frozen by the time he succeeded in stirring the watchman at Norfolk Inn. The servants were all in bed. So was the Duchess, the watchman warned him; but Will brushed him aside, insisting that his message was urgent.

He was not sure by now whether it was, or whether he was claiming so merely to save face. A solitary ride through a devilish night with a drunkard's meaningless letter in his hand was not what he had intended at all, though it was pleasing to think that he might see Jeanne while he was at the Inn. It half-pleased him, too, to think that he would see the Duchess; but he had no idea, now, what he would say to her. He did think of sending the letter in to her without requesting an audience, but that seemed to him a poor solution to his dilemma.

It also crossed his mind that she might in any case refuse to see him before the morning; but she did not. The sleepy page he had sent to her quarters came back to the guardroom to announce that he was to present himself there immediately.

'In her quarters?' Will said stupidly.

'That was the message.' The page went back to his pallet and promptly fell asleep.

Will took a taper and lit it from the guardroom fire. He walked alone through the shadowy corridors of Norfolk Inn, stopped in front of the door that led to the Duchess's quarters and knocked. He meant the knock to be quiet, but it sounded alarmingly loud in the still corridor.

Jeanne opened the door and came out into the corridor.

'Jeanne! Such a tale! You've no idea . . .' His voice faded away: her scowl had killed it.

'Through there,' Jeanne said curtly.

He went into the room.

'Close the door behind you,' the Duchess's voice said.

Will glanced behind him. He expected Jeanne to have followed him in, but there was no sign of her. He closed the door, then turned and looked around him.

The room was not large. There was a bed with heavy hangings, a pallet at its foot, a small table cluttered with jars and bottles, and a carved chest set against the far wall. In the hearth, a fire was burning low; on the table there was a candle in a silver holder. The air seemed to be thick with a rich, musky smell.

There was also the Duchess. She was quite alone, standing near the fire.

Will felt acutely uneasy. He should have changed his clothes before coming to her, he thought suddenly. He had thrown off his sodden hat and cloak in the guard-room, but his doublet was damp and his hose were positively dripping, and his boots were thick with mud: it had been too dark on the road for him to avoid the puddles. He was conscious of the taper he held in his left hand and had no idea what he should do with it.

Lady Katharine seemed to sense his awkwardness. She walked across to him and said in a businesslike voice, 'Quench the taper and put it there. You will need it when you go back. You have an urgent letter for me?'

'Here, Your Grace.'

'Then I shall read it.'

She took it out of his hand and went towards the table. She broke the seals, unfolded the letter, lowered the sheet so that the candle shone on it and began to read.

Will watched her. He had never seen her like this before. Her hair had been loosed from the tight head-dress in which – like all ladies of fashion – she confined it in public. It was darker than he had expected it to be and drifted in soft uneven waves down over her shoulders. As she moved her head to follow the finger which traced the words, it glinted in the candlelight. She was wearing only a nightgown, its laces so loosely fastened that he could glimpse the undercurve of her breast.

'You will be pleased with what I tell you tomorrow,' she repeated out loud.

He knew that was the end of the letter: he had written down the words barely an hour earlier. He met her eyes as she raised them from the page.

'Even John can hardly believe that,' she said in the sarcastic voice he had heard her use with Gloucester.

John? Will shook his head: the combination of his exhaustion and the heavy perfume that filled the air seemed to be working on him like strong ale.

'I am sure he does,' he managed to say.

Lady Katharine smiled slowly. 'Let me guess. Howard and Digby are to get good appointments with salaries, and half a dozen of the others are to be Royal Grooms and Gentlemen of the Bedchamber.'

'A dozen others, Your Grace.'

'A dozen? How generous of the Cardinal! Though, of course, it is not his own money that he plans to spend.' She grimaced. 'The sanctimonious old schemer. How much ale did he shovel down – no, it would be wine, wouldn't it?'

'It would.' He thought of adding 'Your Grace', but somehow it no longer seemed appropriate.

'You look quite sober, Calthorp.'

'Most of the rest drank faster.'

'Is that why John chose to send you?'

She said this with a frank curiosity that disarmed him. 'No', he said in a quiet but firm voice. 'I chose to send myself.'

'Did you, now? Because you would prefer to see John keep to Gloucester?'

'That was one reason for it, yes.'

'I think I can guess the other.' She smiled again her conspiratorial smile. Jeanne, he thought: she knows I came to see Jeanne. He felt that he should have thought of a witty response, but his tongue seemed to have stuck to the roof of his mouth.

The Duchess waited for a moment, then she casually tossed her husband's letter down on to the floor and moved across the room towards him. She stopped a bare pace away. 'You are on my side.'

Will swallowed hard. 'So I am, Your Grace.'

'And you will do all that I ask you to do?'

He swallowed again. 'Everything you ask.'

'Everything?' Her eyes held him. They looked very dark in the firelight. She smiled once more and his gaze moved to her lips, red and moist. 'Then kiss me.'

Will did not move. On one level of his mind he had known that this was coming, known ever since he had entered the room, if not long before; but on another, it surprised him almost to panic. She was not like Jeanne, or any of the other girls he had tumbled: he felt himself in deep water, without a safe footing. Even to kiss her: he had kissed a dozen girls, but never a woman like this one, and his usual easy confidence seemed to have deserted him.

'Like this,' said the Duchess. She covered the short space between them in a single movement, pressing up against him and wrapping her arms around his neck. For a moment his senses seemed to be filled with the smell of her: it was warm and spicy, the smell of the room intensified a thousandfold, civet and cinnamon and oranges. Then her lips met his and her tongue snaked into his mouth.

It teased, it promised. Her hands drifted slowly down his back. Instinctively he moved his arms around her, to complete the embrace.

The kiss took forever, and yet all too soon it was over. The Duchess lingered in his arms for a moment, holding his eyes, then she moved back a pace and began to unlace her nightgown.

109

Will did not pause to consider whether he wanted this: he knew only that it was going to happen. He began to unfasten his own clothes.

The Duchess glanced over her shoulder at him. 'No,' she said, 'leave your boots on.'

'They are muddy right up to the thighs.'

She finished with the laces; she shrugged the gown casually off her shoulders and turned, naked, to confront him.

'Then I shall be muddy too.'

She reached out a white hand to the damp leather, streaked a finger through the mud and brought it up, very deliberately, to brand Will's cheek.

Morning came soon. Too soon, it seemed to Will; it was no time, surely, since he had found himself a pallet and fallen asleep in a corner of the guardroom. Now the shutters were being flung back and there were cries and sounds of running feet. He surfaced uneasily into wakefulness, conscious of a heavy head and dry mouth.

'The bridge!' someone was yelling. 'Down at the bridge!'

It was a crisis, that was clear; but what kind of a crisis? He stumbled to his feet, brushed a hand down the crumpled front of his doublet and went out into the corridor to see if someone could tell him what was happening.

A couple of esquires rushed past, ignoring his muttered request and dodging his outstretched arm. Then a groom; and this time, Will managed to trap him against the wall. 'What is it? What has happened? Is it a French ambush?'

'Saints, no. The Duke's barge. He hit the bridge last night, late. They say he went into the water, and Howard and the rest with him.' The groom ducked, slithered under his arm and dashed out of the open door of the Inn.

The Duchess, Will thought in a panic: I should go to the Duchess. He turned towards her quarters, was almost knocked down by a couple of pages hurtling along the corridor, and then thought again. Decidedly it would not do for him to go to the Duchess.

110

Then he should go to the Duke. Heavens, the barge! To hit the bridge, on a night like that . . . A wave of black horror washed over him. Holy Jesus, was the Duke dead?

He dashed back to the guardroom, pulled on his mud-encrusted boots and tossed round his shoulders the still-sodden weight of his cloak. A moment later he was weaving and dodging through the morning crowds along Thames Street.

He glanced, as he ran, at the alleyways that led to the wharves. Should he go down to the river there? No, he could do nothing there. He took the corner into Fish Street in a tight curve and dashed towards the long expanse of the bridge.

The bridge was even more packed with people than the streets had been. Shopwomen, maidservants and messenger boys stood about in tight knots, whispering among themselves; the water sellers and orange sellers and piemen circled around hoping for extra custom; and through the crowd flowed a steady stream of city masters and apprentices, late already for their morning's work. Will stopped dead in his tracks, panting. He gazed around. The houses and shops formed a solid row on either side of him: as he should have guessed, he could see nothing at all of the river.

'Calthorp!'

The voice was that of Gilbert Debenham, standing with Hugh Austin, another of the Duke's men, outside a butcher's shop. Will hurried to join them.

'Did you bring the litter?'

'The litter? No, I came . . .'

'Never matter, he's not ready for it yet. Drinking hot ale, he is, and warming his feet, snug as a bug in there.'

He? 'The Duke?' Will hazarded. 'He's not harmed, then?'

'A graze on his elbow, no more.'

'And the others?'

'Howard's with him, and Digby, and a few of the rest.' Debenham gestured at the butcher's counter. Will stared at it. The counter was scrubbed, but the meat had not been set out; peering beyond into the shadows of the shop, he could see moving figures. Evidently the butcher and his wife had abandoned their usual trade and were making the best of the strange fortune that had driven the Duke of Norfolk to take refuge in their front parlour.

'There's a few at the goldsmith's there, and a couple breakfasting with the chandler,' Austin added.

'They're safe, then, all of them?'

'Not all. I heard they'd taken up a couple of bodies.' Austin's expression sobered, and Debenham hastily crossed himself. 'We're to wait here for the litter, but you could go to . . .'

'I'll go now,' Will said quickly. But where? He felt only that he should be away from the Duke, away from Debenham and Austin, and he dashed off along the bridge without any clear idea of what he might usefully do.

He must see more, that was it. He caught at one of the apprentices and asked where he might get a view of the disaster.

'You'll get a glimpse from my dormer,' offered a smaller boy standing next to the apprentice.

'You'll show me?'

'Go on, Johnny, show the fine man. Mind, it'll cost you, sir.'

Will fumbled in his pockets. 'I've a farthing.'

'That's kind of you, sir.' The apprentice grabbed at it before he could change his mind. 'This way, sir.'

The boys led him to the attic of an eelshop, a low-ceilinged, dark room with a narrow gable window that looked upstream. Will pushed his way past the scanty furnishings and flung open the shutters. He leaned out and looked down.

The view was not as good as he had hoped: it was not really worth a farthing. But by craning out as far as he dared he could glimpse the base of some of the piers and see the wreckage caught around them. There was a stretch of canvas canopy, mudstained but still defiantly gay, flapping in the wind. Broken stays, a length of rope.

A rowing boat was tethered to one pier, stacked high with strips of painted wood; a couple of haulage barges were approaching downstream.

'I reckon they have all the bodies now,' the apprentice said from behind him with gloomy relish.

The bodies. There was nothing to be done on the river: the boatmen would salvage whatever was still to be found. That was what mattered, the bodies.

'Where? Where have they taken them?'

'The Chapel. Another farthing, and I'll take you there.'

'I've paid you plenty. Show me now.'

'That was Johnny's farthing, sir. A farthing for me too, that's fair, sir . . .'

'I'll find it myself.'

Conniving brats, he thought angrily, as he clambered down the attic ladder and hurried through the eelman's gloomy rooms. He pushed past the counter and on to the road. That must be it, the stone building with a crowd of men muttering around the doorway. He strode across and shoved his way through them.

Inside, the Chapel was almost deserted. There was an atmosphere of stillness, of silence. Will's haste faded: he had no idea now why he had felt such urgency. A priest was standing by the altar, setting a taper to a candle; a door in the corner stood open.

'Norfolk's man,' Will said awkwardly. 'I am Norfolk's man.'

'In the vault,' the priest replied, without turning round.

Will made for the door and went down the steps beyond. The stairwell was dark. The vault was a hemisphere of unpainted grey stone, cold and cheerless. A stretch of dark canvas had been spread on the floor, and on it were laid a row of corpses. Three or four candles, set in brackets on the wall, shed an uncertain light on them. In the corner another priest was on his knees, reciting prayers in a low monotone.

So many! A couple, Austin had said, but there were many more than two. Numbly, Will counted. Fourteen.

He took a step forward and bent to look at the first body. It was one of Norfolk's oarsmen: he knew that from the tattered livery. The corpse had a grey look to it, sodden and battered.

The second body was that of a young page; the third was another oarsman; the fourth was one of Norfolk's grooms, a man he had often laughed and joked with at Framlingham.

The fifth was John Itteringham.

Will's knees sagged. He knelt down on the canvas next to John's body.

A long time passed. Will looked, without seeing, at John Itteringham's face: a pair of open, dead eyes, an expanse of damp, cold, pallid flesh. He won two shillings last week from me at the butts, he thought; did he spend the money?

He could feel the chill from the floor, working its way up from his knees. The priest came to the end of his prayer and started on another with barely a pause. Will thought of joining in, but the words did not come out of his mouth. He got to his feet, clumsily. There was a candlestand in the corner. He walked over to it, fished out two pennies from his pocket and took two candles. He lit them. One for John Itteringham, one for the rest. He watched until the flames were burning steadily, then he turned and went to the stairway without a backward glance.

The priest in the chapel had finished his task and was talking with two of Norfolk's grooms.

'. . . the tides . . .' Will heard, as he walked past them. '. . . treacherous . . . washed downstream . . .'

He went back to the butcher's shop. Debenham and Austin were still there, but the litters had come now. There were half a dozen servants clustered around the empty meat counter.

'Fourteen,' Will said to Debenham.

'Fourteen?'

'The bodies. Fourteen bodies.'

'So many? That's bad. Oh, I was told that if I saw you I was to tell you to attend the Duchess. She's coming here, to the Chapel; must be on her way by now.'

The Duchess. There did not seem to be room in his mind for the Duchess: it was still full of what he had seen in the vault. But he walked, in a daze, to the end of the bridge and out along Fish Street. It was there that he met up with her litter. He turned and walked back alongside it, slowly this time, to the Chapel.

The bearers set down the litter and the Duchess swept the curtain aside. Will moved forward and offered her his hand, but she did not take it, or even glance in his direction. She went into the Chapel; Will followed her. He did not follow her down to the vault; he waited in the upstairs chapel. It was not empty any more. Three priests were there, negotiating in low voices with half a dozen of the Duke's men about the burial arrangements, the memorial services, a service of thanksgiving for the Duke's safety.

The Duchess stayed in the vault for a long time. When she emerged she brushed past Will without a glance and stepped back into the litter. They made their way in silence back to Norfolk Inn. As soon as they arrived she retreated to her quarters.

Had she known John Itteringham? Will asked himself. Had she known any of them, their names, their thoughts, the food they had liked to eat and the girls they had loved? He wanted to tell her about John, what a hand he had been with a bow, how drunk he would get on feast days, the knack he had had of juggling with wooden balls, with apples, even with daggers one time. He held these conversations in his head, but he did not see the Duchess at all.

She reappeared in the hall the following day and Will approached her, but she turned her head away as soon as she saw him coming. She began to talk to Jeanne and the two of them moved off in the opposite direction. After that he did not try to talk with her again.

At least there was no more intriguing with Beaufort. Messengers came repeatedly from the Cardinal, but the Duke and Duchess both sent them away without replies to the letters they brought. Less than a week later they and their retinue were on the road to their castle at Framlingham in Suffolk.

Framlingham Castle was a great hoop, its curtain wall studded with towers, sitting at the top of a massive mound that had been humped spadeful by spadeful by the Normans' villeins out of a marshy river bed. It looked down on the tower of Framlingham church, its aisles and chapels stuffed full of the tombs of the Mowbrays, and on to a little market town whose inhabitants were most of them Mowbray retainers.

The Duke of Norfolk took to his bed when he reached there; he remained there for the whole of that week, and the next, and the next. At first this caused a minor panic amongst his servants. After a few days the panic died down. The Duchess gave the Chamberlain his orders; the Chamberlain gave the rest of the servants their orders. Everything ran as smoothly as before; indeed, rather more smoothly.

Will wandered, a little aimlessly, across the inner bailey of the castle. It was late November. A fitful sun had abandoned the unequal struggle with a gathering mass of clouds. Rain threatened.

He saw a figure emerge from the base of the tower that held the Duchess's private apartments and paused to look more closely. It was Jeanne. He veered cautiously towards her. Jeanne glanced his way and he knew that she had recognised him. She carefully redirected her steps so that she would circle past him, just out of speaking distance.

Bloody woman, Will thought. Still sulking. And for what? He had not tired of her; he had not deceived her with another of the maids. What had he done? Gone to the Duchess when she had called for him, just once,

116

almost a month before. That was all. Three weeks they had been at Framlingham now, and the Duchess and Jeanne between them had barely exchanged a dozen words with him.

He drifted towards the mews. It would be no day for hawking unless the storm clouds blew over quickly, but he could at least remind his new kestrel that he existed. He could tell the austringer to keep it hungry, then if the weather cleared he would be able to fly it the following day. He pulled open the door and looked inside.

It was gloomy in the low-roofed building, and silent, but for a faint fluttering of wings. Will peered through the shadows. Was the austringer there? He could see no sign of him. The only person in sight was a young boy whom he recognised, without pleasure, to be John Mowbray, the Duchess's son.

Perhaps he should stay and be polite to John, he thought; he could give him some advice about that merlin he was having trouble in bringing to the lure. John was not the sort of lad to take advice kindly, though, nor the sort of company to raise Will's low spirits. He closed the door again, as quietly as he could.

Boring, boring. There was nothing to do at Framlingham. There were no errands to be run for the Duke; no important visitors at the castle. There was no prospect of trips to London, Greenwich or Windsor, or of encounters with Gloucester or Beaufort. It had rained almost every day, so there had been little opportunity to hunt or even to practise with a bow. None of the esquires seemed to do anything but drink.

Perhaps he too should go and drink, he thought. It gave him a lugubrious pleasure at that time to souse himself into a stupor, and nurse his sore head afterwards. Nobody would miss him if he went down to the Duck and Mallard. He might find a couple of the others already there, and if Jeanne did not want him, at least Mary did. It was no good trying to tease Mary — first she would look blank, then her eyes would fill with tears —

117

but she was prettyish in a plump, fair way, and undeniably accommodating.

He went for his cloak and set off down the hill.

Christmas came. The Duke did not leave his bed, but the Duchess declared the mourning period over; she engaged extra musicians and admitted the jesters and jugglers who called at the gatehouse. There could be masques, she said, and dances.

Will had always enjoyed masques. This year he played a devil, with a black mask over his face and a long forked tail. He pricked the angels in the backside with a toasting fork and leered at the Duchess. She did not leer back, but she did smile. Afterwards she congratulated him on his performance. She was pleasant and friendly. That was something, Will supposed, but it was not enough. It was not as if the Duke had died that night in the barge: he had only taken a ducking. Will felt that he had suffered more than she had: after all, he had lost John Itteringham, and she had lost nobody that she cared a fig for. If he had set the incident behind him by then, so should she have done. She should have called him to her rooms at least once more. He could not understand why she did not. He had pleased her that night, he knew he had.

His relations with Jeanne seemed to be mending more promisingly. On New Year's Eve she let him kiss her under the mistletoe, and the following evening she came up to him and asked him to partner her in the dance.

He grinned at her and cheerfully agreed. She had been unfair to him, he reckoned, but he did not believe in nursing grudges. Anyway, it would be snowing soon; it was getting to be too cold for late-night trips to the Duck and Mallard, and there were no other girls at Framlingham who had taken his fancy. He danced with Jeanne three times, and though she went off arm-in-arm with another of the maids afterwards, he felt sure that soon things would be back as they had been between the two of them.

The following day, just before dusk, he saw her in the inner bailey as he was riding back from a hunt. She did not avoid him this time: she came over to greet him as he dismounted and walked with him towards the stables.

'I went to the armoury for the Chamberlain this morning,' Will said, 'to fetch some swords for sharpening. And do you know, I forgot to give him back the key.'

'Then you should give it back tonight,' Jeanne said.

'I suppose I should.'

'But not too early.' She looked up at him, half teasing, half defiant, as if to make sure that he understood her. He did. He almost laughed out loud with relief.

He had to wait a while, in the dark with the rows of pikes and helmets. The candle stump he had purloined from the pantry was only half an inch long, so he did not want to light it until she came. At last he saw her, running across the bailey, and opened the door wide to welcome her in.

He watched her as she undressed: not uncritically, but with pleasure nonetheless. She did it well. Mary had always been one for pulling her skirts up with a grunt, but Jeanne toyed with her laces, fluttered her lashes and gave a teasing little wriggle as she shrugged off her shift. Her breasts were on the small side, but set high: they tilted upwards like her nose. She was bony to embrace, but he liked looking at the spare lines of her body.

'I missed you,' he said.

'Did you?'

'Certainly I did.'

'Sometimes I missed you too.'

'That's good.'

The armoury floor was of beaten earth, and not the most comfortable of beds, but there was a good expanse of it, which was as well, since they used every inch. Jeanne was greedy for him; she sighed and panted and urged him on. Not that he needed much urging: a quick poke with Mary at the back of the inn stables had been a poor substitute for this.

The candle flickered; the remnants of the wick were all but drowning in a little puddle of wax. Will sat up and reached for it and carefully propped up the wick so that they would have a moment's light in which to sort out their clothes. He pulled on his hose and began to relace his points. From the corner of his eye he could see Jeanne dressing too. Her movements were swift and efficient now, with all the coquetry abandoned.

'She,' Jeanne said quite suddenly, 'has missed you not at all.'

She, he assumed, was not Mary at the Duck and Mallard. 'Not at all?' he echoed in a teasing voice.

There was just a hint of sulkiness about the way in which Jeanne pulled her kirtle over her head. So that is why she came round so quickly, Will thought: because she saw the way the Duchess smiled at me, and she was reckoning to beat her to it. But what difference can that make? If Lady Katharine calls for me again, then I shall be obliged to go. Jeanne will grouch, but she'll not be able to stop me. And she'll not spurn me afterwards, either: she enjoyed tonight too much.

Anyway, she was lying. Of course the Duchess had missed him.

To punish her, he said wickedly, 'I kissed her too, under the mistletoe.'

Jeanne tied her belt in a bow, in a tight little movement, and glanced sideways at him. 'So you saw it not.'

'Saw what?'

'Hugh Austin.'

For a moment he did not understand her. Then the candle gave a last dying flare and in the light he saw the expectant look on her face.

Hugh Austin? But he was no more than a boy! He was younger than Will, a year younger at the very least, and the girls had never looked twice at his crooked nose and the wart on his chin.

He produced a fair semblance of a smile and said lightly, 'Now if you had said it was Debenham or Orford, I might have believed you.'

'She danced with him four times last night. And when she reached her room she pleaded a headache and dismissed us all.'

Jeanne slipped her feet into her pattens and reached for the latch.

Will reached out his hand, meaning to keep her a moment. He wanted to see her smile with him, and whisper that she knew her jealousy was stupid. Then his hand fell. It is true, he thought to himself. Damn it, she's telling the truth.

Jeanne opened the door and turned to look at him. She smiled cruelly. 'You'll not forget to give back the key.'

That is why she came, he thought. She came to take her pleasure, true, but most of all she came to tell me that, and watch me wince. The bitch. The bloody bitches, both of them.

'I'll not do that,' he retorted. He would give it back first thing in the morning. He knew he would not be needing it again.

He had to get away from Framlingham. There had to be a way. There was nothing for him to do at Framlingham, anyway. The Duke had too many esquires, he needed barely half as many while he was an invalid. There was no sign of his recovering, so surely he would not object if Will asked for leave. He would still be the Duke's retainer, but he had to go somewhere else, to get away from Framlingham.

The problem was, where was he to go? He had neither excuse nor inclination to return to London, Westminster or Greenwich. He could always become a soldier, he supposed, get together a small company and sail for France. But he liked his comfort, he still liked to have women, he liked music, and all these facilities, he reckoned, would be in short supply in the army.

That left only one option: to go home to Norfolk. Bloody Norfolk. Burnham Thorpe Hall it would be: that was the main Calthorp manor, the heart of his inheritance. He had spent a year there before rejoining the Duke's household the previous autumn, and a dull, lonely year it had seemed after the bustle of a page's life at Framlingham. There were a lot of sheep at Burnham Thorpe; there was precious little else.

Even Norwich was more – that was it, he could go to Norwich! There were Calthorp estates and properties all over Norfolk, and all of them had been his since his grandfather and father had died in close succession seven years earlier. Surely he possessed a house in Norwich? He could go there.

The estates and properties were not his to run as he chose yet: they would be in the hands of trustees until he came of age. But the trustees expected him to show an intelligent interest in them (indeed, rather more of an interest than he had yet been inclined to muster) and they would surely agree if he suggested that he might stay in Norwich and travel from there to inspect the rest of his lands?

The more he considered this, the more the idea pleased him. It was years since he had been to Norwich. Then he had been a child, now he was a man. He could drink at the inns, make new friends, find new tricks to play, and perhaps a new girl to tumble too.

He went to the Chamberlain and asked if he might be given leave to pay a visit to Norwich.

The Chamberlain told him to speak to the Duchess.

That was not what Will had had in mind. But he did it, anyway. He spoke to her after supper in the Great Hall.

She listened, with apparent interest.

'Mowbray Inn is shut,' she said, when Will's explanations trailed to a halt.

Was this a veiled plea to him to stay at Framlingham? He stared at her. She looked back at him, her brown eyes wide open, her expression guileless. He remembered Hugh Austin, and decided that it was not.

'I had not thought to stay at Mowbray Inn. I would ask my trustees, I thought, to reopen my grandfather's house . . .'

'Totally unsuitable.' The Duchess frowned. Will waited. 'I have it,' she said, with an air of decision. 'You shall write to Judge Paston. Mowbray Herald will travel to Norwich the day after tomorrow; he can carry your letter.'

Judge Paston! Stay with the Pastons, that sour old man and his wife! That was not what he wanted to do, not at all! He opened his mouth to protest, and then shut it again. Paston was one of his trustees: after spending the last ten minutes explaining to the Duchess how anxious he was to oblige them, he could hardly say now that he was determined not to stay with Judge Paston.

At least it will be better than Framlingham, he thought. And if nothing else, it will put the wind up Walter Aslake.

'I shall do that, Your Grace.'

As he was bowing and making his retreat, it struck him what the Duchess had said. Not Serjeant Paston; Judge Paston. So Gloucester had not just been teasing Norfolk: he had done it after all, got old Paston his place on the Bench.

Just what, he wondered afterwards, had Judge Paston done in return?

123

4

FRANCE

Secret set off on the journey back to France in mid-November. He had lingered in London for a week more than he had originally intended so that he could travel with Suffolk Herald, whose master was also with the army outside Orleans.

Each day they found new groups to share their journey: other heralds and poursuivants, small troops of soldiers, knots of merchants. Before they reached Paris they heard that the Earl of Salisbury had been killed in a freak accident involving a cannonball.

They learned this from a couple of Italian silk merchants, who knew the bare fact of Salisbury's death but none of the details. The next day they fell in with a band of Flemish mercenaries. These knew no details either, but unlike the silk merchants they were anxious to discuss the news, and in particular to discover who was likely to succeed Salisbury as commander of the siege operations.

Secret was unwilling to voice his opinions on this question, though, and it did not surprise him when Suffolk Herald too proved reluctant to be drawn. There was little to be said for promoting their masters' qualifications for a command which those masters might not receive, and might not even desire, and there was nothing at all to be said for outlining their disqualifications to these strangers.

The mercenaries appeared not to appreciate these niceties, but eventually they gave up the attempt to prod their new companions and settled for mulling loudly – and with no attempt at diplomacy – over their own opinions.

Would it be the Earl of Suffolk? He had acted as Salisbury's second-in-command, and was now the highest-ranked English noble in France, bar the Regent himself. But his record as a general was variable, to put it kindly: he had presided over a fair-sized disaster at Montargis, and another at Mont-Saint-Michel. At Pontorson he had been removed from his command, though as his herald bestirred himself to remind the Flamands, it was Bedford's wider strategy, rather than any explicit distrust of the Earl, that had prompted this action. Suffolk was also known to have been opposed from the start to Salisbury's decision to besiege Orleans.

Therefore it might instead be Sir John Talbot, a fine (though sometimes rash) strategist with a formidable reputation amongst the Valois soldiers: Talbot's name alone, it was claimed, could set them to flight. Or if Talbot were reckoned insufficiently aristocratic to head the pack it might be Lord Scales, who was dull but reliable.

'It might be Sir John Fastolf,' one of the Flamands suggested.

Sir John Fastolf? His colleagues laughed out loud. Who on earth had heard of Sir John Fastolf? Fastolf's proposer was not so easily discouraged, though, and he treated them all to a lyrical account of that knight's ability to make money out of soldiering; but in the end the mercenaries unanimously agreed that though it might be Suffolk, Scales or Talbot who picked up Salisbury's banner, it would certainly not be Fastolf.

Though Secret did not trouble to tell them this, he was of the same opinion. He reckoned it would be Suffolk. He cast a few secretive glances at Suffolk Herald, wondering if he also reckoned so, but he knew from experience that Suffolk Herald's well-worn, sharp-featured face was not as easy to read as strangers tended to assume, and as usual he learned nothing from it. Nor did he ask the herald his opinion when the Flamands had parted company with them.

The following day he and Suffolk Herald reached Paris, and there they called on Anjou. The King of Arms immediately told them the answer. The Earl of Suffolk had already been appointed to take temporary command of the siege.

The Earl of Suffolk's herald showed little visible emotion at the news. It was not in his nature to crow; but still, Secret thought, he is not pleased by it. He could not unravel the herald's thoughts and feelings by guesswork; he would only be able to do that by learning more. But he would not enquire in front of Anjou: he would wait until they were alone.

He chose their night's lodgings with this thought in mind: a small, scruffy inn just off the Rue Saint Germain where they could have the attic to themselves, except for a copious insect population. They retired there, with the one short stub of candle the mistress provided, immediately after supper.

'I'll take this one,' Secret said, pointing to what looked to be the cleaner of the two tattered mattresses. He sat down on it to reinforce his claim and removed his boots. He scratched his toes. And said, 'I reckon that will mean more work for you.'

'The Earl's appointment? Aye.' Suffolk Herald inspected the mattress he had been allocated, without enthusiasm. 'Bloody fleapit,' he said morosely. He picked it up – it was too thin to be heavy – and inspected the underside. He moved it nearer the candle, dangerously near. Secret reached out a hand and guided it away. The herald shook it, hard, and a cloud of black dust spread across the attic and over Secret. 'I've no objection to more trips to London, you understand,' he went on. 'But I mislike this news.'

Secret nodded. 'A difficult task, for a man who is against the siege.'

'Against the siege? He's that, and more. I reckon he's against the war.'

126

The herald spread the mattress on the floorboards and lay down on it, on his back. He stared up at the rafters, shrouded in shadows.

'He's a fine man, the Earl, mind you, and a fair master, but he has no stomach for this kind of action.'

Against the war, Secret thought. Against the war. Many men are against the siege. Fastolf for one is so; he has written his opinion to the King's Council, and I have repeated it to other men many times over. Neither he nor I see blame in that opinion; he accepts Bedford's orders nevertheless, and fights as fiercely as ever he might. But against the war! Those are strong words; those are dangerous opinions both for an Earl to hold, and for his herald to impart, even to colleagues such as me.

He said in a deliberately casual voice, 'Maybe now he is in command he will choose to withdraw from the city?'

Suffolk Herald turned and gave him a wary look, as if he were wondering if he had spoken too freely. 'Maybe Bedford has threatened to appoint Talbot in his stead if he makes any move of that kind.'

It was a reasonable suggestion. Once, men had hinted that Bedford opposed Salisbury's determination to pursue the siege; but that had been before the army became committed to it. The Regent often favoured caution; he rarely if ever favoured retreat. Nor could he now support a withdrawal without leading men to deduce that he had allowed Salisbury to override him initially.

'So the Earl would take that ill? If he were to be replaced as commander?' he asked.

'His men would take it ill,' Suffolk Herald said. 'Me included.' He reached a hand behind his back and wriggled a little. He withdrew the hand and deposited something on the floorboards between the two mattresses. Secret did not look. 'And I would take it none too well,' he continued, 'if you were to repeat this conversation to your Burgundian friend.'

Secret considered. 'Now why should I do that?'

'Even at second hand.' Suffolk turned his back to the poursuivant and within minutes he was making puffing noises, apparently intended to suggest that he had gone to sleep.

For a moment Secret listened to him; then he snuffed out the candle and settled down in the darkness.

Fastolf's troops were stationed in an abandoned farmhouse beyond the Fort de Paris, the last of the sequence of Lancastrian fortifications that circled around the north-west of Orleans. It was crumbling, rat-infested, stinking – and by the standards of the siege, a very comfortable billet. The inhabitants of the city had razed the outer suburbs and very few buildings still stood in the war zone.

It was late in the afternoon when Secret pushed open the door of the narrow barn that now provided quarters for Matthew Gough and his esquire George, Christopher Hanson, Peter Basset, Jean de Waurin (now seconded to serve under Fastolf) and his esquire Nicolas – and that would, while he was at Orleans, house him too. Outside the day was still and grey, its dullness broken only by the irregular booming of the Orleans guns a mile and more away. Inside there was a powerful smell of salt pork and cabbage, and a thick fug of smoke. Hanson had broken a hole in the thatch above the cooking fire, but most of the smoke evaded it.

Secret threw his heavy pack towards one of the far corners. He watched it skid to a halt and then sat down on a bale of hay. He glanced around. Nicolas was stirring the cooking pot. Hanson and Basset and de Waurin had been playing at dice, though they had paused when he came in.

'De Waurin will pay for the spices,' Christopher Hanson said sardonically. 'As usual, only he has any money left.'

De Waurin gave an apologetic half-smile and pushed a few coins from his pile across the cleared circle of earth

128

on which they were playing. 'Eight saluts you owe me now, Christophe. You brought the nutmeg?' he continued, turning to Secret.

'A little,' Secret said. 'And ginger, and pepper. Welles had no cinnamon to spare.'

Hanson groaned: No surprise, this. But Hanson had only wanted the cinnamon, Secret thought, if it could be had at Welles' price; and this time it could not. Hanson never seemed to understand that if Welles supplied them at cost, he would supply them only with goods of which he had an excess.

It was good that Hanson cared about food and saw them all fed – direct from the supply trains – at a standard the common soldiers dared not even dream of. It was fair that he should ask for extra spices to barter with the other troops. But it would be bad if he became greedy. Secret endeavoured to ensure that he did not by always failing to bring at least one of the items Hanson had requested. Even for Christmas he saw no reason to make an exception. There were pudding recipes that did not require cinnamon.

Peter Basset abruptly changed the subject. 'Have you seen Sir John?'

'Not yet,' Secret answered. 'He is at the house, I think?'

'He and Matthew were with Suffolk earlier this afternoon. You heard of Salisbury's death?'

'A cannonball, we heard. The tale made little sense.' Secret turned to Hanson. 'You will explain for me, Christophe?'

That would appease Hanson, he thought. Christophe liked to tell him news. They all did, Christophe and Peter and Jean de Waurin. It would probably have appeased Hanson even more if Secret had distributed his letters, but it was a ritual with him never to produce them until after supper.

Hanson got to his feet and went to a barrel that was propped in the corner where Secret had thrown his pack. He lifted the wooden cover and dipped in an earthenware cup. When he had filled four cups he brought them over to the others. Nicolas raised his brows and Hanson nodded to confirm that the boy might take a cupful of ale too.

He sat down on the bale next to Secret's. 'You heard we took the little fort, the Tourelles? That cannot have been long after you left. Salisbury's men attacked from the south, beyond the earthworks, and drove the Frenchies right over the river. They broke two arches of the bridge behind them.'

Secret had come from the north, and the Loire was to the south of the city, so he had seen neither the river nor the bridge since he had arrived. But he had reconnoitred the entire area around Orleans on his previous visit, and had listened to many analyses of the situation while he was away, so the picture was clear in his mind. The broad river, broader even than the Thames at London Bridge, but shallower, with many islands; the handsome wooden bridge; the fortifications to the south, and the Tourelles, a tall, gaunt fortress.

'The Tourelles must be out of gun range from the city walls,' he said thoughtfully.

'Our cannon can't fire across the river, but the Valois two-hundred pounders can manage the range. The earthworks are safe from bombardment. Salisbury made a great commotion about taking them, but it seems to me they're bloody useless: too far distant to make good cover for archers or siege engines.'

'But the fort is tall . . .'

'Oh, the Tourelles was worth taking, no doubt. Makes a damn good observation post. Matthew's been to the battlements. You can see the full sweep of the city walls, he says, and along the river almost to Meung and Jargeau.'

'That is good. But I do not understand. The Earl was killed on the south bank?'

'In the Tourelles itself. He went up the main tower at the dinner hour, when the French guns were quiet. There's a sizeable window overlooking the river, and he

130

stood there. Framed in it, admiring the bloody view. One of the French gunners had aimed his cannon dead on the window. Guyenne Herald claims the gunner had gone to lunch with the rest, but he left his boy to guard the cannon. So the boy saw Salisbury standing there like a bloody picture and set a taper to the fuse.'

'At a range of close on four hundred yards,' de Waurin added laconically. 'Guyenne calls it skill, but the English prefer to think it luck.'

'Which it was,' Hanson retorted. 'You'll not have me believe even a master gunner can calculate an angle to such perfection.'

'A direct hit?' Secret asked.

'Better. The ball struck the edge of the window and the force of it dislodged an iron bar. Salisbury ducked in the wrong direction.'

'And it took him . . .'

'In the face. By all rights he should have dropped dead there and then, but the poor bugger took eight days to go. Time enough for Suffolk's appointment to come through.'

The poor bugger. Death came to all men: that in itself was only a small sorrow. But for a good man one hoped for a clean death. Eight days was a long time. Secret crossed himself and spared a moment's thought for the Earl of Salisbury, a dour man but a clever one, and one not above showing kindness to pages, dogs and poursuivants. Then his mind moved on, inexorably, and focussed on the tone in which Hanson had mentioned Suffolk's appointment.

Not contempt, no: there was no cause for that, as Hanson knew. They had agreed among themselves many times that they had found Suffolk to be a better soldier than his reputation had led them to expect. But there was a certain weary resignation in those words, which told him that whatever Hanson and his friends had hoped for, it had not been this.

This. He already had a good idea of the consequences of Suffolk's appointment. Since he had last been at Orleans, the troops had pulled back. He had left his friends in a safe billet, one well to the rear of the army's main position. Now they were in the same billet, but now it was less safe. It was well out of gun range, true; but the bulk of the army had retreated beyond it, even further out of gun range.

'So it was Suffolk who withdrew the troops?' he asked.

Nobody answered him immediately. They exchanged glances, Hanson and Basset and de Waurin, as if this were an issue on which the arguments between them were still warm embers and they hesitated to choose this moment to fan them back to fire. Eventually Basset replied. 'It was, no question. Fastolf reckons he'll move most of the men back as soon as they've finished building winter quarters. He has them doing that now, out of the rubble.'

'But there is disagreement?'

'Matthew says the same,' Hanson said. 'He and Fastolf claim to have heard it direct from Suffolk. That's how he persuaded his commanders to stage the withdrawal, by promising a return after the quarters are completed. But the whole army knows that to Salisbury, Suffolk had been arguing for a full withdrawal. They're not fooled so easily. He played for time, for Bedford's permission to abandon the siege.'

'Ah, Christophe,' sighed Jean de Waurin. 'Never you are convinced. It matters nothing what Suffolk desired before he was commander. It matters nothing, even, that he had reason once to think that Bedford might support him. Now everyone knows that Talbot is arguing against withdrawal, and Scales. Suffolk has no option but to change his line, or he will lose the command.'

'You do not think, Jean, that the Duke of Burgundy will weigh in with his support for a withdrawal?' Secret asked.

The Burgundian's dark brows lowered – just a fraction, but enough to tell Secret that the question annoyed him. He should not have asked it. He had been asking too many questions too soon after his return; he should have been content to keep quiet and to listen until he had their attitudes straight in his mind. But he had not thought that this particular question would bring on a heavy silence. He thought, suddenly: none of the others have asked Jean that.

De Waurin said carefully, 'I do not think the English commanders would bow directly to Burgundy's pressure.'

'And Saint Rémy does not think so either?'

It was Saint Rémy who would be responsible for conveying Burgundy's messages to the English commanders. He had thought that Jean would answer him directly, this time; but there was more subtlety to his question than he had consciously put into it, and Jean was on guard now. He gave a half-smile, acknowledging that Secret had meant this to defuse the tension, and yet warning him that it did not.

'If you were to read my letters to Saint Rémy, Secret Poursuivant, you would know that I advise him never, never to come to Orleans.'

Never come to Orleans. Sane advice, Secret thought, on waking next morning to a flurry of hail and a wind that sneaked like a thief through the cracks in the barn. He had come with a light heart and a simple eagerness to be once more with his friends, but already he sensed the desperation that plagued the siege army, and he knew that there would be little joy to be found at Orleans that winter.

He had woken late; the barn was already deserted. He scraped a bowlful of porridge from the bottom of the cauldron Hanson had left over the embers of the fire, drank another cupful of the ale, unpacked his tabard and dragged it over his head, then made his way across the stretch of churned-up mud which separated the barn from the handsome old farmhouse where Fastolf himself had his quarters.

Fastolf was there, holding court at the far end of the hall. His backside was settled into an old carved chair and his feet rested on the immense oak trestle that reached from one end of the hall to the other. Rumour had it that Fastolf slept on the trestle, to protect it from the soldiers who coveted it for firewood. At his side stood Matthew Gough, his beard grown shaggier, his eyes wearier than when Secret had last seen him two months before.

'I hope Welles sent paper,' Fastolf greeted him. 'Not a damn sheet to be had in the Orleanais, and my last batch melted away like snow in a furnace. And cinnamon. I'm partial to a good spoonful of cinnamon in my plum pudding.'

His servants never said a direct no to Fastolf. That way, explosions lay.

'Welles sent his own recipe for the pudding to your cooks, sir,' Secret said. 'Ginger it contains, and nutmeg too. He sends to you two letters, and there is one from Serjeant Paston.'

'You mean to say, you rascal, that Hanson has already bartered all the cinnamon to Scales' men.' Fastolf reached out a large red hand for the letters. 'There'll be no chance to lay your hands on more before Christmas. I'll not send you back to London till my next report to the Council is ready.' His eyes focussed on Secret's face. 'That mispleases you, does it? Does it not suit your private transactions?' He lingered fractionally over the word 'private' and leaned forward, letting his feet slide off the trestle with a thud. 'Never forget, Secret Poursuivant, that it is me you serve.'

And me not paid a penny by you since Michaelmas, Secret thought to himself. 'I am not like to forget it, sir.'

'And I am not like to pay you, Secret.' Fastolf leaned still further forward. 'Do you know why, poursuivant? Because the Duke of Bedford has not paid his captains since midsummer. Did they tell you that in Paris?' He sat back with an air of bitter satisfaction at having frustrated his servant's expectations.

It was true, as Secret knew very well. All the same, it

angered him that he should not have been paid. Fastolf had money, much money: that was a poor excuse.

He did not show the anger. To do so would have gained him nothing but curses.

'I bring despatches, sir, from the Duke.'

'Ah,' said Fastolf. 'Gough!' He gestured to Matthew Gough to take the second bundle of papers. As he did so, he stood up. 'Not now. When we are alone.'

He stalked down the length of the trestle. Secret watched him. Not now, he thought. Damn Fastolf: the knight never opened despatches in front of him, never even discussed military tactics while he was within earshot. Fastolf would dictate letters on business in his presence, but not letters on politics and the progress of the war; those ones were always sealed before they were handed over.

Fastolf distrusted him and did not trouble to hide it. Secret found that offensive. He had no objection to caution, but this was more than that: mere caution did not demand that a man distrust his own servants. He had done nothing to merit this obstinate distrust. In any case the elaborate precautions Fastolf took were pointless: what Fastolf did not tell him, Gough invariably did.

Fastolf paused at the far end of the trestle and rotated on his heels. He set his hands on the grooved oak surface and glared right down its length. 'It will suit Welles none so ill,' he said, 'to have you stay at Orleans. That way you can watch Suffolk for him.'

'Are those your orders, sir?'

'My orders, poursuivant? You want *my* orders?' Fastolf stared balefully at his servant. 'My orders are to find enough cinnamon for my plum pudding. Dismissed.' He snapped upright and then glanced down at the letters in his fist. 'Send Hanson to me,' he added off-handedly. 'And Secret . . . what you learn about Suffolk, you will also convey to me.'

'As you wish, sir.' Secret dipped his head in a half-bow, partly to Fastolf and partly to Gough, and backed out of the farmhouse door.

135

Christopher Hanson was writing, with his elbows in the dust and his paper resting on a slab of wood that he had acquired for just this purpose, and now guarded jealously. In a leather package by his side were wrapped the remaining sheets from the sheaf of paper he had managed to spirit from Fastolf's campaign chest. As Secret watched he laid down his quill, picked up a spare one and carefully flicked a spider from the sheet with the feathered end.

'You hate to kill spiders, Christophe.'

Hanson glanced up. Secret was the only other person in the barn.

'It gives me no pleasure to kill them.' He finished writing his sentence, then looked up again and said, 'Did they tell you anything in Paris of the news from Normandy?'

'Only a little. Scales' men could probably tell you more than I can.'

Hanson glanced down at his paper. It was part of the journal of the war, Secret knew, that he and Basset were writing together. The two of them argued sometimes whether it would be better to publish it in the guise of a Life of Sir John Fastolf, or of a Grand Chronicle. In order to leave both options open, they gathered as much news as possible of all the military activity in France.

They loved information, Hanson and Basset. That, to Secret, was both fascinating and appalling. He loved information himself in a way; but his way was different.

Information was his own stock in trade. He could get money for it, and save that money with the Italian bankers to whom Welles had introduced him. Over the three or so years since he had entered Fastolf's service he had built up a very useful balance with the bankers. He sensed that information was a practical commodity to Fastolf and Gough, too: they wished to know things in order to further their careers. But Hanson and Basset did not reckon up the value of information in this manner; they seemed to love it for its own sake. They never played entrepreneur with the facts they acquired; their only trade was in tangible goods. If they looked for any gain from their knowledge, Secret thought, it was a distant and insubstantial one. He suspected that publishing their journal was infinitely less important to them than writing it.

'If I cared to ask Scales' men,' Hanson said carelessly.

Oh, Hanson cared: Secret knew that. But he would not ask, not Scales' men, and nor did he possess Secret's own painfully acquired knack of learning things without asking.

'I think sometimes, Christophe,' Secret said quietly, 'that it makes you and Peter disliked by the other soldiers, that you share a billet with Jean de Waurin.'

Hanson looked up with a half-frown. It gave Secret a moment's apprehension. Even to Hanson and the others he rarely chose to reveal his own thoughts. Relating facts was so much safer.

'It is hardly fair to blame Jean. Because he is Burgundian? You might as well say we are disliked because you are a Norman–Breton, or because Matthew has Gascon blood.'

'Perhaps that is true also.'

'Doubtless it is.' Hanson shrugged his shoulders. 'We are liked by the men we wish to like us.'

True. There was a tight coterie of them: the men in the barn, and perhaps as many again outside it. Without each other they could never have learned so much, or dared to discuss so much openly. But in biting one side of this coin, Secret thought to himself, they bit also the other: there would always be people from whom they could not learn, people from whom everything they discussed was best kept hidden.

He was always careful to keep to himself the opinions that Hanson and Basset, Gough and de Waurin expressed within the barn. To do otherwise would have seemed to him a kind of betrayal.

He thought a lot about betrayal. More than most other men, he suspected; though perhaps not more than other officers of arms. He believed Saint Rémy thought of these things, Anjou too. Perhaps Suffolk Herald also thought of them, though the Englishman was, Secret reckoned, a man less given to abstract thought.

All the time heralds and poursuivants were asked what they knew. They had perpetually to decide how much to say, and to whom. There had been a time, Secret thought, when he had believed that donning a tabard would in itself define his loyalties. He knew now how wrong he had been.

He said slowly, 'Does it trouble you, Christophe, that Jean de Waurin writes to Saint Rémy all that you learn?'

'Does he?' Hanson looked up as he spoke, but his expression was non-committal. Perhaps he had intended his reply to be ironic; perhaps not.

'Much of it, I think.'

'Ah, much of it.' Hanson paused. 'And do you tell much of it to the Duke of Alençon?'

That question shook him. It was a sly one, and he did not expect slyness from Christopher Hanson.

No; perhaps it was not. Perhaps Hanson did not know. For much as Alençon had occupied Secret's thoughts over the years with Fastolf, he had never discussed the Duke with Hanson or Basset or even with de Waurin.

Perhaps, he thought, Hanson genuinely did not know even the fundamental fact that had so altered his own position, three years and more before. In which case – in either case – it was now necessary to tell him.

'But Christophe, Fougères is no longer Alençon's town. He sold his estates there, to pay his ransom from Fastolf.'

Hanson barely reacted. Maybe he had already known. Maybe he did not understand that this was important. Englishmen did not think of overlords as Frenchmen did. English dukes and earls exerted influence in different ways to French dukes and counts. In England men did not pay homage to their overlords.

'Did he, now? Sold them to whom?'

'To Brittany: to Arthur de Richemont, the Duke's brother.'

Christopher Hanson considered this in silence. 'At least,' he said eventually, 'Burgundy is an ally of the English.'

Secret frowned. Slowly, he worked out what Hanson meant. He was contrasting Jean de Waurin's position, Jean de Waurin's loyalties, with Secret's own.

It was not a pleasant contrast. He had deserved to have it made, he supposed; it was a punishment for his remark about Jean. He thought of pointing out that Burgundy was an increasingly unreliable ally of the English. But Hanson already knew that. Instead he said, 'They say the Lancastrians count Duke Jean of Brittany as an ally.'

'But you know as well as we do that there are a bare handful of Bretons in this army.'

Secret hesitated. He did not like the way this conversation was progressing. He did not like to think too hard about his attitude to the old and new overlords of Fougères. His life was complex. He had meant to simplify it when he had decided to serve an Englishman: it was a cruel irony that Anjou's sending him to Fastolf should have had the opposite effect.

He had been a fool in the days before Verneuil, a mixed-up fool. His hatred for Alençon had burrowed into his mind, when it should have lived in his dagger hand until he had exorcised it. He had wanted vengeance, but had lacked the cold urge that brings a man to make the killing thrust, so he had told himself that there were other, bloodless ways of taking vengeance. If there were, though, he had not yet found them.

Perhaps he had never really thought to take vengeance when he turned to the English, but only of escape. But while Marianne's dishonour stayed unavenged he could never escape Alençon's shadow; except that now, bizarrely, it was a double shadow. He was bound to the Frenchman he hated, but he owed homage also to a Frenchman for whom he had no hatred at all. And there was his oath of loyalty to Fastolf: that made three bonds, all potentially incompatible, all equally indissoluble. It was not a situation that gave him pleasure.

He said, 'There are many thousands of Bretons, under Richemont, in the Valois army.'

Hanson nodded, as if that answer pleased him. 'He interests me, the Count of Richemont. He too is a man of complex loyalties: so complex, indeed, that one wonders sometimes whether he owns any loyalties at all.'

'That is true.'

'He is bound by blood and homage to his brother the Duke. But he acknowledged Henry once as his King by fighting for his cause; and now he fights to win that same title for the Dauphin. Which of them does he truly serve? Or is it that he serves his own self-interest throughout?'

'Perhaps,' Secret said, 'he tries to serve France.'

'Perhaps. But there are many ways of serving France; and it is no coincidence, I suspect, that the Count of Richemont always chooses the way that looks likely to gain him the most.'

Secret did not know if that was true; but he did know that it was often said, and that it fitted the facts he knew. After Agincourt Richemont had been a prisoner of the English. Set free on licence, he had broken his oath to his captors. He had tried to redeem himself subsequently by fighting for Henry of Lancaster, father and son, but without success: Bedford had never forgiven him for that breach of the chivalric code, and from him Richemont had won no high titles, no supremacy over rival commanders. So Richemont had defected to the Valois cause after Verneuil, when Buchan was dead and the position of Constable of France in the Dauphin's gift once more.

'Richemont interests me too,' he said.

'Have you encountered him?'

'Once or twice.'

'As a poursuivant?'

'And once before.'

'Is he as ugly as they say?'

That was an odd question. No, perhaps it was not. It was Hanson's way of easing things, of taking the

140

conversation back to shallow waters. There was plain curiosity behind it, too.

'In a sense. He has a strong face.'

'He has a strong presence, they say, and a quick mind. Though as a commander he is less effective than one might have expected.'

'I think that is true.'

'That is often the case with men of divided loyalties. Jean was arguing yesterday that it is the root of Suffolk's failings, that he is failing to take proper hold of the siege because he is uncertain whether he should be serving Bedford, England, France, or his own conscience.'

'And did you agree?'

'We all told him,' Hanson said, 'that he passed beyond bravery and towards foolhardiness to speak of such a thing even among us.'

'Then,' Secret said, 'we shall speak no more of it.'

Suffolk Herald rode for Calais ten days later with a large pack of letters to be delivered to addresses in London and Westminster. Among them were two letters from Matthew Gough.

That made Secret aggrieved. The letters had not been urgent, as far as he could tell. Gough could have waited for his own next trip to England. He needed Gough's business. He needed his bank account to grow. It gave him a warm feeling, the thought of the money being kept for him in London.

It was a small thing; and yet it was not such a small thing, because it tied in with other little signs. Gough was eating less often with the men in the barn, more often with Fastolf. When he came to the barn it was frequently with orders from Fastolf. Gough had for a long time been bringing them information from Fastolf, but to bring orders was different. Secret had thought of Gough as their intermediary with the knight, as, he reckoned, had Hanson and Basset. But now they spoke of Matthew almost as if he were Fastolf's representative among them, Fastolf's spy.

Gough was not like the others: Secret had always sensed that. Hanson and Basset had neither material resources nor ambition. De Waurin was not a poor man, but he too had no great ambitions as a soldier. Gough also was far from rich, but unlike his friends he was steadily growing richer. He was likely to rise, men now said, from man at arms to knight, perhaps even to high command. Soon perhaps he would name his own poursuivant and cease to use Secret's services at all.

That thought hurt. The group in the barn could not persist forever: Secret understood that. Men joined and left even the tightest company of men. But this company was at the core of his life. He could not imagine what would happen to him when it broke up.

In other ways, though, it suited him to see the back of Suffolk Herald. The herald would have given him no more revelations about his master; come to that, Secret would never again have fished for any. Now that the Earl of Suffolk's herald was not at Orleans, the Earl would cast around for other messengers. Perhaps his eye would light on Secret Poursuivant.

Sometimes it did. When Secret travelled to Paris with the supply train he took messages from Suffolk for Bedford. But the messages were sealed when he received them; they were sealed when he delivered them, and read only after he was dismissed. He learned nothing.

He saw Suffolk frequently about the camps that surrounded Orleans: the Tourelles, the Fort de Paris and the other fortifications. But the commander's handsome, long-boned face was not naturally expressive; his words were almost invariably neutral. His manner was not diffident, but neither was it forceful: there was something distant about him, as if he were permanently preoccupied with thoughts other than those he voiced. Indeed he seemed rarely to express thoughts: he asked for facts, gave orders, kept his opinions largely to himself. He never laughed. Secret understood that. There was little to make a man in his position light-spirited.

Secret never saw the commander watching him: that was not surprising since he did his best to avoid being watched and was by now skilled at such evasion. But Suffolk had taken careful notice of him, he soon realised. To the English-born soldiers the Earl spoke in English; when addressing Secret he switched naturally to French, as he did with Guyenne Herald and the other Frenchmen he encountered. His French was not only fluent, it was well accented. Secret knew that Suffolk Herald carried few personal letters to England from his master; he thought to himself that Suffolk must have been in France a long time. He asked the Earl's valet. Years and years, the valet said: ever since he was a young lad. Did he ever go back to England? Never, as far as the valet could recall.

Secret wanted to see inside Suffolk's quarters. He was living then in a farmhouse bigger than Fastolf's, and a mile or so further from Orleans. He had a private room upstairs. It was closely guarded by his servants. Who went into it? Secret asked the guards. They shrugged. Nobody, most of the time. True, the Earl had two of his brothers serving under him, but even they rarely went inside his room. Fastolf? No, not he. Mind, said the guards, that Burgundian – friend of yours, isn't he? – he's been here a few times.

Secret was not pleased to hear this. After some thought, he asked de Waurin. Did he not know? De Waurin said. He and Suffolk had served together in the Nivernais a few years before. So you know him well? Secret said. I knew him then, de Waurin replied. He is different now. He would not say any more.

Christopher Hanson had heard that the Earl wrote poems. He was curious to read them. So was Secret. He asked the servants again, asked Suffolk's valet. They all agreed that there were poems, but none of them produced copies of them.

That was something: the Earl's servants were loyal to him. They all spoke of him as his herald had done, as a good master. Among the army as a whole, though, the

Earl was not liked. It seemed to Secret that he did little to make himself liked: he showed no humour, no personal interest in the common men. Men found him hard to fathom.

Once Suffolk's apppointment as commander was formally confirmed, men soon ceased to credit him publicly with the conviction that it would be best if the siege were abandoned. But increasingly Secret heard mention around the camps of the old disasters, Montargis, Mont-Saint-Michel and the rest. He wondered sometimes if Suffolk knew of this propaganda. He thought that perhaps the Earl did; but he made no visible attempt to suppress it.

In the barn, Hanson and de Waurin were speculating by early December that Suffolk would be demoted. As usual they were correct. In the middle of the month Sir John Talbot and Lord Scales were appointed to share Suffolk's command. By then there seemed to be a fine inevitability about the announcement.

Talbot and Scales were out-and-out supporters of the siege and it was soon resumed in earnest. It was more difficult, however, to revive the spirits of the army. Dysentery was whipping its way through their bedraggled ranks. Everyone knew that the Valois were quietly provisioning the beleaguered city through the yawning gaps in the Lancastrian lines. Orleans could not be taken by storm; it was far too large and strong a city, and the Lancastrians had far too weak an army. It could not be starved out in those conditions, either.

But the guns continued to boom, the engineers to plot and plan in their dugouts. The triple commanders publicly argued among themselves. In private, as far as Secret could tell, they did not communicate at all.

Suffolk seemed to grow more and more remote, more isolated. If he had confidants other than his brothers (and neither of his brothers appeared to be the kind of thoughtful or cunning men who might have advised him well), nobody seemed to know who they were. Secret listened to see whose names the heralds men-

144

tioned in connection with his. There was only one name that recurred frequently; that of the Bastard of Orleans, half-brother of the captive Duke, and commander of the city's defenders. That was not so odd, it seemed to Secret. He reckoned any commander, particularly one who kept his distance from his men, might well share an affinity with his opposite number.

They exchanged letters, the Bastard and Suffolk. So Secret learned from Guyenne Herald, the Bastard's envoy. Guyenne knew the contents of the letters, at least of the Bastard's letters, but it would have been impolitic to ask him about them. Secret did ask Suffolk Herald, returned from England, but he did not know the contents of Suffolk's letters.

Suffolk Herald grumbled continually those days. Secret understood from this that the herald cared about his master's reputation. The herald clearly realised – as did Secret himself – that whatever the outcome of the siege, the Earl could not now emerge from the affair with credit.

The Bastard's letters were not particularly secret. Heralds were conspicuous: everyone in the camp knew when they arrived and departed. It was not clear, though, whether Talbot or Scales ever read the letters. De Waurin and Hanson reckoned that they did not. Their thesis was that Suffolk was trying to persuade the Bastard to surrender peacefully, while the Bastard hoped to create sufficient dissension in the English camp to see the siege abandoned.

Of the two, the Bastard looked marginally the more likely to succeed. There was no real prospect that the defenders of Orleans would surrender, not unless the besiegers managed to tighten their grip on the city's supply lines. Though the Bastard would be in no position to launch a real counter-attack unless he were relieved by a full Valois army, he appeared to be conducting a very satisfactory defence. His reputation as a commander was steadily growing.

Fastolf spent most of his time away from Orleans,

escorting supply trains with his own troops and with any men he could press into service from the Paris militia. He distanced himself – deliberately, Secret suspected – from all three of the joint commanders. He rarely spoke to them. His reputation changed not one jot.

In early December Secret travelled with Fastolf's men to Paris. It would have been two days' journey for horsemen travelling light, but it took four to escort the heavy wagons that were trundling back empty, ready for refilling in the capital.

Supplies for the army were to have been waiting for them, but they arrived to find nothing prepared. It was impossible, Bedford's under-stewards protested to Fastolf: the Parisians asked more and more money for each load of grain, and grew increasingly reluctant to supply any at all.

Fastolf spent nine days proving them wrong, dredging up wagon-loads of hay, corn and flour from merchants all over the city. De Waurin disappeared each day to talk with his Burgundian friends. Hanson and Basset explained to Secret how they usually filled their time in the city. They knew only small areas of it. The whores in the lawyers' quarter were both plain and expensive, Secret patiently explained to them: far better to go to the university quarter. He took them there and showed them the inns where they would find clean girls. He did not stay with them. That would have been a waste of money: there were plenty of women in the city who would oblige him for free. But then, he was a Frenchman. The English were not popular in Paris at that time. The Parisians reckoned the taxes too high, the food prices astronomical; they even blamed the English for the bad winters.

'So Fastolf refuses to send you back to England?', drawled Anjou King of Arms.

'It is rather, sir, that he has no cause to send me.'

'This then is not Fastolf's business?' Anjou tapped the seal of the letter that Secret had put into his hands.

'No, sir, it is not.'

'Yet it is addressed to Fastolf Place in Southwark and sealed with Fastolf's seal.' Anjou turned sharp eyes on Secret. 'Who wrote the contents?'

'They were written for me, sir.'

Anjou's high forehead wrinkled.

'You may read them if you wish,' Secret said.

Anjou's frown faded and his eyebrows lifted to warn that this was a gauche offer.

'You may tell me them,' he said dispassionately, turning to gaze out of the window. They stood in a small room high in the Hôtel des Tournelles, Bedford's Paris residence.

'I write mainly of the grain prices, sir. The Paris merchants overcharge Fastolf. John Welles, his London agent and a grocer by trade, could undercut them by twenty per cent or more. It would be to the army's advantage.'

'And to Fastolf's; but most of all, to the advantage of this man Welles. Who will, I take it, pay you for this information?'

'That is so.'

Anjou gave no immediate reply. He held the letter by one corner and tapped its edge, rhythmically, into the palm of his other hand. 'You write of what else?'

'A little of the Earl of Suffolk, sir. Suffolk has interests in the county of Norfolk, and Welles also.'

'And Welles will also pay you for this.'

'No, sir. I have no hard information, only impressions. They will earn me gratitude perhaps, but not payment.'

Anjou smiled thinly. 'What would you say, Poursuivant, if I were to carry this letter to Fastolf?'

'I would say, King of Arms, that Sir John knows I write such letters. He might guess its contents for himself. There is nothing in it that he does not know.'

Anjou stilled his hand and looked down at the letter. In a swift, confident movement, he ripped off the seal.

Secret held his breath for an instant, then exhaled, telling himself he had told Anjou no lies; more, had told him all the truth.

'It is not proper to send such a letter under Fastolf's seal,' Anjou said coldly. 'I shall reseal it myself.' He gestured to his clerk, hovering in a corner of the room, who scurried forward and took the letter. 'It will be delivered within a month.'

'I should pay you, sir.'

'Not so. I am paid by my lord of Bedford. I do this because it is in his interests.'

Secret did not answer. He and Anjou watched the clerk melt his sealing wax and drip red drop after red drop on to the fold of the torn letter.

'You do not tell this man Welles of Bedford's negotiations with Burgundy?'

'I know nothing new of that matter, King of Arms.'

Anjou gave him a sideways glance and wrinkled his nose. 'It is known to Saint Rémy.'

'Is it, sir?'

'Burgundy asks to have the Duke of Orleans transferred from his English prison to his own custody.'

Had he indeed? Then he was proposing, as he had proposed before, to do something that would place him in the position of neutral third party between the Valois and the Lancastrians. This had always been unacceptable to Bedford and his men, since Burgundy was supposed to be their chief ally.

'This was proposed by whom, sir?'

'By Burgundy himself.'

'And my lord of Bedford considers it?'

'My lord of Bedford's anger scorched the walls of his great hall. But he will negotiate for as long as possible.'

'And when he ceases to negotiate?'

'Do not act the fool, Poursuivant. And do not speak of this yet to anyone.'

Secret was subdued as he made his way back to Fastolf's Paris quarters. If Saint Rémy knows about

Burgundy's plan, he thought, Jean de Waurin surely knows it too.

Jean's position was delicate: they all understood that. But they understood also that Jean told them all that he learned from Saint Rémy. In a week or two this matter would be public knowledge. Why had de Waurin kept it to himself?

I never did know, Secret thought – as he had thought before – whether Jean de Waurin was seconded to serve Fastolf by chance, or for a reason.

He liked Jean de Waurin very much; and where a man liked, he did not easily suspect. He had never forgotten that de Waurin was a Burgundian; but even so he had tended to take it that de Waurin's deepest loyalty was, like his own, to Hanson and Basset and Gough. Perhaps it was not. Perhaps Jean de Waurin's overriding commitment was to the Duke of Burgundy.

'More wine, Matthew?'

'Fill it up.'

Matthew Gough held out his cup. Christopher Hanson lifted the flagon and poured, with the exaggerated carefulness of a very drunken man. He had been drinking all day; they all had. They had bought the wine in Paris, and saved it for Christmas. Now Christmas had come, and they would not stop drinking until every flagon was empty, or until they were all incapable of downing a drop more.

Secret watched Matthew and Christophe, through an inebriated haze, from where he sprawled in a corner of the barn. He would not have cared to predict which would happen first. There was at least one more full flagon. Only George was yet snoring. It was late, very late. It was dark in the barn beyond the reach of the firelight; it was nearly but not quite as dark outside, where a sickle moon shone down on an uncut field of snow. But inside it was peaceful, and outside the guns were booming. The guns had started up again before dusk: the truce had lasted for only six hours.

They had been in the barn since dusk. They had eaten their Christmas dinner with the rest of Fastolf's men, but the rest of Fastolf's men had not had the benefit subsequently of Christopher Hanson's pudding – Welles' recipe, with no cinnamon – or of the flagons of wine.

Peter Basset sighed, and then let out a loud belch. 'Quant je fus prins ou pavillon,' he sang, in a tuneless voice.

'English songs,' murmured Hanson. 'English songs.'

It was a gutless protest, and nobody backed it up: so Basset went on to sing the rest:

> Quant je fus prins ou pavillon,
> De ma dame, tresgente et belle,
> Je me brule a la chandelle
> Ainsi que fait le papillon.
>
> Je rougiz comme vermillon,
> Aussi flambant que une estincelle,
> Quant je fuz prins ou pavillon.
>
> Se j'eusse esté esmerillon
> Ou que j'eusse eu aussi bonne aille,
> Je me feusse garde de celle
> Qui me bailla de l'aguillon
> Quant je fuz prins ou pavillon.

> [When (like a bird) I was caught
> In my lady's trap, she most fine and beautiful,
> I burnt myself on the candle, like the moth.
>
> I blushed bright red,
> Blazing like a spark,
> When I was caught in the trap.
>
> If I had been a merlin
> Or had had as strong a wing,
> I would have kept myself from her
> Who stirred me with a goad
> When I was caught in the trap.]

150

It was one of the songs the minstrels had played on the broken bridge that afternoon. They were the Bastard's minstrels, trumpets and clarions and four boy singers. That little concert was the Earl of Suffolk's doing, Secret thought sleepily. At least one tiny good thing had come out of Suffolk's dealings with the Bastard of Orleans.

'I wish,' Gough said with drunken solemnity, 'I had that fur coat.'

So he was thinking of that too, of Suffolk and the Bastard. It had been Suffolk's Christmas present from the Bastard, the fur coat. The Bastard, rumour said, had received a plate of figs in return.

'I wish we had the minstrels still, and not that bloody booming,' said Hanson.

'I'll sing you another song,' Basset offered.

Hanson sat up. Very deliberately, with intense concentration, he threw the rest of his wine in Basset's face.

Basset lay there, for a moment, with the drips running down the furrows of his cheeks. His eyes opened wider; but he was too befuddled to respond. He gave another belch, turned over on to his stomach and promptly went to sleep.

Secret and Jean de Waurin cleared up the barn in the morning. The squires were feeling too sick to do the work; Hanson and Basset and Gough were not there, as they had all been scheduled for guard duty. De Waurin did not appear to be suffering from any after-effects. The Burgundian made a quiet drunkard, Secret thought to himself. It had been Matthew Gough, to his surprise, who had eventually become loud and belligerent. Gough had tried to pick a fight late the previous evening, but he had found no takers.

There was a strong smell of stale wine and a noxious patch near the fire where Nicolas had been sick. De Waurin worked neatly and rapidly, sweeping the debris out of the door and strewing fresh straw over the beaten earth.

'Low, the supplies,' Secret said.

He meant their private supplies. Hanson had almost finished the spices; there was a bare handful of salt in the wooden pot. Fastolf had still not spoken of sending him back to England. But it was true, he thought as he spoke, of all the army's supplies. Fastolf would have to make another journey to Paris soon.

'That is so. Men were saying even before Christmas that we are like to break from hunger before the Orleanais do.'

'No doubt; unless Fastolf manages to squeeze the Parisians even harder.'

'He will.'

'You truly believe it possible?'

De Waurin gave him a thoughtful look. 'Burgundy will make sure of that. The Duke has no wish to see the siege lifted.'

'You surely do not reckon he supports it!' Secret put open contempt into his voice. Jean is duping me, he thought with weary anger; and he does it poorly, too.

De Waurin eyed him again. He straightened, then he took a couple of strides and sat down on a bale with his makeshift broom still in his hand.

'I thought,' he said, 'that you saw that, Poursuivant.'

'Saw what?'

'Burgundy's policy.'

'The goddamned negotiations over the Duke of Orleans?'

De Waurin shrugged. 'That is no policy. Burgundy hopes to get custody of the Duke, perhaps, but he has never expected it. Neither Bedford nor the Dauphin would permit it: it would put him in a stronger position than either of them could endure. But naturally he wishes the siege to continue. His reasons are no secret, any of them: any man can see them if he considers.'

'I have considered,' Secret said belligerently, 'and I see no reasons.'

'Then consider again. Burgundy now hates both sides. He will never become an ally of the Valois unless the Dauphin publicly acknowledges responsibility for his father's murder, and pleads forgiveness from him. Of which no prospect appears. Nor is he a friend of the English now, for he is Gloucester's enemy, and that will keep him from winning great favour from Bedford or the King. Why then should the siege displease him? So great an undertaking, pursued through a hard winter and beyond . . . You know what damage it has inflicted already, to besiegers and defenders alike. You know how few of Burgundy's men are here at Orleans. You know, too, that Bedford pays every last sou of their wages.'

He knew all this. And he had truly thought on the matter, thought long and hard. And yet, he realised, torn between admiration for his friend and disgust at his own blindness, he had been a hundred miles from this neat – and now so obvious – conclusion.

So that is why Jean never spoke of the negotiations over the Duke of Orleans. Relief dawned in his mind, a rising sun of sheer joy. He did not keep them from us for the sake of Burgundy; it is just that he knew from the start that they would change nothing.

He grinned at Jean, his hangover temporarily forgotten. 'All the same,' he said cheerfully, 'that is the view of a cynic.'

Jean de Waurin responded with a lazy smile. 'If I were a cynic, Poursuivant, I would predict that Burgundy will change his policy just as soon as Bedford runs out of the funds to pay his Burgundian soldiers.'

Secret frowned. A cloud of darker realisation filmed his golden sky. You are indeed a cynic, he thought silently. And so am I by that token; for I can believe that only too well.

And he could see what would follow. The last Burgundians, then, would withdraw from Bedford's army; and had he not always known that Jean de Waurin was a Burgundian?

5

ENGLAND

Agnes was pretty once, Will thought to himself.

The thought surprised him, because this had not been his first impression of Agnes Paston at all. But from where he was sitting, on the bench that ran along the side of the fireplace in the hall at Princes Inn, he had the opportunity to look closely at her without her noticing, and it came to him that this was the key to her appearance. She was not young any more – though it had surprised him to discover how much younger she was than the Judge – and she was not pretty any more, but she still had the pert self-confidence of a woman who is used to being admired.

Agnes was standing in the middle of the hall, scolding Jennet the housemaid. She was a shortish woman, slim, with well-shaped arms. Her neat figure was marred by the generous bulge of her stomach; her child was due in the spring. Her features were regular. On either side of her mouth were scored two deep lines, and there were fainter little lines drawn around her eyes. I did not think her pretty when I first met her, Will thought, because it is so clear from her face that she is a chronic scold.

Jennet was taking the scolding quietly. Jennet took most things quietly. Jennet was like a mouse, all shades of brown: pale brownish skin, sleek mid-brown hair, dull brown kirtle. Her eyes were brown too, bright little mouse eyes. They had shone out at him when he had run slap-bang into her in the corridor the day before. Those

154

eyes had held his then for a moment, but in Agnes' company nothing about Jennet held Will's eyes: they kept drifting back to Agnes.

He did not like Agnes, but he rather admired her energy, her indomitable determination to see everything in her house perfect. It reminded him of the Duchess of Norfolk. The Duchess was a very competent housekeeper too, he thought, though she never stooped to scolding the housemaids.

'. . . out in the yard!' Agnes ended with a flourish. She turned from Jennet and marched towards the yard door. There was something bouncy about Agnes' walk, even with the weight of the child in her belly. The bunch of iron keys at her belt gave out a rhythmic clank. Her skirts brushed the rushes on the floor, making a swishing noise. Spring-cabbage green, Agnes' skirts. Agnes liked green, and scarlet, and acid-yellow. She would have looked prettier in softer colours.

She would have looked prettier in a new gown. He had never seen her in a new gown. She still wears her trousseau gowns, he thought. Perhaps if she had known that she would wear them for so long, let them out and take them in so often, she would have chosen less fashionable styles. The fashions of close on ten years before looked faintly ridiculous by now: or would have done on anyone less assured than Agnes.

Was it Agnes herself who chose not to buy new gowns? Or was it the Judge? He suspected they shared a tendency to string their purses tight. Mind, they were not mean to their visitors: the hall of Princes Inn was generally full, and the trestle creaked from the weight of the food.

Jennet gave a little sigh. Will turned from the yard door, which he had continued to watch after Agnes' exit and looked at her. Was she about to cry? A sniff followed the sigh, but that was all, thank heavens: she straightened her shoulders, went to the far corner and picked up a birch broom. She approached the fireplace, hesitantly, not meeting Will's look. She began to sweep the stone

155

slabs of the hearth, on the other side to where he was sitting.

'Sharp tongued, isn't she?' he said in a cheerful voice.

He half expected Jennet to jump, but she didn't: simply turned to him and gave him a shy smile.

'She grumbles, sir, but she never beats me. And I reckon 'twould be a thousand times worse to have a mistress who cared nothing for her household.'

'That's true.' Agnes is not a cruel woman, he thought: just a discontented one. What she needs is a good tumbling by a young lover. The Judge must be getting past it. Not that he was tempted to try her himself. Princes Inn was hardly the Pleasance, and he doubted if the Judge would prove a complaisant husband.

Ten days in Norwich, though, and not a girl in his bed during all that time. Bloody women: a man might hate them, but it was no fun to do without them.

His eyes rested, almost absently, on Jennet. It was soothing watching Jennet. There was nothing about those gentle shades of brown, those slow steady movements with the broom, to remind him of Jeanne or the Duchess or the other bitches at Framlingham. A very different kind of girl, Jennet. He mentally removed the dull brown kirtle and realised to his surprise that the body underneath was not scrawny at all, but had some very appetising curves.

Jennet swept all the ashes into a metal pan and carried it off to the yard. She reappeared a moment later and went back to the corner for a long feather duster. He watched her reach her arms upwards, straining towards the rafters.

'You'll never reach those topmost cobwebs,' he said, rising from his place by the fire and walking towards her. 'Here, let me help you . . .'

'I still think those Calais merchants are growing too greedy. A great mistake, to fix the Staple permanently . . .'

Will stifled a yawn. I'll bet Judge Paston does it on

purpose, he thought. He picks the biggest bores at the Guild meetings, drags me over to be introduced and then walks off, trapping me with them.

Sir Brian Stapleton and Sir Henry Inglose droned on and on about wool prices, the spring clip and the autumn kill, bales and broggers and taxes. Will glanced around surreptitiously. He had not contributed a word to the conversation for ten minutes or more: perhaps they would not notice if he were to drift away.

He inched towards the window of the Guildhall. A cool shaft of winter sunlight shone through it, highlighting the heads of the two men standing in front of it. That was the Mayor on the left, surely: Thomas Wetherby. Judge Paston had told him to keep away from Thomas Wetherby. He did not recognise the other man, a fair-haired, chubby-faced man in a lawyer's gown.

The two broke off their conversation as he approached and both heads turned towards him.

'Calthorp, is it not?' Wetherby asked in a rich, hearty voice, holding out his right hand. 'Would you not be Sir William's son?'

'His grandson, sir. Sir John was my father.'

'Ah. Good man, Sir John.' He turned to his companion. 'You remember Sir John Calthorp?'

'I know the name, but no more. It's seven or eight years since he died, surely: I was no more than a boy then.' This man too held out a hand to Will. 'John Heydon, sir.'

'I'm sure I'd know your name too, if I were not such a stranger to Norwich.'

'You'll know of my master, Sir Thomas Tuddenham.'

Will did indeed know that name. Tuddenham was the Judge's bogey, worse even, if the Judge was to be believed, than Thomas Wetherby. He could not remember why either man was to be distrusted. Some kind of shenanigans at the Shire Courts, most likely. The Judge would not have told him the details, anyway: when he spoke of his cases it was in dark hints and mild curses.

'I shall hope to know him better in future,' he replied.

Wetherby said, 'You've left the Duke of Norfolk's service, then? And plan to run your estates yourself?'

Will's eyes narrowed. At Framlingham people had known his name and face but cared nothing for his business. In Norwich the reverse seemed to be true: a string of total strangers had tried to discuss his estates with him, most of them with an expertise that he could not possibly match. He liked these conversations even less than he liked keeping silent and listening to bores.

'I've not left it permanently, sir. The Duchess gave me leave to come to Norwich, but I'll be back in her household before the year end.'

'The Duchess?' Wetherby echoed, in a tone which told Will he should have said 'the Duke' instead.

'The Duke was still in his bed when I left Framlingham,' he said hastily. 'Doctors' orders.'

'A wasting sickness, I heard?'

'Colds on his chest, and other ailments.'

Wetherby and Heydon exchanged a glance. Will thought for a moment that they, like everyone else, would ask him whether he reckoned the Duke was ever likely to leave his bed. So far he had avoided giving any opinion on this subject, not least because he did not have one to offer. But instead Heydon said, in a cautious voice, 'I heard the Duchess is administering the Mowbray estates . . .'

'She does so temporarily, I understand, with the aid of a very efficient set of bailiffs.' The Judge's voice acted on Will's spirits like a set of handcuffs. Curse it. He should have been keeping one eye on the Judge; he should have known the Judge would be keeping one eye on him. That was the end of that conversation; not that he was sorry, except that he felt sure the Judge would punish him for his disobedience by delivering him next to the oldest and dullest fogey he could track down.

But John Heydon was not prepared to let him go yet. 'You're planning to spend some time on your estate this summer? Burnham Market, is it not?'

'Burnham Thorpe,' he corrected automatically.

'That's no distance from Brancaster, surely. I travel regularly to Brancaster on business.'

And what was that to – Jesus, was Heydon fishing for an invitation to the Hall? What should he reply? He had never entertained visitors on his own account, he had no idea –

'Then you'll have met the agents the trustees engaged to handle Calthorp's affairs,' Judge Paston said briskly. 'First-rate men, all of them.'

A shutter seemed to fall over Heydon's pale eyes. Will frowned. Agents? Holy Heavens, he thought, was he looking to get work from me?

'Damme's in charge, isn't he? A good man,' Wetherby agreed.

'Come on, Calthorp. I want you to meet Richard Purdance, one of the City Aldermen. He has some very interesting ideas.'

Will dutifully bowed his head, excused himself from Wetherby and Heydon, and trailed after the Judge. How old will Purdance turn out to be? He wondered. Sixty? Seventy?

The Judge turned and glanced at him. He gave into temptation and scowled back.

'Stapleton's son Miles must be about your age now,' the Judge said in a mildly reproving voice. 'Sir Brian said he'd be in Norwich by the end of the week. I have asked them both to come and dine at Princes Inn.'

'That's good of you, sir.'

The Judge nodded, as if he knew it was.

'I had thought you might have met young John Heydon before,' he continued.

'How might I have done that, sir?'

'Why, through Walter Aslake and his men. Heydon is a great friend of Aslake. So is Wetherby, from what I hear.'

Will swallowed. 'I'll remember that, sir.'

John Heydon called at Princes Inn three days later. He went to the clerks' room on business, then knocked at the door of the hall. Agnes received him politely, but not warmly. Heydon invited Will to join a group of his friends that evening, drinking in the Popinjay. Will told him that he had already arranged to meet Miles Stapleton at the Boar's Head.

'Had you,' Agnes asked, when Heydon had bowed his way out, 'made an arrangement with Stapleton?'

He and Miles had met the previous day and taken an immediate liking to each other. Miles had turned out to be a tall lad with an unruly shock of brown hair and a ready grin, as unlike his pompous father in temperament as he could be. They had planned to meet up again, but not that evening particularly; not at the Boar's Head.

Will shrugged. 'If I go to the Boar's Head, I dare say I might find him there.'

'Heydon's the kind of man who would check such a thing.'

'I'll remember that.'

Agnes nodded and picked up her embroidery. 'A lout, Heydon,' she said calmly. 'Drinks too much.'

Will did not answer her; she did not seem to expect him to.

Typical of Agnes, that verdict, he thought. Her judgements were generally terse and rather aggressive. Lady Morley, according to Agnes, was punctilious and dull. The Yelvertons were over-zealous and humourless. Thomas Wetherby was loud-mouthed and untrustworthy.

He thought this mean-spirited of her. But though she judged harshly, his impression so far was that she was all too accurate.

What was he, he wondered, to Agnes? Young and insignificant? That was what the Judge seemed to reckon him. The Judge had been a dutiful host: he had taken Will along to Guild meetings, introduced him to his future neighbours, invited friends to Princes Inn to meet him. But he had given Will no indication at all that he enjoyed his company.

160

He thinks I am frivolous, Will thought to himself, because the wool trade bores me. He seems to think that politics bores me too, but that is not true: I care nothing for the issues, but I am interested in people, in power, in intrigue. I may not be eminent and busy and purposeful like the Judge, but he is wrong to think me a fool with nothing more serious on my mind than the problem of when and where I might catch Jennet alone.

It was, however, true that he had devoted a large proportion of his time and thought to Jennet; and he had succeeded in catching her alone several times, with very satisfactory results. Did Agnes know about that? he wondered. She had given him no indication of it if she had.

Jennet was not in the hall. She would probably be in the solar. Folding sheets, perhaps: it was washday. It should not be too difficult to make his way up there without Agnes noticing . . .

He got up from the bench, quietly, keeping half an eye on Agnes. Agnes reached for a new length of thread from her workbasket. Will moved casually towards the inner door and the stairs.

And down them, at a bound, came young John Paston and his brother Edmund. They tumbled at Will's feet, like a pair of young puppies, with Kate the nursemaid following more decorously behind them.

'Will! Will!' they chorused. 'Tell us that story again. Please! The one about Jonah and the whale . . .'

Will sighed. 'Come on', he said. 'Let's go and sit near the fire.'

The long black drapes stirred. They parted and were swiftly drawn together again. Then a new gap appeared between them; and slowly, a dragon's head poked out. It was red, with scale-markings of gold and huge, luminous green eyes; long-snouted, with a mouth full of teeth. The lower jaw sagged and then snapped shut with a little click.

'Moooooo . . .' The noise that emerged was something like a howl, rather more like a lovesick cow. Will, who had been watching straight-faced till then, doubled up with laughter.

'Well, I don't know,' grumbled Miles, dropping the mask and stepping out from behind the drapes. 'What kind of noise does a dragon make?'

'You were at the procession last year. I was not.'

'Yes, but the crowd were so noisy; I cannot recall the dragon sounding at all. It did breathe fire. How did they contrive that, I wonder?'

Miles glanced across at the overflowing chest that held the Guild's processional props. The two of them were in the basement of Saint George's House in Tombland. They had offered to clear out the room and take an inventory, but so far the contents had been more laughed over than itemised.

The dragon's rear-end, in papier-mâché, lay on the floor. Next to it was the beaten silvered armour that Saint George wore, his scarlet gown and blue garters, and his silver-gilt chaplet. There were two enormous cloths, painted with scenes of the saint's martyrdom; half a dozen banners with images and arms of the saint; trumpets, imitation swords, trappings for the horses; but nothing, as far as Will could see, for the production of clouds of smoke.

Will himself was dressed in one of the attendants' white gowns and an improbably vast pair of silver gauntlets. 'I think,' he said, half seriously, 'they must do it with smouldering cloths. I bet it's uncomfortable playing the front end.'

Miles picked up a sword and gave an experimental slash with it. 'If you reckon so, then I shall play the front, and you may take the tail. And I shall make my dragon roar. With gunpowder.'

Will rounded his eyes theatrically. He half believed Miles. There was something cheerful and reckless about Miles: he could get away with such a stunt, if anyone could. 'I was growing fond of this gown,' he said in a mock-rueful voice.

'Mmm. It is rather fetching, I agree. I shall allow you to be a nymph if you prefer.'

Will inclined his head in acknowledgement and gave a little twirl. It was tempting, the thought of playing a nymph; more tempting to be a dragon with Miles. But unfortunately it looked as if he would have no chance to play either part.

'The problem is,' he said, 'that Judge Paston has no intention of staying in Norwich till Saint George's Day.'

'That is no problem. You can stay on when the Pastons leave. My father would put you up, or Inglose, or – oh, a dozen others.'

'I have to go with them to Oxnead.'

'You cannot bear to leave Agnes?'

Will grinned. Miles knew how untrue that was; but then, he also knew about Jennet. 'I should be heartbroken to say goodbye. Seriously, though, the Judge offered to escort me from there up to Burnham Thorpe. He is one of my trustees: I can hardly refuse to go with him.'

'You plan to stay all summer on your estates? Holy mother, how boring!'

'You planned to go somewhere truly exciting yourself?'

'Orleans. Real gunpowder. God, I hope the war lasts until I get to France.'

Miles really did plan to be a soldier, as Will already knew. But he also knew it would be another year, perhaps two, before Sir Brian allowed his son a horse and armour of his own. 'Well,' he said, 'if you just happen to spend a week or two in Norfolk before you leave – at Ingham, maybe? – I'll not complain if you come to call on me.'

'Checkmate,' Miles said with a laugh. 'I promise to come.'

Oxnead Place was the Pastons' second manor, Will knew; it had been part of Agnes' dowry. The house was almost as low as the church, built of a warm brick that glowed in the red light of the setting sun. Beyond it, Will could glimpse a tiny huddle of cottages, and the thread of the track, narrowing still more and finally breaking up into a mass of footpaths that wove through the fields and down to the river bank. There were two, no, three boats moored at the bank: low-lying barges, set with tall black sails.

The first of the baggage carts that carried the Pastons' furnishings from Norwich was still lumbering to a halt when Agnes clambered down from her less sturdy cart and strode into the house. Will, encumbered by Edmund, whom he had taken onto his horse to curb his restlessness, could only sit in his saddle and watch her until Kate came to retrieve the boy. By the time he had stabled his horse and reached the hall, its mistress was in full flood.

'. . . fresh rushes,' she was screeching at Jennet and Cook. 'Here, and in the parlour, and the solar. I want that spiderweb cleared from the beam. I want another load of wood brought in for the fire. And I want a hot posset brought me right now in the solar.'

She swept off, her posture a blend of weariness and peremptoriness, towards the stairs to the solar. Will subsided on to the floor, indifferent to the age or cleanliness of the rushes covering it. There was as yet no furniture in the hall. He cast a rueful glance at Jennet. Jennet gave him a tired smile and disappeared through a door: to prepare Agnes' posset, presumably.

Nobody else was sitting down. Will sighed and got to his feet. In the yard, he could hear the servants pulling the canvas covers off the baggage carts. He went to help.

Will had liked Princes Inn. It was not an elegant house, but he did not care about that. It was efficiently run, the beds were comfortable and the hall was not too draughty. The beds were the same at Oxnead; but he did not like the place. At Oxnead, he had a continual feeling that the natural processes of decay were only just being kept at bay. Leave Oxnead for a year, he thought, and the weeds would be high around the walls; five years, and moss would be growing over the ruins.

This was in no way Agnes' fault, as far as he could tell. Her efficiency was as much in evidence as ever – though it grated on him more in the peace of Oxnead than ever it had at Princes Inn. The fires never went out, the dinners were well cooked, the servants were industrious and well behaved. The herds and flocks were healthy, the fishponds well stocked and the larder was full of bottled plums and salt pork and well-matured cheeses. But it was alien to him; it was not home, and he had a feeling that it never could be.

It would never have occurred to him to class Framlingham as his home, though he had spent almost half his life in the Duke of Norfolk's household. He supposed Burnham Thorpe was home. He wondered if Burnham Thorpe was damp. It was not, as far as he recalled: the Hall stood high among chalky meadows. He could not imagine the walls there feeling clammy with wet mist from the river; they would be whipped by fresh wind from the sea. At Burnham Thorpe, Will thought, a man might leap and stride; while at Oxnead Agnes grew fatter and fatter, and slower and slower, and the household seemed to slow and fatten around her.

Even Jennet, normally as industrious as she was insignificant, was slowing down. Agnes shouted at her daily and she looked permanently wan and miserable.

Will found her, one morning, being violently sick in the sluice behind the kitchens. He fetched her a cup of water. 'Must have been the pheasant we had last night,' he said, as she sipped it, whey-faced. 'I could have sworn Cook left them hanging days too long.'

Jennet stared at him, wide-eyed.

'My monthlies haven't come,' she said in a whisper.

'Your what?'

'My monthlies. You know, sir. The bleeding should have started last Tuesday.'

Will stared back. Last Tuesday, he thought. 'That is only five days ago. Perhaps it will start today, or tomorrow.'

'Oh sir, I do hope so. But what if it does not?'

What then? There was something women did, surely, in these situations? Only stupid women were caught: the sensible ones knew about the remedies. 'Then you – oh, Jennet, I've no idea. There's a draught of herbs, surely, or something the midwives can do. It's not my business, I'd not know. That's women's stuff . . .'

''Tis never so easy as that, sir.'

'It must be,' Will said in an odd, harsh voice. He turned and walked away fast, round the side of the barns. He did not stop, or even slow down, until he was beyond the furthest barn. The winter fields, the earth dark and shiny, spread out before him. A sky of fat white clouds seemed to press down on him. Bloody Oxnead. Damp, fertile, oppressive Oxnead. He had to get away. He had to get to Burnham, had to get right away from the house and Jennet and Agnes Paston and the Judge, had to get home.

How long before Agnes' child came? It would be days, surely, rather than weeks? And then the Judge would want to go. He had to; had to want to ride with Will to Burnham.

Will went back to the house. Agnes was sitting in a low armed chair near the fireplace, her sewing in her hands. The vast mound of her belly ballooned out in front of her. He stared at it in fascination. Agnes gave him a curious glance, but he could not bring himself to look away.

Jennet might grow like that too. There might be a child already in her belly: his child. A little flame of exultancy lit inside him. His first child.

No, no. It couldn't be so, couldn't. He had never meant to ruin Jennet, never meant to get a bastard on her.

There had to be a remedy.

6

FRANCE
Spring, 1429

It was growing dark and raining heavily. Drips fell from the rim of Secret's hat, on to his nose, his doublet, and in a damp trickle down his back. His horse barely walked, its head lowered, the rain slithering off its flanks and darkening the leather of his saddle. He rode in a semi-stupor, conscious of little but his discomfort, with Matthew Gough, a few paces behind Fastolf. Behind them were four hundred wagons, and the fifteen hundred men, Fastolf's troops reinforced by the Paris militia, who were escorting them to Orleans.

A heavy stench of fish hung in the air. Half the wagons held flour, the other half pickled herrings. Fastolf had taken eighteen days to assemble these supplies, which were intended to last the army throughout Lent.

They had been travelling three days. The previous day, at Etampes, they had heard rumour that a Valois army was riding to relieve Orleans. An hour before they had left the little village of Rouvray-Saint-Denis, and now they were making for Janville. Perhaps they would be there by dark; perhaps not, though Fastolf was hurrying the wagons as much as possible.

'I think,' said Matthew, drawing his horse a pace nearer to Secret's nag, 'we may have a problem.'

Secret pulled out of his stupor and looked up. Two new horsemen were riding with Fastolf, their mounts close together, their heads even closer. Scouts. As soon as he heard the rumour Fastolf had redoubled their number.

Fastolf reined in and turned his head. Gough and Secret spurred their horses and rode up to join him, as the scouts galloped off towards the rear of the procession.

'They found the Valois,' Gough said.

'Five, perhaps ten thousand men, under the Constable. Less than two miles away. We'll form up here.' The road was narrow, but the ground either side was flat, rough grassland.

Already the wagons were jostling to a halt, the wagoners and soldiers shouting to each other. 'Get that bloody noise down,' Fastolf said to Gough.

Gough disappeared. Secret thought: a battle by night, heavily outnumbered, with the wagons to protect, and the wagoners already grumbling every step of the way. Then he thought: this will be no running fight but a pitched battle. No herald rides with this wagon train. I shall have to parley. Another rivulet of water ran down his neck and a shiver followed it.

Fastolf began to bark out orders. They would form the wagons into a tight three-sided square, making an enclosure for the draught animals and the wagoners, and a narrow defensive position for the troops. The Paris archers and crossbowmen would take the left wing; the few men at arms the centre; the English and Welsh archers the right wing.

It took a long time to carry out these dispositions. Occasionally more scouts reported. The Valois scouts had found them, the Valois army was coming. It had artillery. It moved slowly, but not slowly enough to be outdistanced.

'You know my terms,' said Fastolf.

Secret nodded. They would fight: they could not afford to surrender the wagons. And with quarter, of course, for Fastolf preferred gain to vengeance.

It was not Richemont, he knew, who led this Valois army. The Breton count to whom he owed homage was no longer Constable; the Scottish noble Stewart had succeeded him. The Valois court was a wasps' nest, no

168

man stayed in favour with the Dauphin for long. Old one-eye the troops called Stewart. He was reputed to be ruthless. Perhaps he would not concede equal terms, since he would know that he had the advantage.

He thought of saying this to Fastolf, but it seemed to him that Fastolf would know it already.

He dismounted and unbuckled his saddlebag. The rain was easing, but there was heavy cloud and no moon. He felt through his sparse belongings—a spare undershirt and hose, a metal comb, a razor—and located the thick stuff of his decorated tabard. He took off his cloak, pulled his plain tabard over his head and dragged on the fancy one to replace it. He arranged the sleeves in the prescribed manner, down his chest and back. Then he packed his spare tabard back into the bag, wrapped his cloak back round his shoulders, remounted and set off to see what he might do to fill in the heavy hours before dawn.

For a while he watched the Paris archers. They had been issued with stakes such as the English archers used and were hammering a stockade into the soggy ground. It was hard, heavy work; they did it sullenly. Then he moved back into the wagon enclosure. In the space between the wagons there was a confusion of men, horses and oxen. The herring smell was strong now; it caught at his nose and made it run.

Dawn came. And with it a new downpour, and the Valois army, marching efficiently up the road from Janville. Fastolf's men were as ready as they could be. They stood and watched its progress in silence.

Secret strained his eyes, trying to read the banners in the dim light. He made out Stewart's colours, and those of a couple of other Scots commanders; but surely those were the Count of Clermont's colours in the vanguard?

'They waited until Clermont had joined them.'

Secret glanced to his side, and upwards. 'Trust you to know, Christophe.'

'It means we're even worse outnumbered, but otherwise it's no bad thing.'

169

'Joint commanders give scope for confusion.'

'True; but not relevant. Clermont will take sole command.'

Of course; he would have taken that for granted had he not grown used to the English system, where command was delegated partly on merit. Clermont was a royal count, son of the captive Duke of Bourbon, so he would take precedence over any mere foreigner, even if that foreigner were Constable, and a far better tactician and leader of men.

Even so, Secret did not like the news. He had prepared himself to face a Scottish herald, and that was daunting enough when he had never even stood by during a parley before. To parley with Bourbon Herald would be a thousand times worse. At least it is not Alençon, he told himself, nor Richemont either.

The realisation that there would be a battle was beginning to sit solidly in his head. He straightened his sleeves. He had discarded his cloak a few moments earlier and already his tabard was sodden, heavy on his shoulders, the gold and azure and scarlet of Fastolf's arms rain-darkened. Christophe to his left seemed huge and placid, intensely reassuring.

'Secret Poursuivant,' Fastolf said. 'Prepare to parley.'

Hanson touched his shoulder. The pressure lingered for a moment, then the archer strode away. The escort fell into place. A bearer for Fastolf's banner and another for the colours of Paris, and six horsemen. The bearers raised their banners and they rode out from the enclosure.

Before they had covered more than fifty paces the far larger Valois negotiating party set off to intercept them. Secret fixed his eyes on the bright patch of colour that was the leading tabard. That would be Bourbon Herald. But as he drew closer, he frowned. The colours were wrong, it looked almost like . . .

It was. Bourbon Herald was to the right, Stewart Herald to the left. And between them, resplendent in the Dauphin's colours, rode Mountjoie King of Arms.

Mountjoie signed to his two trumpeters and they sounded the parley. The King of Arms bowed. 'Secret Poursuivant.'

'Mountjoie King of Arms. Bourbon Herald. Stewart Herald.' To Secret's relief, his voice was steady.

'My Lord of Clermont demands the surrender of your wagons and supplies. You must abandon your artillery, but you may keep your personal weapons. On these conditions, you may ride for Orleans in safety.'

Your artillery? A supply train? That was a pig's bladder of a joke. Mountjoie surely knew that they had not so much as a culverin.

But this was a formal confrontation: a time for bravado, but not for bluff or buffoonery. These were Clermont's instructions, repeated by his Dauphin's King of Arms – though moderated by Mountjoie's own good sense, doubtless, since he knew his principal for a fool. Could both Mountjoie and Clermont truly believe that their opponents had guns? And if not, why set forward such a condition?

Secret thought hard. Better to let the silence grow than to answer recklessly: it was vital that he take from this confrontation all that he could. Do they hope that I shall deny it? he wondered.

'Your answer, Poursuivant?' Mountjoie's voice was high and held a hint of a quaver. He is scared, Secret thought suddenly. Incredible, but true. He and Clermont have made up this talk of guns because they wish to be reassured that we have none. Five men to each of ours, and guns large and small; and even so, they have no confidence.

Mind, the Valois were the losers at Verneuil; at Cravant; at Agincourt. But they were the victors . . . He searched his mind, but he could recall no Valois victories in a pitched battle of any size within his lifetime.

Such a weight of tradition, all falling on Fastolf's sturdy shoulders. Fastolf cannot hope to win, he thought, glancing past the King of Arms at the mass of the Valois army. They are too many, too strong. But they believe the English do not lose, and it is not for me to dissuade them.

He took a deep breath. 'Sir John Fastolf declines to accept these conditions.'

'He chooses to fight? You are outnumbered, you cannot hope to prevail.'

'He chooses to fight and offers quarter to all those of the rank of esquire and above.'

'Should Fastolf choose to fight, my lord of Clermont's words are these. May God never help his lordship again if a hair of his enemies escapes. He will permit no quarter: those men he captures shall all be put to the sword.'

Secret bowed. 'I shall take these terms to Sir John Fastolf, and return with his response.'

'My lord of Clermont's final words are these. He will permit one parley only. If the English heralds return, he says, they too are to be put to the sword.'

The brutal words were said calmly, but they unnerved Secret even so. For a moment he could think of no answer.

'You have spoken well,' Mountjoie said suddenly. 'But you must see that it is useless.'

Useless? No. On the contrary, this parley had been remarkably useful. He had done well, Secret thought with a rush of inner pride. Mountjoie had not discovered from him that behind the stakes waited a rabble of terrified Parisians and a pack of wagoners who had to be guarded with swords and staves lest they break out and flee with their beasts. And he had learned from Mountjoie something of great value.

He squared his thin shoulders and said in a loud voice, 'Sir John Fastolf understands these terms and accepts them. His own terms will be different. He will allow quarter to your men.'

'Secret Poursuivant,' drawled Stewart Herald, 'you serve not a knight, but a goddamned merchant.'

'And you, Stewart Herald, shall shortly be the servant of Sir John Fastolf's latest source of income.'

172

He pulled on his reins as he said this and turned his horse sharply. He spurred it into the nearest thing to a gallop that it could manage. After a moment he heard the sounds of his escort following him. And further behind his back, faintly, were the sounds of the Valois gunners, readying their weapons; the sounds of the Valois army, preparing to charge.

He was shaking by the time he reached the safety of the wagon enclosure.

'No quarter,' he said to Fastolf.

'I thought as bloody much,' Fastolf replied.

It would have been useless to look for a vantage point. The light was bad; the ground flat; there was nowhere safe. He thought neither of looking nor of running. His place was among the wagons, with Fastolf, Jean de Waurin, Christopher Hanson and the rest. He would even have fought, he thought, had he had a bow and the skill to use it. But he had neither weapon nor skill, so he withdrew to the rear of the space between the wagons. He put a hand on his nag's neck and tried to calm her. All the animals were restless.

His momentary beautiful conviction that Fastolf had a chance of winning the battle was rapidly slipping away. How could they win? The Valois had not only culverins, but two heavy serpentines. The siege-guns were generally useless in pitched battles, but against this square of wagons they would be the perfect weapon. Once the gunners had the range they would be able to fire and fire. They might force a surrender simply by firing, without taking the trouble to charge. But there could be no surrender now. No quarter.

As a poursuivant he would be spared, if the cannon balls did not take him. But he did not think he would wish to live on, if Jean de Waurin and Matthew Gough and George and Nicolas and the rest never came back with him to Orleans. He did not think he would wish to live on to see Sir John Fastolf go down in history as the great failure amongst Lancastrian captains, the one who had lost a battle and brought about the turning point in the war.

It would not be yet, he told himself. First there would be the waiting, as there had been at Verneuil. More, it was not yet fully light.

He was wrong. Men at arms might have waited; gunners did not. The first crack of gunpowder came long before he was expecting it, crashing across the low-muttered prayers of the troops and the whinnies of the horses.

He waited to hear the smash of wood splintering, the scream of men. He waited, and waited, and then another crack came. Perhaps they had misjudged the range; perhaps the first shot had missed the enclosure.

Perhaps he should have gone somewhere else after all: somewhere he could see the gunners set their tapers to the barrels, somewhere far from where the guns were aimed, somewhere from which he could run. He could not run at all from where he was. He could not see anything, bar his horse, a wagoner whispering Hail Marys under his breath and the stout wooden side of a fishwagon.

He closed his eyes. In his mind he could see the gunners cursing, repositioning their weapon, priming it with more gunpowder, ramming home the next cannonball . . .

Another bang. Some packhorses screamed; the oxen lowed. A crash: a hit on one of the wagons. A smell of herrings, overpoweringly strong now. His eyes were still closed, screwed tight. He could picture that too: the gash in the side of the wagon, the silvery herrings spilling out of their boxes and over the coarse grass.

Another bang, and another. The nag jumped and whinnied, jerking the reins in his hand. He opened his eyes. All round him the wagoners were fighting to control their animals. A horse reared; under its belly, Secret glimpsed men manhandling a wagon sideways, making a small gap through which to flee. He saw this

174

without thought or emotion: his head was full of the reverberation of the cannon, the sound of the trumpets, the heavy thundering of cavalry charging.

Cavalry charging. Valois cavalry. Fastolf's men at arms had dismounted. The guns should have taken the victory alone, but the cavalry were charging already. Now the guns will have to stop, he thought with sudden clarity, or they will hit the wrong men.

The guns had stopped, but the noise of the charge was deafening. It seemed to approach him, come level with him, pass him without growing quieter. Then he understood. The cavalry were not charging, but riding round to the back of the wagons. The arrogant Valois bastards! They had seen the guns fire, decided the victory was theirs. Now they were looking for plunder.

The crazy fools. What did they imagine was in the wagons? Guns, a king's treasury, the army's pay? Could they not smell the herring? Secret could smell it, a sickening smell of seaweed and decay. All my life, he thought, when I smell pickled herrings I shall remember this moment.

Another crash. The gunners had seen where the cavalry were aiming, seen that they were no longer between guns and wagons. A scream, and another. He felt a shudder from the wagon at his back. He turned. The next wagon had been hit; a wheel had been knocked loose, the body slumped crazily. Another crash, another shudder. The wagon slowly, slowly keeled on to its side. One of the ropes holding the tarpaulin gave way; herrings spilled out almost to his feet. His nag jumped again; he reached out to reassure her.

His hand came away sticky from her coat, covered in something pale and glutinous. He looked down at his tabard and saw that it too was covered in the pale sticky stuff. It took him a moment to realise what it was. A cloud of flour from the blasted wagons had billowed upwards and was settling on the men and the horses, turning to paste as it touched the rain on their coats.

175

Trumpets, more trumpets. Another charge. The back row of wagons seemed to be holding; some of Fastolf's men had secured the gaps. He had no time to think now, for the nag had reacted with terror to the trumpets: she was thrashing on her short rein, her eyes rolling back. He held hard on to the reins, all his mind fixed on keeping the horse from kicking free.

The reins were digging into his hands, cutting deep. The pain was almost reassuring. Over the sound of his own voice repeating soothing words, meant for the horse, that barely reached his own ears, he heard the shouts of the Lancastrian captains.

The archers were firing now. He recognised the rapid regular swish and twang of the bows, only paces from him. They were firing because the Valois were within range. The noise of the charge was greater than before; it was deafening. They would come, come. They would break through the thin English line, and come charging right over his position.

All his strength was pitted against the horse. He felt nothing but this certainty that they were coming. It was like standing in the sea, seeing a wave approaching, too large, too fast to escape. It would break over his head, it would drown him.

He was holding his breath, waiting for them to come. His head felt as if it were bursting. He hardly felt the nag give up her private battle and subside, mastered. His breath exploded out of him. Through the rushing in his ears he could hear the Valois cries now. 'Mountjoie', that was what they always cried, and 'Saint Denis!' He heard them crying these things. And another cry, even louder. 'Viras!' it sounded like. 'Viras!' He was not drowned. The thought surfaced: that meant 'Go back!'

They were not going back. They were coming forward. He could hear them, wave after wave of men at arms, every instinct urging them forward. He could hear the horses blindly surging onwards. He could hear something else, too: the song of terror. The high, white, blinding sound of men and animals in agony.

176

The stakes. The Valois had charged straight at the stakes. They had not stopped when they reached the stakes: they had hurtled straight on to them, through a storm of arrows.

Secret stood there, his hand still fiercely clenched around the reins, oblivious to the raw pain of his palm, oblivious to the fact that the reins were now loose, the horse quieted. There was nowhere for him to go. There was nothing for him to do but stand and let his head fill and overflow with this chaos and terror and agony.

He continued to stand there for a long time. The sound of the battle faded. A cold wind swirled into the enclosure from between the shattered wagons. The Paris militia were still fighting, butchering the Valois troops, but Fastolf's men had gone, clambering over and between the wagons, swords waving, chasing the Scots down the road to Janville. The men at arms returned for their horses, mounted and rode after their enemies.

A long time later, when he was helping to clear the debris and pack what was left of the herring boxes into the few surviving wagons, Secret turned to find Christopher Hanson at his side.

'Some stupid bastard,' said Hanson, 'killed old one-eyed Stewart.'

These words entered his head and began to make sense there.

'That was a foolish thing to do,' he said.

'Damn foolish. Fastolf has the word out already: he wants the man who claims to have done it. Get him while he's high on bloodlust, that's the idea. Then the damn idiot won't realise he's not claiming bounty, but losing a week's pay.'

A week's pay was cheap, Fastolf's poursuivant thought. One-eyed Stewart would have fetched a good ransom.

'What happened to Clermont?' he asked.

'Escaped, damn it. We've a good few prisoners, but none in that league.'

'So the ransoms will be none so large.'

'Just about large enough to pay for new wagons. And a new load of pickled herrings.'

Two days later, the remnants of the supply train arrived at the English forts outside Orleans. The following morning Secret rode for England.

He went to the court first and recited his news to Garter King of Arms. From there, he went to Southwark to repeat it to Welles. With an armful of letters and a head full of messages, he set out for East Anglia. He told his story again to Norfolk's Duchess at Framlingham, then rode on to Norwich. He stayed at Fastolf's Norwich mansion, Samson and Hercules House, and rode out from there to deliver letters and messages to Thomas Wetherby, Sir Thomas Tuddenham and half a dozen other aldermen and merchants. Finally he set out from Norwich towards Oxnead, the manor where, he had been assured, he would find Judge William Paston.

Secret stopped when he reached the gates to Oxnead Place. The red brick of the house caught and amplified the miserable ration of sunlight that to the English made a fine day. He gazed on the house, the barns and stores that surrounded the yard in front of it, the meadow beyond, broken by a spiderweb of trails and the hollows of half a dozen fishponds, the silver trail of the river with its burden of black-sailed barges. He thought: Paston spoke of this house as if it were set to the seaward, but in fact it lies ten miles or more from the open sea. All the same, though, it belongs to the queer lowland world of the Norfolk waterways; it does not seem part of the landlocked world at all.

He kept to his horse as the mastiffs rushed out at him and the stable boy came to drag them away. He watched them disappear, then turned to find another boy, younger, with a square, freckled, brown face and a clean tunic, almost beneath the hooves of his mount. The boy strained up, catching at the bridle, and twitched the hem of Secret's cloak till he could make out the device on the little enamalled badge he wore on the left shoulder of his grey tunic.

'Or and azure, quarterly. Sir John Fastolf's colours,' the boy said.

Secret smiled. 'On a bend gules, with three cross crosslets argent.'

'Do you have a tabard too? In or and azure?'

'In my pack.' A battered tabard, marked by water and flour and the silver scales of pickled herrings. 'I will show you later, if you wish.' He dismounted. 'I am Sir John's poursuivant. Men call me Secret. And you are . . .'

'John Paston of Paston. And of Oxnead.'

'Your servant, John Paston.'

The boy looked to be seven, perhaps eight years old, a sturdy child, but with something hesitant about his broad face.

'James will take your horse,' the boy said. 'Does Father expect you?'

'They told me in Norwich he was here.'

'He came for the baby. It was born yesterday.'

'Your brother?'

'Sister, worse luck. I already have a brother. He is just four, and I am seven.'

'So I guessed.'

John nodded as if he had expected no less. 'Do you have news of the wars in France? Of the siege at Orleans?'

'Of that, and more.'

The great hall was crowded for supper, though the Judge's wife was still confined to the solar. Secret knew only a scattering of faces at the high table. He recognised the sparse red hair of William Yelverton, the young lawyer, sharp and fast-rising, who had acted for Fastolf on some land purchases. Will Calthorp, normally merry company, but for once subdued. John Damme, a neighbour and agent of Paston's. Sir Brian Stapleton, a landowner from Ingham in East Norfolk.

The family chaplain, and a gaggle of monks: Cluniacs from Bromholm, the great priory hard by Paston village, and Franciscans from the Norwich house.

As soon as he had eaten he began to tell his news. He began by summarising the progress of the siege from Christmas onwards. The men round the trestle listened in silence until he came to Fastolf's action. Their faces lightened then. No wonder, Secret thought. He knew what dealings each man had with Fastolf. He knew how large a share each one hoped for of Fastolf's profits.

He told the story of the battle quickly and simply. It was not a matter he enjoyed. He could still smell the fish and the stale blood and the gluey flour. He had no wish to boast of his own small role; he would have preferred his hearers not to realise that he himself had been at Rouvray.

When he finished there was silence. He looked at the Judge. The Judge gave a short bark of laughter. 'What a perfect battle for Fastolf. Not a Duke in sight to steal the ransoms from him.'

Secret understood this reaction: he had heard much the same elsewhere. He had realised long before that nobody ever thought Fastolf heroic. The knight was admired for his hard-headedness, but this great success of his had elicited no awe, and much amusement. This saddened Secret. It seemed to him that it was not the fault of his account: men to whom he had said nothing spoke not of the Battle of Janville, but of the Battle of the Herrings.

'The ransoms were none so great,' he said quietly. 'Stewart was killed, and Clermont escaped.'

'Even so, this'll line Welles' pocket and buy Fastolf another mile of Southwark High Street.'

Yelverton said this; and it pleased Secret even less. A stupid, facile reaction he thought it. He considered explaining the likely real outcome of the battle. He had left Orleans too soon to see it unfold, but he, Hanson and the rest had all agreed what would happen. There would be short rations for the remainder of Lent; empty bellies and busy tongues in the Lancastrian camps. There would be great bitterness in Paris, since many of the militia had been wounded and a handful killed. The Orleans commanders would appropriate what ransom money there was, giving Fastolf the smallest share permissible. The rest would go towards paying off the massive backlog in the soldiers' wages: towards keeping Burgundy content for another month or two.

He said none of this. These were Englishmen; they did not wish to hear soldiers' grouches. If they thought the news he brought them bad, they would feed him the worst cuts of meat and the thinnest ale.

'Fastolf still buys land in Normandy,' he said.

'All the same, Welles must be doing damnably well out of this,' said Sir Brian Stapleton. 'He probably supplied half the grain in the first place. I wonder he and Fastolf have not thought of lending money to the Council. Surely Gloucester would find him an earldom in exchange.'

The Judge glanced at him with obvious surprise. 'It's the last thing Fastolf wants, to play at Beaufort's game and win English titles for it,' he said tartly. 'Especially when French titles can be had so cheaply.'

'I had not thought even you, Judge, would care to speculate on what Fastolf truly wants,' William Yelverton said.

John Damme gave a slow smile. 'He wants what every one of us wants. Money, a great house, influence in the country.'

'Perhaps we all do,' the Judge agreed. He looked at Secret. Secret did not meet his eyes. He means to change the subject, he thought. He was not sure what was coming.

'And what,' the Judge asked, 'does Fastolf think of the Earl of Suffolk?'

Suffolk. That was predictable: everyone in Norfolk had asked him about the Earl of Suffolk. What the Earl planned to do at Orleans; what he thought of the siege; what men thought of what he thought of the siege; even whether he might abandon the entire operation and come home to England. He had given many replies to these questions, but few answers.

What does Fastolf think? That was a new variation: he had not been asked that one before. He considered what to say for a long time. Too long. The volume of conversation round the table fell; his hesitation was becoming conspicuous.

At last he said, 'His Lordship of Suffolk was taking his pay in grants of land the year before last, and before that. Last year it is said that he did not take it at all.'

'Maybe he saves it to mend the roof at Wingfield?' Yelverton suggested. 'Great leaky barn of a place, and nobody has touched it for fifteen years or more.'

'Suffolk will never come back to England,' Stapleton retorted. 'He's like Fastolf; his life is in France now. A Lancastrian Frenchman, that's what he's become.'

Judge Paston slowly shook his head. 'You will never persuade me that that can be anything but a contradiction.'

He presumably intended it as a goad. Yelverton and Stapleton leaned forward to pursue the argument. Secret drew back and dropped his eyes to his ale. He could feel Paston watching him, but the other man did not intervene again, did not press him for a response. A reprieve; but he suspected it would prove to be only a temporary one.

'This way,' said John Paston.

The two boys were dressed in countrymen's clothes: short tunics and hoods in coarse brown woollen cloth, and thick breeches tied around their legs to protect them from the long grass and the sharp reeds. Secret had done his best to imitate them and an old and faded tabard topped his woollen hose.

They took the path past the cottages, and then a narrow track that led towards the river bank. On this they walked in single file: John leading, with little Edmund a few paces behind him, and Secret bringing up the rear. A plough team were at work in one of the nearer fields: the ploughman and his boy looked up briefly and gave a cursory wave, which Edmund returned. After that they saw nobody. None of them spoke.

There was a raised path along the river bank, perhaps a man's length from the open channel. Between it and the river were the reed beds, a jumble of last year's browned stalks and this year's new growth, a pale, tremulous green, with the occasional bright touch from a clump of marsh marigolds. The path was of trampled earth; to the other side a slight drop led to the water meadows, still marshy after the spring floods and empty as yet of cattle and sheep.

John turned and made a gesture for silence – hardly necessary – as they approached a point where the river curved round and a little tributary fed in from across the meadow. The boys did not stop but turned up the tributary, where the path narrowed still more and became overgrown. The stream here was thin and torpid, the reed beds were choked with weeds. Ahead, a dense band of trees cast a long morning shadow. John stopped, waiting for the other two to catch up; and they moved on more slowly and cautiously, in a half-crouch that made them all but invisible among the dense vegetation.

The marshland birds and animals seemed unaware of their presence. The sedge warblers sang their mocking tunes; a bittern boomed from a nearby patch of dense reeds. Frogs croaked their courting song. Coming to a sudden halt behind John, Secret found that they were almost at the edge of a wide, shallow pond, and that the straggling path petered out into a morass of reeds and mud.

In the shallow water at the edge of the pond a dozen herons stood, motionless in the morning light. John caught at his sleeve and brought his gaze upwards to the nearest trees, where he could make out the shaggy outline of the herons' nests in the topmost branches.

At John's gesture, the three of them slipped to the

ground. They inched forward, parting the reeds in front of them with their hands and flattening them to make a thin carpet above the mud, until they were almost at the water's edge. Then they stopped.

Secret could feel the mud, cold beneath the reeds under him. He could hear the light, steady breathing of the two boys. He felt a little ripple of wind pass over him and pleat the surface of the pond. He glanced sideways and saw John and Edmund still and intent, their elbows set and their faces propped steady. They waited for a long time.

A heron moved, its long neck uncurling, and dipped its beak swiftly into the water. It drew out a tiny silver fish, impaled sideways; and with a rapid, practised movement the great grey-white bird tossed it high into the air and caught and swallowed it whole.

The three waited again, until a second bird made a catch; and again, for a third.

It was the sudden contrast, Secret thought to himself, that made the action so striking. The birds were so still, so patient; and then suddenly so fast, so aggressive in their movements. The model, perhaps, of a Norfolk man's way of life. He glanced again at John; and this time John felt his glance and gave him a smile that flashed as brightly and suddenly as the heron's beak.

The following Thursday morning, Secret was called to the parlour to speak alone with the Judge. It was their first private interview since his arrival at Oxnead. Paston had been away in Norwich one day, busy on his lands, caught up with the neighbours who had come to admire the new baby. All the same, Secret reckoned he had been given a free rein deliberately; and that the Judge had been watching to see how he used it.

He had used it carefully; and though what he had learned had done nothing to increase his liking for the Judge, it had enhanced his respect for him. Paston was harsh with his children, but what father was not? He showed little mercy when his tenants did not pay their rents. But he ran his estates with considerable skill, and his wife, even confined to her bed, was a powerful presence in the household and a constant check on the servants. Welles was right, Secret thought: Judge Paston is a formidable man.

And he has, I trust, seen that I am a careful poursuivant. I have spoken with none of his enemies; I have done nothing to stir his old suspicions. Perhaps he will give me work. Perhaps he will ask me for more information – on matters at Framlingham, for instance – and perhaps I will give it to him.

It took him aback when the Judge said instead, 'What were your orders from Fastolf? When you came here to Oxnead.'

'Why, to deliver the letters I brought you. And to receive your replies, and return them to him.'

'Fastolf did not order you to ask the questions you have been asking? Of John Damme? Of young Calthorp? Of Brother Francis? Of my sons?'

This last was said with a slight menace, as if the Judge expected him to feel guilty. It annoyed him. 'Nor did he order me to give you and your friends news of the war.'

The Judge waved a hand impatiently, as if he were swiping this argument away. It was customary for all travellers to provide reports, and they both knew it. He persisted, 'How much of this do you intend to tell Fastolf? Of what you have discovered in Norfolk?'

'As much as he wishes to know.'

The Judge's face flickered with annoyance. He thinks I am baiting him, Secret thought. And it is not so; but I cannot see that I can reply otherwise.

'I was not aware that Sir John had so great an interest in Norfolk politics.'

Secret considered. 'He does not always wish to know all that I might tell him.'

'So you learn these things for your private satisfaction?'

'I learn them because it is my job.'

185

The Judge was silent for some time. Perhaps he was considering whether to ask more questions. If so, he decided against it. He crossed to a low trestle, where his clerk had laid out his letters. He handed them to Secret one by one. Letters to Fastolf, ready sealed. One to John Kirtling; several to John Welles. A letter to the Duke of Gloucester, and others to his own agents in London. Most of these latter documents did not concern Fastolf's business; he pointed this out and they negotiated a price for their delivery.

Secret stowed all the letters away carefully, bowed to the Judge and backed out of the parlour. Then he went to make his goodbyes around the household. He bowed gravely to John and Edmund, wondering fleetingly whether the little they had told him would earn them a beating. He kissed Kate the nursemaid, who had proved very amenable to his advances; kissed Cook as well, to her loud amusement. He mounted the steep stairs to the solar and made a flourishing bow to Agnes Paston and baby Elizabeth. He nodded at Harry Holt and William Taverner, Paston's groom and bailiff, keeping out of speaking distance for the Judge's benefit. Then he mounted his dun mare and rode for London, wondering as he rode whether he would repeat that last conversation, as well as all the preceding ones, to John Welles.

7

ENGLAND

Jennet's pregnancy was annoying, but once his initial shock had faded Will realised it was not really a tragedy. He wished she would see sense and go to a wise woman, but he soon despaired of the whispered arguments during which he had to keep glancing up to the solar window to make sure that Agnes could not overhear, and resigned himself to the fact that by the late autumn his first bastard would be born.

Obviously it was out of the question for him to marry her, and to his relief she realised that. Nor did he particularly want to keep her as a mistress. She was such a funny, plain, mouselike thing: he could not understand now why he had ever been attracted to her. He knew he ought to make some sort of provision for her, but he still did not have control of his estates and his fortune: he had only a scanty allowance from his trustees, and no inclination to turn a large part of that over to Jennet.

He supposed he ought to talk to the Judge, as the chief among his trustees, but he could see the awkwardness of this and finally decided to postpone the confession until after he had left Oxnead. But he still did not know when that would be.

It would never do to go without the Judge's blessing: he would have to wait until the Judge was willing to accompany him to Burnham Thorpe. It would be a disaster, though, if he was forced to stay for so long that Agnes discovered Jennet's condition before he made his confession.

He was fairly sure Jennet would tell nobody until she was forced to, but he did his best to make it still more certain by continuing to meet her, to listen to her tearful outpourings, and to reassure her as best he could. She would not betray him out of spite, not while he whispered words of love and she whispered more in return. But she was no heroine, and he knew that when Agnes found out she was pregnant she would waste no time in discovering who the father was.

Fortunately the imminent birth of Agnes' own baby meant that she was paying less than her usual close attention to household affairs. With luck she would not notice until she returned to the hall after the birth. Cook would notice sooner, doubtless, and the other female servants; but he doubted if any of them would trouble to tell Agnes.

It was a fine spring, but the days hung heavily for Will. He went hawking; he went rabbiting with the bailiff; on market days he rode into Aylsham and drank in the Red Lion with John Damme and his friends. The Judge rarely spoke to him.

At last Agnes went into labour. She gave birth easily. Her pains started late one night; by the following evening she had produced a daughter.

That surprised Will. He had taken it for granted that the child would be a son, and so, he suspected, had Agnes and the Judge. They had no reason to be put out, with two healthy sons already, but he sensed that they were both disappointed. It took him only minutes to calculate that this was likely to be to his advantage. Judge Paston would have no inclination to stay and admire this unwanted daughter. He might be willing to travel to Burnham Thorpe as soon as the midwife confirmed that Agnes was out of danger.

Will's cheerfulness at this thought lasted only until the arrival of Secret Poursuivant the following afternoon.

There was news of the French wars over dinner that day. He found that interesting, and heartening. There was talk, mingled with the news, of the financial entanglements of Sir John Fastolf and John Welles and half a dozen Norfolk men whom he knew casually. He took little interest in this. He assumed that the poursuivant would hold no interest for the Judge either once his news had been related. He soon found that he was mistaken.

He asked Harry Holt when the Judge might think of going to Burnham. After Secret Poursuivant leaves, Harry told him. This struck him as incredible, so he asked the Judge himself, much more tentatively. The Judge was vague and evasive. Will tried to think if there was some other reason why he might wish to stay on at Oxnead, but none came to mind.

All the same, he could not believe that the poursuivant was dictating the Judge's movements. The Judge seemed to ignore Secret almost as completely as he ignored Will, and protocol did not demand that he stay at Oxnead for the entire visit of a lowly poursuivant.

Being curious – and short of other entertainment – Will began to watch Secret. He followed the poursuivant around the house and its lands, and tried to eavesdrop on his conversations.

Secret gave the superficial impression of mooching around at random, but Will soon realised that his actions were almost all purposeful. When he lingered with the grooms he induced them to talk of the state of Paston's horses; when he chatted with Cook he learned about the pantries. People talked to him; they talked very freely. This was no accident. Secret not only listened to long tales of people's troubles, he also performed little services for each one. He told them stories, he carried messages for them. He even mended their shoes.

Not even the Paston children had been spared this treatment. Will realised belatedly that John and Edmund had not begged him for a story for days. He told himself he was relieved to be rid of their pestering, but he was also a little annoyed at their defection.

He did think of pouring out his own troubles to Secret. He would not have trusted anyone else to keep the information from the Judge. But what use could Secret be on such a matter? The poursuivant was so ugly, with his greasy, cheese-coloured hair and his clownish face and his runtish little legs. He would surely know nothing of mistresses and bastards. This reassuring thought also helped to persuade Will that Jennet could not possibly have confided in Secret.

He thought to himself: so the poursuivant lives up to his name. No, perhaps that was unfair, for it hinted at the underhand, and Secret was not that, merely so unobtrusive that only a man watching him carefully would have realised what he was up to.

Judge Paston had fitted the pieces together, Will thought then; had done so long before he himself had. Perhaps Judge Paston also knew why Secret was gathering information. He himself did not.

He began to feel a grudging admiration for Secret Poursuivant. There was an uncomfortable contrast between Secret's methodology and his own noisy blundering around Norwich – where he had enjoyed himself greatly but had, he now realised, learned very little. There was a contrast between Secret's quiet interest in everything, and his own rapid boredom when the conversation turned to wool and land purchases and lawsuits. There was a contrast between his own loud talk and laughter, and Secret's habitual silence.

He felt a grudging admiration for Judge Paston too.

At last Secret departed. Two days later, Judge Paston announced that he would now accompany Will to Burnham Thorpe.

Will did not tell Jennet he was leaving, but she learned it from the grooms. She came into the stables as he was rubbing down his horse and promptly burst into tears. She looked ugly when she cried. Her sleek brown hair had turned into rat's tails and her little eyes were red and swollen. His longing to be gone from Oxnead was so strong then that it was almost unbearable. He gave Jennet two crowns, all the money he had with him. He did not like the look Jennet gave him, or the look she gave the coins. He meant to do what he could for her; had he not reassured her of that time and again?

Judge Paston travelled with a couple of grooms: necessary security, considering the state of the Norfolk roads. He and Will were also accompanied by a pair of maidservants whom Agnes had offered to loan to Will until he could engage more staff to supplement his skeleton household. Jennet was not one of them. They were both middle-aged, and very plain.

To Will's surprise the Judge allowed the servants to ride on perhaps fifty paces and then drew his own horse close to Will's. Was he actually to be treated to a conversation? He could only recall ever having had one serious conversation with the Judge. That had been made up mainly of pious platitudes after the death of Sir William.

'Of course,' said the Judge, 'the Duchess will see you married this year.'

That was an alarming start. Not only had he not expected the Judge to say that; he had not even thought of it before. 'Do you think so, sir?'

'No doubt of it. I take it that it will be the Duchess' decision?'

And not the Duke's, Will assumed that he meant. 'Almost certainly,' he said.

'That is fortunate for you. Lady Katharine is hardly penniless. She will want to make her small profit, naturally; but I trust she will moderate her expectations.'

Will knew it was normal practice for guardians to marry off their wards while ensuring that the settlement was to their own advantage. Margaret had suffered from it; he had expected to suffer too. All too often the resultant marriages were disastrously inappropriate from every other viewpoint.

'I hope so, sir,' he said.

'It should be to your advantage. You may find the Hall tedious until you have a family to fill it.'

'Perhaps so, sir.'

They rode on in silence for some minutes, but the Judge did not pull his horse away. Will wondered if he was expected to produce a topic of conversation. None of the subjects that came to mind seemed remotely suitable.

The Judge said, 'There is a farmhand at Oxnead who may be willing to offer for Jennet. I do not expect him to take her without a dowry in the circumstances. I assume you are disposed to do whatever is necessary. I shall discuss it with the other trustees when I meet with them in Lynn next week.'

Will went cold. He managed to say, 'That is kind of you, sir.'

'Nonsense,' said the Judge. 'It is merely practical of me.'

Burnham Thorpe lay in the great curve of northern Norfolk, where the county pushes out into the sea to form the eastern side of the Wash. It was one of a little group of seven villages: Burnham Thorpe, Burnham Market, Burnham Deepdale, Burnham Norton, Burnham Sutton, Burnham Overy and Burnham Overy Staithe. None of them consisted of more than a couple of rows of flint and rubble cottages; though Burnham Thorpe lay the furthest inland, even it was no more than three miles from the sea.

It was a region of open fields and salt marshes, all of it good grazing for sheep, and some of it good farmland for wheat and barley. It was a region of mud flats and low offshore islands and little staithes, harbours where the channels silted up every season. Undeniably remote, it was nevertheless rich.

Will Calthorp and Judge Paston arrived at Burnham Thorpe on a brisk, bright afternoon. They came to the village first, a cobbled street lined with cottages. A painted sign creaked outside the Goat and Donkey inn.

Trails of smoke snaked heavenwards from the blacksmith's forge and the chimneys of the baker's ovens. The Judge spurred his horse to the front of the little procession and the grooms and maidservants moved aside to let Will follow him. They turned up a path that bisected a green hill, where tethered goats nibbled at the spring grass. At the top of the hill was the church; and behind its thrusting tower, the gaunt square shape of Burnham Thorpe Hall.

Will could smell the sea: an inshore wind carried the salt that far inland, and with it the hint of a mist. The pattern of the twisting chimneys, the stony courtyard, the fields stretching as far as he could see, all woke echoes in his memory. He could not have described his home if asked the day before, but all the same the knowledge of what it was like had been somewhere in the recesses of his mind. The sight pleased him.

It was less pleasing to see Judge Paston ride over to a stretch of fence, reach out his stick and prod at a broken rail.

Will trotted after him.

'It's to be expected,' the Judge said brusquely, 'that the place will need some attention.'

'I imagine so, sir.'

'Damme's done a fair job, but there'll be no money to be spent until you come into your inheritance.'

'I suppose not, sir.'

'And little enough after that. My, this wind catches at me. Let's get into the hall.'

The grooms had already dismounted. The door of the hall, its oak blackened with age and sea salt, stood ajar, and just outside it waited Jack Hannant, the bailiff John Damme had engaged for Will, with his wife and small son at his side. Will rode across, swung from his horse and went to take their hands and accept their greetings.

'It's cold in the house, sir,' Mary Hannant said with an apologetic smile. 'We lit a fire this morning, but the chill's in the walls. Give us till Whitsun, though, and snug won't be the word for it.'

'There's nothing to apologise for, Mary. It's good to be home.'

He slept heavily that night and rose to the sound of the gulls overhead and a lightening of his heart in the knowledge that he was at Burnham. He quickly pulled on his doublet and hose and was down in the hall before the Judge, though Paston apeared before he had finished the huge breakfast Mary had set before him.

'You can be patient and wait for me, boy,' said the Judge, settling heavily on to the bench and wrapping his hands round a wooden bowl full of porridge. 'I'll not be long. Then we shall look the place over together.'

They began with the house: the hall, the solar, the kitchens and pantries, the stables, the sheds and the yard. They wandered through the tiny walled orchard, where Jack joined them, and he and the Judge argued over the pruning of the pears and medlars. The three of them tramped the inner fields, checking the rows of spring shoots that would grow to provide the estate with barley, beans, cabbage and onions and leeks. Then they walked back for their horses and rode together across the broad expanses of sheep pasture.

Jack and the Judge talked constantly: of what had been done; what must be done; what could be done, with money and men. The bailiff did not grumble, but he spoke with bleak common sense of tools almost past mending, of oxen nearing old age, of hedges that needed trimming and barns with roofs that leaked. Will spoke very little, but he followed their words with his eyes as well as his mind. Against the picture before him he set his memories of Oxnead and of the Duke's farms at Framlingham. It was clear even to his inexpert eye that though Burnham Thorpe was far from being a ruin, it was also far from being in the prosperous state of those other places.

After dinner the Judge's attitude changed. He was still not friendly to Will – who was painfully conscious that he had not yet been forgiven for Jennet – but he became more cheerful, almost hearty. His next outing was on

194

foot, and in the other direction, towards the church and the village. He strode up to the church gate; unhooked the latch; walked through the churchyard and up to the low flint porch.

Will trailed after him. The Judge turned the heavy ring of the door latch, pushed the expanse of solid oak inwards and went down a shallow step into the nave. The priest was not there: the church was deserted except for an old lady in a black dress who dropped a brief curtsey and then scurried out past them.

'You have seen all this before,' the Judge said, with a sideways glance, 'but it will do you no harm to see it again.'

With long unhurried steps, he covered the length of the church and stopped in the chancel. Will followed. The Judge knelt down at the feet of the huge brass image of Sir William Calthorp.

Will paused for a moment, then he stepped self-consciously around the edge of the brass and knelt down by the Judge's side.

As likenesses went, it was poor; indeed no likeness at all, since the artist had never seen Sir William. But he had been well briefed, and everything else was right: Sir William's armour, the collar of Ss that marked him out as a supporter of the House of Lancaster, his shield, his hawks and his dogs.

Sir William had seemed a stern and intimidating man to Will as a boy; this image of him was no more than a few lines on a flat plate of brass, inert, its hands clasped in a lifeless semblance of prayer, its eyes unseeing. But as he gazed at it, it seemed to him almost as if he were back sitting at his grandfather's feet, listening to the gruff voice telling him that one day the Hall and its lands would all be his.

Burnham Thorpe Hall had not been dilapidated in those days. The comparison with Oxnead would have been all to its credit.

He put his hands together, like the hands in the brass, and he prayed.

They left the church through a side door and walked round the east end, taking a path between the graves.

'Thirty years ago that chequerwork was done,' the Judge said. 'To match the chequers on your arms.'

'It was done well.'

'The flint on Norwich Guildhall was cut squarer. But still, this is not bad; not bad at all.' He turned to Will again and gave a brusque nod. 'In the morning, lad, we shall go over the accounts.'

The accounts took them two days to set straight: Jack Hannant was a good solid farmer, but no hand with a pen. The Judge pushed him hard to explain the entries and spent a long time setting them down for Will in columns and totals. So much for the spring kill; so much for the malt shipped from the staithe; so much for the rents from the cottagers. This was the income for last year, lad; now let us reckon up your outgoings. They reckoned them many times over, and each time they came to more than the income. They went over the income again. This flock gave less wool than it might; this field lay fallow when it might have been planted. This rent was low: it should be checked, more money might be squeezed out of the tenant. It's tight, lad, the Judge pronounced, but worse estates than this have been turned around in less than ten years.

Less than ten years! It sounded to Will like a dozen lifetimes. But he kept his thoughts to himself and concentrated on following each figure as the Judge set it down. He asked questions: a few on the first day, many on the second.

'I should know something of the malt trade,' he said to the Judge over supper.

'So you should, and the grain trade too.'

'Is there much you can tell me? Or is there somebody who might . . .'

'I'll tell you what I know, lad; but I can do better than that. Tomorrow we shall go to the staithe and see for ourselves.'

The next morning was fine. They rode, with just Harry Holt for company, down the long slope of land that eased away to the north, over the sheep meadows, over rougher marshy meadows that were no more than a tangle of thistles and long coarse grass, to the flat, endless expanses of salt marsh and mud flats that stretched out to the sea.

They joined the track that led from Burnham Norton and Brancaster to their west and skirted the edge of the sluggish little channel of water until they came to the huddle of cottages that was Burnham Overy Staithe, to the timber wharf, the maltings and the high blank-sided warehouses. They tied up their horses outside the Jolly Sailors and went down to talk to the sailors, the children who tended the mussel beds, the maltsters and their boys. In the warehouseman's office they looked up the accounts of the Burnham Thorpe estate and Will traced the twins of the figures he had read in Jack's books the day before.

'Come, lad,' said the Judge.

He crossed the track and walked to the edge of the water, where he bent to talk to a boy in a rowing boat. He climbed into the boat and gestured to Will to follow. The boy took his oars and they set off down the little channel.

It seemed to Will that they went a long way. They passed endless expanses of mud and reed and low, low islands knitted together from mats of grass. Curlews strutted across the sands, terns wheeled in the sky and a soft wind sang its salty song to them. The buildings of the staithe dwindled into the distance. Finally the water roughened beneath them and they moved out of the channel and into the open sea.

'Thataway, boy.' The Judge gestured.

The boy pulled the boat round, bringing them parallel with the outermost bank of saltings. He took maybe a dozen more strokes, then the Judge said, 'Enough. Stop now.'

The boy shipped his oars and sat panting lightly.

Judge Paston turned his gaze to the mud flats. 'Look there. Do you see them?'

The flats were alive. Seals basked in the spring sun; seals flipped their ungainly way along the shore; seals dipped down, into and under the cold grey water of the North Sea.

'I see,' said Will.

They sat there in silence for a long time, watching the terns wheeling and the seals romping, as the boat rocked gently beneath them and the waves slapped against its side. Finally the Judge said, 'Enough, boy. Take us back now.'

Why did we come? Will wondered for a second. Then he knew the answer. We came to see this.

The Judge stayed at the Hall for three days. On the fourth day he and Will rode to Lynn and ate together with a group of Lynn lawyers at an inn on the Tuesday Marketplace.

It seemed to Will that he needed to find a way to express his gratitude, but it was difficult to decide what he should say. The question troubled him all the time he was eating his pigeon pie. He wanted the Judge to know what a revelation his return to Burnham had been to him, but at the same time he would not have wished the Judge to understand quite how mean his inheritance had seemed to him at the Pleasance.

He could not find words subtle enough to express this, but perhaps the Judge understood anyway – or would have, had he troubled to think about it. 'Keep an eye on the under-bailiff at Calthorp,' he said as they parted in the inn yard. 'The yield from that flock should be twice what it was last season. Talk to Stapleton first, mind, if you think of dismissing him.'

'I'll do that, sir. You'll carry my thanks to Mistress Paston for her hospitality, and to William Taverner for all that he taught me?'

The Judge nodded a trifle impatiently: the lawyers were waiting for him at the gateway. 'A gentleman always repays his debts,' he said. 'It would be to my advantage to be spoken well of to young John Mowbray.'

The Duchess's son was rarely at Framlingham. Will had never before troubled to think seriously of him, or to envisage the time when he in turn would be Duke. He felt the blood rise to his face. Another bloody put-down; and another one he deserved, at that.

'I'll not fail to tell the Duchess of all you have done for me, sir.'

The Judge moved a pace closer and lowered his voice a fraction. 'You are surely not such a fool,' he said, 'as to imagine young Mowbray will look to his mother when Norfolk dies.' He did not wait for a reaction but touched Will's arm, then strode off to join the other lawyers.

Will stayed at Burnham Thorpe Hall till the harvest was in. He travelled sometimes to his other estates at Cockthorpe and Calthorp and East Barsham, learning the land, taking as much interest in the accounts as his trustees would allow, and entertaining some of the country landowners who had been pleasant to him in Norwich. He saw nothing of the Pastons, but did ride twice to Ingham to visit Miles Stapleton.

Those visits brought home to him, more clearly than anything else, the change that the summer had wrought in him. In Norwich he and Miles had been fellow schemers in every piece of mischief going, fellow chasers after maids, fellow drinkers at every tavern. They had laughed together at the pomposity of the Judge, of Miles' father Sir Brian, and of all the other elderly landowners who grouched at their exploits. Will was not laughing any more. He reckoned now that he had been a fool not to listen harder when his neighbours had tried to give him good advice. He could see now how much work would be needed before his own lands reached the same thriving state as Sir Brian's, or Sir Simon Felbrigg's, or Sir Henry Inglose's.

He tried to explain some of this to Miles, but Miles looked at him as if he too had turned into a bore.

At harvest time all his neighbours went home to their own estates. Will joined in the festivities in the village, and he enjoyed being feted as the new master; but when he came home to his empty hall it seemed to him that Burnham Thorpe was a very lonely place. He remembered the Judge's words then, about the Duchess seeing him married.

On that subject too, he could see now that he had been frivolous. He had always been interested in women, but his eyes had been for serving girls and married women, not for marriageable young virgins. No suitable girls had made any impression on him. Not that he would have been able to choose his own wife; but he thought he might have tried to influence the Duchess to choose a girl he liked while he was at Framlingham. Now it was probably too late. She would most likely have picked a wife for him that summer. He hoped she would have chosen someone young and pretty and good-natured. He thought she might. If he had won her displeasure, it had not been done deliberately; on the contrary, he had always tried to do just as she asked.

He would know when he returned to Framlingham. The thought of this made him ambivalent about the prospect of returning, when in other circumstances he would have been enthusiastic. By October Burnham Thorpe had begun to bore him. Even in the most positive frame of mind he could muster, the sheep were still sheep; neither they nor the servants shared jokes with him. He had plans for the estate, but as yet he had neither the freedom nor the money to carry them to fruition. It was irksome to him, too, to feel the eyes of the Burnham cottagers on him all the time, and to know that if he took a single step out of line it would be known throughout the village and beyond. He could not have seduced the housemaids even if Agnes had provided him with young and pretty ones.

200

In early October he wrote to the Duke of Norfolk's Chamberlain, asking when he should return. Three weeks later he received a visit from Mowbray Herald. This constituted his reply. He was to travel to Framlingham immediately, in the herald's company.

They set off the following morning and reached the castle three days later. Will deposited his belongings in the room in the gatehouse tower to which the Chamberlain directed him; then (also as directed) he made for the Great Hall.

He knew from the herald that the Duke was still in his bed. His health had deteriorated further and nobody now expected him ever to leave it. It was to find the Duchess that he was going to the Great Hall.

He pushed open the door, nodded to the Steward and stood for a moment looking about him. It seemed a long time since he had last been at Framlingham. The hall seemed larger than he remembered it, dark and echoing and crowded with people.

A large fire blazed in the hearth; a boy crouched by it, next to the log pile. A couple of hounds were scrapping over a bone, egged on by the pages. A lutanist was playing his instrument in a corner, though nobody appeared to be listening to him. Hugh Austin and his friends were playing at dice. And on the dais at the far end sat the Duchess, surrounded by a throng of her ladies.

The Duchess turned in his direction and he knew that she had seen him. She stilled her conversation and watched him approach. He weaved self-consciously through the crowd, aware all the time that her eyes were fixed on him.

He stopped at the foot of the dais and she stood up and moved forward. She stretched out a hand in a graciously condescending gesture. He took it and bent his head over it.

She is not pretty, he thought. She's all but pop-eyed, and the skin under her chin is sagging. Under the paint she is growing old. I was a fool ever to desire her. He had

201

noticed Jeanne by her side, but he did not look at Jeanne.

'Calthorp,' said the Duchess in a mildly flirtatious voice.

'Your Grace.'

She motioned to him to come up on to the dais. She sat and indicated the place beside her.

'I'm glad you came so promptly. Now you will have time to come to know Mistress Grey before your betrothal.'

'My betrothal?' The surprise in his voice was genuine, though it was also what he sensed she required from him. He had expected this, but not so soon.

'I have arranged the ceremony for Friday. The wedding itself, I think, should be just before Christmas.'

So soon! A sense of dismay flowered inside him, but he said, in a level, polite voice, 'That is most thoughtful of you, Your Grace.'

'I am glad you think so, Calthorp.' Lady Katharine gave him a narrowly appraising look, as if she had expected a different reaction. 'You shall meet with the Duke's secretary after supper. He will read over the deeds of settlement to you.'

'I shall look forward to that.'

'Shall you now?'

'I shall practise my lawyer's Latin on them.'

The Duchess laughed. It was a pleasant sound; it made Will forget that he had thought her plain. His mind was only half on the Duchess, though: the other half was on the deeds of settlement. There would be little or nothing he could do to alter them, but he was more than eager to know what they contained. Whatever he made of his wife, he would welcome her dowry. Would there be much money; would there be estates that he could readily sell for cash? He would need plenty of money if he was to do all that he planned to do at Burnham Thorpe.

'And on the lady herself . . .' Lady Katharine added.

Hastily he brought his mind back to the Duchess. He looked full into her eyes and gave her his most winning smile. 'On her, I shall practise my charm.'

Lady Katharine smiled back at him. Beyond her, he could see Jeanne from the corner of his eye. She was scowling. That was nothing to him; he wouldn't have given a fake farthing for Jeanne.

'I shall expect you to like her,' said the Duchess.

Her. She meant his betrothed – or nearly so. Mistress Grey, she had said. Did he know any Mistress Greys? He searched his mind, but he couldn't place Mistress Grey.

But still, the Duchess expected him to like her, did she? The Duchess was no fool, so he could reckon from that that Mistress Grey was no female equivalent of Walter Aslake. She must be young and presentable, unless the Duchess was leading him on only to laugh at his let-down. He held her eyes and decided that it was unlikely.

He liked most people, he thought to himself; he would probably like Mistress Grey. The Duchess might have expected him to love her. It was as well that she did not. Desire, yes: all his experiences had not killed that in him, but he knew now what bloody bitches women were when you got to know them. He was never going to fall in love.

'How very realistic of you,' he said.

'Is it?' asked the Duchess, in a tone that made him wonder if he had been rude. 'You may find her a little quiet, but that will probably change when she leaves here.'

That struck him as realistic of the Duchess, too: any young woman might be stunned into silence by her presence. He had the sense to realise that it would be tactless to say so, and said instead, 'I shall make allowances. Am I to meet her now?'

'Let me tell you about her first.'

The Duchess told him. Elizabeth, her name was: Elizabeth Grey. She was a younger daughter of Lord Grey of Ruthin. Will had heard of Lord Grey, but had never met him as far as he could recall. Lord Grey had not troubled to journey to Framlingham for his daughter's betrothal. Grey's political intrigues were notorious, the Duchess reminded Will; but they, like his estates, were on the Welsh borders. She clearly reckoned this fortunate, and so did he, on reflection. He was coming to accept his own ignorance about the business of managing his estates, and was prepared to set about remedying it, but he did not like the thought of parading his inevitable mistakes in front of a father-in-law.

Elizabeth was seventeen. The Duchess said nothing about her appearance, except that she was pretty. Instead she told him the dowry. It surprised him to learn that she knew all the details of the settlement. She recounted them in a concise way which told him that as well as being intimately involved in negotiating this match, she had weighed the advantages of it very hard-headedly.

He weighed them too, as she spoke. The settlement disappointed him. Mistress Grey's dower portion was adequate, but not generous. She would bring him a couple of estates, but they were both firmly entailed. There would be little in the way of ready money.

He did his best to keep his disappointment to himself, but the Duchess seemed to sense it and she pointed out to him, not rudely but unambiguously, that this was the penalty he would pay for marrying a young and pretty wife. An older and plainer woman might have brought him more, but he would not have wanted that, would he?

'Not at all.' Will smiled broadly and tried to tell himself that it was true. Perhaps it was. He found it hard to know: he had never thought about marriage in those terms before.

'And now,' said the Duchess, 'I shall take you to meet her.'

She rose and held out her arm as if she expected Will to take it. With her other hand, she gestured to her ladies to follow her.

For a moment Will sat rooted to the bench. It had dawned on him quite suddenly what the Duchess intended. They would all come, every one of them. The

Duchess meant him to meet his future wife for the first time in front of the assembled female population of Framlingham Castle. She meant to watch herself, to see what he made of Mistress Grey and what she made of him; she meant Jeanne to watch too, and all the others as well.

The Duchess smiled, a sphinx-like smile of sheer mischief.

You bitch, Will thought. You bloody bitch. For a moment I almost fooled myself into liking you again. But you've spelled it out now: you're as much of a bitch as ever you were. You use me, that's what you do; you mean me to provide your entertainment. Damn you, I'll not do it!

He knew as soon as he thought this, though, that he had no option. Protesting would have achieved nothing, except to provide the Duchess with some more fun. And to annoy her. He could not afford to annoy her. This marriage would not make him rich: if he was to keep his estates going he would need her patronage for years to come.

'I shall be delighted.' He rose and took her proffered arm. He even smiled, though this time without meeting her eyes.

'She is waiting for us in my chamber.'

He knew where that was, though he had never entered it. The Duchess and her ladies had private quarters in one of the tall square towers that punctuated Framlingham's curtain wall. He led the Duchess there: up the hall, through the great carved doors, across a courtyard lit with late summer sun, and towards the narrow door of the tower.

She loosed her arm then and led the way herself up the winding stairs. Will followed. His stomach was churning his insides to butter. Don't react, he told himself. Don't even look at her; just look in her direction and smile. He prayed she would not come as an unpleasant shock to him. Imagine the worst, he thought. A wooden leg, a crooked back, a cast in one eye, rabbit teeth: tell yourself she has the lot. His mind was still full of a cold anger against the Duchess. She always does just as she chooses, he thought; she never hides her feelings. He was not used to hiding his own, he had always tended to give vent to them freely. He wished he had had more practice in dissimulation.

Lady Katharine pushed open the door at the top of the stairs. She entered the room into which it led. Will followed her. He stepped a pace sideways when he was through the door, to let the ladies follow him, and looked around.

The room was larger than he had expected from the outside of the tower. It looked out to the north, away from Framlingham town, and even the reds and yellows of the tapestries could not make it seem warm. He recognised the furnishings from his visit to the Duchess's room at Norfolk Inn: the bed with its sumptuous hangings, the table with its clutter of jars and bottles, the carved chest. There was the smell he remembered too, the musk and spice smell of her perfume.

A maid sat in the corner, sewing. Lady Katharine ignored her and headed straight for a girl who was standing alone in the centre of the tower room.

Will followed her across the room. He was concentrating so hard on maintaining an easy manner that he barely took in the girl's appearance, barely heard the Duchess's words of introduction. He bowed, smiled and held out his hand. Elizabeth Grey took it.

Her hand was cold and it shook in his. Will tightened his grip to still the shaking. He did not let himself think. He heard his voice saying lightly, 'The Duchess told me I would like you, but she could not begin to tell me how charmed I would be.'

He realised that she would not manage a reply: realised it, he hoped, before it was too apparent to the Duchess. He said some more things, he had no idea what. He smiled again. The Duchess said, 'I shall leave you to become acquainted,' and withdrew to her ladies. Will felt a wave of relief work upwards from his feet.

He was still holding Elizabeth Grey's hand. He drew her further into the room, towards the deep window enclosure. 'Look up at me and smile,' he said in a low voice. 'The Duchess is watching you.'

Elizabeth Grey's face slowly lifted to his. She did not smile, but she met his look. Her eyes were blue, wide and guileless. Her hand clutched at his.

She's like a trapped rabbit, he thought, staring at the trappers through the net. Like a frightened mare. He had calmed mares before. The thing was to talk, keep talking in a low, level voice. Any rubbish would do, it was the tone that counted.

He talked. He did not try to be bright or witty, as he had with the Duchess. Instead he told Elizabeth Grey about his ride that morning, about Mowbray Herald's baby son, about a couple of soldiers he had met at the inn in Thetford where he had lodged the previous night.

The grip of her icy fingers eased a little, so he talked some more. He told her what he had learned about sheep farming, how much his agents hoped to get for the autumn clip. He told her about the staithe at Burnham Overy, the malt stored in the warehouses, the ships that came in from Norway and Flanders. He told her about the seals basking on the mud flats.

It calmed him too, talking to her. When he came to the seals she managed a shy smile. He smiled back. He looked more carefully at her.

No unpleasant surprises: none at all. She was perhaps a head shorter than he was, slim and fragile-looking. Her hair was very fair, neatly coiled behind a small head. Her gown was grey, high necked, with a pale green underdress that showed at the sleeves. Her face was dominated by those large blue eyes. It was a gentle face. He liked her face. He thought about kissing her lips and feeling them tremble under his. My wife, he thought. It seemed an oddly familiar thought.

He glanced over to the doorway. The Duchess was deep in an argument with Jeanne. He and Elizabeth had evidently proved less entertaining than they had expected. Some of the ladies were beginning to slip away.

'Now we shall return to the Duchess,' he whispered, 'and tell her that we have made each other's acquaintance and mean to do very well together. Then I shall make my goodbyes. And tonight, in the hall, will you look for me and smile?'

He focussed on her face until her eyes met his again. She gave a little nod. He squeezed her hand and then, impulsively, lifted it to his mouth. When he lowered it he saw the confusion on her face. He grinned. To his surprise her expression dissolved into a smile. It lit up the depths of her blue eyes and brought sunshine to the cold, cluttered room.

The last thing Will had expected was his summons to the Duchess's rooms that night. Jeanne came to him with it. She was pouting and sulky.

She is jealous, Will thought: jealous of the Duchess. It struck him that it would take very little to bring Jeanne back to his bed. He did not feel inclined to try.

Jealous of the Duchess? No, that was ridiculous. The Duchess was nothing to him, nor he to her. This could scarcely be an assignation: the Duchess doubtless wanted to talk to him about Elizabeth Grey. Of course, that was it: Jeanne was jealous of Elizabeth. Obvious, this answer, but somehow it failed to carry any conviction.

He was wrong about the Duchess. She did mean the summons as an assignation. He was also wrong about himself. He had thought himself so taken with Elizabeth Grey that he could not possibly have desired another woman. But as soon as he had shut the door to the tower room behind him, and he met Lady Katharine's knowing, dark eyes, he discovered that he wanted her very much indeed.

At their previous coupling it had been she who was in control. She had artfully half undressed, leading him on; she had shown him just how to take her; she had even despatched him immediately afterwards before he could make a fool of himself with ardent declarations of love. This time it was different: Will was the master. He let himself be eager and urgent and even a little brutal. Lady Katharine was eager too, eager for everything he could do to her.

This time he was in no danger of mistaking it for love. And she knew it. When they were both satiated, she turned to him on the big canopied bed. 'I was right, wasn't I?'

'Right?'

'When I told you she was pretty?'

He was only momentarily disconcerted. 'Indeed, she is very pretty.'

'And you thought me very cruel.' She gave him a mischievous smile.

'Yes, I did.'

She laughed. 'Perhaps I was.' She stretched her arms and then swung her feet round and clambered out of the bed. She was completely naked. Will watched her as she walked over to the fireplace. Her skin was very white all over, and her figure was still good, but her breasts sagged slightly. It was not really her looks that had attracted him, he thought objectively, so much as her air of immense self-confidence.

The fire was low, but the room was warm. Its atmosphere, too: in firelight it did not seem like the room in which he had encountered Elizabeth Grey that afternoon.

'She needs to be toughened,' Lady Katharine said, 'but not terrified. I had not meant to terrify her.' She glanced back at Will where he lay on the bed. 'If your neighbours tell you to find a strong housekeeper to guide her, do not listen to them.'

His first thought on leaving the tower room that afternoon had been that he would need to do just that.

'I think I understand you,' he said slowly.

'At least you have more sense than to think of giving up your mistresses.'

'I do not doubt I shall think of it.'

'Nobody will tell her of them. Not even Jeanne. Elizabeth may be a goose, but she is a sweet-natured goose. There is little pleasure to be had in goading her; she never seems to bite back.'

'I should not care for a wife who bit back.'

'Oh, you should,' said the Duchess. 'But you may turn out a better man if you do not get one.'

8

FRANCE
Summer, 1429

'Jhesus, Maria.

'King of England and you, Duke of Bedford, calling yourself Regent of France; you, William de la Pole, Earl of Suffolk; Lord Talbot and you, Thomas, Lord Scales, calling yourselves lieutenants of the said Bedford . . .

'. . . give to la Pucelle who has been sent here by God, the King of Heaven, the keys of all the good towns you have taken and violated in France . . .

'I was sent here by God, the King of Heaven, body for body, to throw you out of all France . . .

'. . . go away, for God's sake, back to your own country, otherwise wait for news of la Pucelle who will soon visit you to your great misfortune.'

Why am I still holding this letter? Suffolk stared at the familiar words in weary half-disbelief, then threw the paper down on to the heavy, battered trestle that was the only furniture in the tower room where he stood. He should have torn it up weeks before, when Guyenne Herald had first brought it to him.

But it could not have been torn up immediately: first it had been necessary to discuss its contents with Talbot and Scales, to have copies taken for Bedford and Gloucester. Then a clerk had returned the original to him, dog-eared and brown-creased, and he had somehow found himself pocketing it. It had travelled with him along the Loire valley from Orleans to Jargeau; as had its writer. She sat somewhere out there, the peasant girl Jeanne who had such a bizarre hold over the Valois troops that their commanders let her ride with them and dictate their actions. Waiting to attack.

A witch, that girl. The Pucelle. Virgin, it meant, though it had amused Talbot to mis-translate it as 'whore', and many of the men had copied him. He had never come face to face with her, though he had glimpsed her many times. But her letters had seeped under his skin and turned the siege from something he had merely called a nightmare to something that had actually seemed one, so great was his sense of unreality.

The nightmare was over, the siege raised. It was quiet in the tower room, quieter than he had ever known it during the siege. No guns were booming. The windows were small, but they let in some of the clear light of a fine summer evening. At the same time he had a sharp sense of danger. He had woken from the terrible dream, but to an even worse reality. The disaster was not yet played out.

He could be alone in the tower room for only a little longer: soon he would have to call in his brothers John and Alexander, and his other lieutenants. They would all discuss the situation, and then he would announce his decisions.

He had not yet decided what to do. Jargeau castle was in English hands, as it had been for some months. Within its walls were the small garrison who had held it since its capture the summer before, and the eight hundred men who had ridden with him from Orleans when the besieging army dispersed. Most of the small town was also still in English hands, but the suburbs were now held by the Valois. The Valois army surrounded both town and castle. A large army: eight, perhaps even ten thousand men. It was commanded by the best of the Valois captains: the Duke of Alençon, la Hire, the Bastard of Orleans. And with them was the witch, the Pucelle.

Less than a thousand men, against ten times as many: and that thousand exhausted and demoralised, that ten thousand buoyed up by the fanatical conviction of the witch. No, there was no justification for a straight assault. He could conceivably remain in the castle, hold out in the hope of deliverance. But from where? It was scarcely imaginable that the Valois would ride on and leave Jargeau in English hands. It was barely more probable that Fastolf's men would come to his rescue: their last orders had been to ride to Beaugency, well to the west. The Valois forces were more likely to be supplemented than were his own. Nor was the castle overly well supplied. There had been no spare grain in the Loire valley with which the garrison could have built up their stocks, and there had been no time to make preparations for a siege, not with the Valois army on his tail all the way from Orleans.

That left a negotiated surrender: best achieved quickly, while the terms might still be reasonable. It seemed to him the only realistic option. He would have chosen it automatically had it not been for Bedford and Talbot, but their reactions had to be considered too. After the siege he would have to justify his decisions to them.

Talbot blamed him already for the disasters at Orleans. Talbot refused to accept what he himself had always known, though he had never succeeded in convincing Bedford of it: that the enterprise had been doomed from the start. Talbot was a great attacking soldier, but he had no patience for defence, no sense of proportion when it came to questions of tactical surrender. Surrender now, Suffolk thought, and he would deepen still further Talbot's contempt for him. He would have to wait until the Valois attacked, and try to surrender then.

Which would be – when? The next day? Possibly, following their fierce assault on the suburbs that afternoon. In other circumstances he would have depended upon it, but with the witch nothing could be certain. Perhaps she would not even allow him to surrender. But if so the Bastard would override her, surely. He reckoned the Bastard was a reasonable man.

He strode towards the door, then stopped, turned and went to retrieve the letter. He tucked it away inside his doublet before calling his lieutenants in. His last thought, in the blank moment while he was listening to them tramping up the stairs towards him, was that he should tell his valet to find him a girl for the night. He needed that: it would calm him.

Not yet. Surrender, but not yet. He repeated this to himself as he moved from wall to wall, embrasure to embrasure. At each place he urged the defenders to resist the irresistible for a little while longer. It was his private token, that word 'surrender': his friend. He spoke it to none of the defenders, only to Suffolk Herald, whom he had already primed to negotiate with Guy-enne Herald when given the order.

Some of them knew it had to come. He saw it in their faces when they turned to him: the knowledge that the attempt was hopeless, the castle as good as lost already. In other faces he saw only blank determination. He knew those men, knew all the men. He had fought with them for years. For years they had attacked. They had not always won their objectives, but they had never been on the defensive before, never faced surrender.

They had never before stood behind a wall and watched and waited while the guns were primed, loaded, fired at them. They had never before felt the foundations shake beneath their feet. They had never fired cannon like those themselves, for the English army had no artillery to match the bombard the Valois called la Bergère. What could an archer, a man at arms, even a handgunner, do against such weapons? They could not intercept the cannonballs; could not limit the damage they were wreaking. They could repair; but for how long? Not long enough, his mind urged. Surrender soon.

He thought: the next shot from la Bergère will come any moment now. The last shot had been a direct hit on the tower where he had spent the previous evening and night. They had the range now. Three shots more, to demolish it beyond repair? Four? It could hardly be more than that.

He was expecting the boom; he was inured to the din of the battle. But it deafened, still: the reality of it was beyond expectation. The crash of the gunpowder; an instant of terrible anticipation; then the smash of the great cannonball into the stone of the tower. He saw a crack weave, lightning fast, down the wall. One more hit and the tower could fall.

Surrender now. He blundered across to where the standard bearers crouched just by the doorway to the tower. He nodded to Suffolk Herald. The herald rose to his feet and gestured to the men. He turned away.

In his gut he felt the sickening cramp of defeat. There is nothing to do now, he thought, but wait. The English guns fell silent. Alexander came to stand by his side. Slowly, the English white flag began to rise on the tower.

It was not even halfway up the pole, was not flapping, before la Bergère roared into life again. Its noise this time was as vicious as a slap across a bound man's face. The ball smashed into the tower wall; there was a short, echoing silence. He saw the wall shift. It seemed to hang in the air, its angle impossible; then to slide and crumble. The heavy beams, the great stone blocks, the flagpole and the white flag, the bodies of the standard bearers, all crashed downwards. A heavy cloud of dust and debris followed them, enveloping the inner bailey. Even visored, Suffolk choked. He staggered as the shock-wave from the collapse reached him. His ears rang.

He could not panic in front of Alexander; he had to think clearly. How else to surrender? The white flag was lost under the rubble. A herald could not call, a trumpet not sound, above the din of the guns. But it had to be ended somehow: there was now nothing to defend bar a yard full of debris and corpses.

John was running up, along with his other lieutenants. He lifted his visor and gave them their orders, sharp, firm. Bring the men down from the remaining stretches of the curtain wall. Line them up. Open the gate. March out in formation. He snapped the visor shut.

La Bergère was still firing, aimed now at the rubble, its stones crashing into the bailey itself. The men were forming up, some running down to the bailey, some leaving their posts reluctantly. With his bassinet closed their shouts came to him as indistinct echoes. The Pucelle; the witch; the whore. She was there, that bitch, mounting a scaling ladder like the men. He would not stay to greet her. Find the Bastard, he thought. Surrender to the Bastard.

Men were straining at the bolts on the castle gates. They rammed them free at last and began to pull the gates open. On the walls, the soldiers who had lingered were skirmishing now with the first of the assault troops. Suffolk saw one man fall back and crash down from the battlements to the earth of the bailey fifteen feet below. He turned away and gave the order to advance.

He marched, at the head of his men, through the gates and into the outer ward. Servants' quarters, storehuts, vegetable gardens, stables and cowsheds; and beyond, the waters of the Loire, sparkling in the sunshine. He could see the wooden bridge that the castle had been built to defend. He could see the troops guarding it. Valois troops. Across the walls of the outer bailey, through the castle gate behind his men, over the bridge, Valois troops were thundering down upon his little army. He stopped. He looked for banners. Alençon's colours, the Bastard's, even that bandit la Hire's: he would have surrendered to any of them.

He could see none of them: no captains, no heralds, no standard bearers. Just soldiers, Valois soldiers with their swords and their crossbows and their pikes. Valois soldiers intent on fighting his men.

A plan flashed through his head: edge the column towards the outer bailey wall, bring the archers behind the men at arms, put up some kind of a last-ditch defence until the Bastard appeared. His mind framed the first of the commands, but it was too late: the enemy were upon them, the column was scattering and many of the archers, vulnerable without armour, were running wildly towards the river.

A soldier fell upon him, axe raised. His own came up to meet it. He had fought often and the motions came as instinct: there was no space in his mind for panic. The axes clashed, clashed again. He sensed, rather than saw, an armed figure move close to his left side. His opponent stepped backwards. He advanced a step, then withdrew. Together with the knight – was it John? The visor restricted his vision; there was no time to look properly – he edged towards the wall.

So many enemies, so many. More were coming, more and more from all directions. There was no core of defence any more, only desperation. He thought: there can be no general surrender now. I could find the Bastard now and give him my axe, my sword; he would take them perhaps, but he could not stop his men from finishing their massacre. All I can do is to save myself, and this knight at my side. Forget the Bastard. Any soldier will do, even this one. Ask him for quarter.

The wall was perhaps ten paces away and there were soldiers between him and it. He tried to shout 'Rançon'; but his voice was trapped by his visor and he dared not lift it. He stepped back a pace, took a hand from his axe and pointed with it to his chest. The advancing men hesitated. The foremost of them slowly lowered his own axe.

Suffolk dropped his axe at his feet and drew his sword from its scabbard. He held it out, hilt first. The Valois soldier took it. The other men at arms slowly circled round, protecting him and the knight with him, their valuable new property.

He gulped air. It was thick with dust. The acrid tang of sulphur burned his throat. He thought for a moment that he would be sick, sick behind his visor. The thought made him feel intensely claustrophobic. He pushed up the visor with a gauntleted hand, momentarily indifferent to the danger.

217

The sickness subsided and he made himself look up. The leader of the men at arms who had taken him was standing immediately in front of him, staring at him. He was a shortish man and his armour showed signs of rust. He wore no surcoat: there was nothing to reveal his identity. This was not the Bastard, not la Hire. It was a man of much more humble station.

'Are you a knight?' he asked.

'Hein?'

'Er, es-tu Chevalier?'

'Lui! Chevalier!' A ripple of guffaws passed through the rest of the men at arms.

There was only one course open to a knight of honour in these circumstances. 'Eh bien!' said the Earl of Suffolk. 'Sois-le de ma main.' He gestured for the return of his sword, raised it and carefully and deliberately bestowed a knighthood upon his captor.

Massacre, a bloody massacre. He saw much, too much of it before the Valois soldiers led him away from the carnage and to the safety of their camp. In the hours that followed he heard more. The Valois soldiers were exultant. They had killed the goddamns, killed them all, and taken Jargeau in the name of the Dauphin. The Pucelle would see the Dauphin crowned now, they said. He would be a prince no more: soon he would be King Charles the Seventh of France.

They had not killed Suffolk. Not yet. Perhaps they still would: the Pucelle wanted him dead, his guards assured him. They had not killed John either. The knight at his side had been John after all. He and John were under guard together, in a tent, in a field outside what remained of Jargeau. He thought: perhaps they are lying. Perhaps there are other prisoners. Perhaps Alexander is still alive somewhere in Jargeau.

Alexander was dead.

The Bastard told him that. He was marched from the first tent to another, larger one and shoved to his knees in front of the Valois captains: la Hire and the Bastard and Alençon. And Jeanne la Pucelle. The Pucelle did not speak to him. She spoke of him, indifferently, as if she thought he understood no French. But the Bastard spoke to him, in a forthright, comradely manner. The Bastard said: it was an accident of war, Alexander's killing. His manner said that he did not regret it, but he did regret the pain it caused Suffolk to hear of it.

There was no pain, yet. In his mind was only a persistent memory of the day when he had found Alexander, aged ten, skinning a cat alive. He did not say this to the Bastard.

Instead he listened, silent, as la Hire and the Bastard and Alençon, pretty as a girl, and Jeanne la Pucelle, plain and forthright as a farmer's boy, discussed what to do with him and with John. The witch was not solely for killing them, she was for asking God: by which she meant, praying at the portable altar that had been set up at the back of the tent. La Hire and the Bastard and Alençon were for keeping them alive and claiming a ransom. There was no particular hazard facing the army, they pointed out, no military reason for ordering their death.

The Bastard won the day. He was given custody of both the prisoners. As soon as this had been agreed, Suffolk was hustled once more out of the tent. He was taken to a house in the town where he found John waiting for him. The two of them were kept there under guard overnight. Next morning more men came, with horses, to escort them to their prison. They would go to Blois, the captain of the guard told him.

There were, he saw, two women with the guard. He asked the captain who these women were. The taller woman then lifted her veil and he discovered to his surprise that he recognised her. It was the girl his valet had found for him the night before the battle.

'The Bastard's orders, sir,' said the captain. 'She is to accompany you.'

He could not even remember her name, but he recalled every detail of the incident. He had meant

George to find him a whore, but instead the valet had brought him the first girl he could find in the town. Always lazy, George. The thought came to him then that George was dead.

He turned his back on the woman and her servant and said, 'I do not wish that.'

The guards spoke in low voices among themselves and then the captain approached him again. 'The lady's father arranged it with the Bastard, sir. He is a merchant, well known in Jargeau.'

'The Bastard has my thanks. But I do not wish the lady to accompany me.'

'As you wish, sir.'

He kept his back turned. He could hear the woman's high, clear voice, protesting; he could imagine her dark, accusing eyes. He felt sick once more. Soldiers did such things, and many worse; it was a small sin to have seduced the girl. But he himself rarely committed such sins, and he felt, just then, that he could not bear to have this woman remain to haunt him.

With immense relief he heard the noise of hooves on the cobbles and realised that she was being taken away.

Blois was some miles further down the Loire valley. Suffolk had never seen the town before: it had never been taken by the English. But he knew of its vast castle, the childhood home of the Bastard, his brother the Duke of Orleans and the rest of their extensive family.

It proved to be a neat walled city, with wooden houses topped with red tiles, a sturdy perimeter wall, buttressed and crenellated, a tall-spired church, a large abbey and a handsome bridge across the Loire, guarded by towers and underscored with mills. He and John were taken to the castle. Their escort departed the following morning. After that the castle held only a handful of Orleans family servants, Suffolk and John, four jailers and the manservants the Bastard had provided as temporary replacements for their dead squires and valets.

John grumbled incessantly. That annoyed Suffolk. Naturally it was not pleasant to know oneself a prisoner, but it was to him a relief to have a respite from the war. He would almost have enjoyed the peace of this echoing shell of a castle, he thought, had John not been perpetually grouching about the goddamned Bastard of Orleans, the cursed Pucelle and the bloody Valois. A week later orders came from the Bastard to his servants, to negotiate John's release on parole so that he could begin the task of accumulating the money for his and his brother's ransom. John willingly made the oaths, and two days later he left Blois.

The following day Suffolk was told by his guard that he might leave his room and walk around within the castle. This too was part of the Bastard's orders, he understood. He was glad: not only for the additional freedom, but to know that the Bastard trusted him this much. He did not think of escaping; that would not have been honourable.

He soon came to know the castle, its towers and courtyards, its storerooms and halls, corridors and arcades and staircases. He avoided only the servants' quarters: he was in no mood for company, least of all servants' company. It was a grandiose castle, its fine carvings and tiled floors speaking eloquently of the formidable family which had built it.

He thought a great deal, in those days, of the Bastard. For months he and the Bastard had followed each other's every move at Orleans. They had exchanged messages and letters, even exchanged gifts at Christmas. They had not met face to face before the encounter in the tent at Jargeau.

Then he had been in no frame of mind to attend closely, or to converse with the Bastard; but he had, he discovered now, taken in every detail of the Bastard's appearance. It had been unexpected to him. The Bastard was a son of Louis of Orleans and a cousin of the Dauphin: Suffolk had envisaged him, over those months at Orleans, to have the hooked nose and thick lips of the

Valois princes. But instead he had a round, battered face, with clear, pale eyes, the squashed nose of a fistfighter and an inelegant slit of a mouth.

A good man, Suffolk thought. An honest man, who would look you straight in the eye and tell you the truth. He had thought the same at Orleans until the strange business of the witch had stirred in him something approaching contempt for all the Valois commanders. Then he had thought: how could any fighting man listen to a cheap peasant girl who claims to hear the voices of the saints? But he had seen Jeanne la Pucelle now, and he understood. He knew how enticing an absolute conviction such as hers could be, when set against the terror and the uncertainty of war. He could imagine looking on her determined face, listening to her harsh, girlish voice. He could imagine drawing strength from her; could imagine doing exactly as she said. He no longer blamed the Bastard, or la Hire, or Alençon: in their position, he knew he would have done the same.

The witch had had orders for him too. She had written them, again and again, in those crazy letters. He still had the letter he had carried at Jargeau. 'Go away, for God's sake, back to your own country.' That was what she had ordered him to do.

But what was his own country? It was thirteen, nearly fourteen years since he had set foot in England. He had spent almost half his life in France, serving men of his own nationality who claimed the throne of France. He had a French title as well as an English one: he was the Count of Dreux. To leave France would not feel to him like going home.

Quite the opposite: it was his arrival at Blois that had felt to him like a homecoming. This was what he had longed for: not to return to England, but to find himself in a peaceful France, a welcoming country where no swords were raised, no guns fired. He had no sword now, no army at his back. He was in France, and he felt astonishingly at home.

The Pucelle would not have understood that. But the Bastard would, he thought; the Bastard would.

Just over a month later, the Bastard sent a poursuivant to Blois. He brought a message for Suffolk: John was dead. He had died rapidly, of a fever, in Rouen.

Suffolk listened impassively to this news, to the Bastard's words of sympathy which the poursuivant dutifully recited. Then he excused himself and went to his room. It was in one of the corner towers and there were windows on every side. He walked first, blindly, to the window that looked out on to the town. He could see the spire of the big church – Saint Saviour, the guards had told him; the square where the market was held; the steps that led down to the quays, and the handsome stone fountain. He knew these sights well now, but he had never entered Saint Saviour's church, never walked in the market square. He crossed to the opposite window. From this there was a distant view across the rolling, forested hills of the Loire valley.

Each bird in those hills was free. Each rabbit was free; each ant, even. He was not free. He was trapped: trapped in the gilded prison of Blois castle. For the first time, the stone walls pressed heavily upon him. For the first time since his arrival at Blois he was conscious of the world outside those walls, and of the fact that he could play no part in it.

John dead. He had had five brothers and they were all dead now, bar Thomas, who had taken orders. The de la Poles had always been a prolific family, with four or five sons to a generation. But four dead, already; and Thomas vowed to celibacy; and himself a soldier, not yet married at thirty-three. He had never felt more alone, and at the same time he had never felt more trapped: not only by stone walls, but by a network of obligations and expectations. The whole weight of his family history pressed hard upon him.

He thought not of John, but of all the others. His grandfather, Chancellor to Richard the Second, who had died in miserable exile; his father, dying of dysentery during the siege of Harfleur. His brothers: Michael, killed at Agincourt; Miles, killed at Targu; Alexander, killed at Jargeau. So much tragedy. So much bloody, useless tragedy. He banged his fist against the rough stone wall of the tower room, again and again, until he saw the blood begin to stain the stones. Then he slumped to the floor, nursing his knuckles, and sat there, unmoving, until darkness came.

More weeks passed. Suffolk walked daily, aimlessly, around the castle. He followed the same pattern through the maze each time, his feet moving automatically, his eyes seeing little or nothing.

It was on the day of the storm that he changed his path. He was halfway across the courtyard when the first drops of rain began to fall from a sky suddenly turned to polished slate. Barely a dozen steps later and the rain was solid, enveloping. He ran, arms flailing through the water, towards the nearest doorway.

He realised once he had pushed open the heavy oaken door that it was the entrance to the Tour de Foix. The Duke's own quarters had been here; in his absence it seemed even more desolate than the rest of the castle. Suffolk had climbed the stairs only once, weeks before. Now he climbed them again.

He did not pause till, breathless, he reached the top of the tall tower. Then he stopped. He opened the door at the head of the stairs just enough to allow him to slip in, leaned back against the inside of it and let it swing shut behind him. He continued to lean there as his breath slowed and a puddle of water formed on the floorboards around his feet.

He did not expect the guards to follow him. They would be in the guardroom, playing at dice or tables together; one of them would come to look for him, perhaps, once the storm abated.

The tower room had glazed windows. Rivers of rain ran down the outside of the thick panes. He looked around the room. The floor was deep in dust. He could still see the footprints he had made himself, weeks before, tracing a path towards the far window and arcing back again.

To his left, out of reach of that trail of footprints, a small wooden chest stood against the wall.

There was little furniture in the castle. Suffolk had, he thought, examined each piece; tried the lid of every chest. He could see, though, that neither he nor anyone else had touched this chest for a very long time. He stood looking at it for a few minutes. Then he walked towards it.

There was a key still in the lock; but when he tried the lid he found that he did not need to use it.

A cloud of dust flew off and hung heavy in the storm-darkened room. He propped the lid open against the wall. He saw then that the chest was perhaps a quarter full of papers.

He took a handful of them and brought them towards the window. The rain was dying already and he could see the writing clearly. He leafed through the sheaf. There were bills for bronze-green silk robes and white kerchiefs, lists of grooms, valets and professional fools, menus for banquets, some of them dating right back to the turn of the century.

Blois had not been an echoing shell then. Louis of Orleans had been alive, and his wife Valentina Visconti. Their children had filled the nurseries. The halls had reverberated with the sound of lutes and giterns. The horror had not begun for any of them.

He went back to the chest and drew out more papers. There was a little book with a board cover. Inside were a child's Latin exercises, written in a big, clumsy round hand. The Duke's, perhaps; or the Bastard's, he thought; or it might be more recent, the work of the Duke's young daughter who had been married to the Duke of Alençon. Amo, amas, amat. Alençon was a sadistic bastard, but handsome with it; perhaps the girl did not yet see his cruel side.

He thought for a moment, with unlikely warmth, of the unknown Duchess of Alençon. Then he laid the book aside and rummaged again.

Another manuscript book came to his hand this time: one more roughly made, its paper jagged-edged, the sheets fastened together with faded red ribbon passed through crudely cut holes. But it was fine-grained paper, his fingers told him, and very white. There were perhaps three dozen sheets.

The light from the window showed him this time that on each sheet was transcribed a poem. The letters were neatly formed, but the writer was no professional clerk: here and there the pen had flooded and the lines thickened. The spelling was erratic, too, and he had to concentrate in order to make out all the words.

The poems on the topmost sheets were simple love lyrics. The later ones were poems of love and despair; they were poems of imprisonment.

> De balader j'ay beau loisir,
> Autres deduis me sont cassez;
> Prisonnier suis, d'Amour martir.
> Hélas! et n'est-ce pas assez?

> *[I have plenty of leisure to write ballads,*
> *Other pursuits are forbidden me;*
> *I am a prisoner, a martyr of love.*
> *Alas! is that not enough?]*

A prisoner I am, and a martyr of love. It could almost have been his own lament. But it was more stylish, he admitted to himself, than anything he had ever written. This writer had a deft touch and an attractive cast of mind: he rarely complained, and when he did so he was never far from laughing at his own weakness.

Suffolk had no doubt who the poet was. These poems were all unfamiliar to him, but he recognised their style. The Duke of Orleans had written them. The Duke was famous as a poet, and equally famous as a prisoner.

The Duke wrote again and again of imprisonment; and this was no metaphor, he knew. This man too had felt the walls press hard upon him. This man too had known long vacant hours, when his thoughts were all of things that he was not free to do.

This man had filled some of those hours with poetry. All other amusements forbidden; plenty of leisure to write ballads. Suffolk himself had not asked once for pen and paper in all the long weeks he had spent in captivity. That thought came and brought a pang of guilt with it.

Of course, he reminded himself, the Duke had had a great deal of time to overcome his initial low spirits. He had spent more than long weeks in captivity. He had been taken at Agincourt, and was still a prisoner in England, thirteen – no, nearer fourteen – years later.

That was almost exactly as long as Suffolk himself had been in France.

It was a strange conceit. The French Duke, fourteen years in England; the English Earl, fourteen years in France. Prisoners both. It was as if the Duke of Orleans were his own shadow; his counterpart, his familiar. Why had he never thought it before? It was so clear to him then that this man, these poems, offered the only means by which he might become reconciled to his own fate.

He thought, briefly, of being a prisoner in Blois for the next thirteen years, and pushed the thought aside. Such a thing happened to more than a few men, but for those to whom it had not happened it was beyond imagining.

He read another poem, and another; reread several of them. Sometimes the poet's voice seemed to offer sympathy, to reveal a unique understanding of his own despair. Sometimes it taunted him, light, witty, seeing a wasted life or a broken promise not as a tragedy but as a casual turn of fate.

Vostre besogne est trop ouverte,
Ce n'est pas jeu d'entrejetteurs.

227

Those were the lines that lingered longest in his mind. What you plan is too obvious. This is not a game for dicers.

He thought: I have known many dice-throwers. Talbot is one such: he is a man who would risk everything on a single throw. Such men have no remedy when fate turns up a bad throw. But a chess player, now: he has plans that buttress him against the blows of fortune. He has subtlety: he can outwit the forces that threaten him with disaster.

He admired that poem, admired that sentiment. But tangled in with it, inextricably, were other sentiments that he found not so much admirable as unnerving. 'Faulz trompeurs': those were liars, cheats, bluffers. Those were the men whom the poet advised to become chess players.

He read it again and again, and still he was not sure if the poem was deeply moral, or deeply amoral. He had no doubt that it was one or the other. He never saw it as no more than a pretty pattern of words.

In the end the paper drooped unnoticed in his hand; he gazed unseeing out of the window of the tower room. A gaudy sunset flared and died over the hills. A guard opened the door, registered his presence, withdrew again. The guard returned with his supper in a dish. He did not uncover it, did not eat.

The guard came for a third time, and this time Suffolk acknowledged him and returned with him to his own room.

He woke the next morning feeling curiously refreshed. He thought: prisoner or not, I have the rest of my life to plan out. I should start today.

There were three difficulties facing him. He enumerated them to himself.

First: his career. He did not think himself a poor soldier, but he could not avoid the realisation that he had been an unsuccessful one. His triumphs had been small, his disasters large. The failure of the siege of

Orleans, and the fact that a girl had played a large part in its raising, would be known everywhere. Bedford would not, perhaps, blame him for what had happened; but Bedford would listen to those who did blame him, and act to please them. He might never again be entrusted with a high military command. If he continued to fight in France he would find himself a perpetual second-in-command, serving under men like Scales and Talbot.

Second, the problem of his ransom. To arrange it was a minor difficulty: he had already written to England, calling Thomas to come and stand surety for him while he continued with the task that John had begun. But the cost would be a major difficulty. The last de la Pole to make money had been his great-grandfather; the succeeding generations had generally depleted the Hull merchant's vast fortune. Suffolk would have to sell some of his French estates; if the Bastard pushed him hard he might be forced to sell his English estates too.

Third, his family. He had no direct heir. It had been just about forgivable for him to remain unmarried while John and Alexander were alive, but now he could avoid the cold truth no longer: he had to find a wife.

The answer, clearly, was to find a rich wife. That would solve his financial difficulties as well as his personal ones. He was too fastidious, though, to contemplate the prospect of marrying only for money. She would have to be presentable and cultured, somebody who could encourage and support him while he attempted to rebuild his life.

How, he wondered, did a man of thirty-three set about finding such a woman? He could ask Bedford, he supposed, or Bedford's Duchess – not that he wished to marry a Frenchwoman. He would have asked Salisbury if his commander had still been alive. He could ask Salisbury's widow.

He could marry Salisbury's widow. Suddenly he saw it clearly. He had never been an intimate of the Countess, but he had always admired her cool, sophisticated style.

Once he had even fancied himself in love with her. Though she was not high-born, she had fine manners, and it would certainly be no disgrace to marry as Salisbury had done. And she was rich. She surely had dower estates from Salisbury, and from her previous husband, and she would inherit her father Thomas Chaucer's very sizeable estates.

The more he considered it, the more perfect a solution it seemed. The Countess of Salisbury had been married to a soldier: she would understand as well as any woman what he had gone through. She had lived in France for many years. He would be able to speak French with her, and to talk to her of people and places they both knew. She was a fine singer, he recalled, and a witty conversationalist. She would make him an ideal wife.

Alice, that was her name. Alice, Dowager Countess of Salisbury. He spoke it out loud, savouring the sound of it.

It did occur to him to wonder whether the Countess of Salisbury would wish to marry him. It was not self-evident to him that she would. He was conscious that, already twice widowed, she would choose her own husband this time; he would need to persuade her, and not her father, to opt for him. She doubtless needed a husband – what woman did not? – but she lacked neither money nor rank. She would choose with thought, with care; with audacity perhaps, but not with recklessness.

Suffolk had never known how to charm women. Though he was an Earl, his earldom held unpleasant associations: his disgraced grandfather was not yet forgotten. And he had a fortune that would in future be inadequate to meet his commitments, three sisters and a score of other dependent relations, as well as a record as military commander that had turned from the indifferent to the disastrous.

A martyr of love. The Duke of Orleans' phrase echoed in his mind as he surveyed these unpleasant facts. No, he would not be that; he would be a good chess player, one who takes stock of his weaknesses but plays on his strengths. He would not despair; he would plan a future for them both that the Countess of Salisbury would find irresistible.

That future would not be as a soldier. It was obvious to him now that his talents were not fitted to warfare. He was a clever and thoughtful man, but in military command cleverness and deep consideration were not what was required. He considered, he read, he planned his tactics in advance; but in battle events moved too fast for him. All too often his plans collapsed and he found himself unable to think on his feet and put new plans in their stead. He was still asking himself what he should do when men like Fastolf and Talbot, pragmatic, blind to half the alternatives, would already have done it.

The alternative was a career as a civilian servant of the King; and at that, he began to think, he might fare far better. At court there would be time to think. Events would be less dramatic, the shifts of fortune slower; his plans might come to fruition.

What would the Countess of Salisbury make of that? She would be satisfied, he reckoned, if he aimed to make his mark in the King's Council. He had noticed that she enjoyed court society, that she was forever in the company of the Duchess of Bedford and the other noble ladies in Paris. She would presumably find a similar position in England equally to her taste. And she was a thoughtful woman: one, surely, who could be fired by great ideas.

He had a great idea. He wanted to bring peace to the whole of France.

The news had come to Blois only days before that the Pucelle had had the Dauphin crowned at Rheims. To him, this seemed a move of vital significance. The French nobles who had crowned Charles the Seventh King of France could never turn about-face and accept Henry of Lancaster in his stead. There was no possibility any more that the Treaty of Troyes which conceded the Lancastrian claim to the throne might be enforced by agreement alone.

Nor could it be enforced by might. Orleans had shown him that, or at least shown him that the cost of the attempt would be too great. He did not believe it could possibly be right for the King to destroy France entirely in the guise of conquering it.

So the war would have to be ended by a negotiated settlement: one that ceded some of Henry's claims, but not the greatest of them. He thought he knew what the English should demand. By birth and by conquest Henry could claim Normandy and Gascony, the Ile de France and parts of Anjou and Maine. The Dauphin would be realistic enough, surely, to grant his title to those lands. He might even be relieved enough not to demand that Henry pay him homage as overlord.

That would not be the glory of which Henry the Fifth had dreamed. But men who have looked into the abyss do not yearn for glory: to them it is a great thing to gain safety and security. Henry had died before he had been able to complete the conquest which, had he lived, might have become reality. Suffolk was convinced it could never be more than a dream to his son. The rightness of Henry's claim to the throne he had never doubted; but he was no longer prepared to support to the last man, the last sou, the attempt to turn a half-empty claim into a reality.

Peace, not glory: that was his dream. To have the English and the French meeting as friends; to be able to shake the Bastard of Orleans by the hand, to stay at Blois not as a prisoner, but as an honoured guest. This was his vision.

There was one overriding problem. He knew well by then that his views were unvoiceable in France. There were many who would take them as evidence of treason, who would think him not a visionary but a mewling weakling, selling out the King's rightful inheritance before he was of an age to claim it for himself. Perhaps the Countess of Salisbury would not be one such; but as this had been Salisbury's own view, he dared not assume as much. It would be foolish even to broach such ideas to the Countess before he had made her his wife. No, he would have to appeal to her on a more material level, and pray that that would be enough to win him her hand.

Then he would take her to England. In England he would explain to her his grand vision, and she would share it with him. In England, surely, the civilians and the churchmen at Westminster would listen to him where Bedford and his soldiers had not. Perhaps it would take time to bring them round to his way of thinking. But he was still a comparatively young man and he could spare that time.

The Bastard was coming home at last. Blois slowly began to waken to his arrival.

There was a shaking-out of bedclothes, a washing of the tiled floors, an uncovering of the stored and dusty furniture. Servants ran across the courtyards, where before they had strolled; they shouted to each other, where once they had laughed.

Suffolk attempted to ignore this activity. He spent most of his days in the room at the top of the Tour de Foix. He had begged pen and paper from his guards and he was steadily making copies for himself of the Duke of Orleans' poems. He was also writing poems of his own: love poems to Alice, Dowager Countess of Salisbury.

On the day when the Bastard was expected he did not go to the Tour de Foix. He spent the morning in his own room. There was no guard on him, but he thought this a wise precaution. From there he could see the Loire Bridge; he saw the small troop of horse, with the Bastard's standard flying over it, ride up to the bridge and clatter over its ageing timbers.

He could not see, but he could envisage, the scenes that followed: the servants lined up in the courtyard, the Bastard dismounting and greeting each one. A special dinner would have been prepared for the Bastard, his bathwater drawn and heated; for in the absence of the Duke, Suffolk had already discovered, the Bastard was treated as the master of Blois.

Suffolk was in no frame of mind to write, so he occupied himself by reading his missal. He read for a long time, but without great success: the noises of the castle, so long silent, distracted him.

It was the music that finally drew him from his missal. The faint strains of a rondeau reached him, played fast and well by lutes and viols. He was very fond of music and he had heard none for months. He guessed that the minstrels were in the Great Hall. He could hear only snatches from his tower room. He opened the door and made his way cautiously down the staircase and across the yard.

The door to the hall was ajar. Through it came the music, clear and precise. He stood outside the door, listening, for some time. Then he set his shoulder to the narrow gap and slipped through.

The hall was empty save for the minstrels. There were half a dozen of them, gathered at the far end, sitting on the newly washed floor. They were playing a rondeau with words he recognised: it was a poem by the Duke, one he had found among the papers in the chest. He knew the tune as well. Half under his breath, he joined in the tenor part. One of the musicians turned his head and saw him standing there. The man turned away and continued his song without breaking the rhythm.

Suffolk watched this man, a viol player. The tune came to its neat conclusion. The minstrel he was watching rose to his feet and began to walk towards him. Only then did he realise that it was the Bastard himself.

It was too late to do more than bow. Suffolk bowed. The Bastard held out his hand.

'Monsieur le Comte,' he said with simple directness. 'We have some business to discuss.'

Captivity was no stranger to many great families, but few had suffered from it as intensely as the House of

Orleans. The Duke had been a prisoner for more than thirteen years; his younger brother Jean, Count of Angoulême, had been a prisoner for even longer than that.

Suffolk had forgotten what little he had known about the debacle that had cost Angoulême his freedom. The Bastard reminded him. There had not even been a battle. Orleans had enlisted an English army to help in his private war against the Duke of Burgundy, and then been forced to send it home unused. Salisbury had extracted heavy compensation for the inconvenience – which the Duke could not pay – and insisted that Angoulême should stand hostage meanwhile.

It had pleased Suffolk to think that his ransom would contribute to the Duke's freedom. He was wrong, he now learned. There was no question of the Duke being freed: Bedford and Gloucester refused even to negotiate a ransom amount. So it was towards Angoulême's ransom that the bulk of his own fortune would be put.

The Bastard explained all this, frankly and without particular malice. It was the fortunes of war. Though the English had not been kind to his family, there was no injustice for him to complain of. It crossed Suffolk's mind that the Bastard had little reason to complain in any case. He had risen a long way, for a bastard: perhaps with two legitimate half-brothers at loose his own career would have been more restricted.

He listened to what the Bastard said with this thought in his mind, but there was no confirmation of it in the Bastard's words or his tone. The Bastard had done everything that could have been expected of him, and more, to try to free his half-brothers and to maintain their lands in their absence.

As Suffolk had anticipated, he liked the Bastard. Allied to the squashed features was a blunt manner which he occasionally found disconcerting; but nevertheless he liked the man.

It was all agreed without too much difficulty. Suffolk's ransom would be 20,000 écus; not enough to secure Angoulême's release, but a substantial sum all the same. It would be paid directly to the Dowager Duchess of Clarence, Angoulême's jailer. He would be released on licence so that he could arrange payment as soon as Thomas arrived at Blois.

Thomas had as yet sent no word as to when that might be. Meanwhile, Suffolk remained at the castle. For several weeks the Bastard remained with him.

Those were joyful weeks. The Bastard and Suffolk hunted deer and boar together in the forests; they flew hawks together in the meadows. They practised rondeaux and ballads together; and they talked.

The Bastard had forgotten the little book of Orleans' poems, he said with apparent sincerity; they had been copied out by the Duke's wife Bonne from rough versions brought back by Orleans' heralds. Bonne was dead now, and her book had been packed away by the stewards, he had not known where.

He had heard before that Suffolk himself wrote poems: it was widely known in Paris and among the army. He asked to see some of them. Suffolk showed him the poems he had written while he was at Blois and wrote out a couple of earlier efforts which he still remembered. Some were in French; those in English were translations of Orleans' French originals. All of them were love poems. He had written one or two poems with political themes, but the Bastard was a Valois supporter, however likeable, and he was not shown those.

'They are acrostics?' the Bastard asked.

'No. My mind has never run easily to acrostics. I have no need to weave in the lady's name secretly: I hope to give the poems to her openly when I return to Paris.'

'Ah. A mistress?'

'A lady I have admired for many years. And now I hope she will become my wife.'

The Bastard considered. 'So this lady is in Paris?'

'Her name is Alice – Alice, Dowager Countess of Salisbury.'

'Ah. The Earl's widow. Then she is rich?'

'She has a dower portion from Salisbury, and another from a previous husband; and she is a very substantial heiress in her own right.'

'It will be a good marriage, then.'

'If I can contrive it, a very good one.'

The Bastard considered again. Then he threw back his head and gave a short laugh.

'How English,' he said, 'to write poems to celebrate a marriage of convenience.'

Suffolk watched him. He reminded himself that this vulgarity in the Bastard had to be accepted; he knew by now that it was not intended to give offence. 'My dear Jean,' he said. 'I plan to marry the lady because she is rich. I write poems to her because I love her. The two are quite different.'

'If you say so, mon cher. And the girl at Jargeau?'

Suffolk frowned. It had been the one cloud over the Bastard's homecoming, the news he had brought about the girl at Jargeau. She had conceived, damn her; and her father was loudly insisting that her plight should not be overlooked.

'She will go to a nunnery. It was a very short attachment: her father can scarcely expect more. I have offered to take the child back to England. The Countess of Salisbury is a worldly woman; she should make no objection.'

'She sounds,' said the Bastard ingenuously, 'like a Frenchwoman. And she is beautiful, naturally?'

'But of course. In many ways she is like a Frenchwoman: she has lived mainly in Paris for some years. She is still young, and she is beautiful, and clever. You know she is a grand-daughter of our great English poet Geoffrey Chaucer?'

'Then she too,' said the Bastard, 'would enjoy meeting my brother.'

Suffolk had seen the Bastard's plan. A similar plan had been growing in his own mind.

'My dear Jean,' he said, 'our growing friendship has been the one delight of this unfortunate period. I will do all that I can to bring the same pleasure to your brothers when I return to England.'

'Charles is a great believer in the cause of peace,' said the Bastard.

'We are all,' Suffolk replied coolly, 'anxious for peace.'

'Then why do you fight,' pursued the Bastard, continuing an old argument, 'when you know that the people of France will never permit the English to win this war?'

There was a dangerous pleasure in arguing about politics with the Bastard. Truth and diplomacy wove awkward strands in the mesh of their friendship. Sometimes Suffolk would find his own arguments coming from his friend's mouth, and in the interests of security he was forced to rebut them. It was good practice, he told himself. War might be a game for dicers, but to contrive peace was the task of a subtle and diplomatic man.

'Jean, you persist in misunderstanding. It is not the English who hope to win the war. It is Henry who has a right to rule over France as its King. We merely assist him to enforce his claim.'

'Ah, you argue, you claim, to be supporters of a French cause. But your baby King has no support among the French.'

'He has the support of Burgundy.'

The Bastard spat on the floor, in eloquent expression of his opinion of the Duke of Burgundy.

'And,' continued Suffolk, 'the Treaty of Troyes gave him an unassailable right to the Throne of France.'

'The Treaty of Troyes was an abomination, forced on the people by a mad king and a witch of a queen. Those who suffered it did so only because they expected to exchange a mad Charles for a strong Henry. Now you try to persuade us to exchange a sane Charles for a child Henry. No true Frenchman will accept such a bargain; no true Frenchman accepts Henry's divine right to rule France. Jeanne la Pucelle proved to us that God is on the side of King Charles. And Henry's Regent has resorted to an army of Englishmen who fight in reality so that they can be granted French estates in France.'

Jeanne la Pucelle was a witch who had proved nothing of the kind. But it was useless to argue about her with the Bastard, as Suffolk had already found to his cost.

'The Valois army, my dear Jean, relies just as heavily upon mercenaries. You load your Scottish and Lombard captains with estates and honours.'

'You would call yourself, then, a mercenary?'

A definite hit: one too accurate to be comfortable. He let himself consider before replying.

'I fight,' he said slowly, 'for the honour of my King, and for love of France. I have been fourteen years now in France. I can barely recall life in England. Can you not believe that I love your country?'

The Bastard perused his face for a long moment. 'The pity of it is, mon cher,' he said at last, 'that I believe you do.'

9

FRANCE

Secret heard from an innkeeper in Chartres that the siege of Orleans had been raised. He had been travelling to the city to bring messages and letters to Fastolf.

His first feeling was annoyance. He had expected to find Fastolf without difficulty, at Orleans. Now he would have to look elsewhere.

Where, it was difficult to tell. The innkeeper knew only that the siege was over, not what the Lancastrian army had done afterwards. There were only a few English soldiers in Chartres. He asked them where he might find Sir John Fastolf, but they could not tell him; even their captain seemed to have no interest in events beyond the city walls.

He returned from the castle to the inn, sat outside on a bench in the sunshine nursing a cup of ale and considered the situation. He was not surprised that the siege had been abandoned. It had always seemed to him a hopeless enterprise and there had been talk for weeks that the Valois were raising a second relieving army. There had been talk, too, of a girl the English claimed to be a witch, but he had made little of that.

He decided to go to Le Mans. There was only a remote possibility that Fastolf himself would be at Le Mans; but the English garrison there was much larger, it received messages from Bedford regularly and the captain would surely be better informed than his counterpart at Chartres.

The journey took him two days. It was midsummer

and hot and he did not hurry his old mare. En route he heard only wild rumours. From the captain at Le Mans he learned that the Lancastrian army had divided into sections after leaving Orleans, and that each section had been despatched to join a different garrison. The captain was not certain where Fastolf's division had been sent, but he suggested that Secret next try Beaugency.

That seemed to Secret to be sane advice. He took it. Five miles from Beaugency – a little town on the Loire, between Orleans and Blois – he was told by a pedlar, travelling away from the town, that it was under siege by a large Valois army.

He was not merely annoyed now; he was perturbed. He had frequently found it difficult to locate Fastolf before, but never had he found himself so completely adrift.

He stopped at the next inn he reached. The windows were shuttered and the passage to the yard was boarded. He called out, anyway, that he was a Frenchman and alone. After a long pause, punctuated by the barking of several dogs, the innkeeper appeared from round the side of the building. He asked if he might eat and the man agreed to bring him out some food.

When it came – a rough sausage, bread and wine – he squatted on the ground to eat it. The innkeeper talked to him from over the barricade. The English had come past that way, he said, marching from Orleans to Beaugency. He had put up the barricade to keep the goddamns out and was leaving it up to keep the bloody Valois out.

But a man must eat, he said, be he innkeeper or soldier. Secret agreed. The sausage was good.

'And when a man shows me the inside of his purse . . .'

'You ask him only what he wishes to buy.'

'Mind, they ate in the road, like you, sir.'

'A wise precaution,' Secret agreed. He thought. 'They say he is a fair man, the English captain.'

241

'Matago? Not bad as soldiers go, from all I hear. Mind, he'll not hold the castle against those Valois cannon.'

'Not for long, I should think.'

The innkeeper's wife brought out a slice of cherry flan. Secret ate it.

He considered. Matago. That must be Matthew Gough: the French always mangled English names. Sir Matthew Gough, rather: he had been knighted at Orleans some months before. Now he had evidently been given command of his own division. He probably wished he had not, wished himself a thousand miles from Beaugency and the Valois cannon. His first major command, and he faced the prospect of losing it within days.

What would Gough do in those circumstances? He would send his new poursuivant, Beul, to Fastolf to beg for assistance. It was stupid, anyway, for the Lancastrians to have broken up their army. Now that they knew the Valois were on the offensive they would surely try to recombine their divisions.

Secret thought of going on towards Beaugency. He even thought of entering the town. If he wore his tabard the Valois would let him through safely. But there was nothing he could tell Matthew; nothing he could do in Beaugency but eat the garrison's rations. And though Matthew was in Beaugency, it seemed to him unlikely that Christophe and Peter and Jean would be there also.

He did not think seriously of riding elsewhere. He reckoned his best chance of finding Fastolf lay in staying close to Beaugency. Perhaps Matthew would negotiate a surrender; then he would ride out of Beaugency with his men and Secret would be able to join them. Surely they would then look to meet up with Fastolf's division.

The innkeeper had disappeared. Secret whistled for him and negotiated a price for his dinner over the barricade. Then he unhitched his mare and rode on.

He rode to another inn, then to another, then to another, none of them more than five miles from Beaugency. Some were barred, some deserted, some

242

crowded with peasants trying to drown their fears in strong ale. At most, he found somebody who would talk to him. Every tale he heard was different. There was a vast English army approaching; the Duke of Burgundy had sent troops; yet more Valois forces had arrived. It seemed as if every soldier in France were coming to Beaugency. He heard mention of Talbot, Matago and Fastolf; of Alençon, La Hire, the Bastard of Orleans and Jeanne la Pucelle.

He saw no soldiers at the first five inns he entered. The sixth inn was different. Its barricades had been smashed. He saw this while he was still fifty yards or more away. He approached only close enough to see the blazons on the troops crowding the yard. They were Breton troops, the Count of Richemont's men.

He brought his horse round, moving as rapidly as the old mare could manage, and took her back along the road from Beaugency to Meung. He stopped in the shade of a ragged copse, in sight of the next inn along the road. It was less than an hour since he had downed the last of his ale there.

He dismounted.

Breton troops. He seemed to be thinking with an unreal clarity; with half his mind, he realised that he was very drunk. It had been necessary to buy at least one cup of ale at each inn he visited; at some, the men to whom he talked had bought him a second cup, even a third. It was a hot, bright afternoon: the sun burned down upon him. Breton troops. Richemont's men. Richemont was his overlord now, the lord of Fougères. They were Richemont's men; he was Richemont's man.

He was also Fastolf's man. But Fastolf was heaven knew where in central France, and a bloody Englishman. He was a Breton, or half of one. He had a powerful urge to go to those Breton soldiers, to talk to them as he had talked to the peasants in the other inns. Because he was truly Richemont's man. No; because he was Fastolf's man, and it would benefit Fastolf, surely, if he knew what the Bretons were planning to do. Because

Fougères was no longer the Duke of Alençon's town, and he hated Alençon. Because Matthew Gough was in Beaugency, looking down the barrels of a dozen Valois cannon. The reasons, good, bad and plain ludicrous, chased themselves around his head.

All the reasons pushed him to the same conclusion. Go to the Bretons. In a daze, he unclipped the little enamel badge that marked him as Fastolf's poursuivant. He opened his saddlebag, took out his formal tabard and his pack of letters, wrapped all these things in his spare undershirt and fastened them into a neat bundle. He remounted, set the bundle between his knees and rode slowly to the inn. He told the landlady a long, confused story (second instalment of the one he had invented earlier) about a sick cousin in Meung and gave her two saluts to care for his horse and the bundle until he returned.

He left the landlady, bestowing a crooked, drunken smile on her, brushed his hands down his anonymous grey-brown tunic, told himself that nothing now marked him out for Fastolf's man and set off on foot to join the Bretons.

They were in the parlour of the inn when he reached it again. They had been drinking strong wine. They were not as drunk as he, but neither were they sober. Secret did at least know that he was too soused to keep his lies consistent, so he told them something resembling the truth: that his name was Laurence de Fougères, that he was a Norman–Breton lawyer's clerk, that he had been living near Orleans. Then he brought out the five saluts that he had left in his purse and called for more wine for them all.

Laurence de Fougères. He had almost forgotten his own name, he thought through a winey haze. He had not spoken it for years. That was a sad thought. He was Laurence de Fougères. How could he have forgotten who he was?

He was a Breton. These men talked like him, they told jokes he understood. They drank wine he liked. They were fools. But Richemont was not a fool, he thought. Richemont was a cunning bastard, just like he was.

And these were indeed Richemont's men, through and through. He soon learned that they had all followed the Breton count in each of his switches of allegiance. It did not bother them whether they fought for King Henry or for the Dauphin. In their minds they fought for neither. They fought for money for their next meal, and for the Count of Richemont.

Secret thought of asking more questions, but the words, so clear in his mind, somehow never reached his lips. He drank some more wine instead. In the end he must have passed out. When he awoke it was morning and he was in a field. The Bretons from the inn surrounded him. Surrounding them was the rest of the Count of Richemont's army.

The army was already striking camp. It began to march towards Beaugency. He marched with it, in the midst of his new Breton friends.

The one called Jules proved to have some sense. Secret walked by Jules' side. He carried Jules' pike. It helped him to feel inconspicuous. He asked Jules all the questions he had not asked the evening before.

At Orleans he had heard that Richemont had been driven from the Dauphin's court in disgrace after losing a power struggle with the rival commander la Trémoïlle. True, Jules said. But Richemont reckoned that la Trémoïlle would last no more than a year or two; he still supported the Dauphin's cause. He was taking his men to join up with a Valois army under the Bastard of Orleans, the Duke of Alençon and the Pucelle. Only a few days earlier that army had taken the town of Jargeau from the Earl of Suffolk. Now, with Richemont's help, it would take Beaugency.

Alençon, Secret thought. I have not only joined Richemont's men: I shall be joining Alençon's army too.

There was nothing he could do but continue. He asked more questions. Would Richemont be welcomed by the Pucelle and the others? Jules shrugged. Why should he not be welcomed? At times of success, quarrels were easily forgotten. The Pucelle was uniting all Frenchmen under the Dauphin: she would rejoice to see Richemont, no doubt about it.

He asked about the action at Jargeau. A crushing victory, Jules said. The Pucelle had God on her side, she could do no wrong. She and her men had killed all the English, every one. Including the Earl of Suffolk? Secret asked. Jules gave him a sly look, as if he did not like to have his word questioned.

So Suffolk was dead; or probably so. He did not overrate Jules' accuracy. The common Bretons cared little for individual English commanders, bar the demon Talbot; probably only Richemont knew the truth for certain. It saddened him to think that Suffolk was dead. He had enjoyed watching the Earl of Suffolk.

He marched on. They were now close to Beaugency. He considered what he should do next. He did not want to fight; he could not imagine using Jules' pike against Matthew Gough's men. He could not run away. The army was loosely organised, but not that loosely organised: with a battle in prospect the heralds were watching for deserters and he dared not risk being brought to their attention.

Even then, he only half regretted his drunken impulse. He reckoned the danger of discovery was slight: many of the troops were dressed little differently from himself, and armed only slightly better. If he stayed, he thought, he would need to lay hands on a bow, and to mark his tunic with some semblance of Richemont's device.

If he stayed, he thought, he would learn more. In time he would be able to tell what he had learned to the English. That would bring him credit, and maybe also money. If he stayed, he might have a chance to watch the Count of Richemont. Perhaps that would earn him neither credit nor money from the English; but he wanted to do it anyway.

He wondered what Christophe was doing. Might he

have joined Matthew's men after all, or would he still be with Fastolf? Were they together, Christophe and Peter and Jean de Waurin? Even if they were, and he were to find them, it would not be as it had been in the barn. It was a lonely thought that none of them would ever go back to the barn. Jules and his comrades were poor consolation. It was not so easy to think of them as his friends now that he was sober.

By mid-afternoon they came to Beaugency. Heralds from the other Valois army rode up to them. The news brought by the heralds spread rapidly. The Valois had taken the town, but the English still held the castle. The guns were firing on it; the English were negotiating a surrender.

The heralds directed Richemont's men to a meadow just outside the town. There (rumour said) the Count was to meet with the Pucelle. It no longer seemed obvious even to Jules that she would welcome him. Her army had no need of reinforcements. A whisper circulated that the Pucelle had threatened to fight Richemont himself, as an enemy of the Dauphin.

The troops waited, in disarray, at the edge of the meadow. Secret could see no sign of the Pucelle, or of any of the Valois captains. He reckoned they would have a long wait. He passed it in negotiating with the Bretons. By the time the Pucelle's escort came into view at the far side of the field he was the possessor of a short sword with a broken hilt.

The Bretons still called him Laurence. It sounded less strange to him by then. But he would not fight with them, he told himself: not against Matthew's men.

There was as yet no need for fighting. He had only to listen to the guns firing, a mile away; only to watch. He watched the Pucelle ride out to the middle of the field, with an armed man at her either side and a row of three standard bearers behind them, heralds, trumpeters and esquires. He looked at the standards. That was the Pucelle's standard, the white one with Jesus and the

247

angels on it. Those were the nettles of the House of Orleans, the Bastard's standard.

That was the Duke of Alençon's standard.

That is the Duke of Alençon, he thought, looking at the armed man to the Pucelle's left. He squinted. Alençon was bareheaded: he could see the Duke's fair curls.

The Count of Richemont's escort detached itself from the mass of his troops and rode out to confront the Pucelle.

Secret's eyes moved from Alençon and to Richemont. Then, involuntarily, his focus changed and he saw the scene as a whole. The standards, the tabards, the escorts: the confrontation. He had last seen such a sight in the rain, in the dawn light, on the road from Rouvray to Janville. Then it was he who had ridden out to parley. He remembered his exultancy; he remembered his terror. He remembered Mountjoie's expression as he repeated Clermont's words. Clermont was not with this army, and one-eyed Stewart was dead.

It seemed to him that it would make a neat resolution to his own dilemma if Alençon and Richemont were to part as enemies. Then he could fight with Richemont's men against Alençon. Perhaps Richemont in his fury would turn his coat again and ride to defend Matthew Gough. That would be better still.

From where he stood with the Bretons, the figures were all indistinct: he had no hope of seeing their expressions. He watched Richemont dismount. The Pucelle dismounted too.

Richemont is short, Secret thought: he is no taller than the girl. That surprised him. He considered it. He had seen Richemont before, but then the Count had been sitting, in the castle at Fougères. He had the long, thick torso of a much taller man; only his legs were little.

Jeanne la Pucelle knelt in front of Richemont on the tussocky grass of the meadow. She leaned forwards. From where Secret stood she appeared to be embracing Richemont's knees. Richemont raised her to her feet.

248

They were talking, evidently, but there was no possibility of his hearing any of their conversation. He hated his ignorance. He hated the speculation of the Bretons all around him, all of it ludicrously ill-informed.

The conversation ended. Jeanne and Richemont walked side by side to Alençon and the Bastard. These men now dismounted. The four of them stood close together. They could not embrace because of their armour, but there was no doubt: Richemont had been accepted.

His soldiers cheered. They then dispersed without waiting for orders. A bloody rabble, Secret thought. He also thought: I was a fool to raise my own hopes, when I knew it would not end as I longed for it to end.

He also thought: I hate the Duke of Alençon. I shall be a spy in his army, but I shall fight with him never. And then he thought, with surprise: I say that, but the hot feeling is not there to match the words.

It was an old sorrow that he had never succeeded in avenging Marianne, but it was one that he had not felt in years, and it came to him now with an unfamiliar sense of bitterness and guilt. It was Laurence de Fougères' sorrow, and he had not been Laurence de Fougères. He had become another man, with another name.

A part of him felt that he should try again: that there should be something he could do to Alençon even now. A larger part of him felt he did not like to be Laurence de Fougères: that it would be more comfortable when he became Secret Poursuivant once more, and he could put this old sorrow behind him again.

The sun was low. The Breton army proceeded to stake out their camp in a meadow adjoining the one where Richemont and the Pucelle had talked. The guns were still firing. Jules came to tell Secret what Richemont was said to have told the Pucelle. He had said: whether you were sent by God, I do not know. But I fear you not if you were, since my heart is pure. And if you were sent by the Devil – then, I fear you still less.

'Crazy, eh?' said Jules.

'Crazy,' Secret agreed. He thought: Richemont is indeed a clever bastard. He only makes himself appear a fool, because he speaks to this witch, the Pucelle.

The Bretons shared their rations with him. As soon as he had eaten he fell asleep. He was tired, very tired; he did not wake till an hour or more after dawn.

He noticed immediately that the guns were no longer firing. Jules and his comrades had no idea what had happened. He had to know, so he asked the men from the next contingent. They told him that Gough had capitulated at midnight, and at dawn the Pucelle and her commanders had allowed the English garrison to ride from Beaugency.

Too late, too late: Matthew was gone without him. He dared to ask no more. He returned to Jules' men and waited. The information that he wanted reached them soon after their breakfast. Gough was withdrawing to Meung, freed on condition that he and his men agree not to fight for ten days.

All the soldiers agreed that ten days was all the time they needed, and more. It would take them less than ten days to find Fastolf's men and thrash them; less than ten days to find Talbot's men and thrash them too.

Secret thought: that will happen. This is a huge army now. It is badly organised, but it has confidence. It will defeat both Fastolf and Talbot, either separately or together. Suffolk's division annihilated already; Gough's little garrison humiliated; Fastolf's and Talbot's men as good as lost. Bedford's treasury already scoured and scoured again of every last sou. Orleans the English could have survived; but all these defeats, put together, will surely mean the end of the English hopes of taking all France.

He also thought: I am glad that Richemont's men did not fight Matthew's men.

He thought of going to Meung. He did not want to go

to Meung. He wanted to see what would happen. In Meung, he sensed, nothing would happen.

So he stayed with the Bretons. The Valois army raised camp and set off north, leaving a small garrison at Beaugency.

Trudging north with the Bretons, Secret watched the Count of Richemont. It was not difficult to watch him. Richemont rode a large black destrier and he stood out against his mass of footsoldiers. Whenever the army halted he would walk around the camp and talk to some of the men. He talked to his lieutenants too, in a loud, deep voice.

What he said was rarely informative. That did not surprise Secret. He remembered his discussion with Christopher Hanson, back in the barn. He thought that many men must have asked themselves what he and Christophe had asked: whether the Breton was a man of confused loyalties, or of no loyalties at all.

He had a striking face, Richemont. No neck to mention; a low sloping forehead; thick overhanging brows; a bulbous nose. Many men called it ugly. Secret privately admired it: to him it seemed to radiate strength and intelligence.

Richemont is powerfully dominant, he thought: men talk of him constantly. And yet he is a strangely ineffective general. He had long known that Richemont was not particularly successful as a commander; seeing him now, with his men, he began to sense why. Richemont's influence stretched no further than his presence, the carrying distance of his voice. He did not transmit it to his subordinates; he had established no network of delegated command.

He looked at Alençon too, cautiously, from a distance. But it was difficult for him to see Alençon. His eyes seemed to be filmed with his sense of his own shame, his bitter knowledge that he would never now do what his honour had obliged him to do.

Of the Bastard of Orleans, la Hire and the rest he

gained only an impression, vague but convincing. It seemed to him that all the Valois commanders shared something of Richemont's quality. They were all brilliant individuals, no less, no more. The Bastard of Orleans, Richemont, la Hire: it was true of each one. And it was true most of all of the Pucelle.

Only in such an army could there have been a role for a peasant girl who wore a borrowed suit of plate armour and claimed to talk with God. Secret had ridden before with armies led by men of deep religious conviction: Bedford was one such, he spent many hours in prayer each day. But he had never before ridden with an army where God was so tangible a force, where men not only hoped, but looked, for miracles. They all spoke of their divine destiny to save France. They swore less than most soldiers; their pillaging of the countryside was modest. The Pucelle had sent away the camp followers and the men had accepted this without demur. And if Alençon and the Bastard and Richemont were less than totally united, at least they did not squabble in public – which, by the standards of French generals, was something truly exceptional.

Secret saw all this; but he saw it with detachment. He was not enthralled by Jeanne: he thought her more likely a witch than a messenger of God. He had no real belief in the rightness of her cause. It was a matter of politics to him, not one of divine right, which man became ruler of which slice of territory. He thought: the English believe in the rightness of their cause too. Whatever Jules and his comrades imagine, I know that Matthew and the rest are not devils.

Naturally he did not say these things to Jules and the others. With them he repeated the phrases he heard them repeat. He prayed out loud, like the Pucelle, to Saint Margaret and Saint Catherine. He talked of boiling up the bones of the goddamns and sending them home in pots.

And as they continued to march north, as the scouts returned with news that they were coming closer and closer to Fastolf and Talbot and their men, he thought: my God, it will happen. They will massacre them all.

He asked himself, almost as if he were discussing it with Jean and Christophe, what he would do if he were in Fastolf's place. The answer was obvious to him. In Fastolf's place he would withdraw. That was the only tactic with any chance of success. The Valois were spoiling for a battle: they would chase Fastolf north rather than stop to pick off the Lancastrian strongholds. If it was thwarted of a fight the jumble of feudal levies might not hold together.

But Talbot was no man for withdrawal. Perhaps Fastolf would see it, perhaps he would argue for such a policy; but Talbot would never agree to it. And Talbot would prevail. They would press onwards. The Valois would find them and they would be mice caught in a trap.

Secret looked at the men who surrounded him. Jules and the other Breton peasants, friendly but stupid. Richemont, dangerous and untrustworthy. Alençon, no longer hated but still despised. The Bastard of Orleans, la Hire, the Pucelle: strangers all to him. And he thought: these men plan to kill Jean and Christophe and Peter.

He was not one of these men, not any more. Even the Breton jokes seemed to him no more than a flimsy disguise. He was the friend of Jean and Christophe and Peter. He thought: I have spent too long on this dangerous charade. Now I must be with my friends, even if it is only to die at their side.

He had been two days with the Valois army, but he had learned only snippets. He had uncovered no fatal weakness, discovered nothing that might turn the course of a battle. Nor would he, now. The battle would come soon. He had to get away. He had to find Jean and Christophe and Peter before the Valois found them.

He listened to the scouts. He learned that they had found English soldiers at Patay, a village on a crossroads where the road from Lignarolles to Coinces intersected an old Roman road. He waited until it was dark. Then he murmured something about going to piss in the hedge and he walked away from the Bretons, away from the guards and the heralds, away from the Valois army.

The army had been moving irregularly and he was no more than seven miles from where he had joined it. He walked till dawn, then slept in a wood till midday. Shortly afterwards he was back at the inn where he had left his horse, his tabard, his badge and his letters.

Would the battle be that day? He prayed not. Even if he managed to spur the mare to a trot, he would not reach Patay much before evening.

He rode along deserted roads, between lines of poplars, past shuttered farmhouses and boarded-up inns. He rode for many hours. He did not stop to eat.

At last he came to Patay. It was no more than a huddle of cottages and a fortified church. He knocked on the cottage doors, but none of them opened to him. He rode through the village and into the fields beyond.

And came across the remnants of a battlefield. Trampled hedges, blood on the cornstalks. Corpses, many corpses. Baggage wagons and artillery. Troops, Valois troops, staking out a camp on a low hillside in the shadow of a copse.

One look told him that there were no living Lancastrians still at Patay. If Jean and Christophe and Peter had been here, they were gone now; or they lay there among the corpses.

A blind horror came over him. He sat there for a long time, astride his old nag on the Roman road, thinking of what had happened there that day.

He had to know what had happened. But there were no Lancastrians to ask, so he would have to learn it from the Valois troops.

He was weary, but a firm decisiveness had caught hold of him now. He rode back to the village and took a series of farm tracks that led him, eventually, to the far side of the copse. There he dismounted. He hid his pack under a thorn bush, hitched the mare's reins to a low branch, rolled around twice in the dust, plunged his arms into the thorn bush and then added some deeper scratches with his dagger. He fought his way through the centre of the copse and walked unsteadily down the hillside towards the Count of Richemont's standard.

Soon he located Jules and his fellows. They were less battered than he. It seemed the battle had been over very quickly. There was blood on Jules' dagger, but there were no scratches on Jules' arm: he suspected the dagger had been plunged into a corpse.

He told them a simple tale. He had got lost in the dark the night before. He had slept with a different division of Bretons. They were good men; he had fought with them.

Jules and the rest questioned none of this. They barely listened: they were too busy arguing about what had happened.

Secret looked around at the battlefield; he listened to their tales. It was a crazy site for a battle, he thought: the cornfield, the road running along its edge, the copse obscuring the ridge, and the view down to the hollow with the little village and the blank-walled church. The fighting seemed to have been a mixture of wild attacks and cautious withdrawals.

He did not dare to ask questions, but slowly, by listening to the arguments, he pieced together the outline of what had happened. The Valois scouts had known that both Fastolf's division and Talbot's were very close at hand, but on the plain of Beauce around Patay, rolling and thickly wooded, they had lost all trace of them. Whie the scouts were searching, Talbot and Fastolf had already chosen their position. The archers were to be stationed along the line of the hedge that straggled out from the copse and along the ridge, to protect the baggage and the artillery. The main body was to make a stand between the copse and the church, and Talbot was to command the vanguard, five hundred men who would block the narrow road to the

Valois, to ensure that the rest of the army had time to form up.

It seemed to him that that had been a good plan. It was a restricted site with plenty of cover, suitable for an outnumbered army forced to fight a defensive action. If they had had time to complete their dispositions the Lancastrians might have stood a chance. But a stag had broken from the copse and run along the hedge, and the stupid English archers had shouted out 'halloo' to each other. The bulk of the Valois army had been close enough to hear the cries, close enough to fall on the archers and on Talbot's men. The vanguard had been quickly overrun, half the soldiers killed, the other half fleeing in disarray.

The Bretons could not agree what had happened to Fastolf's men. Some of them swore that every one had been killed. Others scoffed at these claims. The men at arms had remounted and ridden away, they said, before the Valois could reach them.

Maybe Fastolf was dead. Maybe he was a prisoner – as was Talbot, the Bretons all agreed. Maybe he had escaped. Secret had to know for certain. He went for another piss. It was twilight. Instead of returning to Jules and his friends he zigzagged through the campfires and baggage wagons towards Richemont's tent.

'Halt.' It was not so dark: the guards had seen him. He moved towards them. He let his jaw drop and smiled the amiable, vacant smile of a simple-minded peasant.

'Looking for Jean from Fougères,' he mumbled.

'Not here, you oaf. This is the Count of Richemont's tent.'

'Oh. Didn't know he had guards.'

'For the prisoners, you fool.'

'Prisoners?'

'The English. Lord Talbot, Lord Scales. The English commanders. Big ransoms.'

'Thought we killed them.'

'Not the nobles, you fool. They mean money. We kill the poor bastards like you and me. Lord Talbot, he gets

256

picked up out of the dust, then they give him a cup of wine and a slice of beef for his supper.'

The other guard spat, silently, on the ground.

'The Count took them all, did he?'

'Damned if I know. They're all in there, that's what I know. The Count, the Bastard of Orleans, la Hire. And the English prisoners. Lord Talbot and Lord Scales. Probably talking about who pays what right now..'

Secret was silent for a minute.

'The Duke of Alençon, he's a good man,' he ventured.

'Your master, Alençon?'

He nodded.

'You keep out of his way tonight. He's roaring mad. He wanted the other Englishman, Fastolf, the one who took him at Verneuil. And damned if he didn't get away.'

'Thought we killed them all.'

'Not that one, curse it. We'll get him next time.'

'That we will,' murmured the other guard.

Both guards fell silent. Secret stood with them for a moment.

'Any wine come your way?' he muttered.

'What if it does, you oaf?'

'My friend Georges. Lost a toe. The wine might . . .'

'All the sodding same, you peasants. Wine, wine, wine. Be off with you.'

This last remark was underlined by a hefty prod from the guard's pike. Secret stumbled. And, muttering that he had meant no harm, he disappeared into the dark.

Fastolf was surely heading north. It would be suicide to ride in any other direction. Fastolf would have to make for Paris and report to Bedford. Secret retrieved his horse from the copse and set out after him.

He soon left the battle zone. Beyond it was just the usual sorry desolation of Lancastrian-occupied France: scrawny cattle, unmended fences, fields already knee-high with weeds. He was less than a day behind the soldiers, but their trail seemed very faint. Twice in the first day he lost it. At each inn, and at most of the larger farmhouses, he asked if the goddamns had ridden that way. Often he was greeted with blank stares. When he did receive an answer it was usually negative.

He did not let himself panic, but he was worried, very worried. He had understood that Fastolf had commanded the largest part of the Lancastrian army: four, even five thousand men. He had seen many corpses at Patay, true, but he had assumed that at the very least a thousand men would have escaped. By the second day he had come to think that the men he was pursuing were much fewer than that. They were a small mounted troop with no baggage, the sort of troop that moved fast and left little trace behind it.

He had no real confirmation that he was on the right road until he reached Etampes, nearly forty miles from Patay. The lieutenant commanding the garrison told him that Sir John Fastolf and his men had stayed there overnight. How many men? He asked. Fifty, sixty perhaps, he was told.

Fifty or sixty. A cold sick feeling came over him.

There would be other survivors, he told himself. But with Fastolf, only fifty or sixty mounted men.

De Waurin had a horse. And Hanson, perhaps: he had been fighting as a man at arms recently. Basset, possibly.

From Etampes they had ridden on towards Paris, to Corbeil. The next morning Secret continued his pursuit.

He reached Corbeil by early afternoon and made for the castle. Perhaps Fastolf would still be there. If not, he would be able to get food and directions.

His badge took him past the sentries and into the castle yard. He looked around for the stables and instead saw Jean de Waurin.

Relief rooted him to his saddle. He sat on his horse and watched in a daze as de Waurin approached him.

'Secret Poursuivant! I did not know that you were here.'

Secret found his voice. 'I am here only by minutes. Sir John is here too? And the others?'

258

'Hanson and Basset, yes. Not Matthew. We thought he might travel this way, but not yet.'

Hanson and Basset. They were all safe, Jean and Christophe and Peter. Weariness hit him as if he were walking into a black oven. He swayed.

'Here,' said de Waurin. 'Take my hand. I have the reins. Just get down.'

He almost fell off the saddle and into Jean's arms. Jean hugged him. He hugged Jean back.

'The horse is tired too,' Jean said in a prosaic voice. 'Let's get her to the stables.'

The distancing tone was what he needed; the action, too. He straightened himself, letting his feet slowly take the whole of his weight. Jean was still holding the mare's reins. He released Secret and began to lead her towards the stables.

Secret followed him. 'Sixty men, I heard, from Patay.'

De Waurin glanced round. He too is tired, Secret thought, seeing the heavy lines etched into the sardonic face. He fought and he has not rested since.

'You heard of the battle? A bad business, very bad. Fifty-four rode with Fastolf. Perhaps a hundred more have joined us since.'

A hundred and fifty-four. Other survivors might have ridden to other Lancastrian strongholds. Men escaping on foot might still be south of Etampes. But that was bad indeed. Very bad.

'I heard only from innkeepers, along the way.'

'Then you must hear the true story from me, and before you see Fastolf.'

They reached the stables. De Waurin handed the reins to the first groom he encountered, with the briefest of orders. He turned and took Secret's arm above the elbow. He walked as rapidly as Secret's failing feet would allow him, towards a long, low building that was set against the inside of the curtain wall.

A barracks. Inside it was bare of furnishings and crowded with men. De Waurin released Secret's arm and pushed his way through to the far end of the room.

Secret stood for a moment in the doorway, watching him.

The Burgundian stopped next to a small group of men who were squatting on the floor. Christophe? Yes, it was Christophe, and Peter too, and Nicolas.

They were getting to their feet already, but there was no need for them to come to him: he was already more than halfway to them.

'Secret!'

The tears were running down his cheeks, but he did not notice them. He and Peter and Christophe were all caught together in a hug of dense relief.

'Here, have my pallet,' Hanson said.

Secret sat and the rest joined him. He could see them clearly now; he looked critically. A bruise was darkening on Christophe's cheek and Peter's arm was bandaged below the elbow. Their faces wore the grey look of total exhaustion. But they were there, all of them.

'You've not eaten?' Basset asked. 'We'll not be able to find you much. But there's something, Christopher?'

'I'll go to see what I can turn up.'

By the time Hanson was back, with a cup of thin ale, a dry bread trencher and a hunk of hard cheese, he had begun to understand. This was a refuge almost as temporary for his friends as it was new to him. They had no posting here in Corbeil, no rations. They had scarcely enough room to lay their bedding. They were here only to recover, then they would move on, they did not yet know where.

He was almost too hungry to eat: he had had no food since the evening before. But he chewed with dull determination on the hard bread and listened as de Waurin began to tell his story.

It was not so very different from the story he already knew. He had guessed right: Fastolf had argued for a withdrawal, but Talbot had refused to listen. The two of them had taken their troops south with the aim of relieving Beaugency. They had heard of the fall of the town when they were still a day's journey from it. They had heard, too, that the Valois army was looking for them. So they had stopped to fight. The outcome was no news to him.

What he had not understood before was that Fastolf had withdrawn fast, very fast: as soon as Talbot's vanguard began to break up under the attack. He had not ridden to Talbot's recue. And this, from a man who had earlier resisted the decision to advance.

'Had he any option?'

Jean de Waurin shrugged. 'Very little. Most of his men were scrapings, dregs of the Orleans army and rejects from the Normandy garrisons: not the men to recreate Agincourt. Talbot's troops were overwhelmed in minutes, they couldn't hold on until we could get to their side. We saw Talbot himself taken prisoner, and Lord Scales. Then we all urged Fastolf to retreat.'

'But he could be criticised . . .'

'No doubt he will be. The rumour's already reached the garrison here: Talbot has accused him of cowardice. If Talbot had been killed it would have been different, but he is alive, and furious. The Valois will demand an immense ransom for him and for Scales, and . . .'

'And Fastolf meanwhile keeps his profits intact.'

'There are many men,' Basset murmured, 'who would not be sorry to see Fastolf in trouble.'

'There are those who would,' Hanson retorted. 'His own men, not least. We all depend on his good fortune: we shall all suffer if the worst comes to pass. Secret, I've already started to write an account of the battle; so has Jean. We'll give you copies before you leave.'

'Leave?'

'That you cannot doubt,' de Waurin said brusquely. 'Sir John will send you to Paris. He dare not go further north himself without new instructions. You must go to justify his actions before Bedford.'

Must go! His weary mind and body told him that he could not, must not go. He should stay here with Jean and the rest. He should sleep.

'It should not be so,' Christopher Hanson said gently. 'But it is.'

It was. He must go now, he knew, to Fastolf; then back, with luck, for a night at least with his friends; then on the road again, to Paris.

He went through the details of the battle again. He told the others what more he knew himself, from the Bretons. He thought of telling them about the Bretons, but decided against it. Now now. He could not survive without their friendship, he did not dare to test it now. Then he drained the last of the ale, nodded to them and went alone in search of Fastolf.

De Waurin had told him where to go. Fastolf had taken over a room at the head of a squat stone tower. He found the right tower, brushed down his tabard with a grimy hand, wiped his mouth with the back of it and set off up the stairs.

The knight's room was circular and bleak. The stone was thick and it was cool inside in spite of the afternoon heat. Fastolf was not alone: the captain of the Corbeil garrison was with him, and half a dozen other soldiers. But to Secret's surprise Fastolf threw all these men out before confronting him.

He watched Fastolf while the knight did this. He too was exhausted. He was looking old. There was a greenish tinge to his skin and his body seemed to have grown leaner. Secret thought: I think this man pragmatic, but defeat came just as hard to him as it did to the others. Then he thought: he is my master, and he is no longer the most successful soldier in France. Then he thought: but he is still my master, even in defeat.

Fastolf slammed the door shut behind the last retreating soldier and paced back to the centre of the room. 'You were a long time coming.'

Hanson and de Waurin had said the opposite: they had told him he had done well, that such a journey might have taken him three, four or even five days longer.

'I was misdirected, sir.'

'Did you hear of the battle?'

'Only a little, sir, along the way.'

'You must know more.'

Fastolf said this in a grouchy tone. Secret thought: he detests this encounter. He does not want to tell this tale, to me least of all. But he knows that he must. He can write letters for me to take to Paris, true, but Anjou and the Duke of Bedford may both wish to question me after they have read them. It would look strange, worse than strange, if I could not give the right answers.

So the dice were shaken again. It was the same story and yet not the same. At some points it meshed with de Waurin's story, with Jules' story, with his own experience; at other points it flagrantly contradicted them. Secret listened carefully, very carefully. He thought: I must tell this version to Bedford and Anjou. Not my story, nor Jean's or Christophe's, but Fastolf's own tale.

There was no mention in Fastolf's tale of the quarrel with Talbot. Secret thought that a mistake. The two men had quarrelled openly before a council of their men at arms: not only de Waurin, but a dozen others had heard them. He would have preferred the quarrel to be in the story: if Bedford did not hear it from him, surely he would hear of it elsewhere. But this was Fastolf's version.

Fastolf carefully numbered his troops. His voice reviled them for trash, but his words said nothing of this. There was no self-pity in Fastolf's version.

He gave a brief but accurate account of the action itself. It had been clear all along, he insisted, that Talbot could not be rescued. It seemed to Secret that this interpretation did not follow as naturally from his account as he seemed to imagine. Perhaps he himself could remedy that, he thought: add some additional details, change the timing a little.

For himself he did not blame Fastolf for withdrawing, and not only because there had been no blame in Jean's story, or in the faces of the others as they listened to it.

At least, he thought, that way something had been saved from the disaster. For Jean and the rest to be corpses or prisoners would have aided nobody but the Valois.

Fastolf came to the end of his account. Secret asked a few, a very few questions. He could sense that Fastolf's patience lay at its very edge: he did not want to tip it over. But in Fastolf's version some of the blame for the decision to withdraw lay on de Waurin, and on others of his own friends. He would not have told this to Bedford. He meant to ride to Bedford with different names, alternative arguments.

'You have it, then,' Fastolf said at last.

'I do, sir.'

'There will be letters too. Tell Bedford only what he asks you: it is all in the letters. You may tell the same to Anjou King of Arms if you wish, but nobody else in Paris is to hear this account. You understand?'

'I think that a mistake, sir. If men hear your side of the tale their sympathy for you will grow, and . . .'

'You are impertinent, Poursuivant. Go now.'

'In the morning, sir. It is late now, and I have been travelling . . .'

'The guards will find you a mount.'

At least he had eaten. At least his poor horse might rest. At least he had seen his friends and knew they were safe. He made for the stables.

The grooms found him a brown mare, even older than the horse that had brought him from Chartres, but well rested and sound. In the castle church the bells were ringing for compline. It was still light, would be light enough to ride for perhaps three hours longer. He rode for Paris.

On either side of Secret the countryside of France rolled out, flat as mangled washing, towards the horizon. Endless miles of neglected farmland, with here and there a cottage or a farmhouse. Above it, the sun slid down an endlessly blue sky. In front of him was an endless straight road. He saw nothing of this after a while. He tried not to think of his saddle sores. His other thoughts were no less painful. The Count of Richemont; the corpses at Patay, piled in the ditches; the barn outside Orleans, deserted now, or reclaimed perhaps by the farmer.

He stayed that night at a tiny roadside inn. There were no fellow travellers. He had no wish to discuss his mission, but he regretted this: it was safer to travel in company. He thought of waiting at the inn until he met other men bound for Paris, but finally he decided to ride on. All the roads in this area were plagued with gangs of brigands, discharged soldiers and starving peasants who had turned highwaymen, but poursuivants and heralds were allowed to pass by many such gangs. Such men did not know how to sell his letters. They knew only that men like him rarely carried much money: only a few saluts, generally, to pay their lodging on their journey. If he rode his mission would be over sooner, and he would be back sooner with Jean and Christophe and Peter.

He was on the road just after dawn.

The morning was uneventful. Just after midday he saw moving shadows under a clump of beeches not far from the roadside. He continued to ride. There was nothing to be gained by stopping. The fields on either side of the road were deserted, their corn grown tall, silk-smooth in the sunlight, unruffled by even the slightest wind. The last village he had passed was perhaps two miles back. There were no farms, no hamlets visible. This might be trouble, he thought. If it was he would have to face it alone.

He was drawing level with the trees. He dared not glance openly at them, but he looked from the corner of his eye. There were five or perhaps six men under the beeches, with a horse, a young black gelding, and two donkeys.

They were not farm labourers who had stopped work for lunch: these men were waiting. For him.

265

He kept his hands deliberately loose on the reins. He murmured quietly to the old brown mare. He thought of whistling a tune, but he reckoned that might provoke the men.

He had almost passed the trees when the men moved. Swiftly. The man on the horse galloped round to block his path; the others rushed out on foot to surround him from behind.

The mare was not up to a gallop, not after a day of hard travelling. Secret reined her in.

'Je suis Poursuivant', he said in a clear, carrying voice. 'Officier d'armes.' No need to say that he served an Englishman: such men would not recognise Fastolf's arms on his badge.

The brigand's gruff words escaped him, but the gesture that accompanied them was clear enough. He dismounted.

Two of the men took him by the arms, while the others made for the mare. His pack, with the letters, his tabard and a hunk of bread for his lunch, was strapped to the saddle. He tried to tell the men that there was nothing of value in it, that he was a poor man.

The blow to his head cut him off in mid-sentence.

He came to in a ditch. It was nearly nightfall. His head hurt, with a thick fuggy ache which focussed into a sharp pain somewhere at the back of his skull. He reached his hand to the pain and felt something damp and sticky. He brought his hand back before his eyes and stared at it, wondering. This dark mess was his blood.

He stood. His legs worked, bar a heavy cramp where he had been lying awkwardly in the ditch. It was lucky that it was midsummer: the ditch was dry. His arms worked too. There were bruises on his back, a graze down his side and on his cheek, but no other fresh injuries. He looked around. A flat landscape, deserted: cornfields, hedges, and just off the road, a clump of beeches. Now he remembered.

The horse. That was the important thing, the old

brown mare he had taken at Corbeil. He did not know its name, if it had one: he had not thought to ask the grooms. He whistled, hoping it might come. The whistle faded away into the empty landscape.

His pack: had they left it on the horse? No, they had been unfastening the straps, surely, before he . . . He looked in the ditch. It was shallow, overgrown with weeds. He walked along it in either direction for perhaps fifty yards. His feet hit nothing, bar a couple of boulders. It was growing too dark to see, but he did not need to see. Such brigands would not have hidden his pack. If they had discarded it they would have done so openly, thrown it empty on to his body in the ditch.

The stars were coming out. It was a clear night with a slim curve of new moon. The road was wide: he could follow it easily in the starlight. How far back had the village been? He could not remember. He began to walk.

A dog barked as he approached the village, but it must have been tied up, for it did not come up to him. There was a bare handful of cottages on either side of the Corbeil road. To his left was an inn. A light shone through the front window and there was a lantern above the archway that led to the stableyard.

He walked slowly, unsurely under the archway. There were candles lit in the stables. He could hear the grooms talking and as he watched a figure left the stables and made for a door in the corner of the yard. He waited in the black shadow of the arch, but nobody else followed. He moved swiftly across the yard and round the end of the stable.

He could smell the rich stench of a midden, just make out the low shape of a pigsty. The grooms' voices were muted now by the thick stone wall of the stable. He leaned against this wall. His breath was shallow and ragged. One of the grooms laughed; the murmur of the voices resumed.

Secret reached for the hem of his tabard and pulled it upwards, bunching the rough frieze around his belt. Underneath he wore a thin undershirt. He felt for the

267

hem of this. It was a deep hem, lumpy and uneven. He slipped his fingers between two of the coarse stitches and ripped.

In the still night, the noise sounded disconcertingly loud. He paused again but nothing happened. Then he dropped on his knees, feeling in the starlight for the coins that had tumbled on to the ground. Saluts that were the basic currency of Lancastrian France; a Louis d'or; a few English marks. He pocketed them, then made his way cautiously back into the yard. Light shone from round the door in the corner; he headed for this and pushed it open.

There was a maid coming along the corridor. She stopped dead at the sight of him and dropped the plate she was carrying. Before her scream hit the air, he had fallen on to the earthen floor in a dead faint.

It was another week before he was fit enough to think of moving. The mistress of the inn had found his money, but had mercifully not stolen it. Once he had paid his bill there was just enough left to hire a nag. He could get to Paris, he thought; but not from there back to Corbeil, unless Bedford agreed to see him without his letter from Fastolf and to loan him some money.

He was in no mood for further heroics. By then, he told himself, plenty of accounts of Fastolf's action would have reached Bedford. He waited until a party of travellers stopped at the inn and then joined them on the road back to Corbeil.

Sir John Fastolf reached out a calloused hand. He caught hold of the little enamelled badge that Secret Poursuivant wore on his left shoulder. He pulled, sharply, and the catch broke, leaving the badge in his hand. He cast a contemptuous glance at the device. Or and azure quarterly, with three cross crosslets argent on a bend gules. Then he threw the badge to the ground and stamped it, very deliberately, into the dust under his mailed boot.

'Your tabard,' he said in an icy voice.

'But sir, I must explain to you –'

'Your tabard.' The knight's voice rose dangerously.

'It was in my pack, sir. The bandits took it, with the letters and the rest of my things.'

'Go and check his pack, Hanson.'

'He had no pack when he arrived, sir.'

'Go and check!'

Hanson went. The men in the castle yard stood in silence until he returned. 'The grooms confirm it, sir. There was no pack on his mount.'

There was a stormy silence. Secret wondered, inconsequentially, if Fastolf was considering asking him for the price of the tabard.

'I always knew you,' Fastolf said coldly, 'for a damn French traitor. Now get out.'

He went.

He dared not stay in the castle, so he went back into the town of Corbeil to look for an inn. At the second one he tried he found a serving girl who giggled when he complimented her. She brought him wine and a meal of bread and cheese without asking for payment in advance. He sat in the parlour of the inn till long after dark.

His thoughts were confused. Fastolf's reaction had surprised him. Fastolf had never hidden his distrust, but he realised now that over the years he had come to take it for granted. The harsh words and secretive actions had angered him sometimes, but less and less so as time passed. On the whole he had thought of them as a kind of bizarre ritual. How strange it was that in some sense Fastolf should genuinely have thought him a spy. That was how he interpreted the little scene. Underneath Fastolf's frustration and justifiable annoyance, the very solidity of the knight's suspicion had come through clearly to him.

He thought: I must stay here, in Corbeil, until I have talked to Christophe. Christophe does not distrust me, I am sure of that. Nor does Peter Basset, nor Jean de Waurin. My friends will help me. Christophe or Peter will come and find me. Not tonight, perhaps, but when Fastolf's temper cools and they can get away unnoticed.

Jean? No, it will not be Jean. He would not be able to come. Fastolf distrusts him too in some measure: for no better reason, perhaps, than that he is a Burgundian. A Fastolf grown even more suspicious than before will watch Jean de Waurin like a hawk eyeing its prey. Perhaps he will even look for an opportunity to drive Jean too out of his service.

The inn grew empty, and still nobody had come. They would not come that night. The girl came across to tell him that she had to shut the parlour. He took her by the hand. She did not object as he led her into the yard. He had her against the wall, in a patch of deep shadow. She giggled at first. Then he grew rough and her fingernails dug into his shoulders, but she did not cry out, did not fight him. He felt better afterwards. The girl showed him where he could sleep, on a pile of straw at the back of the stable.

It was late on the second day that the huge figure of Christopher Hanson darkened the inn door. Secret rose up from his seat in the corner and came to the doorway. They clasped hands and stood there for a moment in silence.

Hanson paid Secret's bill at the inn and stood him supper, a very good supper such as they had not eaten for many months. They ate capons in a sauce of ceps, good white bread and yellow peaches. They drank a great deal of Touraine wine. Hanson was subdued, watchful, though there were no soldiers at the inn.

'He made us swear, Peter and I, that we would give you no commissions. Jean de Waurin he has already sent back to Bruges. This should get you as far as Welles.'

Hanson threw a small leather bag down on the table. Secret decided it would be politic to check. It contained five saluts and a couple of Burgundy riders. It would be enough to get to Calais, if he hired cheap mounts; and there he could probably beg a passage across the Channel from a shipman who had carried him before.

'You think I should go to Welles?' he asked.

'Had you another plan?'

'I had thought to try once more to reach Bedford . . .'

'You thought better last time, when you turned back. Bedford's guards would never let you see him without a badge or a letter from Fastolf.'

'Has Bedford acted?'

'We heard two days ago. Talbot sent his herald, after he was captured, with his version of what happened at Patay. He made it clear that he blamed Fastolf for the defeat; that he reckoned Fastolf could have saved his men if he had attacked right away.'

Secret considered. 'That is questionable, at the least.'

'It is more than questionable, but Bedford has accepted it now. He has publicly accused Fastolf of cowardice.'

'I could go, nevertheless . . .'

'If you insist.'

'Insist? Why, Christophe, would I be wrong?'

Hanson shrugged. 'Bedford will soon see sense, I suspect. He cannot afford to drive Fastolf back to England. With Talbot in captivity, Scales and Suffolk too, he has few other captains, and none as good as Fastolf. Even Fastolf does not believe Bedford will go through with this threat to strip him of his Garter.'

'His Garter!'

'Just so; it has gone that far already. And it will take time to bring things back.'

'But I could help, I could tell Bedford . . .'

Christopher Hanson quietly shook his head. 'There is much that you could tell Bedford, but Bedford will not listen to you, not yet. And Fastolf will give you no thanks for trying. You'll not win your badge back in that fashion.'

'And by going to Welles I shall?'

Hanson ignored the bitterness in his voice. 'Think it through,' he said.

Secret thought. He could see now what Christophe had in mind. Welles was a born tactician. It was to his advantage to see Fastolf in favour, and to have an intermediary with Fastolf whom he knew well, and could also use for his own business. It was true: Welles would do what he could.

He trusted Welles, within limits. He had done favours for Welles many times, and been paid in cash, but he had never been obliged to ask the grocer for this kind of help before. It was not that which made him hesitate, though: it was the thought that already he was pledged to too many masters, and that by taking this path he would commit himself to yet another man. He had served Welles before, but only when what was in Welles' interest had seemed to him also to be in Fastolf's interest.

This too was perhaps in Fastolf's interest, but Fastolf would not see it so. More: if he took such help from Welles then Welles might give him other orders which he did not think to be in Fastolf's interest, and he would be in no position to refuse to carry them out.

And what is that to me? he asked himself. It is not I who spat in Fastolf's face: Fastolf has spat in mine.

But he wanted to regain his place in Fastolf's service, and not only because Christopher Hanson seemed to assume that that was his intention. He had turned his back already on one life, one set of loyalties and obligations. He had been Laurence de Fougères, and then he had been Secret Poursuivant. And afterwards? He did not want to live under yet another name.

The more he thought, the more the uneasiness grew in him.

'You do not think,' he said slowly, 'that Welles will refuse to see me?'

'Welles?' Hanson gave a curt laugh. 'Oh, Welles will see you. He'll not like it when you explain, but he'll not turn you away. Most likely he'll find a way to turn it all to his advantage. I'd stake a Channel crossing on that. But Matthew's here now; if you wish I'll ask him to write you a letter for Welles. Or I could do so myself.'

'There is no need for that, I think.' Christophe is so certain, he thought. And what alternative is there?

Hanson drank some more wine. 'You had not thought,' he said cautiously, 'of going to the French? To Richemont, say? He is a Breton commander, is he not?'

Yes, he had thought of it, many times. And decided against it, out of love for this man who sat across the trestle.

'No, I had not thought of it.'

Hanson shrugged. 'No offence.'

'I have taken none. And you go?'

'Perhaps to Le Mans. Who knows what will happen in the wars now?'

'I doubt if the Dauphin has the will even now to drive the English back any further.'

'His commanders are quarrelling, from what we hear. And they too mislike this business of the girl.'

'They say she is a saint.'

'They also say,' Hanson replied, 'that she is a whore.'

10

FRANCE
Winter, 1429-30

Alice, Dowager Countess of Salisbury, fingered the keys of her keychain. Most of them were heavy: keys to the buttery, the larder, the money chest. Her fingers stopped at a lighter key, more fragile, one of the smallest on the chain. She inserted it into the lock of the little cedarwood box that sat on the inlaid table in front of her.

She unlocked the box and glanced over her shoulder at her audience. Eight women were watching her: Anne, Duchess of Bedford; her stepdaughter Alice Neville, the new Countess of Salisbury; her maidservant Lucette, and Anne and Alice's servants and ladies-in-waiting. She withdrew from the box a fat sheaf of papers and glanced down at it with a smile.

'*All* love letters?' Lady Anne asked.

'Oh no, not letters. I keep only poems in this box. Letters I generally throw away. Unless they contain offers – and then I send them to Father.'

'Very wise. And are they *all* from the Earl of Suffolk?'

Alice gave a light laugh. 'That would be telling you far too much!'

In fact they were not all from Suffolk. She had persuaded both her husbands to write her poems on occasion; there had been an elegant missive from the Duke of Burgundy (composed, she assumed, by one of his minstrels, to make amends after the clumsy pass he had so publicly rejected); there were half a dozen from other suitors, and one or two from Parisian gentlemen with less honourable intentions. Most of those were extremely bad, she thought privately; but she enjoyed weighing this pile and had never even considered throwing any of them away.

She picked up the paper which lay on the table. On it was inscribed Suffolk's latest effort, which she had already shown to Lady Anne and was now about to add to the collection in the box.

Lady Anne had admired it: politely, but with apparent sincerity. And why not? As love poems went it was more than adequate. The Earl of Suffolk had a sense of style. He wrote on good white paper, with good black ink, and if the hand was not his own (she thought it more than likely he had used a secretary for the fair copy) it was nevertheless elegant rather than clerkly. The words themselves were not embarrassing, and one really could ask no more than that from a love poem, unless it came from the hand of a genius.

The Duchess was not the first lady to whom she had read it out loud, and the words her eyes drifted over had a comforting familiarity to them:

> Ou que Ie suis, ou que ie vais,
> Quoy que ie dis, quoy que ie fais,
> Vous auez le coer que fuit mien.

> [*Wherever I am, wherever I go,*
> *Whatever I say, whatever I do,*
> *Yours is the heart which puts mine to flight.*]

Admirable sentiments. It would be possible to take pride in a husband who wrote poems like that. She picked up the page and held it briefly to her lips before adding it to the sheaf. Then, becoming suddenly businesslike, she arranged all the papers back in the box and turned the key once more in the lock.

'So,' said the Duchess, as she was doing this, 'have you forwarded a letter to your father?'

Alice considered whether she should answer this frankly. She decided she would. Lady Anne was kind and discreet, so the news would go no further until she was ready for it to do so.

'Ten days ago.'

'Naturally he will favour the suit.'

'I have reason to hope he will.'

In fact she had the best of reasons, though she would not have told the Duchess that the marriage had originally been Thomas Chaucer's idea. He had advised her to look to Suffolk as soon as he had received the news of Salisbury's death. In other circumstances Alice might have been offended by this pragmatic haste, but by the time she received her father's letter she had conceived the same idea for herself, so the advice had instead come as welcome reassurance to her. She liked to please her father. And she was anxious to remarry quickly: it did not suit her self-image to be a dowager.

Nor did she particularly mourn the Earl of Salisbury. She had admired him, but she had never managed to love him. His successor was more handsome, more cultured. She thought it might prove possible to love him.

She glanced at Lady Anne. So plain, Anne: she must be a saint, Alice thought, not to be jealous of all my admirers. She knew that the Bedford marriage was said to be happy, but looking for love, she cared little for mere happiness and saw this as no compensation.

'I do hope,' she said, 'that the Duke of Bedford will also favour the suit.'

'We should both be delighted,' Lady Anne said. 'Though you do realise that it is not to John that you must look for permission to remarry?'

'But as the Regent in France . . .'

'He controls only the affairs of the King's French subjects. You are an English subject of King Henry, so you must look for your permission to his Lord Protector.'

'To Gloucester!'

'Why, Gloucester is a great romantic, they say,' murmured Alice Neville.

'This is hardly a matter for romance, my dear,' the Duchess said briskly. 'It is a question of money and politics.'

Yes, politics. Gloucester versus Beaufort: the great quarrel at the heart of the English government. Political wrangling bored Alice, but as Thomas Chaucer's daughter she had been brought up to take such matters seriously. She had not considered this angle before, though, because it had never occurred to her before that her permission would have to come from Gloucester.

She herself was by birth and obligation connected to Beaufort's party. If Suffolk had been Gloucester's man she would have accepted that, but she knew that it was a bonus in her father's eyes that he should as yet be a member of neither party. When – if – they returned to England together, Chaucer and Beaufort would both expect him to ally himself to them. Gloucester would expect it too; and Gloucester would scarcely welcome it.

Alice mentally doubled her estimate of the indemnity she would have to pay to secure her freedom. Gloucester might even be reluctant to grant her permission at all. That was a dismaying thought. But she did not want Anne of Bedford to see her dismay, so while her mind was absorbed in making these calculations she managed to give a light smile and to point out that she barely knew the Protector.

'Perhaps you will come to know him,' Lady Anne said. 'He is a cultured man, Gloucester, a patron of the arts. His Duchess is not all one would wish, but I hear she is a charming lady nevertheless. I hope you and Suffolk will become their friends. Taking that with your father's connections with the Cardinal, you may soon be in a position to ease some of the tension at Westminster.'

Was that why Bedford favoured the marriage: because he hoped it would help to keep the peace at Westminster? What cheek! It was flattering to learn that the Regent thought her capable of quelling such a notorious storm, but that was not why she was choosing to remarry. This was her romance: her friends should have gloried in it with her, not tried to make use of both her and it, she thought with mild annoyance.

'My dear Duchess,' she said lightly, 'I shall be so absorbed in my handsome husband that I shall have little time to visit Greenwich.'

The Duchess laughed and rapidly changed the subject.

In the early months of 1430 the Earl of Suffolk called daily at the Hôtel d'Arras on the Rue Saint-André-des-Arts, the episcopal residence which had been Salisbury's home in Paris and was now granted to Alice. It was a proof of considerable devotion since he was living at the Hôtel de Clisson, well distant on the right bank. He was newly free from imprisonment and very much at liberty in Paris. He had not yet been released from his command, but he had now no troops of his own and had been assigned no new military post.

Alice soon realised that Suffolk's freedom suited Bedford: the Regent was genuinely happy to pave the way towards their marriage. It did occur to her that he was also happy at the thought that Suffolk would leave the army and return to England with her. She did not like to dwell on this, though. It seemed unfair that her handsome, eligible, high-ranking suitor should have the most appalling reputation as a military commander.

She was also aware that since paying his ransom the Earl of Suffolk was no longer a rich man. He had no influential relatives, no great expectations — except from her. However, this did not trouble her; she had always had enough money to buy all that she wanted, and it simply did not occur to her that Suffolk might be marrying her primarily to gain a share of it. He loved her: that seemed to her self-evident.

This pleasant conviction was reinforced by his poems, though they had to compensate for the fact that in person words of love seemed to come to him less easily than they did on paper. He had a fine mind but an awkward manner; with women especially he was clumsy and uncertain. If his verbal lovemaking was sometimes hesitant, though, at least he had better taste than to speak to her of the war.

There was a lull in the war that spring. The strange witch-woman Jeanne la Pucelle had proved less successful after the Dauphin's coronation and the previous autumn her army had been disbanded. The Duke of Burgundy's attention was centred on his forthcoming third marriage to Isabella of Portugal, and Bedford had done no more than attempt to consolidate his hold on Lancastrian territory.

The talk in Paris was all of Bedford's plan to bring King Henry to France and see him crowned in the city. Paris was not the traditional site for such ceremonies, but as the Dauphin had been crowned at Rheims it was necessary for the Lancastrians to choose a different location for their rival king. The coronation would be a grand affair, designed to display the solidarity of the House of Lancaster's supporters, and to counter the propaganda effect of the Dauphin's coronation.

Alice rather liked the idea of remaining in Paris until the King arrived. She would welcome him in person in her new guise as the Countess of Suffolk and enjoy the coronation feasts, the masques and the dances before moving on to conquer London society. She suggested this to Suffolk, so prettily that she had no real doubt that he would assent. He replied in carefully convoluted phrases. It took her some time to realise that he had in fact rejected her suggestion. He was prepared to remain in Paris only for as long as it took to arrange their wedding and his own discharge from Bedford's forces.

She found it disconcerting that he should thwart her. Salisbury had not always done as she wished, admittedly, and nor had his predecessor, Sir John Philip; but both of those men had drawn a clear distinction between women's matters such as new gowns, over which she would invariably get her own way, and men's matters such as their absence on military duties, over which she could exert no influence at all. Suffolk had somehow treated this request as those men had treated women's matters – and still refused her.

She told herself that she was simply unused to his manner. She could readily understand why this was important to him: it might affect his future career. He had told her that he was anxious to enter the King's service in England, and she could see that it was necessary to make it clear to all the world that he was not being rejected by Bedford, but was responding to Westminster's urgent call for his services.

Gloucester's reply came quickly. The marriage would be permitted – at a price. Thomas Chaucer advised Alice to pay it. She could afford the fee; he could not afford to antagonise Gloucester. She instructed her bankers, and sent her father word that she had obeyed him, along with two of Suffolk's latest poems.

She had been sending him copies of Suffolk's poems for years. Though Suffolk's love lyrics were conventional, his political poems were much less so, and sometimes she had wondered about their phrasing. What was the phrase that had struck her? 'Out spying this or that': that was it. She had thought twice about sending the poem that said that to her father, but Salisbury had read it and seemed quite unconcerned by it, and she had thought that it might appeal to him. Clearly it had. Now she admired her own foresight. How pleasant it was to know that the two most important men in her life were in perfect accord with each other.

Gilles Binchois, young, slight, thin-faced, bent his head to his lute and struck a gentle note. The lutanists in his little band echoed it with mild variations, and then proceeded to eliminate these. When they were all ready Gilles looked up and caught the nod from Suffolk which told him to proceed.

They would be love songs that night, all love songs: for the betrothal had taken place that afternoon, the papers had been signed, and this was a banquet to celebrate it. Alice had planned everything herself. It was a white and yellow banquet: a spring banquet, with the hall of the Hôtel d'Arras decorated in daffodils and the food spiced with saffron and lemon. The centrepiece was a subtlety made from meringue, with a lion and unicorn couchant (the emblems of the Chaucer and Burghersh families, Alice's ancestors) arrayed around an ape clog, Suffolk's rather prosaic badge.

The lutes began. And Gilles' strong tenor voice, alone, sang the first verse of Suffolk's rondeau:

> Lealement a tous Iours mais
> Depieca & plus qu'onque mais,
> Ie sui vostre, & vostre me tien,
> M'amour, ma Ioye, & mon seul bien,
> Mon coumfort, mon desyr, ma pais.

> *[In good faith for ever more,*
> *For a long time and more than ever,*
> *I am and have been yours, and consider*
> *myself yours,*
> *My love, my joy, and my only good,*
> *My comfort, my desire, my peace.]*

Alice watched Gilles for a few moments, then she turned to look at her betrothed. He was sitting between herself and Anne, Duchess of Bedford. He was silent, listening intently. She knew already that he loved music quite as much as she did herself. It was no accident that he employed Gilles, who wrote the prettiest tunes she had ever heard. He was a worthy patron for the minstrel. Though she would go one better, she said to herself: she would be Gilles' inspiration.

How handsome the Earl of Suffolk was. His tawny hair hung almost to his shoulders: that was so much more flattering than the crude basin-cut Salisbury had favoured. He had a long, loose-limbed body, a longish face with heavily hooded eyes and a sensitive mouth. One could not marry a man merely for the pleasure of looking at him, but it was pleasant, to be sure, to marry a man whose appearance gave one satisfaction.

Of course, there was more to admire in him than his mere appearance. She admired his learning; she admired his skill with a pen. She shared his taste in music, in fine food; she liked his choice of clothing. She admired his ideas and opinions. Such as . . .

Such as his interest in French politics, she finished, after much thought. It was difficult to think of any other subjects on which he had expressed his opinions to her.

But they were well attuned, she had no doubt about that. In the preceding weeks she had learned a great deal about him. She knew, for instance, that he was not a man given to gossip. He had shown no interest at all in the Duke of Burgundy's much-trumpeted wedding plans, and no more than was necessary in their own. A little more interest would have pleased her, but she had always rather despised chatterboxes, and Suffolk's reticence struck her as proper and manly.

He was a serious-minded man, but he was not fervently religious: that was good, she too was no lover of mournful monks and chilly chapels. He doubtless mourned the brothers who had been killed the year before, but he was not given to dramatic expressions of grief – or, indeed, to dramatic expressions of any kind. He seemed to her to have a very self-contained character. Reserved, that was the word that came to mind.

That would suit her well. She too had a cool temperament. She disliked people who seemed to invade her, who asked her impertinent questions about what she was thinking, who stood too close and threatened to mess up her gowns and crumple her headdresses.

He had never been less than attentive, she thought, but his love was founded on admiration rather than on passion. He did not grope at her, he was content with appraising looks. She reckoned there would be less to endure in private than there had been with Salisbury.

She had been gazing at him for a long time. Suffolk

could not have failed to be conscious of her inspection. He turned slowly to meet her gaze.

Alice had looked only rarely into his eyes. They were pale brown, long-lashed, deep-set. The intensity with which they looked into her own was all the more alarming for being unexpected. This was not the aloof stranger she had been describing to herself: this was a man who would soon have licence to know her intimately.

It was not only, she suddenly realised, a matter of her acquiring a new husband. This man would also be acquiring her as a new wife. She would become his property, his possession, to use as he would.

That was an unnerving thought. Fortunately Gilles' rondeau came to an end just then. She looked away from Suffolk, with feigned casualness, and applauded the minstrels.

Now that she had broken free of that disconcerting look, she did not find it difficult to dismiss her sudden apprehension. Of course she had always known that in theory a woman was completely subject to her husband's will, but all the same no wife did exactly as her husband wished; the clever ones generally did just as they wished themselves. She had done that herself throughout two marriages. If she had succeeded in manipulating the shrewd and forceful Earl of Salisbury, she should have no difficulty in doing the same with his one-time subordinate.

There would be intimacies, of course: that was as necessary as it was, to her, undesirable. But they could be endured, as she had endured them before. It would not happen often. Soon she would find ways to set him at an acceptable distance from her.

If only her father were there! If only he had been able to come to Paris for the wedding; but it had never been remotely conceivable that he would. He had come to Paris two years before, with Cardinal Beaufort, but since then the pains in his back had grown worse and the dangers of the journey greater. She had written once to beg him to come, but she had read from his reply both what he said and what he did not, and she had not written on those lines again.

Still, she would see him when she and Suffolk reached London. And then from London they would go to Ewelme. A faint smile stirred her mouth. Perhaps she would miss the coronation in Paris, but it would almost be worth that sacrifice to be back at Ewelme.

Her father's Oxfordshire manor had been the magic home of her childhood. She had spent many long summers there when her mother was alive. The world then had seemed a safe and welcoming place. War and death had been no more than words in sermons. Marriage had conjured up to her not the indignities of the bedroom, but a picture of a woman in a pretty gown of satin, standing by a handsome man and smiling as she received the congratulations of her friends.

She would be that woman, at Ewelme. The servants would bow before her and kiss her hand. There was something to be said, she thought, for being the richer partner in this alliance. Instead of being banished to her husband's estates she could expect him to live with her at Ewelme.

All that would happen soon. The wedding ceremony itself would be simple and would follow quite quickly on the betrothal. This was her own choice. Her wedding would come so shortly after the Duke of Burgundy's that it could not conceivably be the most splendid of the season, so instead it would be quiet and stylish. Like this party. Only the vulgar would prefer fountains flowing with Rhenish wine to a serenade by Gilles Binchois.

Then before the autumn was over they would leave Paris; they would spend the winter in Rouen; and the following spring they would be in England.

'My Lady,' said the Earl of Suffolk.

Alice turned back to him. She gave him a pretty smile, but this time she kept her eyes lowered.

Suffolk took her hand. He brought it slowly to his lips and let them just graze the back of it.

284

A little shiver ran through her: she had always hated even the most casual of touches. She tried to ignore it. The kiss was no more than a courtly gesture, she told herself. It was a compliment, an acknowledgement of her beauty. The Duchess was watching, and Alice Neville, and the rest of Paris society. She smiled again and leaned forward to whisper to her betrothed how much she admired Gilles' setting of his poem.

'Si belle, madame.'

As she spoke, Lucette set down the comb with which she had been arranging Alice's hair. She bent to pick up a little silver mirror with a frame of ebony and held this in front of Alice.

Alice craned forward and looked carefully at her reflection. Her honey-gold hair had been loosed and it fell down in flattering waves past her shoulders. Her almond-shaped green eyes (her best feature, she had always thought) had been accented with a touch of kohl, her skin whitened and her lips reddened. Lucette had done everything perfectly. Yes, she was beautiful. She had all the still elegance of a van Eyck Madonna.

'Merci, Lucette.' She put a hand to her hair and flattened a loose strand. Yes, she was nervous too. She was trying not to think about what would come next; while Lucette had been doing her work she had been reliving the beauties of the wedding ceremony, held that morning among the towering splendours of Notre Dame de Paris. But seeing her own face reminded her that her new husband would soon come and see it too. It will be over quickly, she told herself. And tomorrow you shall begin in earnest your new life as the Countess of Suffolk.

Lucette set down the mirror on a little carved table by the bed, picked up a silver snuffer and started to extinguish the candles. Alice watched her. Lucette knew just what to do. She had been with Alice for seven years: she had done all this before.

Lucette stopped when just two candles were left. It was a large room, and they barely lit the centre of it, but they would serve to welcome the Earl and to show off her handiwork. Then Suffolk would snuff out this final pair himself.

'C'est tout, madame?'

'Oui. Merci, Lucette.'

'Alors, je dis à monsieur le Comte.'

The door closed behind her. Alice sat alone, in her thick white silk nightgown, among the heavy green draperies of the carved and pillared bed. She shivered. Though it was still summer it was cool in the room: the Hôtel de Clisson was a thick stone building, almost a castle, and it had the chill of little use about it.

Several minutes elapsed. Then there was a double knock, short and confident, at the door.

'Come in,' she called.

The Earl of Suffolk came into the room. He was still dressed as he had been at supper, in a short houppelande of blue velvet, its sleeves and neck furred with marten. He crossed immediately to the bed and reached out to her with both arms. She could smell the wine on his breath. His face was flushed and his eyes were bright. He has been drinking, she thought, with an involuntary upsurge of disgust: all the time I was getting ready for him he has been drinking.

'My darling. At last.'

He pulled her to him, firmly, and a hot male mouth descended on hers. His hand ran down her body in a confidently possessive motion, briefly cupping one breast through the thick silk of her nightgown, then moving on to caress the curve of her hip. He pushed her back on to the pillows and his body covered hers, heavy and insistent.

Alice had a moment of sheer panic, then she pulled herself together. She closed her eyes and searched her mind for something to distract her. The wedding ceremony, that was it. The high soaring arches of Notre

Dame. The endless row of columns, the light flooding through the windows behind the altar.

Suffolk's weight eased and she felt him fumbling with the laces of her gown.

'Help me,' he muttered in a thickly slurred voice.

Help him? No, she couldn't, it was too much to ask, she would be sick, she . . .

'Damn these laces!' He pulled, hard, at the thick material. Her shoulders jerked under the strain, and then the silk gave and there was a harsh ripping sound.

Automatically Alice opened her eyes and glanced down to see what damage he had done. He was tearing at the gown now, dragging it off her to expose the pale expanse of skin beneath.

The candles! The last pair of candles were still lit! How could he! She must snuff them out, she . . .

'Oh my darling, you're so beautiful.'

He had mistaken her movement, he thought her eager to embrace him and he pulled her to him, greedily, the gown falling away behind her and his lips searching for hers.

Alice twisted her head sideways. 'Please! The candles . . .'

'Leave them. I want to see you, all of you.'

See her! This was worse than Salisbury, it was worse than anything! She struggled frantically, desperate now to get away from him, but he seemed not to notice her terror, or to take it for something else. A tiny core of reason within her mind told her that there were limits beyond which she must not fight him, and at length she subsided, aching and exhausted, and left him to take his pleasure as he chose.

On a bright autumn afternoon, on a day of blue sky and cold, clear air, the Duke of Bedford and his party rode through the drifts of red and gold leaves that carpeted the Bois de Vincennes. They had been hunting, with much success: the grooms who brought up the rear of the loose procession carried the carcases of three well-grown does and two heavily antlered bucks.

Ahead of the grooms, but perhaps thirty paces from the Regent and his Duchess, Louis of Luxembourg, Bedford's Chancellor, and the rest of his court, rode the Earl of Suffolk and his new Countess. It was precisely four weeks since the day of their wedding.

Alice's spirits were high. She always enjoyed the excitement of the chase, and it had been a particular pleasure to see her husband's first arrow strike the bigger of the bucks full in the flank, and to hear the Regent's loud congratulations. The crispness of the afternoon pleased her, the sound of the Duchess of Bedford's laughter, the subdued yapping of the hounds, the smooth, regular motion of the fine mare she rode; she liked the feel of her green gown, part of her trousseau and worn for the first time that day, and of the light tug of the wind at the folds of the thin veil that draped her headdress.

She did not notice how far Suffolk had drawn her from the rest of the group until he brought his mare closer alongside hers and reached to take hold of her reins. Their trot subsided into a walk and she turned to glance at him, wondering what it was that he wished to say. They spoke alone together very little. After that first terrible night he had understood that he did not please her. He had begged to know why, again and again, but she had been unable to tell him and finally he had ceased to ask. He seemed to have withdrawn into himself. He came to her at night – twice each week precisely, as if he thought this the minimum he was entitled to expect, and always stone sober – but he rarely sought her out in the daytime.

'There is something you should know before we leave Paris.'

'Is there, my Lord?'

'There is a child.'

This statement made no immediate sense to her. That did not concern her unduly: she frequently found Suffolk's comments elliptical. But she considered it and still had no clue to what he was telling her. 'Whose child, my Lord?'

'As yet she is only weeks old. She will not be fit to travel for some months. But she is strong, the nurses say, and it is likely that she will survive. Next summer I shall have her brought to England.'

Alice frowned. Whose child was he speaking of? He had not answered her. It surely could not be – holy Mary, was he trying to tell her that this child was his?

'I trust you have no objection,' he said in a cool, reasonable voice.

'I . . . er . . . I did not . . .'

'I have engaged wetnurses, naturally. The child's mother is to enter a convent, a Carmelite nunnery near Meung. You shall not see her and I shall have no further dealings with her. But it was agreed with her father that I should take the child.'

The bright afternoon faded, grew distant. The wind still ruffled her veil; the Duchess laughed again and Louis of Luxembourg joined in; but she was no part of it. She rode out of the day, and into a nightmare.

'I felt sure you would be reasonable,' Suffolk was saying in the same calm voice. 'It is not what either of us would have chosen, but it is a situation that must be accepted. Before long I hope we shall have children of our own. But I already have an obligation to this one, and I look to you to help me fulfil it.'

Children of our own? But did he not know? He knew, he must know, that she had been twice married before. And there had been no hint of a child, never the slightest reason to hope. She could not conceive, she was certain of it.

But this other woman had. This nameless woman had given her husband a child: a healthy child, who looked set to survive.

Her stomach seemed to have cramped into a hard ball of pain. There was a high buzzing in her ears. A woman, a woman she was not to know, in a Carmelite nunnery near Meung. And a child – who was to come to England.

'Has she been named?' Her voice was tight; it sounded strange to her.

'I have called her Jeanne. In England, naturally, her name will be Joan.'

Jeanne. But that is the witch's name! The witch has joined a new company of soldiers. Bedford was talking of it this afternoon. She is riding towards Soissons. We spoke of her today, and laughed, and cursed. Jeanne. Why has he called it Jeanne?

'Obviously we shall not have the child with us in London,' Suffolk went on. 'I doubt if Wingfield is in a fit state to be lived in: it is many years since I was there. So I intend her to be sent to Ewelme. I have written to your father. He accepts my reasoning and has given his permission.'

To Ewelme! Magic Ewelme, polluted by the presence of this little bastard! Her own father, agreeing that this witch-child should go to Ewelme! The cramp inside her seemed to explode into a fireball of horror and anger and pain.

She pulled on the mare's reins, brutally, bringing her up sharp, and stared wild-eyed at Suffolk. For a moment he did not notice her movement: he rode on for several paces. Then he reined in his own horse and turned to face her. They stared at each other for a long moment, a raw, naked stare. Then Suffolk set a spur to his mare's flank and rode back to her.

'I have upset you,' he said. He caught at her reins again. 'Please forgive me. That was not what I intended.'

He had upset her. He had done worse than that: he had ripped away her pretty façade and gazed on the writhing mass of terrors and uncertainties that lay beneath it. And nobody, nobody did that to Alice Chaucer!

The shock and anger solidified into a new mask. With a heroic effort, she slipped it into place. Once more she was Thomas Chaucer's daughter and heiress; once more she was the public Alice, the beautiful, sophisticated Countess of Suffolk.

'Not at all', she said in an odd, level voice that she scarcely recognised as her own. 'It was most considerate of my father to agree.'

11

ENGLAND
Summer, 1431

'Alice Chaucer', the Duchess of Norfolk repeated. 'Alice
– Chaucer.'

Will Calthorp had not been listening to her up till
then. He had been in a daze of boredom, as he frequently
was on the long afternoons when the Duchess summoned him and Bess to Mowbray Inn, but his attention was
drawn instantly by that name. He moved away from the
stretch of wall where he had been leaning and took two
paces towards the circle of Norwich ladies surrounding
the Duchess, stopping just on its perimeter.

'You call her Mistress Chaucer?' he asked teasingly. 'I
had thought the lady would prefer to be known as the
Countess of Suffolk.'

Lady Katharine glanced up at him. Their eyes connected momentarily, then she restored most of her attention to the ladies.

'Oh,' she said, 'she may be an expert at making good
marriages. Three of them, and not yet twenty-seven!
Lady Philip, Countess of Salisbury, the Countess of
Suffolk – she can call herself what she likes. But I can
assure you, underneath it all she is still plain Alice
Chaucer.'

The ladies murmured and giggled. Curse it, Will
thought, I reckoned for a moment that I was going to
discover something useful, but all I'll learn from this
conversation is the depth of Kitty's prejudice against
upstart Mistress Chaucer. He had already gauged that
fairly accurately. Nor was the prejudice only Kitty's:

Bess had already grumbled to him at length about the prospect of Suffolk's low-born bride presiding over a generation of Norwich social gatherings, and he knew she was the least catty of the Duchess's coterie.

'They say,' Jane Yelverton offered, 'that she is rich.'

'Oh, undoubtedly she is,' the Duchess agreed. 'When Thomas Chaucer goes to his Maker she will have Ewelme, and a dozen other estates almost as fine. Salisbury left her more than my brother Richard would have liked. He'd reckoned on the bulk of the estates coming down to his Alice and it turned out a good half of them are settled for life on her stepmother. And I suppose Sir John Philip provided his halfpence too.' She grimaced. 'What a pity she is said to be beautiful. If she were plain, everybody would reckon Suffolk had married her for her money.'

'Is she beautiful?' Bess asked innocently.

'So they say. Not that I have seen the lady, as far as I can recall. She has been in France ever since she and Salisbury were married. Richard told me she was rather tall.'

'Perhaps the Earl of Suffolk is tall too,' Bess suggested.

'Perhaps he is.' Lady Katharine paused and then gave a wicked smile. 'Never fear, ladies, we all have one unassailable advantage over Mistress Chaucer.'

Will could not for the life of him think what it could be. Even their greatest admirers would not have called Kitty, Bess, Jane Yelverton or any of the other ladies present outstandingly clever or particularly accomplished, as Alice Chaucer was reputed to be. A few of them were pretty; but so, evidently, was the Countess of Suffolk; several of them were passably rich, but she was considerably richer than any of them bar Kitty herself.

Evidently Bess could not follow the Duchess's reasoning either. 'Which is . . .' she asked tentatively.

'Why, my dear, she is barren. Two husbands dead and buried, and not a child to her name.' The Duchess smiled triumphantly. 'Which is why I have no doubt that the Earl of Suffolk has made a great mistake in marrying her.'

'How sad it must be for Lady Suffolk, if she really cannot have children,' Bess mused.

She and Will were riding back to Calthorp Inn. It was only a few streets away from Mowbray Inn, but they needed to wear their finest clothes when calling on the Duchess, so instead of walking they rode the short distance to avoid muddying their hems and their best leather shoes on the filthy Norwich streets.

'You do now know that she cannot,' Will responded. His mind was only half on the conversation. 'Plenty of women bear children when they are older than she, even after years of barren marriage.'

'But imagine! Imagine how miserable we should be if we did not have Amy; if we did not know there was another child on the way, and hope for still more. I should be wretched if I prayed every month for a child and every month my prayers were not granted.'

'I dare say you should.'

'And you would too. Would you not, Will?'

'Of course,' he said vaguely, glancing at her. Something in her expression caught at him, though, and he turned back to her for a second, longer look. She was gazing at him earnestly, almost worriedly, as if his response to the trivial question mattered intensely to her.

Bess loved Amy; she looked forward to the birth of the next baby. She cared about children and everything to do with them; but more than that, she cared that Will should share her absorption in their little family. When the midwife had first set Amy in his arms, six months before, he had made a facetious remark about skinned rabbits. Bess's expression had told him what a disastrous mistake he had made, and since then he had never repeated it.

He did his best to live up to her expectations. He listened when she talked to him, he cuddled Amy when the nursemaid brought her to them. But even then, he

294

sensed, it was barely enough to reassure her. He wanted to reassure her: he did not like to see her worried. A baby was a baby, and a man could not be expected to feel passionately over a tiny scrap of a thing, but a wife was a wife, and his was the centre of his life.

'That reminds me, Bess,' he said gently. 'I think you should ride no more until after this next child's born. I know old Blackie's steady, but they say the motion's bad for women in your condition. Now that you're certain of it you should stay at home, or travel by litter when you must go out.'

Bess gave a little frown. 'How right you are, Will,' she murmured. 'It was thoughtless of me. I should do nothing that might endanger the baby.'

They rode in silence, and only moments later they turned into the courtyard of Calthorp Inn, a low-lying house, secluded, set down by the river not far from Norwich Cathedral. It was small compared with Burnham Thorpe Hall, but well proportioned and pleasant to look upon, with low gable ends outlined by old and worn carved timbers.

Bess reined in Blackie and Will dismounted rapidly, throwing his reins to the groom and striding across to help her down. There was just a fleeting moment when he felt her weight, before her foot touched the cobbles of the courtyard. How light she is, he thought. How fragile. They walked arm in arm across the courtyard, towards the hall door.

'Then I suppose I should visit the Duchess no more.'

'I doubt if that would be wise; I'd not wish to have you offend her. In any case she should be leaving Norwich within a week at most. It must be more than a month since she was last at Framlingham.'

'Then perhaps it will not hurt the baby so much if I . . .'

He cut into her sentence, momentarily exasperated. 'You shall take the litter, as I said. I'll ask Jack to prepare it for you.'

'Oh. Of course, Will.'

She did not look at him as she said this. He knew the tiny criticism had hurt her. He had not meant to hurt her. But it did annoy him that he should need to spell out to her what she should do, even that he should have ended up offering to speak to Jack himself. That should have been her own task. It was not that she deliberately shirked tasks like that, she was not lazy, but she was so retiring by nature, so disorganised, that he found himself doing more and more of the little jobs that should have been hers. And why not? he reminded himself hastily. She was not well, the baby was making her sick every morning, and it was not such a great hardship to him to make life easier for her.

As she tried to do for him. It crossed his mind that Bess might have no real inclination to visit Kitty even once more before the Duchess left Norwich. No; that was not it. As far as he could judge the two women were on genuinely good terms: even close terms, as far as the difference in their stations and temperaments permitted. He had never had the remotest reason to suspect that Bess knew about his private relationship with Kitty. He was certain he would have been aware of it if she had known.

'Will you miss the Duchess when she leaves?' he asked more cheerfully as he pushed open the hall door and saw her through.

'I shall be a little sorry to see her go. But I think it will be more of a loss to you, Will, than it will be to me. You always enjoy seeing Lady Katharine so much.'

There were few things Bess could say that could drive Will to silence; but that was one of them.

By the time he had seen Bess to the low settle by the fire, he had recovered his wits.

'In fact,' he said, coming to sit by her side, 'there is a reason why I should particularly like you to visit Mowbray Inn at least one more time. It would be to my advantage to learn as much as I can about the Earl and Countess of Suffolk.'

Bess looked at him and frowned. 'About the Countess

296

of Suffolk? But we talked of her this morning, Will. You heard what the Duchess had to say, surely?'

'I did. But another day she may have a little more to relate, when I am not there to listen.'

'And if she does, you would like me to remember it and tell it to you.'

'Just so.'

'Then I shall do so, naturally.' She gave him a little smile. It was a trusting smile, with a touch of the conspiratorial in it: it was as near as Bess ever came to looking coquettish. 'I had not thought it would interest you to hear of Paris gowns and headdresses.'

He framed a vicious retort, but he managed to bite it back before it reached his lips. 'You would be surprised, my dear,' he said lightly, 'to know just how many things do interest me.'

When the cook came for her orders shortly afterwards Will left Bess and retreated to his counting house. This was a rather grand name for a small shed off the back courtyard. It was a shabby place, poorly fitted out, its only furniture a high desk he had bought second-hand from Judge Paston and a battered oak chest, and its heating non-existent. But he liked the counting house, liked the smell of ink and newly pressed paper, the neat row of wooden boxes on the shelf. When he opened the shutters he could look over his garden and that pleased him too, for he and Bess had worked long and hard to plan their garden, and now the gardeners were working on turning those plans into reality. As yet the nearer half was little more than an outline of sanded paths and empty beds of earth, and beyond there was a tangle of bushes leading down to the water meadow and the river beyond, but he had the picture clear in his mind of how it would look one day, when the low hedges were grown, the frames for the roses were set and the roses climbing round them, and the meadow was sweet with long grasses and bright flowers.

He paused for a moment, gazing down to the river and

thinking – with considerably less pleasure – of Bess's words earlier. Then he set to business. He unlocked the chest, drew out his sheets of accounts and spread them carefully over the top of the high desk. His eyes scanned the columns of figures rapidly until they came to the ones he was looking for.

His interminable hanging-around that morning had been repaid in the end: Kitty had given him another commission. He picked up his quill and began to ink in the details. The fee would pay the wages of the second shepherd he had hired at Burnham and there might be just enough money left in the coffers to hire Mistress Dawson for Bess's lying-in that winter.

He would manage; but as always, it would be tight. Very tight. Life seemed to be a perpetual round of hard decisions. Pay the bailiff's wages or mend the barn roof? Have the carthorses shod, or buy a good thick cloak for Bess? There was never enough money for everything.

So many problems – and he could share none of them with Bess. He had to protect her, had to keep her away from the realities of unpaid bills, cruel bailiffs and tenants evicted when they could not pay the rent. Bess needed to live in a tranquil world. She should think only of him, and the babies.

But Paris gowns?

If she had understood him, he knew, it would have been because she was as cynical and knowing as Kitty and the rest. He did not want that: he loved her for her innocence, for her simple, honest heart. It was a lonely business, though, acting always as his wife's protector. He could not help longing sometimes for a partner in whom he could confide.

He had Kitty, admittedly. Kitty was hard-headed where Bess was not, just as Kitty was an uninhibited bedmate while Bess was shy and loving. He could not always have been so gentle with Bess, he sometimes thought to himself, if he had not been able to work off his aggression in Kitty's bed. But Kitty was not his wife: she was his patron.

Kitty had a fascinating mind and he found it a perpetual challenge to duel with her. She was undeniably sharp-witted, but it seemed to Will that she rarely thought deeply. Her mind was a butterfly's: skittering, lightweight, its interest in the odd connections she made between ideas and people, and not in her depth of deliberation.

He had heard men criticise her for being casual about financial matters, but he knew that they were mistaken. She ran Norfolk's massive estates more than adequately. But she took a personal interest only in small pockets of the dealings: her real knack was for picking good stewards and bailiffs, men she could trust to work well with the minimum of supervision.

Men like him. He enjoyed working for her. She was not over-generous, but neither was she mean. She never interfered unnecessarily or countermanded his decisions; she always took a friendly interest in his personal affairs. He reckoned he was doing better with her than he could have hoped to do with any other patron.

But . . . but. His first and deepest loyalty was not to Kitty, but to Bess. He had no intention of letting his fondness for Kitty override his judgement, and his judgement told him that while at present he was managing, and indeed doing steadily better for himself, this state of affairs could not continue for ever. Kitty was only in charge of the Norfolk estates because the Duke was bedridden. Any possibility of the Duke's recovering had faded long since: the question was how long he would survive.

Five years, Will reckoned, was the outside. And when the Duke died, every instinct told him that things would happen precisely as Judge Paston had hinted to him long before. Kitty's son John Mowbray, Earl of Nottingham, would inherit both title and estates and he would promptly move to oust his mother from her comfortable position.

Will did not like John Mowbray; John Mowbray did not like him. John Mowbray would perhaps continue to employ him as steward at least for a while, but he would show him no favour because he knew him to be his mother's man.

Will had no intention of waiting until all this took place, and he was confronted with a steadily worsening situation. He had been making contingency plans. He had been setting a part of his mind to this problem for some time, but so far he had been able to see only one solution. He would have to leave Kitty's service when – or even before – the Duke died. He could only do so if he first found a new patron. There was only one suitable candidate: the Earl of Suffolk.

So he badly needed, not gossip about Paris gowns and headdresses, but hard information about the Earl of Suffolk. Only when he knew more about the man and his associates would he be able to gauge how best to play off Norfolk and Suffolk against each other.

He could tell Kitty many things, but he would never have told her this. Kitty's interest in his affairs was sincere, but it was based entirely upon the assumption that he was her creature. Perhaps she looked ahead to the Duke's death (though he suspected that she did not), but he could not believe that she looked still further and saw this possibility – no, probability – on the horizon. He would not have raised the subject; he would not have reassured her falsely; though he knew she despised her son, he would not have taken as read her approval of his plans.

Mind, she had been thoroughly catty about the Countess of Suffolk. There is jealousy there, he thought. Does she see a time when the Suffolks will reign supreme in Norfolk and she herself will be reduced to the unappetising role of dowager?

No; he did not believe her bitchy remarks had been fuelled by future jealousy: present greed lay behind them. Kitty needed to be the permanent hub of her circle; she needed to be reassured that she was not only the highest-ranking lady in Norfolk and Suffolk, but also the most intelligent, the most beautiful, the wittiest:

everything, in fact, with the possible exception of the most devout. She comfortably outranked the Countess of Suffolk, but she had no inclination to submit to being set in the shadows even temporarily by the other woman's arrival.

Would she be? He did not know the Countess, but he doubted it. Kitty may not be accomplished, he thought, but she is a good conversationalist: Alice Chaucer will have to work hard to outshine her there. Her intimates are most of them musical philistines: they will care nothing for the Countess's skill with the lute. The squires are tied to her and in any case they enjoy her attentions quite as much as she enjoys theirs. And the fawning flatterers like Yelverton will not swap a duchess for a countess: they'll most likely look down on Alice Chaucer quite as thoroughly as she does herself.

Outside Kitty's little circle there was another Norwich; there were many other Norwiches. There was, for example, the Norwich that consisted of serious-minded people who cared about politics and religion – as Kitty did not. It seemed to Will that the Earl and Countess of Suffolk might totally dominate that Norwich, that East Anglia even, and it would discommode the Duchess of Norfolk not one jot.

He liked that thought. That East Anglia had suffered the most from the Duke of Norfolk's incapacity. That East Anglia still felt acutely the absence of men such as Sir John Fastolf, away for so many years in France. That East Anglia might be revitalised by the Earl of Suffolk's return to England.

He himself might become Suffolk's retainer; he himself might become a part of that East Anglia. That thought rather unnerved him. He had always looked on with mixed emotions when men had tried to tell Kitty about the running battles among the Norwich Aldermen, the extortion at the tolls, the unchecked bribery at the Sessions, and had been repulsed by her sharply phrased indifference. Suffolk, he thought, might react differently. Suffolk might expect his retainers to attempt to correct these wrongs, as Kitty did not.

He knew Kitty would have laughed at any suggestion that Will Calthorp would find the prospect of intervening in such trivial intrigues anything but boring. But the Will Calthorp who had once thought the wool business boring (and who now spent much of his time running his own and the Norfolk estates, without any visible sign of boredom) was not sure that he shared Kitty's opinion. He was not only Katharine Neville's lover, after all; he was also Bess Calthorp's husband.

And for Bess's sake he must learn more about Suffolk; but not through Bess herself. Who else could he ask? He had asked Judge Paston, but Paston had had nothing to tell. He could think of nobody who might tell him more.

He finished his sums; he sanded his ink, gathered his papers together and shut them all in the chest. Then, thoughtfully, he left his counting house and went to see what Cook had prepared for dinner.

As usual, the shutters of Fastolf Place were firmly shut. Behind the closed gate that led on to Southwark High Street one-legged Harry swept the yard, grumbling, with an old birch broom. In the stables three grooms drank ale and three horses water. In the kitchens Meg stirred cinnamon and ginger into a large iron pot half full of wine. And in the hall, under the row of high windows, behind the trestle, sat three men.

In the centre was John Welles, the peacock feather in his hat nodding, the rings on his fingers winking as they caught the narrow shafts of sunlight. On either side of him were two men in the long grey gowns of lawyers: to his left William Yelverton, and to his right Judge William Paston. And on the trestle, the results of their afternoon work made three neat piles. One pile of letters to Southwark men; one pile to Norfolk men; one pile for Secret Poursuivant to carry to France.

They were ready now for the other business of the

afternoon: to discuss the news of the Earl of Suffolk's imminent return to England.

'I cannot see,' Yelverton said, 'that it will make any difference in Norfolk.'

Then you are a fool, William Paston thought silently to himself. As usual you speak too quickly, and with too little forethought. Yelverton was wrong, he had no doubt about that; but he was not yet sure where the truth lay. Perhaps a good argument would tell him.

'Not so,' he said bluntly. 'It will make a very great difference, I've no doubt of that. As for the precise effect it will have – that depends very much, I think, on what Suffolk makes of Tuddenham and Wetherby.' He turned, as he brought out these names, to look at John Welles.

Welles did not reply. William's look turned into a glare, but Welles seemed not to notice. Instead Yelverton persisted, 'If Suffolk behaves anything like the Duke of Norfolk he'll never even speak to Wetherby.'

Welles suddenly bestirred himself. 'But,' he said, in a satisfied voice, 'he will certainly speak to Tuddenham.'

'He'll do more than speak, I sincerely hope. I'd hope to see him back me in quashing Tuddenham's gang of extortioners.'

Welles smiled. 'I doubt he'll do that, William. He'll use Tuddenham himself as a land agent.'

There was a little silence after this remark, broken only by the persistent wintry snuffle of Welles' heavy breathing.

William said slowly, 'Are you telling us you have firm information that Suffolk is planning to use Tuddenham?'

'He's not committed yet, but I understand it's probable. And it's a natural choice, surely?'

'Natural? If he cares nothing for the morals and methods of his agents; if he reckons to need a land agent of that calibre. The latter is certainly unlikely. He'll spend most of his time at Wingfield and Cossey; a good bailiff will prove more than adequate. Bailiffs have run his estates up till now.'

'And done it appallingly,' Yelverton said. 'Half the cottages are falling down and the only rents collected regularly are those Lady Morley enjoys. I see your point there, John: Tuddenham would transform those estates.'

'I heard much the same,' Welles said. 'In any case, William, your premise is doubtful. Why should Suffolk wish to live in East Anglia? You think in terms of political influence, but we have no reason to think that Suffolk cares in the slightest for the Norfolk Knights of the Shire. He has no acquaintances in the county, barring his sister, and Lady Morley is a bore by all accounts. His new Countess is heiress to Ewelme, which is in much better repair than Wingfield. My guess is that she and Suffolk will live mainly in Oxfordshire and London.'

Your guess! Damn your guesses, William thought. Especially when they are so bloody convincing. You have no right to know so much about Norfolk affairs: it must be more than ten years since you last set foot in Norwich.

He knew why Welles knew so much. The unscrupulous bastard got his information from the likes of Thomas Wetherby. He despised that tactic, and yet he envied it. He himself could not afford to deal with villains. John Welles could, and did. So Wetherby had told him what Suffolk planned . . .

No, it wouldn't wash. Suffolk was not in Norwich yet: Wetherby could not have met him yet. Wetherby might have told Welles of Tuddenham's hopes, or Tuddenham himself might have told him that he had written to the Earl, but they must all have learned of Suffolk's own plans from a different source. From France. Which meant: from that accursed little poursuivant, Secret.

An uncomfortable memory surfaced in William's mind: of the day almost a year before when he had received a sealed letter from Sir John Fastolf, written in Christopher Hanson's big rounded hand, and with a postscript added by Hanson himself: 'I, Christopher Hanson, ask this thing of you, sir.'

The thing: to aid the poursuivant after his dismissal from Fastolf's service. To tide him over with commissions, to intercede with Fastolf and ask the knight to take him back. Naturally he had torn up the postscript and thought no more of it – until he had heard that Secret was indeed back in Fastolf's service. Then he had begun to wonder which other of Fastolf's associates might also have received such notes from Christopher Hanson.

John Welles had, no doubt. And Welles' subsequent actions could be deduced from the facts that the grocer's information on affairs in France, always good, had become even better thereafter, and that Secret was regularly seen to be going about his private business in Southwark and London.

Secret had sources in Paris and Rouen, where the rest of them did not. If this information had come through Secret, there was all too good a chance that it was correct.

He said slowly, 'If you are right, it will be a disaster.'

'It'll be a kick in the backside for Suffolk's tenants,' Yelverton said cheerfully. 'But for the rest, I stick to my case. Suffolk's return will make no difference to the rest of the county.'

'Use your brain, man. Think, think what such an arrangement would mean. Think of the power Tuddenham would gain in Norfolk; think of the court connections Suffolk would bring him. Think of Tuddenham's brutality, of the complaints you've heard from the manor courts. Imagine him employing his ruffians not only on the Duchy of Lancaster estates, but on the de la Pole lands as well.'

'But even then . . .'

'What's that? Half the county, if not more. Tuddenham's methods are reckoned exceptional now, but then they would seem like the rule. Think of Suffolk and his men presiding at the courts: there would be even less redress for ruined men. Think of what that alliance would do for Wetherby and his crooked Aldermen, for the Aslake gang and the Nowell gang.'

He was ordering his thoughts as he spoke, his case gathering momentum by the moment. But he did not forget himself: he said these things because he wished both Welles and Yelverton to hear them.

His attention was focussed on Yelverton, but he glanced often enough at Welles to see the fury staining his face. He judged his moment carefully, moving his gaze to Welles before an explosion came, and continuing, with the brisk determination that a lifetime's experience of riding out interruptions actual and potential had given him, 'You can't deny it, John: they're a pair of villains, Tuddenham and Wetherby. They each back up every one of the other's vicious schemes. I know you sup with Wetherby, I know you hear his gossip and sell his goods, but even so, that is the plain truth.'

'You are biased, William,' Welles said vehemently.

'Not so. I merely read the evidence, and decide upon it. I had no quarrel with Wetherby until I learned of his misbehaviour. His stance over the church cases I approve of, and I have told him so. But there is plenty to dislike in his choice of associates. Read my papers again, John. Read the depositions I have in my chest.'

'So you have more? You have evidence enough to convict him now?'

There was a sly note in Welles' voice, which angered William intensely.

'Convict him?' He spat out the words. 'Damn it, it's not evidence that convicts such a man. It's the weight of the opposition against him. Small men will not bear witness in open court when they've seen knives drawn and cudgels raised against them, had their barns fired and their sheep poisoned. I tell you again, John, there is no other way. You, and men like you – like Suffolk too – must read my papers. You must unhorse Wetherby. Then, when he's down, it'll be the time to set the lawyers on him.'

Welles had been leaning forward, his hands on the trestle, listening carefully. Now he sat back stolidly and leaned against the wall. 'So you do not have more.'

'I have enough. I can show you lists of names, dates, places; I can show you papers. They would be proof to any reasonable man of forgery and evasion at the tolls. I can show you evidence that he and Tuddenham have met many times with Aslake's men, and with the Nowell gang down at Ipswich. Between them they know every damned ruffian in either county. You'll not persuade me that they meet such men so as to urge them to save their souls.'

'I'll not try, William.' Welles shook his head. He fished a disreputable scrap of cloth from his pocket and wiped his nose on it. 'But this is small beer. Every county has its ruffians. There are robbers everywhere. I've never known a customs man who's failed to take his cut of the tolls.'

'Not to this extent.'

'To this, and greater. To my mind Wetherby and Tuddenham are no worse than dozens, hundreds even of others. Norfolk must have some men in control. Today it is men such as those who fill the void. Surely it will be no wonder if the Earl of Suffolk chooses to patronise them?'

'In control! Thomas Wetherby applies no firm ruling hand: he's a Lord of Misrule if ever there was one. I live in Norfolk, John: and I would see it for a disaster if Suffolk set himself behind the lot of them. Tuddenham already has too much power in the county; Wetherby and his cronies are the same in Norwich. They are pushing now to have Heydon appointed Recorder.'

'So I heard,' Yelverton said.

'And you know the consequences, William. Heydon in that post will do just as they choose. A nod of the head, and Wetherby and Tuddenham will name the sheriffs. The Mayor, too. Not once only, but year upon year.'

He had to convince them: to convince Welles above all, for Yelverton already accepted his case against Wetherby and Tuddenham, even if he was being blind-eyed on this question of Suffolk. His arguments seemed to him unassailable; the evidence was clear. If this were a law court he would surely have won.

But he was not winning. He was entrenching them both in their opposition. Through all the force of his persistence he sensed this; he saw the looks of collusion, of amusement almost, that told him he had pushed them too hard.

It caused him annoyance, but no surprise, when John Welles rose to his feet while he was still speaking. Welles pushed past Yelverton, lumbered to the door to the kitchens and called down the corridor to Meg.

William Yelverton said earnestly, 'You are too pessimistic, William. We know nothing against Suffolk. Even if he does appoint Tuddenham, why shouldn't we expect him to keep the man decently in line? True, whether he lives at Wingfield or not he can hardly avoid serving on local law commissions, but that's all to the good: he should add more than a little weight to them. Wetherby's verdict on the church cases has failed to stand up, but Suffolk would have the clout to enforce an unpopular decision. I'm damned if I can see the Duke of Norfolk ever making the effort.'

'But could he enforce decisions against his own men? That's none so easily done. And if he is not the man we hope him to be, disaster will be a mild word for what follows.'

'Catastrophe?' Welles asked in a cheerful voice, returning to the trestle with Meg close behind him. 'An uprising? A revolution?'

'At the worst it could come to that, if these wrongs persist unchecked.'

'Why, William, I never knew you before for such a doom merchant. Take some wine and wipe that chill from your soul.'

'I'll drink, John, but I'll not be persuaded to agree with you.'

'Then we shall agree to disagree.'

Meg doled out the mulled wine from her pitcher into three cups. They drank.

Welles is no fool, William thought to himself, but on this I cannot budge him. I might even think myself biased, had I not looked over every scrap of evidence and seen for myself that I am not. He had an urge to persist, but he knew that the time for argument was past. If he were to pursue it further it would have to be on another day.

'It's an even more interesting question,' Welles said ruminatively, 'what Suffolk will do on the King's Council.'

William drank some more; then, as Yelverton was not speaking, he found a reply. 'Interesting? But John, it's all but certain. He'll favour Beaufort. I know Thomas Chaucer: he plays incessantly on his Beaufort connections. He's a stubborn old bird and he'll make damn sure his daughter's husband supports the Cardinal.'

'Will he?'

'Suffolk's no churchman,' Yelverton said. 'Nor his Countess either, it seems. Jane's last letter was full of Lady Morley's gossip about the Countess: her beauty, her wit, her French gowns, her poets and her musicians. But not a word that I can recall about her priests and chaplains.'

Trivial stuff, William thought contemptuously. He glanced at Welles and caught for once a hint of agreement in the grocer's expression.

'Women see these things differently to men,' he retorted. 'Agnes' letter was the same. She had a strange fancy it was a love match: passion flowering in Paris. Personally I'd have thought Suffolk could weigh Alice Chaucer's estates just as carefully as Salisbury did. Mind, it would be interesting to hear how much they paid Gloucester to get the dispensation for her to remarry.'

'Arguably they paid him nothing,' Welles said.

Both the Williams turned to stare at him. It was Yelverton who said, in a wondering voice, 'Are you suggesting, John, that Suffolk will turn out a Gloucester man?'

'Is that so strange a thought? He's a bad soldier and a fair poet. I've heard both descriptions applied to the Duke of Gloucester too.'

What an interesting idea: a very interesting idea. William played with it, in silence, as he drank the rest of his cup of wine. He filled the cup again and thought some more. He did not believe it – quite – but it was a pleasant possibility: he wished he could believe it.

The wine was beginning to sit warmly inside him. The light was fading outside: it was not dim now in the hall, but positively dark. Meg reappeared with a taper and went round the walls, lighting half a dozen fat tallow candles. In their warm light the hall of Fastolf Place looked far less squalid; cosy, almost. The sharp edge of William's annoyance blunted into something resembling satisfaction.

He might curse John Welles, he thought, but there was no denying that he could be useful. Nobody else could annoy him quite as thoroughly as this old moneybags, not even young Yelverton; but when it came to it, he trusted Welles' information, and his judgement too. There were times when he would have preferred a different route to Fastolf, but he could have done far worse. They worked well together, the two of them – the three of them.

And since he would be leaving for the Inner Temple before the dusk turned to darkness, and he had no intention of leaving on other than friendly terms, he could afford to say lightly, 'Now if Suffolk were to establish himself as a Gloucester man, then there might be an opportunity . . .'

'For you,' Yelverton finished for him.

William raised his cup to them both. 'Not that I have anything against Beaufort, bar a wish that he and Gloucester would stop squabbling and get on with the job of running the country.'

'Not that you have anything against the Earl of Suffolk either.'

He inclined his head in acknowledgement of this and

smiled. 'I have nothing against any of those men,' he said quietly. 'But I have much, John, to hold against Wetherby and Tuddenham.'

Could it possibly be true that Suffolk would favour Gloucester? Did Welles really know enough to tell? These questions filled his head as he and Harry rode in silence back over London Bridge.

He certainly did not know enough himself. He had been angling for weeks for information about Suffolk and had learned little more than that a hundred other Norfolk men were busily engaged on the same mission: all doubtless hoping, as he was, for work from the Earl, or for him to support their policies, or for a favourable judgement from him in their lawsuit. All of them pretended to tell each other all that they knew: most hoarded every scrap of information, he suspected, in the hope of winning an inch of advantage over the rest.

Mind, he thought, even when you know a man as I know Welles or Yelverton, it is no easy thing to tell what choice he will make in such a situation. But knowledge helped. Even women's information helped. In fact it helped a good deal, for women chattered less cautiously than men.

What exactly had Agnes said about the Countess of Suffolk? He had read her letter two days earlier; only the outline of it had stayed in his mind. Maybe it would be wise to read it again.

By the time he and Harry turned down Thames Street he was certain of this; impatient, even, to have the letter in his hands. As soon as he arrived at the Inner Temple he left Harry with the horses and hurried to his quarters. He indulged himself by lighting two candles instead of his usual one, took the sheets out of the little box he used for papers when he travelled and unfolded them once more.

A new dress for Lady Morley's reception? Extravagance! But no, no; if Jane Yelverton was indeed to be in satin, then Agnes must be in satin too. Another sugar loaf: yes, he must tell Harry to buy that before he returned. Here was the piece. The Duchess of Norfolk had told Jane Yelverton . . . the Duchess of Norfolk had told Bess Calthorp – need she phrase it like that, curse her? It was no fault of his that he and Agnes were so rarely invited to Mowbray Inn – that she heard the Countess of Suffolk to be . . .

It was women's gossip, but Agnes had conveyed it skilfully. The Countess of Suffolk was said to attend mass no more than she was obliged to; to sing French songs to the lute; to favour wide headdresses over narrow chaplets. She had virtually no acquaintance in Norfolk: Lady Scales had met her once, Lady Fastolf not at all. So there would be no favourites whose causes she would push, no enemies she would seek to punish. Every phrase set her down as a frivolous lady of fashion. He was willing to bet she would exert no influence over her new husband, even if he were truly as besotted as the gossips seemed to think.

And of the Earl himself? Of the Earl, the ladies with whom Agnes had chatted had said nothing.

None of the information in the letter was of any real assistance to him. Still, he thought to himself, that was no fault of Agnes'. She had done a thorough job. She was clever, Agnes, and observant. And her tongue was as sharp as a clerk's best quill; but perhaps in the presence of the Countess of Suffolk she would manage to curb it, and win favour.

She had done all he asked of her, and much that he had not: she understood him well on matters such as this. He was fortunate in Agnes, but he desperately needed other sources too.

Not Tuddenham, though. John Welles had called him biased, he thought, but it was not bias that set him against Tuddenham. It was right judgement. He would not have let the desire for advantage blind him to the realities of right and wrong, and by every standard of his Sir Thomas Tuddenham was a man to be despised. Even in his private life he was a reprehensible knave: he had abandoned his wife, rumour said, and was now talking of divorcing her. Wetherby and Heydon were no better. Whatever these men knew of Suffolk, he would not speak to them.

Mind, they did not know much. The more he considered, the more he was sure of this. Welles' real information came from Secret.

He too saw Secret regularly. The poursuivant delivered letters and accepted replies; he recited tales of sieges in Normandy and political wrangles in Paris. But any private information the poursuivant possessed was reserved for men such as Welles.

And he knew why. He did not trust the poursuivant, and Secret knew that. He did not like Secret, and it was no revelation to him that Secret did not like him.

Was that bias? Perhaps it was; although, he thought, John Welles, so loud in defending Tuddenham and Wetherby, had never complained about his attitude to Secret. In any case this suspicion of his was shared by other men; not least, by Fastolf himself.

Not Secret either, then. He would have to wait until Suffolk himself arrived in England.

And in the morning, he would call at a draper's and buy the satin for Agnes' new dress. And ribbons, scarlet ribbons, to trim it – and ribbons for little Lizzy, too. Barely two years old, and talking already so clearly that he could understand every word she said! Bright as a brass button, Lizzy was. Brighter than Agnes, he would swear; brighter than either of the boys.

If only the boys were even five years older, and capable of keeping their own eyes and ears open about Norwich; he might have had two fine spies to work for him then. But they would grow: into sense, and if he himself had even moderate good fortune, into the Earl of Suffolk's favour.

12

ENGLAND

When the great Italian banking families set up shop in
London in the time of Edward the Third, hoping to make
massive profits from the King's borrowings to finance his
campaigns in France, they established themselves in a
wide cobbled street that became known as Lombard
Street. When they left, bankrupted and disillusioned by
the King's failure to sustain his conquests or repay his
debts, their houses, balconied, carved and turreted in
the style of the south, were taken over by English
merchants who were canny or foolish enough to believe
that they would prove more successful.

William de la Pole, merchant and shipowner of Hull,
was as audacious as any, and more successful than
most. He bought the house of the Bardis and turned it
into a banking empire of his own. His son Michael lived
at Bardi Place when he rose to be Chancellor to a later
king, and Earl of Suffolk. After his exile the house stood
empty; and it remained empty for almost fifty years.

The de la Pole bailiffs repaired the roof occasionally,
and relatives of the absent Earls (three of them, in
succession) sometimes stayed at Bardi Place. It took a
flurry of activity in the early spring of 1431, however, to
make the house look remotely habitable; and there was
still work to be done by the time the current Earl of
Suffolk and his new Countess arrived in Lombard Street
on a fine March morning.

Suffolk told the masons, the carpenters, the plasterers
and the glaziers that they might leave off work for the

day; the servants who had accompanied them that they might retire to the Cardinal's Hat until he called for them. He waited outside with his Countess until Bardi Place was empty. Then he carried Alice over the threshold and into the hall of the house that was to be their home together.

It was a large room, surprisingly light, with two big windows looking out on to Lombard Street. The walls were covered in frescoes, thinly overlaid by the dust the workmen had created. The woodwork was carved and painted in faded shades of pink and white; the ceiling was plastered; the floor was paved in pinkish-grey marble.

Alice's eyes opened wide. 'My Lord!' she breathed.

Suffolk smiled at her wonderment.

'I thought the same, when I came here yesterday. I had almost forgotten what the house was like. Even as a child I stayed here only briefly, two or three times.'

'So beautiful.' Alice gave a little sigh of pleasure. She released his hand and started to move around the room. She ran her hands over the carving around the doors; she traced the outline of the dolphins that supported the mantle; she wiped some of the dust from the frescoes and frowned with concentration as she made out the details of the scenes of Florence and the Tuscan countryside.

He stood by the doorway, watching her every move. She seemed totally absorbed in her exploration, genuinely excited by her discoveries. There was an extra lightness in her step, a liveliness to her movements. He had always thought her beautiful, but she had never seemed lovelier to him than then, in his house.

She belongs here, he thought to himself. It is the right home for her; she is the right mistress for this house. Her style and its, strong and unusual both of them, complement each other well. She is the one person who could transform Bardi Place from a curiosity into a wonder.

She was paying him no attention, but he did not care, so long as she was captivated by his house. He watched her move over to the far door, which led to the back offices and the yard. She peeped down the corridor and then turned and faced him for the first time since the beginning of her exploration. 'But my Lord, surely we cannot live here!'

Cannot? He did not understand her. Her tone, light, almost teasing, made no more sense than her words. This was a reality, not a dream: the carpenters and glaziers had been solid proof of that. But perhaps, he told himself, she was misjudging the practicalities.

'In a few days it should be possible. You see the dust, I know, and the peeling paint: you smell the damp of disuse. But those are surface things. The Bardis built solidly. The house may be old, but it is still sound. I saw the schedule of works yesterday: there is less to be done than you might think.'

Alice did not reply. Her eyes were still fixed on him. So beautiful, Alice's almond-shaped eyes; so expressive. But at that moment they held no message that he could read.

'Lombard Street,' she said eventually, in a cool, neutral voice.

Lombard Street. So that was it. Two weeks in Westminster, staying with her father, had served to teach Alice where fashionable people lived in London. They did not live in Lombard Street. Suffolk knew that perfectly well; but he had not expected her to mention it.

'I know it is not in the best part of town.' He hesitated. He had not thought he would need to plead for Bardi Place: he had believed the house would speak for itself. But the magic was gone now: Alice had destroyed it. 'It is hardly a palace by the river. But it will suit us very well, will it not, for now?'

She appeared to consider this. Her eyes fell. It had been a mistake to plead, he thought momentarily: he should have dictated to her. Then she lifted her face again and gave him a flirtatious smile.

'My Lord,' she said, 'it will suit us wonderfully.'

He had the impression for a moment that she was

316

putting on a façade for him. He pushed the thought aside. Her first enthusiasm for Bardi Place had surely been genuine. Her turning against it could have been no more than a momentary impulse: she was thinking the better of it already.

'Come and see the rest,' he said.

'Now?'

'Yes, now!' There was a tentative quality in her voice that told him she was willing to be persuaded in the house's favour; so now he would persuade her. He crossed the room in a couple of long strides, took her arm and led, almost pulled, her towards the door.

There was a wide staircase that led from the hall up to two smaller chambers above; and another small staircase that led from there to three still smaller rooms; and a ladder that led from there to a long, low attic. They looked at it all. Alice was lively again now; she was treating it all as a wonderful game. She held his hand. They peeped together round doors and into cupboards, edged cautiously on to the little balconies, leaned from the attic dormer and looked out over the roofs of London.

He saved until last the room at the back of the house on the first floor. The builders had not yet touched this room. It was darker than most of the rooms in Bardi Place, with painted oak panelling and heavy shutters over the windows. An old bed frame, bare of draperies, sat in the midst of an expanse of dusty floorboards. But in spite of the dust, the air of neglect, this room had charm. This was the room he remembered best from his childhood. He had thought from the first that he wanted it to be Alice's room.

He stopped by the door and let her loose his hand again and walk in alone. She took a few short steps, then paused and looked around her. She said nothing, but this pleased him: he wanted a genuine reaction from her, one that would come after she had taken time to absorb the atmosphere.

How self-contained she is, he thought suddenly.

Behind the gay façade she is a very private person. He wanted the room to break down her guard and show him something of what Alice was like when she was alone.

She still did not look at him and he could no longer resist the temptation to speak. 'I intend this for your room: your withdrawing room.'

She glanced his way, but only quickly. She turned from him and he saw a little frown mar her clear profile. She went to one wall and tapped the panelling. She paced out the length of the room, very deliberately. The frown faded and a look of concentration followed it. Finally she turned to him again. 'I can see how it could be done. The Duchess of Bedford had a room in Paris I always admired, with a low bed, and stools, and pots of marjoram and thyme on a shelf by the window. Perhaps the light here is not so good for sewing . . .'

She spun round, turning her back on him, and made her way to the window. Her hand reached for the catch of the shutters.

'Not now.' His movement was so rapid that he reached her side before her hand had closed on the catch. He put out his own hand and closed it around her wrist.

They stood there, frozen, for a moment. He could feel her rapid pulse under his fingers. Slowly, deliberately, he drew her round to face him. His arms slipped around her back, holding her tight against him.

'There is no mattress on the bed,' Alice whispered.

'We can manage without. Please. For me.'

He lowered his head and tried to look into her eyes. He was so close to them that he could see every speck in the green irises, but she did not seem to be looking back at him. There was something opaque about her eyes: Alice had withdrawn behind them to a place which he could not reach.

Even here; even in this room. It had always been like this once they were alone; but here, he had thought, he might manage to break the spell. Instead he had once more pressed her too far, once more destroyed the fragile accord he had worked so hard to build up.

Perhaps he should not have touched her; but he had to touch her. She was his: his woman, his wife. He had to possess her. He had to find a way of breaking through her shell, so that instead of embracing an empty husk of a body, forever out of touch with the Alice who cowered somewhere within, he made love to a woman who responded with eagerness and joy.

For this there was never any eagerness. This she did not even feign. She hated it, he knew. He knew that; and yet he found it inexplicable. He was not an ugly man, not dirty or deformed. Other women had responded to him. Every time, when he drew away from her afterwards, sickened by the knowledge that she had found his every touch repulsive, he told himself that next time, surely, it would be different.

There was something appalling in the half-formed thought that it would never be so. He sensed that in time he might come to face up to that. His ardour might weaken. He might find it possible to play the abstemious husband, trouble her only sufficiently to give her a chance of conceiving, and take a mistress for his pleasure. But for now that was too much to ask of him. He had to have her. He would not be cruel: he would plead, not demand. But if she could not welcome him, she must at least accept him.

Through his arm, he could feel the tenseness in her back. Her hands on his shoulders had no more life than a doll's hands: they neither clutched at him nor pushed him away. The only movement was in her lower lip: he could see it trembling slightly. He fought the temptation to quell the quivering with his own mouth. His eyes were fixed on her lips: he was waiting, as he tried always to wait, for the signs of her acquiescence.

It seemed to him that he waited for a very long time. Then Alice's body seemed to grow heavier, its weight against his arm more real. Her lashes fluttered. Her lips parted into a languid smile. 'The floor is very dusty.'

'Then take off your gown.' His hand brushed across

the folds of the blue satin gown and came to rest on the laces that fastened the front.

'No; no, I shall do it.' In a swift movement, almost panicky, she pushed his hand from her and drew a pace away. She gave him another nervous smile, as if to soften the blow of her instinctive rejection. She turned her back on him. And slowly, her movements self-consciously awkward, she began to unlace her gown.

London seemed to Suffolk to be strangely provincial after Paris. It was the richer of the two cities: unlike Paris it had not been ravaged by nearly a century of war. It had as large a population as Paris, it had more trade. But in Paris the buildings, the people, the music and the paintings had all spoken to him of high civilisation; and here everything seemed crude and basic in comparison.

He believed Alice saw this too. He did not mention these thoughts of his to her, though. It was because of their marriage that she had left Paris and come to London: he did not want confirmation that she too regretted the exchange. And it pleased him to think that on this subject they had a deep and silent accord: that they were both at heart Lancastrian French.

The court at Westminster dismayed him. It was dominated by Warwick, the King's tutor, a formidable old soldier but no courtier; Gloucester rarely troubled to go there at all. The Pleasance he found to be an improvement, but Gloucester's reputation as a man of learning seemed much exaggerated. Gloucester read, true, but only in Latin and in English translations: he had barely any French and no Italian. He wrote scarcely at all. There seemed to be no good poets in England, no good musicians. Everything was second-rate.

At least he had managed to persuade Gilles to come to London: at Bardi Place, if nowhere else, the music would be superb. But that one green shoot was not enough to enliven this cultural desert. He needed more.

He knew already what he needed; who he needed. He needed to meet the Duke of Orleans.

It was not enough merely to read copies of the Duke's old poems. That was a thin satisfaction for him, and none at all for Orleans. That cultured Frenchman, that fine poet, had been shut up for years in a desolate castle in the wilds of Lincolnshire. If he himself found life at Bardi Place to be barren and frustrating, how much more must the Duke of Orleans be suffering? Perhaps it was necessary to keep him a prisoner; but if so, surely, he could be a prisoner at Wingfield or at Ewelme, or even at Bardi Place itself. There he himself would be able to talk with Orleans, to read poetry with him, to write with him. That would be a source of delight to them both.

Even to speak in French, he felt, would be a relief. In London few men spoke the language well, and even those few looked askance when he used it to them.

With Alice he did speak French – but rarely. Thomas Chaucer invariably grumbled when he switched to that language; Alice generally made a token attempt to respond to him, then reverted to English to please her father. Alice did a great deal to please her father. That had surprised Suffolk. He had thought that he and Alice were both returning to London as strangers. Not so, he now discovered. Alice had resumed her place in a small but close family; only he was alone.

He told Alice nothing about Orleans. It seemed to him that in spite of her years with Salisbury, she had no appreciation of the nature of a soldier's life. He did not think she would understand if he tried to explain to her what it felt like to be a prisoner. Orleans' poems she would appreciate, true; but he did not feel ready to show them to her.

He thought more often, strangely, of telling Alice's father. Thomas Chaucer would perhaps have comprehended the fascination that Orleans held for him; but he would not, Suffolk suspected, approve of it. So he did not tell Chaucer, knowing that it would not be wise to fuel Chaucer's disapproval of him.

He had uncovered only slowly the full extent of that

disapproval. At first he had not even suspected its existence. His few dealings with Chaucer prior to his marriage had always been amicable. He had known that Alice sent her father copies of his poems and had assumed that the other man admired them; he had known that Salisbury's good opinion of him had been relayed to Salisbury's father-in-law. It had been clear from the start that Chaucer had welcomed the marriage. Since his return to England, though, their relations had deteriorated.

He knew now that it had been a mistake to arrange to send the baby Jeanne to Ewelme; a mistake, indeed, ever to mention her to Chaucer. He had thought Chaucer would sympathise, as one man of the world with another, caught in an awkward predicament. His confidences on the subject had been deliberately planned; he had thought it a good tactic to set himself in Chaucer's debt. But Chaucer's attitude to this little debt fell short of the chivalrous; instead of camaraderie he showed something verging on contempt.

Chaucer did read his poems and comment on them; but in a cool, critical way that reminded him that though they were competent, they were far from being works of genius. Chaucer made references – slighting references – to his military career, when he would have preferred to bury that subject completely. And though Chaucer had endowed Alice with some additional estates as part of her new marriage settlement, he had made it clear that he intended to continue to control them himself, rather than allow Suffolk to do so.

Chaucer did not even treat him with the deference he considered to be his due. The older man was invariably polite, but he showed every inclination to act as Suffolk's superior, not as the inferior he actually was. He had evidently expected to introduce Suffolk to London society as his own protegé, though Suffolk soon scotched this misconception. Chaucer was also free with his advice on political issues, and free with his annoyance when Suffolk declined to take it.

Had Chaucer's opinion of him really undergone a drastic revision in just a few weeks? Suffolk could not see why it should have done. Chaucer had known of his faults and failings earlier: most of them much earlier, well before the marriage had taken place. There had been no new disasters, no new causes for disapproval. But though from a distance the two of them sustained something resembling a friendship, at close quarters they persistently grated on each other. It was uncomfortable, too, the way in which they competed for Alice's attention.

The move from Westminster to Bardi Place improved things a little; but not enough. Suffolk soon came to fear that unless he was careful, he and Chaucer would come to a serious falling-out. He knew what issue would cause this. They would argue over Cardinal Beaufort.

He was sure it had pleased Chaucer as well as it had suited his own plans when he had accepted a place on the King's Council. But he had realised almost immediately afterwards that Chaucer had welcomed this move solely because he had expected him automatically to strengthen the ranks of Cardinal Beaufort's supporters. Suffolk had no intention of allowing himself to be tagged as a Beaufort man. The Cardinal was not in England then and Suffolk had had no chance to discover yet whether he was likely to favour a negotiated peace in France.

And even if Beaufort did support his own policies, he thought to himself, it was not certain that he would ever be in a position to guide them towards fruition. The Cardinal was wrapped up in his attempts to gather an army for a crusade against the Hussites, his interest in English politics seeming clearly subordinate to his interest in Papal affairs. It was Gloucester who wielded power in the Council. If he were to take a stance as Beaufort's man he would be setting himself in opposition to Gloucester. He was not prepared to do this, merely to oblige Thomas Chaucer.

It was not easy to ignore Chaucer's advice when Alice became visibly upset each time the two of them argued. It was not easy to ignore Chaucer's advice when he was dependent upon Chaucer's money to refurbish Bardi Place and Wingfield Castle. It was even less easy to ignore Chaucer's advice when it ceased to be advice and started to take the form of orders: politely worded orders, but orders nonetheless.

He could not afford to defy Chaucer; he was damned if he would obey him. The only alternative, he decided, was to escape. He would leave London for a while. He would go to East Anglia.

By early summer Suffolk's plans were complete. He had engaged an agent, a man who would first introduce him to Norfolk society and subsequently remain in the county to oversee his affairs while he was more profitably occupied elsewhere. He had finalised his itinerary.

It was necessary to go to Wingfield, but briefly, since the castle was by all accounts a disastrously uncomfortable place. Then he and Alice would spend a few days in Bury. Finally there would be a long stay, several weeks, perhaps a month or more, in Norwich. He possessed a substantial deerpark just outside Norwich, at Cossey. He envisaged himself and Alice staying there for much of the time, going hunting and hawking together.

He told Alice of these plans one morning in May. It was a bright, warm morning, and larks were singing, swallows dipping and swooping even among the chimney pots of Lombard Street. His enthusiasm for this East Anglian trip was by no means wholehearted, but it was easy to imagine Norfolk on such a day as a place of blue skies and yellow cornfields and white sheep, a place where no man could fail to be happy.

Unfortunately these were not the images he evoked in Alice's head. She heard him out in stony silence.

'I had not realised, my Lord, that you wished to be away from London,' she said when he was done.

'That is not what I said. We have both been well occupied in London, but we cannot stay here forever.'

Alice greeted this statement with a dubious look. It occurred to him then that whatever the shortcomings of London, she had in fact enjoyed their time there. She had thrown herself energetically into making over Bardi Place, ordering hangings, buying benches and tables and beds and dishes, setting the kitchens to rights and engaging armies of servants. Her misgivings about living in Lombard Street had not been mentioned again.

He steeled himself for a plea that they remain in London for a few weeks longer; but instead Alice attacked in an unexpected direction.

'Then we shall go to Ewelme.'

Shall we? he thought. It was the first time she had mentioned her father's estate since he had spoken of sending Jeanne there. He knew now what a blundering fool he had been; he understood now that she herself could not conceive. That realisation had pained him: he had expected, even needed, his marriage to bring him an heir and had cursed his blindness in failing to consider Alice's history more carefully. He believed he appreciated how much her inability must hurt her and how bitterly she resented the very existence of Jeanne. He had done what he could to try to win her forgiveness, but he had thought himself unforgiven.

To go to Ewelme before the child arrived might act as a poultice to this hidden wound. Alice's suggestion might even be a sign that she had forgiven him, would help to prepare for the child's arrival – no, he should not expect that of her, he told himself hastily. But whatever he might or might not read into her suggestion, it was evident that she wanted to go to Ewelme.

'I wish we could do so,' he said gently. 'But alas, I have business to attend to in Norfolk.'

'In Norfolk it will be *cold*.'

It was a facetious complaint and it annoyed him. It annoyed him that she should complain at all, that his gentleness, his attempts to sympathise, were being met

– as Alice so often met them – by a cold unwillingness to consider his point of view. He tried to keep his annoyance to himself. It is not that she wishes to anger me, he told himself; not that she is determined to thwart me. It is simply that she does not wish to go to East Anglia.

One possible reason for her attitude entered his head. He went to sit beside her on the little padded bench that she had placed beneath the windows of the hall.

'You are offended, I fear, because I did not consult you sooner. I apologise. There have been so many men for me to see, so many decisions I have had to take. I did not wish to bore you by discussing them all with you.'

He was careful not to touch her, not to sit too close. He did not try to hold her eyes. But he sensed from her rigidity that she had no intention of submitting yet, and it was no surprise to him when she said, in a pettish voice, 'I cannot understand why it is necessary for you to go to Norwich.'

'Then let me try to explain to you.' His hand reached instinctively for hers; with an effort, he moved it back to rest in his lap. 'In France, when I thought of England, I thought almost invariably of London. The things that happened in England, the things of importance to me, all occurred in London and Westminster. The King's Council meets here; they form their policies here. To men like the Cardinal, the Duke of Gloucester, your father too, life centres around London and Westminster. Though I have estates in East Anglia and in the North of England I rarely gave a thought to those places. They were no more to me than names in letters written by my agents. Norwich, Ipswich, Bury: I know no one, and am known by no one, in any of those towns. But – wait, and I shall show you something.'

He rose, leaving her in the hall, and hurriedly made his way upstairs to the small room he had given over to his herald, his secretaries and agents. There was a table under the window, awash in papers. He grabbed a handful of them and dashed back to the hall. He dropped the papers, in an extravagant shower, on Alice's lap.

Alice stared blindly at them. He knelt down at her feet and picked a paper at random from her lapful.

'Look at this.' He unfolded the sheet and glanced briefly down the lines of writing and at the signature. 'This one is from my agent at Dedham. He wishes to know whether I desire him to have the great fishpond drained this year, and whether he should engage John Makepiece to do the work.' He dropped it back in Alice's lap and took up another. 'This is from a man named Hubert Smallbone. He tells me that one of my keepers at Cossey is turning a blind eye to poachers and begs to be given the man's job once I dismiss him.' And another. 'And this from Sir Henry Inglose, asking whether I shall attend the meeting next month of the Guild of Saint George in Norwich.'

'But these are trivial,' Alice said in a firm little voice.

'I know they are trivial! But see how many there are! Some more serious, some even less so. All of them demand that I make a decision, all of them that I act in some way.'

'You did not go to Norwich for such reasons when you were with the army in France.'

'I did not receive such letters when I was in France!'

'What, none?'

'Never so many, never letters such as these. When I was in France I told my agents to handle such matters for me. But now my agents come to me and insist that they be given my authority and backing before they act.'

'Then give it to them in London.'

He rose to his feet. Alice was annoying him intensely; the letters annoyed him too. He was beginning to find it difficult to contain that annoyance. He paced up the room, his hands behind his back, then returned and stood in front of her. 'I understand what you ask, but it is not possible. I must begin by showing myself in Norwich and Ipswich and Bury, by meeting my tenants and my bailiffs. I have done all that I can do from London. I have engaged a land agent, a man called Tuddenham,

Sir Thomas Tuddenham. He was well recommended to me; he is used to acting alone. He too begs me to make this visit. There are other men, men Tuddenham has recommended to me, and whom I have yet to meet. I shall never gain any understanding of Norfolk unless I go to Norwich, and join the Guild of Saint George as Tuddenham advises me to do, and speak to all the chief men in the county.'

'So this is what you wish, my Lord?'

He sighed. 'I would not phrase it so. It gives me no pleasure to read such letters. So many of these men, judges and sheriffs, bishops and abbots and landowners, seem to expect me not merely to take an interest in their county, but positively to run it for them. I have no desire to do that. I did not return to England so that I might sort out petty squabbles over fishing rights and gate tolls. I came back with the intention of playing my part in the government of the country. My wish is to help determine the Council's policy in France. But I cannot do that while I am continually deluged with letters such as these.'

There was more that he might have said, much more. Above all, there was the problem of his finances. He had to have more money. He had read with growing disquiet not only the letters from his agents, but the many letters from men who were not his agents, criticising those who were, pointing out the failings in their husbandry and promising that in the same position they could increase his yield from his estates severalfold. But he did not wish to mention these matters to Alice. He knew already that Alice's solution to every hint of financial difficulties was to turn to her father.

'So we shall visit Norwich just this once.'

'We shall visit this once, and then I shall delegate as much of this business as I possibly can.'

He phrased this answer carefully, though without any real doubt that she would take in its evasion. She sat for a moment, hands neatly clasped in her lap, eyes lowered slightly, looking beautiful and composed and so damnably self-contained. Then she said, 'Alice Neville thinks you misread the role of the nobles in England. She says you have been too long in France and you imagine you can act like a French Duke with a fiefdom of your own.'

And I think, he said to himself, with a sudden hot flaring of temper, that you say this to annoy me. Your father the Speaker of the Commons; your cousin the Cardinal; your stepdaughter the Countess of Salisbury; you talk of them all, again and again. You are no fool: you know I have few family connections, and that at this game I cannot rival you. You know that John is dead, and Alexander too, but you never think of my pain and loneliness, or show me even the commonest kind of consideration.

He turned from her sharply and paced the room once more, striding up and down its length until he had the anger under his control. Then he returned to her and said, with no more than a touch of acidity, 'Your stepdaughter is mistaken: I imagine nothing of the kind. I have always known that England is very different from France; and in France too I was largely among Englishmen. But I do believe that it is to my benefit to establish my influence over my tenants.'

'So that you can nominate a couple of Knights of the Shire to Parliament?'

'Is that so insignificant a thing? I thought your father was a great champion of the rights of the Commons in Parliament? And a great exponent of their power to bring down even the greatest nobles, when it suits them to do so?'

This argument had hit home: Alice gave a little nod of approval, and seeing it, he felt himself relax. He would be able to persuade her; of course he would. He would not be forced to demand that she obey him, he would win her round to his own viewpoint.

He must not rush her. He told himself this every time he left her side, angry and frustrated and bewildered by her obtuseness; and every time he found it hard to keep to his resolution. He had to give her time, give her space in every aspect of their life together. If he did not do this, he had no doubt that the barriers she kept so high would never be lowered to him.

Alice said quietly, 'Then we shall do as you suggest, my Lord. But may we go to Ewelme after midsummer?'

Ewelme in the late summer? By then he would have been away from London for vital months. Beaufort and the King would still be in France. There would be no better time to work to win Gloucester's confidence, or to establish himself as a regular – and independent – member of the King's Council. He had reckoned to be in London then, and maybe to return to France himself for a short while before the winter came.

But he needed Alice's approval, needed it so much. He needed to conciliate her, even if it did oblige him to sacrifice other aims. He wanted, too, to give her happiness for its own sake, and he understood that it would make her happy to go to Ewelme.

'You shall go to Ewelme, if that is what you wish. Perhaps I shall be unable to join you there: but in that case you shall go there with your father.'

Alice lifted her face to him. He saw the sheer pleasure written on it; then, in an instant, it was as if she had lowered a veil. She said, in a dutiful voice, 'My Lord, I should not wish to go anywhere without you.'

Oh, you wish it, he thought, with a sense of dismay. You wish to go to Ewelme far more than you wish to be with me. And if you do offer to sacrifice Ewelme to me, I'd swear you reckon on my rejecting your sacrifice.

But he would not. After all, Alice was only doing as any decent wife would do, after arguing with far more persistence than most husbands would have tolerated.

'Then perhaps you will manage to find Norfolk perfect with me.'

Alice's green eyes flared for a moment, as if his response surprised or even angered her. He held them, trying to catch the spark that lit them; trying to catch Alice and bind her to him. But the spark was gone in an instant and there was no more to be seen than her beautiful façade.

She gave him an empty, compliant smile.

'For you, my Lord,' she said, 'I am sure I can manage to do that.'

To Suffolk's mild surprise, Norwich proved to be a pleasant city. The Wensum, though a small river, was a busy one which curved pleasingly round the white bulk of the castle on its mound, and between the open expanses of the Cathedral meadows and the slopes of Mousehold Heath. The walls were in passable repair and the market was thriving. The towers and spires of the fifty or more churches almost all had bells, which rang out brightly to call the merchants and the apprentices and the priests and monks and friars to worship. From Conesford Street to Tombland to Upper Newport, the houses of the richer citizens were large and handsome. There were dozens of inns and shops and stalls, and a man could obtain anything that he required, so long as he did not require books or music or good French gowns. Suffolk Inn was thoroughly uncomfortable, admittedly, but it was only a short ride from the city to Cossey, and the keepers there had worked well in his absence: the hunting was superb.

His only disappointment was in his new servants. He had met Sir Thomas Tuddenham only briefly in London and gained but the sketchiest impression of the man. Now he was thrown into Tuddenham's company for long hours; and before long he came to the ineradicable conclusion that he did not like his land agent.

He could not recall who had recommended Tuddenham to him. Whoever it was had enthused about Tuddenham's skill as an estate manager; and they had told the truth, since Tuddenham was very knowledgeable and could show figures to prove how he had increased the yield from the Lancaster estates. But they had not mentioned Tuddenham's cold eyes, or his pockmarked face, or his over-trimmed doublets. They had not mentioned the fawning, obsequious manner which grated so. Nor had he heard any hint in London of the unpleasant rumours which reached him from several quarters in Norwich: of Tuddenham's disastrous marriage and scandalous divorce, of his questionable judgements at the manor courts, and of his brutal treatment of tenants who could not pay their rent.

It had been a mistake, he now realised, to take on so many men on the sole basis of Tuddenham's recommendation. That decision had made such sense in London. Then he had thought above all of the pressure of business encapsulated in those endless letters; but now the realisation came home that he had committed his reputation and his fortunes into the hands of a group of strangers.

Few of them were what he had expected. He had had an impression from Tuddenham's description that John Heydon was a formidable lawyer, but the City Recorder proved to be as brash and naive and aggressive as he was young. He had imagined Thomas Wetherby to be a merchant in Chaucer's class, but instead he found a countryman with no idea of court manners, no learning, and the scantiest of contacts in London.

These were small disappointments, but real ones, because his commitment was firm: he had lost his opportunity to make his own choice among Norfolk men. Strangely, Alice seemed not to share them. She scoffed at the Norwich ladies and their little old-fashioned headdresses, but she laughed at Heydon's jokes and chattered with Tuddenham of clothes and music. Wetherby she did not care for; but she acquired a taste for being escorted around the city by Tuddenham when Suffolk was closeted with his bailiffs and estate managers and representatives of the Norfolk guilds.

They were boisterous company, Tuddenham and Heydon; and Alice seemed rather to heighten than to dampen their spirits. She encouraged them to ape the Duke of Burgundy and play practical jokes on the servants at Suffolk Inn; once she rode with them through the streets singing loudly, long after nightfall.

Several of the representatives of the Norfolk guilds mentioned these and similar incidents to Suffolk. They did so with the greatest deference; but it was significant, he knew, that they should have done so at all.

He found it discomfiting. In London Alice had rapidly established herself in a prominent position in court circles; he had never thought her anything but a social asset to him. In Norwich, he thought uneasily that she was rapidly coming closer, if anything, to being a liability.

Nothing seemed to have gone right for Alice. From the start the ladies of Norwich had treated her with a sort of defensive truculence, as if they had all decided in advance not to like her. He could not understand it. True, Alice's tastes and experiences were very different from theirs; true, she seemed to make considerably less effort to charm them than she had made to charm Lady Warwick; but that should not have made so very much difference, surely.

All her life, wherever she went, Alice had been admired; but in Norwich she was not. Suffolk sensed that she could not understand it either. He assumed that her behaviour with Tuddenham and Heydon was her way of coping with an uncomfortable situation; and in that light, he chose to tolerate it without making any comment to her.

There was a stretch of scrubland, perhaps four hundred yards of it, separating Lakenham Woods from the city wall of Norwich. The wall was set low at that point, with the ditch beneath it, and it was a fairly steep walk to the edge of the woods.

Alice was breathless, almost panting by the time she reached the first oak trees. She threw herself on to the coarse grass. She was wearing the dairymaid's spare kirtle: no need to worry about staining it. Her companions reached her a moment later and dutifully plopped down next to her. It had been her choice to make them walk fast, almost run. Outings like this needed zest: doing everything fast was one way of adding it.

She was feeling lively; she was feeling mischievous. Norwich was only tolerable to her for as long as she warded off her depression in this manner. She was confident that Sir Thomas and Master Heydon would support her in any mild mischief she indulged in. She liked neither man as well as her husband appeared to suppose, but they were passable company, so long as she resisted the temptation to bait them. Provincial, correct in their manners before the aristocracy, they had never dared to bait her back, and her taunting only made them edgy.

She sat up. She glanced briefly at Tuddenham and Heydon, did not glance at all at Lucette. She looked backwards along the path she had taken. The point where she was sitting was just high enough for her to be able to see most of the city. It was almost midday on a summer day; the sky was greyish, filmed with high cloud, but the light was clear.

Norwich. Somehow she had never imagined, in those days in Paris when she had waited for the messenger to bring her Suffolk's latest poem, when she had listened to Gilles' serenades beneath her window, that the choice she made would bring her to Norwich.

But there could have been no other choice. And things could be worse, she told herself firmly. Though her husband was more demanding than she could easily tolerate, he was also thoughtful and well-intentioned: he was not a cruel man, and that, in such times, was a rare virtue. Norwich was not Paris, but there were worse places on God's earth; indeed from a short distance Norwich looked positively attractive. She had no real cause for complaint. And she was not complaining: she was trying, in her way, to make the best of her situation.

'Do you see the gate to your left, my Lady?'

It was Sir Thomas who spoke. That was no surprise. Alice's silences generally made Sir Thomas nervous: he felt it necessary to entertain her all the time. He was

334

fond of explaining things. Now he would explain the view to her. No better diversion then presented itself, so she decided to do her best to enjoy Sir Thomas' explanation. 'That fat, ugly little gate?'

'Just so. They call it the Iron Gate. It is a postern, as you see: too low and narrow for carts or wagons. The road beyond leads up to the swinemarket.'

'And the tower, where the walls arch round?'

'That is the Broad Tower. Then Berstrete Gate you recognise, of course.'

Of course: they had left their horses there with the gatekeeper, only a few minutes earlier. It was the gate guarding the London road, she realised; she and Suffolk had come by that route into the city three weeks previously. Distinctly odd, Berstrete Gate: lopsided, with a round tower propping up one side and a portcullis that announced its pretensions. No pigs waddled through Berstrete Gate; the King's servants came that way to the Castle, looming white and forbidding on its bare green mound.

Her eyes moved on and Sir Thomas continued with his commentary. The wall seemed to hang at the top of a cliff, then snake down, uneasily, to the valley of the Wensum, joining the river just before it began its great loop around the castle and the Cathedral. There stood the Black Tower, lofty and intimidating with its facing of shiny black flint, a prison below and a watchpost above. More towers marked each turn in the wall until it levelled into the square protrusion of Conesford Gate, hard by the river, and the little pair of boom towers that guarded the river itself.

'You know Norwich well, Sir Thomas.'

'That I do, Lady Alice. And Heydon too, no doubt. Between us we could tell you the name of every gate, every tower in the wall, every church. And there are fifty or more of those, not counting the friaries and the Cathedral.'

It was true: the space inside the walls was thick-studded with towers and spires.

'I think that would be a little excessive, Sir Thomas. But tell me, where is Suffolk Inn?'

'Look right between the Broad Tower and the round tower of the gate. Do you see the spire of Saint Michael Conesford?'

'I think so. And the red-tiled roof, just this side of it?'

'That is Suffolk Inn. See, the Austin Friars behind, between it and the river?'

'I do.' Alice was silent for a moment. She gazed at the red-tiled roof. She imagined the Earl of Suffolk beneath it, dutifully closeted with the Bishop and the Prior. He was pleasant to look upon; Norwich was pleasant to look upon. Enjoy them, she told herself. Find things to enjoy.

There was more to enjoy. Though the dairymaid's spare kirtle was a little scratchy, it was comfortably loose in contrast to her tight-fitting silk gowns. There was a certain harmless amusement to be derived from Sir Thomas, who looked endearingly silly in the coarse hooded tunic and rough leather sandals he had put on to oblige her. He would never be handsome, Sir Thomas, with his rutted face and severely cropped black hair, but he was chivalrous, and though he was not witty he was working hard at entertaining her.

Her eyes drifted from the red tiles to the spire of Saint Michael, from the spire to the grey stone of the wall, from the wall to the ditch. They focussed on a dark shape in the ditch. She kept staring at the dark shape until she was sure what it was. It was a dead horse. And at the rim of the ditch stood a ditcher, with a long ditching shovel in his hands, who was grubbing away at it rather ineffectually.

The sight did not disgust her. The ditcher and the horse were both some distance away; they were no more real to her than figures in a painting. That was what it was: a macabre painting. Masquerade with ditcher and dead horse.

She looked at this for a long time. Then she recollected herself, turned her back on the ditch and switched her attention to John Heydon and Lucette. They had brought the food, packed in rush baskets; already they had half unpacked the contents on to a length of checked cloth.

'What did Cook provide, Lucette?'

Heydon answered. 'Just what you ordered, my Lady: simple country fare. Spiced pigeon pie. Cold roast peacock. Amber jelly. Spiced oranges. Honeyed sweetmeats.'

It was not so very funny, but Alice laughed loudly. Heydon was a vulgar man, but at least he had some spirit about him. He was not at all lawyerish, even in his choice of clothes: she would have taken him, had she not known his profession, for an innkeeper or perhaps a tanner. He was a heavy drinker and a voracious eater. The signs of his indulgence were already clear: his eyes were bloodshot, his waistline was flabby. In ten years, perhaps, he would be repulsive; but he was still young, and still passably handsome in a coarse-grained way.

'Do have some claret.' Heydon uncorked a bottle of ale and proceeded to pour its contents into four small cups.

Alice accepted hers from him and raised it. 'Country life.'

'Country life,' Heydon, Tuddenham and Lucette dutifully echoed.

The baskets proved to contain a large hunk of yellow cheese, two halfpenny loaves and a large pat of butter, four cold chickens well roasted with tarragon, a fat plum pie and a great quantity of ale. This was precisely what she had ordered. At least, she thought, the cook at Suffolk Inn had had sense enough to listen to her.

She ate. They all ate, enthusiastically. And drank. The ale was strong: she had instructed Cook to buy it in from the Popinjay. They emptied a dozen bottles in quick succession and the easy stupor of a summer afternoon began to settle on them.

'Do you sing, Mr Heydon?'

'Alas, not even for you, my Lady.'

'Then we shall entertain you. Lucette, *tu connais le petit rondeau que Gilles nous donnait hier?*'

Lucette nodded. Alice began to sing and Lucette joined in. Their voices weaved neatly in and out of each other. Alice and Lucette had sung together often. The ale slurred their timing, but their pitch was perfect. The sun sneaked through a gap in the cloud; the afternoon mellowed.

They sang three songs and then Sir Thomas offered to contribute one. He embarked on a spirited rendition of 'Merry it is while summer ilast'. The sheer volume of his voice more than compensated for the defects in its tunefulness. Alice glanced at Lucette and saw her own amusement reflected in her maid's face.

She did not notice the ditcher until his shadow came over Sir Thomas. Nor did Sir Thomas. 'Ei! Ei!' he sang. Then he fell abruptly silent.

They all stared at the ditcher. His legs were muddy and his tunic was filthy. His face was half-hidden by a floppy straw hat. He was not a flat figure in a painting any more: he was large and real, and he exuded a strong smell of stale sewage.

A momentary unease came over Alice. She giggled and that served to suppress the unease. The ditcher was not threatening: he looked stolid and reliable. He was a family man, no doubt, with a dozen children at home in some hovel down a back alley. Perhaps he would divert them even more effectively than Sir Thomas had done.

'What for do you folks be eating on the common?'

'We do be having a picnic, my man,' John Heydon said. Alice giggled again.

'Not on the land by my ditch, you don't.'

'We are well away from your ditch, you can be sure,' retorted Sir Thomas.

'Well, you do go and eat your supper someplace else.'

'We are eating our supper here. Now please go off and leave us in peace.'

'Folks are not allowed to eat on the land by my ditch.'

Slowly, with a great deal of drunken dignity, Sir

Thomas rose from the ground. He reached out as if to take hold of the ditcher, then clearly thought the better of it and withdrew his hand.

'My good man. My companions and I intend to enjoy our picnic in this precise spot. You are spoiling our enjoyment. Now please return to your ditch, and leave us alone.'

The ditcher stood his ground. ''Tis the town ordinances,' he said stubbornly.

Alice stood up too. 'Do let me introduce myself,' she said. 'I am the Countess of Suffolk.'

'Oho, and I be the Duke of Norfolk,' retorted the ditcher.

'Can you not recognise a masquerade when you see one, you oaf?' Sir Thomas spluttered.

Alice glanced at Sir Thomas. Two red spots had appeared in the centre of his sallow cheeks. That unnerved her a little. In her experience anger and amusement did not sit well together. The interlude had already persisted for longer than she would have liked; she began to sense that it might not end pleasantly.

'Long words don't fool me,' said the ditcher. 'Now will you folks go quietly, or shall I call the guards at the gate?'

No, it was not funny any more. Even as a novel form of entertainment it left a great deal to be desired. She had an uncomfortable and growing suspicion that the ditcher would prove incapable of seeing the joke; and she was not confident that Sir Thomas saw it, either.

'Pay no attention to him,' she said, mainly to Lucette. She sat down again by the rush baskets and turned her back on the ditcher.

She knew, not least from the smell, that the ditcher was still there behind her. She heard Sir Thomas say, 'Be off now. You are upsetting her Ladyship.'

'She be no Ladyship in a kirtle like that, no more than I be a Duke. I be Thomas Aylmer the ditcher, and I have my job to do.'

'Then you can do it,' retorted Sir Thomas, 'in the ditch.'

These words were followed by scuffling sounds. Alice turned round again, just in time to see Sir Thomas crash to the ground with a startled yelp. A rational part of her mind told her that he had not actually been struck by the ditcher; he had stumbled over a tussock, probably in the course of an attempt to hit the ditcher himself. But this thought was faint and barely coherent.

Sir Thomas staggered back to his feet, turned and rushed at the ditcher again. She saw his heightened colour, the sweat shining on his forehead. She saw the ditcher throw his spade to the ground. He met Sir Thomas' approaching right fist with a counter-punch, a good deal more efficient. It sent Sir Thomas to his knees. Sir Thomas wavered there a moment, astonishment on his face, and then keeled slowly to the ground.

Alice stared at his recumbent body. She did not feel afraid. It was amazement that she felt chiefly: amazement at an unreal scene, as if the gargoyles on a church had suddenly come to life and were cavorting in front of her. It did not occur to her to react.

John Heydon did react, and fast. He was on his feet before Tuddenham hit the ground. He took the ditcher from behind with a brutal punch to the side of his head. It was the ditcher's turn to look astonished. He fell more dramatically than Tuddenham had done, sideways on to the rough grass.

There was a moment's heavy silence. Alice became aware of a noise, oddly loud. Eventually she placed it: it was Heydon's breathing, hard and erratic. The sewage smell seemed to hang in the air. A tableau, neatly posed, met her gaze. John Heydon standing, legs akimbo, over the ditcher's body. Sir Thomas Tuddenham, now on his hands and knees like a startled dog, staring blankly at the two of them.

Heydon moved. He began to kick the ditcher. He aimed two strong kicks at his ribs, rolled his body over with a fastidious toe and kicked again. The ditcher gave no sign of life. His body rolled a little, down the slope. Heydon slipped his foot under it and gave another kick.

It rolled some more. He went on rolling and kicking, rolling and kicking the unconscious man down the slope towards the ditch.

He reached the ditch, more by chance than judgement, at the spot which boasted the rotting horse. He slipped his foot under the body once more and gave one final, powerful kick. The ditcher fell into the ditch. He seemed to land on top of the putrid carcase. Heydon spat contemptuously after him, then turned and, without a backward glance, started back up the hill.

Alice watched all this; watched it so intently that she did not think to check on Sir Thomas' welfare until Heydon was halfway up the slope. She thought about it then and turned guiltily to him. There was no cause for great alarm, she saw immediately. Lucette was seeing to him. She wiped the dust off his tunic and hood; she set about rearranging his liripipe. Sir Thomas accepted these services with an air of mild embarrassment.

Heydon reached them. He stopped by the ditcher's spade, picked it up and threw it wildly in the direction of the ditch. He retrieved the battered straw hat and sent that flying in the same direction.

'More ale, my Lady?' he asked Alice.

Alice shook her head. 'Sir Thomas,' she said, her eyes still fixed on Heydon, 'will you take me home, please?'

Suffolk had had a wearing afternoon. The Bishop and the Prior had stayed at Suffolk Inn for twice as long as he had anticipated, and even before they departed other callers had been queuing up to claim their share of his attention. Sir Henry Inglose and Sir Brian Stapleton, urging him to stay in Norwich for the next Guild meeting; the wife of a man accused of poaching a deer at Cossey, pleading for mercy; a discharged soldier looking for work as a groom, and a dozen others. All petty tasks, all necessary, all timewasting. His head began to ache, his limbs to feel heavy.

He thought sometimes of Alice out on her masquerade picnic. It had been Heydon's idea. He had considered forbidding her to go when she had first mentioned it the day before, but in the end he had said nothing; though the idea was unconventional it had seemed harmless enough, and Alice was so clearly looking forward to it. He had watched her leave that morning, looking younger and more vulnerable, somehow, in the clumsy kirtle and apron than she appeared in her Paris gowns.

He was in the hall, going over the accounts with the bailiff from Hellesdon, when he heard her voice in the yard. It gave him a little start of pleasure; and one of surprise. It was still early: he had not expected her to return before dusk.

He dismissed the bailiff and went into the yard to greet her. He saw her standing there with Tuddenham and Heydon, with Lucette hovering behind her, and the grooms and horses around them. He stood in the doorway for a moment, watching her. She seemed so lively, such a contrast to all his sober and worried callers. She was laughing at something – he had no idea what – with Tuddenham.

Then she sensed his presence and turned to him. Her eyes met his, as they so rarely did. They seemed to him very bright, almost unnaturally so. For a moment, he thought he saw panic in her expression.

He moved forward, and so did she. By the time she reached his side the odd expression had faded so completely that he wondered if he had imagined it. She caught at his arm, almost clinging to him. 'Oh my Lord, such strange happenings in the woods!'

Her tone was cheerful, almost teasing; she smiled gaily at him. But he was sure now that something was wrong. Alice would never normally have run to him, or touched him in such a way. He slipped his arm about her waist, and she did not protest; she leaned against him, as if she were grateful for his presence.

He looked down at her for a moment, but he could read nothing clear in her face, so he looked instead at the others. This time he saw the bruise darkening on

Tuddenham's cheek, and the mudstain, dried and dull against the shiny flat stuff of Heydon's doublet.

A moment later Alice had pulled away and Heydon and Tuddenham crossed the yard to join them. They all explained at once: all determinedly light-hearted, all insisting that it had been a great joke. There had been a silly incident with a ditcher who had complained when they picnicked too close to his ditch. It was nothing for him to worry about, Alice repeated insistently: Sir Thomas and Master Heydon had taken excellent care of her. They had soon sent the ditcher on his way.

With force, to judge by the bruise, Suffolk thought to himself. He disliked that thought. He disliked the merry explanations. He sensed that underneath her gay façade Alice was close to hysteria. But he did not dare to alarm her further by demanding explanations in front of her, so he laughed with Tuddenham and Heydon and contented himself with making sure that Lucette accompanied her when she retreated to the solar to change into her day dress.

From the corner of his eye, as he was watching her make her way up the steps to the solar, he saw Tuddenham make a furtive movement towards the gates.

'Wait,' he said.

Tuddenham and Heydon turned guilty faces to him. He led them into the hall. And he demanded to know what had really happened.

The story soon came out. It was not so very different from the story he had already been told, but under pressure Tuddenham admitted that it had ended in violence. The land agent insisted that even so, it was nothing more than a joke; but Suffolk did not share that opinion. It sounded to him like a silly, sordid incident which could easily have been avoided. He suspected Tuddenham and Heydon had mishandled it. They could surely have sent the man away more gently. And to use force, in front of Alice: that was disgraceful.

He meant to say this to them, but it was not easy to

343

frame his annoyance into words. He was still unnerved by the thought of Alice's bravely hidden distress; his mind kept straying to her, when it should have concentrated on the conversation. Tuddenham talked insistently in a low voice and it was difficult to find a moment at which he could interrupt.

'So there really was no danger to her Ladyship, my Lord,' Tuddenham repeated yet again. 'And we have it all in hand, you can be sure. Heydon will go now to speak with Wetherby. By nightfall, the ditcher will be in the Castle dungeons.'

The Castle dungeons? That was not the outcome he had expected from what had gone before. 'Is that necessary?'

Tuddenham and Heydon both nodded earnestly. 'Very important, my Lord,' Tuddenham said. 'You must show the city you mean to use a firm hand. It would not do at all to let the man off. He insulted Lady Alice!'

That was true: it was the ditcher who had brought about the incident. He was most directly to blame for Alice's unhappy experience.

'Perhaps you are right. I can see a night in the dungeons would do the man no harm.'

'You can trust Wetherby to take care of it, my Lord.'

'That is good to know.' Suffolk withdrew a pace. Perhaps Tuddenham was not such a fool, he thought. The land agent had done his utmost to protect Alice, even if his methods had been questionable. Now he was acting firmly and capably, and without any need for prompting. Was this not what he had wanted most: strong servants who would take the weight of Norfolk affairs off his back? Tuddenham did not really deserve censure: he was a very able man. His personal dislike of the man should not blind him to that fact.

He said, 'You will call on us at Cossey tomorrow, Tuddenham, to discuss the rents?'

'I'll do that, my Lord. And my Lord: please believe that to upset Lady Alice was the last thing we intended.'

'Think no more of it.'

The same advice should apply to himself, he thought wearily, as he made his way out of the hall and up to the solar. It was a trivial matter. His life was full of trivial problems. He should try to forget them: he had important things to do.

Ten days after the ditcher's imprisonment, Suffolk learned that there were protests about it in the city. Sir Brian Stapleton told him this; he had heard no hint of it from Tuddenham and Heydon. Indeed he suspected, considering the matter afterwards, that they had been doing their utmost to keep it from him.

Stapleton's view was forthrightly expressed. It was unfortunate that the ditcher had not recognised the Countess, but hardly surprising in view of her masquerade clothes. Perhaps he should have been more circumspect, but he had been within his rights to ask the picnickers to move. It was his job to keep the scrubland clear. To punish him at all had been harsh, when he had already felt the force of Heydon's fist and, rumour had it, the toe of Heydon's boot. By then he had been overpunished by any standards.

'A night in the dungeons was not so excessive,' Suffolk remonstrated.

'One night would have been tolerable; but by now he has been in the dungeons for ten nights.'

'Surely not. I understood he was to be released the following morning.'

'Not so, my Lord.'

'Then I shall look into the matter immediately.'

'Thank you, my Lord.'

Damn Stapleton, Suffolk thought, as he gestured to his chamberlain that his visitor was leaving. No; damn Tuddenham. Ten nights in the dungeons: the land agent knew very well that that had not been his intention. Now he was in danger of gaining a reputation for brutality, and not just among the ditcher's friends and relations, but among men such as Stapleton whose opinions carried a deal of weight in the county.

This little matter was rapidly ceasing to be trivial. It had to be terminated. He called Tuddenham to him and told the land agent to see that the ditcher was freed immediately.

Sir Thomas reacted with polite surprise. He gave the impression that he thought it none of Suffolk's business. This did not please Suffolk. He pressed Tuddenham for an assurance that it would be done.

Tuddenham apologised obsequiously, but Suffolk did not get his assurance. The matter was out of his hands now, the land agent insisted: the ditcher would have to wait until the jail delivery.

Was it so? Suffolk wished he knew more of English law, so that he could judge. But he did not, and he could scarcely ask Heydon in the circumstances. Indeed he could not see that he could do anything more at all. Tuddenham had made it perfectly clear that he would be offended if his judgement were to be overruled.

And he could not afford to offend Tuddenham, he reluctantly decided. If he did, he ran the risk that Tuddenham would resign his service. However unpleasant an individual Tuddenham was, he was a more than competent land agent. His resignation would be a real loss; and it would take weeks to replace him, and all the men who had followed him into Suffolk's service. Suffolk could not spare those weeks; and anyway, he told himself, to do anything of the kind would cause a stir in the county far greater than the stir the ditcher's imprisonment was causing.

Tuddenham would have to be left to handle affairs as he saw fit. There was no real reason to doubt his judgement, there was only the word of Sir Brian Stapleton to set against him. If Sir Brian was wrong, there was nothing to trouble himself about; if Sir Brian was right Tuddenham would have to find his own way out of the situation. It was time for his master to leave Norwich.

He would be heartily glad to be gone. He had seen more than enough of Tuddenham and Heydon and Wetherby, more than enough of Lady Morley, Lady Rothermere and a great many other elderly Norwich ladies. He had done his duty, but he had derived little pleasure from his visit to the city, and, neither, he suspected, had Alice. She deserved compensation. He would take her to Ewelme after all.

13

ENGLAND
Winter, 1431-32

In the hall of the Mansion House, official residence of
the Lord Mayor of London, John Welles sat in state in a
vast carved chair with a scarlet cushion. Behind him
waited two valets, one of whom held, like a trophy, his
hat with its peacock feather; at his left hand stood his
clerk, Giles, and at his right, looking incongruously
scruffy in his worn grey tabard, Secret Poursuivant.
Through the hall, in a never-ending procession of gaudy
liveries, drifted other members of the Mayor's household: his sword-bearer, his crier, his water bailiff, his
serjeant carvers, his serjeants of the chamber, his
yeomen of the chamber, yeomen of the waterside and
yeoman of the fishmarket, together with representatives of the Grocers' Guild and the other London
guilds, clerks, messengers, grooms, lesser servants and
curious passers-by.

John Welles paid no attention to this incessant
activity. His eyes were fixed on the paper in his hand,
which was liberally covered with notes and drawings,
done in a spidery, inexpert hand.

'And at the drawbridge on London Bridge,' he said,
glancing at Secret, 'I thought we should have a giant.'

'On a pillar,' Secret suggested helpfully.

'Oh yes, a pillar. Or perhaps two pillars, one for each
leg. Decorated, properly decorated. Ivy, or vine leaves.'
Welles gestured to Giles to make another note. 'And he
must carry a sword.'

'Offering to vanquish the King's enemies.'

'Vanquish?'

'There was a Latin phrase they used in Rouen. What was it – "Inimicos eius induam confusione."'

'Ini – yes, that has a fine ring to it. Mind, I was thinking of the giant who frequents the Boar's Head, and I doubt if his Latin is all it might be.'

'I could tutor him,' Secret offered. He had long since ceased to pretend to Welles that he had no Latin.

'Perhaps that would be the answer. 'Tis none so easy to lay one's hands on giants and dwarves, particularly when we need so many of them.'

They did need very, very many of them, as Secret well knew. John Welles was determined to see the King's return from France celebrated and feasted even more gloriously than his coronation had been. When the King had been crowned in London, after all, he had not been so fortunate as to have Welles as Mayor of the City; but now, in the year of the French coronation, the grocer had achieved his greatest ambition.

His naive openness about the pleasure this gave him, the smile of glee with which he tossed his hat to the valet, his exclamations of delight every time he put on his cloak of crimson velvet, his hat furred with beaver, his golden girdle and baldric and his great mayoral chain, still surprised Secret. He had never realised before that John Welles was a man who lusted after power and position.

Money, yes; he had known Welles cared about money. Knowledge, too. He had always been aware that Welles was capable of manipulating men in little ways, that he liked to play a prominent role in his own circle. But power, the wider political power that is grounded in public position: strangely, in the years before Fastolf had turned him off after Patay he had barely noticed Welles' urges in that direction. He had never even thought of Welles as a London man: in Fastolf Place the talk had been of Norfolk, and the politics of Langbourn Ward had barely received a mention.

But he noticed Welles' urges now, because a large part of his life was spent in helping the grocer to fulfil them.

'Should I go to the Boar's Head, then, and suggest –'

'Yes, soon, soon. Let me just check . . .' Welles' eyes returned to the paper. These were no more than the previous day's notes; the full details of the arrangements covered not one sheet of paper, but many fat sheaves. Already there had been months of planning, and there were still weeks to go before the celebrations – perhaps many weeks, since it was difficult to be certain precisely when the King would return.

There was more to be done than Welles could himself grasp, let alone perform, but his interest in every detail was intense. His entire official household was wrapped up in the preparations, and dozens of other men had been pressed into service. Welles' fellow Aldermen would pay their part; his colleagues in the Grocers' Guild, and men from all the other London guilds; his messengers and apprentices; the King's Master of the Revels and his men; the Monk of Bury, John Lydgate, who would write the verses; the Deans of Saint Paul's and Westminster Abbey, who would hold services; the Duke of Gloucester's musicians, who would provide the music; Garter King of Arms, who would organise the ceremonial; and an army of jesters, minstrels, carpenters, painters, seamstresses and pastrycooks.

For all of this, John Welles would pay. It had been an even more startling revelation to Secret that John Welles was not merely comfortably off, but an extremely rich man.

'The Black Heath – we have that settled now?' Welles looked up at Giles and received an encouraging nod. 'The tableaux are coming along. Mind, I must press the Serjeants for the details of theirs. Must check with Lydgate, too – Secret, you do that, ask for a copy of everything he's written. The church services, yes, yes. By Saint Laurence and his gridiron, what a lot there is to do. Oh, the coins, the gold coins. Must speak to the Italians, make sure they send me the new minted ones.'

'Shall I do that?'

Welles glanced Secret's way, then frowned. 'No, I shall do it myself. Go now and find the giant. Now, Giles, my speech, my speech to the King . . .'

My speech to the King. Secret smiled, secure in the knowledge that Welles' eyes were not on him, as he made his ceremonial bow and withdrew in measured backward steps. For this the grocer was willing to pay out hundreds of pounds from his private purse: for the pleasure of shaking the Duke of Gloucester's hand and bowing to the King. He might appear to the outside world as a hard-dealing merchant, but to those who had seen him caught up in these preparations he was like a small boy given a wooden sword for Christmas.

Such pomp, such unabashed glee, such shameless self-importance. Welles' own tableau had been the first to be settled. It would be at the Great Conduit, where the grocer reckoned the crowd would be thickest. The Master of the Revels had personally devised it for him: Mercy, Pity and Grace, drawing up the wines of temperance and good governance from a well set in a bower of fruit trees.

Wells for Welles. The grocer might not carry arms, but he was proud of his device. He had dressed his servants in a livery patterned with wells, he had written into his will a legacy for a new well to be built for the city, and another for a window showing a well, for the new Guildhall. He had handed a suit of the well-patterned livery to Secret Poursuivant and told him to wear it.

Secret Poursuivant had refused. He had considered the matter, but he had refused.

It was not that he disliked this work for Welles. On the contrary, he enjoyed it. He was worked hard, but he had a fondness himself for ceremonial, and it was good to know that while he was about these errands there was no need to watch his back, no need always to think before he spoke, no need to distrust the people around him. But even so, he had reason for disquiet.

He had known, of course, that Welles would demand recompense for the trouble he had taken to intercede with Fastolf. He had judged this matter, at Corbeil and after, and had decided nevertheless to ask Welles for help. His fear then had been that Welles might ask him to undertake tasks that were against Fastolf's own interests. Not so: Welles had his own sense of justice, and every task he had specified had been as innocent as that day's tasks were. But there were so many tasks, many more than Secret had bargained for.

There were tasks for Hanson, too: Hanson had taken much trouble, and Hanson too expected to be rewarded. Hanson and Fastolf and Gough: each man now served with a different garrison, each man wished to send messages to each of the others, to his family, to business contacts in London, in Paris, in Rouen. Beul Poursuivant carried some of these messages, but Secret carried many more.

It was not that this angered Fastolf. Rather, it was upsetting to him that Fastolf accepted his pattern of work so readily. The knight had taken him back, if only to appease Welles and the others. Once again he wore a tabard of or and azure; but he was no poursuivant in the real sense. He was a messenger boy, carrying messages and performing errands indiscriminately for Fastolf and Welles, Hanson, Basset, Gough and a score of other men.

And it was not for this, he sometimes thought to himself, that he had schemed to put himself in Anjou's favour. He wore his tabard, he kept his name, but he had no firm place in Fastolf's household, or in any other man's. He had no household of his own. Much of the time he was on the road, or in strange inns; for the remainder, he was a perpetual visitor in the houses of other men.

He thought all this, but he was no more than middling low-spirited as he made his way from Thames Street to London Bridge, and down Southwark High Street. It was a fine, clear day. This was territory he knew, and he would eat, drink and sleep that night in the company of old Harry, John Payn and other men he knew. Christmas was coming soon, and there were many worse places to spend Christmas than Fastolf Place. But he would have swapped Fastolf Place for a barn outside Orleans without a moment's hesitation; and he would have turned his back on all Welles' fees and ceremonials, his meetings with the Duke of Gloucester and his intrigues with Norfolk men, if he could have had in return even a hint that Fastolf trusted him.

Alice was sitting in the panelled upper room at Bardi Place, which she had now turned into her withdrawing room. The bed was draped in yellow damask; pots of marjoram lined the windowsill, beneath which was placed the bench on which she sat. The shutters were thrown open and through them came the cool, fresh air of a fine December day, and the faint cries of the street traders along the Cornhill. Lucette sat in a corner with another of the maids, embroidering a length of the fine white linen that Alice used for petticoats. Alice was reading one of the Duke of Orleans' poems. She read it several times over, silently mouthing the words as if she were sensing how it would sound when set to music.

Then she looked up at Suffolk, who was standing before her, waiting for her response.

'No,' she said. 'No; this one I never saw in Paris.'

'Nor did I read it until I came to Blois. But it is well written, is it not?'

She glanced down at the sheet of parchment again; and again, Suffolk's eyes followed hers. He had written out the poem himself. It was still his favourite of the poems he had found at Blois. 'Ce n'est pas jeu d'entrejetteurs.' He knew the words by heart.

And in a strange way, he had taken them for his guiding rule. It pleased him to think that he was no dicer. Each move in his game was planned: not least, showing this poem to Alice on this fine December day.

'Yes, my Lord, it is very pretty. And you have more?'

'A few. I shall show them to you, but not today. You should savour them, not devour them at a single sitting.'

'I should like that.'

That was a plain response. And the poem was not pretty: it was both more and less than pretty. But he knew Alice, and he was not disappointed by her reaction to it.

'Of course,' he said, deliberately, 'I have copies only of the poems Orleans wrote before I was at Blois. No doubt he has written many more since.'

'No doubt. Could you learn where he is now; the Duke?'

'They move him regularly, but he is most often at Bolingbroke in Lincolnshire.'

'Then we could write to him perhaps; or call on him when next we travel north.'

'That would not be possible,' Suffolk said curtly. 'The Duke is a prisoner. He does not receive letters or visitors except by special permission.'

'How unfortunate.'

'Not necessarily. There is a way by which we might come to make his acquaintance.'

The almond eyes narrowed a fraction. 'Tell me, my Lord.'

'I have thought to offer to take over as Orleans' jailer.'

'His jailer!'

'There is no cause for alarm. I would act as his custodian, be responsible for his safety; naturally I should not guard him in person. It is an honourable post. Sir John Cornwall holds it at present, but the contract is renewed regularly: there is an opportunity for others to bid.'

'And you think to bid for it?'

'It is a matter I have considered.'

Alice did not reply. Her eyes drifted to the parchment once more.

Perhaps I chose the wrong poem, he thought. He had known this one to be subtle and cynical, but he had not chosen it only because of his own pleasure in it. He had

354

thought hard about showing Alice one of the love poems that she had not yet seen, one that was truly pretty, that she could ask Gilles to set to a tune. He knew why he had rejected it. He was jealous. He did not wish Orleans to speak to his wife through love lyrics neater and more resonant than his own.

So instead Orleans would show her – if she wished to see – something of his own motivations. He knew himself to bite the green blackberry, and he had not yet given up hope that Alice would understand this, and show him where to find the ripe fruit.

Alice looked up, with all the calm of a good decision clear on her face. 'I shall speak to my father.'

'No. Do not do that.'

'But my Lord, my father has friends at court, he understands such matters, he can advise us . . .'

'I forbid it.'

This he had foreseen. He had planned his reaction: that was why the firm refusal had come so rapidly and easily to him. His experience had been that Alice never defied him when he gave her an unambiguous order.

He had seen as far as Alice's frank astonishment, her blind inability to understand his response. And he had tried to plan his next moves, but at this point the game had blurred into myriad uncertainties in his mind.

He moved clumsily, coming to sit next to Alice on the bench by the window. 'Forgive me; I should not have spoken so roughly. But you should understand that this is a delicate matter. The Duke is an important nobleman in France. If it becomes known that I wish to become his custodian, it could cause comment at court. You and I appreciate that we wish only to read Orleans' latest poems, to speak to him of literature and music, but others may interpret our moves differently. We must act with circumspection.'

'Certainly, my Lord. But my father . . .'

'Your father is a good and wise man. But he has been very little in France; he does not value things French, as you and I do.'

Alice's smooth brow creased, her eyes darkened. Suffolk felt his muscles tense. He was certain that she did not realise yet how deep the rift was between him and her father. He did not want her to realise it.

Slowly, Alice turned to him. He met her gaze. Her eyes were wide open, and very green.

'Then what should I do, my Lord?'

It was an effort to him not to sigh with relief. For once, he thought, he had judged right: this far, she was his.

'It would be to our advantage if you were to show this poem, and the others I shall give you, to Eleanor Gloucester. And to the other ladies at court: to Lady Warwick, Lady Salisbury and the rest. There is no need for you to tell them that I gave the poems to you. Say merely that you have received them. Give them copies, if they ask. Tell them how anxious you are to make the acquaintance of the Duke of Orleans. Then, in time, you may tell them that you are pressing me to bid for Orleans' custodianship.'

'That I am pressing . . .'

He tried to hold her gaze, but the green eyes clouded and the frown returned, deeper this time on her brow. She rose to her feet abruptly. 'My Lord, this is subterfuge.'

Calm; keep calm. Show her no sign of alarm.

'I would not call it so. It is a ruse, a small ruse of a most innocent kind. We have no cause to hide our true motives; it is merely that we do not wish others to misinterpret them.'

'I can see no reason, my Lord, why they should do so.'

'But I can.'

He too came to his feet. He took her hand – she accepted this, now, without ever pulling away from him – and drew her back down to sit beside him.

'Small things, my Lady, cause comment at a court such as Westminster. That you and I speak the French of Paris, and not the French of the English army, is enough to disturb those who can barely greet a stranger in that

356

language. You wear your gowns in the Parisian style; my doublets were styled likewise until I sent for an English tailor. Men notice such things, and ladies too. It is a small step from there to the suspicion that we favour the French too greatly.'

'We do, surely, favour the French. But not the Valois. We favour Henry as King of France, not Charles.'

'To us that is clear. But it is not so for those to whom all things French are foreign. To such men it could seem suspicious that I wished to know the Duke of Orleans.'

Alice frowned once more. Her eyes fell to her lap. Suffolk kept looking at her. He tried to work out how she might be thinking, but he found that difficult. He did not yet understand her political opinions. He had assumed at first that she had a deep interest in politics, not dissimilar to her father's. The suspicion had grown since that her interest was in reality much more shallow and intermittent, but he still found it difficult to act on this assumption.

'I think, my Lord, that you would be wise to forget this plan.'

'But I do not wish to forget it.' He said this with all the conviction he had put into his earlier refusal of her suggestion that she speak with Chaucer. And when she did not reply, he judged the length of the silence, and then said in a low voice, 'You will do this small thing for me?'

'If you wish it, my Lord. But I do not like it.'

'You will like it well enough when Orleans writes his poems to you.'

This response disgusted him even as he said it. It had come to his mind a dozen times before, and every time he had told himself that he would not say it to her. But it was too late: it was said now.

He could not bear to watch her reaction. He rose immediately and walked rapidly out of the room. Then paused; then, with renewed decision, made his way to the room he had once allocated to his secretaries.

That had been before he had felt the need for a private

refuge. On their return to London from Ewelme that autumn – after a visit cut short, because neither of them had found it comfortable to be with Jeanne and her nursemaid – he had reclaimed that room for himself. He spent some time there almost every day: writing, thinking, doing nothing but being alone.

He strode across to the narrow window, set his forearm across the top of the frame and rested his forehead on it.

It was done: he had her promise. But how difficult it had been. Every step of the way he had had to judge her, to manipulate her, to coax her. And for what? So that she would perform for him the kind of minor service that many wives would do without a second thought.

Questions, always questions. She never accepted his orders immediately, but always made suggestions of her own. She argued with everything. Eventually she obeyed him, true, but in a way that made him never confident of her continuing obedience. They had been married for a year and a half and still it did not seem to him that she was his.

It had taken a year before he had risked ordering her to come with him to the Pleasance and make the acquaintance of Gloucester and his Duchess. (Chaucer had not forbidden her to do this, but he had made his dislike of it evident.) Then he had delayed and delayed again, and only now had he dared to speak to her of his desire to meet the Duke of Orleans. He had not spoken to her at all as yet of his ambition to bring about a negotiated peace in France. And that was not for lack of longing. He wanted to tell her of these things that mattered so much to him. There was nobody else he might have told.

That thought made him sad; it made him lonely.

'Back to the cells with him,' William Paston said in a weary voice. 'And the next prisoner.'

The jailer grabbed the prisoner, an old one-armed beggar, and gave him a rough yank in the direction of the courtroom door. As it opened, a second man strode in. Something about his motion made William sit up a little straighter and take a careful look.

This man was not the usual drunken layabout. He stood upright, had no obvious deformities, wore a decent tunic and was suspiciously clean: he must have bribed the jailers to let him wash. He inclined his head decorously to the assembled justices. 'Your honours,' he said strongly.

William turned to William Yelverton at his side and raised his brows slightly to ask whether Yelverton knew of the man and his circumstances. Yelverton shook his head.

'Master May?'

John May, the master jailer, had entered behind the prisoner. He scratched a stubbly head as he moved forward.

'Greenwood, your honours. James Greenwood. Charged with coining false pence and halfpence.'

'Pardon me, sirs. 'Tis Geoffrey Greenwood. My name, your honours.' The prisoner spoke again, loudly and confidently.

Thomas Wetherby leaned over from the far end of the bench. 'Well known in the city,' he said quietly. 'Runs a smithy off Nether Newport.'

William nodded. It was not uncommon for smiths to smelt down scraps of brass and copper into counterfeit coins as a sideline. He looked at the prisoner again. Geoffrey Greenwood seemed quite unabashed by the inspection and met his eyes briefly; but he focussed his attention on Wetherby and on Sir Thomas Tuddenham, who sat on William's left. William knew those signs. The bribes had gone to Suffolk's men.

'And the evidence against him?'

A succession of stallholders, innkeepers and small shopkeepers rose to give evidence of counterfeit money passing through their hands. The under-sheriff related his visit to the smithy, and his discovery of moulds for coining pence and halfpence. The justices and court officials wriggled and shuffled. They all preferred assaults and murders.

'Anything to say for yourself?'

'I have a wife and seven children, your honour. I have been in jail since the Bartholomew fair.' Greenwood paused and added, 'I have three sureties who will vouch fo me now.'

'Thank you.' The weariness had come back into William's voice. It was a foregone conclusion, he could tell; Tuddenham and Wetherby would insist on the man being released.

'Will the justices now retire to consider their verdict.' He rose and led the other men into the justices' parlour.

'Seven cases,' Thomas Wetherby said. The justices' parlour boasted a fire. He moved over to it, rubbing his hands together. Yelverton followed, while Tuddenham drifted towards the window. 'Not bad for a jail delivery. I dare say we can agree to free Greenwood with a caution, and then I think we can call it a day.'

William frowned. It was annoying, Wetherby's habit of taking the initiative from him. As the only judge on the panel of justices he nominally controlled the jail delivery himself. Not that he cared particularly about the fate of Geoffrey Greenwood, but it was dangerous to set a precedent.

Anyway, he was not yet ready to call it a day. There were other cases to be reviewed, other men in jail, and he did care about some of them. Indeed there was one case he had been particularly anxious to see come up before the justices: the ditcher, Thomas Aylmer. He had a suspicion that this was not what Wetherby and Tuddenham wanted.

'Not so soon. We must see the man Aylmer. I've heard a number of complaints about his jailing.'

Wetherby looked round. His hands mechanically continued their rubbing notion. He gave a slight shrug.

'Form complaints. I know the case you mean: a load of grumbles from the man's friends and relations.

There's no substance to them. I know the feeling of the city. Aylmer knocked down Tuddenham and offended the Countess of Suffolk. We had no option but to clap him in jail.'

'Perhaps so, but he has been there – what, twenty weeks? Thirty? That is more than long enough. His case should come before this commission.'

Yelverton's sparse red hair poked in between the two of them. 'I think we might try a private word with the Earl before taking any action on that case,' he ventured.

William glared at him. Why did Yelverton always have to pick such inopportune moments to assert his independence? And was he actually in a position to have a word with the Earl? He certainly was not himself. Suffolk had barely spoken to him when he had visited Norwich, and had not returned there since the spring. Nor did they frequently cross paths in London.

'There are proper channels for these matters,' he said. 'Justice should be seen to be done.'

Thomas Wetherby raised his heavy brows and opened his eyes wide.

'Judge Paston,' he said, in his rich, firm voice, 'you've always impressed me as a sensible man. And you're a firm believer in jailing wrongdoers to bring them to their senses, are you not? There was that man Aslake with his threats and bills; we had him in the Guildhall for ten weeks or more. And the widow who brought a petition, the one you had put in the pit at the Castle . . . ? She never came before a jail delivery till she had been there nigh on three years.'

William glowered. He did not like to be reminded of those particular cases; he did not like to be threatened either, even in a veiled way. Anyway, there had been considerably more than a few form complaints. Sir Brian Stapleton had taken up the ditcher's case, and several Aldermen opposed to Wetherby had mentioned it to him.

He was opening his mouth to retort that he had every intention of calling Aylmer and hearing his side of the story, when Sir Thomas Tuddenham stepped across from

361

the window and intervened. 'As it happens, the Earl of Suffolk will be in Norfolk next month to chair a session of the Assizes. I think that might be a suitable occasion to bring up the case. Then if the Earl wishes, he can show his clemency towards the man who insulted Lady Alice.'

'You feel no inclination to show clemency yourself? Towards the man who knocked you down in Lakenham Woods?'

Yelverton stepped in hurriedly. 'I think Sir Thomas has made an excellent suggestion.'

William began a scowl; and then, thinking, suppressed it. He was in a minority, a clear minority. With Yelverton's support he could have forced his view on the rest of the justices, but he could hardly do so without it. Damn Yelverton. A fawning flatterer, who dared not stand up for his own opinions and risk offending Tuddenham and Wetherby. Most likely he was getting work through them: from all accounts there was plenty to be had.

He himself had no particular qualms about antagonising either Tuddenham or Wetherby. They would never push work in the way of his clerks. They surely knew about his file of names, dates and places, knew he was out to make an unanswerable case against them. He had talked to too many people – not least, to John Welles – to imagine that it was still a secret.

But Suffolk; it would be a different matter to antagonise the Earl of Suffolk. He had no quarrel with Suffolk.

'In that case,' he said brusquely, 'it should be me who discusses the matter with the Earl.'

Tuddenham opened his mouth, as if to argue, and then carefully shut it again.

Shortly afterwards the justices dispersed, with Geoffrey Greenwood freed and Thomas Aylmer left to simmer in his dungeon. William strode down the Guildhall steps, in a thick humour, and found Harry Holt waiting for him, two pairs of reins in his hand, at their foot.

The Guildhall stood part-way up a shallow hill. To either side, straggling up the hill, was the maze of stalls and alleys which made up the city markets: the fishmarket, pungent and slippery, the shambles and the little row of stalls leading off it which sold black pudding and tripe, the malt market, the spicery, the herb market, needlers' row, ironmongers' row, the net market and the ropery, skeppers' row with its piles of rush baskets, the feather house with its bales of duck, goose and chicken feathers for mattresses. It was mid-afternoon, and the shouts and bangs, the smells of meat and fish and straw, of cooked pies and fresh-baked bread, all carrying sharp and strong to him on the chill winter air, seemed to proclaim the pleasures of freedom, and to set in stark contrast the horrors of the Castle pit.

'You freed the ditcher, sir?' Harry said in an eager voice.

'It was not so simple a matter,' he retorted. He took Blazon's reins and busied himself in mounting.

'Sir Brian will be sorry to hear that, sir.'

'I am sorry for it myself.'

That drove Harry to silence. As soon as William was comfortably settled, his grey skirts arrayed over the saddle, the groom mounted his own horse and they began to ride together back to Princes Inn.

How true, he thought: it had not been simple at all. He knew there had been a time when his concept of justice had been as sharp and bright as Geoffrey Greenwood's counterfeit halfpennies. No more. The writing on this coin was blurred with long use. He knew now that it was no easy business to establish guilt and innocence, right and wrong.

The ditcher had hit Tuddenham, no doubt about that. Thus far, Tuddenham's spite was justified. But he had had good reason for hitting Tuddenham, if the tales told in the taverns were to be believed. And even if it had been a crime, what punishment fitted it? Thirty weeks in the pit with the rats? Or a return blow, a great deal harder, from John Heydon, that upstanding young lawyer whom nobody appeared to think had committed a crime?

He picked up these issues and tried to weigh them. But they were slimy: they slipped through his fingers.

In any case it was not, curse it, a question only of proper verdicts and fit punishments. It was a question of enforcement. When justice was not backed by might it was no better than a deed to a property on which another man was firmly installed.

His thoughts turned naturally from the ditcher to Tuddenham; and from that crater-faced individual to the Earl of Suffolk. It was not corrupt, he thought, but realistic, to make efforts to appease powerful men. Do otherwise, and he would lose all his authority. He could not lose his position as judge, but he could find himself overlooked when commissions were drawn up, find the doors of men such as Gloucester and Beaufort shut fast against him.

I sit in judgement at the courts, thought William, and I feel the sensation of absolute power; it seems to me then as if I alone can control men's destinies. Men see that, men like Harry: they see me give verdicts and pass sentences. What they do not see is that it is an illusion. I look at my chest full of indictments against Thomas Wetherby, and I know that in truth I have no power at all. The real power lies where it has always lain: with men such as the Earl of Suffolk. I am merely its instrument.

He needed Suffolk. He had survived the loss of Norfolk as a patron, but he could not survive if he incurred Suffolk's enmity also. It seemed to him, though, that Suffolk also needed him.

This was at the heart of his annoyance: the feeling that the Earl should have courted him, and the knowledge that he had done nothing of the kind. Outright bribery was not necessary (though a man who wanted a judge in his pocket naturally had to pay to put him there), but Suffolk could have paid him attention, flattered him, given his clerks occasional work, shown favour to his sons. He had done none of this.

William reckoned he knew why. Tuddenham was to blame. Tuddenham was his enemy and he believed that Tuddenham was doing all he could to ensure that he and Suffolk should find themselves at cross purposes, and remain so thereafter.

Tuddenham had to be outwitted, that was what it came to. Strike a deal with Tuddenham and he would be demeaning himself, setting at risk his hard-won reputation for fairness and independence. But perhaps he could strike a deal with Suffolk himself? That way he might even win a chance to engineer Tuddenham's downfall.

He had dimly sensed this at the end of the argument in the justices' parlour, but now he saw it clearly. He had to win Suffolk's support, and from that everything else would come. If he had Suffolk's ear, he could both make fair judgements and enforce them. If he had Suffolk's ear he could set his folder of names, dates and places in front of the one man who would not only appreciate its contents, but be able to act on them.

If he had Suffolk's ear, then he could see Thomas Aylmer freed. No; no, freeing Thomas Aylmer might lose, not gain him Suffolk's favour. Instead he should show Suffolk that he had the power to determine Aylmer's fate, should discover what the Earl's real wishes were – and then enforce them, whether it came down to freeing the man or to hanging him.

Heroic? No. But what was Thomas Aylmer's fate to a man who had dedicated himself to a fight against Tuddenham and Wetherby, against the Aslake gang and the Nowell gang, against the truly powerful forces of corruption and brutality in the county? Thomas Aylmer was small beer. If necessary he could be sacrificed.

He and Harry turned down Elm Hill and a moment later they rode through the gate and into the yard of Princes Inn. They dismounted and Harry took the horses. William hesitated. He thought for a moment of going to the clerks' room. He wanted to talk to someone, to test out these newly formed ideas; but he could not conceivably talk to the clerks. It would have been Yelverton once, but no more, no more.

He had it. He should talk to Agnes.

He found Agnes in her usual place in the hall, sitting in a comfortable chair with one eye on the servants and the other on the mending she had taken from the overflowing basket at her side. She dismissed the servants when she took in his expression, but the mending she kept working on while she heard him out. He watched her. Her fingers flew in and out of the flimsy material: she was darning one of little Lizzy's dresses. Every thrust of the needle was forceful, every thrust accurate.

He watched her face, too. She muttered under her breath as she worked. He thought at first that she was repeating his arguments, but then he realised that she was merely counting her stitches. He could see the deep lines around her mouth that made it look as if she were scowling even when her face was in repose. He caught occasional glimpses of her predatory pink tongue. That sight aroused him, but it was less than a month since her last miscarriage: no prospect of satisfaction there.

He told her everything, accurately and at length, from Geoffrey Greenwood's first appearance to his final thoughts as he turned into Princes Inn. She did not interrupt him at all, though she nodded occasionally to show that she was listening.

She came to the end of her thread and bent to bite short the loose end.

'I thought at first to make an appointment with Suffolk when he comes to Norwich, but I'll not risk Tuddenham edging me out. I'll be travelling to London next Monday. He has a house in Lombard Street, I'll call on him there.'

'No.'

'No?'

Agnes measured another length of thread off her roll, bit it off and guided the end through the eye of her needle. She knotted the end. And looked up at him

366

again. This time, she met his eye. 'You are a fool, William Paston.'

Damn the woman. Nobody else spoke to him in such terms. But he waited, to see how she would justify her verdict.

'You saw it, and then you overlooked it. You can get the better of Tuddenham in another way. It is all plain to see.'

'It is?'

'There is no real need of a jail delivery to see a man such as Aylmer released?'

'No, not in this case. No formal charge has been brought against him. There are other ways of freeing him.'

'Then you free the man.'

'Free the man?'

'Quite so.'

'And if that proves to anger the Earl of Suffolk?'

Agnes turned over the little mass of cloth, searching for the right spot. She plunged in her needle; not angrily, but with the same sharp competence she always showed. 'If the Earl of Suffolk wished the man to rot in the pit, then doubtless he will be angry. But with you?'

Slowly, he came to it. 'With Tuddenham.'

'For failing to prevent it. Quite so.'

The thought flowered in his mind. It was a beautiful argument. Quite, quite beautiful.

'Agnes Paston,' he said, 'you are a marvel.'

Agnes looked up at him. She smiled, then widened it, then let it turn into a laugh. William found himself laughing too. They sat together, in the hall at Princes Inn, with the sound of that marvellous laughter echoing in the air around them.

14

ENGLAND

In the upper room at Fastolf Place which he shared with
Harry, John Kirtling and the rest of Fastolf's Southwark
servants, Secret Poursuivant knelt over the leather pack
which he always carried with him. He unfastened the
buckles, drew back the straps and flipped up the flap
that held its contents safe.

He pulled out his best blue and gold tabard and shook
it. He took it to the narrow dormer and opened the
shutters so that he could look it over. It was undeniably
grubby. He gave it an experimental whack against the
rough brick wall. A cloud of dust flew out. He whacked
again, and again, then rechecked it at the dormer. That
was marginally better; but there was still a winestain on
the sleeve, mud near the hem.

His fault. He had only possessed this tabard for the
two years since Fastolf had reinstated him; its predecessor, grubbier still, had been lost to the bandits between
Corbeil and Paris. That one had lasted for six years, so
there was no looking to Fastolf to order him a replace-
ment for a long time to come.

And no time to spend his own savings on such a thing,
even had he the inclination to do so. It would have to
suffice: he would have to hope Garter was too occupied
to notice its condition. He went down to the kitchens to
beg a cloth and water to scrub at the worst stains.

He washed his face too, even doused his head under
the pump and rubbed some black soap into his hair. Meg
hacked the front into a straight, short fringe. He dressed

in a newly washed undershirt and clean (though darned) hose, slipped the offending tabard over his head, arranging it in the prescribed fashion for poursuivants with the sleeves hanging down his chest and back, and went down to the stables. He had already negotiated with John Payn: a fifth of his fee for the loan of the best grey mare.

Fastolf Place was very quiet. Harry and the rest had all been commandeered by John Welles to help erect the tableaux. Welles had tried to enlist him too, but he had bluntly refused. He was a poursuivant, and on state occasions poursuivants had a prescribed role to play. They received good fees, also. He had only to find Anjou or Garter at Deptford, persuade them that his appearance passed muster, and that fee would be his.

The grey mare was taller than the nags that were his usual lot, but docile and a pleasure to ride. He smiled to himself. It would be rare entertainment, the trip to Deptford and back.

It was a cold but fine February day, and it was still early when he reached Deptford. The High Street was crowded, though the King's procession had not yet come into view. It would be a small procession, he knew: the King was riding this far with only the escort that had brought him from France. Then at Deptford he would be joined by the multitude of monks and priests who would accompany him through Kent and into the City, by trumpeters, heralds and poursuivants, and by a thousand more curious souls of both high and low estate.

He edged the grey mare past a flock of Benedictines, through a gaggle of Carmelites. Ahead of him he saw a bright golden flash: the metallic thread of a herald's tabard, catching the sun as he moved. He made for this and found that it was Suffolk Herald, mounted on a good black gelding.

Suffolk stared at him appraisingly and then nodded.

'They told me Anjou was this way.' Suffolk turned the gelding and rode off. Secret followed.

They soon found Anjou and the other officers of arms, except for Garter, who was riding with the King. Anjou gave them a brief glance, then turned to them again, his face showing surprise that Secret should be there, hesitated and turned away. It hurt Secret, but he had expected it. At least he had his acknowledgement.

Anjou had with him a clerk who wrote their names on his list and told them in a surly manner that they could collect their fee at Westminster two days hence. He told them where to wait. They waited.

'They say,' said Suffolk Herald, 'that the boy has grown tall. I've not seen him since the English coronation.'

'Nor I.' That was more than two years before. Henry had been in France for most, but not all of that time, but it was no matter: they would not have seen him if he had been in England.

'Curious?' the Herald asked.

'A little.'

He was by no means as awestruck as John Welles, but it was true, he was curious. Power and money fascinated him, and King Henry was a potent symbol of both. Thousands of men had died already, that Henry of Lancaster might have his dual crown; thousands of pounds had been expended so that the boy could be crowned in Paris. He wondered, in a detached way, whether these events might have succeeded in gilding with a kingly aura what he recalled as a rather unprepossessing child.

There was a power to the occasion, at least: to the priests murmuring their Ave Marias, the guildsmen resplendent in their processional gear, even the ordinary citizens of Deptford shouting cheerfully to each other across the road which the serjeants had cleared and roped for the King. There was a sense of expectation, not so different to the dead hour before a battle.

And the trumpets, when they sounded, faint down the Kent Road, were not so different from battle trumpets. There was the familiar cloud of dust, though

Henry's procession moved far more slowly than a line of men at arms on the attack; the familiar thud of massed horses' hooves. It was beginning: the King was coming.

The King came. He rode past the spot where the heralds waited and stopped to receive greetings from the Deptford guildsmen. Anjou rode up behind Suffolk and Secret and told them to move further down the road, but they risked ignoring him: they could see well from where they were positioned, and they wanted to see.

It seemed to Secret that Gloucester was the dominant figure. He sat astride a huge black destrier, several hands higher than the rest. His fur-lined cloak was thrown back to show off a doublet of blue and yellow velvet figured with gold and thick with jewels. His hat, blue velvet too, dipped down over his forehead. At his side sat Eleanor his Duchess, that scandal personified. Her cloak was of scarlet, her tall hennin was veiled in white gauze and her gown was of gold-encrusted white satin.

There was Garter King of Arms, the golden lilies and leopards of his tabard vivid in the sunlight. Archbishop Kemp, the Chancellor and senior cleric in the escort, wore his finest robes. The bishops, the squires, the trumpeters: all was magnificence and colour. All, except for the small boy who sat between Gloucester and Kemp, on an improbably large white mare, his hands clenched on the reins. He wore a sober tunic of dark blue, bare of adornment, cut long over his knees. A narrow circlet of gold was set on his neat brown head.

Secret was close enough to be able to make out his expression. It was gentle, rather blank. He thought to himself that young Henry was not overawed by the tumult around him. The boy seemed subdued, rather; slightly detached.

The cheers of the crowd were thunderous. The guildsmen stood speechless; a multitude of monks and nuns fought with each other to reach the small space in front of the King and do him reverence. Henry sat looking down on them all; and his only response was this expression of gentle indifference.

There was, thought Secret, nothing feigned about it. The boy was just that: indifferent to it all.

Garter was a fine judge of the moment when the crescendo peaked. He motioned to the serjeants to clear the road once more. Secret and Suffolk Herald followed his signal and made their way with the other officers of arms, Exeter Herald, Clarenceaux King of Arms, Bien Alaunt, Warwick's poursuivant, Gloucester Herald, and a dozen others, to the head of the procession. Gloucester, Kemp and the rest drew the King back into their midst. The monks and nuns slowly fell in behind; the trumpets and clarions sounded; and at a slow walking pace, the King of England and France and his vastly expanded retinue continued on their way to London.

Suffolk Herald nudged his gelding into a pace closer to Secret's mare. There was noise all around them: the heralds chattering, the monks reciting their prayers and thanksgivings, the nobles whispering to each other. Any conversation they held would not be overheard.

''Tis true, then: he has gained no taste for it.'

'For statecraft? He looks a solitary boy. One to take more pleasure in his toy soldiers than his real ones.'

'Aye, and in going to mass with his chaplain. Mind, they should never have banished his mother. An unsuitable influence, they said, but she might have made something of him, and Warwick has scarcely done that.'

'He is still young.'

Suffolk shrugged. 'He's a twice-crowned king, and now he must act like one. Not that this farce has done anything to appease the French.'

'It was not intended for the French.'

'You think not? Then you misread Gloucester and Bedford. I have it from Anjou that they invited every nobleman in France. And how many came?'

None. Or none that counted, in any event. Everyone now knew that, in France and in England. The Valois sympathisers had scarcely been expected, and it had been no great surprise when the Duke of Brittany had declined his invitation; but it was far more significant that the Duke of Burgundy, England's chief ally in France, should have chosen to stay away, leaving Louis of Luxembourg, his Anglophile liegeman, as his most senior representative.

Suffolk knew all this, doubtless, so Secret did not trouble to mention it.

'They say the food at the banquets was atrocious,' he said instead.

'The army stewards arranged it. Cooked days in advance, most of it, and stinking even before they set it on the table.'

'And there were riots on the streets . . .'

'Aye. After the banquets, and later, when the King left. They expected him in Paris to abolish the salt tax and release prisoners, and he did nothing such. Some men even believed he would throw money into the crowd as he rode past.'

'That shows a sore lack of understanding.'

'Aye, but starving men do not think like chancellors. I take it that Mayor Welles has a better understanding of what is required of him?'

Secret looked Suffolk over carefully. Suffolk looked innocently back.

'I take it,' Secret said, 'that he has.'

Half London, it seemed, had followed the Mayor to the Black Heath. The serjeants had shuffled the crowd into some kind of an order, drawing those who had obeyed the order to wear guild livery to the front, and banishing the most disreputable to the fringes. Between the two banks of spectators, a long passage had been carved. The King would be sucked like a honey bee into the heart of a hybrid rose in shades of red and white with flashes of gold.

Secret knew every detail of the dispositions, for he had seen Welles going over the plans again and again with the serjeants. Nearest the Canterbury road waited the Sheriffs and Aldermen of the City of London, resplendent in furred scarlet with sanguine hoods. The guilds-men were in white gowns with scarlet hoods, their devices embroidered on their sleeves. At the rear lingered the merchants from Florence, from Genoa and Venice, Pisa and Milan, brilliant in their national costumes.

The officers of arms fanned out into a semicircle, with the trumpeters at either end. The nobles took their place in the centre; the monks and nuns and onlookers shuffled to a halt behind them. The trumpets sounded triumphantly. And a plump figure in scarlet spurred his brown mare and galloped towards them, across the springy grass of the heath, with his attendants at its heels.

Secret had rarely seen Welles on horseback; never before seen him exceed a leisurely amble. He hoped Welles was not aware that he cut a ridiculous figure.

The Mayor was gasping with the exertion by the time he reached their position in the vale. Garter took pity on him and ordered another blast of trumpets to give him time to recover before greeting the King.

By the time the last blaring note had faded away, the redness in Welles' face was subsiding, though his breath was still laboured. He brought his mare round and stopped it a pace in front of the King. He reached out a hand to his furred hat and swept it low to one side, bowing as deeply as he dared without risk of losing his balance. He had no intention of dismounting, Secret realised: this was his moment of glory and he intended to keep the centre stage. The King gave him a grave nod in return, and the Mayor, following Garter's signals, turned to lead the procession across the heath.

When they reached the London crowd they halted for the speeches. Welles repeated his bow. And with hat in hand and hands clenched on his reins, he recited the words that Secret had heard him practise so often: 'Sovereign Lord and noble King, Ye be welcome out of your Reign of France into this your blessed Realm of England, and in special unto your most notable City of

London, otherwise called your Chamber. We thank God of the good and gracious arraigning of your crown of France, beseeching his Merciful Grace to send you prosperity and many years, to the comfort of all your loving people.'

The crowd could not have heard a word, but they clapped and cheered wildly. John Welles, his cheeks growing still redder, bowed in gracious acknowledgement. Secret thought to himself that there was no doubt in the grocer's mind that the cheers were primarily for him.

'He is with the King now, my Lord. He left his room not five minutes ago.'

'Thank you.' Suffolk dug into his pocket and withdrew two pennies. 'You will show me the way?'

'Follow me, my Lord.'

The page cast a furtive glance up and down the corridor, then set off at a fast trot. Suffolk followed. They turned a corner, and another, ascended a flight of stairs, and another.

'In here, my Lord.'

'Thank you.'

As the page seemed to be waiting expectantly, he dug again and produced another penny. The page bowed and withdrew. He pushed open the door.

It was a small room, at the very top of one of the towers of Westminster Palace. The walls were entirely covered in hangings. There was a fire, lit much earlier in the day from the look of the embers, and now banked high to await Gloucester's return. At one side of the fireplace there was a low chair, padded with purple cushions; at the other, an even lower footstool. A small carved table stood against the wall. There were no other furnishings. But still, he thought, it was furnished more richly by far than the rest of the palace; and it was warmer, too.

He was cold from his wait in the corridor: he went to sit in the chair. Then it occurred to him that Gloucester might return very soon, so he rose and walked to the window. He began to pace up and down, slowly, abstractedly.

Would the King question the appointments? He found it hard to tell. From all accounts Gloucester found it difficult to deal with the King's childish idealism, but Henry was still too young to show real independence, and in no position to question the Lord Protector's judgement when it was backed up by the Council. Nor would he fully understand the implications, surely. Gloucester kept him under tight control: even Suffolk himself had had no opportunity to speak privately with him since his return from France four days earlier, and Lord Cromwell, the most vehement opponent of the changes (he was to be deprived of his post as Chamberlain) had been kept out of the palace completely. Nobody would have been able to take Henry aside and explain to him that his uncle was packing his Household with his own supporters in order to strengthen his position against Cardinal Beaufort.

Still, Gloucester would be nervous until everything was signed: he could not afford to incur a setback. Then when the appointments were confirmed he would return to his room, full of relief, and find Suffolk waiting there for him. He would know instinctively that Suffolk had come to demand his own reward for the support he had given in the Council – on this, and on various other issues – and he would not be pleased at that thought. Then Suffolk would outline the favour he wished to receive, and Gloucester would be so relieved that it involved no financial outlay, no further reshuffle of appointments, that he would surely grant it without further question.

So Suffolk had calculated. But he too was nervous, for he too could not afford to incur a setback. He had tried several other channels, and he knew now that he could only achieve his aim with Gloucester's assistance.

He stopped his pacing and reached into his pocket for the poem. He glanced at his hand and realised to his annoyance that he had pulled out two papers: one was the poem, the other the letter Chaucer had written him, begging him to oppose Gloucester in the Council.

Damn Chaucer. He could not afford to oppose Gloucester. He was still working to prove that he was not Beaufort's man, and to do that it had been necessary to set his course towards Gloucester's side of the stream. Even then he sensed that Gloucester felt no warmth towards him – and he himself felt a certain contempt for the Duke, which Gloucester quite possibly sensed – so whatever Chaucer imagined, the two of them were not intimates, or even natural allies. If he had voted against the appointments Gloucester would have taken him to be an enemy, and he could not afford that, even if Beaufort were to return to England and regain a share of the power. Beaufort might not return. Bedford had obliged him to divert the army he had assembled for his crusade against the Hussites to guard Paris while the King was there. The Cardinal desperately needed to appease the Pope, who had not taken this well.

He shoved the letter back among the folds of his doublet and unfolded the poem. Alice had written it out for him: he had thought even of this small detail. 'Quant je fus prins ou pavillon': it was genuinely Alice's favourite.

My lady, fine and beautiful. Alice had worked hard to help him get Orleans. She had made many copies of the poems he had shown her, and given them to Eleanor of Gloucester, to Lady Warwick, and to a score of other influential court ladies. She had had Gilles set several of them to music and had practised singing them with Lucette. He did not pretend to himself that he was doing this for Alice, but he was glad to know that it would bring her pleasure too if he succeeded.

A door banged, not far away. He jumped and folded the sheet in two. He heard footsteps scuttling down the corridor. The door opened. The page slipped through and held it open for Gloucester.

Gloucester saw Suffolk as soon as he entered the room. He cast him a look of mild annoyance and dropped into

377

the low chair. He gave the page a terse order for mulled wine and the boy disappeared.

'The King signed?'

'Naturally.' Gloucester set his feet on the fender and reached out his hands to the fire. 'Chilly in the King's rooms,' he said. 'They are all good choices. He has no grounds for complaint.'

'I am sure it gives him just the Household he wishes for.'

Gloucester did not look up again. 'And so he should have. There is no reason why Parliament should dictate these appointments now that the King has been crowned.'

'None at all. I am sure nobody will say a word against your arrangements.'

Gloucester turned limpid grey eyes on him. 'How pleasant to be reassured of your support.'

Suffolk gazed back. He went to sit on the stool at the opposite side of the hearth. 'Of course,' he said softly, 'there is the matter of my own recompense.'

Gloucester's face froze, barely perceptibly. He permitted himself to frown. 'The court positions are newly filled. I cannot conceivably make changes now that I have the King's approval. And Parliament is likely to protest if the Crown makes any more grants of land this year.'

'My dear Humphrey, you know I have no desire for a court appointment at present.'

Gloucester gave him an irritated look, as if to say that though he had frequently been reassured of just that, he had never quite succeeded in believing it. 'Forgive me,' he said, 'if I find it difficult to guess what other recompense I could give you.'

'My fault entirely. I believed I had mentioned it to you. It is for Alice. I promised her I would tender for the guardianship of the Duke of Orleans.'

Gloucester reacted slowly. He opened his eyes wider. Then he lay back in the low chair, half closed his eyes and appeared to consider this suggestion.

'Orleans will never be set free. Certainly not until the King is of age; and not even then if I have my way. In France he would be too powerful.' He opened his eyes a little more and focussed his gaze on Suffolk. 'It could be dangerous to know him even as a prisoner.'

'I had not thought of it as a political matter. Alice values Orleans' poetry. She covets him as part of her literary circle. She sends you a copy of one of the Duke's poems, which she has written out herself.'

'Indeed?' Gloucester's hand barely reached out: Suffolk had to lean well forward to put the paper into it. The Duke unfolded it with one hand and glanced dismissively over the lines of the rondeau.

'I admire it too.'

Gloucester looked at the paper again. He read some of it aloud, slowly, in a heavily ironic voice:

> Je rougiz comme vermillon,
> Aussi flambant que une estincelle,
> Quant je fus prins ou pavillon.

He let the sheet drop on to his outstretched legs and raised his eyes to Suffolk.

Caught in the trap, Suffolk thought. He imagines that of me. He thinks I truly have some political reason for wishing to meet Orleans; he thinks he has seen through my smokescreen of pretty poems and glimpsed a plot with the Dauphin's supporters, or something such. Gloucester is a fool; his hatred for all the French is the thing that maddens me most about him.

Gloucester rose to his feet, leaving the paper to fall to the floor. 'You should look to the Italians, Suffolk. That's where my interests are moving these days. The French are old-fashioned in comparison.'

He went to the window, turning his back on Suffolk. Suffolk stared at him. Gloucester's legs were set slightly apart. He was growing fat about the middle. His chin was tilted upwards: he was not looking out of the window, simply turning his back to express his contempt. A flame of anger stirred inside Suffolk, not on his own account, but for Orleans, and for the poem so carefully composed and so lightly discarded.

It was ironic, and worse than ironic, that Gloucester should be so completely mistaken. He had had neither the time nor the information to think beyond Orleans' poetry. He had no idea whether gaining access to the Duke would help or hinder his peace plans. Gloucester knew little about those plans – he had realised months before that the Duke was completely unsympathetic to them, and had kept his confidences to a minimum – but now the Duke was suspicious. He knew he ought to abandon the plan to get Orleans in order to allay that suspicion. But he could not bring himself to do that.

'Alas,' he said as lightly as he could, 'there are no distinguished Florentine prisoners to bid for.'

'True,' Gloucester murmured in an abstracted way. He turned and stood for a moment staring at the door. The page returned with a tray and two cups of mulled wine. He placed these on the table, bowed and withdrew again.

'You know what Cornwall receives? As his fee?'

'I have made enquiries.' That was easily checked; no sense in denying it. 'It is a fair price for the contract, but I believe the Duke's security could be improved. For the same fee I shall provide two more jailers.'

'The same fee?' Gloucester went to the table. He picked up the cups and presented one to Suffolk. His eyes met Suffolk's. They were cold and hard as two pebbles on the beach. 'But it is normal, I believe, for a competing tender to set a lower fee?'

Yes, it was normal. But he asked this as a favour. Gloucester knew of his financial problems. It would not suit Gloucester either if he was forced to look for help from Thomas Chaucer to solve them. He had been prepared to settle for a level fee, but a reduction would hurt. 'I could ask my secretary to consult the records.'

'That will scarcely be necessary. Shall we say, a ten per cent reduction? I think that is fair.'

It was not fair, it was hard. But he could not afford to say so, and they both knew it.

'Then it is agreed? I shall talk to the Council Clerk tomorrow.'

Alice came to Suffolk, a month later, in his upper room at Bardi Place. She rarely interrupted him there. He turned with surprise when he heard her footsteps on the stairs, laid down his pen on his table and waited until she knocked quietly on the door and pushed it open.

'Yes?'

Alice came into the room. She was wearing her green gown, one of his favourites, and a simple headdress that framed her neat features like a halo. A little frown puckered her forehead.

'My Lord, I have heard a disturbing tale from your herald.'

He rose to his feet. 'What tale is that?'

'About the Cardinal. They say that Gloucester had his baggage searched at Sandwich and has seized plate and jewels that he claims do not belong to him.'

'I too have heard that tale.' He crossed to where Alice stood and took her hands. 'It is disturbing, but there is an explanation. Gloucester claims the plate was taken illegally, as surety for a loan. The Cardinal may take the matter to the courts. If the plate is proved to be his it will be restored to him.'

'But even so, this comes so soon after the Serjeants petitioned to have him resign his see. It is true, surely, that Gloucester is plotting to see him ruined.'

'I doubt it will prove so easy to ruin Cardinal Beaufort.' Suffolk gave an uneasy laugh. 'Gloucester plans no more, I suspect, than to weaken the Cardinal's position in the Council. But it is disturbing, even so, and I have begun enquiries already to discover what lies behind this.'

'My father relies upon you to defend the Cardinal.'

'I am aware of that.'

'So I may tell him that you will do all that you can?'

The frown was fading; Alice looked up at him trustingly. He hesitated: he did not want to lie to her. 'You may tell him that I am investigating these matters; and that I shall discuss them with him shortly.'

Alice's eyes dropped. He sensed that she was measuring this response. 'He will be glad of that, my Lord,' she said in a low voice. 'And you will tell me, if you discover any more?'

'If you wish to know.'

'I do.' She gave him a gay smile. 'Now I shall leave you to finish with your papers.'

'I'll be down to the hall shortly to hear your new song.'

'Do. Lucette and I have been practising it all morning.' She leaned forward and kissed his cheek, swiftly, awkwardly. Then she loosed her hands and left the room.

Suffolk stood there, looking at the door, after she had gone. Damn the herald. He should not have told her that. Though someone else would have done, he knew, if the herald had not, for the tale was spreading fast. Damn Gloucester. He never acted with moderation. He had already strengthened his position, he was firmly in control of the Council, but he was pressing on and on with his attacks against Beaufort.

And why? Had these new attacks not been made it was conceivable that Beaufort would have stayed on the continent and attempted to patch up his relations with the Pope. Now he would be forced to return and defend himself. He was a rich man, but he was also a covetous one: he would never submit to resigning Winchester and losing six years' back revenues, on the flimsy excuse that a couple of earlier bishops had resigned when they received their red hats, fifty years and more before. He was proud: he would not tolerate being treated as a common smuggler.

Surely it was against Gloucester's interests, though, to have Beaufort return? Surely he was not such a fool, and his advisors too, that he had failed to think the matter through?

It was four days since Suffolk had heard of this latest attack, and ever since he had been investigating, as he had told Alice, to discover what lay behind it. His enquiries so far had told him little. Men at Westminster murmured that destroying Beaufort's fortune was a popular move: wealthy churchmen were not loved. They whispered that Beaufort would be left with fewer resources with which to bribe his supporters. Both of these were true, but it seemed to Suffolk that they were insufficient as explanations. There had to be a deeper reason.

He returned to his table and sat down once more. His account books were spread out in front of him. He looked at them and frowned. Whatever difficulties Beaufort faced, the Cardinal's financial position could scarcely be as disastrous as his own.

Matters had been growing steadily worse ever since his return to England. That was not Tuddenham's fault. The agent had done well in increasing the revenues from his estates, but his expenses had also increased. From every side new claims were being laid on his funds and his attention. Nor was Alice merely careless with money: she was appallingly extravagant. Chaucer had taught her to enjoy the best, but he had not taught her to weigh the cost when choosing clothes, furnishings, or servants. Bardi Place had cost a fortune to refurbish; the roof at Wingfield was still leaking and urgently needed replacing; every trip to Ewelme, to Cossey, to his other estates, involved a huge caravan of men and possessions that seemed to consume marks, nobles and pounds with every step it took.

He had been slowly coming to the conclusion that he could not afford to remain neutral any more. When Chaucer died and Alice came into her inheritance his problems would be solved, but he could not wait until that happened. He had to have a patron. He had to have money, and he could only obtain that money either from Chaucer and Beaufort, or from Gloucester. But Gloucester's distrust of him, first made apparent when he had asked for Orleans' custodianship, seemed to have intensified since; and he hesitated to choose to submit to Chaucer's pressure, or to support Beaufort when the Cardinal was in such a weak position.

Why was Gloucester attacking Beaufort so intemperately? Why? He stared at the grim rows of figures and suddenly an idea came to him.

He played with this idea as he went down to the hall; it filled his head as he listened to Alice and Lucette singing their songs. When their songs were over he called for his grooms, had his horse readied and set off for Westminster.

He went to the Treasurer of the King's Council and asked to inspect the accounts. This he knew to be a privilege open to any Council member, though few used it. He looked carefully at the figures. He wrote many of them down, returned to his upper room and made some calculations of his own. Then he sat back, satisfied. He understood now.

It was so simple, so obvious, though he had heard it said nowhere in London or Westminster. The exchequer's annual deficit was running at around twenty thousand pounds a year, several times the King's regular annual income. Gloucester had to take drastic measures, or a financial crisis would bring an abrupt end to his administration. He needed Beaufort's fortune.

It struck him as a pretty irony that Gloucester should be in worse financial straits even than he was himself. He found it only too understandable that Gloucester would act in strange and vicious ways in order to obtain money. He had come close to doing the same himself. Why, when Gloucester had bargained down his fee for guarding Orleans – but that had not after all been malice, he now realised: the Protector was using dirty tricks against friend and enemy alike.

It was, Suffolk thought to himself, Gloucester's great weakness that neither he nor his King should be a rich man. The Duke's moderate fortune had all been squandered on the Pleasance; Henry of Lancaster's father had expended his on the fields of northern France. And Gloucester had to maintain his and Henry's position in the face of opposition, overt or covert, from two very much richer men: one, Cardinal Beaufort, the other, the Duke of York.

Stinging Beaufort, paring fees, would do no more than win Gloucester a few months. It would take more than that to end a crisis of such proportions.

The situation would ease once the King was of age. Taxes would be easier to raise then. The King would marry and his wife bring him a dowry. The Valois prisoners – including the Duke of Orleans and the Duke of Bourbon – could be ransomed. But these events were still many years off. How did Gloucester plan to survive those years?

If he negotiated with the Valois, Suffolk thought, he might persuade the Dauphin to provide money in return for territorial concessions. It was an interesting thought that while reason alone might not lead Gloucester to the negotiating table, the need for money might. He himself would not have supported this policy, however: he detested the thought of bargaining away the King's French inheritance. He had never wanted Henry to lose France: his aim was to see the King secure what he could of it in the only practicable way.

He could see only one other possibility. Various rich lords and merchants might help His Highness by lending him substantial sums: with good security, naturally, and at very acceptable rates of interest.

There were large profits to be made in that game: was Beaufort himself not proof of that? Suffolk needed to make large profits. It occurred to him that he might present his findings to Gloucester and suggest to the Duke that he might make his share and more of these loans. He might present his findings to Gloucester, and suggest to the Duke that it would be inadvisable for them to be made public. He might indicate a certain wardship that he would be glad to be granted; an estate or two over which he would happily act as trustee.

In this way he might obtain Gloucester as a patron, in spite of their mutual dislike and distrust. Mind, that would not gain him an ally who would further his aims for France. Gloucester had made it very clear that he was opposed to negotiations: he still believed that Bedford's forces might one day take the whole of France. Gloucester knew – Suffolk had told him, and so had many other men – that it was only a matter of time before Burgundy deserted Henry for the Dauphin. The signs were clear: Burgundy's failure to attend the coronation had been only the last of many. But Gloucester still refused to accept that it was vital to negotiate before this disaster took place.

Gloucester had to be persuaded, though. Negotiations over France could not be pushed through in the teeth of Gloucester's opposition. As for Beaufort: he had still had no opportunity to sound out Beaufort's attitude to France, since the Cardinal was not yet back in England. If Beaufort were to lose his power and influence, though – as he might well do, if Suffolk did not defend him – his attitude would come to be of no importance.

It was apparent to Suffolk that to lean on Gloucester was an unsavoury course of action, but nevertheless it tempted him. But then he remembered Alice's little frown as she had spoken to him of the Cardinal, and he thought to himself that if Alice were to discover what he planned she would be deeply upset.

Should he swallow his pride and go to Chaucer after all? He might undertake to defend Beaufort against Gloucester, in return for the promise of money from the Cardinal or from Chaucer himself. He might tell Chaucer what he had learned of Gloucester's motives and leave Chaucer to make good use of that information. Gloucester might be discredited as a result; but it was difficult to imagine his being so thoroughly discredited that his attitude to France would become an irrelevance.

At any rate he would have to speak soon to Chaucer. He had promised Alice that he would.

*

Suffolk knew that it had cost more than he could easily afford to win the contract to guard the Duke of Orleans, but by early that summer it was all agreed. Orleans would come first to Bardi Place. Then, once the castle repairs had been completed, he would be moved to the greater security of Wingfield.

Alice was elated. With every poem of the Duke's that she read, she became more enthused at the prospect of meeting him. She continually repeated to Suffolk, to Thomas Chaucer, even to Eleanor of Gloucester, Suffolk suspected, that it was above all her efforts that were bringing Orleans to Bardi Place.

Did she truly believe this? He honestly did not know. He never suggested otherwise to her. He wanted her to feel that she had been useful to him. But he suspected that Alice knew – as did everybody else whose judgement mattered – that though they both wanted Orleans, it was he who had bought them the Duke. The price had been his, and his alone, to pay.

His uneasiness at Gloucester's suspicion of him and his motives clouded his enthusiasm at the prospect of Orleans' arrival; but even so, he looked forward eagerly to meeting the Duke. He found it difficult to be patient, to keep his distance while Orleans was being installed in Lombard Street.

He had to be patient. He dared not let anyone, least of all Orleans himself, know how much the approaching meeting meant to him. He forced himself to create business at Westminster and Eltham and Windsor, so that he would be away from London for the vital two weeks while the Duke was settling in.

And while he was at Westminster, he went to visit Thomas Chaucer.

'In here, my Lord. Master Chaucer will be with you shortly.'

Thomas Chaucer's boy ushered Suffolk into the front parlour of Thomas Chaucer's Westminster house. He closed the door behind him. Suffolk was left alone.

Chaucer knows this to be damnably discourteous, he thought with annoyance. It is contrary to all social practice for a merchant to keep an earl waiting. But every time I come to his house he does it.

As he had done before while waiting in Chaucer's parlour, he went to the window and looked out. On the road below, a continual stream of the traders and servants of Westminster passed by. Down there it was all bustle. It had been all bustle in the Palace, too; but it was pleasantly peaceful in Chaucer's parlour.

He turned his back on the bustle. He moved a pile of cushions and sat down on the window seat in the space he had cleared. He looked at the cushions, heaped opposite him. On each one was embroidered either Chaucer's unicorn couchant or the lion couchant of the Burghershes, Alice's mother's family.

Everywhere in this house, he thought, I see symbols of the harsh reality that Chaucer is never so vulgar as to put into words, but never so unworldly as to ignore: that my family fortune was lost at Jargeau, and that his estates will eventually go to make up the deficiency.

He did not hate Thomas Chaucer, he reminded himself. Chaucer was not his enemy. Chaucer was a supporter of Henry of Lancaster; Chaucer was the father of Alice. They were players on the same side in the same game. It was in Chaucer's interest, too, that the Earl and Countess of Suffolk should thrive.

It was in his own interest to appease Chaucer. He would have to be deferential to Chaucer and bury his exasperation. He would have to provide the explanations that Chaucer demanded, though he would certainly tailor them as he saw fit. He had begun to feel revolted at the thought of cooking up an underhand deal with Gloucester; in many ways, he felt, it would be better to agree to act as Beaufort's champion. But he would not come hat in hand and offer this: he would wait for Chaucer to set down his terms.

He waited. Shortly afterwards, Chaucer came.

They worked dutifully through the social preliminaries. Chaucer's boy poured wine. Chaucer asked some general questions, to set the scope of his enquiries. Suffolk embarked on his explanations.

They were long explanations. Chaucer drank three glasses of wine. He rarely interrupted, but he appeared to listen intently to them all.

Suffolk spoke honestly about the policy he had pursued in the Council. To lie would have been foolish: it was not long since Chaucer himself had retired from the Council, and he still had excellent sources of information. He spoke of his hopes for France, his conviction that an outright victory over the Valois was now no more than an impossible dream. He explained his view that a negotiated settlement offered the only chance for an honourable end to the war. He related the substance of his few unproductive discussions on this subject with Gloucester. He had tentatively raised the matter with Lord Cromwell, with Archbishop Kemp, and with half a dozen other Council members; he outlined these discussions too.

He spoke with honesty, and with a large degree of openness. He had told this tale in its entirety to no one else. There had been nobody else to tell. Except Alice; but there were reasons why he had not told all of this to Alice. There was nobody else he could trust now that Alexander was dead, and John. He did trust Chaucer. Chaucer would do or say nothing that could harm him, because to harm him would be to harm Alice. And Chaucer's attentive silence, Chaucer's occasional probing questions, even Chaucer's steady consumption of wine, all somehow prompted him to share confidences with this man who did not like him.

His confidences were not boundless. He did not outline the precise terms on which he believed the King should make a settlement with the Dauphin; and he made no mention of the Duke of Orleans.

Chaucer swirled the last half-inch of his third glassful of wine around the inside of the glass. He glanced at the half-empty pitcher, as if he were considering another refill. It was not yet midday. Had Chaucer always drunk as heavily? Suffolk looked at his face, at the broken veins on his cheeks, the dark bags beneath his eyes, and thought: I have seen this man age, even since I brought Alice back to England. Was the wine a cause of the ageing? Or was it merely a palliative, a way of making bearable some source of pain? He had no way of knowing.

Chaucer finished his glass of wine, but he did not refill it.

'So,' he said, looking down at the empty glass in his hand, 'you still do not support Beaufort's men.'

'Not so, sir. I have done nothing directly contrary to the Cardinal's interests. I suspect you mean that you wish I had opposed Gloucester more forcefully. But I dislike this business of opposing factions in the Council.'

'You may dislike it, but it is there, and can hardly be ignored.'

'Ignored, no; but it can be resisted. If we are to move towards peace in France we must agree among ourselves. Burgundy is neck-deep now in schemes and truces with the Valois. For the Council members to squabble at such a time is a luxury we cannot afford.'

'Gloucester has always had less faith in Burgundy than Bedford has.'

'True. But Gloucester refuses to draw the natural conclusion: that we must negotiate before, and not after, Burgundy changes sides. The disaster of the Coronation has more than half-persuaded Bedford of that. Perhaps Beaufort sees it too. Gloucester, though, still imagines that the English alone could hold France.'

'And you hold yourself out as his supporter.'

'Not so. I take an independent line. On some issues I have supported the Protector, on others opposed him. It would gain me nothing to take a stand as his opponent. While I am seen to be neutral I can find opportunities to work on him, to try to convince him of his mistakes.'

'His mistakes,' Chaucer echoed. He fell silent for a moment. His forefinger tapped the side of his glass in a regular, insistent rhythm. It annoyed Suffolk; he was tempted to reach out and still that tapping finger.

'Mistakes like Gloucester's treatment of the Cardinal?' Chaucer asked, with sudden vehemence.

'Not all men see that as a mistake. Some believe that the Cardinal would have been wise to resign his see six years ago.'

'Some men have nothing to gain from seeing the Cardinal in a position of power.'

'I am not certain yet that I have anything to gain from that myself.'

He said this cautiously, hoping to move on to a veiled negotiation. But Thomas Chaucer simply stared at him. 'Henry Beaufort is my cousin.'

'True, sir, but he is not my cousin.'

'He is Alice's cousin.'

'I am well aware of that; but my understanding is that my wife has no financial expectations from the Cardinal.'

'Expectations? Perhaps not. But she has commitments. And so do you, as her husband.'

'I do not consider that I have a commitment to support Beaufort in the Council.'

'Then I tell you that you have; that I expect you to oppose Gloucester's petty schemes with every scrap of marrow in you.'

Tell me! Damn Chaucer! He would not be told what to do! He was prepared to discuss supporting Beaufort for money, but he would not do it merely as a favour, a 'commitment'. He could not afford to do that. If he did, he could see himself spending his life fawning to two old moneybags, looking over his shoulder to see their reaction before he made any move, eternally begging for loans that came each time weighted down with conditions. He had to be made a clear offer, one that would ensure his financial security, before he would agree to back the Cardinal. Otherwise, he told himself, he would leave Beaufort to stew in his own pit and settle for pressing Gloucester.

'I shall do nothing that is against my wife's interests,' he said in a cold voice.

'You are angering her father!'

'And you, sir, are angering her husband.'

Chaucer's face grew redder and redder. His eyes bulged. He heaved himself to his feet and slammed his wineglass down on the little silver tray that held the pitcher.

'Goddamn you, man, you are using my Alice as a pawn in your sordid little game! Playing off Beaufort and Gloucester against each other! Do you seriously imagine you have the power to get away with that? They will squash you like a fly on the wall! And you imagine that will not hurt my Alice!'

Suffolk too rose to his feet; he too slammed down his wineglass. Then he turned, hot with anger, to confront the shorter, older man.

'My game, sir, is not sordid! I work for the good of my King and country. I play my game so that the Council shall adopt the policies I know to be right. And I expect, and receive, the wholehearted support of my wife.'

Chaucer glared; Chaucer glowered; Chaucer scowled. Then Chaucer subsided. He seemed to sink into himself. The redness of his face faded; his eyes dwindled in their sockets. And there he stood, a tired and ageing man.

'I did not marry my Alice to you for this,' he said in a defeated voice.

'Then you married her to me for what? For the greater glory of Cardinal Beaufort?'

'For her happiness, damn you! To win her happiness!'

'To hell with Alice's happiness! You married her to me so that you might have another earl as your creature!'

'My God! You truly see it so.' Chaucer's face changed. From anger, from defeat, it switched imperceptibly to an expression of pure hatred. 'To hell,' he repeated, in a low hiss, 'with Alice's happiness.'

For all his fury, Suffolk could not escape a moment's

unease. 'I never meant it so,' he muttered. 'Damn it, sir. You know I never meant it so.'

'You think her happy now? You truly think you make my Alice happy?'

'I do everything I can to make her happy.'

'Not so. You use her, man. You use her.' Chaucer strode to the door. He opened it. 'Get out,' he said, in a low voice.

Suffolk did not move. Chaucer turned to him again. 'Get out,' he repeated. It was a yell this time. 'Get out!'

Suffolk went to the river. He dismissed the grooms and squires who had been waiting for him in Chaucer's yard, sent them back to the Palace and went there alone. He walked, alone, past the King's bridge and the jetties with their barges, past the mills and wharves, and on to the stretch of open land they called the mill bank. It was a dull day. The mill bank was deserted. He walked there for a long time.

Alice's happiness. It was a foolish notion, of course, that he should have married Alice for the sake of her happiness. Even more foolish to imagine that Thomas Chaucer had encouraged the match for such reasons. They were both of them pragmatic men: the marriage had been for reasons of politics and finance.

But that old fancy of years before, that he loved the Countess of Salisbury, had turned to a very real knowledge that he loved the Countess of Suffolk. Desired her, true; but it was more than that. It meant much to him that he should ensure her happiness.

And he had done all he could, damn it, to ensure Alice's happiness. He had not obliged her father, but even so there was nothing for her to object to, and much for her to admire, in his political ambitions. He had been a considerate husband. She was mistress of a fine house, she had fine clothes, fine music, too. She had freedom to choose her friends and behave with them as she chose.

And yet; and yet. Alice was not happy. She was

bright, she was gay, but that had fooled him no more than it had fooled her father. Under the gaiety she was not happy.

He believed he knew why. It was not her dislike of his embraces: it was something deeper than that, something that explained all that and more. Alice wanted something that it seemed neither he, nor any other man, could give her. She wanted a child.

Did Chaucer not see that? Was it not clear as the nose on his face? It should have been. But, thought Suffolk, Thomas Chaucer was in his way as blindly self-centred as was his daughter. He wanted his daughter happy for his own satisfaction: that he might show her off to the world. See, my daughter, the Countess of Suffolk! See my beautiful, accomplished, happy daughter!

But it was not to be. Happiness was nobody's right. Alice had as much cause as anyone to be happy, more cause than most. If Alice was not happy, then that had to be accepted, as had so many harder things. If Alice was not happy, that was no reason for him to abandon his own great cause.

All the same, he thought, he should tell her about his hopes for France.

The sky grew dark. Storm clouds threatened, and evening was not far off. He shrugged his cloak tighter round his shoulders and began to walk, slowly, towards the Palace.

He thought only afterwards of the original cause of his visit. It should not have ended as it had: he had expected to leave Chaucer with a commitment to support Beaufort. But it was too late now. He would go to Gloucester, with the figures in his pocket.

15

ENGLAND

Seventeen years. It was seventeen years since Charles, Duke of Orleans, had been in France. It was seventeen years since he had been free. That was very nearly half his lifetime.

He remembered – oh, in snatches. There was the nightmare. He had it less often these days, but still he woke sometimes, his body cold and damp, thinking for a moment that he was back in that muddy field in Flanders, the stench of blood in his nostrils, awakening slowly and painfully under a pile of sodden corpses that only his armour kept from crushing him.

There was the pleasant dream of Blois, of larks singing in the trees and fountains playing, of flying a falcon in a sky blue as the sky in England never could be, of Bonne – poor Bonne, the wife he had never wanted, dead now after all those years of pointless waiting. He could not remember her face, but he had written an elegy for her, mechanical in its mourning.

Mostly, the old memories and the fresh news jostled together in his mind. He heard and understood only fragments about the war. It was a source of wonder to him that it should have continued for so long. After Agincourt, he had thought the Dauphin's cause completely lost; and yet men had continued to fight – and to lose, for the most part – without ever conceding a final victory to the English.

He wondered sometimes whether the English had completed their victory over him. He would occasionally catch himself thinking unawares in English rather than in French. For seventeen years the women he had loved had been Englishwomen. He had loved no men. The only Frenchmen he ever saw were his servants, Robert and Jean; and he was a Duke, to whom familiarity with servants was unthinkable. He wrote poems of longing for France, but he was no longer sure in his own mind what it was he longed for; what he would find, were he ever to go back.

Meanwhile, this was life: his room. A room changed once more. It was good to know himself in London. In London he might have more visitors, might be able to order some new books. About his new custodian the Earl of Suffolk he knew nothing, bar the little the jailers had told him on the journey from Lincolnshire. There was one jailer who spoke French. He had wondered if the man was a spy, but had soon told himself that the suspicion was ridiculous. All the jailers worked for the English, they all watched him, this one no more than the others.

This room was set high in a tall house: almost pretty as English houses went, in something of the Italian style. The room faced to the rear; the window was barred in iron so that he could not lean out, but he could see rooftops, hear the noises of a stableyard somewhere down below. It was a plain room, not large, but with a fireplace of its own and – a wonder, this – a shelf on the wall where he might set his books.

He spent two days supervising Robert and Jean as they arranged his things in the room. Every object mattered intensely to him. Almost everything came from Blois. On the small table was his leather dressing case, with two combs, a mirror and two razors with ivory handles, all decorated with the arms of Orleans in coloured enamel. Next to this were arrayed a chessboard, ready set with cool ivory chesspieces, a board for the game of tables and the two little booklets into which he had copied the rules of each game.

In the chest by the window were folded, in layers

separated by thin paper strewn with rosemary, dozens of pairs of bronze-green hose, sets of the fine linen under-clothes he always wore and two warm robes embroid-ered with his device, the nettle. An armory held a supply of nougat from Lombardy and half a dozen pots of the quince marmalade that was his particular passion. He had wine delivered to him too, sweet white wine from the Loire valley, but that was stored in his custodian's cellar: only one flagon sat on the top of the armory, next to a pair of silver goblets.

The books mattered most of all. He had been building up his library ever since he had arrived in England, begging some volumes from France, persuading English visitors to give him others. He had psalters, missals, books of hours and lives of the saints. The works of Saint Augustine, Saint Gregory and Saint Jerome, Hugh of Saint Victor and John of Hovendene. Seven books on medicine – his health worried him. And his manuscript books.

He was a methodical man and liked to use two manuscript books at once. He had a second table at which to write. At the centre of it was a little notebook, slightly dog-eared at the corners, which he generally left open at the page on which he had been working. His handwriting was even, rather square; but the neat effect was marred by dozens of crossings-out, insertions and notes in the margins. To the right of the notebook were set his pens, sharpened each day and laid out in a file, and a pot of newly made ink, with its bitter, slightly musty smell.

The bigger book was set to the left of the table. Its vellum pages within the calf binding were immaculate. The clasp was silver, imprinted with his arms. Jean polished the clasp weekly. Jean called this the Book of My Lord's Ballads. His lord had no name for it.

For four days nobody came but for the guards who brought his meals and a dour French-speaking Benedict-ine who celebrated Mass for him each morning. Jean and Robert had been free to go outdoors at Bolingbroke, but here they too were confined, for fear (he assumed) that they would bring him news he was not to hear.

He was used to the silence; his routine was long since established. After Mass he sat at his writing table until dinner. Usually he wrote a little; often he sat dreaming of nothing in particular. He ate whatever food was brought, ending the meal with a small piece of nougat and washing it down with one glass of wine. Then he read until the light faded. He rarely lit candles: his custodians did not normally supply such luxuries, and little money was sent to him from France.

On the fourth day he had a visitor. He knew at a glance that she was a lady of quality. She was tall, with a high, smooth forehead, wide, almond-shaped eyes that sloped upwards slightly at the outer corners and a neat, self-possessed little mouth. Her dress was of green damask, with sleeves and underskirt of cream lace; the horns of her headdress were draped with a thin creamy veil. The maidservant who accompanied her, he could tell, was a Frenchwoman.

This lady did not attract him physically: his passion was fired only by short, dark women. But she was a visitor, and there was refinement and intelligence written in her face. He rose to his feet and bowed.

She greeted him in very good French, introducing herself as the Countess of Suffolk. This he had guessed: it would have been out of the question for any other lady to visit him before he was properly established in this household.

It was pleasant to sit with the Countess and talk, while her servant embroidered napkins in the corner. The Countess talked well and wittily, but he found he had been deceived by those almond eyes: though her look at first had seemed to promise it, she was not at all flirtatious. It was strange, a little unnerving, to discover how well she knew his poems, even some of the ones he had never set in public circulation. Her husband, she said, had found copies of them at Blois.

This too was an unnerving revelation; he did not ask her to expand on it.

The Countess did not talk to him of politics or personalities, and this he accepted. They spoke of poetry and of music. The Countess did not write, but she sang, and sang well. On subsequent visits she brought with her a small lute and sang some arrangements of his own poems, and some English songs he had not heard before. There had been little music in his life. He enjoyed these interludes.

It was on her fourth or fifth visit that the Countess made a remark which betrayed that she was disobeying her husband's orders. The Earl of Suffolk had intended Orleans to be kept alone until his return. This was a trifle disconcerting, but the Duke had faced worse embarrassments. At least he understood now why the lady never spoke of her husband to him.

Two days later, Suffolk returned.

He did not come to Orleans' room, but the Duke was summoned to meet him in another room of the house. It was an upper room that, in the fashion of English houses, appeared to have a variety of uses. There was a table set under the window, at which someone – a secretary, perhaps – was clearly accustomed to write: it was strewn with papers, there were pens and a rather grubby inkpot. This was no woman's room. There was a bed: not the best bed, he judged, but a second- or even third-best one with hangings of embroidered dornick. A small chest; no other furniture.

The Earl of Suffolk was already there, waiting for him.

He had been told that the Earl had been a soldier in France; but this man was at heart no soldier, he sensed immediately. Suffolk's face had none of the blank decisiveness of a successful commander's face. His eyes were hooded, but when he raised them their expression was surprisingly open; their colour, a pale brown. The mouth spoke of sensitivity; the lines etched round it, of a man who frowned more often than he smiled. He was tall and held himself well, with just a hint of the soldier in his bearing; his clothes were elegant. Every feature was good, but they were combined less than perfectly: it seemed to Orleans that the overall effect fell just short of handsomeness.

'My dear sir,' said Suffolk, coming forward with hand outstretched, 'it is a pleasure to make your acquaintance at last.'

Conventional words, but spoken with a slight suggestion of uncertainty, as if more than might be expected rested on this meeting.

'At last?' Orleans echoed. Conventionally polite in return, he took the outstretched hand and bowed.

'It is three years now since I was at Blois: as a prisoner of your half-brother Jean. I promised Jean then that I would endeavour to meet you when I returned to England.'

'Then you have more than fulfilled your promise.'

'Not entirely.' Suffolk smiled. It was a bright smile, brighter than Orleans had anticipated from his face: it transformed him, made him the handsome man he had not quite seemed before. 'Jean was, and is, my friend. I hoped then, from what he told me of you, that I might become your friend too.'

A Duke, even in captivity, receives approaches of many kinds, from men of many different tempers and stations in life. Orleans had been treated in England with deference, with contempt, with indifference and with admiration. He had been urged to support the Lancastrian cause, invited to betray secrets; he had been asked (expected, even) to spy for the Dauphin. Some men had appeared to trust him, others had doubted even the most innocuous words he spoke. But friendship? He had not reckoned such a thing possible under such circumstances.

All his life he had been schooled to react with polite indifference except when he was confident in a different reaction. He had no confidence here. But it was disturbing to see the bright smile slowly fade from Suffolk's face and a bland mask come to overlay it.

He spoke, almost at random, to halt that process. 'Can you tell me of Jean?'

'Why, certainly. He must have been a child when last you saw him?'

Suffolk took his arm and drew him over to the window. They stood in the shaft of light that streamed through it. Orleans had calculated as he was being led to it that the room was at the front of the house, but his attention now was focussed not on the world beyond, but on the other man who shared that little space with him.

These were things that had been kept from him throughout his captivity. Few people had ever spoken to him of the war, and those few had mostly been ill-informed; nobody had spoken to him of Blois or of his family, beyond the terse notes that had told him of their deaths. And now the Earl of Suffolk was talking freely, of the siege of Orleans, of Jean's career as a soldier of the Dauphin, of life at Blois.

Orleans' private terror was that he should inadvertently reveal how extraordinary this was to him. Suffolk spoke of friendship; but perhaps he did not know how other custodians dealt with their prisoners? Perhaps he imagined that Cornwall and the rest had spoken with the same openness? He himself knew so little, far less than was sufficient to enable him to ask the right questions. This business of the girl soldier Jean had followed, for instance: he could not comprehend it, it made no sense from the snatches he had overheard. He dared ask nothing, for fear he should reveal the true extent of his ignorance.

Unprompted, Suffolk spoke at length. These were, it was clear, matters on which he had thought deeply. But his account was difficult for Orleans to follow: Suffolk assumed so much, he talked of tactical subtleties when Orleans was unfamiliar with even the bare outlines of his story. And he spoke of these men, Jean, Guyenne Herald, Richemont and the rest, as if they were intimates of Orleans', when in fact they were strangers,

401

all of them, to him. Even Jean: the awkward, wayward boy he had known at Blois had no connection that he could see with the formidable commander of Suffolk's acquaintance.

He concentrated fiercely, trying to stow away what were to him largely disconnected scraps of information, in the hope that later he might succeed in piecing some of them together. He dared not assume that this conversation would be a precursor to others. Custodians were unpredictable. He thought that even if he were to spend years in Suffolk's custody, his jailer might never speak with him so openly again.

Such effort was unfamiliar to him. For years his life had been lived with infinite slowness. Each thought had been turned in his head until he knew it backwards, each of the rare letters he received savoured for days. This man lived at a far faster pace; he could not keep up. His eyes closed momentarily; he swayed slightly.

Suffolk saw immediately and took his arm once more. 'Forgive me, I have been thoughtless. I should have invited you to sit; I should have offered you wine. Come, there are no benches here, but we shall sit on the bed.'

He saw Orleans to the safety of the mattress and left him to recover, in the gloom of the heavy hangings, while he went to the door to call a servant. A moment later he returned and sat by Orleans on the bed. They sat in silence for several minutes, until a boy came with wine and wafers.

'I value your kindness,' Orleans murmured. The wine was good: drier than he liked, but of fine quality.

'Not at all.' Suffolk rose to his feet: edgily, as if he disliked being still for too long. 'I had intended,' he said, 'to invite you to dine with us tonight. But perhaps you would prefer to be alone? Then you shall meet my Countess tomorrow, and the rest of my household.'

'That is most thoughtful of you.'

'Not at all,' Suffolk repeated. He paced to the window and back. 'We shall be in London for several weeks,' he said. 'Then we travel to Suffolk, to my estate at

Wingfield. I hope to permit you more freedom there. In London, you understand, it is wise to be discreet.'

'I understand.'

'May I call on you tomorrow? Forgive me, I did not ask the servants your routine; I shall be free early in the morning, then I have business to attend to in Westminster.'

This was an unusual courtesy. A prisoner could not demand privacy: most visitors came to him as the Countess had done, uninvited, assuming their absolute right to enter his room.

He thought for a moment of refusing. This man was pressing him hard; he was not sure yet that it was only for friendship that he looked. Then he remembered the mask that had been drawn over Suffolk's face when he had hesitated to respond earlier. He himself was lonely. Reject the Earl of Suffolk now, he thought, and he might be given no further chance.

'After Mass . . .' he said.

'Naturally. After Mass.'

16

ENGLAND
Autumn, 1432

It was a dull autumn, the weather so damp and listless that it discouraged everybody from more than a minimum of thought and action. In a great canopied bed in the keep of Framlingham Castle, the Duke of Norfolk lay in a state a little removed from death. It seemed questionable whether he would ever find the strength to make a move as positive as dying.

The Duke was expected to die. A thousand relatives near and distant, retainers, pages and squires, pastry-cooks and gardeners had been summoned to Framling-ham to attend his deathbed. After three weeks during which the Duke seemed to have moved not a finger closer to heaven or hell, they were becoming as argumentative as bees caught in the keeper's net.

William Paston was feeling particularly restless. He had welcomed this invitation to Framlingham, but he had not expected to enjoy his stay at the castle; and so far his expectation had proved correct.

From his point of view there was nothing to be gained by prolonging John Mowbray's life; indeed he looked forward to the Duke's approaching death, as far as proper piety and politeness permitted. He had never quite forgiven the Duke for his lack of support over the Aslake affair; and the Duke, he suspected, had never quite forgiven him for thinking him so clearly in the wrong. After persisting for six or seven years, the coolness had seemed unlikely ever to evaporate entirely; while a new Duke would mean a new slate, new opportunities. The old fees would be paid, and there would be a fat new fee for acting as one of the Duke's executors.

This job, however, would not necessarily increase his popularity with the new Duke, since most of the estate proved to have been dowered on his mother. William's preliminary tussles with the Mowbray papers had left him with an enhanced respect for Ralph Neville's powers of negotiation.

He had hoped rather that his visit would bring him an enhanced respect for the Earl of Nottingham, John Mowbray junior. Surely the lad could not really be as unappealing as everyone made him out to be? Alas, he was. Admittedly he was only seventeen, and might yet improve; but he struck William as a mope of a boy. He seemed as little interested in serious matters as his mother, and he had far less prepossessing manners than the Duchess. William could not imagine his making any impression upon affairs in East Anglia for years to come.

For the Duchess herself he had never felt more than a cool respect. She was so bright, so boisterous, so talkative: exhausting company, and for all that so uninformed about the political situation. He had heard that mother and son were on poor terms. He watched carefully to see if this report, too, was accurate. It was. But this did not cause him to dismiss the Duchess from his mind: the size of her dower estates had made too great an impact upon him.

And even if the new Duke seemed set to dispense with his mother's advice as soon as possible, she had a great many other useful connections and was clearly on excellent terms with most of them. Ralph Neville had had fourteen children by his two marriages and a remarkable number of them were now making their mark on the world. Any woman closely related by blood or marriage to the Duke of Buckingham, the Earl of Westmoreland, the Earl of Salisbury, the Earl of Northumberland, Lord Fauconberg, Lord Latimer, Lord Abergavenny and the Bishop of Durham demanded careful attention. And there was more. There was the Duke of York, who was, to William's genuine surprise, in temporary residence at Framlingham.

He found Cecily Neville, Duchess of York, to bear only the vaguest of resemblances to her boisterous sister; and even less resemblance to her nephew, though she was exactly his age: seventeen. She was a large, plain young woman who attended Mass at least three times a day. She had been married off to York as a child, but the marriage had only recently become a reality; as had York's position of power, after his successful petition to Parliament to restore to him his family estates.

York's position was delicate, as every man knew. His descent from Edward the Third was superior to that of Henry of Lancaster, and it was inevitable that he would provide a focus all his life for those discontented with Henry and the men who governed in his name. But Henry had succeeded to the throne without incident, even though he was a baby at the time; and if York's very existence was troublesome, he had as yet done nothing to cause concern among supporters of the House of Lancaster. At twenty-two he seemed scarcely more than a boy: shortish, he had a round face and a slight body that looked as if it too might in time spread into roundness.

William hesitated to be seen to favour York, even in this company. But York sought him out and talked seriously to him, and he was flattered enough to talk back. The Duke was no Norfolk man, he would cause no havoc in the county; and he was, after all, a nobleman of considerable estates who might prove useful to John or Edmund, might indeed provide the odd commission for his clerks.

They both measured their talk carefully. York spoke with concern about the situation in France; he expressed a desire to participate at some time in the war, but this was all but obligatory for a man in his position. He had no reason to favour either Gloucester or Beaufort, and it was no surprise when he proved tight-lipped on the subject of their quarrels. He was not yet an active member of the King's Council. William eventually realised that York was even less well acquainted with either man than he was himself.

So why had the Duchess of Norfolk invited him to Framlingham? William spent several days mulling over this question. Eventually he decided that it was ridiculous to try to read a political significance into York's presence. The Duchess's lack of interest in politics was no feint. York and his wife were there purely to strengthen her position should her son turn against her.

The rest of the company held few surprises, and even fewer attractions. Most were male and most were young. William knew many of the names, fewer of the faces: these were the sons, grandsons even, of the men of his generation.

Will Calthorp was one of them. That was understandable. Calthorp had turned from esquire to land agent in the era when the Duchess held the reins and the Duchess might reasonably consider him, too, as one of her own allies.

Strange, William thought: he had cultivated young Calthorp in the expectation that the lad would be a useful contact for him in Norfolk's household. He had even thought to gain some work by this method. He had dropped hints to the lad, and watched him take them up; had seen Calthorp transformed from an uncertain heir into an assured landowner. But he had had no return on this small investment of time and trouble. Calthorp was never rude to him, never other than mildly deferential, but there was no warmth between the two of them. Calthorp had ventured nothing to him: no opinions, no scraps of private information. He seemed totally loyal to the Mowbrays.

What would Calthorp do, William wondered, after Norfolk's death? Would he stay with the Duchess – the Dowager Duchess – or would he choose to serve her son? Assuming, that was, that her son would keep him on.

Perhaps Nottingham would not. He wondered if Calthorp had allowed for that possibility.

William was crossing the inner bailey one afternoon, making for the stables, when he saw Calthorp emerge from them, mounted, with his hawk on his fist. He hailed the lad. 'You aim to hunt?'

'Just so.'

'Then you'll not refuse my company?'

There was a barely perceptible pause, then Calthorp gave him a pleasant smile. 'I'll welcome it, sir.' He dismounted. 'I'll await you here.'

William sent Harry to the mews for his goshawk; while the groom was gone, he saddled his horse himself. Mustn't keep the lad waiting too long, he thought.

Harry reappeared. He got Harry to help him mount inside the stable: he did not want Calthorp to see the grimace when his bad leg took his weight for a moment. He pulled on his long leather glove, let Harry set the goshawk on his wrist and twisted the jesses around his fingers. Then he rode out.

They rode together, he and Calthorp, with their grooms following behind, through the great main gateway and across the drawbridge. It was a warmer day than most had been that autumn, dry, with a sky of high, fluffy clouds. They turned to the north, across the rough grassland that surrounded the castle.

'Good to get out,' Calthorp said.

'You find the castle stifling?'

Calthorp turned and gave him a careful look, as if he were trying to judge just how idle this question had been. 'I find it crowded, after Burnham.'

'So you choose to hunt alone.'

'Sometimes. Other days I ride with Austin, or Debenham; I've been out with York and his men once or twice. The Duke has a fine pair of falcons here: young birds, but well trained. Maybe you've seen them in the mews?'

William nodded. His mind was on the names that had been omitted from this list.

'No lack of company here,' he said.

'Far from it.'

'Seems the Duchess has a fondness for surrounding herself with young men.'

Calthorp gave him another quicksilver glance. 'You set that to the Duchess, rather than to Nottingham?'

'I do. They none of them look to me like young Nottingham's choice. He's a cygnet amid ducklings in the company of all these young gallants.'

He meant this to goad Calthorp and he could see that it did. But the lad did not leap back; he considered first. 'Nottingham has a fondness for Bacton and one or two of the others. But there's truth in what you say: it cheers Kitty to be surrounded by handsome young men.'

They reached the end of the meadow and skirted round to find a gate into the apple orchard beyond it. It was cool in the orchard. The air was thick with the sweet smell of windfalls rotting in the long grass.

'You must admit,' Calthorp went on, 'that Kitty behaves admirably. She shows her tedious husband every consideration, summons the best doctors, mops his brow in person. She is careful never to create a whiff of serious scandal. And she remains cheerful throughout the most trying circumstances.'

Kitty. Calthorp had used that name twice, and with a cadence that proclaimed it to come naturally to him. And yet few men to William's knowledge called the Duchess of Norfolk by that name, even behind her back. 'A damn sight too cheerful for my liking,' he said in a consciously grumbling voice. 'Am I to take it that she plans to remarry as soon as is decent?'

'I doubt it,' Calthorp said airily. 'Though some of the young men certainly hope otherwise. She has found her husband exasperating – why should she look to replace him? She is perfectly capable of managing her own affairs. I take it the terms of her settlement were generous?'

William decided to ignore that question. 'She will have no political influence in the county unless she remarries.'

They had reached the far end of the orchard. There was no gate to be seen in the fence. Calthorp looked pointedly at Blazon and led them to a spot where the top rail of the fence was broken. He let William take a low jump before him.

There was a strip of long grass between the orchard and the edge of the oakwoods that surrounded Framlingham. Good country for goshawks, William thought. A good day for hawking. They might catch blackbirds or pheasants, even a rabbit or a hare.

'You plan to fly her to the quarry?' He said this before Calthorp could suggest otherwise. He liked the prospect of the random ease of a hunt on good land, where the hawk could be released to find its own game. He wanted to hear more. He did not want to waste this opportunity for talk in beating up their prey, just for the sake of taking an extra rabbit back to the castle kitchens.

'If you prefer.' Calthorp licked his forefinger and held it out. The wind was light, variable. It had to be judged right: released downwind, the hawks would catch nothing.

They rode to the far edge of the grassland, unhooded the hawks and released them. Calthorp's went first, William's own a moment later. The birds rose a little and hung in the air, almost motionless, looking for prey.

The men sat side by side on their horses, watching them.

'Of course,' said Calthorp, 'you saw so little of the Duke. He never really recovered from his ducking in the Thames. It was that, Kitty reckons, that broke his health. Sailing back to Greenwich at night from Southwark. Winchester Inn. He had to get back, you know, for fear Gloucester would learn he had been intriguing with Beaufort.'

'So the Duchess blames his illness on Beaufort.'

'In a way she does. Illogical, of course, but she'd worked so hard to keep him from Beaufort, and she reckons the accident would not have happened had he not defied her.'

'And why,' William asked, 'should she have wished to keep him from Beaufort?'

Calthorp did not answer immediately. William kept his eyes on the hawks. Perhaps he had gone too far. Perhaps the lad was wondering if all this really was new to him? In fact it was. There had been a deal of gossip about the accident itself, but little speculation on its causes. He had never thought about it before: he had never reached beyond his wicked pleasure at Norfolk's downfall.

'I doubt if it was a question of policy. She simply dislikes political intrigue. Most women do, do you not find?'

'So she has come to the conclusion that not possessing a husband will suit her better.'

'Just so. When she tires of widowhood she will look instead for one with no political ambitions; but she sees no urgency in that. I suspect she still hopes to fall in love, and she has much better taste than to do so over John Mowbray's deathbed.'

The hawks had still not swooped. William took his eyes from them for a moment and looked at Calthorp. Calthorp looked back. William thought: he has weighed every word he has said.

The sun was shining. The horses were at ease in the meadow. William was rather enjoying himself. So was Calthorp, he sensed. William decided to goad him some more. 'What a pity she married you off to Bess Grey. You might have had her yourself.'

Calthorp's eyes narrowed. Kitty, William thought. He did not weigh that: that was a slip. And now he knows it.

But he was a sharp lad: he did not give William time to dwell on it. He went on, with only the shortest of pauses, 'Of course, she completely fails to see how badly her scheme will imbalance Norfolk and Suffolk affairs. Nottingham will have no influence for five years, perhaps ten. If Kitty has no husband to meddle in county politics there will be nobody to oppose Suffolk.'

'There is some truth in that, but you put it too strongly. There might, for example, be Sir John Fastolf?'

411

'I hardly think so. Fastolf may be coining it in France, but he is no more than a knight. The old Norfolk families do prefer to answer to a duke, or to an earl at the very least.'

One of the hawks had sensed its prey. William caught the motion from the corner of his eye and he turned away from Calthorp to watch it.

He was too far away to tell which bird it was. It was swooping low, tracking over the long grass barely a couple of handspans from the top of the stalks. Then it pounced, disappearing into the lush green of the meadow as it finally overtook its quarry.

'Mine, I think,' said Calthorp. He waited for a moment, then set his fingers to his mouth and whistled a few clear notes.

At the third whistle the bird rose. There was a limp grey bundle in its talons: the carcase of a small rabbit. It flew, low and arrow-straight, across the meadow towards them. It was quiet in the meadow and William could hear the hawk's bells as it came closer, jingling, faint and discordant.

Calthorp's groom reached in the pack fastened to his saddle. He handed his master a small cube of meat. The hawk dropped the rabbit at Calthorp's feet and landed on his gauntlet; he fed it the meat neatly.

'Mine has it now,' William said.

They watched the second hawk. It was a little further away from them, repeating the same motions: the pause, the swoop, the low tracking flight. But it came to the hedge at the edge of the meadow without pouncing. It rose again, talons empty, into the sky.

William watched it recede until it was no more than a speck of brown silhouetted against the clouds.

'So,' he said, his eyes on the speck, 'you plan to stay on with young Nottingham when his father dies?'

Silence, broken only by the murmur of the groom as he played austringer and hooded the hawk, by the rustle of the breeze in the oak trees. It hung lightly on them. But William was waiting. He thought for a

412

moment that Calthorp would pretend he had not heard.

'No,' the other man said. 'I shall part company on amicable terms, so that I can review my commitments in a few years. But by the end of the year I shall be wearing the livery of the Earl of Suffolk.'

William started. He moved so suddenly that Blazon jerked in response beneath him and he was forced to grab at the reins to hold the horse back. That was a possibility he had not even considered.

He considered it now, rapidly. It was not really so unlikely, he supposed. There would be disadvantages for the Duchess's old favourites in cleaving to either Mowbray faction after the Duke's death. But there were disadvantages in serving Suffolk, too; grave disadvantages, in his opinion.

It struck him as a stupid move: all the more so, because Calthorp so clearly thought it a clever one.

The boy was no match yet for Tuddenham. He would find himself outmanoeuvred; and that was a pity. He was a likeable enough lad. He deserved a better fate. If nobody had warned him yet how foolish his plan was, then he deserved to have William warn him.

'I thought you hawk, not rabbit in your soul.' The harshness in his voice got across: a shiver seemed to pass over Calthorp's face.

'I cannot see that such a move will make me less so.'

'Then you see too little, boy.' William pulled on his reins. He brought the mare round, confronting Calthorp head on, his back to the grooms. 'Men surely say even at Framlingham that Suffolk's men have a reputation for extortion and intimidation?'

Calthorp grinned, disconcertingly. 'Men say that you hate Sir Thomas Tuddenham, and I guess they speak true. I do not doubt you have reason. But for me, it is a great advantage of Suffolk's retinue that he already has so many specialists in that department. He needs no other such. It is Kitty who presses me to lean on her tenants; with Suffolk I shall have the pleasure of knowing that other men deal with such matters.'

413

'They will make you the bait in their trap.'

'Not so, I reckon. Indeed, there is no trap. Tuddenham and his men seek for nothing but fair returns for their lord. And while they gather in the rents, I shall dance attendance on the Earl and Countess. I shall be a regular attender at the Guild services and a flatterer of the gentry. Suffolk needs such men, also. Men see him as a harsh lord, but that can be changed. Servants such as I shall show the kinder face of Suffolk's rule.'

'My Lord Justice . . .' Harry murmured, pulling on William's gown.

'You call her, Harry,' William responded without turning. 'You reason very prettily, Will; but I still like this not at all. Tuddenham and Heydon have blood on their hands. Join them and you will be tainted by its stench.'

'That is not proven,' Calthorp said stubbornly. 'And not for lack of your trying, I hear. In any case, you cannot say the same of the Earl.'

William clenched his teeth. There was plenty he would have said of the Earl; but he realised that to Calthorp he could say none of it.

And for a good reason. It was an impression he had, no more: it was not evidence that would satisfy a lawyer, or even a man such as Calthorp.

An impression: an impression gained largely, he admitted to himself, from what he knew of Tuddenham and Heydon and their associates. This was all he had against Suffolk, the fact that the Earl was master of such men. Perhaps it was true, as he had heard men argue, that Suffolk himself was a good man. Perhaps Calthorp himself had seen enough of the Earl to judge him soundly; to judge him favourably.

And if Calthorp did have faith in Suffolk's own integrity, then perhaps his argument was a valid one. It was only if one questioned that integrity, only if one rated the master as no better than his more questionable servants, that the other man's decision would prove to be a massive misjudgement.

He knew he had not said enough to make the lad reconsider his stance; but he sensed that he had already pushed him as far as, and further than, he was willing to go. Their basis of trust was shallow. Calthorp had no reason to trust his judgement over Suffolk's, or over that of the other men who had doubtless advised him. If he did say more, he might destroy every trace of the flimsy bridge he had built that afternoon.

And he needed that bridge. He needed, badly needed, an ally in Suffolk's household. At least, he thought, Calthorp might prove to be that.

He glanced at Harry. The groom had the hawk now: she had come readily to the call. He had her catch, too. It was nothing but a fieldmouse.

Calthorp said, 'Shall you fly her again? My bird will do no more: I flew her yesterday, and look to fly her again tomorrow. But it is early. We can move to the farther field if you wish, and see if we find better sport there.'

'No. Let us ride back now.'

They rode in silence back through the orchard. It was still a mellow afternoon, but William's mind was disturbed, his pleasure gone. He had made this expedition because he wished to learn something; but it had not been this that he had wished to learn.

He still had an urge to say more. It would have to be said before they returned to the castle. He took his chance when they reached the orchard gate. He set his hand on the gate and paused, holding the other man back. 'I know nothing against the Earl himself,' he said in a measured voice. 'And I should well like to believe him to be the man you think him to be. But take care, Will; take care.'

Calthorp showed him just a flash of annoyance – deliberate, he thought – and then drowned it in a grin.

'Never fear,' he said merrily. 'I shall.'

The Duke of Norfolk died that October. There was a funeral, large and pompous, in Framlingham Church. Then the relatives, their retainers, their pages and

415

squires all departed, and there was left at Framlingham only the sparse and bony skeleton of a ducal household.

October and November were cool and squally months. Will counted the days until the Duke of Norfolk's month's mind was kept. He played his part at the sombre service. He told himself that the next day he would seek out Kitty.

In fact she beat him to it: she called for him that night. Though she had continued to see him throughout the Duke's last illness, she had kept his month's mind resolutely: it was the first time they had been together since the funeral.

And Will knew, if Kitty did not, that it would almost certainly be their last. He made love to her not with his usual agression, but with lust and with affection. He thought to himself that he would miss her.

The candles were burning low, the fire no more than fading embers, and the night more than halfway through, by the time they lay satiated in Kitty's great bed. Kitty turned to him then and said, in a low voice, 'John will call for you in the morning.'

He glanced at her and frowned. She seemed perfectly at ease. John, he thought. Then you mean me to serve him, and not you. That surprised him.

'I need to speak to him,' he said cautiously.

Kitty gave a half-frown. They rarely spoke of her son when they were together; he wondered for a moment if she thought he had been over-familiar.

'You'll not be disappointed. His terms are good: I've made sure of that.'

'Kitty,' he said, with sudden awkwardness. Curse her! He had meant to break his news to them both in the Great Hall, where the audience would mute their reaction; he did not wish to explain to her now. But he could see that he was left with no alternative. 'It was good of you to arrange it. But after serving you, I could not go on to serve John.'

'Don't be ridiculous.' Kitty swung her feet round and

clambered out of the bed. She took a couple of logs and arranged them on the embers. She reached for a flagon of wine and poured two glasses, which she brought back to the bed.

'I know John's failings far better than you,' she said sharply, handing him one of the glasses. 'But you'll find him a fair master.'

You are wrong, Will thought silently. True, you despise John's laziness; but I'd swear you are blind to his depravity. You are too grateful that he tolerates the young men you bring to Framlingham to notice that he uses them himself. This was one reason why he did not wish to take Nottingham's livery, but it was only one. There were others that Kitty would understand; he saw no reason to explain this one to her.

'I don't doubt I would have done,' he said quietly. 'But I have thought long and hard, Kitty, and I have decided to make my career elsewhere.'

'Elsewhere?'

'I've a wish to play my part in Norfolk politics, and you know as well as I that there will be little scope for that if I stay at Framlingham.'

Kitty frowned, biting her lower lip. He kept his look steadily on her. She might find this incomprehensible, he thought, but she knew him well enough to understand that it was the truth.

'If that is important to you, then I dare say it can be arranged.'

'I have arranged it, Kitty.'

'You've spoken to John yourself?'

Bloody woman. How obtuse she could be. He swallowed his annoyance as best he could, and said again, 'Kitty.'

She caught his tone this time. She turned to put her glass on the thick wood of the bedhead, then she confronted him, suddenly serious. 'Tell me.'

'I plan to serve the Earl of Suffolk.'

'Suffolk? Will, you're not serious!'

'It is all arranged. I had intended to tell you tomorrow, but it's as well that you should know now. I'll finish my work here, and then in one week, or perhaps two, I shall ride for Wingfield.'

'I cannot allow this,' Kitty said with vehemence.

You cannot stop it, Will thought, with a private surge of pleasure. I shall be your servant no longer, Kitty.

'I am committed now,' he said quietly.

'But John needs you!' She stared at him, her brown eyes wide and prominent, her hair a wild tangle after the fury of their lovemaking. She made a fist and hammered it into the mattress. 'He's a fool, you've no need to tell me that, but he'll grow into sense. He needs men such as you. He must have agents he can trust. You cannot leave him now! I tell you, you cannot!'

'Kitty.' He moved to take hold of her shoulders and tried to pull her to him, but she resisted furiously, transferring her pummelling fists from the mattress to his chest. Finally he managed to pin her against him. He could feel her heart beating, feel the surge of blood in her.

'Kitty,' he repeated. 'Believe me, I had no idea that you would arrange this for me, and I am truly grateful. I believed that John would have no wish for my services. If I had known what you intended, I could have planned things differently. But it is too late now. I have made a commitment.'

'Then you must break it.'

'I cannot do that.'

'But you have a commitment to me!'

'I shall always be your friend and your devoted admirer, Kitty. But I am bound to you no longer as a servant.'

It sounded pompous to him even as he said it. It must have sounded pompous to her too, because she reacted with rage. Before he could stop her she had pulled away from him and leapt off the bed. She grabbed the wineglass she had set on the bedhead and with a sudden violent gesture she threw it to the floor. It shattered, spectacularly, on the flagstones of the tower room, and spatters of red wine rained on the heavy hangings and the thick linen sheet.

The echo filled the room for a long moment. Then there was silence.

Kitty reached for her nightgown. She shook it over her head and with shaking fingers she began to lace it up. By the time she had tied the bow her fingers were steadier. Will lay on the bed, watching her. He did not think to move.

She went to the door and opened it. She leaned out and called for Jeanne.

He moved then, grabbing his hose and his doublet and scrambling into them as best he could. He was less than half-dressed by the time a sleepy Jeanne appeared at the door.

'Master Calthorp is going now, Jeanne,' Kitty said in an icy voice. 'He will leave the castle at dawn. And you will tell the Chamberlain for me, please, that he will never be welcome here again.'

How wrong Judge Paston had been, Will thought. The Judge had pointed his finger at Tuddenham and Heydon, told Will that his troubles would come from them. But at Wingfield and at Bardi Place, neither man was in evidence. He rarely gave them a thought. His preoccupation was with Cardinal Beaufort, the Duke of Gloucester and the Duke of Bedford. It was a source of endless fascination to him, the complex nature of the Earl of Suffolk's relations with these great men.

How strange it now seemed that he should have thought it scandalous for the Duke of Norfolk to call on Cardinal Beaufort behind Gloucester's back. How naive he had been then; how naive Kitty had been in such matters. As a member of Suffolk's household, he rapidly came to think such niceness little short of laughable.

Suffolk was nobody's man but his own. He was no lapdog, as Norfolk had been. He bowed to no other man's opinions. He called on them all, spoke with them all: with Gloucester, with Beaufort, with Bedford too when the Regent returned to England that year. Will thought that an admirable policy. And it seemed to him, watching and listening to Suffolk's complex discussions with these great and powerful men, that he had made a very wise choice in selecting this man to be his master.

'Six thousand pounds,' said Suffolk Herald. He sat down on a stool by the hearth and took a deep draught of the warm ale that Ann, the Cook's girl, had just handed to him. 'I saw it,' he continued, 'written in black and white in the Cardinal's letter to the Earl.'

Will shrugged. He was already installed on a second stool, in the opposite corner. 'That is no news, Herald. We heard as much back in the summer.'

'No, you have me wrong. This is another six thousand pounds.'

'Twelve thousand in total.'

'Aye. And they say the Cardinal was due to be repaid thirteen thousand marks this year, which he had agreed to forego.'

A weighty total. Will gave a little nod to show that he appreciated that. 'So the crisis is over.'

The herald shook his head. 'Not so. That will cover the King's deficit for this year, but his other debts remain. I hear they are now nigh on a hundred and sixty-five thousand pounds.'

A hundred and sixty-five thousand pounds! He had known, as every man who cared about such matters now knew, that the King was deeply in debt. But a hundred and sixty-five thousand pounds! He had never heard such sums mentioned before, never.

'Even so,' he said slowly, 'that will be sufficient to keep Gloucester safe for the moment.'

'Not that the Cardinal intended it for that. He was careful, mind you, to keep from making this last loan until Bedford was here to take the credit.'

'But he did it, no doubt, to keep Gloucester off his back: to redeem his jewels and secure his see.'

'No doubt. And mark you this: the Cardinal has demanded in the Council that Lord Cromwell be appointed Treasurer.'

That was interesting. Will had gained a reasonable grasp by now of the characters and allegiances of the Lords of the Council. Lord Cromwell he knew to be a sharp, independent-minded man who had fought bitterly when Gloucester removed him from the prestigious position of Chamberlain. It was no surprise that Beaufort should move to have him reinstated; indeed, promoted. But it would anger Suffolk, he thought. There was bad blood between Cromwell and Suffolk.

'How has the Earl taken that?' he asked.

'Coolly.' Suffolk Herald gave a tight grin.

'He did not covet the Treasurership for himself?'

'I reckon he did. But he looks to Bedford, not Beaufort, to find him a Household salary.'

The door to the kitchens swung open and one of Suffolk's valets stepped in. 'More wine,' he said, 'for Master Chaucer.'

Ann moved, grumbling from the marble table where she was rolling pastry. 'I sent up a flagon not an hour ago.'

'And now it is empty.' The valet was holding it; he upended it and let a couple of purple drops fall on to the marble.

'Not there! You'll stain it,' Ann scolded. She bustled off to the pantry.

'Chaucer's with the Earl?' Will asked.

'I reckon so,' said Suffolk Herald. He got to his feet. 'We should move before anyone looks for us.'

'We should,' Will agreed.

He followed the herald to the door that led into the hall and the main part of Bardi Place. In truth, he did not expect anyone to be looking for him. His own duties were various: he reported only to the Earl himself, and if the Earl was closeted with Thomas Chaucer he would be safe for hours. But Suffolk would be in a high temper, he thought, by the time Chaucer departed: a temper all the more high for being suppressed during his father-in-law's visit.

He knew why Chaucer had come, since he had lingered in the room during some of Chaucer's conversations with the Earl. Chaucer came to remonstrate with Suffolk over his attitude to the Cardinal. And Suffolk calmed him, not by undertaking to follow the policy he advocated, but by pressing on him large quantities of wine. After a lifetime in the wine trade Chaucer was used to strong drink: he was never seen blind drunk or totally incapable, but often his eyes were clouded, his speech was slightly slurred, and his attention appeared to wander.

In the kitchens, this fact was well known. Clearly Suffolk too was conscious that Chaucer was slowly drinking himself to death. But Will suspected that his Countess did not realise it. Beautiful, self-centred Alice lived at a frenetic pace; though it was she, and not Suffolk, who invited her father to Bardi Place, she rarely troubled to give him more than a swift embrace and a moment's conversation before returning to her own affairs.

The Countess travelled almost daily to Westminster or to Greenwich, to visit the Duchess of Gloucester, Lady Warwick and her other notable female acquaintances. Suffolk appeared to encourage this. It seemed to suit him for his wife to cultivate as wide a range of noble ladies as he himself did men.

It seemed to Will, though, that both Suffolk and his Countess had few close friends. He had acted as the Countess's escort on occasion, and he had noticed that she showed little inclination to make opportunities for private conversation with Eleanor of Gloucester and the rest. Her visits were public affairs. She would play and sing in the summer hall; she excelled in exchanging the inconsequential, slightly acid gossip that was the hall-mark of the Pleasance.

The Countess was a good musician. Will admired her for this. There was invariably music to accompany dinner at Bardi Place; often the music continued all evening. Nor was it the casual lute-strumming that he had come across at Framlingham and the Pleasance: it was skilled playing, always. He had never heard a better lutanist than Gilles Binchois; never known a man with such a gift for setting words to music. Gilles was diplomatic, too: his men made light work of subduing their talents and acting as a backdrop when the Countess chose to sing, alone or with her maid Lucette.

Will enjoyed these performances. So, clearly, did Suffolk. And so too did the Duke of Orleans.

This was another interesting feature of life in Suffolk's household: the enigmatic presence of the captive French duke. Orleans kept to his room during the day, but he dined with the household in the great hall; at least, he did so when Suffolk was present at Bardi Place, and when there were no important visitors.

Will had had no previous dealings with captive French dukes, but it had slowly become apparent to him that this one enjoyed unusual freedom. It was not precisely a secret, the manner in which Orleans was treated; but it was, he understood, a matter that Suffolk preferred not to have discussed.

He suspected it would have appalled the Earl if he had realised how freely his Countess spoke of the Duke when she was with Eleanor of Gloucester and her cronies. It would probably have appalled him even more had he realised how frequently the Countess called on the Duke in his rooms when he himself was absent on business. Nobody told him of these matters, though they were mulled over occasionally in the kitchens.

Curious, that, Will thought. Suffolk talked, talked at length and to many people; he was not ill-informed. But he did not invite confidences: though people answered his questions, they rarely volunteered him anything.

In the early spring of 1433, Suffolk moved his household to Wingfield once more. Will accompanied him, but stayed for barely ten days at the castle. He had taken a rapid dislike to Wingfield. The low-flying flint quadrangle in its moat struck him as cold and damp, and the grumbles of Suffolk's tenants seemed tedious to him after the political intrigues of London – as, he suspected, they did to Suffolk himself. He asked permission to return to Burnham Thorpe and was given it. By mid-April Suffolk planned to be at Norwich; Will was told to rejoin him there.

To Burnham; to Bess. He had not seen Bess since the previous summer. He had missed her so much. It was a joyful prospect, to be exchanging the stiff formalities of the Earl's household for the simple pleasures of his own. To hold Bess again; to hug Amy and little John; to tell Bess all that had happened to him, all he had learned: how wonderful it would be!

He rode fast to Burnham Thorpe, with only a groom for company. The journey took him a bare two days: one day to travel from Wingfield to Norwich, and one from Norwich to Burnham. It was late afternoon when he arrived.

His horse was tiring, but he spurred it to a fast canter down the cobbled street of the village. Up the hill; past the church; and there on the hilltop was the Hall, square and plain and, oh, so dear to him, with the green meadow, dotted with sheep, wrapping all around it.

Dusk had fallen; there was an uncertain flicker of candlelight from behind the mullioned windows of the hall. He drew his horse up in the yard and rapidly dismounted.

A tiny figure came hurtling across the expanse of stony ground. 'Father!'

'Amy, my lambkin!' He caught her in his arms and brought her up high for his kiss. So heavy she had grown! So tall! Nearly three years old now. It was six, seven months since he had seen her, but she had known him straight away.

'Come back here this instant, Miss Amy!'

That was the nursemaid: a new one. Bess had spoken of her in her letters.

'I'm bringing her, nurse.' He lowered Amy to the ground, bent to deposit another kiss on her forehead and let her pull him across the yard.

The nursemaid was in the doorway, next to Mary Hannant. In her arms was a big laughing baby who was surely John. Will would not have recognised him; but how fine he looked! To think he had once thought babies all the same, miserable mewling little creatures. This one looked so sturdy and healthy and happy. He exclaimed over it, one hand still held fast in Amy's tight little grip.

'Where is your mistress?'

He said it in slight puzzlement that Bess too should not have run out to greet him.

'In the hall, sir, waiting for you. 'Tis not so easy for her to move just now.'

'Of course, the baby.' She had written that she was with child again, but it had not sunk in properly that he would find her swollen-bellied and weary. Easter, it was due: less than a month away.

He hurried down the corridor to the hall, with Amy skipping along at his side and Mary and the nursemaid following after him. There was the candle he had seen from the window, set in a bracket on the wall by the settle. And there was Bess, just getting to her feet as she heard him coming.

He caught her and hugged her to him, cheerfully oblivious to the servants, before he looked at her. But he felt immediately her ribs clearly moulded under his fingers, beneath the soft material of her dress, and when he lowered her back to the settle he could see the hollows around her eyes and beneath her cheekbones.

'Oh, Will,' Bess murmured, 'it has been a long winter.'

By daylight, next morning, Bess looked to him to be even worse than he had thought her on his arrival. There was a greyish tinge to her skin, and her neatly coiled fair hair was thinned and faded. Her joy at seeing him was genuine, he felt sure, but all the same, it seemed to him that it cost her an heroic effort to be cheerful in front of him.

He felt sympathy, of course, but also a kind of impotent horror; and anger at his own impotence. He should not have been gone for so long. But it had been necessary for him to be gone, necessary for him to establish firmly his place with Suffolk; it was by Bess's own choice that she had not come with him to London.

A wrong choice, perhaps; but he could understand why she had made it. To conserve her strength, in part; and in part, to express her disapproval at his decision to abandon Kitty.

She did not say this now – she did nothing deliberate to mar his homecoming. But he knew that he was not forgiven, because she asked no questions at all about his new master and mistress. He remembered her innocent curiosity when it had first been learned that Suffolk was returning to England, and knew that this was deliberate.

He should not have allowed her to conceive again, so soon after John. There was nothing to be done now; he should have acted the summer before, to prevent it. He could not blame it on his ignorance: Kitty had told him, forcefully, that it would do Bess no good to bear another child. She conceived so readily: once a year, ever since their marriage. It pleased her so that she should, but he knew that it was destroying her.

Amy and John were so fit, so strong, he thought, as he kissed her goodbye and made his way to the counting house where the bailiff was waiting for him. There was nothing of Bess's weakness reflected in them. But there had been another child, too: Richard, buried now under the flagstones in the Greyfriars in Norwich. The memory came back to him, stark and clear, of the terrible days when he and Bess had watched their baby sicken and die.

Then he had felt the same sense of hopelessness, the agonising knowledge that he would have done anything to prevent it, but there was nothing he could do. But Bess would not die, surely. Bess could not die. He could not bear to watch Bess die as Richard had died.

He pushed open the door to the counting house and set a smile on his face to greet Jack Hannant.

A strange person had been at work on the account books: Will saw immediately that many of the entries were not in Jack's writing, clumsy but solid, nor in his own. The numbers were formed carefully, but there were ink blots and smudges, one or two crossings-out, as if this other person were not familiar with the task facing them. It disturbed him. He took a pride in his account books: he did not like to see the entries botched. And it was Jack's job to keep the accounts in his absence: he did not like the thought that some other person had intervened.

'You have a new assistant, Jack?' he asked.

'Only old George, sir.'

Old George was a farmworker: hardworking, but uneducated – illiterate, surely?

'George made these entries?'

Jack peered over his shoulder at the book and Will pointed to them.

'Why, no, sir. That is the mistress's hand.'

The mistress? Will turned and stared at Jack. 'You mean my wife?'

'Just so, sir.' Jack looked uneasily back at him. 'I took it to be your orders, sir. Every week, since last autumn, the mistress has gone over the books with me.'

Every week, since the autumn? Bess, who hated to use a pen, and invariably asked Jack to write her letters to him; Bess, who had always professed herself muddle-headed when it came to figures?

He could not ask more questions, not of Jack.

'Stupid of me, Jack. I quite forgot that she mentioned it to me. Now let me see . . .'

There were more puzzles when he came to check the figures. 'This entry here, Jack: what is that?'

Jack looked. 'Why, the pigs, sir: the ones we sold on Burnham Market.'

'You sold the pigs?'

'Last October, sir. I know you said in the summer that you meant the meat for the household, but the mistress said . . .'

'Quite so, Jack,' he said hastily.

There was more. Slowly, over the course of a long morning, he uncovered it all. The sheep had been sold; not half the autumn kill, as he had intended, but all but a couple of carcases. Ducks and geese, too, on the Burnham Market. The money had all gone towards repaying his debts. Bess's orders, every one.

Had she meant it to please him? His deficit was down, well down; his finances were a great deal healthier than he had anticipated. But at what a cost! He had intended her to have meat every day during the hard weather and she could scarcely have eaten it twice a week. That was not what he had intended, not at all.

He confronted her about it, as gently as he could, that evening after supper when the servants had gone off to their quarters and they were alone in the hall.

Of course she had meant him to be glad; he sensed that, and did his best not to show her how much her intervention had dismayed him. But he soon realised that she had acted for a more selfish reason, too: to quell her own worries about the state of their finances.

How had she known, when he had done his best to keep his difficulties from her? It was not hard to worm the truth out of her. Kitty had told her. She had told Bess how much Will would have earned had he stayed on in Nottingham's service – and led her to believe that he had budgeted to receive such a sum. She had somehow discovered, and told Bess this too, how much Suffolk was paying him.

The interfering bitch! No wonder, he thought, that Bess had taken so hard his decision to leave Norfolk's employ for Suffolk's. For every letter that he had written to her telling her how good a move he had made, Kitty had written her two assuring her that it had been a disaster.

It was not a disaster. Patiently he tried to explain that to her. Eventually he went to fetch the account books, lit a second candle and showed her the entries detailing the investments he had made in the previous three years, in sheep and pigs, in hedges for his fields and new farm tools. He explained to her the pattern of return on his crops, showed her how the effect of his investments was slowly becoming apparent, described how he planned to repay his outstanding debts. This last was not his priority, but he did not dare to frighten her further by telling her about the additional money he had planned to borrow, so that he might do more to improve his lands.

She was still frowning when he came to the end of these explanations, so he went on to tell her something of what he knew about the Earl of Suffolk's finances. It had in fact been an unpleasant shock to him when he had realised that in spite of the lavish way in which the Earl's household was run, his new master was in real financial difficulties. When he had joined Suffolk he had thought airily of asking for more money as soon as he had given the Earl time to judge his worth; he had assumed that he would only need to request a loan to have it granted. This he did not tell Bess. But he did tell her that Suffolk had expectations of gaining a Household appointment through Bedford, and that the Earl had received some valuable grants of land from the King's Council in recompense for his loans to the exchequer. In the autumn, he reckoned, when he had been serving Suffolk for a year, it would be reasonable for him to ask for a raise in his fee. 'So you see, Bess, there is no cause for worry. None at all.'

'I see. Oh, Will, but it troubled me so, that I had done so little to help you! And the new cook, the one Lady Felbrigg recommended to me, seemed to think I had been so extravagant in the kitchens, and . . .'

'Then the new cook is a fool.'

Bess's face fell and he thought immediately that he had been too sharp with her.

'Or at least,' he hastily amended, 'the new cook did not realise that I wanted the best for you, Bess, regardless of the cost. A stronger woman might eat plainer food, and thrive on it, but you are not strong, and with the baby coming you need good meat every day. I want to see you well, Bess. I want that most of all.'

'I shall be, Will, as soon as the baby comes.'

He wished he could believe her.

Will fell easily into the rhythm of life at Burnham. There was so much to be done. Jack worked well, and the men under him, but the estate needed his own attention and it galled him that it should not have it. One day, he thought, when the sheep runs were paying off properly, he would cut down his commitment to Suffolk and spend half the year there, or even more.

Most days he rode across the fields, checking on the flocks and the state of the new hedges. Twice he went to Burnham Overy Staithe; and once, in a strange, restless frame of mind, he persuaded one of the boatboys to take him out to see the seals. He went to the Burnham Market and talked to the stallholders; he negotiated with the blacksmith and the carpenter and the other village craftsmen for the work that needed to be done that summer.

He saw few of his neighbours. Walter and Margaret Aslake called once, and he did his best to make them welcome for Margaret's sake, but could find little to say to his sister, and it gave him no pleasure to see the lines of discontent on her face. Sometimes it occurred to him that Bess rarely had visitors, but he was glad to have her to himself, and so tired at the end of each day that he never wished for other company.

It was a surprise little short of astonishment when one day, as he was in the counting house going over the rent returns from Cockthorpe with Jack, the stableboy rushed in to tell him that a knight had just ridden into the hall yard. On a great warhorse, the boy exclaimed, with a sword at his side and a dagger tucked into his belt; and a page trailing after him on a smaller mount.

Will rushed out immediately, eager to see who it might be. Halfway across the yard it had struck him that he was wearing his working doublet, which had seen much better days. He must cut a very ordinary figure in contrast to the splendid knight. He told himself firmly that he had no cause for humility: he came from a long line of knights himself, and he set a smile on his face and turned his scramble into a jaunty walk.

The knight was dismounting by the time Will reached him. The stableboy had not exaggerated: he was a fine sight, tall and straight, his tunic surmounted by a bright surcoat, and his crested helmet on his head.

He set a second foot down from the stirrup and turned towards Will.

'Miles! Miles Stapleton!'

'Hello, Will,' Miles said quietly.

When their hugs and exclamations were over, Will set his visitor at arms' length and looked him over. No wonder he had not known him until he was close enough to touch him: this was a Miles weathered, toughened, grown from boy into man.

'Heavens,' he said, burying his sudden sense of confusion in another smile, 'it must be three years since we met. But come in, come in. I'll call Bess and have Jack go for ale and cakes for us.'

They made their way side by side into the hall.

'Father told me you were at Burnham,' Miles said, 'and I thought to ride over and tell you my news.'

'I would have ridden over myself if I'd had any idea you were at Ingham. I heard you were in France, Miles, with Lord Arundel's men.'

'So I was. But I sailed back with Sir John Fastolf, some weeks ago.'

'And are you to stay?'

'Until my marriage, and a little beyond. I take up a

431

new posting after Easter with one of the Normandy garrisons.'

'Your marriage!'

It seemed just like the old Miles, the man who gave that bright laugh at his surprise. 'Just so: my marriage. But – why, you must be Bess . . .'

Will turned, following Miles' gaze. It was Bess, making her way down the steps from the solar. So slowly; so painfully, clutching the bannisters with every step. Hastily he dashed across the room to help her and to bring her to meet his friend Miles.

They had never met before, but he sensed immediately that they liked each other. There was a brightness in Bess's eyes, as if she were as delighted as he was by this unexpected visit; more liveliness in her manner than he had seen since his return to Burnham, as she told the housemaid to go and make sure that Jack had given the proper orders to Cook.

It was such a pleasure to him to have Miles there; but at the same time, there was something hurtful about the sight of Bess and Miles together. They belonged to such different times of his life, the laughing, careless knight and the woman with hollow cheeks and swollen belly. It had been a joy to him to get back to Burnham and Bess, but it struck him now that there had been no laughter since his return.

'Miles is to marry, Bess. Imagine, his bringing us news such as this!'

'Congratulations, sir. Is it a Norfolk lady that you are to marry?'

'It is. You know her, surely, Will: Elizabeth Felbrigg.'

Elizabeth: Sir Simon Felbrigg's daughter. He did indeed know her: as a pretty child, red-cheeked, dark haired, full of life and mischief. So Miles was to marry this merry girl, while he . . .

He promptly pushed the thought aside and echoed Bess's congratulations as effusively as he could. He genuinely was pleased for Miles: it was a good match for him, in every sense.

Then Cook arrived, with the cakes and ale, and his unease was gone for good, and they were laughing and drinking together, the three of them.

'From Ingham!' Bess exclaimed. 'You rode today, all the way from Ingham? You cannot possibly ride back tonight. So you will stay here with us? You must! For tonight, at the very least.'

'Alas, it can only be for tonight. I have to ride to Lynn in the morning. But I shall be more than glad to stay, if you will have me.'

What a day it was! The accounts were forgotten; he did not even remember to go back to the counting house and stopper his inkwell. There was so much to show Miles, so much to tell him, so much sheer pleasure in drinking and talking and walking with him.

The hard things, the worries, he would not have talked of to Miles. But no matter; it was as if the years fell away from him, it was like a festival, to glimpse even a shadow of the idle, merry times they had had together in Norwich. He could not remember when he had last laughed like this with anyone; could not remember, even, when he had last drunk cup after cup of ale without counting each one. There had been much to enjoy at Framlingham and at Bardi Place, but never a time when he could relax, never a moment when he could safely forget to mind his tongue.

There had been just that instant, when he had stood by and watched Miles and Bess greeting each other in the hall, when the knight had seemed like a stranger to him. But by the time supper was over and they were sitting side by side in the hall, the ale warm in their bellies and their feet propped up to feel the heat of the fire, that was scarcely even a dim memory in the back of his mind.

'I should have known,' he thought out loud, 'that you were at Ingham. How strange to think you have been there for weeks. I've heard not a word from your father.

When I think, I cannot remember when I last saw your father, or Sir Henry Inglose, or any of those men. They've not called on me here since I came from Wingfield; and I saw no one in Norwich when I stopped there on the journey.'

Miles did not answer him. He did not notice this immediately: they had been talking so easily that it seemed no more than a casual pause in their conversation. But the pause grew into a silence, an odd silence. He turned his face from the flames and glanced across at the other man. Miles looked back at him. Not with anger; not with contempt, or any other unasked-for emotion. But he knew all the same, knew beyond doubt, that something was wrong.

'My father will always be your friend, Will,' Miles said awkwardly. 'But he has taken it hard to see you turn into Tuddenham's man.'

'Tuddenham's man? But I am none such. I am the Earl of Suffolk's man, it is his apeclog that I wear.'

'But this is Norfolk, Will; and in Norfolk men take what Tuddenham does to be what his master does.'

There was a little silence, and Miles went on, 'You have not heard, perhaps, of Roger Watson of Lessingham? His sheep took the rot last summer. And when he could not pay his dues to the Duchy Tuddenham's men threw him from his land, fired his barns and hacked down his rooftree.'

'I had not heard.'

'But there are others such, many others; and you have heard of some of them.'

Of course he had. He had even seen a barn burned out on his journey to the staithe, asked what had happened and received nothing but nervous stares in response. In Suffolk the Earl had received a stream of complaints of just this kind: some not so bad, some worse. But in Suffolk Will had been able to think them merely annoying and tedious; while at home, when they touched Miles' neighbours and his own, they somehow appeared in a different light.

'You should know, Miles,' he said, a shade resentfully, 'that such work is not my work.'

'But do you plead for such men? Do you oppose Tuddenham and his curs? Do you speak with the Earl of such matters?'

'I have been so little time in his service, Miles. Tuddenham I have seen not at all, in London or at Wingfield. In time, when I am established, when my worth is known . . .'

'In time,' Miles said curtly, 'you will find it too late.'

'I hope it will not be so. You must tell your father, Miles, that I am no henchman of Sir Thomas, that I do none of his dirty work.'

'That I will,' Miles agreed. He changed the subject and began to speak of Normandy. There was still a warmth between them, in the candlelight; but there was a shadow, too, that lingered. And when Miles mounted his warhorse the following day, doffed his helmet and waved it to them, the crest streaming in the sunlight, he did not offer to call at Burnham Thorpe again.

It would have been safer, Will reckoned, if Bess had been in Norwich for the birth. She had given birth there to her other children, but she was determined that this Easter child should be born at Burnham Thorpe. It was too late, in any case, to alter that decision: she was now in no condition to make the journey back to Norwich.

The waiting came hard to him; and not just because he saw how hard it was for her. It seemed as if he had perpetually to rein himself in. Bess did nothing to offend him – indeed, she did everything possible to try to please him – but he could not be natural with her. He was afraid for her. He felt that he needed to keep all his stronger thoughts and emotions from her. The Bess he saw day by day, sitting in the solar with Amy and John at her feet, humming to herself and hemming endless napkins for the baby, had no connection, somehow, with the woman who had blotted those stumbling entries in the account book. This was a fragile woman, one who had to be protected. He dared not shout or swear in front of her, dared not grumble to her about the misdeeds of the farmhands and the ill effects of the cold weather on the wheat crop.

He missed Miles. Miles' wedding day came and he sent messages of good wishes from them both; but he could not leave Bess to go to Felbrigg for the wedding.

He thought a great deal, too, of Kitty. With anger, often. Her meddling seemed to him to have caused such harm to Bess. But oh, he would have been glad to see Kitty, if only to shout his fury at her. Oh, for a night with Kitty, to act her master between the sheets, to take his pleasure freely. He fought these thoughts, but still they came back to him.

On Good Friday Bess went into labour. It was an inauspicious day. Nobody spoke of this at Burnham Thorpe Hall, but he saw the maids in a huddle together whispering and knew that they too were thinking it.

He sent his groom for the midwife. He would have gone to sit with Bess till the midwife came, but she sent the nursemaid down to say that she would rather not have him there. He mooched around the hall, alone, for a while. Then he went in search of Amy. The nursemaid was still with Bess; the children had been handed over to the housemaid for minding. He took Amy and walked with her down to Burnham Thorpe Church.

By the time he arrived at the lych gate the church was filling fast for the Good Friday Mass. The miller and the innkeeper were standing on the path outside the porch, arguing; a dozen village children were playing at tag around the gravestones. Will caught one of the older girls and told her to mind Amy for him. He went into the church alone.

The Calthorp family pew was empty. He unlatched the door, went into it and sat down. He prayed a little; for much of the service that followed, he simply sat and thought. Two living children, he repeated to himself;

and a third who had been born alive. But Bess should have been stronger.

She was still in labour when he returned to the house. He left Amy in the dairy with the cook and went to saddle his mare. Only when he reached the stable did he remember that it was a Holy Day and he should not ride. He had thought of going to the sea, anyway, and on reflection he could see that it would have been too far: she might call for him when it was over and he ought to be near.

The iron latch on the stable door was broken. He decided to carve a new one out of yew. He reckoned the wood would be strong enough: it would save a few pence from the blacksmith and last for a year or two at any rate.

It was a fresh day, with a salt wind running off the sea and just the hint of a mist. He worked till dinnertime, then went into the hall and ate a frugal meal of black bread and herring. He could hear footsteps from the solar above; once or twice a woman came down to fetch hot water.

He went back to the stable, finished the latch and fitted it. He picked another branch of yew from his woodpile and began to carve a spoon. He was hollowing out the bowl when the nursemaid came running over the yard to him.

He stood up slowly. 'Is it over?'

'All over, sir. You have a fine son.'

They called him George. He looked to Will to be strong, but he sicked up the wetnurse's milk and did not thrive. Two weeks later he was dead.

Bess lived on, a pale wraith. She cried for two days, then she stopped her tears and called for John and Amy.

She did not call for Will, but he came to her anyway. He soon realised it was a mistake. Bess was grieving for George. He was not. They had Amy and John; it was a small sorrow to him that George was dead, but it mattered little when set against the fact that Bess was alive.

He wanted her to be more than alive; he wanted her to be strong and happy. If he had known what to do to make her so, he would have done it; but he could find neither words nor actions to which she would respond.

Bess had moved from solar to hall, and was sitting with the children, when the carter's boy came with a letter. Will was down at the staithe, so she took it for him. She gave it to him when he returned, and watched him turn it over in his hands. 'The Earl of Suffolk's seal?'

'That it is.'

'You should read it, then.'

'So I should.'

He did not want to read it in front of Bess, but she was sitting there looking expectant, so he broke the seal and unfolded the single sheet of paper.

'Does he call for you to attend him?'

He did; or at least, his clerk did so for him. There was no other cause for the Earl to write; he could see no sense in denying it.

'He calls, but he does not demand. I can be in Burnham for days, even weeks more; until you are strong enough to walk, at least.'

'I would rather you heeded his call.'

He let his hand drop, with the letter in it. He looked at Bess and she looked back at him. Her look was gentle, weary; but there was something stubborn lurking beneath the gentleness. 'We cannot afford to give offence to the Earl.'

It would not have caused so much offence, he thought. And he would have afforded it, had he thought it right for Bess. But he knew that it was not right for her. She wanted him gone.

She loved him still, he thought; but there was a gulf between them, and he could see no way of closing it. Except by time, perhaps. By giving her time and space.

'Then,' he said, 'I shall ride for Cossey tomorrow.'

17

ENGLAND

On a cold day in March a small procession of men rode
with military precision along a rutted track, across a
drawbridge that spanned a wide moat, and up to the tall
flint gatehouse of Wingfield Castle. At its head was
Secret Poursuivant, wearing his best – though extremely
shabby – blue and gold tabard. Behind him rode Sir John
Fastolf, flanked by esquires; and at the rear, two grooms
and a valet.

The portcullis began to creak upwards when they
were halfway across the drawbridge; it was still reced-
ing as Suffolk's Chamberlain appeared in the gateway.
Secret dismounted and nodded to the Chamberlain. The
esquires too dismounted and hurried to assist their
master; but Fastolf, still agile, was already on his feet
and holding out a calloused hand.

'We are not expected,' he said bluntly, 'but I have
news that the Earl will wish to hear immediately.'

The Chamberlain managed to keep an unperturbed
expression. He bowed and gestured to one of the pages to
take this information to the Earl. Secret, unobtrusive in
spite of his colourful attire, melted into the shadows. He
knew the castle well, knew where to find Suffolk Herald
and his other acquaintances. Fastolf and the remainder
of his escort waited with barely concealed impatience.
They did not have to wait for long. A steward appeared
only minutes later and invited them to follow him
across the broad, grassy square of the inner quadrangle
to the winter hall.

It was a low room, its flint walls supporting a steeply sloping roof, with a row of arched windows looking out across the moat and the meadows beyond. A pair of hounds lay stretched out in front of the fire, but every other inhabitant of the room stood at the doorway, with the Earl of Suffolk and his Countess at the forefront.

Fastolf strode forward and, ignoring Alice, took Suffolk's right hand in both of his.

'You'll not believe this,' he said, 'but Bedford plans to remarry before Easter.'

For a moment Suffolk was disconcerted; he had expected surprising news, but not of this nature. But he recovered quickly.

'You were right to come immediately. Let us find food and drink for you and your men, and then you must come with me to the solar and tell me more.'

Suffolk learned the core of the tale as Fastolf and his men were eating. This was not yet public information, but according to Fastolf it was all round Paris, and before long it would be all round London too. It would cause a scandal in both countries, for it was less than four months since Anne of Burgundy had died, and it had been generally understood that Bedford and his Duchess were a devoted couple.

And now, if Fastolf was to be believed, the Regent was panting to get into the bed of a seventeen-year-old: Jacquetta of Luxembourg, daughter of Jean of Luxembourg, a staunch Anglophile among Burgundy's lords, and niece to Louis of Luxembourg, Bedford's Chancellor. He planned to marry her fast: not least, because he did not want to give the Duke of Burgundy any opportunity to express his opposition to the match.

Burgundy's attitude was an issue to be discussed with Fastolf in private. In the hall, Suffolk turned instead to Alice and said, 'You remember the girl from Paris?'

'Only as a child. A pretty child with winning ways; but still, a child.'

'She's no child now,' Fastolf retorted. 'I never knew a woman so conscious of her own beauty, or so certain how to use it. Bedford is besotted. We've spoken to him, all of us, but he's beyond all appeal to reason.'

'You've spoken; to oppose the match?' Alice asked with frank curiosity. 'It sounds to be too hasty, true, but surely there is no other objection to it? Surely it's understandable that the Regent should be anxious to get himself an heir at last?'

Suffolk met Fastolf's eye. He tried to convey a warning and he sensed that he was receiving one in return.

'Marriages of state are always complex matters,' he said deliberately. 'There are arguments for and against even the best of them. You've finished your supper, Sir John? I have some finer wine in the solar, if you'd care to accompany me there.'

'All in good time.' The knight set down a chicken leg and wiped his mouth on his sleeve. 'Where's that damn poursuivant?' he asked. 'I'll have him ride to Caister tonight, to warn the servants: I'll be leaving for Norfolk in the morning.'

Secret materialised out of the shadows. 'I thought to sleep here tonight, sir, and ride at dawn.'

'Not so. You've supped, haven't you? Suffolk's man will find you a new mount. Let me come with you to the gatehouse and give you my message for the bailiff.'

The knight lumbered to his feet and marched off, leaving Secret to trail after him. Suffolk stood watching them retreat through the door. Then Alice touched his sleeve and said quietly, 'So this is a serious matter, my Lord.'

'It may be so.'

'The Cardinal too should know of it.'

She said this almost as a question, uncertainly.

'If there is reason to think that he does not, I shall ride myself in the morning and speak with him.'

Fastolf accepted the finer wine almost suspiciously, as if he had been expecting to call at a barracks and was disconcerted to be accorded the courtesies of a country house. But he drank it anyway, with frank enjoyment.

Suffolk watched him. He had not seen Fastolf since Orleans. He remembered what he had heard of Patay and the years afterwards, and he thought to himself that Fastolf had weathered them well. He was fast passing beyond a vigorous middle age, but his body was still stocky, as hard and sturdy as a treetrunk, and his eyes were sharp and watchful.

Fastolf set down his cup and met Suffolk's eyes.

'The Duke of Orleans was not in the hall,' he said brusquely.

'The Duke is my prisoner. He has a room in the west tower, and two jailers guard him constantly.'

'So he does not come to the hall?'

Fastolf said this with more than suspicion; almost with disbelief. Somehow he has learned how Orleans is treated here, Suffolk thought; and he did not like that thought.

'He comes sometimes, when there is music, and when there are no visitors. If you wish, you may meet him and talk with him.'

'Later, later.' He paused and drank again. 'Has he agreed to speak for us in the negotiations?'

'I am discussing the matter with him.'

'Then tell me what I should say, and I shall say it to him.' He paused once more. 'Bedford lets those who will, believe that he's marrying the Luxembourg girl so as to gain a new intermediary with Burgundy; but I doubt the Cardnal is fool enough to swallow that story. You should tell him that the Regent writes off Burgundy as a lost cause and is making shift to tie lesser allies to his side.'

'The Luxembourg men would barely furnish him one garrison. And they are Burgundy's vassals. Would they take the King's side if he were set against their lord?'

'I reckon they would. Better men that Beaufort have believed as much.'

'But you do not?'

442

'Bedford himself would like to believe it. But the plain truth is, he's not marrying the girl for that reason. He's marrying her because he's besotted.'

By the time Fastolf rode off the following morning Suffolk knew that neither he, nor any of the men who had come with him from France, had yet called on Cardinal Beaufort. He had his own horse saddled and his grooms prepare for the journey, and just before midday he set off on the long ride to Southwark. He reached Winchester Inn late on the following day and asked immediately for the Cardinal.

He had not made this journey only to please Alice. He had discovered, over the preceding year, that Beaufort was prepared to give limited support to his own policy for a negotiated peace in France, and in the wake of this discovery he and the Cardinal had found themselves in loose alliance. Beaufort was a pragmatic man. He understood at least in part why Suffolk had earlier supported Gloucester, and he bore only a slight grudge against him for failing to oppose Gloucester's savage attacks, particularly since Bedford's arrival had eventually served to neutralise them.

Indeed, Bedford's return to England had done much for Suffolk's causes. It had won him an appointment as Steward of the King's Household, and further eased his financial problems; but more than that, it had seen the formation of a faction who were openly committed to negotiations with the Valois. Bedford and Fastolf in France, Beaufort and Suffolk in England, were the leaders of this faction, though Suffolk knew that none of the others would have advocated peace except on terms that he believed they would never succeed in obtaining.

Gloucester remained their most vehement opponent. He would countenance nothing but outright capitulation by the Dauphin. And Suffolk was uneasily conscious that after a long period of under-the-counter trading of loans and privileges, Gloucester now had as much hold over him as he had over Gloucester; if not more, for the details of the King's financial crisis were no longer secret.

He, Beaufort and the rest all knew that while Gloucester maintained his opposition it was unlikely that any negotiations would come to fruition; but even so, they had been working towards a first meeting with the Valois that spring. Bedford's remarriage might change the situation drastically, so it was a matter of genuine urgency that Beaufort should know of it. But the Cardinal treated urgent news more casually than Suffolk did and he had to wait far longer in an anteroom at Winchester Inn than Fastolf had waited in his own gatehouse.

At last a priest appeared and guided him up to the hall, where the Cardinal sat, red robes arrayed in elegant folds, in a high chair under the rose window. He greeted Suffolk curtly, though not aggressively, motioned him to sit and listened intently to his story.

'You think Fastolf's information reliable?' he asked when the tale was told.

'I think him no man to see such matters where they are not plain to be seen.'

'Perhaps so.' Beaufort frowned as he said this and Suffolk added, 'Nor do I think he could have invented such a thing.'

'It dwarfs the imagination of a man like Fastolf; that is true.' The Cardinal frowned again and thought for some time. Then he said slowly, 'If he does this without Burgundy's consent, then it can be with no hope of pleasing, or even appeasing, Burgundy. True, Burgundy too has known what it is to lack an heir; but he will be in no frame of mind to sympathise. So we must believe, I suppose, that Bedford is choosing to strengthen his ties with the Luxembourgs in the hope that they will stay with him when Burgundy changes sides.' He lifted his pale blue eyes to Suffolk's. 'But to think this is to set Bedford down as a fool.'

Suffolk thought of Fastolf's opinion of Bedford's motives; for a moment he considered telling it to Beaufort. But he felt himself more truly Bedford's man than Beaufort's and it seemed to him that that would have been disloyal.

'To my mind, Bedford is caught in a trap. He watches it closing on him, and he looks for ruses which might spring the jaws open. I doubt if he really believes that this particular ruse will prove his salvation.'

'It is perhaps wiser than to depend upon the negotiations. Have you yet made Orleans see sense?'

'I have the statement drafted. By Easter, I reckon, I shall have persuaded him to sign it.'

'And it is clear?' In acknowledging Henry, he meant, as King of France.

'It is.'

'Then bring it to me as soon as it is signed. Richemont, Bourbon and the rest will take it for a sham; but even so, it may serve our purpose.'

'Fastolf was in England!' Judge Paston exploded.

'True, sir, he was.'

'In Suffolk!'

In Norfolk too, Secret thought to himself; but he did not say this.

'True, sir.'

'And now he is gone.'

There was a note of sheer despair in Paston's voice. Secret did not feel sorry for him, but he thought it politic to appease him and he said levelly, 'His visit was short, sir, and he had many men to see, and much business to attend to.'

'Oh yes, much business,' the Judge muttered with heavy irony. 'No matter. Come to me tomorrow after Mass, and I'll have my letters ready for you to carry.'

'I'll do that, sir.' Secret backed out of the hall of Princes Inn; and as he reached the yard, came flat up against young John Paston.

'Secret Poursuivant!' John exclaimed.

'Your servant, Master Paston.'

'Secret, you must come to the woodshed and see. Edmund has two tame rats and we race them through mazes. Can you come to see now? And have you news, news about the wars?'

'I have news, and I will come; but first I must see Kate, and Harry, and Cook.'

'We'll be there till suppertime. You know the way?'

'I know the way.'

John paused for a moment, then ran off across the yard. Secret stood watching him. He was no child now but a lad, of eleven or even twelve. A kind-hearted lad, full of enthusiasm, though not over-fond of his Latin. Sturdy and tall, though he could be clumsy and his face was plain as a barn door.

He thought to himself for a moment that there would be worse masters than John Paston when he was grown; and then he thought to himself that he had too many masters already and went off in search of Kate.

Fastolf come, and Fastolf gone! Damn that beggarly Breton! When Secret was out of sight – and, with luck, hearing too – William indulged himself by slamming his fist, hard, against the rough brick of the chimney-breast.

So many years since Fastolf had been in England; and now to come and go without a word! It was almost too much to bear.

It was his hopes that were dashed, admittedly, not his real expectations. He could not complain about the share of Fastolf's business that came to him and his clerks. But he looked for more than business: he looked for a patron for John and Edmund, and he could see no alternative but to allocate that role to Fastolf, though he was realistic enough to admit that Fastolf himself most likely did not intend this. The new Duke of Norfolk had put little business his way, the Earl of Suffolk none at all. Agnes' plan over the ditcher had seen the man freed from jail, but it had gained him nothing beyond this small satisfaction; though admittedly it had not, he judged, hurt him either. He remained on good terms with Gloucester, but his access to the Duke was strictly limited and Gloucester had flatly refused to give John a place in his household. Only Fastolf was left.

He could guess where Fastolf had gone, whom Fastolf had seen. He had seen John Welles. He must have come to renew the contracts to provision Bedford's retinue, and Welles' contract was the largest of all.

It was too late to catch Fastolf now: according to Secret, he would be at Dover already. But he had to go to London soon; and there would be something to be said, he thought to himself, for paying a visit on John Welles.

William had never visited John Welles' house or his shop: he invariably met the grocer at Fastolf Place. But three visits to Southwark, on successive days after his arrival in London, failed to turn up Welles; so after much deliberation, he decided to hunt out the bear in his cave.

He and Harry rode along past the haphazard sequence of taverns, stone churches and graceful old houses that lined Lombard Street on a drizzly April morning. They found Welles' premises without too much trouble. There was a double-fronted grocer's shop below, redolent of flour, spices and black soap. Above, the building reached up to two and a half storeys of brick-and-timbered parlours and bedrooms. The alley at the side showed glimpses of a busy confusion of yards and storerooms. They rode on past without stopping. William left Harry to stable the horses at the Cardinal's Hat and walked back alone.

He asked for Welles in the shop and after some whispering among the apprentices he was shown up to a parlour immediately above.

It was a dark room, empty of people and stuffed with furniture, all padded and carved and jumbled together. Welles' wife, presumably, had the taste for polished oak, for fringes and tassels. She must have chosen the shining silver dishes that crowded each shelf; she must nag the housemaids to maintain the artful level of tarnish on the pilgrim badges laid out on the armoury.

Welles' wife. He had never met Welles' wife: Welles kept her hidden away. Ill health, he told his friends, but in a tone which told them that it was ill temper, too, which kept him away so much from Lombard Street.

He considered what he had heard of Welles' wife. Like Fastolf, the grocer had married late in life. Again like his cousin, he had married for money. But where Fastolf had selected an aristocratic wife, John Welles had opted for a widow whose previous two husbands had been a stockfishmonger and a fellow grocer. There were children by the grocer – five, or was it six? – but Welles never spoke of them. There had been no children by Welles.

There were footsteps on the stairs. Would he meet the wife now? No; it was Welles himself who pushed open the door and sailed into the room, muttering apologies for keeping him waiting. He was in outdoor clothes; he slung his hat over the back of a chair and threw his cloak at an apprentice who had followed him in, and who was already encumbered with a wineflask in one hand and two cups in the other. He poured the wine himself when the boy had gone and handed one cup to William. They were very fancy cups: half coconuts, set in wrought silver stands.

Then he descended into a cushioned chair, settled himself comfortably and demanded to hear William's news.

William found the surroundings unnerving; and it was also unnerving, somehow, that John Welles should appear so much at home among them. He had never envisaged the grocer in a room like this, but the hat with its nodding peacock feather, so casually perched on the chairback, Welles' heavily beringed fingers curled around the fancy cup, the faint reflection of the grocer's plump figure in the polished surface of the little table: everything proclaimed that he was perfectly at ease in this tasteless little parlour.

He had come to glean news, not to provide it, but he searched his mind for something he might tell Welles. It was not easy. Welles would know all the news from

France; he would know about Wetherby's latest dealings on the Norwich Council; he doubtless had his sources at Westminster. William told a scurrilous tale or two from Framlingham. He mentioned the Duke of York with elaborate casualness. Welles did not react at all.

'York says,' he prodded, 'that he hopes for a commission in France.'

'He'll not get one. Neither Bedford nor the Dauphin will make a move now until Burgundy makes up his mind.'

'Makes up his mind? Burgundy will keep at his game until he dies – or till all France is his alone.'

'If you reckon so, William, then I guess you've not heard about the Lady Jacquetta.'

The Lady Jacquetta meant not a jot to him, but there was a touch of glee in Welles' voice that told him this was a part, at least, of what he had come to Lombard Street to hear. He listened. Welles told him.

'They say,' he concluded, 'that she is very beautiful.'

They? It did not sound like Fastolf's verdict. It had been Secret, presumably: this must be one of the (how many?) things Secret had not told him. 'Bedford surely has more sanity than to marry her for that reason.'

'Gloucester's brother? And good King Henry's?'

'Well, if he does so, he is a damn fool. But at least Fastolf is none such: I never knew him to look twice at any woman. And now we should reckon, perhaps, that this will bring him back to England for good?'

Welles shook his head. 'Not so. Bedford will not build up his forces, but he dare not reduce them either. He'd not release Fastolf, even if Fastolf were of a mind to come back. Not that he is.'

'I thought the messy business at Patay had broken his prospects.'

'True, it killed his reputation with the common soldiers. Mind, even after the herring fight they never thought him a Talbot. But Bedford . . . doubtless he'll not forget it altogether, but Fastolf's style of fighting suits him none to ill. Containment, that's his policy

449

now. He'll wait until Burgundy forces a move out of him – or until he faces the Dauphin across the conference table.'

'Nonsense. Bedford plays with that idea only to pacify Beaufort; and Fastolf, I'd swear, will have none of it.'

'Not so, William. Fastolf has put his weight now behind these planned discussions at Dover.'

'To sign away the King's lands? To accept the Dauphin as King of France? Christ in heaven, John! No sane man in England would stand for that! Nor any Englishman in France, neither.'

Welles did not reply. He simply sat, in his comfortable cushioned chair in his ghastly, overstuffed little parlour, drinking his wine from his fancy coconut cup.

At last William faced up to the unpalatable truth. 'You know this for certain.'

'Fastolf supports negotiation. Not surrender, William; but negotiation. And I support it too.'

'But Agincourt, man! Think of Agincourt!'

'I do. And of the Treaty of Troyes. But those are history now: pages in a chronicle, written long since and browned with age. Agincourt was close on twenty years ago. It must be ten years since Verneuil. What victories have we seen since then?'

'True, none to light bonfires for. But even so –'

'So turn the page. Think of Orleans; think of Patay. You should have talked to Fastolf. Think of Fastolf, in the days after Patay. He was a careful man before; now he is fenced high with caution. And this is the course of a cautious man: to work to secure what we have in France, and not risk all for the sake of gaining everything.'

He should have talked to Fastolf. But damn it, it was Fastolf who had chosen not to talk to him! 'A pity Fastolf does not choose to be cautious in Norfolk.'

Welles' bushy brows lifted for a second, and fell again. 'You have the Earl of Suffolk, now, in Norfolk.'

'And a damn disaster he has been.'

'So you wish you had Fastolf too; and why? So he might serve as Suffolk's opponent?'

'Jesus, man, we do not fight a war in Norfolk! These are not Bedford, Burgundy and Charles of Valois! I talk of an English county, of priests and farmers and dealers in wool. I talk of men who cry out for leaders to set a firm hand against insurrection and injustice. One powerful noble; even two, competing: that is not enough. We need many lords and knights; and not men such as Suffolk and Fastolf who think always not of their own country but of France, who pay their bailiffs and send their messengers home with shopping lists; but men who know what happens in the county.'

It was growing dark in the parlour. Welles had made no move to light a candle. A shadow fell over his eyes, obscuring their expression.

'Insurrection and injustice,' he repeated.

'And smaller misdeeds. There is too much bribery, too much intrigue, too much favouritism.'

'Too much power for Thomas Wetherby?'

'You know I think that, John; and for Tuddenham and Heydon.'

'Of course, Heydon is the Recorder now . . .'

'You know him?'

'He's never in London, but I hear tales of him. And what I hear leads me to reckon him too young and too brash to have any real influence.'

'But you are never in Norfolk, John. You see even less than Suffolk does. Alone, Heydon would be a nobody; but he is not alone. He is buttressed by Wetherby, Mayor again, and by Tuddenham, High Sheriff now of Norfolk and Suffolk. A strong Recorder might curb the Mayor's actions; this Recorder is the Mayor's puppet.'

'So the Mayor has at last pushed through rulings in favour of the Prior?'

William grunted. 'So the Mayor uses his power. Sometimes wisely, I grant you, but all too often for bad purposes.'

Welles frowned, as if to say that this was stale beer, and William persisted, 'Yes, John, there *is* proof. Still not enough to indict any of them, in a county where they dominate the courts; but enough to persuade men with open minds. Judges and jurors boast openly of being bribed. Men come to me over and over again with tales of intimidation and violence.'

'Involving Wetherby himself?'

'Involving Heydon, some of them. Involving the Nowell gang, and other associates of Wetherby's.'

Welles gave a little hiss: an ambiguous sound which might have indicated annoyance, or disapproval, or disbelief.

'Does Suffolk know this?' he asked.

That was an unexpected question; was it meant as a diversion, William wondered, or as something more? He thought about it for a while, then said carefully, 'He knows, perhaps, to the extent that you know it yourself. He must receive petitions from men wrongly imprisoned and fined, from tenants evicted and workmen threatened.'

'And he appears not to heed them.'

'He has his reasons, doubtless. Tuddenham and the rest are his retainers; I hear men praise him for backing them up. But this is not France. In Norfolk he heads no army of occupation. He should uphold the rule of law in the county.'

'Men might argue, William, that that is your own role.'

'It is a role I might play more effectively if I had the backing of men such as Suffolk and Fastolf.'

Welles did not reply. William looked at him. His face was almost lost in the shadows now, his expression hidden.

He felt a twinge of unease: he did not like to play the self-righteous moralist. Of course he had taken bribes himself: no man who refused them could have reached so high a position. It seemed to him, sitting there in the half-dark and thinking, that his own actions and judgements – like Fastolf's, though in a very different way – were hampered by the past. He had neither the right nor the inclination to play the hero, even had he been certain that heroics were required. He would exert his own authority, if at all, only when he was backed by men of position and influence.

'Of course,' Welles said, quite suddenly, 'Wetherby cannot stand again for Mayor. Not for – what is it, two years?'

'Three, but the latest Charter. He has a candidate lined up to succeed him, but perhaps he has not yet gauged the depth of opposition.'

'And you have?'

William took a sip of his wine and swirled the lees of it around the coconut cup. He said slowly, 'It would hardly be tolerated in London if the King or his Council were to interfere in the choice of Mayor.'

'Nor in Southwark, if Cardinal Beaufort, say, expressed a preference.'

'Nor in Norwich . . .'

'If a Judge, or the Earl of Suffolk, or the Duke of Norfolk, played a direct part in the proceedings.'

William nodded. 'The High Sheriff, naturally . . .'

'Has very considerable influence. And Suffolk influenced Tuddenham's appointment, just as he saw Tuddenham through as Shire Knight in the last Parliament.'

On this line Welles lumbered to his feet, went to the door and called down to a boy to come and light the candles. He poured more wine while the boy was passing round the room, and when the boy left he crossed over to the window and looked out. On to Lombard Street, that unfashionable thoroughfare which was still a centre of power and commerce; still the home of the Earl of Suffolk.

'Do you not agree, Judge Paston, that the merchants of this country hold far more real power than the Council and the King? When they choose, they can make or break a king. Let alone a man like Suffolk.'

'I doubt if Suffolk would agree with you there.'

'I suspect that with half his mind he would. And with the other half he would deny it just as vehemently.' Welles turned, an unexpectedly quick and decisive action. He lifted his cup to William. 'To Mayday,' he said.

Mayday. The date of the elections in Norwich. What did he know? What did he think would happen on Mayday? It was less than three weeks away.

Very slowly, William raised his own cup. 'Mayday it is.'

18

ENGLAND

In a room high in the west tower of Wingfield Castle, an Englishman who had spent most of his adult life in France sat over a chessboard with a Frenchman who had spent most of his adult life in England. They talked as they played, slowly and thoughtfully, moving effortlessly and apparently at random between English and French.

Suffolk set his hand on the black king and moved it one square to his left. 'The divine right of kings,' he murmured.

'Which providentially attaches to whichever man his subjects maintain in that position.'

The sardonic response surprised him a little, though it was perhaps a tactic he should have anticipated.

'You do not mean that, Charles,' he replied evenly. 'You fought for the Dauphin, did you not, because you genuinely believed that it was right for this man to reign as King of France?'

Orleans had not actually fought for the Dauphin. He had been a captive since long before the death of King Charles the Sixth of France, and it had been for that King that he had last fought. He did not point this out.

'Among other reasons. I believe it is wrong for kings to usurp their position by force.'

'Or to obtain it by treaty? But Henry of Lancaster has a good claim to the throne by inheritance – a better claim, many would say, than does the Dauphin.'

'Which is why,' Orleans responded, advancing a

pawn, 'there are the two kings on one board. The two opposing armies.'

'In which the kings are the weakest pieces.'

'And yet,' Orleans replied, his eyes tracking a weak diagonal, 'the most important.'

'How true. How different the game would be if either king were a powerful piece, dictating the pattern of the game, attacking forcefully. That is the irony of our chessboard, is it not? That men fight for the right of two kings to obtain a position that neither of them particularly desires for himself. Henry would just as well learn his lessons and read his missal at Westminster, while Charles of Valois looks only to maintain his comfortable little court at Bourges.'

Orleans gave him a careful look. But it was no news, Suffolk thought: it was nothing they had not said to each other before; though before, perhaps, it had been said in words more elegantly veiled.

'But that,' said the Duke, 'is not what they were born for.'

'So they must be made to compete. And if they will not do so themselves, their supporting pieces must advance their claims for them.' Suffolk reached out to move a bishop to command the dangerous diagonal – and to pose a threat, though he expected his opponent to have anticipated it.

'We do.' Orleans made the inevitable countering move.

'How different the game would be if either side possessed a piece with overwhelming power: a queen, say, who could dominate the board. True, the Valois did seem to have one for a time with the Pucelle, but they drove her into a corner and sacrificed her. Maybe not deliberately, but predictably, because it was so clear that they feared and distrusted her. And now they, like the English, are more concerned to maintain the balance on their own half of the board than to attack their opponents.'

'Your move,' Orleans reminded him.

They sat in silence for some moments, staring at the board. Then Suffolk looked up and at the other man. He wanted his gambit to be seen for what it was: a carefully thought out, deliberate move. He set his hand to a knight and brought it out to the centre of the board. Threatening, exposed. He and Orleans had played many times together; when he concentrated, he knew, the edge was his. He doubted if Orleans would be able to decide whether this was intended as a simple sacrifice or as a trap.

'Perhaps you think to yourself that after all it is politic to allow me to win this game?' Orleans said half to himself.

'Or perhaps I am aware that you are likely to win it anyway?'

It might have been true: the game was still quite evenly poised. But Orleans declined the gambit. He moved a rook to protect his threatened bishop.

'Of course,' he said, as he made the move, 'sacrifices are often a sign of poor strategy. In a well-planned game each piece advances only to protected squares. Each piece is buttressed by its lesser supporters.'

'Of course.' This time Suffolk moved fast. He wanted to make it clear that he had anticipated Orleans' last move all along; that it had suited his strategy admirably. He brought out his queen. Now Orleans could not fail to see the inescapable checkmate three moves distant.

He did see it. He did not even pause to consider all the possible counter-moves. He rose abruptly from his low stool, felling his king with a casual, almost impatient gesture as he did so.

'Your game.'

He stalked to the single arched window. Suffolk spun round on his own stool to watch him.

It had all turned out just as he had planned; but now he felt a momentary – not unease, but sorrow, that it should be so. He had no shame. He was acting from the best of motives, and without deceiving Orleans in any way. He had meant it to be a bargain, and it was: a fair bargain. But there was no honour in it for the other man. To him, it could only appear as a trap. It was this thought that made him say, impulsively, 'Naturally I would not dream of enforcing our agreement.'

'But you had my word.'

True. He had earned it through honest and open discussion. If Orleans still felt some uncertainty in his heart, in his mind he knew this to be the way forward. Suffolk, too. But it was a hard way to use a friend; and he needed this man as his friend even more than he needed him as a political ally.

He had schemed, planned, risked much to gain custody of Orleans. But that had not been for the sake of the peace negotiations: that had been that he might come to know the poet. Except that the poet was born French, and a royal duke; and he himself was English, and a servant of King Henry. They could not change these things; he knew now that he should have faced up much earlier to the realisation that they could not ignore them either.

It was much, he told himself, that they should have become friends at all. He was confident that they were. Their trust in each other was true, though limited; their loyalty to each other was real, although as honour demanded it came second to their loyalty to their kings. Their talk was sometimes barbed and guarded, but it was nevertheless frank considering that they had been made by circumstances to be each other's enemies. It was unfortunate that he should need to make use of Orleans, but he did not doubt that if their positions had been reversed, Orleans would have made similar use of him. At least the whole matter had been carefully measured and laid open.

So, in friendship and with resignation, Orleans would sign. He had to sign; for without his signature there would be no peace negotiations, no chink in the wall of his cell, no prospect, however distant, of one day regaining his freedom.

Orleans moved. He crossed to a carved desk, set by the wall of the room. In silence he selected a quill, uncorked a pot of ink and dipped in the tip and scratched his signature on the last sheet of a lengthy document. Not bothering to sand his work, he left the topmost sheets folded back and moved to a table. This was his room. On the table his servant Robert had set out on a silver platter a flagon of wine and two silver cups. Robert was not with them, so Orleans poured the wine into both cups himself.

Suffolk watched all these operations with an intentness that was betrayed only by the expression in his light brown eyes. He watched in silence, until Orleans was pouring the wine. Then he said, with elaborate casualness, as if he had not noticed any break in the continuity of their conversation, 'Naturally I appreciate that a wise man puts only limited faith in promises obtained from prisoners.'

It was not really intended as a concession. This was one of the unspoken premises upon which they had negotiated the bargain; the only difference now was in its being spoken out loud. He meant it to reassure Orleans. And he suspected from the other man's slight change of posture that it did, though no more open acknowledgement was made. Orleans picked up one of the cups and drank deeply. He turned his head and looked back at the desk.

They were both too distant to read the words, but either of them could without over-much effort have recited them from memory. The proposals were decked out in legal jargon, set forward in Orleans' name. Signed in that room, by that man, they could be taken to mean everything or nothing. For in the midst of the meaningless phrases were embodied the Duke of Orleans' acknowledgement of Henry of Lancaster as King of France and England and Lord of Ireland; his enumeration of the French nobles who would, he believed, assist in peace negotiations; and the offer of his own castles of Blois, Orleans and Chateaudun to the English.

Orleans gave this document no more than a brief glance, then he turned again, to look Suffolk straight in the eyes for the first time since he had known the game was lost. 'Do you know,' he said, in the voice whose gentleness Suffolk now knew to be a deceptive indicator of his inner strength of purpose, 'I believed once that you expected your companions to accept my sacrifice.'

'Did you so? I thought you believed only that I expected them to believe you in offering it.'

'And you think even now that they will?'

'Perhaps not. But it is has a certain value to us, nonetheless.'

'As an illusion?'

That was what it was, Suffolk thought wryly: a pretence, shadow-thin, that Orleans might be counted as Henry of Lancaster's supporter. Gloucester would not believe it; Burgundy would not believe it; Charles of Valois might let out a token curse when he heard of it, but it was hardly conceivable that he would take it seriously either.

'Perhaps so,' he said. 'But in negotiation we hide behind illusions. We set up shadow puppets and let no man walk behind the curtain and touch the pieces themselves.'

'No man? No opponent, true; but what of the men on your own side?'

'Not even them.'

'Not even yourself?'

That was a bee sting of a question. He had thought himself on the same side of the curtain as Orleans. But no; it came to him clearly now that he had passed only one barrier, and that there was an infinity of barriers set up around this man's heart and mind. He crossed the room, reached out without touching Orleans and picked up the second cup. 'Just so,' he said. 'Not even me.'

19

ENGLAND
May, 1433

It was May Day. Underneath the chequered flintwork of the gable end of Norwich Guildhall, the pillory stood empty. The cage for prisoners below the pillory stood empty too, and the stocks. Even the adjacent well was unusually deserted. The gable end stared blankly down its hill towards the second hill topped by the huge white bulk of the Castle.

A few boys guarded the piles of baskets, the haunches of beef, the clucking chickens and the bales of rope that bordered Norwich Market. A scant handful of customers shouted and argued at the stalls, munched pies and disappeared, laden, down Gentleman's Walk. But around the scaffolding surrounding the porch leading into the Guildhall, where a small tower was half-built, a thick knot of men crowded.

They could not enter the building, not because the double doors were locked – on the contrary, they stood wide open – but simply because it was already crammed solid with people. Men were pressed shoulder to shoulder along the corridors and up the stairs. In the great hall the crowd was so dense that men hung from the narrow windows, gasping for breath. Men jostled around the foot of the dais, the sole spot at which the floorboards could be glimpsed, heaving and shouting at its serried rows of occupants. Sweat glistened from a thousand faces. The weak drooped, overcome by the powerful stench of over-excited, underwashed humanity.

Had there been less chaos, the sheriffs might have

checked the credentials of those entitled to vote. In that case Secret Poursuivant would never have succeeded in taking his place at the back of the hall, just out of range of the surges that periodically swept through the doorways, packing the crowd even tighter. Had this possible drawback occurred to John Welles, he wondered?

Welles had been vague, suspiciously vague, when Secret had asked whom he was to watch, what he was expected to learn. He was not even, he thought with more indifference than exasperation, a particularly suitable observer. He knew only a few of the men in the hall even by sight. His regular trips to Norwich had told him only a little about the rivalries on the City Council. The grocer could scarcely look to him for a deep analysis of the situation.

But Welles had known something, that was obvious. This was no run-of-the-mill election; it was evident even to him that political passions in Norwich were at their spring tide and threatening to flood. Welles had known that, though he had not ventured north of Shoreditch in all the time Secret had known him. Did Welles also know – or guess – just where the banks would break? He wished he knew himself.

But he did not, so he stood in his inconspicuous position at the back of the hall, reacted not at all when his neighbours jostled him and whispered in his ears, watched and waited.

Most of all he watched the men he knew: the men on the dais. At the centre sat Thomas Wetherby, the outgoing Mayor of Norwich. He wore a scarlet cloak and about his shoulders was draped the mayoral chain. Their crimson gowns trimmed with beaver marked out the twenty-three men who sat on either side of him, and in a second row behind, as the other Aldermen, from among whose ranks would be chosen the next Mayor; but Secret knew the names and faces of only two or three of them.

With these men on the dais were the other City

officials: on the left, the mace bearer and sword bearer, and on the right, the coroners, serjeants and sheriffs. Tuddenham was at the very end. He seemed to shrink inside his gown, as if he wished he could fade inconspicuously into the shadows; but that was no realistic aim for a High Sheriff of Norfolk and Suffolk. Wetherby kept glancing at Tuddenham, though the Sheriff's constantly twitching face turned in every direction except the one which would have brought it into confrontation with the Mayor.

Suffolk's men, Secret thought. Tuddenham was openly so; Wetherby by repute, as he had learned long before in the taverns. And Heydon, too, enjoyed the Earl's protection by all accounts. Superficially at least, Norwich had become Suffolk's city, Norfolk Suffolk's county. Suffolk himself was in Norwich, men claimed – or at least, within an easy ride of the city, at Cossey. Was this the reason why men appeared to hope and fear so much of this particular election: because they expected Suffolk's men to use it to try to tighten their stranglehold, their rivals to use it to try to break it? This was the closest he had come to a thesis; but in the taverns, the men to whom he had talked had been uncharacteristically tight-lipped when he tried to press them.

Heydon was talking – speaking officially, as Recorder of the City. In his hand, clenched in front of a sizeable pot belly, was a sheaf of papers. He stood with his legs slightly apart, as if he had settled his weight comfortably on them in preparation for a lengthy harangue. His voice rose and fell in a dull, irregular rhythm. Nobody was listening. Heydon surely realised this, but the knowledge did not appear to discomfit him. He spoke pompously and (thought Secret) badly. His Latin epithets were mangled, his French proverbs worse than bizarre. His English words contained no message that Secret could discern, certainly no clue to the mysteries behind the election.

Secret's eyes drifted back to Wetherby. He saw the

Mayor exchange nods and glances with a couple of the other Aldermen, as if he were checking on agreements that had already been made. Heydon's voice, meanwhile, droned into the final formal phrases of his oration: 'So, in accordance with the Charter given to this City by King Henry the Fifth, and with the amendments to the Charter agreed under the seal of King Henry the Sixth, I now pronounce that the proceedings for the election of a new Mayor shall begin.'

Heydon gestured to another man, who scrambled from the front of the crowd and up on to the dais. 'John Querdling shall be your speaker.' He peeled a couple of papers from his sheaf, handed them to Querdling and turned to lead the Mayor and Aldermen from the room. They retreated through a curtained doorway at the rear of the dais, which gave, Secret knew – he had checked out the layout of the Guildhall the previous day – on to stairs that led both down to the street and up to the Mayor's parlour.

This, surely, was where Welles really needed a spy – behind the hangings in the Mayor's parlour. But the grocer had not implied to him that he should go to such lengths. Perhaps Wetherby himself would tell Welles what took place there? Perhaps he had bribed one of the other Aldermen?

His eyes fixed on the curtain, he woke only slowly to the realisation that Heydon's arrangements had run into a slight hitch. There was a rustling and stirring among the crowd immediately below the dais. 'Hey!' one man shouted. 'We'll not have Querdling.'

'We choose our own speaker,' another echoed him.

But Heydon had already disappeared; and Querdling, a plump tanner, paid no attention. He had an extremely loud voice. He bent his eyes to the topmost paper and began to read out the proclamation: 'Sirs and friends, for the love of Jesus Christ in proceeding with this present election, behave yourselves goodly and honestly, and without love, hate or dread, choose and name two sufficient persons for the office of Mayor, such as are

464

honourable and profitable for this city. Of which each of them shall previously have been Mayor or Sheriff of this city, and of which neither shall have been Mayor less than three years before.

'The Aldermen eligible to be Mayor this year are Richard Purdance, John Manning, John Gerard, John Asger, William Grey, Gregory Draper, John Wilby, Robert Topps, Richard Moseley and John Copping.

'May I have your shout for Richard Purdance . . .'

So this was how it was done. Secret had asked, but the accounts he heard had made little sense. He had not expected anything so crude. But it was, he now realised, an effective procedure. Querdling prompted the crowd to cheer for each of the candidates. He then decided which names had received the loudest acclaim and retired to put these forward to the Aldermen. These latter voted more decorously, in the privacy of the parlour, for one of the Commons' two candidates.

Querdling appeared to be either unable, or unwilling, to impose any kind of order on the crowd, let alone silence. Everyone was shouting all the time, though they did shout perceptibly louder when Querdling yelled the names of their favoured candidates. As far as Secret could judge, the outcome would be self-evident. The loudest shout of all was for a man named Richard Purdance. He knew the name, though not its owner; knew him for a rival of Wetherby. Would the second candidate be Wetherby's man? It would be John Gerard, he reckoned, but he knew nothing of Gerard.

With much shoving and pushing, the process staggered to a close. Querdling plucked a little group of men from the crowd – how he chose them, Secret could not tell – and strutted self-importantly towards the doorway.

The noise level fell momentarily as he disappeared through it, and then rose again. There would be a wait, presumably; a long wait. A thousand arguments resumed among the crowd.

Secret listened to the chatter he could easily hear from where he stood. To his left, a shipman was relating to his companions a tale of skulduggery at the tolls. 'So I told the gateman,' he continued, 'that three bales I brought in, and three bales I would pay for. But he claimed they weighed as four, and . . .'

To his right, two masons were arguing about the strength of the ale at the Popinjay and the Rising Sun. Though vehement, their conversation seemed perfectly apolitical. In front of him a priest was whispering in a tailor's ear. 'Gerard', Secret heard, and 'Wetherby'; but he could not piece the tale together.

The curtain over the doorway flickered and was then swished aside. A group of men emerged from behind it. They were the men who had left with Querdling; but not Querdling himself, not the Aldermen. As soon as the curtain had fallen behind the last of them the conversations started up again. 'So I drew my knife, and he called in his clerk, and . . .'

John Querdling reappeared. He strode across the dais and slipped down into the thick of the crowd. There was another long hiatus. Then at last the curtain was pushed aside again, and in the darkness behind it, Secret glimpsed the bright scarlet of the Aldermen's cloaks, the gleam of Wetherby's chain.

With measured strides, Thomas Wetherby led the Aldermen and John Heydon back on to the dais. He moved to the front, turned and watched as the rest of the men seated themselves. Then he swivelled back to face the crowd; and waited, silently, until the volume of noise fell around the hall.

'Sirs,' said Wetherby in his treacle-thick voice, 'we the Aldermen of the City of Norwich received as your nominations for the position of Mayor of this City' – he paused theatrically – 'the names of Alderman John Gerard and Alderman William Grey. We have voted accordingly. And I hereby pronounce that the new Mayor of the City of Norwich will be Alderman William Grey.' He turned to the clump of Aldermen and reached out his hand as if in welcome. The Alderman who rose to his feet was one of the men to whom he had been nodding earlier. He was short, bald, with a smooth skull and a creased face beneath it. He crossed the dais and took Wetherby's hand. The two men bowed to the crowd. 'And now,' continued Wetherby, 'I shall complete the proceedings by leading the new Mayor home.'

'That's not what we said!' a man shouted near the dais.

'It was Purdance we wanted. Purdance and Gerard.'

'Master Sheriff.' Wetherby turned to his left, with a small nod, and the two city sheriffs moved smartly forward, sticks in their hands. 'The nominations we received were for Gerard and Grey. And the election has been performed in accordance with the rules set down in the Charter of the City.'

'We'll not have Grey!' shouted the crowd.

'Purdance!' voices yelled. From the corridor, Secret could hear the beginnings of a rhythmic shout. 'Purdance! Pur-dance!'

Wetherby's small figure seemed to puff and grow. His cheeks expanded, his lips thinned. He turned to William Grey and spoke in his ear, inaudibly. Then he turned back to the crowd. 'Grey it is for Mayor,' he shouted.

'We're having none of him!' the crowd yelled.

'You'll have who Mister Wetherby says,' shouted the mace bearer, jumping to his feet and swinging his mace with both hands, 'or I'll crack your damned head open!'

'And I'll cut off yours!' retaliated a butcher, leaping on to the dais and waving his cleaver in the air.

As the sheriff reached to grab the butcher's wrist, Thomas Wetherby gave a tug to Grey's arm and turned in a sudden movement towards the curtained doorway. A clerk whipped aside the curtain and the two men dipped under it. Wetherby paused, turned once more and cried, 'Grey it is for Mayor!' Then, pushing the hesitant new Mayor in front of him, he beat a hasty retreat down the stairs.

Secret, pinned against the back wall, saw the cleaver fly from the butcher's hand and transcribe a wide arc across the room, smashing the glass of a window in the far wall. The mace bearer was wielding his mace like an axe, crashing it down on to the heads and shoulders of the men near the dais. A sheriff crashed to the floor. A couple of Aldermen surged to the front; a dozen workmen vaulted on to the dais from the floor. John Heydon and Sir Thomas Tuddenham, their faces whey-coloured, joined the stampede to the far stairs.

A pair of apprentices pinned the mace bearer to the floor and a tall, fat Alderman, grabbing the mace, jumped with unexpected agility on to the Aldermen's bench.

'Who's for Purdance as Mayor?' he yelled above the mayhem, twirling the mace in his hand.

'Pur-dance!' The thunder of the crowd was his reply.

'And who's for Grey?'

A hiss came from a section of the crowd, and a rotten egg, badly aimed, exploded on the wall behind the dais.

'Then I declare that Richard Purdance is Mayor of this City.'

The shout that greeted this declaration was so loud that Thomas Wetherby and William Grey could have heard it halfway across the market place to Rampant Horse Street. Secret cheered with the rest, calculating as he did so the odds of his succeeding in extricating himself from the crowd and catching up with Wetherby. He decided they were minimal.

The fat Alderman rapidly restored a kind of order. Purdance, a tall, thin man, joined him on the bench. They argued together for some time, then the fat man announced that the election would be repeated.

It was, to the accompaniment of a thousand arguments as to whether it would be valid if conducted without Wetherby's presence. The fat Alderman once more declared Richard Purdance to be Mayor of Norwich. The arguments continued. Some men did not want Richard Purdance as Mayor; many more argued that he would never succeed in acting as Mayor after such an election. Purdance and the other Aldermen, visibly uncertain, whispered in gaggles on the dais. Finally Purdance stepped once more to the front and announced to the crowd that he was sending for the Bishop of Norwich.

The Bishop! The commons erupted in a mixture of amazement, relief, disgust, fury and – from more than a few – hilarity.

It was, thought Secret, an incredible move. More practically, he reckoned it would be a slow one. Perhaps Purdance would manage to persuade the Bishop to come, but he would hardly succeed in bringing him to the Guildhall at a trot. And if he did come surely Bishop Alnwick would not be either brave or foolish enough to announce a verdict immediately, and in public.

The hall was already emptying; men who had attended out of no more than idle curiosity, or who despaired of seeing a resolution that day, were drifting homewards. Secret joined the movement towards the door.

There was more to know; more to happen. But it would not happen in the Guildhall. It would happen at Wetherby's house; in the Bishop's Palace; in the inns and parlours of Norwich; perhaps even at Cossey Lodge or Suffolk Inn. Within a day or two every whisper and nod would be related in the taverns. That was where he should go if he wished to learn the rest of the tale.

Did he wish to learn it? He ought to find out, he knew, for the sake of his good relations with Welles. But he was conscious that the excitement and fury of the crowd had not caught him up; it had merely pointed up to him the gulf between himself and those who cared intensely about the affairs of this city. Norwich was no home to him: he had never thought that more clearly than now.

A poursuivant: a pursuer. But it was a sad thing, Secret Poursuivant found himself thinking that May Day, to pursue nothing but information. A riot, a battle, a disputed election, a robbery or a murder: all were to him facts. He was an eternal witness, matching other men's endeavours, cataloguing their passions and their loyalties. And feeling, he thought in that moment of desolation, scarcely more than that most shallow of loyalties himself: his allegiance to any man who paid his fee.

He would tell any man, at a price, what he had witnessed in the Guildhall; tell them true, as far as his eyes and ears and mind could piece the story together. He would even tell that harsh, distrustful old Justice, William Paston. How furious Paston would be, he thought viciously, when he learned that the Aldermen had sent not for him to adjudicate on the legality of their election, but for the Bishop. No; perhaps not so furious. It was a dangerous business to confront Thomas Wetherby at his most ruthless: perhaps Paston would think himself well out of it.

Should he go to Princes Inn? Should he tell Paston before any other witness could beat him to the account, and watch the Judge's face as each twist and turn of the tale unfurled? It was a wicked temptation. But he remembered, belatedly, that Judge Paston was one of the many men to whom John Welles had not wished him to advertise his presence.

And his commitment to Welles was not, perhaps, as mean and shallow as he had thought it; for he kept to the orders Welles had given him, and with a little sigh, set out instead for the Popinjay.

The parlour of Cossey Lodge was decorated with may. The Countess of Suffolk had ridden out that morning with her ladies to gather it, and she had arranged it in great bunches, foaming white, in the unlit fireplace and on a small side table. Alice herself sat sideways on a high chair by the fireplace, drumming her fingers on the carved oak of its back.

She was irritated, Will knew, because Tuddenham had not arrived. She had calculated on his appearing before Gilles began his songs. It had passed the stage when they had murmured that Tuddenham was rather late. They had already voiced, in cautiously general terms, some of the reasons why Tuddenham might be delayed. Now they were beginning to be anxious.

Will glanced around the room. Suffolk was standing by the hearth. Every few moments he glanced across at Alice. There was affection in his look but also, Will decided, more than a touch of exasperation.

Gilles was tuning his lute yet again; he was alone at Cossey, for the rest of his band had remained at Bardi Place. And Lucette was concentrating fiercely on her embroidery, as if to ward off with the little square of linen the sharp edge of Alice's growing displeasure.

He himself was the only other person in the parlour. The household servants were in the great hall, and Alice had invited nobody else but Tuddenham.

Will had thought once to take Suffolk's livery so as to involve himself more deeply in Norfolk political affairs; yet on the day of the Norwich elections he found himself trapped three miles away in Cossey Lodge, exchanging light banter and waiting to listen to songs.

He had tried to tell himself that he had thought of throwing himself into larger issues than squabbles on the City Council; but he had sensed, from the many whispered conversations he had stumbled on since his return from Burnham Norton four days earlier, that the question of who would succeed Wetherby as Mayor was considered far from trivial in the city, and in the county too. And what else had he had in mind? Roger Lessingham's fallen rooftree? He had not spoken to Suffolk about that, and he knew it to be a poor excuse that Lessingham had been a Duchy tenant and not one of Suffolk's own, and a little better excuse that Suffolk had been preoccupied with waiting for news of the peace negotiations.

He was glad, in a sense, that he had been expected to stay at Cossey and not to appear in public with Tuddenham and Heydon. He would be glad of Gilles' music, which had done much to soothe his mind since his return. But all day he had had an uneasy feeling that he should know more, should be doing more, and this had intensified with Tuddenham's continuing failure to appear.

'I think,' Alice said just then, with a bright, decisive air as if she were conscious that it was good of her to take the little disappointment so cheerfully, 'that we should forget Sir Thomas and go on with the music.'

Suffolk nodded, but made no comment. He turned to the lutanist. 'Something merry, Gilles.'

Gilles bowed his head and settled the lower edge of his lute more comfortably on his legs. Will watched the expressions flicker across his face as he considered what to play. It would be something to please Alice: Gilles cared a great deal about pleasing Alice.

He began with variations on an Italian tune, fast and fiery; but he seemed to recognise that Alice remained fidgety and soon slipped smoothly on into one of her favourite songs, a ballad with a maying theme. Alice joined in the last verse, her light, clear voice blending with his handsome tenor; then she turned abruptly to Suffolk, before he could begin another.

'If you are really concerned,' Suffolk said, 'then I shall send one of the grooms to Norwich for you.'

'Sir Thomas is usually so reliable.'

Will said, 'Almost certainly he had been delayed on sheriff's business. There may have been trouble in Norwich after the election.'

'There is too much trouble around Tuddenham,' muttered Suffolk, half to himself.

Alice's gaze flicked over to Will and then back to her husband. Will had heard; he did not pretend otherwise, though he did his best to keep the full extent of his surprise to himself. 'I could ride across now, my Lord. It's still light outside; I would be at Suffolk Inn before dusk.'

'If you could . . .' Alice began; but Suffolk interrupted her ruthlessly. 'Thank you, Calthorp, but I shall go myself. I wish to speak with Tuddenham. Tell James I shall want horses and two – no, perhaps three men to accompany me. I shall leave as soon as I have dressed for the journey. Alice, my dear, you will forgive my entrusting you to the present company?' He crossed to take Alice's hand as he spoke and fixed a deliberate look on her, as if he were expecting her to make up for his little indiscretion. Alice evidently recognised at least part of its message. She lowered her eyes and murmured her thanks.

Will went in search of James, the head groom. Suffolk go to Norwich! So he too has sensed something, he thought to himself; and he too, perhaps, feels that he should be doing something. He felt relief at that thought. Since his conversation with Miles Stapleton he had thought at length about Suffolk's attitude to Tuddenham's misdeeds, and his thoughts had not been confortable. He was anxious for proof that his master was capable of decisive action on local affairs.

He lingered in the yard until Suffolk appeared, cloaked and spurred for the ride. The Earl glanced around the yard, taking in the waiting men and horses, and then, to Will's surprise, made for him. He took Will by the sleeve and drew him aside so that they could talk without being overheard. 'Where should we find him, do you think?'

'At Intwood, perhaps; more likely in the city. Doubtless they'll know at Suffolk Inn. You'll stay there tonight, my Lord? Shall I bring Lady Alice to join you in the morning?'

Suffolk hesitated for a moment, then he shook his head. 'She should stay here. Come yourself, before midday, unless I send word earlier.'

Bishop Alnwick moved rapidly to quell the unrest. He demanded a second, carefully supervised election to choose the Mayor of Norwich. The Earl of Suffolk supported him in this demand and made no protest when Richard Purdance was belatedly established as Mayor of the City.

Wetherby and Tuddenham both came to Suffolk at Suffolk Inn. He saw them in private, in the solar. They emerged with long faces. Will observed this with pleasure. Neither man subsequently questioned the Bishop's verdict.

Purdance also moved promptly. A few days later he appointed his own men, Robert Laudersdale and William Hempstead, as sheriffs. He went on to have John Heydon deposed as Recorder, and William Yelverton set in his place. Wetherby and Tuddenham came to Suffolk Inn again, and this time John Heydon was with them. Again, Suffolk spoke to them in the solar. The conversation went on for a very long time. Will waited in the hall below. From time to time he heard raised voices. All four men emerged this time with long faces.

The following day Suffolk returned to Cossey Lodge; two days later he and Alice set off for London.

Will remained in Norwich, on the Earl's instructions. The Earl ordered Tuddenham to give him work to do in and around the city, but he made no move to speak to him of the events of the election and its aftermath, and neither did Will himself raise this topic before he left.

Will hoped that the issue was now dead; but it was not. Now that his supporters were established in all the vital positions of power, Richard Purdance set about destroying all vestige of the Wetherby faction's influence in the city.

He chose to do this publicly. Open government was what Norwich needed, he insisted, after years of Wetherby and his cronies plotting in dark corners and making secret agreements in taverns and corridors. The evidence was clear enough against Wetherby's men for legal redress to be taken against them. Purdance had the cases discussed before the Council and the verdicts sealed with the Great Seal of the City of Norwich. Thomas Wetherby was displaced as Alderman of Conesford Ward, banned from taking up any other public position within the city and fined one hundred pounds for wilfully and maliciously acting against the Charter and the city liberties. John Querdling was disenfranchised for carrying a false report from the commons to the Mayor and Aldermen. John May the jailor was fined for being a common rogue, coming into the hall at the election armed, raving and bawling out, 'Varlets, I shall break your heads and put you in Pentney', and striking many men on the heads with his mace. Only Tuddenham, of the men who had supported Wetherby at the election, retained his position untouched; and that was merely because, as High Sheriff, he was beyond the jurisdiction of the city.

The day after these verdicts were pronounced Tuddenham came to Calthorp Inn and cornered Will in the counting house. He told Will that he and Wetherby and Heydon planned a meeting the following day at Intwood. Will retorted that he would be at Hellesdon that day on the Earl's business. Not so, Tuddenham said quietly. While Suffolk was in London, he himself had the power to give Will orders; and he was ordering him to come to Intwood.

'So,' said Agnes Paston, 'that nasty little man Wetherby has been given his comeuppance at last.'

'For the time being,' her husband agreed.

'And there was no need for you to stir yourself at all.'

'So it seems,' said the Judge, thinking regretfully of his chest packed full of the papers he had been collecting about Thomas Wetherby and his dealings.

'So it is,' retorted Agnes.

'If you say so, my dear.'

William was happy, for once, to appease Agnes. She had reason to be unhappy: she had miscarried for the third time in succession only weeks before. And before that, a dead child. He would have let her be now, settled for poking the dairymaid at Oxnead occasionally; but Agnes was adamant that she wanted to try again for a child as soon as she was recovered. She was recovering fast. A strong lady, Agnes, with a will to match.

And a sensible head on her shoulders; though this time he doubted if she was right. Certainly it had pleased him to see the affair handled entirely by the city officers. He had not wanted to make a greater enemy of Wetherby by sitting in judgement against him, and he was still uncertain whether any of his own evidence would stand up in court against the flood of bribery and intimidation that Tuddenham and his men would undoubtedly have unleashed. That far, it had been well done. But it was going too far now.

The Duke of Gloucester had made the same mistake when he had tried to end Cardinal Beaufort's power. William had warned Gloucester against it, but in vain; he tried to warn Purdance now, with no greater success. He had generally found in the course of his long career at law that guilty men accepted fair punishment. But when the punishment was much too severe to fit the crime they became not repentant, but indignant: they fought back.

Purdance's men had made their sentences very severe, their verdicts publicly humiliating. Thomas Wetherby was not the man to take such punishment lying down.

It was true, as Purdance pointed out to William, that there was nothing that Wetherby could do in the City Council. His power there was lost completely. But Tuddenham was still High Sheriff; the Earl of Suffolk's influence was undiminished, and wearing his livery counted for a great deal. By late summer, many men who had remained neutral in the earlier tussles were beginning to mutter that Wetherby would be ill-rewarded for his loyalty if Tuddenham and Suffolk did not exert themselves on his behalf.

Whatever his faults, Tuddenham was loyal to his friends. He protested Wetherby's innocence throughout and complained loudly and long that the former Mayor was being appallingly misused. Wetherby waited for the complaints to gather force; then he too acted. By that September he had begun his campaign in earnest.

476

Wetherby took his protests at the scandalous misgovernment of the city of Norwich, and the gross misuse of its Great Seal, to the King's Council. This audacious move led William, and many other men, to assume that he had been assured of the Earl of Suffolk's backing.

Suffolk, however, absented himself from the vital Council meeting. None of the remaining Council members professed themselves capable of judging the situation. They took refuge in the traditional resort of those unable, or unwilling, to make their own decisions: they appointed a Commission of Enquiry to look into Wetherby's complaints.

Lord Cromwell respectfully suggested that the Earl of Suffolk would be the perfect man to head such a commission. Suffolk politely declined the offer. It was a matter for Norfolk men, he protested, and a minor one at that: a matter of the city, not the county. At Suffolk's instigation a very modest commission was drawn up. There were no great lords represented on it at all. It consisted of four local landowners and one judge: William Paston.

William resisted the temptation to point out to Agnes that she had been mistaken. Her temper was sweetened then in any event: she was pregnant once more.

He was sorry to have been chosen, though he admitted to himself that he would have resented it even more had he been passed over. At the same time, he found his appointment intriguing. He thought that Suffolk had surely been in a position to pack the Commission if he had wished; but he had not done so. Was this an indication that he would turn his back on Wetherby if the Commission chose to dismiss his complaints?

It was certainly tempting to test that theory in the only way possible. But on reflection William felt that it would be rash to do so. He decided to play out a holding action, to persuade his fellow Commissioners to defer giving their verdict for as long as possible, and to make soundings in new quarters.

20

ENGLAND

Hugues de Lannoy, Seigneur de Santes, Councillor Chamberlain to two generations of Dukes of Burgundy, Chevalier of the Order of the Golden Fleece and Ambassador Extraordinary, set foot on English soil on a cloudy day in the early summer of 1433.

He was in a good humour. He had met the Regent by chance at Calais while he was looking for a ship to transport his party across the Channel, and Bedford (who was also coming to England, but more slowly) had had his steward arrange a balinger for them.

He learned in Sandwich that a variety of prelates and nobles were travelling to Dover in order to greet Bedford and his new wife. Nobody was travelling to meet his own party, but he did not take this amiss: he had become accustomed, after years of experience, to indifferent receptions. He knew, too, that it was by no means certain that the King would receive him immediately. He needed to know where the King was, and what his attitude might be. So after asking what route the dignitaries were likely to take, he set out to intercept them.

This he did on the road between Sandwich and Canterbury. When he made out the banners and tabards of the procession in the distance, he drew up his men and sent his poursuivant on ahead to announce him to the English heralds.

The English procession, full of elderly churchmen, was moving slowly. As de Lannoy watched, a small group of men detached themselves and rode at speed down the road towards him, with his poursuivant following close behind them.

He saw while they were still perhaps fifty paces away that they were led by the Earl of Suffolk. A couple of grooms were riding with him, but no other nobles of consequence. De Lannoy motioned to his own men to draw back a pace and rode forward to meet the Earl in the middle of the road.

They had known each other in Paris, as members of Bedford's Council, where they had been on formal but friendly terms. The Seigneur de Santes valued formality. He went through his bows and greetings with as much care as if they had been in a throne room. Suffolk returned them cursorily, with half an eye on the approaching procession.

De Lannoy outlined his encounter with Bedford. 'And his charming new Duchess,' he continued. 'So enchantingly pretty. Almost as beautiful,' he added with conscious tact, 'as your own Countess. I trust Lady Alice is . . .'

'She rides with us,' Suffolk said, 'to greet the Duchess.'

'But of course. They will have known – no, perhaps they will not have known each other in Paris. Lady Jacquetta is so young . . .'

'Perhaps not,' Suffolk agreed.

'And the Cardinal . . .'

'In Southwark. You have letters for him?'

'Naturally. And for your good self, from my Lord the Duke.'

'You will call on me in London then, and deliver them.'

'They can be delivered to you now.'

De Lannoy motioned to his poursuivant. He could see from Suffolk's face that the Englishman was annoyed. Suffolk had made a calculated gesture, perhaps, in riding to meet him: he had thought it pointed enough without receiving a bundle of letters from Burgundy in front of Gloucester, fast approaching, and the rest of the procession. However, it suited his own purposes to see Suffolk as clearly marked out as a pro-Burgundian in the English court as he himself was known to be pro-English among Burgundians. He signalled imperceptibly to the poursuivant to take his time sorting through the letters.

'The Cardinal would perhaps appreciate it,' Suffolk said, 'if you were to attend early mass at Saint Mary Overy.'

He took that to mean that he should deliver the Cardinal's letters in more privacy. 'Then I shall do so before I attend His Highness.'

'The Earl of Warwick is in London. He will undertake the arrangements for you.'

He knew that the elderly Warwick was the King's tutor. He said cautiously, 'I had hoped to call upon your own good services in obtaining an audience with the King.'

'It will be my pleasure, if you find it necessary. Which I trust you will not.'

The poursuivant, fumbling, extracted a couple of letters from the batch in his hand and held them out just as the trumpeters were drawing up to them. Suffolk drew on his reins and pulled his horse to the side of the road to receive them.

There were other matters de Lannoy wished to bring up, but this was not the occasion. He too drew back. He raised his hat again and swept it down with a low bow as the Duke of Gloucester, his Duchess, the Archbishop of York and the rest of the dignitaries rode imperiously by.

Suffolk let the last of the procession pass them; then he turned to de Lannoy, raised his own hat once more and without another word rode off to resume his place with the Englishmen.

As he rode on, rapidly, to escape from the dust stirred by the procession, de Lannoy thought about Suffolk. It was five years or more since they had last met: before the disaster at Orleans. They had spoken French in those days, and Suffolk had used the same language this time, with an unconscious ease which suggested that he spoke it regularly still. With Lady Alice, perhaps? Or with the Duke of Orleans? In Paris, though, Suffolk might have been taken for a Frenchman; and on this occasion he had looked emphatically – deliberately – English. His doublet had been well-fitting, the deep blue velvet stylish and discreet; but there had been nothing French about its cut, or about Suffolk's low-brimmed hat, or his heavy cloak trimmed with ermine.

Suffolk's look had always been thoughtful, often distant. Now there was something contained about it, wary even. De Lannoy thought that he would have expected him to have lost the harshness of the soldier and taken on a courtier's expansiveness. Not so. Suffolk's gestures had all been measured: he had given the impression of a man who rarely if ever loosened his control of himself. Why? Did he have more enemies in the English court than he had had in France? Was his marriage perhaps not entirely the success that it was reputed to be?

He had had only a brief glimpse of Lady Alice, but he judged from it that the changes in her were less marked. He had known her better than her husband during the years when she was largely in Paris, sometimes at Hesdin and Bruges; and in those days he had admired her beauty and her taste while regretting a certain obtuseness about her. It was this that had caused him to be surprised when Suffolk had married her.

Lady Alice was not so young now, he thought: it was close on ten years since he had first met her, and she had been a grown woman then. There had been no signs of wear on her face, though; he had sensed the same freshness about her manner.

He suspected he might learn more from the Countess of Suffolk than he would from her husband. He had decided from what he had heard in France that the Earl should be useful to him, but he thought now that Suffolk was unlikely to let himself be caught off guard. He would learn only what the other man intended him to learn.

He and his colleagues had come to England largely in pursuit of information. It was proper for Burgundy to send regular envoys as a sworn ally of the English; it was necessary for him to do so while the alliance remained prickly as a sour chestnut.

Of course, he thought, the English King's Council could not be totally unaware of Burgundy's dalliances with the Valois. They must assume that Burgundy in turn knew which of them now advocated a negotiated peace. But perhaps they had not yet realised what steps the Duke had taken to sabotage the planned negotiations the month before, and to prepare the ground for a settlement that would please him better.

Burgundy's concern was that the English might learn this and retaliate by performing a wrecking manoeuvre of their own. There was, for example, the rumour that King Henry envisaged a marriage to one of Charles of Valois' daughters. That could bring about an agreement behind Burgundy's back. Burgundy had been adamant that it must not happen.

The Seigneur de Santes' personal inclinations did not always precisely match those of his master. He had never hidden his fondness for England and the English, and that always left open the possibility that the Duke might have anti-English plans he did not know about. But he believed that this time the English interest was fundamentally the same as the Burgundian interest: to see tripartite peace negotiations, held preferably under Burgundy's auspices, which would lead to a realistic settlement acceptable to all parties. If such a thing was possible: and that was something any man would have questioned.

On his first morning in London de Lannoy went early to Mass at Saint Mary Overy. The Cardinal received him, very briefly, after the Mass in the vestry. He accepted the letters and hinted in a polite way that it would be convenient to him if de Lannoy communicated through the Earl of Suffolk in future.

De Lannoy accepted this suggestion with equanimity. He thought it of overriding importance to maintain Beaufort's goodwill.

He called next on the Earl of Warwick, who informed him that the King was to be found at Guildford, at his hunting lodge.

He was not over-fond of hunting, but he had no other objections to travelling to Guildford. The court there would behave more informally than at Westminster: there might be many more opportunities for private discussions, perhaps even with the King himself. The following morning he and his companions set out with the guide and escort Warwick had provided, through Westminster and down the broad and badly kept roads of Surrey to the lodge in Guildford Forest.

Warwick had not offered to accompany them, but he was at the King's left hand when they were announced: perhaps he had taken a better-kept road. Bedford's party had also arrived at Guildford. The Regent stood at the King's right, displacing his brother Gloucester who hovered a pace behind, with a hint of a sulk on his handsome face.

De Lannoy gave the usual bows, made his formal greeting, presented his letters of credence and the rest of his party and was pleasantly surprised to be greeted in French by the King. The boy spoke the language in the style of the English soldiers, but fluently. Then the rest of the court were summoned to the hall.

While they were assembling he looked carefully at the King. He had heard that the boy was sickly. It would solve many problems, he had often thought, if the King were to die, and his claim to the French throne were allowed to rest with him. Henry looked, however, to be in remarkably good health. His thin, serious face was a good colour; there was flesh covering his ribs. His voice was quiet but steady, and though he said nothing to suggest incisive intelligence he was evidently not the halfwit the French made him out to be.

He also commanded proper respect from his fledgling court, at least in the presence of foreigners. The assorted nobility dutifully descended to their knees as Burgundy's letters of greeting were read out. The letters were in French and de Lannoy amused himself while their formal phrases rang out over his head by attempting to judge which of the noble lords could understand them. Warwick nodded in the right places. Gloucester did not, which did not surprise him: he had heard that for all the Good Duke's book-learning he had never troubled to master the language. He was well aware that Bedford spoke good French. York, Northumberland and the very young Duke of Norfolk appeared not to follow at all. It was no more than a matter of curiosity. Naturally there would be a formal translation later.

When the greetings gave way to the more pointed inanities, de Lannoy and his colleagues were ushered off to an anteroom. It was to the north of the lodge, cold and cheerless in the late afternoon light. There was a wide, low window through which he saw a meadow, the grass just risen to ankle height and dotted with celandines, and the edge of the forest beyond.

A moment later there was a commotion as the doors to the hall were thrown open and the courtiers began to spill out. De Lannoy moved forwards, to see if he might snatch a private audience with the King; but the squires of the Household blocked his path, and instead Suffolk came across to take his arm. 'The King has withdrawn to his private quarters. He plans to hunt early tomorrow and will not appear again today. But there is still some time before we dine: shall we walk outside?'

They walked in silence down a narrow corridor. It led to a door that gave on to a back courtyard. To their right was the meadow and they made in this direction.

'You saw the Cardinal at Southwark?' Suffolk asked.

'Briefly, yes, to deliver my letters. He has not come to Guildford?'

'He rarely hunts. The King will stay here only two, perhaps three days; then his court will move to Sheen or Windsor.'

De Lannoy wanted to arrange his private audience without moving further from London and Suffolk reassured him that it should be possible the following evening. They discussed Gloucester, briefly and cautiously; they talked of Warwick and of the Archbishop, Kemp.

It was cold in the meadow: the last of the sunlight had gone and a stiff breeze was blowing up. They turned and began to move back to the lodge.

'And the Duke of Orleans . . . ?' de Lannoy began.

Suffolk gave him a veiled look. 'The Duke is held in custody in England, like the Duke of Bourbon and the other prisoners taken in the wars. It is not usual for captives to appear at the King's court.'

De Lannoy had discussed Orleans with Saint Rémy – now known as Toison d'Or, King of Arms of Burgundy's new Order of the Golden Fleece – before he left Arras. It had been an illuminating conversation, for the King of Arms evidently had a useful source of information in English circles – though he would not give its identity. He had learned that Orleans and his jailer were on warm terms; and he had since come to think that possibly Suffolk would permit him to meet Orleans. It would be irregular, but Suffolk might think it to be in his own interests.

'So he is to be found at your residence in Suffolk . . . ?'

Suffolk walked on. They reached the courtyard; and with barely a break in his stride, the Earl turned not to the door they had come through, but towards the mews opposite.

There was a falconer at the far end of the mews, attending to a falcon gentle. Otherwise the mews was empty of men. Suffolk stopped by the stand of a peregrine falcon and unhooded her gently.

'Your own bird?'

'She is old, this one, and wily. My falconer brought her down from Ewelme. She dislikes this countryside: it is more wooded than I expected, I should have sent for a goshawk instead. I flew her in the far meadow this morning, but she caught nothing for me.' He bent to the bird, ruffling the short buff feathers of its breast with a long finger. 'If you and your companions were to present yourselves at my London house,' he continued, 'I think you might find the company of interest to you.'

'You return to London . . .'

'When the King rides on.'

'And a suitable hour for such a visit . . .'

'It is the habit of my household,' Suffolk said, 'to dine early.'

De Lannoy decided it would not have been subtle to invite himself to dine at Bardi Place. He suspected Suffolk had been ambiguous on purpose; and he chose to call after dinner. Orleans would not dine with the Earl, surely, when there were visitors: it would raise too many difficult questions of precedence. But he meant to arrive only just after dinner, since he was curious to know how Suffolk and his Countess ate at home.

They ate lavishly, he found. There had been a sucking pig and a peacock, cooked in all its feathers; a dish of larks and one of pigeons, a lêche lombard and a blanc manger. There had been pastries and jellies and dishes of small, sweet strawberries. There was a lingering rich smell of almond and ginger and nutmeg and mulled wine; and though the lutanist who played from a corner of the dais that day was not Gilles Binchois, he was very nearly as good as Gilles.

He took in all this while the chamberlains conferred behind their screens, and while Suffolk strode down from the dais to greet him. Then pages led him and his men to a withdrawing room, pillared in pink marble.

For the first time, he felt apprehensive. He had for many years been Burgundy's regular ambassador to the English court and his commission from the Duke was by now couched in very general terms. There had been a friendly and informal discussion with Duke Philip in his garden at Arras. Many subjects had been mentioned; the Duke of Orleans had not.

Nor was it at all certain that Orleans would be well disposed towards Burgundy. Burgundy's father had after all murdered his own father, and he had never succeeded in taking proper revenge. True, John the Fearless had himself been assassinated by the Dauphin and his men, but for quite different motives, and several years later.

Just then a young esquire slipped into the room. He held a silver salver containing lozenges of Lombard nougat. The Duke of Orleans' sweet tooth was notorious. Were these sweet gifts meant to signal a sweetening in his outlook towards old enemies? Perhaps so; but de Lannoy was not fond of nougat. He chose the smallest piece on the tray and was still attempting to swallow the final fragments when he heard a flurry of activity from the hall.

Suffolk Herald entered first. A number of liveried servants – all in Suffolk's own colours – followed him and the Herald arrayed them carefully about the walls of the small room. Then came the Earl himself, ushering in a slender man in black. Lady Alice did not accompany them.

But he is old! That was de Lannoy's first thought. The Duke was grey-haired and walked with a slight stoop, as if his imprisonment had been spent in rooms with ceilings too low for him. He would have taken him to be a contemporary of his own had he not known that Orleans was more than ten years younger, around the same age as Suffolk himself.

Suffolk Herald had barely completed the introductions when Orleans crossed to take him by the hand. 'You have news of his Grace the Duke of Burgundy? He is in good health?'

'In excellent health when I left Arras.'

'I am most anxious to commend myself to his good graces.'

De Lannoy gave his habitual oblique nod. 'I shall be

delighted to convey that information to him. His Grace recommends himself very earnestly to you and desires to know of your own state of health.'

'I have received . . . close attention. My bodily health, as you see, leaves nothing to be desired.'

Suffolk broke in, with a hint of sharpness. 'You have not had the pleasure of an interview with the Duke of Bourbon?'

Bourbon was the other Valois Duke who was held as prisoner – even more closely than Orleans, by all accounts – by the English. He had not even attempted to see Bourbon, as Suffolk doubtless knew and he took this to be not so much a question to him as a careful rebuke to Orleans. 'Not on this visit, no.'

Orleans glanced briefly at Suffolk and gave a gentle, careworn smile. 'A sadly weakened man. I saw him myself for the first time since I left France, at Dover these past few weeks. His health is failing fast. I fear he despairs of ever playing any useful part in the affairs of the world.'

He certainly might have despaired of the puny peace initiative, de Lannoy thought to himself. By now his first shock on seeing Orleans was giving way to a more measured appraisal. He could see no sign of harsh living or ill treatment on the Duke's face. There was the paleness, the infinite, painfully won patience of the long-term captive; but if Charles of Orleans had ever known despair – and surely he was well acquainted with it after nearly twenty years as a prisoner – he had learned to live with it. No, unlike Bourbon, this man was not finished yet, not to be dismissed as a cipher in the game of nations.

'God willing,' he began cautiously, 'good can come even from a lot as difficult as that of yourself and the Duke of Bourbon. The opportunity to become a mediator in the cause of peace between two great kingdoms . . .'

A small muscle snapped in Orleans' tired face; and the Duke's body straightened, as if the impulse had carried through him. 'God knows,' he said vehemently, 'I have offered myself to the King of England and his Lords as an intermediary. My Lord of Suffolk knows this as well as any man. But so long . . . I am a sword shut up in a scabbard, never drawn even in practice, for so long that no man recalls clearly how it appeared in action. I say again and again that it will never be possible for me to be of any use unless I have liberty to converse with my friends in France.'

'If it were clear,' Suffolk murmured, 'that your friends in France did indeed desire peace as earnestly as you do yourself . . .'

Orleans gave a small sigh, as if the argument between the two men had been well rehearsed. 'My dear sirs. I believe there are even today those among the greatest lords in Charles of Valois' court who would be glad to listen to me, and who would follow me in what I advocated.'

'And you would advocate peace?'

'I would welcome the opportunity to act as the means of obtaining peace even if it were to write my own death sentence no more than a week thereafter.' He turned deliberately to Suffolk. 'And let me repeat to you, my dear Suffolk, that my cousins of Burgundy and of Brittany can do more in this cause, after the Kings themselves, than any person now living.'

'No one could be more anxious than the Duke of Burgundy to promote the cause of peace,' said de Lannoy.

'My Lord Duke, I have always assured you that Burgundy is well disposed towards peace,' Suffolk said.

'I have no doubt of it,' said Orleans, with only a shade more intensity than the words merited. He turned once more to de Lannoy. 'I have long been persuaded, my dear sir, that neither his family nor mine are the cause of the evils that have troubled France for so long. Believe me, sir, I speak sincerely.' He caught de Lannoy's arm and squeezed it, as if to emphasise his conviction. A second squeeze, hard on the heels of the first, seemed to suggest that he would have said more if Suffolk had not been there.

It was to this that de Lannoy's thoughts returned, once the formal protestations had been repeated thrice more and he and his men had taken their leave with a promise to repeat the visit before they left London. There had been something a little theatrical about the gesture. And it had been done in full view of Suffolk, who was not, he knew, a slow-witted man. If his distinguished ward declined to lay the blame for the French troubles on the houses of Burgundy, Brittany or Orleans, on whose doorstep was he setting them? Surely Suffolk was not incapable of arriving at the obvious answer.

Was Suffolk disturbed by the obvious answer? Or was he convinced that peace with France could be achieved only at the expense of uniting the French dukedoms against the House of Lancaster?

He did not seriously doubt that Suffolk sincerely wanted peace. It had been one of the minor revelations of his visit that the peace party was better established, and Suffolk more influential within it, than he had previously suspected. And beneath Suffolk's veiled words and gestures he believed he had glimpsed honesty. But whether Suffolk fully understood the price the English would have to pay for peace, and would advocate their paying it . . . that was a very interesting question. If he did take that line he could scarcely fail to be in a very small minority in the English Council. It had been made politely clear that public mention of the meeting with Orleans would destroy any chance of a second interview.

The question became still more interesting when the following morning the footman announced a dapper, pale man who declined to give his name.

'Let him enter,' de Lannoy said thoughtfully as he set down his pen and sanded the latest sheet of his voluminous notes.

The man entered, hat in hand, like a superior servant – which he proved to be.

490

'Jennin Cauvel, sir. Barber to my Lord the Earl of Suffolk.'

The man spoke in rapid Flemish, in a low voice. De Lannoy automatically switched to the same language. 'You had a message for me, my man?'

'From the prisoner . . . that is, from the Duke of Orleans, sir.'

'You have access to the Duke?'

'I act as one of his jailers, sir. The Earl uses me because I speak French.'

De Lannoy let no trace of interest show on his smooth Flemish burgher's face. 'And the message?'

'The Duke said I was to mention the rumour, sir, as he hated the Duke of Burgundy, and was threatening to make war on him if ever he got free.'

'And?'

'And to tell you, sir, that that is no truth. As long as I have been near him, sir, I have heard him say marvellous much good of my Lord of Burgundy. He says he loves him with all his heart, and he has spoken more of him than of all the rest of the Lords of France.'

'Thank you, Cauvel. You have this in writing?'

The barber shook his head. 'No, sir. He does not write letters, sir. But if you were to provide a letter from the Duke of Burgundy, I could charge myself with making sure that it reached him, sir.'

'Indeed.' De Lannoy resisted the temptation to add a 'sir' of his own. 'I regret I have no such letter to entrust to you at this moment. But I will give you a message for his Grace the Duke. Please inform him that the Duke of Burgundy returns his generous sentiments.' He paused and pursed his lips. 'And that he can depend upon the Duke's utmost assistance in attempting to procure his release.'

'Yes, sir. Thank you, sir.' The barber bowed obsequiously and kept on bowing as he retreated towards the door.

De Lannoy did not share the contents of this little

discussion with his fellow ambassadors, but he did glance around the guards when he returned to take his farewell of Suffolk and his captive. The barber Cauvel was among them, and there looked to be just a hint of dampness on his forehead.

Charles of Orleans seemed pathetically reluctant to see the back of his visitors.

'My dear Suffolk,' he said in an openly pleading tone, 'if I might just write a letter to my cousin of Burgundy?'

Suffolk reached out to take his arm. 'I think it might be as well,' he said courteously, 'if you were to deliberate over the matter this evening.' He turned to look over Orleans' shoulder at the grouped embassy. 'It is tomorrow that you leave?'

De Lannoy inclined his head very slightly. 'Early in the morning.' He took Suffolk's words to be a polite rejection of an audacious request.

Cauvel was announced once again that evening, late. De Lannoy had him admitted immediately. He glanced nervously around the room, then reached into his tunic and pulled out a sealed document.

'A letter to the Duke of Burgundy?' de Lannoy asked quietly in Flemish.

The barber nodded. 'For me to deliver to you in person, sir.'

'From my Lord of Orleans?'

'Oh no, sir. My Lord of Suffolk wished you to know that the Duke of Orleans may not have leave to write to you or to his Grace the Duke.'

For once de Lannoy's diplomatic coolness came close to deserting him. 'Then the letter?' His voice had dropped to a whisper.

'Why, from my Lord of Suffolk, sir.'

21

ENGLAND
Winter, 1434-35

The winter of 1434 was the coldest that men could remember. In London, the Thames was frozen solid for months. In Norfolk ice lay thick on the rivers, on the desolate expanses of the peat workings, even on inlets along the coast.

Paston village was close to the coast, in the flat, featureless plain of north-east Norfolk. It lay in a dip, out of sight of the sea; but there was nothing but sheep in the mile between the village and the sand dunes, bound fast with marram grass, that kept the waves from flooding in across the low-lying land. Two miles to the south the great towers of the Cluniac priory at Bromholm punctured the skyline. The monks at Bromholm guarded a small piece of the True Cross, brought to England generations before by a chaplain to Baldwin, the Emperor of Constantinople. Greater monasteries had declined to pay the exorbitant price asked for a dubious little splinter, but the monks at Bromholm had seen their faith rewarded, for the tiny relic in its jewelled box was said to have worked miracles. Through its influence the blind had regained their sight, the crippled walked again, lepers had been cleansed of their blight; it had even, men said, brought the dead back to life. It had certainly brought the remote abbey kings in pilgrimage, and earthly riches.

It was an inhospitable stretch of shoreline, with treacherous currents and deceitful sandbanks well off-shore. At Happisburgh, just south of Bromholm, a light shone on dark nights to warn the ships off Happisburgh sands, the long sunken hill nine miles out to sea that claimed, nevertheless, a rich harvest of wrecks every season. The men of Paston and Bromholm, Happisburgh, Trunch and Gimmingham did not engage in smuggling; they simply waited like vultures for treasures to be washed up by the tides.

There was only one harbour in the entire twenty-mile stretch of coast between Cromer to the north and Caister to the south: at the tiny fishing port of Mundesley, just north of Paston itself. It was here that William Paston was having thick timbers and good blocks of stone shipped from Newcastle for the building of his new mansion at Paston. In Norfolk no stone was to be had but flint, and now that he was in a position to replace his father's modest house he had no intention of making his grand new manor of flint.

A frosty hand had sketched the outline of William's house-to-be on the hard ground just by Paston church. It had rimed the piles of grey stone blocks and red bricks that sat at strategic points within and around the outline. It had given an ethereal look to the heavy timbers. The site resembled a sugar conceit, half assembled by the confectioner.

William Paston aimed a morose kick at the nearest beam.

'It will be two years or more, at this rate, before the house is fit to move into,' he grumbled.

He was with William Yelverton, whose sparse red hair was shrouded in a grey frieze hood, and whose pale eyes were screwed up against the sharp winter light. Yelverton mentally measured the foundation trenches and then frowned, as if he were trying to work out how to bring William back into the right frame of mind for the conversation he intended to pursue.

'Stone foundations?' he asked.

'Four courses, then brick above.'

'How thorough. And you'll lay a park over there, leading behind the church?'

'Here. I want it facing south. I shall move the road.' Meeting a quizzical glance William added, 'I have all the necessary permits.'

Yelverton's button of a nose gave a little twitch. How, he wondered, could Judge Paston still retain that old-fashioned lawyer's certainty that nobody could possibly object if he was able to produce the requisite number of pieces of paper? He had seen the hostile glances of the village men and women they had passed on their walk from the old house. Moving the road would mean changing the path men had trodden for generations, even altering the route of church processions; and that was the kind of thing that raised tempers to boiling point in small villages.

Paston should have known that. He had seen men come to blows over such matters often enough in recent years. It was the kind of thing Thomas Wetherby excelled at, settling on an audacious solution to a long-standing problem and forcing it through on paper. Getting papers signed rarely raised more than vocal opposition; but men who neither knew nor cared about papers and permits would make their feelings known much more clearly when it came to solid changes that affected their lives.

'Talking of permits,' he said, 'is your Commission going to revoke Thomas Wetherby's fine?'

William did not respond for a moment. He glanced at Yelverton and mentally reconstructed – accurately – most of his train of thought. Other people had made similar comments about his plans and he acknowledged the truth of them. But the house and its grounds had to be made quickly and well, because he felt himself to be growing old, and he was not prepared to see John inherit a second-rate estate. Nor did he trust John – yet – to obtain his own permits, or fight his own battles afterwards; but he would not have explained this to anyone.

He gave a little scowl. 'I would hardly call it *my* Commission,' he grumbled.

'You are the Judge; everyone takes it for granted it is your Commission. And,' added Yelverton with the complacency of one well out of the argument, 'that you can determine the outcome.'

'Now that I certainly cannot do. Felbrigg and Stapleton and the rest have their opinions too.'

Yelverton considered this and decided it was best ignored. 'I find it hard to believe that you would go against the Wetherby party while Suffolk is giving them his support.'

'And Suffolk is giving them his support?'

'So I assumed.' Yelverton shrugged.

That response did not displease William. He reasoned that if Yelverton knew, he would have said so. 'Tuddenham is giving them his support?'

'You know he is, William.'

'And you have assured them of your support?'

Yelverton frowned. 'It would hardly be appropriate, while I am Recorder.'

'Hardly, since it was Purdance who had you appointed.' This was intended to goad, and it did: Yelverton's face wrinkled in annoyance. William knew the younger lawyer had been embarrassed to find himself Purdance's choice. The Mayor was well intentioned, but at heart a little man: he had no powerful patrons. For all his many friends in the city, he had managed to build no depth of support in the county. Yelverton could not have refused the post without destroying his reputation for impartiality, but by accepting it he had offended Wetherby and Tuddenham, and had made an enemy of the displaced John Heydon. William strongly suspected that he had privately reassured them of his support in order to restore his position.

Perhaps Yelverton realised that he had deduced all this. Certainly Yelverton understood at least part of his own dilemma. William hated Wetherby and his cronies as strongly as ever: he had no relish for rescinding their punishments, though he wished (for practical reasons) that they had been more temperate. But if the Commission did give a verdict, he wanted it both to be, and to be thought by others to be, fair and correct. And he was anxious to win Suffolk's approval, without destroying his reputation with the other powerful men of the county. No easy combination, even if Suffolk were prepared to see Wetherby kept down; a virtually impossible one if (as Yelverton evidently believed) Suffolk was not.

He had found this a problem of hideous difficulty; and he knew that though Yelverton was not directly implicated, he too was not merely curious, but seriously concerned. Why else would the Recorder have made the journey to Paston along treacherous lanes where the cart-ruts were frozen solid and the dips held pools of ice?

Indeed, to make such a journey in such conditions indicated more than concern: it suggested an urgent need to know. Why? Was Yelverton acting as an agent for Tuddenham? Or was he just worried he might be driven into committing himself before he knew which side was going to win?

With Yelverton riding so far, he could not be sent away too dissatisfied. William needed Yelverton's support, however much it wavered; he needed Yelverton's information. He also needed, though, to make sure that his plans would not become known to Tuddenham.

'It is difficult,' said Yelverton, 'to judge who is supporting Purdance, except for plain men such as Stapleton and Inglose.'

'It is a difficult situation in many ways. There is much to be said for trying to clarify it.'

'Clarify it?'

William took a brave step. 'For example, by encouraging the Earl of Suffolk to make his position clearer.'

He watched Yelverton mentally absorb this. He did it passably. 'You plan to ask him privately what outcome he favours?'

'These things must be done openly.' It was Purdance's catch phrase.

Yelverton greeted it with a short bark of laughter. 'So you intend to co-opt him on to the Commission?'

'Would you recommend that?'

Yelverton's face wrinkled still more. 'It strikes me as an excellent plan, William,' he said at last. 'Clearly the best alternative.'

The best alternative! God, how second-rate Yelverton could be! Three or four alternatives had competed in William's mind, and he had thought this one of the poorest. Still, Yelverton's answer told him all he needed to know about his colleague's own position.

'I thought, rather, of persuading the King's Council to recommend a new Commission.'

'Do you have the power to do that?'

The power? Of course he had the power. He had not thought Yelverton would ever doubt it. But then, he thought to himself, Yelverton often acted these days as if the two of them were equals; perhaps he almost believed it. He had been lulled himself into almost believing it from time to time. But it was not so.

There had been a time when, thwarted by one noble, he had been able only to plot with his inferiors, in Yelverton's little way. Now he had access to other nobles. A judge, even a lowly Judge in the Court of Common Pleas, could take his own soundings among the King's Council. He could measure the influence of a man like Suffolk, even of a man like Gloucester. He could find their enemies, and make use of them.

'It is not so much a question of power,' he said quietly, 'as a question of persuasion.'

Yelverton thought. 'So my Lord of Gloucester might well be persuaded . . .'

'He might.' It was true, William told himself. He did not add that he was saving Gloucester's favour for future insurance, and that this time he was putting his faith in Lord Cromwell. 'Damnably cold out here,' he went on. 'Come and watch the boys skating for a moment, and then we'll make our way back to the old house for dinner.'

'I'll look forward to that, William.'

'I'd look forward to a good haunch of beef myself, but we can offer you none such today, I'll warn you, not with even the brine tub frozen over. And the stewpond, too.'

'Pickled herrings?'

'Just so. Pickled herrings, every damned day. Another ten days without a thaw and we shall all look like pickled herrings. Agnes looks like one already. Elizabeth, now – you've see my little Lizzy?'

Yelverton's face betrayed him. William gave a wry smile. 'No beauty, that's what you're thinking? Maybe not. But she has spirit, man. The life in that child. Pity she was not born a boy.'

'And your boys?'

He shrugged. It would never have done for him to admit – even to Agnes – that his boys were a disappointment to him. He rarely even let himself think as much. But once he had thought a son a malleable creature, who could be made into the shape his father chose; and instead his sons had emerged from their cradles ready formed. He had thought to write the book of their lives, but he found himself reading a book with words he would not have chosen.

They were not bad boys. They were no more disobedient than the sons of other men. They tried hard to be what he wanted them to be; John, especially. The boy worked hard, even his least enthusiastic tutor had said so. But what to William had come as easily as breathing came to John only with the labour of a long-distance runner. His studies seemed to light no fire in his soul. Little in John's life did rouse his spirit, as far as his father could tell. Compared to little Lizzy, he seemed at times barely half-alive.

It had certainly not been a part of William's plan that he should favour his daughter over his sons. This truth which he only half admitted to himself caused him deep disquiet. It was for John that he had laboured so mightily, for John that Paston Hall was being built, for John that he had worked to build contacts with the great men of the land. His love for Lizzy was a diversion; and he felt at times that he could ill afford it.

He said cautiously, 'I have John's time at Cambridge set for next year. He has more to learn still at the Norwich school, and he's useful at times on the estates. But I think sometimes that I would have sent him from home before now, if there had been anyone to send him to. Not that I ever intended him for a squire: it must be Cambridge, if I'm to make a lawyer of him. So I shall send him to Trinity Hall; and from there, if he does well, to Peterhouse. Then by the time he gets to the Temple . . .'

What might have happened? Suffolk's downfall? Some signs of life from that morose boy Norfolk? Or from that even more morose boy, the King? Fastolf's return? Nothing certain, much that was possible.

'By then,' said Yelverton, 'I reckon he will have need of a little law learning.'

'Aye,' said Thomas Wetherby. 'You take the spring clip as sold, Sir Thomas. Cossey, and Hellesdon, and any of the other estates: I'll warrant I'll find you a better price for all of it than any of the Lynn merchants could run to.'

'I'll warrant you could,' Sir Thomas Tuddenham agreed. A thin hand snaked out from the ruffles of his fancy cuff and across the trestle that separated the two of them. They shook on the deal. Tuddenham rose to his feet as he withdrew his hand and said briskly, 'Such a deal should be sealed with strong ale. I'll stand you one, sir. And for you, Calthorp?'

Will started a little, to find himself addressed. 'Not this time, Sir Thomas. I should be making my way back to Suffolk Inn.'

'But you'll not leave till I'm ready to come with you, and that'll give you time and more to down a cup.' He gave Will no time to protest, but set off towards the doorway that led to the back room of the inn and the cellars.

Will watched him retreating. It was damnable, the skill Tuddenham had at this. It always started with a little request, the kind he could not easily refuse. 'You'll walk with me to the Castle, Will? I'm travelling your way, I'll be bound', or something like that. Then there was a small bribe, a hint of a useful commission to draw him more firmly into the spiderweb. And then he would be caught fast while Tuddenham cocooned him round, spinning Wetherby, Heydon, Walter Aslake, Charles Nowell and half a dozen similar men into a sticky shell around him.

There would be a casual meeting – except that it was never, surely, truly by chance that Tuddenham ran across these men when he was in Will's company; an invitation to drink a cup of ale, or sample some newly imported wine, or look over some stocks in a warehouse; and then a deal, struck in front of him before he could make his excuses and leave. The deals were not illegal, not scandalous, but the effect was always to implicate him, to mark him out as one of the circle of men around Tuddenham and Wetherby.

As a result, all Norfolk now had him set down as Tuddenham's henchman. Sir Brian Stapleton and Sir Henry Inglose did not cross the road to talk to him any more; Miles Stapleton had not visited Burnham when he had last come back to England. A dozen good, solid neighbours had ceased to send invitations to him and Bess; and half a dozen doubtful men, the kind his father and grandfather would never have hobnobbed with, had taken up the slack in his life.

Nor could he honestly say now, as he had said with such conviction eighteen months before, that he did none of Tuddenham's dirty work. The good commissions only came his way if he accepted his share of the rougher business. He had managed to draw the line at acting the ruffian – not that Tuddenham or Heydon would ever have been caught with firebrands in their hands – but he had been obliged to press men, again and again, to pay dues beyond those they could reasonably

501

tolerate; to fix the bribes in local sessions; to take a harsh line when tenants in distress pleaded with him for time to pay.

And now he found himself sitting with Thomas Wetherby in the front room of the Bess of Bedlam, with a dozen curious tanners all glancing their way and Wetherby leaning over the trestle wearing a conspiratorial look that told him that the next subject would be the campaign against Richard Purdance.

Wetherby was almost certainly about to ask him to do something he would be wiser not to do. He could hardly refuse if he was asked outright, so he decided to avoid being asked. He jumped to his feet and exclaimed, with as much conviction as he could muster, 'Holy Moses! I swore I'd meet John Damme at the Guildhall more than an hour ago! You'll excuse me, sir, and pass on my apologies to Sir Thomas.' Before Wetherby could frame even a word of answer he was out in the street and making his way along it at a fast jog-trot.

He did not slow down until he was approaching the river. It was still barely mid-morning. It was unlikely that John Damme was at the Guildhall; possibly he was not even in Norwich. Tuddenham and Wetherby would see through the excuse in a moment. Still, it was no news to them that he wormed out of such requests whenever he had the chance.

He had already mentally written off the morning and he had no pressing work at Suffolk Inn. He reckoned he could afford to go home, surprise Bess and tell her Suffolk Herald had promised to attend to her order for a dozen yards of grey worsted at London prices.

A whistle, barely audible, came from his mouth as he turned down the towpath towards Calthorp Inn: an echo of one of the songs Gilles' men had been practising for Christmas. It was a clear, cold day, and with the Wensum still frozen from bank to bank, there was not a soul in sight. His even temper was rapidly restoring itself: it was not a day for holding a grudge. He nodded at a robin on an overhanging bough and turned to cross Whitefriars Bridge.

It was only a few yards from there to the narrow gateway that led into Calthorp Inn. But as he approached it, a sense of uneasiness came over Will; a suspicion that something was not as it usually was. His feet quickened, then slowed; and he came to a full stop on the icy pavement just outside the gateway.

The courtyard was crowded: not just with the usual coming and going of his and Bess's servants, but with four or five unfamiliar horses, and with a couple of grooms in a livery that was not at all unfamiliar. Mowbray livery.

The Duke would not pay his household a visit, surely, unannounced and at an hour when he was unlikely to be at home. But the Dowager Duchess – curse her, she would!

He moved into the shadow of the gateway. At least, coming home on foot and alone, he was not obliged to face Kitty unprepared; he could take a moment to consider why she had come, and to prepare answers to the questions she might ask.

He watched the grooms. They were leading the horses to the stables. There were Kitty's own dapple-grey mare; two other mares, probably her ladies' horses; two heavier-footed geldings that the grooms must have ridden. The grooms knew the way to the stables, though he himself did not recognise the men. The horses knew the way, too; and Kitty's grooms and his own stable hand were bantering together in a manner that told him they were no strangers.

But it was – heavens, it was two years or more since the Duchess of Norfolk had called on him to his knowledge. Even when he had served her she had come only rarely to Calthorp Inn: when she wanted to see him she had generally summoned him to call on her. Since he had left Kitty's service he had had no direct dealings with her at all.

Bess had: he had known that ever since his stay at

503

Burnham. But he had made his annoyance clear, and he had thought that Bess had since kept her distance from the Duchess. Now, though, an unnerving suspicion grew in him – and slowly hardened into a conviction, as he watched the men in the yard disappear, laughing together, through the stable door – that this was no exceptional visit, and that it was not by accident that Kitty had chosen to call at a time when he was unlikely to be at Calthorp Inn.

His feelings hardened too – from mild consternation to a full-blooded fury. Kitty and Bess, conspiring behind his back! This, surely, was behind Bess's stubborn refusal to resign herself even now to a graceful acceptance of his position in Suffolk's household. He strode across the yard and pushed open the iron-framed oak door with such force that the hinges screamed their protest.

The scene that confronted him was a blur of motion, quickly resolving itself into a still life. Bess, standing where she had leapt up from the wooden settle by the fireplace, her hand raised to her mouth in a gesture that clearly proclaimed her guilty embarrassment; Kitty, still sitting, her skirts spread wide about her, only her quivering headdress betraying the rapid motion that had swung her head from fire to door; Jeanne and another maidservant, both of whom had automatically jumped for the safety of the shadows in the far corner of the room; even Bess's little lapdog, which had spilled off her lap and stationed itself protectively in front of her in a crouch, ready to bark the rafters down, before it recognised him.

Will bowed very low. 'What an unexpected pleasure, Your Grace. And a rare honour, to have you call on us in so informal a manner.'

Kitty inclined her head very slightly and her veil quivered once more.

'It is a fine morning. Might I persuade you to walk with me down to the river, while my wife arranges for some refreshment for you and your ladies?'

Kitty was still silent and he thought for a moment that she was going to refuse. He sensed Bess's deep breath, as if she were gathering her courage to intervene; but before she spoke Kitty rose to her feet and said in a gracious voice, 'I should be delighted, Master Calthorp.'

He moved a few paces forward and held out his arm. Kitty took it and nodded for Jeanne to follow. In as stately procession as was possible in so cramped a space, they made their way along the narrow corridor that led past the kitchens, and out of the house in the direction of the river.

She had seen this too before, he thought, or surely she would have exclaimed at the expanse of garden that greeted them. The neatly trimmed low hedges, the tight clumps of the perennial herbs, the sanded paths: everything was now in its place. An arch of briar roses, stark and forlorn in midwinter, separated off the herb garden from the water meadow, where the long grass was rigid still with the morning's frost, and the paths were clearly traced down to the waterfront.

He had been told many times that it was the finest garden in Norwich; but Kitty did not stop and stare, certainly did not exclaim. She did shiver a little, since she had taken off her travelling cloak in the house and followed him – for the sake of effect, presumably – without stopping to replace it.

He noticed the shiver, but he did not even think of lending her his own cloak.

'The path is quite dry,' he said.

'But the long grass will dirty Jeanne's white skirt. You may wait for us here, Jeanne.' Kitty loosed her arm and strode off alone towards the river. Grudgingly, Will admitted to himself that whatever her failings were, cowardice was not one of them. He nodded curtly to Jeanne and set off in Kitty's footsteps.

She stopped only a couple of paces from the water's edge. It was a quiet stretch of the river, even in summertime; that day it was totally deserted. The opposite bank was a thick tangle of bushes. By the small wooden jetty at the foot of the garden were moored a couple of Will's barges, frozen solid into the water.

'She has stopped the vinegar douches,' Kitty said. She did not look at him and it took him a moment to realise that she was talking about Bess. He cursed under his breath. He had meant to attack her immediately, and on totally different lines; but now he could scarcely avoid answering her.

'Only this last month,' he said grudgingly.

'Last month, this month, next month!' Kitty exclaimed. She did turn to him now, her face vivid with annoyance. 'It makes not a jot of difference. It would be insane, Will, to let her conceive again!'

'That is not so, Your Grace. Last winter, yes, or the summer before, but it is eighteen months and more now since she last gave birth, and the doctors say she is completely recovered.'

'Then you see the wrong doctors,' Kitty retorted. 'Never again, that was Master Ascham's verdict.'

'And a damn-fool, catch-all verdict it was! Three doctors she has seen, Kitty, and two of them have attended the Countess of Suffolk herself. All of them say that her health is much recovered. You can surely see that for yourself. She's not so thin now, not so pale, and if she conceives now the child would be born in August or September . . .'

'Not so bad a time, but still more than she could stand for.'

'But she is determined to stand for it.'

'Then you should be determined to stop her!'

Kitty glared at him. Will glared back. They stood there, their anger freezing them almost as firm as the barges on the river, the winter sunlight striking down on their faces.

Kitty was the first to melt. She said in a low voice, 'Surely another son would not mean so very much to you, Will.'

She frowned as she said this; and Will felt something stir inside him. His temper evaporated. He realised, belatedly, that she had not just been trying to divert him: she genuinely was deeply concerned for Bess.

'No, it would not; and I did not press her to do this, far from it. I should be glad to settle for the family we have already. But to Bess, Kitty, it is life itself. She has tried to resign herself to Ascham's verdict and she cannot do it. She knows the risks, knows them well. But if they were ten times as great she would still take them.'

'Knowing that it could mean being lost to the children, to Amy and John? Being lost to you?'

But she was lost to him without, Will thought ruefully. Friends, midwives, Kitty herself had all explained to Bess about the vinegar douches, but she had never carried them out consistently, complaining again and again that the process was confusing, was messy, that she couldn't do it right. After months of arguments he had simply ceased to make love to her, and she had taken this hard. He was not prepared to tell Kitty that, or to explain the joint misery that had led him to reverse his decision.

'Even then.'

Kitty's frown deepened and there was a short, heavy silence. But she did not press any further. Instead she caught her skirts and swirled round, back towards the house. 'Then you must send word to me,' she said, 'once she conceives. There is an excellent midwife in Oxford. I shall send her up to you.'

'Oxford?' Will asked, curious, as he followed her through the grass.

Kitty swung round again. This time there was a wickedly triumphant smile on her face. 'I called on your wife, Master Calthorp, so that I might tell her my news in person. I have been much in Oxford recently. And a week next Tuesday, I marry an Oxford man.'

An Oxford man? He frowned. 'But the Earl of Oxford is already married,' he said slowly.

507

'My dear Will,' Kitty said, 'I am a Dowager Duchess already. What should I want with an Earl? Oh, no. My husband-to-be is Master Thomas Strangeways.'

Strangeways? *Master* Strangeways? The name meant nothing to him. And yet he had a wide acquaintance in London and had heard the name of many Oxfordshire men since he had taken Suffolk's service. He looked into Kitty's eyes. She looked straight back at him, but her eyes narrowed slightly and he sensed something tense in her posture. This was not Kitty's usual boundless confidence: it struck him more as defiance. It came to him that she was on the verge of making a disastrous misalliance.

'You have the dispensation already?'

Kitty held his look for a moment longer, then she glanced upwards, as if in amusement. 'Imagine, my dear!' she said lightly. 'I called on Humphrey, and he told me that he handles such matters no longer.'

Of course not; for the Duke of Gloucester was Protector no longer, the King in control of his own business. Kitty would have had to travel on, to Westminster. He guessed immediately that she had not done so.

'They say the King is a trifle lacking in a sense of humour,' he remarked.

'Do they indeed? But he is not cruel; and if I tell him after the ceremony, with many apologies, what can he say?'

'He can impose a fine on you.'

'Ah, but my dear, they say he is in such desperate need of money that he is certain to charge me a fortune in any case.'

End of conversation. Kitty's choice, firmly imposed, since she was already approaching Jeanne and holding out her arm. Jeanne took it and the two of them moved rapidly down one of the little sanded paths towards the door to the house.

Will stood for a moment, by the blackened stems of the briar arch, watching them. Kitty's admonitions, Kitty's news, swirled round his head. From beneath them, though, surfaced his original annoyance: surfaced the thought that he was still far enough from the house for a private conversation, and that if he called her back he might tackle her over the tales she was telling to Bess.

But what could he say? She had told Bess some uncomfortable truths, but no lies to his knowledge. She had acted cannily, but not dishonourably. She was still a Dowager Duchess, and not the woman to submit to his demand that she speak differently to his wife. To raise the subject would only renew their old enmity, and lose Bess a good friend.

He moved hastily after her and reached her at the doorway. He supplanted Jeanne, taking her arm himself until he handed her over to an anxious-looking Bess. The cook had produced her refreshments. He stayed and politely ate two honey cakes and drank a cup of milk. Then he made his apologies and went to pursue his business at Suffolk Inn.

It was dark when he returned home and all trace of the Duchess and her servants was gone from the yard. Bess was waiting for him in the hall. She was sitting on the settle by the fire, mending a pair of Amy's hose by the light of a couple of candles. She looked up as he slammed the door and smiled uncertainly at him.

A returning smile came easily to his face, though behind it were a number of uncomfortable thoughts. Hang Kitty, he said to himself, crossing over to join Bess on the settle. We have made our decision now, to risk another child. It is too late to go back upon it; and to fret over it will only make things worse.

22

ENGLAND

'Not that damned water,' whispered Thomas Chaucer.

'Of course not,' Alice replied briskly. 'You shall have wine, Father, if that is what you wish.' She threw a withering look at the maid who had brought the water and sent the girl back to the cellar for good Gascon wine.

'It eases the pain', Chaucer murmured. 'Bloody priest. Said I should be sober to take the sacrament, but I told him, I can think when I have wine. I think well then. But the pain, the pain – when the pain is there I can think of nothing but the pain.'

'The priest came this morning, Father?'

'Every morning. Tells me I should confess again, but what damned chance do I have to sin, lying here in bed?'

Alice forced out a laugh. 'I dare say you have your chances, Father. The maid is pretty enough.'

Chaucer gave a cracked smile. 'Aye, and there are sins other than those of the flesh. Pride. I can lay claim to that. And my damnable curiosity. The passion dies, my dear, but the curiosity . . . some of that remains in me still.'

Bending over the bed, Alice did not hear the footsteps of the maid until she was halfway across the room. The girl set down the flagon of wine with a flounce that verged on the insolent and withdrew without asking for permission.

Alice damped down her impatience at the girl's manner and poured the wine herself. She swirled it slightly round the tall Venetian glass and gazed for a moment into the clear purple depths.

'Shall . . . have to . . . sit up, my dear.'

She set down the glass and turned to her father. His body was light, now: it was not so great a task to pull him upright and set the pillows behind him. She smoothed the heavy embroidered coverlet over his legs and placed the glass in his hands. He sipped. And though he tried to hide it, a little grimace creased his face.

'It is not turned to vinegar, Father?'

'No, Alice.' Chaucer's painful smile appeared again. 'I tell myself to savour each sip in case it is my last. And yet it never tastes as good as I intend it to.'

'But this shall not be your last glass, Father. Far from it. In a few days you will be up again, and walking.'

Chaucer's eyes, fixed on her, were dark. The pain, Alice told herself, though a part of her knew it rather for a kind of dumb misery.

'Shall not do that, Alice. Not even for you.'

'Drink the wine, Father,' she said, a little brusquely to hide her unease. 'The next sip will taste sweeter.'

Her father drank. And, released for a moment, Alice crossed the room and looked from the window. They were high up in the Westminster house, in a bedchamber that looked down on the Abbey churchyard.

For her. A part of her, a part of the Alice that had always shrunk from the sick, the decayed and the ugly, would have seen this invalid die as soon as might be. It was an effort that strained everything in her, to hide her disgust at the state into which her father had fallen. And yet another part of her willed him to live on, and on: to live for her.

Thomas Chaucer had been the hub of her life; the still point to which she could always look, however the wheel turned; the one enduring constancy that had taken her through marriage and widowhood, through joy and bitter disappointment. He had been her guide, her standard. Her justification, as she was his. He had loved her always; judged her, never.

And nor should she judge him, she scolded herself; only love him, be to him the daugher he needed at the last. She set her face back into the serene mask that she meant him to see on her and turned once more to the interior of the room. Everything was as it should be. The boards had been swept clean and strewed with sweet herbs to take away the smell of sickness. The apple logs she had ordered specially burned in the little hearth. On the windowsill, a sleek-coated black cat licked its paws. The hangings round the bed were part drawn to cut off the draught from the door; her father's nightshirt was clean that morning. She had no cause to hide from him in housewifely tasks, least of all when those agonised eyes pleaded with her to talk with him.

She took the stool from under the little table by the bed and came to sit at his side.

The glass was empty. She offered to refill it for him, but Chaucer shook his head.

His voice, when it came, was a whisper so low that she had to strain closer to hear it. 'Should have chosen a better husband for you, Alice.'

A little shiver of surprise ran through her. That was totally unexpected. Her father had never criticised her husband to her; she had not thought that he harboured any criticism unspoken.

'Not so, Father,' she said softly. 'You chose very well.'

'Not a bad man,' Chaucer whispered. 'But I meant him to love you best, Alice. And he loves his causes more.'

'I do not understand you, Father.' It was true: she did not.

'Then,' he whispered, 'you are too young. Get to my age, Alice. You know then that causes matter nothing. People, only people. Never use people to further a cause.'

Alice frowned. A tiny part of her sensed that there might be something to this; but it was no argument to fall into at such a time, she told herself firmly. Her father had no real desire to play with philosophical

512

notions; what he needed was reassurance. So she said –
not heartily, he would see through that, but in the same
soft voice – 'There is no reason for you to fret, Father.
The Earl of Suffolk treats me very well.'

'He uses you, my dear. Uses everyone around him.'
Chaucer seemed to attempt an ironic smile; but it
turned into a grimace of pain. 'He is not the man I once
thought him, Alice. And his causes are not the answer
he thinks them to be.'

'He is my husband,' Alice replied, gently but firmly.
'You drink your wine, Father, because it is such, and do
not let yourself call it vinegar. I love my husband
because he is such. And he is no vinegar to me, but as the
finest wine from Burgundy.'

'Aye,' Chaucer murmured. 'As it should be. And he
should work for the King's glory, even if his King be a
fool of a boy. But sometimes, when you see . . . when
you see clearly, when you see the King to be a fool, the
cause turn to writing on the wind, it is hard to love them
as you ought.'

'I see no such thing, Father.'

'Then see it not,' Chaucer whispered. His head fell
back against the hard pillows. 'I see you, Alice, see you
clear. And yet I love you still.'

There were many answers she could have given; only
one that she could be sure would not be hurtful to him.
'And I love you, Father,' Alice Chaucer dutifully
replied.

'Aye,' murmured her father once more. 'As it should
be.' His eyes closed. Alice waited for some time, in the
silence of the little bedchamber, broken only by the
crackling of the apple logs on the fire. But he had no
more to say.

It would be better, William Paston thought to himself, if
he could resolve the Commission of Enquiry into
Thomas Wetherby's complaints without taking advantage of Lord Cromwell's willingness to oblige him. It
was not that he doubted Cromwell; merely that he

preferred to leave this small debt, like so many others, unpaid for as long as possible. And on reflection, he thought that there might be another way to deal with the problem of the Earl of Suffolk: one not underhand, but a little more subtle than his original plan.

He let it become known among his acquaintances at court that he and his fellow Commissioners were having difficulty in reaching any conclusions. That much had been apparent to Norfolk men for months; but if Suffolk heard this tale repeated in London, William reckoned, he would read more into it. He would perhaps realise that it had been intended to reach him. He might then realise that the Commission were not prepared to deliver a verdict until they learned something that they did not yet know. And what could that be but his own attitude to the verdict, or verdicts, they thought of delivering? Whatever verdict Suffolk hoped for, he was surely anxious to have the entire matter done with; so if he succeeded in reasoning this far, he would take the necessary next step and arrange to speak to William himself.

The plan worked. On William's next visit to London he found a letter waiting for him at the Inner Temple. There were some matters the Earl of Suffolk wished to discuss with him, the letter said; would he please be so good as to present himself at Bardi Place?

This formal little note rather pleased him: not only because it was proof that he had planned well, but because he relished the forthcoming meeting. At last he would have a chance to confront Suffolk, to duel verbally with the man, to make up his own mind about the Earl's worth. At last he would have a chance to indicate to the Earl the things he could only reveal face to face: the favours he believed he could do, and the payment he would wish to receive. At last he would have Suffolk's attention fixed on him for long enough for him to be able to work John's name – perhaps even Edmund's, too – into the conversation.

This did not blind him to the knowledge that it would

514

be a very uncomfortable meeting if the Earl proved to be determined to see Wetherby vindicated. He had already decided that he would not find against Purdance, even to oblige Suffolk. But he could offer various compromises.

The crudest of these, and the one he favoured least, would be a reprise of his earlier plan: an undertaking not to find for Purdance either, but to have his commission disbanded and a more conciliatory one set up. He hoped this would not be necessary, partly because he knew it would do nothing to enhance his reputation in the county, and partly because he genuinely wished to see Purdance vindicated and Wetherby humbled. So he would set out his other suggestions before raising this possibility. He was, for instance, prepared to find for the Prior when the Priory's case against the City next came up. John Heydon was facing accusations of bribery, and he was willing to do what he could to ensure that this suit was resolved favourably. Perhaps Suffolk would be able to add to this little list of favours.

He rode to Lombard Street, in the company of his clerk James, who had been well briefed about his plans. They stabled their horses at the Cardinal's Hat and walked up past Welles' grocer's shop to Bardi Place. William paused for a moment outside, staring at the balconies and the turrets of the Italian bankers. Then the main door opened, an earlier visitor departed and he found himself being ushered into a vast hall.

Fancy frescoes, a painted ceiling, vast empty expanses of marbled floor: it was the most outlandish room he had ever entered. And not to his taste at all, but he had discrimination enough to recognise that it was remarkable of its kind, and curiosity enough to give it a good look before bringing his attention to bear on the occupants.

There were half a dozen men in the hall, though these were all but lost amid the huge expanse. Suffolk Herald and Will Calthorp were lingering by the fireplace, propping up a dolphin apiece. There were the Chamberlain who had shown him in, a couple of pages and clerks, and the Earl of Suffolk himself, standing near the windows with his hands clasped behind his back and an abstracted look on his face. Like his servants, he was dressed in mourning: his father-in-law had died only days earlier.

'Judge Paston, my Lord.'

Suffolk turned, slowly, to look at him and nodded his head.

The Chamberlain guided William and James towards a long trestle set close to one wall. James delved into his bag, drew from it a bundle of papers and spread them carefully across one end of the trestle. William settled himself on the bench that ran between the trestle and the wall; James sat down next to him; and Suffolk, without comment, placed himself opposite them.

William glanced cautiously past the Earl. He could see most of the hall from where he sat, including the fireplace and (by moving his head a little to one side) the main doorway. Calthorp was looking in his direction; William gave him an unobtrusive nod. He wondered whether the lad would be able to overhear their conversation. That was difficult to judge without knowing the acoustics of the hall. Suffolk presumably knew them intimately, but he appeared to have taken no notice of Calthorp.

He rapidly decided that it would be best to follow suit. It was not as if he was sure that Calthorp would prove his ally. He had no more idea of Calthorp's opinion than he had of Suffolk's, and he was considerably less concerned about it. It was annoying, mind, that Calthorp had not proved more helpful to him, had not visited him in Norwich or given him any hint which might have resolved things sooner. But it was too late to worry about that, and he could not afford to distract himself from the immediate task of taking control of this encounter.

Speak first, that was important: set the first line of attack. He launched in immediately, speaking in a rapid but carefully judged lawyer's pace, designed to discourage any potential interruptions.

He spoke for a long time. He summarised every aspect of the case before the Commission. Purdance's complaints against Wetherby, and the findings. Wetherby's complaints against Purdance. Purdance's defence of his actions to the Commission. The legal niceties of the use of the City Seal, and the position of the City Clerk. He did not pause until his account was complete.

Suffolk said, 'I was already aware of the facts. I am waiting to hear your opinions.'

That grated on William. In other circumstances he would not have taken it to be rude, coming from a superior, but it was hardly the note he had wished to strike. Annoying, too, because he could scarcely avoid giving some kind of direct answer and he had not wanted to make his own opinions clear until Suffolk had revealed his – if then.

He said, cautiously, 'Speaking strictly as a lawyer, I consider that there were grave irregularities in both of the elections for Mayor.'

'And not only at the elections, that is clear. These fines and disqualifications are quite outrageous.'

That remark was even more alarming: it had all the subtlety of a knock on the head with a wooden mallet. It was not what he had expected from what he had previously heard and seen of Suffolk. Just one response, in what he intended for a long conversation; but that alone had removed the bulk of his space for negotiation. Another like it, and the meeting he had planned so carefully would be virtually wasted: he would be forced to resort to his last-ditch plan and might not even gain anything in return.

'If you look, my Lord, you will see that they are all correctly engrossed and sealed with the City Seal.'

Slowly, deliberately, he selected four of the papers, folded them so that the seal was uppermost and pushed them across the trestle to the Earl.

Suffolk barely glanced at them. He is not interested, thought William: he did not call me here to negotiate. He simply plans to state his position. Perhaps Yelverton was right after all: perhaps his support for Wetherby has never wavered. But even so, if he is determined to see a verdict for Wetherby he has taken a strange approach. It is more as if the whole matter bores him, and he wants it done with and me away again as quickly as possible.

'My sources suggest to me,' Suffolk said, 'that the seal has been used improperly.'

'There is nothing in these depositions to support such a view.'

'Then may I suggest that your Commission should look to obtain further depositions.'

The Earl drew back a little. His eyes were not on William; they had drifted down to the trestle and its litter of papers. His expression was quite indifferent.

While absorbing all these little signs, William made a show of considering this advice. He did not take it seriously: none of the men on his Commission would ever contemplate doing anything of the kind. But he did need to consider what lay behind it.

Is it possible, he asked himself, that Suffolk is telling me to do this, not because he is determined at all costs to support Wetherby, but because he believes this to be the fastest and easiest solution to our dull little Norfolk squabbles? If so, he is making a grave mistake. In fact a double mistake; for it is one mistake to aim for the easiest solution, and a far greater one to imagine that it consists of finding for Thomas Wetherby.

It bores him, the whole matter: that is clear. He has called me here so late, tried to handle me so brusquely, because he has no interest in it. But he is a great nobleman in Norfolk, and prominent in the King's Council: these things oblige him to play a large part in the county's affairs. No doubt they are small beer when set against the Council's deliberations on the war in France; but Norfolk is his backyard and it will reflect ill on him if his cocks and his mongrels scrap there so fiercely that all England comes to hear of it. He may live in Oxfordshire if he wishes, but Norfolk needs him nonetheless; and he needs Norfolk. He needs even me.

To make an enemy of a reputable Judge? That is the act of a fool. I too have my little share of influence on the Council. I know what audacious policies the Earl of Suffolk tries to pursue there; I know how badly he needs support. Men such as I should be at its core, but the core of this man's apple is rotten with corruption and neglect.

In any case neither we nor Suffolk could now hold down a verdict for Wetherby. Things have gone too far for that; we could see real insurrection if any Commission were to try. Fights in the street, battles at the bridges, affrays which would make the little tussle at the Guildhall look like lads playing in the schoolyard.

'I doubt,' he said slowly, 'whether it would be helpful to do that, my Lord.'

Suffolk looked up. 'Might I ask why, Judge Paston?'

'Because it is our understanding that if we uphold Wetherby's complaints, Purdance and the present sheriffs are like to call upon Norwich men to resist their reinstatement.'

Suffolk met his eye this time. William watched the Earl's attention focus around his steady, light brown gaze. Doubtless he was still exasperated with the whole matter, but he was not bored, not now.

'That can easily be handled,' he said softly.

'With respect, my Lord, you are not often in Norwich. Our belief is that it cannot.' He said it levelly, his eyes still on Suffolk. Suffolk stared back. 'There could be a serious threat of civil unrest in the city,' he added.

'Are you trying to tell me, Judge Paston, that Norwich is so ungovernable that it is impossible to redress outrageous irregularities such as these?'

'There is a great deal of ill feeling in the city against Thomas Wetherby.' Suffolk did not make an immediate reply, and he rashly added, 'John Heydon, too; and Sir Thomas Tuddenham. Hard things are said about all of them, and their associates.' He felt, rather than saw, James react at this; instinctively, he gave the clerk a sharp kick on the shins.

There was a hint of a frown on Suffolk's face, but he showed no other reaction. I hear often that he is an unresponsive man, William thought: and that at least is true. Of course all this is no news to him, though no judge can have told it to him before. His indifference comes automatically: it will take more than a few words to shake him into a changed attitude to his servants.

He had no intention yet of offering more. This was an earl, a man of fortune and influence: he had come to conciliate him, not to act as avenging angel. He waited patiently for Suffolk's reply.

'There is always resentment against strong rule,' Suffolk said at last. 'But are you trying to suggest to me, Judge Paston, that the remedy for that is weak rule?'

Was he? Scarcely. He had never seen the problem in those terms. This was an unexpected approach, in a discussion hardly distinguished as yet for its subtlety. In a different situation he might have enjoyed exploring it, ironing out the ambiguities, trying to make sense of the Earl's values and attitudes. But his hold on Suffolk's attention was still fragile; foolish, he thought, to risk expending it in such a manner.

Foolish to reply, come to that; for he could think of no reply that would neither directly contradict Suffolk, nor play into his hands. So he let a silence fall between them. Suffolk waited for several moments, then he answered himself. 'Clearly it cannot be. It is necessary to take a firm line. Wetherby and his men must be confirmed in their offices; the fines must be cancelled. Wetherby is no sapling, to bend under pressure. He has influence in the city; he knows how to take control, and Tuddenham will support him. You may make it known that they have my support also. That should be sufficient to ensure that Purdance accepts the verdict.'

He stood, abruptly. He picked up a couple of the papers and fiddled idly with the seals. One broke as he picked at it, cracking open to expose a thick wavy line of red wax. He looked down at William through hooded eyes. 'Your fellow Commissioners will do as I suggest?'

William looked back for a moment. Then he set his hands on the trestle top and pushed himself slowly to his feet. Careful, he told himself; don't overdo it. Old and distinguished, that is your role; you must not appear decrepit, not in front of this man. No sapling, true, but you are not yet dead wood either. He kept his hands on the trestle, kept bending slightly forward and deliberately looked downwards as he replied. 'I think, my Lord, that it would be necessary to look directly to the King, or perhaps to a great lord such as yourself, in such a case.'

The words and manner were as conciliatory as he could make them, while ensuring that his message was unambiguous. If he could salvage nothing else, he thought, he would at least try to leave without pushing Suffolk into showing overt anger.

'I see.' Another silence, which lasted long enough for William to give into the temptation to look up. Suffolk had not moved. He was still fiddling with the seal. His face had acquired its half-frown again, as if he did not see it at all. He seemed to become conscious of William's look and a moment later he returned it. 'I am disappointed in you, Judge Paston.'

'I am sorry to hear it, my Lord.'

'You will be.'

No; no anger. This was said coolly. Suffolk turned his back on William and glanced round the room. He settled his gaze on Will Calthorp. 'Calthorp, you may show Judge Paston the door.'

Judge Paston bowed and murmured the conventional phrases he would have murmured whatever the outcome of the meeting. James was still sitting, apparently enthralled by the duel. William kicked him and he scrambled hastily to his feet and bowed. Then William turned to Calthorp, who had moved a few paces closer to them. He gave the younger man a very deliberate smile. 'Why, Will,' he said. 'I have some messages to pass on to you from young John and Edmund.'

It was a hollow gesture, to get in their names when everything else was lost. Calthorp responded more rapidly than he had expected. So he has been listening, William thought: he has taken in all of it.

'How long it is since I was in Norwich. Young John must be well grown now. Bound for Peterhouse, was it, or Magdalen College?'

They talked, in middling loud voices, of the boys and of Agnes as they strode together down the long room, with James a pace behind them. Neither of them glanced back to see if Suffolk was paying any attention.

They passed through the door, into the archway that led from Lombard Street to the stableyard, and out into the street. Then they stopped.

I did wonder if he was indifferent, William thought; but he is not. He cares about the outcome, no doubt of that. Not a word, though, not a gesture that I noticed in all that interview, to tell me what line to take or hint what result he hoped for. Why? Was Stapleton right: has he really become Tuddenham's man? That would explain it. He is no fool, not blind or deaf: he would feel some shame, surely, if that were so.

Calthorp said in an undertone, 'You came with the impression that it might be possible to push through a verdict against Wetherby.'

'I thought I had cause to suspect it.'

'It would have been, I think, had the Commission decided against him immediately. Then Suffolk would have accepted it; but now Wetherby and Tuddenham have their campaign too well set, and they have pushed him into declaring his support for them.'

William stared at him. Tuddenham's man, Wetherby's man – no, Will Calthorp was neither, to judge from the contempt he put into his voice, from the level gaze that returned his own. But he did not yet understand. 'You thought this then? When the Commission was set up?'

'I – I suspected it. No more, then. It has become clearer to me since.'

'Since it has become too late to do anything.' His sarcasm was blatant; he had lost his appetite for subtlety.

Calthorp's cheeks reddened slightly and his gaze fell. But he replied with spirit, 'It is easy, sir, to say that now. But at the time, I thought it necessary to do nothing. The Commission went to you; all Norfolk knew you for Wetherby's enemy. I knew you so myself, beyond any doubt: you have talked to me, talked plain, of your opinion of Wetherby and Heydon and Tuddenham. Why then should I doubt that you would find against them?'

'Why doubt? Because, you damn fool, I can afford to anger the Earl of Suffolk no more than you can yourself!'

The red had drained now and it was a blanched face that glanced towards the high windows, warning William that his voice had risen too loud for safety. He half thought that Calthorp would hurry him away, push him from the stable arch. But the younger man held his ground and in a moment he said, more levelly, 'We have both misjudged, sir; and we both regret it. But you clearly think now that it would not do to find for Wetherby; and so do I. So what should be our plan?'

'Plan? It is too late, lad, for any plan. My men cannot find for Purdance; Wetherby and Tuddenham would wreck any such verdict. There is nothing to be done but what I said to the Earl.'

'To make him give the verdict? I swear to you, he will not give it against his own men.'

'Then the worst may happen. There will be revolution in Norwich. And men will lay the blame at the Earl of Suffolk's door.'

'We cannot let that happen.'

It was a boyish plea, more full of disbelief than of determination. But Will Calthorp was no child, William thought viciously to himself. No lad, even, though habit made him call him such: he was a man of twenty-four or so, with a wife and children of his own. He bore his own share of the blame. Let him weigh it, then, feel it heavy on his shoulders. Let that handsome face with the ready grin learn what it was to frown. Let that careless soul learn what it was to regret. Why should he himself shoulder all the risk, all the burden?

'Ah, man,' said William, 'we already have.'

23

ENGLAND
Spring, 1435

His disappointment at the Duke of Bedford's remarriage was not the only reason why the Duke of Burgundy was considering making his peace with the Valois by the end of 1434. Perhaps, though, he would have set about the matter differently if his sister Lady Anne had still been alive and available as an intermediary, or if Bedford had made more effort to appease him.

Not that Bedford was against peace. In fact, he was one of its strongest proponents in the Lancastrian camp; at least as strong as Beaufort, and stronger than the Archbishop of York and the other churchmen who professed to want to end the war. It was Gloucester who stood firm for war, who refused to consider ending hostilities until all France was under Lancastrian control.

If Gloucester was – to Burgundy's mind – entirely unrealistic, however, Bedford also was lacking in reason. He appeared to want peace only on terms that could never possibly be acceptable to Charles of Valois. He not only expected Henry of Lancaster to be confirmed in his title over territories that he had never held more than tenuously; he also insisted that Henry would not under any circumstances pay homage to Charles for his French territories. Burgundy, who had always held his own formidable territory as a nominal vassal to the Valois King, had no sympathy with this ludicrous demand.

Over the winter the Duke of Burgundy exchanged a

long series of messages with the Valois leaders; and in January this clandestine activity culminated in a very public conference at Nevers. The outcome was not for public consumption; but it did not displease Burgundy to think that the English knew he had come to terms with the Valois.

At the same time, however, the Duke was the sworn ally of Henry of Lancaster, and he accepted his obligation to put a public gloss on these harsh private realities. In the spring he set his energies towards organising a serious peace conference. It would be held under his patronage, and on his territory, at Arras. He demanded of the Valois that they should put in an appearance in strength, and not pull out at the last moment however strongly the English provoked them. And he hinted to the English, surely as clearly as was necessary in the circumstances, that this would be the last chance to salvage the Anglo-Burgundian alliance. Oaths could be broken, after all, with the connivance of the Pope; and at that moment the Pope had little sympathy for the English.

Burgundy sent Toison d'Or, his King of Arms, to England that February to deliver the invitation. But the herald was taken sick on the journey and he was reluctant to entrust such a message to any lesser ambassador, particularly since he was not sure how efficient the English spies had been at Nevers. In consequence he did not deliver his message to King Henry's Council until May. It then belatedly occurred to Burgundy that the English might become so enraged at his treatment of them that they would refuse to come to Arras. He had no intention of permitting that to happen. In that case the outcome might well have been war between England and Burgundy, while the Duke remained convinced that at Arras he would be able to arrange everything to his greatest convenience. He decided to send Hugues de Lannoy back to London, to keep a watchful eye on the English preparations and to press home the Burgundian viewpoint in the more sympathetic quarters.

On a cool and still day in the late spring of 1435, a little procession of barges was making its way down the Thames towards the Duke of Gloucester's Pleasance. They were a gay sight, with their striped red and gold awnings, their painted sides and the bargemen in Gloucester's red and gold livery, but the faces of those on board, for the most part, hinted at a serious, even solemn mission.

In the first barge sat the Earl of Suffolk and his Countess, with Will Calthorp and half a dozen other retainers.

Alice's gown was of yellow satin, figured in gold. Cut deep at the neck, it rose to a high waist. The veil over her horned headdress, sheer and long, drifted down across her shoulders. Her hand trailed languorously over the side of the barge, so that her fingertips just touched the water.

She watched her fingers for a moment, disappearing into the murky depths of the Thames. Then she turned her head and glanced at her husband. His posture was almost as casual as hers, but she could read his tension from his stiffly set shoulders and the way his foot tapped on the boards of the barge-bottom.

'I still do not understand,' she said, 'why you wish to bring the Burgundians to Greenwich.'

Suffolk shrugged. 'Because it is necessary that they meet Gloucester.'

'But everyone says that Gloucester is opposed to this conference.'

'They say it, true, but not before the Burgundians.'

'Will Gloucester not say it himself to the Seigneur de Santes?'

'No,' Suffolk said shortly.

That 'no' had a ring of conviction about it. Alice did not know why Suffolk should be so certain, but she did not trouble to question any further.

She glanced round warily at the silvery head of the Seigneur de Santes. He and his companions were following in the second barge. He was looking in her direction; in Suffolk's direction. He unnerved her. In Paris, she had always found him coolly indifferent to her. Now, on his visits to London, he sought her out, but his conversations were more like interrogations. Polite, apparently pointless interrogations; for she had never managed to fathom what it was that he hoped to learn from her.

And her husband, she thought, exasperated, did not attempt to explain, but merely issued orders. Do not speak of the Duke of Orleans. Ridiculous, that: she knew nothing of Orleans' politics, so she could hardly reveal any secrets that would help the Burgundians. Say nothing of arguments in the King's Council. That was insulting to her intelligence: she would not have dreamed of doing so. Give him no hint of why it is that you come with us today to the Pleasance.

At this thought, Alice felt a twinge of uneasiness. Her relationship with Eleanor had always been more of a social friendship than an intimate one, but this visit threatened to change that. True, she had spoken with Eleanor before of her longing for a child: it mirrored Eleanor's own longing. She had tried Eleanor's remedies before, as Eleanor had tried hers. But never before had she tried anything like this remedy.

There was something reckless about Eleanor, she thought. She could imagine Eleanor as a pretty, wilful child, creating havoc at home – uprooting flowers in the garden, perhaps, or chalking on the walls – while the adults muttered that she would come to no good. Eleanor had risen high, but only as the result of an act of outlandish daring: few women, and even fewer men, would have wagered that Humphrey would eventually marry her after she ran off with him. And though she behaved decorously in public as a royal duchess, she seemed still to court danger and excitement. Mistress Jourdemain was not the first witch she had invited to the Pleasance. More than a few people privately called her a witch herself.

Which she was not, Alice thought prosaically. As

much was said of any pretty woman who managed to marry above herself; the whisper now, for instance, was that Lady Jacquetta had used witchcraft to ensnare Bedford, when any fool could see he was simply besotted with her beauty. But becoming the Duke of Gloucester's wife did not set Eleanor Cobham out of reach of accusations. If Queen Joanna had been imprisoned for consorting with witches – and that well within men's memories – then Lady Eleanor might be, too.

And Lady Alice, for that matter. Alice did not relish the thought. She was no danger-lover. Her first thought – her first action, indeed – when Eleanor had whispered her news had been to refuse to meet Mistress Jourdemain. No matter what potions and spells she could offer; it was not wise to dabble in such things. But Eleanor had pressed her, and Suffolk, told of this, had unexpectedly pressed her too. Using her, Alice thought, with an uncomfortable memory of her father's words. He wished to see her conceive, naturally; but he wished too to conciliate Gloucester and his Duchess.

And, to be fair, he wished for her happiness and safety, and had planned the visit carefully. If any busy tongues muttered that the Countess of Suffolk had called at the Pleasance while Mistress Jourdemain stayed there, then other tongues could retort that her visit had been a formal one, to accompany the Burgundian delegation.

What would Mistress Jourdemain do? Alice wondered. Would she examine her? Prescribe a potion? Perform a spell in front of her, or present her with a recipe for one to do herself at midnight? Perhaps it would work. There had been one or two months recently when she had had cause to hope for two or three days, before the inevitable disappointment came.

Perhaps it would work for Eleanor. Alice gave a bitter little smile. That would please neither her husband nor Cardinal Beaufort – nor the Burgundians either, presumably. From what Jacquetta had told her, there was little likelihood that the ailing Bedford would get his longed-for heir, so any child of Gloucester's would become heir to the King, at least until he married himself. That would strengthen Humphrey's position immeasurably; that would destroy any remaining chance of a negotiated peace with France.

Was there really any hope, even at that time? She did not know. Suffolk was worried, she knew. But she also sensed that he was not despairing.

The Countess is restless, thought Hugues de Lannoy. No wonder that they are all on edge: they know that it is both necessary that I meet with Gloucester, and entirely conceivable that Gloucester will say or do something to wreck my mission. But even so, I find her restless.

His methodical mind cast back, for the umpteenth time, over the progress of his mission so far. His formal tasks were completed. He had spoken before the King's Council, reminding them of King Henry the Fifth's sincere wish for peace, of the sufferings of the French, and of the agonies of the Duke of Burgundy himself. He had eulogised Pope Martin the Fifth and his legate, Cardinal Albergati, who would preside at Arras, though he had sensed no corresponding English enthusiasm for either man. He had talked in private with Cardinal Beaufort. Beaufort had shrivelled, he thought: was drying up as he moved into old age. But he had influence still, and was closer to being Suffolk's master than his ally.

To Gloucester he had not yet talked – hence this outing. He had seen the Duke at Westminster and in the Council, though. Where Beaufort had shrunk, he had found Gloucester expanded: grown fat about the middle, sagging about the chin. He was much younger than the Cardinal, but he seemed to be ageing more rapidly and less gracefully. Perhaps he would die first. Not soon enough, though, to alter the outcome of the conference. However shallow his support in the Council, however little favour the growing King showed him, the Duke of Gloucester still had power enough to veto a negotiated settlement.

And a negotiated settlement it would have to be: that, or no settlement at all, no hope for the English in France. In truth, de Lannoy thought with a touch of sadness, Burgundy would prefer the latter. Duke Philip had no friends now among the English. He himself had tried to persuade the Duke that Suffolk could become his friend, but it was a feeble effort: the two men were not similar in character, and Suffolk lacked the power and position that might have stirred Burgundy's interest in him. There was no time, anyway. Even if Suffolk were conciliatory at Arras – even if all the English were conciliatory – Burgundy already had his mind made up.

I try, thought the Seigneur de Santes. I have made every effort possible, since my arrival in England, to ensure that the Council will select a delegation which might conceivably salvage something from the situation. But there has never been any real possibility of that happening; and even were it to be so, I know in my heart that it would only anger my master.

I court Suffolk, have done throughout this embassy and previous ones, because I find him to be a thoughtful and reasonable man. Given the power that he does not yet have (and perhaps never will have), he might have forced through the solution that I favour myself. I find him devious sometimes, but he is no fool, no liar. I admire him, I even like him. But even as I court him, I know that I am setting him up as a sacrifice to Burgundy's ambitions. My deeds, above all, will mark him as a Burgundian; Burgundy will betray the English; and Suffolk will be destroyed. Orleans, too. If I persuade the English to bring him to Arras, I shall be writing his life sentence in English captivity. True, Burgundy says he will work thereafter to see him freed; but I find it hard to believe in the strength of Burgundy's conscience.

He found that sad. But what other option did he have? Still, it passed through his mind that if the afternoon brought him any notion of how he might destroy Gloucester, it would have served both the English and the French causes very well.

'Let me warn you now, Suffolk. I will not agree to send Orleans to Flanders. You may affect to trust Burgundy, but I know better.'

'The Valois will not negotiate seriously unless Orleans is made available. There is no doubt of that.'

Gloucester snorted. 'The Valois will not negotiate at all. Not on the sovreignty issue, and we cannot possibly come to terms unless they concede that.'

It was a blunt attack; it was brutal. It made no concessions from Gloucester's previous position. It was precisely what he had feared and expected. His only relief was that it was, thank goodness, being made out of the Burgundians' hearing.

There, Suffolk had not been mistaken. Gloucester could be foolish, could be impetuous, could be arrogant and aggressive; but he had been raised as a prince, and he was enough of one to know that in front of a foreign embassy English nobles must never, never air their differences. So he had treated the Burgundian delegation all day with icy politeness, and had let loose his anger only now, when he had succeeded in drawing Suffolk away from de Lannoy's side and into a little enclosed courtyard, fragrant with pinks and overlooked only by the kitchens.

Suffolk had no hope that Gloucester's mind would be changed: he had been fixed firm in this attitude for many years. But it was necessary, all the same, to strike back. 'True, there is no hope of the Valois conceding that; but you draw the wrong conclusion. It achieves nothing to demand the impossible. The King's Council cannot act like mystics praying for miracles. We must be reasonable men. We must choose between the possible outcomes; and there are only two. We settle, on the terms that the Valois are willing to concede; or we hold out, and find our last French allies deserting us, our last chance of securing our existing territories destroyed. That would be the true disaster: to stand by, whining of thrones and coronation oaths, while Burgundy comes to terms with the Dauphin and goes on to grab Northern France for his own.'

'We should never have used Burgundy in the first place. I always maintained as much. And to play into Burgundy's hands now? To sign away the King's inheritance in France, because this is what Burgundy wishes? Only a knave would think this possible!'

'We should sign away nothing, my Lord, but what the King does not in truth possess. The title you talk of is hollow. What is it to be king, if the King's subjects would rather fight him than bend their knee to him? A sham, no more. I talk of estates: of fields and towns and rivers. Your estates, and mine, ravaged by war and threatened always by the Valois armies. To secure the King's lands, to see his lesser titles to them acknowledged by Frenchmen great and small, by the Pope, by all Europe: surely this would be wise.'

'Wise? Wise! Let me tell you what would be wise. An attack would be wise! We had the Valois on the run back in '24, and what happened at Orleans and after? Fools and knaves ran our campaigns, and led the army to disaster after disaster. Stupid, incompetent, misguided, every one of them. We should have pressed home our advantage after Verneuil. Then we could have dictated our own terms and sent the Dauphin packing to his bloody Spanish allies.'

Fools and knaves. Gloucester knew it was he who had commanded the army at Orleans and Jargeau: he meant it to bite. And damn it, it did. Even now, the memories were red-raw, the anguish cut deep. He had learned to bury the images – he could not have functioned otherwise. But he had no defence, even now, against any man who tried to exhume them.

No defence; but he could attack. The anguish surged into anger. A film of red spread behind his eyes. Dissolute, indolent Gloucester had been dallying with his mistress at the Pleasance, while he himself was knee-deep in mud at Orleans. Fools and knaves? Had Gloucester ever tried to run a campaign with an empty purse and an emptier store? Had he tried to keep men in good heart when the bloody flux had them doubled up in agony? Had he ever tried to counter cannon with arrows, to persuade a company of hundreds that they stood a chance against thousands? Then what damn business had he to criticise those who had, even if they had failed at the impossible?

'Pressed home?' he almost shouted. 'Pressed home! With men on their knees, and horses fit only for the knacker's yard? With not a penny to pay the troops we had, let alone to muster more? In a country full of brigands, where every farmer cursed us, and even the whores turned away our custom? That is the talk of a fool, sir; the King's generals were none such! And now matters are worse. Then we served a penniless child of a king; now we serve one plunged into a sea of debt, and sinking fast. And you speak of standing by while Burgundy leads his men to take the Valois banners; of attack! Such talk is lunacy, sir, and not fit for a king's counsellor!'

Gloucester's heavy face reddened. He raised his hand and Suffolk thought for a moment that he would strike him for his insolence. Then he lowered it and said instead in a low voice piled thick with menace, 'These are bad times. No man disputes that. But better times must come, even if we cannot yet tell when or how. Remember Crécy, and the old victories. Remember Agincourt. A miracle, men said, and yet it happened. It was after Agincourt that my brother set out his negotiating table. And you tell me that we should sit at one now, with our fortunes at their lowest ebb? You tell me that we should sign away the titles that once were not empty; titles that could one day be filled once more? You tell me that we should tell a king not old enough to remember his father's glory that neither he nor his heirs should ever again claim the throne of France? No, sir. A thousand times no. It would be a scandal and a disgrace.'

'It would be so, perhaps, were our fortunes truly at their low point. But that is not so. We hold Normandy still, and Maine, and other lands. Refuse to negotiate now, and we shall lose them all. You talk of past glories; I talk of present possessions. Small perhaps, but more than our King can afford to surrender.'

'He will not surrender them!' Gloucester roared.

'You aim to hold them for him?' Suffolk sneered in response.

There was a moment of terrible silence. Then Gloucester said, 'Just so, sir. That I do. Your precious Burgundian friend in there wishes to know my position? Then you may tell him this. If the Duke of Burgundy reneges in any way on the Treaty of Arras, then I will personally lead an attack on Flanders. And if the Duke of Orleans has any hand in these negotiations – any hand at all – then I will make damned sure that you and your accursed French friends have no contact with him whatsoever for the rest of his natural life. Is that understood?'

It was not believed. Gloucester was a blusterer; a maker of hollow threats. But a royal duke, nonetheless, and one whom Suffolk had already opposed far more openly than was wise. He did not need Gloucester's money now that he had Chaucer's inheritance, but there were years of dirty dealing he dared not risk seeing Gloucester reveal; he could not afford to turn their open rivalry into enmity. He stared back for a few seconds, then said slowly, 'That is clearly understood.' And turned to go back to the Burgundians.

They had been in the summer hall when he left them; it was empty now, but for a small orchestra dutifully playing English serenades. The doors that led out towards the river had been thrown open. He made for them, and through them. The music of the lutes and viols followed him, drifting out over the parterre, across the lawns that swept down to the river, past the butts where a group of pages were practising with their longbows, and far, far out across the water.

They were there, on the terrace. Lady Eleanor, her dark face flushed with laughter; Alice, a smile lighting up her paler, smoother face; their ladies, the esquires, de

535

Lannoy and his men. He stood on the step for a moment, watching them. The joke had been Calthorp's, addressed to Lady Eleanor, he could tell. De Lannoy had laced his fingers together and stood watching the two of them, his fingers flexing rhythmically, his eyes moving from one to the other and back again.

Alice saw him a moment later and moved towards him. She took his arm and led him towards the others, saying, in a bright teasing voice, 'My Lord, you are to have your fortune told. Lady Eleanor had planned it for us all. I have had it done, and Calthorp; even the Seigneur has obliged us, so it would be quite improper for you to wriggle out of it.'

The Seigneur heard this. He turned his attention to Suffolk and, without unlacing his fingers, inclined his upper body in a polite little bow.

'A fortune teller?' Suffolk echoed uneasily. He was unnerved; coming from the argument with Gloucester, he had expected nothing so high-spirited. He had left the Burgundians with Calthorp and with Gloucester's men; he had not thought that Eleanor and Alice would join them. They were supposed to be in the Duchess's private quarters, with the witch. Christ in heaven, surely the witch had not . . .

He turned abruptly to Lady Eleanor. 'You have engaged an astrologer?'

'Too slow for a festival,' Eleanor replied gaily. 'Mind, Sir Roger Bolingbroke, my clerk, is skilled at reading the stars; I will ask him, if you would care to have it done. Dangerous, for a man born under the Scorpion?' She set her head to one side and examined Suffolk as if she were reading his fortune from his face.

'I was born too early for the Scorpion. On the sixteenth of October, under the Scales.'

'Justice and proportion. How suitable,' Eleanor said with just a shade of irony, 'for an ambassador. But today you must submit to Mistress Jourdemain. She shall read your hand and tell you wonders.'

He sensed, rather than heard, footsteps behind him.

'My Lady,' he said in a deliberately light voice, 'I have already heard many such today, from your husband.'

There was a short bark of laughter, almost in his ear. The Duke of Gloucester slipped past the little group without pausing again and moved on towards the river.

Suffolk gazed at him. It was a slouch, Gloucester's movement; almost a waddle. How long, he thought, since the Duke of Gloucester had even mounted a horse? He travelled almost everywhere by barge, litter and carriage. He was not old – forty-five perhaps, certainly less than fifty – but it was laughable to envisage him as a general, pitted against Burgundy's army. Bitterly laughable.

'My Lady, you should detain your husband. To learn his fate would surely fascinate us all.'

Calthorp said this, in a decent attempt at a diversion, but Eleanor was not to be distracted. 'Mistress Margery has read his hands before,' she replied. She brought her eyes to Suffolk's face. 'Alas, sir, there is no escape for you. But you need not look so apprehensive: we shall let you learn your fate in private. So long, that is, as you tell us everything when you return.'

Calthorp laughed at this, and Alice, and some of the Burgundians. 'I shall show you the way,' said Eleanor. She gave him a mischievous smile and held out her hand. He forced a smile of his own; he took the offered hand and slipped it into the crook of his elbow.

She led him back into the house. And through it, further than he had expected. They walked through tangled passages of the old house and fresh-plastered halls of the new, through anterooms and stores, across a small courtyard. He knew then where she was taking him: to the winter hall, at the other side of the palace. So Mistress Jourdemain is not even in the Duchess's rooms, he thought, and possibly has not been all day; so de Lannoy and the other Burgundians have seen her, and spoken to her. And her remedy? That was why Alice came, the cure for barrenness that Eleanor spoke of. But

Alice would surely have said nothing of that, not once she had realised how Eleanor had planned it all.

Eleanor might have mentioned it, mind; or teased him, or flirted as she generally did. Her maidservant was following them, but she was surely used to Eleanor's behaviour. The Duchess's hand was quite still on his arm, though, except for the occasional pressure to guide him; she said nothing at all.

They came to the heavy pair of doors that led into the winter hall. Eleanor paused and before he could move forward himself the maid had slipped past them and was opening the doors. She left them ajar, then moved back, as Eleanor slipped her hand free. 'To knowledge and truth,' she whispered and slithered away with the maid into the shadows of the corridor.

He stood there for a moment once they had gone. A ridiculous business. A dangerous business, even: stunts like this could trap a man with accusations of treason. Might Gloucester himself have planned something such? Should he go back, even now? No. Not only would he risk looking a fool; he might expose Alice to danger, since she had already done just this. He pushed the door open a little wider and strode into the room.

He saw the witch almost immediately: sitting in a low chair by the window, her face turned towards him. He moved towards her. She was not young, he saw as he approached; even elderly. Not a scrawny witch, rather a plump one. And as neat and clean as her surroundings merited, in a frilled green gown, adorned with a great many necklaces, brooches and chains.

She was much as he had told himself she would be, when he was trying to persuade Alice to come and call on her. She was no fairytale crone, but a wise woman, red-cheeked and mild-eyed, who would have been better cast as a loving grandmother. Behind her, through the window, the sheep grazed across the steep expanse of Greenwich Park; by her side was a plain oak stool.

'Do come and sit by me, sir,' she said in a warm voice

538

with a touch of a Suffolk accent to it. 'Forgive me if I don't rise, I suffer dreadful from rheumatism in the knees.'

How prosaic. He had imagined a meeting full of dark terrors, but here was the kind of fortune teller who told young girls of their husbands-to-be, penniless peasants that they would find a fortune. He sat and held out his right hand.

'No, sir. I see you do this none too often. 'Tis always the left hand that gives a clearer picture.' Mistress Jourdemain reached out to take it as she spoke. She uncurled his palm gently. With the forefinger of her free hand, she traced its lines. He had heard vaguely of their meaning; even done this once before, when he was a child, before he had gone to France. The lifeline, wasn't there, and the heart line; and what was the deep one that curved round the base of his fingers? He could not remember.

And she did not speak. At last he said, edgily, 'So? Shall I have many sons?'

'Never see children in a gentleman's hand, sir.' Mistress Jourdemain did not look up. 'I see a life quite long. Your lifeline is strong: you will enjoy good health until you die. I see riches and success. See, the line here, how it twists and turns? There was a crisis in your life, was there not – five, ten years ago? And there will be another crisis, perhaps as far in the future; but this time you will emerge from it strengthened.'

Suffolk murmured a reply and the witch lifted her head and gave him a wide-eyed, disarming look. 'Was there anything special you wished to know, sir?'

He shook his head.

Mistress Jourdemain splayed his hand a little wider, pressing down on the thumb. She was not so gentle now; the pressure was uncomfortable. She turned the palm towards the window. 'See here, the line that curls around your thumb? It is long: that is the sign of a sharp brain. Sometimes you think too hard, sir. Intrigue can be dangerous.'

This time he did not reply and Mistress Jourdemain

loosed her grip. She murmured some commonplace remarks about loyalty and the love of God. There was nothing specific in her words, nothing to catch his interest. He had the impression that she had drifted into a standard speech that she gave to all her customers. He was relieved when her voice slowed and finally came to a halt.

'That is all you have to tell me?'

'Unless you wish to ask me more, sir.'

'No. No, I have nothing to ask.'

'Then I shall call a boy, sir, to show you back to the ladies.'

'I can find my own way.' Suffolk stood up and flexed his knees: the low stool had cramped him. He dug in his pockets. He brought out a shilling and a silver penny; he gave her them both. 'Thank you,' he said curtly. He nodded and made for the door through which he had come into the room. It seemed very quiet: he could hear the dry rushes that covered the floor rustling about his feet with each step he took.

'Sir!' He was almost at the door, well into the shadow of the gallery, when her voice stopped him. He turned. She had not moved: she was still in the low chair by the window.

'I see your death, sir.'

Involuntarily he took a couple of steps back towards her.

'Such honour, such riches. But you will die a shameful death. And you should beware, sir, of the Tower.'

There was nothing dramatic in her tone of voice, but the words shook him. He stood there for a moment, rooted firm. Then the life came back to his legs and he all but ran from the room.

He did not stop until he had turned a bend in the corridor. His breath was short and shallow; to his annoyance, he realised that he was shaking. There was a little alcove a few paces further along; he made for this and stopped there, leaning his shoulder against a pane of the side window.

It looked out on to the park, an expanse of rough grass, studded with grazing sheep. He looked blindly at this for some time. Then he had the sensation that a voice was calling him: Alice's voice, raised high as if in a child's game of hide-and-seek. 'I'm coming,' he answered, though in an undertone, and set off to rejoin the game.

Under the rose window of Winchester Inn, Cardinal Beaufort dropped his head on to his clasped hands. He sat there for several minutes, his eyes closed; then raised his head abruptly, opened his eyes and looked full at the Earl of Suffolk.

'It will be necessary,' he said, 'to keep you and Orleans apart.'

It was a fortnight after Suffolk's visit to the Pleasance. There had been a Council meeting the day before, which had succeeded in bringing to birth a compromise agreement on the invitation to Arras. It was now confirmed that a delegation would be sent. It would not be as glittering as those that the Burgundians had intimated that they and the other French nobles would assemble: that was scarcely avoidable, since Gloucester was not prepared to attend and Bedford lay sick in bed at Rouen; but it would consist of more than the usual collation of heralds, council clerks and clerics. In keeping with tradition it would be led by a churchman: by John Kemp, Archbishop of York. But Suffolk was to be Kemp's chief supporter, nominally second-in-command of the delegation, and in a position to undertake his own private negotiations with the French lay ambassadors. The Burgundians would be there, of course; and in a formal sense (or so the Council was obliged to assume) as supporters of the Lancastrian cause. There would be other Frenchmen in the Lancastrian delegation, headed by Pierre Cauchon, Bishop of Lisieux. Buttressing these principals would be close on two hundred lesser lords, bishops and priests, countless knights, heralds and hangers-on. And as a final concession to Burgundy, the Duke of Orleans would travel to France.

From whom, Beaufort judged, Suffolk should be kept apart. Suffolk found that no great surprise.

It was two years, no more, since Beaufort had leaned on him to persuade Orleans to sign the paper in which he acknowledged Henry of Lancaster as King of France. Then, Beaufort had been convinced that the little charade would help the Lancastrian cause. It had been intended to enhance the illusion that Henry had solid support among senior French nobles; there had even been the suggestion that it might have helped to bring Burgundy more firmly into line, as leader of the French supporters of the Lancastrian cause.

Now only a fool would take Burgundy to be any such thing. This new conference had been staged to provide Burgundy with an opportunity to change his colours: there had been scant need of the spies at Nevers to tell the English that. And if Burgundy demanded that Orleans make an appearance, it was not so that Orleans might have a chance to reconvert him to Henry's cause: it was so that he might make for himself an opportunity to explain to Orleans how he, too, could safely reconvert to Charles of Valois' cause.

Thus far, Suffolk and Beaufort were agreed. But beyond this point, they differed; for Suffolk trusted Orleans, and Beaufort did not. That Orleans might be a genuine supporter of Henry was barely conceivable, even to Suffolk. But he took the Duke to be an honourable man nevertheless, and valuable for that simple reason.

For honourable men, whatever their allegiance, could be trusted to negotiate fairly; and here, he believed, Orleans had a vital role to play. The initial Valois demands would doubtless be as ludicrously over-optimistic as the demands that Henry's Council had drawn up. If there was to be any hope of an agreement – perhaps at Arras itself, more likely at a subsequent round of negotiations – then they, as well as Beaufort and Gloucester and the King, must be made to see reason. There would have to be intermediaries: informal intermediaries, not that old maid of a Cardinal and his supporting cast of monks. Suffolk believed that Orleans could be such an intermediary. He could think of no other man who could play that part.

Orleans was not a perfect choice, true. He was a Valois, and that had to be counted as a disadvantage. He had English enemies as well as English friends – indeed, many more of the former. He was a stranger to many of the younger Valois nobles; little better than a stranger to his own generation. But there was no one else.

And there could only be Orleans if the English took a risk and put their trust in him: not as their supporter – that had never been more than a hollow sham – but as a man of integrity who understood the real strengths and weaknesses of their position. There could only be Orleans if he were thoroughly and frankly briefed on every tiny change in the Lancastrian position. There could only be Orleans, Suffolk believed, if he and Orleans worked closely together throughout. Nobody else could play the role of informer; for nobody else understood, as he believed he understood, where the boundaries of trust should be drawn.

Nobody else would risk such a scheme. That was the hard truth behind his plan: that if it were done at all, it would have to be done surreptitiously. Every other Lancastrian – even Beaufort – would have to believe that Orleans was travelling to Arras only to appease Burgundy. Beaufort could be told afterwards what part the Duke had played, if he did succeed in mediating an agreement; Gloucester would not be told even then. And if he did not succeed? That would be no shame, unless he actually betrayed the English. Betrayal, admittedly, would destroy both Suffolk's own career and the English hopes of a lasting presence in France.

It was a risky scheme, but he thought it an honourable one; after all, the greatest risk would be his own. But if he and Orleans were kept apart it could not work.

So he had to dissuade Beaufort, but without explaining exactly what he was planning.

He said carefully, 'I do not think it necessary. It is known already that Orleans is my friend. If I am seen with him at Arras it will doubtless become known more widely; but such friendship is no disadvantage, surely, when it comes to negotiations.'

'No disadvantage?' Beaufort made a kind of humphing noise. 'Kemp distrusts you already; Gloucester whispers that you plan to commit treason, and sell the King's heritage to the Valois. Consort with Orleans – with any of the Valois princes – and you walk into a nest of vipers.'

'Then I shall step carefully, and with my hand to my sword. I alone can commit the King to nothing; I cannot even persuade the Archbishop to step beyond the conditions the Council has laid down.'

'In public, no; but in private you could do more, and that is what men will suspect, if you and Orleans are seen together.'

'Let them suspect it.'

Beaufort frowned. His pale blue eyes narrowed. 'You plan to negotiate through Orleans.'

'I plan to make soundings through Orleans,' Suffolk said cautiously. 'Negotiate – I would not call it that.'

'The Council did not agree to send Orleans to France for that.'

'The Council agreed because you urged them to send him, and I also.'

'True; but I urged it only to appease Burgundy.'

'We can scarcely come to any agreement by antagonising Burgundy.'

Beaufort frowned again. He thought. And said, 'I do think it wise to appease Burgundy, whatever Gloucester argues. And Orleans shall go to France – must do so, now – for that purpose. But your plan is not to appease Burgundy, but to appease Charles of Valois' ambassadors.'

'I think that necessary, too.'

'I think that impossible in such a circumstance. And to put your trust in Orleans for such a purpose is a risk I cannot countenance.'

'There is no better intermediary.'

'Not so. There is Isabella.'

'Isabella!' Suffolk echoed in disbelief. Beaufort meant Burgundy's Duchess. She was also Beaufort's own niece, and sharp-witted, men said, but Suffolk had never even considered her as a potential go-between.

'Just so. Isabella. With Isabella, we shall have no need of Orleans. He must go to France, true, but he shall not come to Arras, and shall play no part in our discussions. He shall stay at Calais and Burgundy and the rest may travel there to talk with him.'

'But I have no acquaintance at all with the Duchess Isabella.'

'It is not necessary that you should.'

'But to use her, to negotiate through her . . .'

'I shall do that.'

That was enough to stun Suffolk into silence. *Beaufort* negotiate? Beaufort? He had been working for months to establish himself not as Beaufort's puppet, but as the leader of the peace party, the man who would represent them at Arras; and now Beaufort spoke of negotiating through Isabella? 'You said nothing to the Council of a wish to travel to Arras yourself.' He tried to speak neutrally, but he could hear the tone of sullenness that he had not managed to eradicate from his voice.

'I have no wish to be tied as you will be tied, with Council proposals beyond which you may not step.'

'So you will go to Arras – as a Cardinal?'

'And defer to Albergati, merely because he won his red hat first? Not so. I shall not go to Arras. I shall go to France; but I shall remain at Calais.'

At Calais. With Orleans. Watching Orleans, though Beaufort did not say it, to ensure that Suffolk would not somehow manage to work around his precautions and use the Duke in spite of them.

He had worked so hard to tie together his negotiating arrangements and Beaufort, the wily bastard, had cut through them all.

'Had you any more to say?' Beaufort asked silkily.

'I must consider this plan of yours.'

'There is no need. I have considered it well myself. Let me call my clerk to show you to the stables. I shall not come down with you: I have some urgent business to attend to.'

And I, thought Suffolk, as he followed the clerk like a sleepwalker down the shallow stone stairs, suddenly find myself with a great deal more planning to do.

It was only as he was riding for Suffolk Inn that he remembered Gloucester's words at the Pleasance. He had considered the threat to take Orleans from him if he took the Duke to Arras as an empty boast at the time. But it had come back to him several times since and he had begun to think that it was possible that Gloucester might do it. To fight against Burgundy, that was laughable, but to find a new jailer for Orleans – that would cause Gloucester scarcely a moment's trouble. And yet to him, it could bring a lifetime of regret.

He had been willing to risk taking Orleans to France, for them both, for the sake of the negotiations. But now, he thought uneasily, he might prove to have risked it not for the negotiations, but for the sake of an empty charade.

24

FRANCE
Summer, 1435

Secret was not familiar with Arras, but the road from
Amiens was easy enough to find. It was late afternoon
when he arrived at the city gates. He asked the
gatekeeper where the best places were to stay and where
the heralds were congregating, and was told to go to
Guillaume de Goneville, Burgundy's Chamberlain, who
was responsible for finding lodgings for the delegates to
the Congress and their hangers-on; and to try the inn on
the corner where the Grand Marché joined the Rue de la
Taillerie.

He chose to do the second of these first. The
gatekeeper showed him the direction. The side streets of
Arras were narrow and rutted; it took him some time to
reach the Grand Marché, which proved to be wide, but
crowded: with stalls temporary and permanent, inhabitants and visitors, goats and chickens, cheeses and
cabbages and garlic. Secret wrinkled his nose. He skirted
round the edge, staying in the shadow of the tall
buildings which lined the marketplace, until he arrived
at the inn.

He stabled his horse there temporarily – inns on
marketplaces were expensive and he planned to find
cheaper permanent quarters in a backstreet – and
pushed open the narrow door that led inside from the
yard.

It was dim and shadowy in the barroom: only one
small window, and the shutters hanging half-closed
over that. Slowly, as his eyes adjusted, he deciphered

the shapes of a row of barrels of Flemish beer, half a dozen large hams hanging from the rafters, a rough assortment of benches and stools alongside a couple of even rougher trestles – and a group of men sitting around a circular table in the corner.

He approached the men. The gatekeeper had told him right: it was Toison d'Or, he saw, sitting with his back to the wall. At first he took the others to be local poursuivants and hangers-on; then one of them turned at the soft sound of his footsteps, and he was face to face with Jean de Waurin. 'Secret Poursuivant!'

'Mon vieux ami!'

They lunged together into a great warm hug, in the centre of the dark little barroom. Even before de Waurin had released Secret, he was exclaiming, 'But it is years! Five years or more, surely . . .'

'Six years, since we were both at Corbeil.'

'Just so. Corbeil, the summer of '29, after Patay.' De Waurin's swarthy face lengthened momentarily, and then he brightened again and said, 'And now in Arras, for the Congress, no doubt.'

'No doubt.'

'So Sir John Fastolf is coming to Arras?' asked Toison d'Or.

'He does not plan so. But he is to present a report to the King's Council this autumn, if the war continues so long; he acts as an advisor now to Gloucester. And they say half the heralds in Europe will be at Arras this summer.'

He said this quickly, but it was a careful answer: he had had it ready prepared. As he spoke the last words he sat, in the space the other poursuivants had cleared for him, and called for ale in a loud voice, so that Toison d'Or would have no immediate chance to question him about it.

Fastolf's poursuivant could scarcely attend a great international congress except on his master's behalf, but it would have been an exaggeration to say that Fastolf had ordered Secret to come to Arras. He did know that Secret planned to spend the summer there and was genuinely interested – though only mildly so – to learn what would happen. He had even expressed a willingness to pay for occasional reports on the proceedings. But there was no prospect of his paying Secret a proper poursuivant's salary, especially in these days of virtual truce. Secret had come to Arras because he reckoned there would be casual work for many messengers and tale tellers there that summer; and also because he reckoned that many men who roused his interest would be in Arras.

'Not half the heralds,' said de Waurin, 'but every one in Europe. Less than a dozen, though, have arrived here yet.'

True; because it would be two weeks, perhaps more, before the Congress officially began. Secret had known this: he had arrived early on purpose. 'I thought to come soon to find good lodgings.'

'You have some already? In the cité?'

'Should it be the cité?'

De Waurin shrugged. 'We hear that de Goneville plans to lodge all the English there.'

'Then perhaps it would be more interesting to lodge in the ville . . .'

'I do not think,' said Toison d'Or, 'that Garter King of Arms would appreciate that sentiment.'

No, he would not. Garter King of Arms did not like his underlings to act unconventionally; he did not like what he knew of Secret's bizarre relationship with his master. He had to be appeased. Therefore, it would be the cité. Secret knew it had been facetious of him, even stupid, to suggest otherwise. Six years since he had seen de Waurin, he reminded himself. He had seen Toison d'Or that spring, but with the King of Arms he had never had more than a nodding acquaintance.

'Perhaps he would not. Then I shall ask Monsieur the Chamberlain for a plump, accommodating landlady in the cité . . .'

'With a plump, accommodating daughter.'

'Or two,' he agreed cheerfully.

The poursuivants laughed, and Toison d'Or too. Secret sat back; accepted his ale from the barmaid; and drank. A dirty inn, he thought; but all the same he was glad to be there.

He lingered in the inn until de Waurin got to his feet. Then he rose too and followed de Waurin to the door. De Waurin seemed to accept, without either of them suggesting it, that they would walk together.

'I heard you joined one of Burgundy's divisions when you left Fastolf,' Secret said.

'For a while. Then I was at court for some time; then I fought again, in Lorraine.'

'And at court, what did you do?'

De Waurin glanced at him, frowned and walked on. He should not have asked, Secret thought: he would not have liked to have such a question asked of him, not after six years.

'I hear still from Hanson,' de Waurin said, quite suddenly.

'He writes?'

'From time to time.'

'And you write to him.'

Silence. They walked on. De Waurin said, 'You should take that road, to come to de Goneville's office.'

'I should like to know first where your lodgings are.'

'Then I shall show you.'

Guillaume de Goneville proved to be a plump little man, with a bald head and a small, bristling beard. When Secret finally reached his office there was a long queue of men waiting to see him: visitors waiting to be lodged, nearly all of them. The Chamberlain was strutting up and down his office, waving his papers and despairing loudly of the impossibility of pleasing them all. Secret installed himself in a corner and watched. He was in no hurry; he was curious about the process.

Ten thousand men, he had learned in the tavern, were expected to come to Arras for the Congress. Ambassadors, observers, clerks, chaplains, heralds, minstrels, knights prepared for the lists, pickpockets, fortune tellers and servants, all requiring accommodation for several months. Naturally quarters had been reserved first for the ambassadors themselves, and for the Duke of Burgundy's retinue. He asked a clerk where these personages were to stay. They would be lodged in the ville, all but the English, in great houses like those in the roads that led off the Grand Marché.

Finally the clerk gestured to him and he moved forward and introduced himself to the Chamberlain as Fastolf's poursuivant. De Goneville showed no interest; he was referred to another clerk; he was given an address. It meant nothing to him, but the clerk told him the way. He bowed his thanks and set off, through the ville – the lower town – and towards the great ditch that separated ville from cité, and the Porte de la Cité.

It was a longer walk than he had expected. And the English would all be in the cité, he thought: all this long walk away not only from the Valois, but from the Burgundians too. There was only one gate that led from cité to ville, only one bridge across the ditch. The ditchers and the gatekeepers would do well out of the Congress of Arras.

The address he had memorised turned out to belong to a tall, narrow house with warped shutters and a rusted lamp bracket by the door. He smiled at the woman who opened the door, but she was thin and careworn and did not manage a smile in return. She offered him a room on the first floor. I would prefer the attic, he said. She shook her head, but she showed him up the main stairs and to the attic ladder.

Secret climbed it alone, leaving the woman waiting at the foot. Bending double because of the low rafters, he made straight for the dormer. He poked out his head, pushing the shutters well apart. It was good. He could see right across the rooftops of the cité, to the ditch, the wall, most of the Grand Marché and an occasional shining glimpse of the river.

Then he turned and gave a cursory glance to the pile of straw mattresses which made it clear that in a few days the inhabitants of the attic would be sleeping shoulder to shoulder, foot to foot, and went down the ladder to check with the woman when dinner would be served.

The next morning he went out early, and the next, and the next. The English, French and the leading Burgundians were not yet in Arras, but there were heralds, poursuivants, travelling men and ambassadors from other territories already installed in the town. He talked to these, at the inn on the Grand Marché, and in some of the other inns; he talked to Jean de Waurin. De Waurin brought him a number of other contacts: servants of the Duke, a girl who served in one of the largest inns, retired soldiers, writers and spies. These disparate individuals all shared one quality: they knew a great deal about what happened in the city. Secret slipped effortlessly into their circle, paying for information from one with information from another.

He went to look at the audience rooms of the Abbey while it was still open for public inspection and glanced at the parallel benches on which the Ambassadors and legates would sit during their negotiating sessions. He tracked down passable food and accommodating women. He learned the streets of the ville and the cité by heart and satisfied himself about the lodgings of the chief protagonists. Burgundy himself, naturally, would stay at the Cour de la Comte, and within a short walk were the quarters allocated to his vassals and supporters, Jean and Louis of Luxembourg, the Duke of Gueldres, the Count Nassau, the Bishop of Cambrai, the Count of Vaudemont, the Duke of Bar and various lesser luminaries. The Duke of Bourbon would take over a grandiose hôtel on a narrow street just off the Petit Marché. The Valois churchmen would be in streets around Notre Dame des Ardents. Arthur de Richemont, Count of Brittany and (once more) Constable of France, would have a commodious hôtel, the yard of which backed on to the Cour de la Comte.

Burying his badge in the folds of his tunic and emphasising his Breton accent, Secret persuaded one of the servants who had come to prepare for Richemont's arrival to show him round this hôtel. He peeped into the rooms that would form the Constable's private quarters; he looked through windows and peered over walls. He thanked the woman graciously and went back to the ville to have his hair cut and his chin shaven, ready for the arrival of the delegations.

The English delegates came early, even before Burgundy himself. Anjou King of Arms was not with them, as he had stayed at Rouen to serve the sick Regent, but Bedford had sent his poursuivant Fleurs de Lys, and Garter King of Arms had come to supervise the ceremonial. Secret, who was still conscious of Garter's strained tolerance of him, filled in the King of Arms with his week's observations; and Garter, who could see no alternative, hurried to de Goneville's office to make a stringent protest at the lodging arrangements. He pointed out that it would be more appropriate for the Lancastrians and the Burgundians to be at closer quarters since they were, after all, allies against the Valois; and that Archbishop Kemp was particularly anxious for Jean of Luxembourg to play a leading role in his delegation. His brother Louis, Chancellor of Lancastrian France, was obliged to remain in Paris, so Jean, Bedford's father-in-law, was the senior of the two Luxembourg nobles present.

De Goneville's expressions of despair intensified. How impossible, he exclaimed, to rearrange ten thousand lodgings, to precipitate an avalanche of objections, to offend (heaven forbid) the Duke of Burgundy himself. Garter staged a dignified withdrawal. The English had forfeited their first piece.

That evening Secret sent his first report to Fastolf. In one of the inns he had met a messenger who was heading for Le Mans – where the knight was stationed, in his capacity as Governor of Maine and Anjou – and he entrusted him with a letter, doubly tied and sealed.

It had been difficult to know what to tell Fastolf. Ever since Patay, most of his work for the knight had been routine: delivering sealed letters, reciting messages of no particular importance, dealing with minor questions of precedence, carrying out ceremonial duties. This half-commission was something different; but it would do nothing, he knew, to alter Fastolf's distrust of him.

He had settled in the end for facts, and for the kind of superficial impressions he had heard discussed and reported all round him. Kemp, he said, looked lugubrious; Suffolk appeared determinedly cheerful and was on good terms, it seemed, with Burgundy's officials. De Lannoy had come to Arras with the English and had lingered, speaking urgently to Suffolk, outside the Earl's lodgings before he withdrew to his own quarters in the ville. Beaufort had not yet arrived and was not expected to appear in Arras itself. Of Jean de Waurin, as of the heralds and poursuivants, Secret did not write.

More heralds and poursuivants were coming every day. They abandoned the inn on the Grand Marché as it grew more crowded and took over a little tavern in the Rue des Augustines. There Secret talked to Portugal King of Arms, servant of Philip of Burgundy's third Duchess, Isabella. He talked cautiously to A ma Vie, the poursuivant accompanying the Breton delegation. He talked to Suffolk Herald, who appeared gruff and unforthcoming; to Huntingdon Herald, who arrived a few days after the rest, wearing the Cardinal Beaufort's colours and charged with sounding out the Burgundians on the Cardinal's behalf.

Burgundy came next, in state. And on the Sunday following Burgundy's arrival the kings of arms, heralds and poursuivants gathered for the arrival of the Valois delegation. Their choice of Sunday was deliberate, Toison d'Or claimed: the Royal Dukes (the King himself would not attend) wanted the people of Arras to be free to greet them with suitable enthusiasm. The

Valois delegates had assembled at Saint Quentin, a day's journey from Arras; and Burgundy had sent the Count of Estampes with a large retinue to meet them there.

The heralds and poursuivants were to go not there, but to the wood of Mouf-laine, a bare half-league from the town, where the procession would be drawn up for the grand entrance. Burgundy himself would ride to Mouf-laine; so would representatives of all the other embassies in the town: those of Sicily, Spain, Navarre, Poland, Asia and Romania – but not the English.

Garter decreed that the English heralds, however, would go, so Secret dusted down his tabard and went back to the little inn where he had stabled Fastolf's black mare. He groomed the mare and polished her harness, combed his own hair and splashed water on his face. He rode at the back of the group of heralds, with Beul, Matthew Gough's poursuivant, and Eagle Vert. Suffolk Herald was immediately in front of them.

They rode to the edge of the wood and stopped. There was no sign of the Valois. Perhaps they had not yet arrived, thought Secret; or just as likely they were waiting in the shadows until their audience was assembled for a dramatic appearance. It turned out to be the latter. Trumpets sounded only moments after Burgundy and his procession had halted; there was a rustle, a flurry of birds from the treetops, and out of the greenery rode the Duke of Bourbon and the Count of Richemont, with their supporters behind them.

The Duke of Burgundy descended from his mount. He walked informally up to the French horses. Bourbon and Richemont too dismounted and Burgundy hugged them both and gave them a peck on the cheek.

The heralds sat motionless and watched this tableau.

'Should we cheer?' Beul whispered sardonically in Secret's ear.

Secret lifted his brows and dropped them again. 'Not unless Garter does,' he whispered back.

Garter did not.

Regnault de Chartres, Archbishop of Rheims and Chancellor of Valois France, dismounted more slowly and he and the Duke shook hands. Then Mountjoie and the other Valois heralds rode up to join them and Garter, Mountjoie and Toison d'Or drew a few paces apart to discuss the details of the procession.

It began with six trumpets and clarions, sending mournful melodies echoing through the dank hills of Flanders. The officers of arms followed. Mountjoie, then Toison d'Or. Malo King of Arms jostled with Bretagne Herald, with Ermine, Feu Gregois and Bar. The Kings of Arms of Brabant, Flanders and Hainault sketched against the pale sky the extent of Burgundy's power. Portugal rose alone, as if to emphasise Isabella's independence. Then came the higher-ranked English: Garter, Suffolk Herald, Huntingdon Herald. And finally a host of lesser poursuivants whose names expressed a variety of unintentional opinions of the forthcoming proceedings: Vostre Veuil, Toutain le Gras, Voit Qui Peut, Vrai Désir, Bonne Querelle, Plus Que Nuls and Il Dit Vrai. Secret, Beul and Eagle Vert, all close together, melted into the middle of this pack.

Arthur de Richemont prepared the way for the other nobles, in the company of the Counts of Vendôme and Estampes and the Lady of Clèves. The three Dukes of Burgundy, Bourbon and Gueldres rode abreast; and from this crescendo the procession tailed off into a less orderly array of minor ambassadors, knights, lesser lords, pages and esquires.

They rode in stately order down to Arras and through the gates. They paraded through both of the market-places. In the Grand Marché the procession came to a halt and the trumpeters played a final fanfare before it dispersed. The greater lords were guided away to pay their respects to the Cardinal, and the lesser submitted to an orderly dispersal to their lodgings.

Secret was not interested for once in the opinions of the heralds. They could tell him only what he had seen for himself: that Richemont looked much as he had done before Patay; that Bourbon looked much as he had done at Janville, when he had been the Count of Clermont and his father the Duke, now dead, had been a prisoner of the English; that Burgundy, after angling to have his two brothers-in-law appointed to the Valois embassy, was planning to butter them up. But it would be interesting, he thought to discover what the English ambassadors made of their heralds' accounts.

With this in mind, he looked for Suffolk Herald the next morning. He was not to be found. Garter told him, eventually, that the herald had returned to Calais immediately after the procession. With a message for Beaufort, presumably, or for the Duke of Orleans.

And what, Secret wondered, would the Duke of Orleans make of Suffolk Herald's account? Perhaps he would not be allowed to hear it.

There were other ways of learning things, however; at least when one was not a prisoner. Secret wandered around the cité for the next few days. He listened outside windows; he bantered with grooms and teased chambermaids. He asked little, but there were chances, many chances, for these servants to tell him without being asked what they had seen and heard.

The servants hired in Arras told him next to nothing: it seemed the English were too cautious to speak freely in front of them. But there was a voluble deacon in Kemp's entourage, a chatty groom who had come over with Suffolk. Suffolk was out of favour, Secret learned. All the other English ambassadors had agreed on a policy designed to show their disapproval of Burgundy's fraternising with the enemy. They were accepting private invitations from the Burgundians, but were refusing to join any party at which the Valois princes would be present. They had even agreed to stay away from the tournament that the Duke had arranged for the end of the week.

Suffolk was refusing to follow suit. He had protested to Archbishop Kemp that this could achieve nothing. The English would not change Burgundy's mind or his

557

deeds in this way: they would simply add to their own isolation and drive Burgundy further into the arms of the Valois. Suffolk had had an invitation from Bourbon to a game of tennis, the groom said: Kemp had forbidden him to accept it, and they had argued violently in Kemp's private room. Suffolk had also had an invitation to act as a supporter of Burgundy's champion at the tournament. He had not told Kemp of this. He had told the groom to get ready his best black mare and her trappings for the first morning of the tournament.

In a chillingly splendid hall at the Cour de la Comte, Duchess Isabella of Burgundy sat on a high-backed chair. Two paces away, on a slightly smaller chair, sat the Earl of Suffolk; a maidservant sat on a stool next to a small inlaid table at Isabella's side; and around the room, formally at ease, stood a brigade of servants in Burgundy's livery of the golden fleece.

In Isabella's hand was the end of a silver chain. The other end of the chain was attached to a collar, studded with rubies, that encircled the neck of a small monkey. The monkey also wore a little red velvet cap. It jiggled and jumped on its chain: from the Duchess's lap to her arm to her shoulder, around the back of her neck, and back again.

Suffolk watched the monkey, drawn in spite of himself by its exhausting, distracting, pointless activity. Sometimes he tried to bring his eyes back to Isabella's face, but he found the stare from her eyes, which were the same cool blue as Beaufort's, difficult to hold. That stare was fixed on him, but in a cold and passive way: when he met it full on he found no flicker of life in her eyes, stirred no change of expression whatsoever.

They spoke, in polite and icy tones, in formally phrased French; it was a conversation punctuated by long pauses. The Duchess Isabella mentioned 'my husband the Duke', 'my uncle the Cardinal' and 'my father the King of Portugal'. Her husband the Duke of

Burgundy, she said, wished for the freedom of the Duke of Orleans. She said nothing further of politics or policies, let alone of negotiations, though Suffolk did his best to lead their conversation in this direction. Had Beaufort actually spoken to her? he wondered. Was Beaufort persisting with his plan to use her as an intermediary? If so, there was clearly no place in it for him. In any case, he would not have put even a sliver of trust in this iceberg of a female.

He could not use her, but it was at least necessary to appease her, to persist with the conversation for a respectful length of time. Eventually Guillaume de Goneville slipped through the door, coughed discreetly and Isabella's frozen stare moved from his own face to the Chamberlain's.

'Your Grace. Cardinal Albergati is now here, and waiting to speak with you.'

Suffolk rose to his feet. 'Madam, I have detained you too long.'

'Not at all.' Isabella extended a long-fingered hand and produced a toothy smile. Suffolk took the hand in his, bowed his head over it and made his obeisance.

As he retreated, backwards, he gave a last glance around the hall. On the low table were the illuminated psalter he had brought as his formal gift, its silver clasp set with pearls, and a silver tray containing the remnants of their refreshments. Suddenly the monkey leapt down from Isabella's shoulder and pounced on a discarded almond wafer. Isabella's blue eyes were fixed on the doorway and she paid no attention to the monkey. The maidservant reached out and cautiously, apologetically, tried to prise the wafer away from its paws.

Suffolk backed out the last few paces and let a valet show him down the stairs. At the foot were his squire, waiting to attend him back to his hotel, two of Burgundy's stewards and Albergati and his attendant monks.

'My Lord.' Albergati gave him a half-bow.

'Your Grace.'

559

Their eyes met. Unlike Isabella's glassy stare, the old Cardinal's eyes reflected every thought of a wise and weary spirit. Suffolk would have made a joke about the monkey if the stewards had not been within earshot; he reckoned Albergati would have laughed.

But even so the Cardinal does not like me, he thought, nodding to the squire and following him out of the carved doors. The Cardinal has no fondness for any of the English.

His groom was already in the street, with the horses. They mounted and began to make their way along the narrow streets to the Porte de la Cité.

I shall send a message to Beaufort this evening, Suffolk thought. No; first I shall speak to de Lannoy. He will be understanding and will make new suggestions to me; he will try to raise my spirits, and God knows, though I try to remain cheerful, they are low enough already. Beaufort will do none of those things.

Beaufort called her clever. Perhaps she is. Perhaps it was by Burgundy's orders that she stonewalled me; perhaps in different circumstances she unbends; laughs, even. What does she make of Burgundy's practical jokes? Has he tried the trick fountain on her; the hidden trapdoor in the corridor at Hesdin? Does she pant, does she sweat when he lies with her?

I wish Alice were here. The thought came, and surprised him; and then did not surprise him at all. Alice was skilled in formal conversation, far more so than he: with Alice there, the conversation would not have been punctuated by such lengthy silences. He could not imagine bargaining with Isabella himself, could not honestly imagine Beaufort doing so; but he thought Alice might have stood a chance. He had chosen not to have Alice accompany him to Arras; but he had been thinking when he made that choice of the secrets she might accidentally let fall to de Lannoy, and not of the secrets she might prise from Burgundy's Duchess.

Too late to alter that decision. Too late to persuade Beaufort to change his mind and send Orleans to Arras.

He had been trying ever since he arrived to seek out other possible intermediaries, but with no success. As he had known all along, there was nobody else.

De Lannoy had tried to persuade him that Burgundy himself might act as an intermediary. Burgundy did not wish to break his solemn oath to Henry of Lancaster, his ambassador had insisted: he had organised the Congress in the genuine hope that it might lead to a tripartite peace between the English, the Burgundians and the Dauphin's supporters. The Duke would do all that he could to help Suffolk meet the Valois princes informally, according to de Lannoy; it was necessary to trust him, and to work with, not against him.

And within limits, Suffolk thought to himself, he had done that. He had accepted Burgundy's invitations to the Cour his request to act at the tournament. Brabant Herald had brought him personal notes from the Duke, and he had sent Suffolk Herald with replies. When the two of them had encountered each other after Mass at the Cathedral there had been smiles and nods. But these public and semi-public interchanges had not led to invitations to private dinners, to surreptitious encounters, to meetings in places where they could speak frankly without risk of being spied upon. They had led to meetings with the Valois ambassadors, but every encounter had been orchestrated by Burgundy, and all of them had been as empty and formal as Suffolk's audience with Isabella.

He had wasted precious days and achieved nothing but to stir the suspicion of Kemp and the other English ambassadors and give them the maddeningly inaccurate impression that he and Burgundy were on close terms.

Damn de Lannoy. It was not that Suffolk trusted him totally; but he had chosen to accept the Burgundian's judgement and to believe in his basic good faith. Perhaps he was wrong and de Lannoy had been working all along to entrap him. Or perhaps it was not as simple as that: perhaps both he and de Lannoy were caught in the Duke of Burgundy's trap.

The more he considered, the more he returned to this thought: that he should take de Lannoy's friendship for the English as genuine, but that he should trust Burgundy himself not one inch.

He could not use either Orleans or Isabella as his intermediary with the Valois ambassadors: what could be done in the way of surreptitious negotiation he would have to do himself, face to face, without Burgundy's intervention or even knowledge. He would have to set up private meetings with Richemont and with Bourbon. That would not be easy, in a city full of Burgundian spies, when he knew so few of the Valois and trusted even fewer.

Could his herald arrange such meetings? No, he was a capable carrier of messages, but no man for subtle negotiations or private intrigues. Was there anyone else he might call upon to arrange it? He thought and thought, and it seemed to him that it could only be done through one man: through Hugues de Lannoy.

On the dead days after the arrival of the last delegation and before the first negotiating session, Secret Poursuivant walked around Arras. He varied his routes, but he arrived again and again at the same places. The Abbey cloisters; the Cathedral, vast and echoing, and its cloisters; a quiet stretch of river bank, down from the quays.

He had marked out these places in his mind soon after his arrival in Arras, by a very simple process. He was a stranger in the city; so were the Earl of Suffolk, the Count of Richemont, the Duke of Bourbon and a number of other men who interested him. Where, he had asked himself, would two strangers go if they wished to meet apparently by chance, and to talk to each other without being overheard? Why, to places such as these: obvious places, easily found by someone not very familiar with the town, and almost invariably deserted.

For days he made these rounds in vain. Then one day,

as he sauntered through the Cathedral cloisters, he saw a sight that caught his interest. The tall figure of the Earl of Suffolk, in a dark cloak and a low-slung hat with an eagle's feather; and by his side, the Seigneur de Santes, his conspicuous grey hair also shadowed and his velvet doublet shrouded. Behind them followed Suffolk's groom, a couple of pages and a Burgundian minor official of some kind.

Suffolk and de Santes were deep in conversation; the servants were kicking stones and scuffling their shoes in the dust of the paths. He doubted if any of them had seen him. Quickly, he moved behind a pillar.

He could hear their footsteps, approaching. He could hear the murmur of their voices, though he could not yet make out the words. He glanced around to see if there were any better hiding places: niches in the walls, or gravestones behind which he might crouch. Nothing.

The sound of the footsteps ceased. Had they stopped? He held his breath and strained his ears.

'Tennis!' It was a shout; unprepared for it, Secret quivered.

'Tennis!' Suffolk repeated. 'A game of tennis? You can suggest nothing better than that? But you know, surely, that Kemp has already forbidden me to do anything of the kind!'

De Lannoy's reply was much lower-pitched: Secret concentrated fiercely, but he could not catch the words. It was appeasing, though: the tone told him that.

'No,' Suffolk retorted. 'Emphatically not. It must be a secret meeting. A private rendezvous, with none of Burgundy's servants involved. Not a damn tennis court, lined with court officials. Nothing that Kemp will come to hear of, or Beaufort either.'

'Then you ask the impossible.'

'I ask what must be done, if you are to prove your sincerity.'

'I have no contacts through which I might arrange it. None of us have. Even Jean of Luxembourg has not been able to –'

The rest of de Lannoy's sentence was drowned by a loud clang. It echoed through the cloisters, bounced from stone to stone. Then before the ringing in Secret's ears faded, it was succeeded by another clang; and then another.

The Cathedral bells, striking for matins, high above them, in the tower. A door opened further down the cloister and a black-robed monk scurried out. Another followed, and another; another door opened.

In minutes, Secret thought with furious regret, the cloister will be crowded. And in minutes thereafter, it will be empty again: empty not only of the hurrying monks, but of the Earl of Suffolk and the Seigneur de Santes as well.

But he had heard something. Enough, he thought, to prime a conversation with Suffolk Herald; more than enough to prime a conversation with the groom.

He leaned his head back against the pillar, considered and slid his body downwards, so that to any glancing monk – or Earl, or Burgundian official – it would look not as if he had been hiding, but as if he were sitting dozing in the summer sun. He closed his eyes to complete the impression. And thought: a meeting, and not with any of Burgundy's men. Who else might the Earl of Suffolk be anxious to speak with in private, so anxious that he asks the Seigneur de Santes to arrange it, even though he openly admits his distrust of the man? There are not so very many alternatives. I shall find the answer somehow.

Hugues de Lannoy sat at his high desk in the Cour de la Comté and chewed the end of his quill. A clean sheet of parchment was laid out in front of him, but for once he had written nothing.

He dared to write nothing. It was – no, he would not call it treason, but it was undoubtedly an uncomfortable situation in which he found himself. He could send no letters on such a subject; he could make no notes to guide himself.

Suffolk asked too much. He spoke of distrust, claimed to be disillusioned; but did he not realise that he, Hugues de Lannoy, had also seen some illusions shattered since he had come to Arras? It had been bad enough when Suffolk had told him in London that Beaufort was to travel to France with the delegation: a body-blow, that, when he had been working from the start on the assumption that Suffolk himself would be the leading lay ambassador, the custodian of the Duke of Orleans. But what had followed had been far worse. That morning Suffolk had freely admitted that he was so isolated from all the other English, even Beaufort, that he dared not tell any of them what he planned! Cautiously to extend one's neck for the sake of a united English peace party: that had seemed to de Lannoy a risk well worth taking. But to lay it on the block, for the solitary sake of the Earl of Suffolk: that was a very different proposition.

Perhaps he should drop Suffolk, de Lannoy thought. Perhaps he should court Beaufort instead. Alas, though: he could see no prospect of Beaufort ever negotiating realistically with the Valois. Suffolk, and Suffolk alone, seemed prepared to consider that.

But Suffolk alone did not have the power to force the English to come to terms: that was painfully apparent. The uncomfortable truth was that there was no prospect, none at all, of the Congress of Arras culminating in a peace between Charles of Valois and Henry of Lancaster. Though to be fair, Suffolk too appreciated that: he held his carrots not at de Lannoy's nose, but somewhere much closer to the horizon.

What might Suffolk realistically achieve? de Lannoy asked himself. Ignoring the circumlocutions, the evasions, the over-optimism, what can he offer?

He chewed his quill some more. He tapped his fingers on the polished wood of his desktop. And he decided: Suffolk offers this. He intends to make it clear (or at least, reasonably so) to Richemont, and possibly to Bourbon too, what terms he personally considers Henry should settle for. Over the next few months and years he will attempt to scramble into a position powerful enough to enable him to force through those terms, even against the opposition of Gloucester and the die-hards in Henry's Council. And he will make use of whatever clandestine help Richemont (and possibly Bourbon) chooses to offer him, in order to reach that position.

Enough? It was something. But it was not enough. Such an arrangement would do nothing to stop Burgundy breaking his oath of support for Henry of Lancaster; and it was this that de Lannoy wanted to prevent, this that he saw as the justification for his not-exactly-treasonable negotiations. No, he thought, I can help Suffolk no further. I shall still work towards my own objectives, with the Luxembourgs and the other men who sympathise with the English; but I shall do no more than that.

'We are', said Jean de Luxembourg, 'moles burrowing in the dark.'

'Just so,' de Lannoy agreed.

'There was a light at Richemont's hôtel almost till dawn that morning.'

'And Rolin, I hear, was invited there to dine last night.'

Rolin was the leading Anglophobe among Burgundy's counsellors. Jean de Luxembourg turned to his nephew. 'When was your last invitation, Louis?'

Louis shrugged. 'Not one, so far.'

'Nor I.'

There I have beaten them, thought de Lannoy. I have been to Richemont's hôtel twice; but in the company of Rolin and a dozen others who say out loud that Burgundy would be justified in reneging on his treaty with the English. We listened to the minstrels; they sang that maddeningly jaunty rondeau of Orleans'. We talked of the shrubs in Burgundy's garden at Dijon.

He said, 'You have no acquaintance, then, among de Richemont's entourage?'

'None whatsoever. Nor you?'

'Nor I.'

'Toison d'Or must be acquainted with Richemont's herald,' Louis offered.

'So he must,' de Lannoy agreed.

'You will speak to him, then?'

'With a view to requesting an interview for us with Richemont?'

Jean de Luxembourg considered. 'Perhaps not so; not yet. Nothing so blatant. We should be cautious, until it is more certain which way the agreement will be set down. With a view, perhaps, to learning something of what is said in Richemont's hall so long after dark.'

Hugues de Lannoy considered too. He would like to know that, he thought. He would like it very much. It would ease his conscience, still grumbling about his refusal to help Suffolk. It would help him to decide how best to act during the rest of the Congress, if only he knew what was being said in Richemont's hall.

'I shall speak to him this evening,' he said.

De Lannoy spoke to Toison d'Or. It was a long and difficult conversation. At length, Toison d'Or grew exasperated with all the diplomat's polite evasions. Did de Lannoy want him to bribe one of Richemont's servants? he asked bluntly.

De Lannoy did not want that. Certainly not. He simply wanted to know . . .

To know what only Richemont's servants could tell him, Toison d'Or retorted.

True; but surely there was some way – some intermediary – some method of discovering . . .

Toison d'Or got to his feet. 'I shall send a man to you tomorrow,' he said.

De Lannoy spent an uncomfortable night. He imagined a man like Jennin Cauvel appearing in the hall of the Cour de la Comte and asking for him; he imagined Rolin observing this man and wondering what his business was. He began to think it would be better to disappoint the Luxembourgs; better to remain a mole, and chew on dirt forever.

In the morning, early, his valet came to tell him that a man had come to call on him.

He cleared his throat uncertainly. 'What manner of a man is he?'

'Why, a poursuivant, sir.'

'A poursuivant!'

'They call him Secret Poursuivant. The servant of Sir John Fastolf.'

'So you ask this,' said Secret, 'on behalf of the Duke of Burgundy?'

The Seigneur de Santes chewed his lips. Secret watched him. He thought: a denial, though a prissy man such as this will not put it into words.

'I would prefer not to disclose the name of my principal.'

'But I may take it that your principal is a Burgundian?'

The Seigneur wriggled some more. 'You may take it that the identity of my principal is known to Toison d'Or, King of Arms.'

To Toison d'Or! That was a surprise. He tried not to show it. 'And I am to report my findings to you . . .'

'Before the formal sessions begin, if that is practicable. Let me see. There is a quiet stretch of the Cathedral cloisters . . .'

A Breton, thought de Lannoy. A Breton! One of de Richemont's own countrymen, and yet a servant of an English knight!

Outrageous, that Toison d'Or should have sent him such a man. But since Toison d'Or had done so, he had had no option but to give the man his commission. Of course, he had told him as little as possible. Too little, doubtless. He would come back with no information of value. That lank, yellowish hair, unwashed for years from the look of it; that patched up tabard: a loser, that man, if ever there was one.

A Breton. He knew few Bretons. But the Bretons are, he thought, in a situation not so dissimilar to that of the Burgundians. Their masters shift from allegiance to allegiance, frequently without warning or explanation; their honest and sincere servants surely sometimes find it difficult, impossible even, to revise their own loyalties at precisely the same pace. They too must at times feel as if they have been torn to rags by the pressure. This Breton serves an English knight; he took that service, perhaps, when the Bretons were true allies of the English. And now? Well, whatever he feels he can scarcely have any allegiance to Richemont: if he had, Toison d'Or would not have recommended him to me.

Moreover, he is Fastolf's man: that speaks volumes. He is no fool, Sir John Fastolf. If he sees fit to put his trust in Secret Poursuivant, then I can scarcely be criticised for doing likewise.

Toison d'Or, thought Secret. So Toison d'Or was behind this.

He had not known that, for he had been given his message by Jean de Waurin, who had delivered it in a friendly but indifferent way that said merely: this is work, and it will bring you money.

Work: to spy on the Count of Richemont. Mind, de Waurin was not to know that he had any lingering sense of allegiance to the master of Fougères. And to spy on behalf of an unnamed man, known to Toison d'Or, who used the Seigneur de Santes as his agent.

He thought to himself: de Santes did not admit that the man was a Burgundian. Is it possible that he asks this on behalf of the Earl of Suffolk?

He found that an interesting thought. He knew already that the Burgundians were divided, that the Seigneur de Santes was a pro-English Burgundian. He knew that Toison d'Or had loftily declined to reveal which of the two Burgundian parties he supported. He had first-hand knowledge that de Santes had considered, at least, Suffolk's request that he arrange a private meeting with an unknown man. But would de Santes have agreed to set spies on Richemont, on Suffolk's behalf? And if he had agreed, would he have told that to Toison d'Or?

Never matter. It was work. Jean de Waurin would not blame him for taking it. He cared little about any other man's opinion in Arras. The problem was, how could he set about it? De Lannoy was a tight-fisted man: he would not pay well for the sort of gossip Secret would learn from listening over the yard wall of Richemont's hotel. He would need to get into the hotel, and at a time when Richemont had important visitors: Rolin, perhaps, or even Burgundy himself. It would be too dangerous to masquerade as a Breton servant or soldier. Too many people in Arras knew his face, knew him for Fastolf's poursuivant. Possibly Richemont was one of them; certainly several of his servants were. Perhaps he could bribe a chambermaid, as he had done before? Late-night discussions, de Santes had said: perhaps he could break in through a kitchen window after most of the servants had gone to bed?

He was halfway down the Rue d'Amiens, absorbed in these deliberations, when a strong hand caught at his arm from behind. It yanked him to a halt.

'The Constable,' said a rough voice with a strong Breton accent, 'wants to see you.'

He could only twist his head, without risking irreparable damage to his arm. He did this, though it was hardly necessary: he had guessed already that the voice belonged to Richemont's groom. The glance showed him an expanse of stubbly chin and a knife, a very well-honed knife.

'It shall be my pleasure to attend the Constable,' he said.

The groom led; Secret followed. No chance encounter in the cloisters, this: they went to Richemont's hotel. The Chamberlain waved them past the door as if Secret was expected. The groom pushed him in the direction of the

570

stairs. He thought: Richemont's private room is at the top, just below the attic. He began to climb.

He climbed, and climbed, with an occasional prick in the ribs to keep him moving briskly. He made as if to continue to the attic when he came to the right floor: it would not do to show that he knew the layout of the hotel. The groom caught the hem of his tunic, hauled him back and pushed him towards the two guards who flanked the door.

These men dismissed the groom – to his private relief. One of them disappeared through the door. Secret recited six Hail Marys under his breath. The door was thrown upon and the guard announced, 'Secret Poursuivant.'

This room had been bare when he had peered through the door a month earlier. Now it had hangings of cloth of gold and a great carved oak chair with a purple cushion. In this chair sat the Constable of France, Arthur de Richemont, master of Fougères.

Secret bowed with a flourish. He raised his head again and contemplated the Constable. The Constable contemplated him.

Distinctive, this face, thought Secret. As distinctive as my own; and almost as familiar to me. He looks to have grown harder, Richemont: the lines around his mouth have deepened since Patay and his chin juts more fiercely. These have been rough years for him, years when fortune has buffeted him like a gull caught in a hurricane at sea. But he has power still. That is what I remembered most clearly, the obscure lust for power that radiates from him.

Richemont still did not speak. Secret thought of himself, of how he must appear to the Constable. He had worn his poursuivant's tabard for the interview with the Seigneur de Santes. He had on his second-best pair of hose. This outfit was barely up to Garter's standards, and it had been well below the Seigneur de Santes', to judge from the wrinkling of his nose; but Richemont showed no sign of contempt. His implacable dark eyes simply moved up and down, as if he were taking an inventory.

Eventually he said, 'You were with my army before Patay.'

'I was, sir.'

'As an English spy?'

'Sir, I am a Breton.'

'From where?'

'From Fougères, sir.'

Richemont nodded. He knew this already, Secret thought.

'And yet you work for an Englishman; for Sir John Fastolf.'

'I do, sir.'

'As his poursuivant.'

'Just so, sir.'

'You took your oath when?'

'Ten years ago, sir. I joined Fastolf's service after the Battle of Verneuil.'

It was honest of him: damningly honest. But what else could he say, when Richemont had known it anyway? Richemont had probably known it for years. Perhaps he had known it since before the Battle of Patay.

'In the circumstances,' said the Constable, 'I think I would be justified in making a request of you.'

If he knew all the circumstances, thought Secret, he would be justified in telling the groom to cut my throat.

'I am listening, sir.'

'You listen always,' Richemont said harshly, 'from what my servants tell me.'

'There are certain things that I can tell you, sir.'

'Doubtless there are. But you are Fastolf's poursuivant and you should tell them to him.' Richemont's eyes flickered. Secret thought: this man broke every chivalrous oath in the book, in the years after Agincourt. He knows that I know that, and think of it. He thinks of it too. With shame? Perhaps so; perhaps not. Perhaps he does not refuse my information because of genuine scruples, but merely because it pleases him to defeat my expectations.

'What I require,' said the Count of Richemont, 'is that you arrange for me a private meeting with the Earl of Suffolk.'

'An attack on Calais?' Beul said. 'A stale threat, that one.'

'Aye,' agreed Suffolk Herald. 'But the Bretons, Richemont and his men, have undertaken to stage a diversion; that puts some meat into Burgundy's pie.'

'Even so, it will scarcely sway Kemp.'

'Nothing,' said Toison d'Or, 'will sway Kemp.'

It was a lacklustre discussion; they knew the truth of what Toison d'Or said only too well. They knew it all: the proposals, the counter-proposals, the promises and threats that backed up both. The following day the formal sessions would start. It was time for them now: the real negotiations were done with.

And after all the tournaments, the dinners, the games of tennis, the casual encounters and the secret meetings by the light of a solitary candle, there remained an unbridgeable gulf between the position of the Lancastrians and that of the Charles of Valois. There remained, too, a firm agreement between Charles of Valois and the Duke of Burgundy. The Congress of Arras would end with the signing of a treaty; but it would be the treaty the English had dreaded, and not the one they had hoped for.

'Just as well,' said Beul, 'that Burgundy sent his carpet for the floor of the Abbot's sitting room.'

An old joke, thought Secret. Why should Burgundy have wanted a carpet set down in the negotiating chamber? Why, to deaden the stamp of Archbishop Kemp's feet, the sound of his voice as he roars with anger. He did not wait for Beul to bring out his punch line; he staggered to his own feet and went to the counter to get some more wine.

He was drunk already. He planned to get very, very

drunk before he left the tavern: for the first time, since he had come to Arras. Always before he had wanted to stay sober, so that he might miss nothing; but there would be nothing to see now, nothing to miss, until the lines had all been spoken, and the play reached its final act.

In the Abbot's sitting room in the Benedictine Abbey of Saint Vaast – a handsome room, thickly carpeted, its walls lined with elaborate tapestries and its acoustics quite atrocious – the Earl of Suffolk sat on a hard wooden bench. The Ambassadors' bench, this; the Cardinal's bench was opposite. There was only one Ambassadors' bench, tenanted in rotation by the Lancastrians, by the supporters of Charles of Valois, and by the Duke of Burgundy's officials, for the peculiar protocols of such negotiations dictated that the opposing parties should never suffer the inconvenience of actually meeting face to face. Except, thought Suffolk, that the deviser of this thoughtful arrangement had failed to allow for the possibility that the ambassadors might find themselves at loggerheads not merely with each other, but also with their mediator.

This was no mere possibility: it was rapidly turning into an actuality. For Cardinal Albergati, he of the mild manners and weary eyes, had on that very day decided to express some opinions of his own. His patience had been exhausted, and no wonder. First there had been the tedious days when none of the parties was prepared to set forward any proposals at all. Then there had been seven offers made by the Valois, and indignantly rejected by the Lancastrians, interspersed with seven counter-offers made by the Lancastrians and indignantly rejected by the Valois. There had been the Duke of Burgundy, stirring and pricking and grouching; there had even been a Valois raiding party, and a little battle on the hills outside the city to enliven the proceedings. And all this had culminated, not in any faint suggestions of an emerging consensus, but in Kemp announcing that he objected so violently to every single one of the French proposals that he and his fellow ambassadors intended to withdraw from the Congress.

Any feeble hope that Albergati might attempt to dissuade him had been evaporated as soon as the Cardinal began to speak. This was no conciliatory effort: this was a prologue, an introduction to the last stage of the Congress. Albergati had begun his speech by expressing his opinion (worded judiciously and delivered in a modest tone of voice) that the offers put forward by the representatives of King Charles the Seventh of France were perfectly reasonable as a basis for a settlement. So King Charles demanded that Henry of Lancaster pay him homage for the lands the latter claimed within his kingdom? A minor request. To pay homage was only a personal matter; this should not have proved a sticking point to serious negotiations.

Now the Cardinal had gone on to consider the English King's claim to the Crown of France. No sensible man, he pronounced, could take it to be as clear or strong as his rival's claim. Might the English ambassadors, he suggested, like to retire and consider these remarks?

Archbishop Kemp rose to his feet and bowed. Suffolk followed suit, and the lesser English ambassadors. They retired to the small room that had been set aside for their use. They waited for a considered fifteen minutes. Then they returned to the Abbott's sitting room and Kemp proceeded to voice – at length, and in a loud voice – their fury and disgust at the attitude the Cardinal had adopted.

The Cardinal heard him out, eyelids drooping and mouth pursed shut. Then he remarked that it appeared to him to be evident that there was no prospect of attaining a general peace. In the event of this happening, his instructions from his Holiness Pope Martin had been quite explicit. He was to attempt to bring about a more circumscribed peace. The Duke of Burgundy had proved less intractable. So the English might withdraw if they wished: negotiations would then continue between the Duke of Burgundy and the representatives of King Charles.

The English withdrew.

It was bad, thought Suffolk; as bad as could be. On his way back to the cité of Arras, he reckoned up the toll. The English had made some small concessions and gained nothing in return. Burgundy and Charles would sign their treaty, and the English would lose their last substantial European ally. He himself had lost much of Beaufort's trust; he had never come close to winning Kemp's. Orleans had been able to do nothing; Isabella, as far as he could judge, had never shown even token sympathy for the English position.

There had been the meeting with Richemont, true; but in the end he had been forced to turn to de Lannoy to arrange it. It had been a relief when, after the Burgundian had initially refused, he had eventually sent Secret Poursuivant with a message giving a time and place; but it had prickled at Suffolk, the knowledge that the Burgundians knew of this meeting, and indeed had most probably stationed their spies where they would over-hear every word. No frankness, no trust had been possible under such conditions.

He had planted a seed, he thought; but if it were ever to bear fruit it would not be for long years to come. Could the English succeed in holding on to any of their French possessions for many years more? He doubted it. It seemed to him then that everything was lost. Yes, it was as bad as could be.

Then he turned the corner and came to the road on which was his hotel. Outside the hotel a man was standing. Anjou King of Arms, in mourning. And he knew that there was still worse news to come.

Over Arras, a damp, thick blanket of grey cloud. Falling from it, filming the town, a cool misty rain. The walls of the cité, the ditch, the Porte de la Cité: all were wrapped in a filmy grey shroud.

Through the rain, heads bowed, dressed in the black

they had donned when they heard of the death of Bedford, rode the English delegates to the Congress of Arras. They reached the gate and the gatekeepers claimed their tolls for the last time. They plodded on, down the road that skirted the ville and led northwards through the mist towards Calais and the English Channel.

They had no eyes, any of them, for the two men who stood just outside the Porte de la Cité watching them. The men continued to watch until the bedraggled banners and the dripping horses had disappeared into the distance; then they wrapped their cloaks tighter round them and set off, by unspoken agreement, for the nearest inn.

It was an unfamiliar one: a mean little one-storeyed hut, frequented, from the look of it, by ditchers and tramps. It suited them well. They paid separately for a cup of ale each and sat down, in their sodden cloaks, on the bench nearest the few spluttering sticks that were the inn's apology for a fire.

'So it is finished,' said Jean de Waurin.

Secret shrugged. 'Not yet. It will not be finished until the English have lost everything.'

'Or until they see sense.'

Secret thought, dispassionately, of the Earl of Suffolk. He thought of the Earl's face, barely glimpsed under the hat with the eagle's feather, as he had ridden past in the rain; he thought of the expression he had seen on that same face when he had come to take the Earl to his rendezvous with Richemont. He had had hope, then, Secret thought; and doubt too. But the morning after he was morose. Did they agree nothing? Perhaps he should have stayed, under the bushes by the river bank, and listened to them. But had he listened, he would have felt honour bound to tell what he heard to the Seigneur de Santes; and on reflection, he had not wished to do that. 'That never was an English virtue. But they will be forced to negotiate again: in a year, or two, or ten. They might perhaps hold on to Normandy and Gascony for that long, if Burgundy remains neutral.'

'Burgundy had never been neutral. He has always been a Frenchman.'

'And you?'

De Waurin glanced across at him. Then he looked down at his murky cup of ale. 'I too am a Frenchman,' he said. 'And my indentures oblige me to fight for Burgundy for another year. After that, I think, I shall withdraw from the army. It would not be comfortable to fight on the opposite side to Hanson and Basset.' He let out a very faint sigh. 'The last battle I fought for the Valois cause was Agincourt. My father died, my brother died, and ten thousand Frenchmen died.'

'Now it is the turn of Englishmen to die.'

De Waurin did not respond to this. He drank a little of his ale. It was sour and thin. He set down his cup, picked it up again and threw the dregs on the fire. It hissed and smoked its protest. 'And you? You are bound to Fastolf?'

'Until he turns me away.'

'You believe he will?'

'Not while he fights in France.'

'He will not fight in France forever.'

'True.'

'And when he does so no longer?'

Secret considered. 'Perhaps I could pass as a Norfolk man. Or perhaps I would return to Fougères.'

'I have an estate at Lisle.'

Secret smiled. 'Perhaps,' he said, 'I shall come to Lisle.'

To agree a peace it is necessary not to cling to one's honour but to accept compromises: to acknowledge that even blood enemies must be forgiven, that even the most sacred oaths must sometimes be broken. Such actions come easily to few men. To some they are impossible.

The Church, always pragmatic, attempts to make these actions possible. It absolves men from oaths, it reassures them of the rightness of their deeds. Cardinal Albergati, preparing for the final acts of the Congress of

Arras, placed the holy sacrament on the altar of the Abbey Church of Saint Vaast and a cross of gold on a cushion. These were solemn symbols to give weight to the solemn acts that would end a series of blood feuds and cause men to renounce their sworn allies and their sworn enmities alike.

The Duke of Burgundy and his entourage took their seats on the right side of the choir and the French ambassadors assumed theirs to the left. The Cardinal celebrated the Mass of the Holy Spirit. The Duke's confessor preached the sermon, on the theme 'Ecce quam bonum et quam jocundum': see, what blessing and what joy. Then Philip Duke of Burgundy rose from his seat. He approached the cross and touched it. On the cross, he swore that he would never again hold rancour against the French because of the murder of his father, and that he would maintain peace with Charles of France and his allies. The Cardinal gave a little nod to the Duke of Bourbon and the Count of Richemont, and these men in turn came to their feet and walked to stand at Burgundy's side. They begged pardon in the King's name of the Duke of Burgundy for the death of his father.

The Duke's confessor brought the gospels. Burgundy and the Valois princes stood to one side. Each pew in turn was emptied. The lords delegated to the Congress approached the Cardinal one by one. On the gospels, one by one, they swore their allegiance to the new treaty, which recognised Burgundy's claim to an immense spread of territories in Northern France, all of which had been under the control of the Anglo-Burgundian alliance, and which recognised, too, the right of Charles of Valois to be called King Charles the Seventh of France. For the Burgundian Lords there was a further ceremony to be undergone. Cardinal Albergati formally absolved each one from his commitment to the old treaty with the English.

There were some to whom the outcome of the proceedings could be neither a blessing nor a joy. Most of them were not in the Church of Saint Vaast. The English had set sail from Calais; Jean of Luxembourg had decided in advance to defy his Duke and had left Arras already. Hugues de Lannoy was in the church, bereft of his natural allies. He had come without deciding what to do. His decision came to him while he was watching the slow file of lords approaching the cushion and the altar; while he listened to Albergati's flat unemphatic voice repeating the words of the absolution over and over again. He stood up when the ushers nodded to him. But he did not approach the altar: he walked in the other direction, out of the church.

It was a gesture made in an undramatic manner, but it was sufficient that it should have been made at all. Burgundy could not let it pass. The next morning Rolin came, and a dozen others, to remonstrate with the Seigneur.

Their arguments ranged from the passionate to the pragmatic. Some were atrocious; some subtle; some plain and full of sense. De Lannoy listened to them all. At the end, he still thought it shameful that Burgundy should have deserted the English. But he could see now that it was pointless for him to have made such a gesture. What good could he do, after all, for even the best of causes if he made himself an outcast? There was still a war to be ended; he still, perhaps, had a part to play in ending it. He told Rolin he would submit. Burgundy did not crow, did not punish: he merely arranged a new ceremony. Albergati had left Arras by then, so de Lannoy gave his oath before the Bishop of Auxerre.

He had invited nobody to this ceremony, done nothing to publicise his intentions; but they had become known nevertheless to the men who care to know such things. Some of these men came to the church. Toison d'Or, King of Arms, attended; Jean de Waurin, too. Jean de Waurin wrote afterwards to Christopher Hanson, and so de Lannoy's unconventional oath eventually reached a still wider audience. 'Here am I,' he said, 'who have already made five oaths for the preservation of peace during this war, and seen not one of them kept. I now swear to God that for my part, I will do nothing to infringe the agreement I now make.'

25

ENGLAND

A fortnight he had had the message. Fourteen whole days, and still he had not had his permission to ride from Ewelme. The bitch, Will thought. The cruel, selfish, rotten bitch!

He banged at his desk with his fist, to blunt the edge of his anger; and then calmed down. Anger would do nothing; more sensible to think how he might approach her next.

He could see no reason why he had to stay at Ewelme. All right, Alice had been justified in keeping him back until he had finished checking out the bailiff's returns; all right, it had been reasonable to make him wait another four days so he could escort her to the Countess of Oxford's house party. But there had been nothing for days now but a series of petty little tasks: check on this servant, read over that letter. It was not that she needed him still, simply that she had not given him permission to go.

He had had only one chance to ask her, two days before; and then, he admitted ruefully to himself, he had messed it up. He had realised too late that she felt neither sympathy, nor any inclination to feign it.

Alice barely knows Bess, he thought; and behind her facade of cool indifference she is deeply jealous of Bess's pregnancy. But she does not hate her, and she is not malicious. It is easy to call her cruel, but it is not that at all: it is surely no more than thoughtlessness. I cannot confront her, though, and tell her of her failings. It will not do to shame her into agreeing: I need to cajole her. I need to make her feel that she is being generous. Perhaps I can play on her liking for me.

Her liking for him. It was no more than that. He had made consistent efforts to charm Alice, and he knew he had to some extent succeeded, but they had never been intimate. Alice did not flirt with him, and he had realised long before that it only annoyed her when he flirted with her. He was certain that she would never have dreamed of taking him as a lover. But she liked him, he thought. She liked to have him around.

Was that it? Could it be as simple as that? Alice had no cause to keep him from Norwich; but she might genuinely wish him to stay with her, at Ewelme.

Alice is lonely, he thought. Suffolk is in Arras, Orleans too in France. Her father is dead, and she has no other family. Little Joan she ignores. She is intimate with nobody else at Ewelme; perhaps with nobody else anywhere. Her heart must be starved, so hungry that it craves even my superficial pleasantries. She does not want me too to go away from her.

He had admired Alice ever since he had first met her, for her gaiety, her stylishness and her musical skill. He had learned to like her, in spite of her faults. But never before had he thought of her with any depth of feeling. Never before had he pitied her.

He stood there for some time, before his high desk, full of a pity for his cool, self-absorbed mistress that struck him as odd even as he felt it. Then he picked up his quill and drew a sheet of paper towards him. He knew now what to do. He would write to Tuddenham and tell the land agent that his mistress needed him urgently at Ewelme. Strictly speaking this was improper of him, since Tuddenham was his senior in Suffolk's household, but he felt certain that Alice would not criticise him for it. And when Tuddenham comes, he told himself, I shall be able to leave her and go to Bess.

It was another week before he was able to ride to

Norwich. All week, his new sympathy for Alice had alternately risen and fallen in counterpoint to his anxiety about Bess. He had woken several times at night, dreaming about Bess. In the dreams Bess had looked as she had looked at Burnham, when he had ridden to join her before George's birth.

At least, he told himself, this time he would not be taken by surprise. This time he would expect to see her with sunken eyes and hollow cheeks. This time he would be able to hide his shock better, and to be a better support to her. She would not turn away from him this time. He understood what this coming child meant to her. He had tried to think of it regularly, to imagine it as a living baby, so he would rejoice with her if it was born alive and well, and mourn as she did if it were to die.

On the journey his sense of guilt came to weigh increasingly heavily on him. Now that he was away from the frenetic, meaningless activity of Ewelme, from the house where everything focussed so inexorably on Alice, it struck him as terribly wrong ever to have thought of putting the happiness of a healthy mistress before the desperate needs of a sick wife. What had he ever gained from his service with Suffolk but a thin living and a barrelful of trouble? He should have risked Alice's fury, he told himself, and ridden immediately to Norwich. But it was too late now. And at least Tuddenham would not be in Norwich: there was much to be said for that.

He arrived in the early afternoon, on a pale, cloudy summer day. The orchards were in fruit; the middens, the fishmarket and the meat market were pungent in the heat. He came to Berstrete Gate and rode at a fast trot up Conesford Street and past the markets before turning round the foot of Castle Hill, towards the Cathedral and the river. He saw nobody he knew, and his mind was on Bess and what he would find at Calthorp Inn, but all the same he could sense the tense atmosphere in the city. Men did not smile on the streets, but kept their heads down and their looks to themselves.

He rehearsed his own smile, and his apologies too, as he approached Saint Martin at Palace, and the road that led to Calthorp Inn. He was not expecting to see Bess at the door: he assumed she would be in the solar, waiting for him to come to her. But there she was, framed in oak and thick summer shadows, with Amy and John at her side.

He pulled his horse up, too disconcerted at the sight to feel immediate pleasure. Then she moved forward and he saw that there was warm colour in her face; her hair was neatly coiled, and she held herself upright in spite of the child's weight. She smiled at him and his face split into joy at this unexpectedly happy homecoming.

His own apologies were not needed, but Bess herself apologised as he eventually disentangled himself from the children and the two of them linked arms and moved into the hall. She should not have let Jack write to him, she murmured, when her illness had not been so very serious, and now she was fully recovered.

'Nonsense; you were right to send for me. Ewelme will not miss me until after the baby is born.'

Bess glowed. 'Only days more, the midwife said. Oh Will, I'm so glad you're here in time for the birth. Last time was so sad, but this time you'll see, everything will go much better. The baby kicks so hard. Here, put your hand here and feel it.'

He did not feel a kick, only a lump; but he exclaimed as if he did. I was right to come, he thought, even though she is well. The unhappiness of last time destroyed so much between us, but this time Bess really is stronger. Surely the child will live and thrive, and that will mend us: we shall be happy together again.

Days more, the midwife had said; but in fact it was only hours, for Bess went into labour that evening. Will was glad. Over supper he had caught himself staring at her, trying to see the traces of her illness beneath the picture of health and happiness she was presenting to him. It was still only three weeks since Jack had written to say that she was seriously ill: he knew the shadow

585

must be there, however bright the sunlight she was standing in. It seemed to him that it was the best possible time for the baby to come. Her fragile health seemed to have reached its zenith: even two or three days more, and she might have weakened again.

Even so, he paced anxiously until the midwives arrived, and almost as anxiously afterwards, up and down the hall, listening to the flurry and scrabble of their footsteps overhead. The pacing, coming after the long, fast journey and two nights of lumpy inn pallets, lulled him into a weary stupor. He did not notice at first when the door opened.

'Father,' a small voice whispered.

'Amy! You should be in bed!'

'I heard the voices, but they told me not to go in to Mother, and I can't sleep, and . . .'

'Here. Come here and sit with me.'

He took her hand and led her to the settle, set against the wall near the unlit fire. She curled up on the seat with her feet under her and he put his arm round her shoulder and told her over and over that in the morning she would have a new brother or sister.

In the morning, the baby was born dead.

Dead. All the games he had played with himself, the hours when he had amused himself thinking up names and nicknames for the child, trying to guess the shape of its face and the colour of its hair, imagining Amy peering over the side of the cot, little John beaming his welcome: and now it was dead. He had told himself he was playing these games so he might share Bess's grief, if it came to that, just as fully as he could have shared her joy; but he had not expected this wave of pain that crested up and swept him off his feet.

Dead. The midwife brought it downstairs, all swaddled up in the cloths that had been set out ready for it. He called for the nursemaid and sent Amy away, trying to avoid the pain and confusion in her eyes. Then he took the bundle, set it down on the settle and gently unwrapped it.

It was a boy. He had meant to call it Thomas if it was a boy. The body looked so tiny, so fragile. It was blue-tinged, but perfect, absolutely perfect, except for the marks the cord had made round its neck when it strangled in the womb. For months this little child had been taking shape inside Bess: and now there was nothing left but a parcel of inert flesh.

He crossed himself, whispered under his breath, 'Goodbye, Thomas' and silently wrapped it up again.

The midwife stood watching him, without comment. She received the body back, brisk and professional, as if this was a daily occurrence to her – as it probably was, he thought with numb astonishment at the idea that any other human being might have known this over-whelming sense of shock and helplessness.

'She's weak, sir, but she coped well with the labour. It was an accident, sir. Everything was going well right up to the end. Ten to one it'll never happen to her again. She'll mend. Leave it till the winter, and she should be fit enough to try again.'

'Oh no. Never again.'

'You must not say that to her, sir. Say to her that you'll try again, I beg you, sir.'

He turned away from her and went up the stairs to the solar. One of the maids was with Bess, sitting on a stool by the bed; she jumped up when he came in and retreated to a far corner of the dim room.

Bess looked now as he had expected to see her when he arrived, a skeleton clothed in skin, and her eyes were still dark with pain. But she grabbed at his hands with unexpected strength. 'Only an accident, the midwife said. It might have happened to any woman. But I was strong enough, Will. We shall be able to try again.'

He forced out a smile. 'As soon as you are recovered.'

'You promise?'

'Yes. I promise.'

She mourned afterwards, but with determined seren-ity. The thought that they would try again had taken firm root in her. She made Will repeat his promise again and again. She told him repeatedly that many women fared worse, had five, six or even more stillbirths, and still managed to bring up a large family. He knew this to be true, but still it filled him with a kind of impotent horror whenever he thought of the promise he had given her.

He took Thomas to the Greyfriars for burial himself. He could not help thinking of the baby as Thomas, though now it would never be christened. On the few occasions he was obliged to mention it to Bess, though, he said 'the baby'. Bess in return said nothing at all.

John was still too young to understand properly, and the servants all kept up a subdued cheerfulness, but it seemed to Will that Amy shared much of his own pain. Six years old: she had understood it all only too well. He could not bring himself to speak to her, but a week later she came to him in the hall and asked to speak to him. He followed her to the attic where she had been sleeping while Bess was sick.

She knelt down and pulled out a little bundle from behind her truckle bed.

'These were for Thomas. Nurse said I should give them to John, but I shan't.'

Will did not reply. Amy put the bundle on the bed and unwrapped it.

There was a little book, a sheet of paper folded and cut and sewed together with clumsy stitches. She turned over the pages to show Will: she had written out an ABC, in big, uneven letters, with a picture drawn beneath each one. There was a handkerchief, hemmed in pink wool; a wooden doll that she had had since she was a baby.

'Can they go in his grave?'

'He's at the Greyfriars,' Will said in a flat voice. 'I'll take them there.'

'Can I take them? Please?'

'No, sweetheart. It's not for you.'

He thought for a moment that this was cruel of him, but afterwards he felt sure it was right. He wanted Amy to keep a picture of a live baby in her head, not one of a stone slab. Anyway, he did not take the bundle to the Greyfriars. He kept it under his bed for a week, then he gave the contents to the nuns.

Ten days later, Sir Thomas Tuddenham presented himself at the door of Calthorp Inn. So soon! Will thought with dismay. He had hoped that Tuddenham would stay at Ewelme for a month at least, for his own sake as well as for Alice's.

'Lady Alice is well?' he asked, as he led the land agent through to the hall.

'As gay as ever. You had the news here? It's said that the Congress of Arras has begun badly, that there is no hope of the Dauphin accepting our terms.'

'So there will be no peace?'

'Between the Dauphin and Burgundy there will be peace.'

'For certain? That's bad.'

'It is.' Tuddenham narrowed his eyes, in spite of the dimness of the hall, and squinted at Will. 'You'll know as well as I how the Earl will take it. But France is France, and England England: our task is to work on him so he'll give the verdict Wetherby looks for, and as soon as may be after his return.'

'I doubt he'll be in a state of mind to think of Norwich affairs.'

'Then you and I must make him think of them.'

'I have no plans to return to Ewelme yet: my wife needs me here. But I shall think on what you say.'

'You shall do more. We have a meeting at Intwood on Thursday night, Wetherby and Heydon and the rest.'

'I shall be interested to hear what you decide.'

'You shall come to Intwood, and share in our decision.'

He knew that tone: polite, almost honeyed, but with a whip hand held in readiness. He knew, without needing to think, that Tuddenham would persist even if he invented an excuse. But he did not want to go to Intwood.

'I'll see if I can manage it, sir.'

Tuddenham's squint intensified. 'I saw Heydon this morning,' he said sharply, 'and he told me you've taken up not one of his invitations since you returned to Norwich, nor Wetherby's either. But this invitation you shall take, if you value your position with Suffolk.'

'I am to take that as an order, sir?'

'You are to take it as an order.'

Will rode to Intwood – late – on Thursday night. The meeting was less dramatic than he had anticipated. Wetherby and his men had had their case against Richard Purdance prepared for months: there was no more evidence to be gathered. They spoke of planning to win Suffolk's ear, but it seemed to Will that they were already confident he would come to Norwich well before the year end and give them the verdict they wanted.

Tuddenham had better access to Suffolk than he had himself: it was not necessary for him to do anything. However, he understood why Tuddenham had ordered him to come to Intwood. Wetherby's group were confident, but not so very confident that they would risk men whispering that some of Suffolk's servants were giving them less than full support. They needed to demonstrate that they had plenty of backing; they needed to be in a position to persuade Suffolk that Judge Paston's dire predictions of revolution in Norwich would prove unjustified, and that they would have no trouble in keeping a firm hold on the city after his verdict was delivered. Will knew that this invitation would be only one of many. Tuddenham would summon him to Oxburgh and to Baconsthorpe. He would watch to ensure that Will spoke with Wetherby and Heydon at Guild meetings and greeted them in a friendly manner when he encountered them in the street.

It would never end, he thought morosely, as he made his goodbyes the following morning and rode, with Tuddenham jailer-like at his side, back towards the city. Each time he did as Tuddenham insisted, he found himself still more committed. Small demands led to large demands. When and if Wetherby did regain control of Norwich, he would keep that control with bribery, fear and violence. He himself might avoid the violence, but at the very least he would be expected to play his part in making threats to men with whom he was far better in sympathy than his present company.

Was there any alternative? Was there, even now, anything he could do? He thought and thought, but he could see no other path than Tuddenham's open to him. He believed Tuddenham's men to be powerful; he found them intimidating. He had had neither the time nor the inclination, since his arrival in Norwich, to sound out the men who formed their opposition; and they had not sought him out either. Most likely they lacked the determination to fight yet another round against Wetherby; most likely it would all come about as Tuddenham intended.

In the weeks that followed he did as Tuddenham asked, by and large, in a spirit of dull indifference.

It was a surprise, and a pleasure, to both Bess and Will when Mowbray Herald presented himself at Calthorp Inn. The Dowager Duchess of Norfolk had arrived in Norwich for a short stay, he announced; the Dowager Duchess would be graciously pleased to receive them both.

Bess was not yet well enough to leave the house, but Will sent back word that he would accept the invitation. He had had a summons from Heydon to a meeting at the Bess of Bedlam the following afternoon; he sent Jack along instead, with a message that he had been called urgently to Mowbray Inn.

Mowbray Inn had once been Kitty's to rule; now she was permitted to stay there only under sufferance from her son. But she was still a rich woman, and the house was almost as crammed with servants as it had been in the old Duke's day.

Will's manufactured sense of urgency soon evaporated as he was passed from Chamberlain to steward to valet. This too had not changed: Kitty had always made him wait. He waited for an hour or more, then eventually Jeanne appeared in the hall and told him, in indifferent tones, that he might present himself in the Duchess's private room.

'Master Calthorp, Your Grace.'

He strode in confidently; and stopped abruptly, in a collision course with two alaunts, big hunting hounds. The dogs did not stop. One of them hurled itself straight for his throat, to the accompaniment of a chorus of loud barks.

'Here, Bellman,' a languid voice said.

Will put his hand up, automatically; he felt the dog's breath hot on it, as the animal leaped high.

'Here, Dancer. Here, boys.'

There was no conventional commanding note in the voice, but the dogs responded immediately: their barking died and they slunk back, growling, to the fireplace.

Will's eyes followed them. They were pretty animals, high-bred and fine faced, but heavens, fierce for parlour dogs. Their master was pretty too. He had yellow hair and thick red lips, a yellow satin doublet and very tight red hose that showed off long shapely legs. He looked young, even younger than Will had expected. He lay back on the padded bench by the fire as if it were a cold day, though it was still September and warm. A lute trailed from one hand. The dogs settled, sprawling, at his feet.

'Master Calthorp,' Kitty said, stationing herself in front of him to claim his full attention. 'Let me present Thomas Strangeways, my new husband.'

It took another hour of inconsequential chatter before Kitty rose from her bench and invited Will to come and sit with her in the window seat. Strangeways did not respond to the invitation; he had taken little part in their conversation. Kitty positioned herself where she could watch him, Will noticed, but he had picked up the lute now and was strumming away, half-heartedly, his eyes on the strings.

'Is she very sick, Will?'

'No,' Will answered honestly. 'Visit her if you wish, Kitty; or in a week or two, she will be able to come here.'

'You were lucky, then. Very lucky. She'll have more sense than to try again; there's every chance she'll live to a good old age.'

He hesitated, then said awkwardly, 'You do know that the baby died?'

'Babies do. And women cry, but life goes on.' She said this almost automatically, then it seemed that her thoughts connected and she turned to him sharply and said in a quite different tone, 'You *have* made her see sense, you and the midwife?'

'The midwife told me, Kitty, that the disappointment was the hardest thing for her. She has to have hope. She needs that, if she is to recover.'

'There are other things that can be hoped for.'

He took a deep breath. 'The midwife told me that I was to promise her we'd try just once more.'

He sensed the string of tension pull taut inside Kitty. 'Sweet Jesus!'

'You've not seen her yet, Kitty. She *is* strong enough, truly she is.'

'She is not, Will. If the midwife told you that, she was a damn fool. You should have let me send you Mistress Allen. She'd never have been so blind.'

'And it is what she wants, Kitty, even now.'

Kitty glared at him. He met her eyes as steadily as he could. He was expecting another tirade from her, another barrage of objections about Bess's fragile state of health; but after holding his look for a long moment, she dropped her eyes.

'Make her wait at least, Will. Make her think again. Give her time to recover properly.'

'She shall have it all, I promise you.'

'You will send her to Burnham?'

'When I return to London; in two weeks, perhaps, or three.'

Another woman might have commented on the household he was returning to in London; on the news that had just come from Arras, of the end of the Congress and the treaty the Duke of Burgundy had signed with the Dauphin. But he did not expect it of Kitty: all this would mean nothing to her.

'I shall be there myself, before the winter sets in.'

'Then perhaps I shall see you at Westminster.'

'At the Pleasance, perhaps.'

'Indeed, or at the Pleasance.'

Yes, he thought: it would be the Pleasance, with Gloucester, and not the King's dreary court. He could have told that himself from his first glance at Strangeways.

He glanced again at the esquire and then turned back to his wife. Kitty was looking at Strangeways, too. She sensed his eyes on her, though, and slowly turned her head to meet his look.

He thought: Kitty has married a fool, and she knows it. But he is a pretty fool, and she chose to do so with her eyes open. She has no illusions, and more, her disillusionment is not fresh: she had his measure when we talked at Calthorp Inn, before they even married.

'We shall be in London till Christmas, perhaps,' Kitty said.

'And then . . .'

'And then in Oxfordshire.'

'So you will not return to Norfolk . . .'

Kitty gave a little shrug. 'Thomas has few friends in Norfolk.'

Even so, his wife could have kept him there for longer, or planned to bring him back sooner, if she wished to see her own friends. Evidently she did not.

Will had come with half a thought of telling her about Wetherby's plottings, about Suffolk's likely verdict and its possible repercussions. But it seemed to him then that none of it would interest her, or her husband either. Like

Alice, they would retreat to comfortable Oxfordshire and turn their backs on this troubled little corner of England.

The thought annoyed him. He said, sharply, 'I think sometimes that I am in the same position.'

To this she did react: with a long look, and then a wicked little smile.

He thought: she cares nothing of the squabbles, but she cares still for me; she has followed every turn in my fortunes. I was wrong in thinking she knows nothing of Norwich affairs. I'd swear that for my sake she has learned all of it: of Tuddenham, of Heydon, of Wetherby; of Sir Brian Stapleton and Sir Henry Inglose and the rest. She knows that what I say is true. And she thinks to herself that it is a result of my choosing Suffolk over Norfolk, and that I have only myself to blame.

'If that is so, Will,' Kitty said with just the tiniest touch of malice, 'then perhaps you, too, should think to spend Christmas in Oxfordshire.'

Alice is older than Bess, thought Will: much older, nearly ten years older. It is not as if she looks young, not any more. But she has not aged in the way Bess has aged, her hair thinning and her face growing faded and puffy and her figure spreading. There is an ageless elegance now about Alice.

So slim, Alice, so straight and self-possessed. There was no line on the smooth expanse of forehead beneath the rim of her headdress; no shadow around her almond eyes. She was beautiful, but hers was the cold beauty of a woman who had never suckled her own child, or sat up all night to nurse it through a fever; of a woman who took an hour or more to dress each morning, without ever being called away from her room by the urgent pleas of a lively family. Coming back to her after leaving Bess at Burnham, Will found her brittle. She was sometimes merry, but she was rarely joyous.

There was a shell around her: she kept the world at a distance. Will wondered, in the heavy autumn days at

Bardi Place when they were waiting for Suffolk to return, whether the Earl would penetrate that shell once he and Alice were reunited. Then Suffolk did return and he soon realised that Suffolk barely noticed the shell and would never even try.

Arras had, of course, been a disaster. Suffolk knew it, and Beaufort, and Gloucester. Alice certainly knew it, though she never spoke of it. Even Kitty and Strangeways, Jack Hannant and the pages in Bardi Place, knew of it. Burgundy had played his game tightly; but now he had moved the vital piece and confronted his opponents with a discovered check.

Suffolk Herald claimed, warm in his place by the kitchen fire, that the real blame lay with those in the English Council who had refused to put forward realistic peace proposals. Will was inclined to agree. But few other men thought along these lines: the criticism in London was directed almost entirely at the pro-Burgundians, and most heavily at Suffolk himself.

Will found this strange. It was no secret that Suffolk had advocated a negotiated peace; a sorrow perhaps, but no shame that he had failed to convince the rest of the Council. Suffolk was hated not for this, though, but because he was being described as a friend of the Burgundians.

A friend? The Earl had talked with the Seigneur de Santes, but not so very much; he had never shown friendship to the Duke himself, and Alice's little contretemps with Burgundy was still remembered and spoken of. Those who had listened to Suffolk had surely known that he had distrusted the Duke of Burgundy for many years.

But now, at the very worst of times, Suffolk had been marked out as a Burgundian supporter. This had not been so before Arras; somehow it had happened in Arras. But what had happened, and why? Had Suffolk intended it? Or had Burgundy and his advisers planned it? The former struck Will as incredible, and the latter as most peculiar. If de Santes and his colleagues had wanted to set up a scapegoat, why had they not attempted to discredit Gloucester? Or failing that, Kemp or Beaufort?

True, Beaufort had taken some punishment: he was in no position now to rival Gloucester in the Council. But he was old, thought Will, and seemed not so very troubled by this. Suffolk was not old; he was ambitious. The failure of his hopes at Arras, and the loud criticism heaped on him after his return to England, combined to press his spirits down, down: down to the ground and below, to well-water level and below.

Alice did nothing to cheer him, made no attempts to open herself to him, as far as Will could judge. Perhaps Orleans would have proved a better source of consolation; but Orleans was no longer at Bardi Place. Gloucester's men had met the Duke's balinger at Dover and escorted him away. Gloucester's servants had come afterwards to collect the Duke's possessions and transport them to his new quarters in Kent.

Gloucester had kept his word and shown a grim sense of humour in finding Orleans a new custodian. He had sent the Duke to Sir Reynold Cobham, an elderly, amiable and extremely drunken Kentish knight, whose chief claim to fame was in having fathered Gloucester's beautiful wife.

Tuddenham called twice at Bardi Place in the fortnight after Suffolk's return, but Suffolk spared him only ten minutes each time, and the careful phrases he and Wetherby and Heydon had composed remained unspoken. Suffolk seemed to have interest in only one thing: in seeing Orleans again.

He sent Suffolk Herald to Gloucester with a polite request that he be allowed an interview with the Duke. Gloucester laughed in Suffolk Herald's face and flatly refused. Suffolk called at Winchester Inn and spoke at length with Beaufort, while Will waited on the stairs; but it was clear from the start that Beaufort could do nothing. He asked Tuddenham, asked Will himself, for their suggestions, but they had few to make, and none of those bore fruit.

He sent letters to Cobham's house in Kent, but they were returned unopened, with Sir Reynold's compliments. When it was clear that these efforts had all hit unyielding rock, he pressed Alice to intercede with Eleanor Cobham. Alice protested, loudly enough for the servants to hear through the walls of Bardi Place. She went to the Pleasance nevertheless and did as her husband requested; but perhaps without great conviction, because Eleanor proved no more obliging than her husband.

Alice's complaints surprised Will, on reflection. He had not expected her to care passionately about Suffolk's disappointment, but he had expected her to regret Orleans' departure on her own account. They had spent so many hours together: she had seemed to have a genuine fondness for the Duke.

But then, Will thought brutally, most likely she had had all that she had wanted from him. She had heard his views, read his poetry, used him as an audience for her songs.

Had they ever, he wondered, spoken of things that really mattered to either of them in those endless private meetings? Had they talked of his imprisonment, of the family he never saw, of the wife who had died back in France? Had they talked of Alice's marriage, or of her longing for a child? He could not believe that they had. He thought: Orleans was no more her friend than Eleanor was or is. They were acquaintances, both of them; no more.

There had been fewer private meetings with Suffolk, far fewer, and Will had always assumed that those few had been largely devoted to political negotiation. It had filled him with uneasy admiration when Suffolk had succeeded in persuading Orleans to sign his deposition. This he had never thought of as friendship. But he sensed now, seeing Suffolk sunk in spirits to the mud of the well bottom, that he had misjudged. Under the shallow pleasantries of those long evenings filled with poetry and music, under the negotiations too, there had been a bedrock of deep feeling between the two men.

Will's sympathy for Suffolk was real; but as the weeks went past and the Earl still summoned enthusiasm for nothing but his efforts to contact Orleans, it began to rub away. He had not expected Suffolk to be enthusiastic either about the slow job of rebuilding his position in the King's Council, or about the tedious task of giving a verdict on Wetherby's complaints against Purdance. But he had expected him to do these things all the same; and he was not doing them.

It was a relief when he was given no opportunity to indicate to Suffolk his support for Wetherby, as Tuddenham expected. But Tuddenham returned to Norwich that October and Will subsequently began to think that there was much to be said for speaking to Suffolk instead on Purdance's behalf. If he was ever to change his allegiance, it was high time that he did it. Perhaps it would hurt himself and Bess financially, but he reckoned he would survive Tuddenham's enmity — with Kitty's help if necessary, or even Judge Paston's. His present course was hurting Bess in other ways. He wanted her to be able to hold her head high in Norwich, to make the friends she chose and not the friends Tuddenham chose for her. He wanted her to be proud of him and he believed that she was not. He no longer had his old confidence that he was a good husband; sometimes he felt as if he were looking at himself through Bess's eyes, and he was less than overjoyed at what he saw.

It had seemed, when Judge Paston had come to Bardi Place almost a year before, that it was already too late for him to act. But with every day that passed he came to think it less inevitable that Suffolk would give a verdict for Wetherby. Low-spirited, vulnerable, perhaps Suffolk might be ripe prey for an attack from an unexpected quarter.

Three times, he approached Suffolk in his upstairs room. He stood by the table under the window as Suffolk fiddled with the mess of papers and broken quills, and he spoke: not with passion, but with quiet conviction, suggesting to the Earl that perhaps Norfolk men were not all mistaken when they came to him with criticisms of Tuddenham and Wetherby. Suffolk heard him out, but he did not respond: throughout these interviews he appeared distant and unconcerned. All through the late autumn Gloucester's resurgence in the Council continued virtually unchecked; and Suffolk visited Norwich not at all.

But these matters could not be ignored forever: the volume of letters and callers from Norfolk grew weekly, even daily. In November Suffolk made his move. He went to the King's Council and persuaded them to commission a different Judge, William Godred, to enquire into the situation.

Godred was no Norfolk man; he knew nothing of the background to the troubles, and he lacked both a high reputation and an authoritative manner. Will was angered and disappointed when he learned what Suffolk had done. He thought it a half-hearted, inadequate response which would solve nothing. He told himself that in a few months Suffolk would surely realise this. Then his pain at losing Orleans would be dulled, and his hope of regaining him faded: Will would be able to approach him again and press him to act himself, with firmness and conviction.

But before this could happen more dramatic events turned Suffolk's attention in a quite different direction. The Duke of Burgundy besieged Calais.

Adam Moleyns, the cadaverous young clergyman who was the new clerk to the King's Council, lowered his eyes to the mass of paper. He lifted a sheet a little closer to them and began to read in a sonorous, droning voice: 'First, it seems well that the King should lay no sieges, nor make any conquest out of Normandy, nor endeavour to make any conquest by way of siege as yet. For the sieges have greatly hindered his conquest in time passed, and destroyed his people, as well lords, captains and chieftains, as his other people, and wasted and consumed innumerable good of his finances, both in England, and in France, and of Normandy. For there may no king conquer a great realm by continual sieges . . .'

'Rubbish,' muttered Lord Hungerford in a low voice. 'What else did his father do?'

Moleyns' voice trailed to a dismal halt and he looked warily at the source of the interruption. The Councillors, who were careful to behave impeccably when the King ventured to join them, tended to the opposite extreme in his absence.

Suffolk took pity on him. 'Fastolf is so concise in speech,' he said, 'and so remarkably long-winded on paper. Moleyns, perhaps you could summarise the rest of his recommendations.'

Moleyns frowned, reminding Suffolk that though the clerk had given him a furtive kind of support, he was still a stickler for accuracy and disliked seeing corners cut. He dutifully skimmed through the rest of the papers, reading out occasional sentences, offering a rare aside when he came to a figure. 'Two leaders, with . . . 750 spears of well-chosen men. To land and base themselves at Calais or Crotay and make forays from June or November. To move forward burning and destroying and taking crops and cattle for sustenance of English-held towns.

'To the intent to drive the enemies thereby to an extreme famine, and to begin yearly at the seasons in the manner above said to be employed in such countries as shall be thought most expedient.

'And in this wise it is thought that the King may make and sustain this said war three year day fully in the seasons aforesaid with the wages of one year and a quarter, to pay for every year five months' wages only . . .'

'Repeat that last piece more slowly,' rapped out Lord Cromwell.

The clerk obeyed.

'Poorly phrased,' Suffolk said.

'Not a badly argued policy, though,' Gloucester said. 'Particularly the financial aspects.'

Suffolk glared at him. 'It is hardly conciliatory.'

'The aftermath of unsuccessful peace negotiations is not the time to be conciliatory,' Gloucester snapped.

Suffolk could not make himself feel conciliatory to Gloucester when the Duke deliberately challenged him. He was working up a stinging retort when Lord Hungerford intervened. 'Has York commented upon the paper?'

The young Duke of York had been appointed the year before as Lieutenant and Governor in France and Normandy. It was an appointment that had taken on an increasingly political aspect following the death of Bedford, since that made York the senior nobleman in Lancastrian France. His long-term opinions on the war were as yet a mystery to Suffolk: as they were, he understood, to most if not all of the Council members.

'York's main concern,' Gloucester said with superbly aggressive tactlessness, 'is to be relieved of his posting.'

'I hardly think Fastolf is reminding us of that,' Cromwell contributed.

Hungerford by now was bent on his own tack. 'Two commanders for lightning scorched-earth raids. That is no task for York. Presumably Fastolf sees himself and Talbot . . .'

'On the contrary,' Gloucester said, 'it will be me.'

There was a dead silence.

Of all the Council members, only Suffolk had had any reason to anticipate it; but he had not believed for one moment that Gloucester would go through with the threat he had made the previous spring. By the time he recovered from his astonishment, Gloucester had assembled the rest of his argument and was starting to present it. 'Naturally Fastolf wrote his memorandum immediately after Arras, and before we knew of Burgundy's intention of besieging Calais; but I consider it remarkably apt in the circumstances. I shall lead a party of reinforcements to Calais. We shall repulse the Burgundians, and if time permits before the winter draws in we shall undertake a short chevauchée through Picardy. It will be a salutary lesson to Burgundy, and a reminder to the French at the same time. Any objections?'

Suffolk had plenty of objections, but he could not voice them, not without the opportunity that he clearly would not be given to think them through and phrase them. Gloucester allowed the rest of the Council only a short silence, then continued, 'I am glad to hear it, since I have already discussed this policy with His Highness, who greatly approves of it. As you are all aware, King Henry was deeply distressed by Burgundy's treacherous behaviour at Arras, and he fully supports my own intention to teach him a lesson. Since this is a matter for urgency, I shall leave in ten days. Suffolk, I would value your support in this.'

The limpid grey eyes met Suffolk's light brown ones full on.

'You shall have it,' Suffolk said.

With only a groom and a valet for company, Suffolk rode back to Bardi Place that afternoon. His anger was too heavy to hide for long: he wanted to be away from Gloucester, and fast.

He arrived just as dinner was being served. Alice was there, but Lady Warwick was there too: he could not speak, except to give them the outline of his news.

'He's a brave man, Gloucester,' Lady Warwick said. 'I know men call him a poor soldier, but it seems to me that he is a brave man.'

It had seemed so to Cromwell, Suffolk knew, and to Hungerford and most of the rest. Gloucester had always had the knack of making popular moves. Perhaps the men of the Council had privately thought his plans rash; but in public, they had all applauded them.

603

'It is understandable that he should wish to act,' Suffolk said carefully.

'I think it is wonderful,' persisted Lady Warwick.

Alice said nothing. Suffolk glanced at her, but she did not look back. She does not understand this, he thought; she does not realise what it will mean to me.

He had its measure himself by then; he had considered it throughout the journey from Westminster to London. Gloucester, damn him, had planned it well; indeed, planned it perfectly. He himself had been invited to act as second-in-command. If the expedition succeeded, Gloucester would hog the glory; if it failed, it would discredit them both. He could not afford to take part and let it fail, not after half a lifetime of military reverses. He could not have refused to go and fight, not after the débâcle at Arras.

What could he do, now that he had accepted? He had thought of asking Beaufort's advice, but he had come to no decisions.

The spices were withdrawn; the meal came to a leisurely close. Gilles took up his lute, bowed and retreated. The ladies departed for the solar and the men of the household gathered round their master, anxious to hear more. Suffolk had little more to tell them. He would have confided in none of them; he trusted none of them to advise him.

He retired early; it was almost an hour before Alice joined him in the great bedchamber. But he was awake and waiting for her. Lucette folded the last of her day clothes and laid them neatly on the chest before withdrawing. Alice sat on the edge of the bed, on the side where he had left the hangings undrawn. She did not snuff out the last candle.

He expected her to speak of Gloucester, but instead she said, 'So they did not discuss the appointments in the Council today.'

'The Household appointments? No, they did not.'

'It surely cannot be delayed much longer.'

'It makes no odds to us, my Lady. With Bedford

604

dead and Beaufort out of favour, I shall be offered nothing.'

'Lady Warwick felt that there was a chance.'

'If I bribed and cajoled, perhaps. But I am not willing to sacrifice everything else to that end. I have other ambitions, as you know very well.'

'You speak of France? But there is no hope for peace in France now.'

'We will not make peace this year; but there will be other years, many other years.'

Alice did not reply. She snuffed the candle and they were in darkness. He could hear her slipping under the covers, drawing the hangings so that they were cocooned.

'Lady Warwick told me today of a house that might suit us. The Rose, that was Sir John Pountney's house, and the Black Prince's. It's on Saint Laurence Hill, just north of the Cold Harbour.'

Suffolk did not reply. He felt anger stir, cold inside him.

'I told her that I should go there tomorrow, to look at it,' Alice persisted.

Still he did not reply.

'I may do so, my Lord?'

'If you wish.'

There was silence for a moment, then Alice said in a high little voice, 'I do wish it.'

They neither of them spoke again. He thought she fell asleep soon afterwards, though he could not be certain: he did not touch her, and she was always a silent sleeper. He himself did not sleep for a long time.

The Rose. He knew the house. It was large and handsome, a low-set stone house with a tall tower at one corner. He had long admired it. But it was not Bardi Place, and it pained him to think that Alice still wished to live elsewhere. This was his home: he cared nothing for palaces near the waterside, and Thomas Chaucer's money made no difference to that.

It made a difference to Alice. He had believed once, he thought wearily, that she would share his own ambitions, that their lives would be centred on a growing family, and on his own great ambitions for peace in France. But the children had not come, despite all the prayers and spells, and they now barely even hoped for them. Alice cared for France, but not for the interminable plotting and planning that would be needed to secure the right peace. Instead she longed for this: for a great house on Saint Laurence Hill, and for her husband to secure a prestigious appointment at court to replace the post as Steward he had held briefly and lost two years before.

In Arras he had been persuaded that he missed her, that he loved her and longed to be back at her side. He did not tell himself now that he did not love her. But ever since his return they had argued: over Orleans, over Tuddenham, over what seemed to him her empty, petty ambitions. He had looked to be soothed, encouraged, but instead Alice had brought him a series of crushing headaches.

Her lack of understanding had always been painful to him, but he had never resented it more than in the dark days after Arras. He was slowly regaining his sense of destiny, but that was no thanks to Alice.

Henry had lost Burgundy; he himself had lost Orleans. But the English still had firm control of much of France; there was still much to be bargained for; to be fought for, even by the Duke of Gloucester. Fighting was no solution, though: he still coveted peace. He still longed to see Englishmen living peaceably in France, and to be one of them himself. But that could only happen if men of vision and determination worked for it to happen, not merely over the short weeks of conferences, but over long years of attrition, of attack and defence, of trust and betrayal. His vision was returning to him: he was no longer the blind man who had stumbled from Arras in the rain. But he needed still to strengthen it.

He wanted to go to France. That was the irony behind Gloucester's insistence: that he genuinely wanted to go to France. It seemed to him then that there was nothing for him in England but mud and ashes. Orleans was in England, but he was past all hope that he would see Orleans again. He believed that in time he would manage to arrange an intermediary to deliver letters – perhaps de Lannoy, or the Bastard, or another Frenchman – but that was no reason for him to linger in England. Once he had thought it might be possible to love East Anglia as he loved France, but Norwich to him now was no more than the scene of a tired tangle of problems which he had neither the interest, nor the time, to set about resolving. He would have done much to get away from the old persistence of Tuddenham, and the new, but equally exasperating, persistence of Will Calthorp.

It was Gloucester who was the stumbling block. Damn his empty posturings, his showy ambitions. If Suffolk had been able to think of any way short of treason in which he could have damaged Gloucester, he would have done it. What he wanted was to be in France, but away from Gloucester.

But why not? he thought with sudden clarity. Gloucester's main aim was to avoid leaving him unwatched in England with the King: he might be persuaded that another deputy would suit him better, if he were assured that Suffolk was elsewhere in France. There were other English armies in France, other postings. He might go to Gascony. He might arrange a posting to Rouen, and watch the Duke of York at work.

It was not so long since he had been in France: he had no illusions about the situation that would face him there. A demoralised army, confronting odds that were now overwhelming; an administration in Rouen still in tatters after Bedford's death; few friends, and those men that he dared not meet. None of it would bring him easy joy. But even so, it was what he longed for.

Alice stirred, murmured and turned over in the high cold bed. Suffolk slid down beneath the covers and felt a warmth begin to come to him. Yes, he would go to

France once more: not out of coercion, but with real, though faint, hopes for the future. But he would not go to Gloucester's France. The France he would go to was his own.

26

ENGLAND
Summer, 1436

With a trundle of wheels and a creak of hinges and a
clunk of trunks and tables and bedframes, a heavy
wooden cart pulled into the courtyard of Calthorp Inn
in Norwich. The carter reined in the horses and they
clattered to a halt; and with a last noisy protest, the cart
lurched to a standstill behind them.

Almost before it was still, a dozen people had surrounded it. The grooms caught at the horses' bridles; the
servants made for the lashings, ready to untie them and
carry in the contents before they were prevented from
doing so by the rain that the purple clouds threatened.
Will Calthorp made for the bench at the front of the
cart. He held out his arms and little John took his hands
and jumped down, laughing and shouting. Amy followed, impatient to see her brother out of the way. Will
passed the children one by one to the nursemaid; and
then he turned to Bess.

Bess climbed down more slowly: there was no spring-
iness in her. She was thin, thinner than he remembered
seeing her, but she felt heavy for the brief instant when
he took her full weight. She leaned against him for a
moment when her feet were on the ground, and then she
pushed herself upright, gave him a determined smile
and walked towards the heavy doors that led into the
hall.

He stood for a moment, watching her; then he turned
and said some words of encouragement to the servants;
then he followed her into the house.

'You should have sent me word, and stayed at Burnham.'

'No, Will; no. It was the journey that made me sick, only the journey. In a day, or two at most, I shall be recovered.'

Will frowned. That thinness was not the result of the journey, he thought, nor the faded colour of her hair, nor even the worn look of her face, like a much-washed dishrag. Those were the signs of a sickness that had persisted for many of the months he had been away from her. Those spoke of broken nights filled with bad dreams, of meals uneaten and rest untaken.

'You shall not leave this bed today,' he said firmly. 'Nor tomorrow either, nor any day this side of Sunday. Even then, I think you would have done better to stay at Burnham, in the country air. Perhaps in a short while you will be able to make the journey back there.'

'Oh no!' Bess's voice was thin, but the vehemence behind her protest was real enough. 'No, Will, I shall stay here with you, in Norwich.'

It was not the best thing for her. But he did not dare to persist when she seemed so weak, so he turned their conversation to lighter things; and after a while, when Bess fell back on the pillows, he left her and went downstairs.

I know why she came, he thought: though she did not speak of it, and nor did I. It was not just to be with me. It was to keep me to my promise, and get another child.

That thought filled him with a great sense of weariness. He had never known how to fight the stubborn streak in Bess, or even how to reason with her. But he believed it would not do to give in to her; for whatever she imagined, she surely did not have the strength to live through yet another childbearing.

It was a warm summer evening. The nursemaid had put Amy and John to bed, but a reddish light was still streaming through the windows of the hall. He made for the doors and walked slowly round the side of the house and into the garden. The briar hedge and its archway were thickly studded with pink roses; beyond, he could hear the shouts of the bargemen as they passed on the river, on their way to their evening's moorings.

It was two weeks since he had left London and come back to Norwich. There had been nothing for him to do in London, little even for him to see, for Suffolk, like almost all the great lords of the King's Council, was in France. Suffolk was in Rouen with the Duke of York, while Gloucester had gone to Calais and the Earl of Salisbury, the Earl of Somerset, Lord Cromwell and Lord Hungerford had all spread themselves across Normandy, heading a campaign to defend Lancastrian-held territory against the anticipated Valois offensive.

Some news would come soon, surely: from Suffolk Herald, perhaps, or Secret, or Beul, or one of the other poursuivants who journeyed sometimes to Norwich. That might provide an excuse for him, once he had exhausted the possibilities of Bess's arrival. He was not prepared to see Tuddenham yet, even if he was driven to lie in order to prevent it. He was not ready to decide yet whether he would agree to be appointed a justice of the peace.

It was a lowly appointment, but an honourable one. Normally he would have accepted it without a second thought, but he had done nothing without second thoughts since his arrival in Norwich. Every meeting with Tuddenham or Heydon, every short exchange with other men at the Guildhall, every visit to his own or Suffolk's estates, especially an appointment such as this one, to which Tuddenham had proposed him: all of them carried weight while the verdict was looming over the Wetherby case.

Judge Godred was in Norwich. He had been taking depositions all that week from the men involved in the Council disputes. Will himself had not been involved and he did not expect the Judge to interview him; but he assumed that the Judge was also beginning to calculate less formally which of the prominent citizens of Norwich were Wetherby's supporters, and which his opponents.

He felt himself to be one of Wetherby's opponents, but he had not yet made his opposition public. Suffolk knew of it, of course, but Suffolk was in France. Judge Paston had once known of it, but he had given no sign that he remembered. And clearly neither Suffolk nor Paston had spoken to Tuddenham, who still assumed that he was Wetherby's supporter.

It was more than time for him to correct this impression, to announce his opposition to Wetherby. But he had been postponing this, and not only because he dreaded facing Tuddenham's enmity and the probable loss of much of his steady work and regular income. There was another, greater difficulty. He was unhappy about what he knew of Purdance's support.

There were opponents to Thomas Wetherby whose identity every man in Norwich knew. As well as Purdance himself there was Robert Chaplain, then Lord Mayor, and John Cambridge, another of the Aldermen. These men were campaigning hard to counteract Wetherby's own campaign. They were small traders, though, and not great landowners in the county.

Many of the county landowners were reckoned to be against Wetherby. The men who had shunned Will himself over the previous three years, men like Sir Brian Stapleton and Sir Henry Inglose, had grumbled about Wetherby's doings and Tuddenham's, and Heydon's and the rest, for years. They had championed the ditcher whom Heydon had thrown in his own ditch and dozens of other men who had suffered at the hands of Tuddenham and Wetherby's henchmen. But they were not in Norwich that summer. Almost all of them were at their country estates, and their servants had assured Will that they had no intention of returning to the city before the winter – if then.

Will had thought William Yelverton to be a firm opponent of Wetherby, but when he had talked to the Serjeant he had soon realised that he was taking no active part in the Purdance campaign: he seemed fearful of doing anything that might prejudice his chances of obtaining a seat on the King's Bench. He had been sure that Judge Paston was an opponent of Wetherby; but after listening and asking in many Norwich inns, he knew that nobody took Paston to be the leader of the opposition to Thomas Wetherby.

The hard truth was that Wetherby's opposition had no clear leader among the great men of the county. It was made up only of little men.

Will was prepared to act as Yelverton's supporter, or Paston's, or Stapleton's, much as he was taken by men now to be Tuddenham's supporter. But he could not do that, if Yelverton, Paston and Stapleton kept silent. Still, he could not believe that they would continue to say and do nothing, when Godred came to the end of his investigation and afterwards. By then, surely, one of them would emerge as Purdance's patron; and he would find himself in a position to approach that man, and through him make his own opinions public.

'I was at Princes Inn today,' said Bess over supper.

Will glanced up warily. Bess at Princes Inn? She had not told him beforehand that she intended to call on the Pastons. Perhaps he would have told her not to do so, if she had asked him. He had not called on the Judge himself; and it was four weeks now since Bess had arrived in Norwich. 'With Agnes Paston? Or the Judge?'

'With Agnes, most of the time. The Judge is in bed. You knew that, Will? His gout, they say.'

'So I heard.'

'But my other news will be fresh to you, I think.'

Other news? Bess? News of Godred? he thought with a stir of apprehension. News of Yelverton, or other of Paston's associates?

'Tell me.'

'Agnes Paston is carrying again.'

She said it in a voice which mixed satisfaction with jealousy, and with a kind of defensive pleasure, as if to say: at her age! Still, I shall be in the same state soon.

Curse her. She thought of nothing but babies. He

knew that through and through, but even so he had let himself think for that instant that she might have something to tell him of serious Norwich affairs. He only just stifled a sarcastic retort.

But it had been news, at that.

'It must be years since their youngest boy was born.'

'There's a girl too, Will. Mind, she's no beauty, little Lizzy Paston. And a saucy child, not like our Amy. I'd be ashamed to take her visiting if she was my daughter. Then since she was born, seven years of miscarriages and stillbirths. But Agnes looks well, Will. The child should come in November, the midwife told her.'

'She's a strong woman,' Will said cautiously.

Bess did not respond directly to this. 'There's a good midwife at Oxnead, she told me. I thought perhaps to visit on my way back to Burnham.'

'You're not sure yet?'

She flushed. 'Not sure, no, Will, but I am beginning to –'

'You'll not have another child at Burnham,' he broke in roughly.

Bess opened her mouth, as if to protest, and then shut it again. 'As you wish,' she said.

He glanced across the trestle at her. She sat very composedly, looking back at him. Her hair was neatly coiled under its little cap, her hands were folded in her lap, her shoulders straight. She had done everything possible, since her arrival in Norwich, to try to persuade him that she was well. But he was not persuaded. Her determination was an eggshell over the runny yolk of her fragility; crack it, and she would fall to pieces.

'Bess,' he began again. 'If you are not sure yet . . . could we not wait awhile? Till the autumn, say, so the child might be born next summer?'

He made his voice as gentle as he could, but he had barely finished a sentence before he saw her lower lip begin to tremble.

'But Will, you promised!'

614

He had. And everything since had urged him to break that promise. Keep it, and he would destroy Bess. But break it, he thought now: that would destroy Bess, too.

'Aye,' he said, 'I did.' He pushed his trencher aside and stood up abruptly, scraping the bench on the floor.

'The Judge asked after you, Will,' Bess said in a louder voice, as he made his way to the door. 'And I said that you would be calling on him shortly.'

On the Judge? And on his wife, obscenely fat already with the coming baby? He had no enthusiasm for doing that. But he knew, even without Bess's prompting, that a visit was already overdue. Two days later he went to Princes Inn.

* * *

Whoso have any quarrel or plea
If in the Guildhall at Norwich it be
Be it false, be it true,
If he but withstand John Hawke, John Querdling,
Nicholas Wales, John Bylaugh, John May, sore shall him rue
For they'll rule all the court with their lawes new.

'Bloody incompetent doggerel,' Judge Paston complained, in the same loud voice as he had used to read the verse. He folded the paper and slapped it down on his outstretched leg. 'At least Aslake always made his verses scan.'

While Richard Purdance's men, thought Will, were emphatically of a lower class. Illiterate, most of them.

'True,' he said, 'it will scarcely sway Serjeant Godred.'

'Pointless, in any case, to try to sway Godred. He will recommend nothing.'

'Sir, that cannot be so. He must make a report to Suffolk. A cautious report, maybe; an uncertain report; but . . .'

'But one insufficient to persuade Suffolk to disown Wetherby and his scoundrels.'

That was Will's own impression, gained from weeks of careful listening in the taverns, and at Intwood and Oxburgh and Baconsthorpe. 'Perhaps so. It will take more than a report from a nobody such as Godred, to make Suffolk change his colours.'

'Will it so? Then what will it take?'

'A strong campaign, led by a man respected throughout the county. That is what is needed, opposition to Wetherby expressed by men with real local influence and determination.'

Paston glanced down at the paper, then up again at Will. He frowned. 'Men like you.'

'My influence is limited, sir. I look to follow the lead of men stronger and more widely respected than myself.'

'Then you underrate yourself. And you underrate your responsibilities, too. If you think that necessary, it is you who should undertake it.'

'I thought it a task for you yourself, sir.'

'Then you think wrong. For years I have set myself firm against Wetherby and Tuddenham, but I am old now, and sick, and crippled with this damned gout. I've not set foot outside this house these past two months. I shall make myself known as your supporter, but I am past acting as the champion of Purdance's men. That is a task for a coming man; a task for you.'

There was a silence in the solar. Will turned his back on the high chair where the Judge sat and he looked out of the window. There was little to see, just the usual stream of priests, friars, clerks and apprentices making their way up and down Elm Hill.

A task for him. It surprised him, for he had genuinely not thought of himself as being in Tuddenham's class, or Paston's, though he knew his estates were larger than either of theirs. And yet it did not surprise him. He had been reluctant to come to Princes Inn, had put it off for week after week. And why? Because he had sensed that he would be told this.

He found the thought alarming. He was not ready to take a leading role. He felt himself to be in no position to take one. He wanted to do something; but he did not want to do as much as that. Damn it, Yelverton should have done it, or Stapleton, or any one of a dozen older and better-established men!

'I have spoken to the Earl of Suffolk, sir,' he said awkwardly. 'But it has achieved nothing.'

'I too have spoken, and Stapleton. And you think we have achieved more than you?'

'No, sir; but there should be larger men.'

'True, there should, but there are not. There is only you. And you must grow, to fill the gap; or shrink, if you do not.'

Will looked out of the window for a moment longer; then, reluctantly, he turned round again. He looked at the floor. He avoided Paston's challenging glare and instead looked past him at the interior of the small room. In a far corner crouched little Lizzy, with a chequer board and a pile of ivory pieces at her feet. Bess was right: she was an odd-looking child, with a mass of frizzy hair and a sharp-featured, bright-eyed face peeping out from within it. She looked up and glared at him, a miniature of her father, and he quickly took his eyes from her.

He sat down on the low windowsill and pushed out his legs in front of him. He looked at his legs. They looked very long, very straight and strong. Judge Paston's leg was propped up on a stool in front of his chair. It was an old leg, mottled and bloated, with the pattern of sinews and veins showing through his summer hose.

He had felt so often, in the previous few weeks, this acute consciousness of his own health and strength: especially when he was with Bess. It never failed to unnerve him.

It is true, he thought: Judge Paston is an old man now. The leg. That voice: it is as if he has lost all sense of volume. The occasional deafness. I'll bet he finds that convenient at times.

'Tuddenham had you made a justice of the peace, I heard,' the Judge said belligerently.

If Paston had heard that, he got his information fast, even when he was confined to bed. It was only a fortnight since Tuddenham had cornered him at the Maid's Head and he had reluctantly agreed to let his name be put forward; the appointment had been confirmed only days earlier.

'I would not call it altogether Sir Thomas's doing, sir.'

'You'd not? That's how Yelverton spoke of it to me.'

Will did not reply.

'If you do not act now, you will be set down forever as Tuddenham's man. You will see Wetherby prevail, and the worst happen in the city.'

'You ask too much of me, sir. Your own position is secure; you need beg work of no man. But I am committed to the Earl of Suffolk. I would risk supporting Purdance, but if I set myself up as the leader of his party I shall surely face Tuddenham's enmity, and he may well succeed in forcing my dismissal from Suffolk's service. I cannot afford to do that. Bess is almost certain she is carrying again; my estates are still not in good order; I have already turned my back on Norfolk and cannot look to him in Suffolk's stead. Make your own position known, and I shall stand behind you. But I cannot, dare not, lead the pack. That is still the place for you.'

'I cannot do that, Will.'

Their eyes met: each man pleading, each refusing. The two reflected each other like a series of mirrors, their images shrinking into infinity.

There was shame in Will, that he was not a greater man than he knew himself to be; but there grew in him too, surging up from somewhere deep down inside, a sense of anger. Paston was ageing, but he was not so very old. He was sick, but not so very sick. He could have done more than he offered to do, damn it! His excuses were no better than Will's own; worse, even.

The sanctimonious old goat! Men think you strong, Will thought to himself, but you are not so, no more than I am. They look at your square jaw and your hard mouth, and they believe that you will set yourself firm.

But you commit yourself only rarely, and then you do not translate your commitment into action. What was your campaign against Wetherby ever but a box full of papers that you kept to yourself? You talk of impartiality, of the need for justice; but your actions speak of greed for approval, of a craven fear of offending great men like Suffolk. You will never be a martyr to justice, and if you have ever thought yourself one, then you have fooled yourself.

'So there is nobody to stop Wetherby,' the Judge said slowly.

A silence.

'No,' Will said at last. 'No, there is nobody.'

Gloucester's campaign in Flanders proved a bizarre kind of triumph. There was no need for the Duke to rescue Calais: on his arrival he discovered that the Burgundian besiegers had been so incompetent that the Calais garrison had been able to repulse them and capture most of their ships without any help at all. Gloucester shared in their celebrations, then he took his army on a quick scorched-earth raid on the rich country and wool towns of Flanders. It gave nobody cause to think him a brilliant general. But it brought him credit, nonetheless; it brought him favour from the King.

Suffolk stayed in France until past Christmas. There had been no glory to win in Normandy: the garrisons had hoped for no better than to hold their ground. On his return, he seemed quiet and withdrawn.

Godred presented his report that January. It was as circumspect as everyone in Norfolk had expected. Suffolk's copy lay among his papers at Bardi Place, but Will never saw him readiing it. In March of 1437, he travelled up to Norwich with only Will and a dozen grooms and servants for company. He did not discuss the Wetherby affair on the journey and Will made no mention of it. Two days later, in front of a full Assembly of the Aldermen and Commons of the City of Norwich, he declared his verdict.

He found for Wetherby, of course: decisively, more decisively than Will had expected, even more decisively than he had feared. Suffolk declared the documents sealed against Wetherby and his men to be void; he cancelled all the fines and disqualifications they had suffered. Wetherby and William Grey were freed to stand again for election as Aldermen; their servants could regain their former posts. Suffolk's only stipulation was that Wetherby should undertake not to sue or vex the Commons of the City in future. His ruling was short: it made no mention at all of Godred's lengthy depositions.

Wetherby, John Querdling, John May and the rest presented themselves at Suffolk Inn the following day. They were turned away by Suffolk's Chamberlain. The Earl was already preparing to leave the city, they were told, and he had made no plans to return.

Will would have chosen to leave too; but he could not, because Bess was near her term. He saw Suffolk and his men through Berstrete Gate, then he turned his back on them, wheeled his horse round and rode alone to Calthorp Inn.

The prospect ahead of him promised to be even more wearying than he had found the task of attending Suffolk and holding Wetherby at a short arm's length. Bess was so gaunt, her bulging body so desperately fragile. She talked incessantly about the coming baby. It would be strong, she said: no doubt of it. Look at Agnes Paston. Seven years of agony she had endured, but now she had a sturdy baby boy. It was possible. It was.

It was not. Will knew it; the doctors knew it; Bess knew it herself, he suspected. They none of them said it to her.

In the next few days he said it sometimes to Friar Brackley, whom he saw every day at the Greyfriars. He prayed every day in the cold echoing expanse of the friars' church. He lit candles for the dead babies. He did not pray for the coming baby: it was not real to him. He prayed for Bess. On bright days, that she might survive and see sense; on worse days, that it might be not too painful, and over quickly.

God is merciful, Friar Brackley assured him. You must have faith. Will had none. He had nothing now but bleak despair.

It was almost a relief when her labour began. But there, he thought grimly, God could have shown more mercy: it started on one of the coldest mornings of that March, and it continued all through that day and far into the night. By the night-time she had not even the strength left to cry out. He had not the strength himself to hope. The fear was not yet real to him.

Towards the morning he fell into a doze on the settle. The midwife had to wake him with the news.

'She is asking for you, sir.'

He jumped to his feet, unsteadily. 'It is over, then?'

'You have a fine son. I told her, it would be best for you to keep out of the bedchamber; I told her I'd bring the child down to you. But she'd have none of it, sir, and I don't like to thwart her, not now.'

'Is she —'

'She's bad, sir.'

He thought, numbly, that he should run, but his feet would not obey him. He picked up the candleholder that he had left on the floor and stumbled to the stairs. He climbed them, holding to the rail at the side. He pushed open the door to the bedchamber.

In the gloom he could see nothing at first but the nursemaid, clucking over the cradle. There was a thick, fusty atmosphere in the room. The hangings were half drawn around the bed; the space within was shrouded in shadow. He walked unsteadily across to it and pulled the hangings back.

A white face, huge-eyed, stared at him from the pillow.

'He's strong,' she whispered.

'That he is.'

'See him. Go and see him.'

He did not want to see the baby. He should have

621

stayed with her, he thought. But he went anyway and peered in the cradle. The baby was swaddled already: a red, angry face peeped out from among the wrappings. He took in a pair of wobbly blue eyes, a tiny tuft of brown hair. The baby yelled.

He went back to Bess. She had not moved. He turned to the nursemaid.

'The midwife should be here, surely. And the doctor.'

The nursemaid stared back at him. She shook her head silently.

On the floor, he saw a heap of old linen sheets. They were stained; in the uncertain candlelight, they looked almost black.

He turned his eyes from them and back to Bess. She knows, he thought. She accepts.

She opened her mouth and he saw, rather than heard, her whisper something.

'It's all right, Bess,' he said, with a vague idea of comforting her.

A hand came up and caught at his arm. He leaned nearer.

'William,' he heard. It was barely more than a sigh.

'William?'

'The baby, sir,' the nursemaid said from somewhere by his elbow.

'Oh. Of course, if you wish. We shall call him William.'

She said nothing, but he sensed that it comforted her. He reached over her body and took the hand that had caught at him. It was very cold. He held it. They sat for some time, without talking, listening to the baby's cries and the murmur of the nursemaid trying to soothe it.

Footsteps on the stairs, alarmingly loud. The door opened, and there was Friar Brackley, with the housemaid hovering behind him.

Will got to his feet. 'Should I stay?'

'If your wife wishes . . .'

Bess's head moved almost imperceptibly, to the side away from where he stood.

'I'll be back soon,' he said.

He went downstairs. It was still not dawn: the house was silent, the children were asleep. He waited. A long time seemed to pass. Then footsteps again, and Friar Brackley made his way downstairs.

'May I go up . . .'

Friar Brackley crossed to him and set a light hand on his shoulder. 'I think we should pray together, first.'

Pray? For a moment, he did not understand. Then he did.

He should have been there, he thought in numb amazement. How could he not have been there? How could she have let herself die, when he was not by her side? It was not fair, not fair.

He took a step towards the staircase. Not fair. Bess couldn't have done this to him, not while –

'My son,' said Friar Brackley, holding him back, firmly but gently, 'first you must pray.'

Will stayed in Norwich for another month, until he had kept Bess's month's mind at the Greyfriars. The baby was thriving by then, and the snow had almost gone from the road to Burnham Thorpe. The riots were beginning in Norwich: Wetherby's men against John Cambridge's men. Richard Purdance was dead: he had died two days after Bess, of a fever.

Will took the road to Burnham, with the baby and its wetnurse, Amy and John, his servants and a strong escort, the day after the service. Thomas Wetherby had come to the Greyfriars, and Sir Thomas Tuddenham, and John Heydon, but he had spoken to none of them. A letter had come from Wingfield to Calthorp Inn that morning, as he was preparing to leave. He had paid the messenger threepence and told him he had arrived too late to deliver it.

623

27

ENGLAND
Summer, 1434

In the hall of Intwood House, on a cool April day, a little group of men sat around a blazing fire, nursing cups of strong ale and talking in low voices.

'Two Serjeants from London to supervise the elections,' Thomas Wetherby said in a thoughtful voice. 'Who will choose them, Thomas?'

'The King's Council,' Tuddenham said. 'They'll make a free choice, but they'll take note that it was Cambridge requested it. I'll do what I can, but I cannot swear to see that they choose the men we'd have picked.'

'And what of Walter's suggestion, that I offer to pay their expenses?'

'They'll take your money, no doubt, Thomas. But I'd not care to say if it would make the Council more likely, or less, to choose serjeants who will do your bidding.'

'It makes no difference,' John Heydon said in a hearty voice. 'Any man will do as we ask, if we line his pockets thickly enough.'

The Guildhall at Norwich, on the first day of May, 1437. At the foot of the stairs, a fat man with one eye and a muscular body stood guard over the pile of knives and cudgels that had been confiscated from the men attending the election. In the hall, the men of Norwich stood silent. On the platform the Aldermen sat in their crimson gowns trimmed with beaver. And at the very front of the platform, surrounded by half a dozen burly men whose cudgels had not been confiscated, stood the two Serjeants from London, flanking the outgoing Mayor, Robert Chaplain.

'I hereby pronounce,' Chaplain stated in a thick Norfolk burr, 'that the new Mayor of the City of Norwich will be Alderman John Cambridge.'

The half-dozen burly men raised their cudgels. There were murmurs, but there was no violence. John Cambridge stepped forward and took Chaplain's hand, and Chaplain proceeded to lead the new Mayor home.

Men rode that night to Ipswich, to Charles Nowell and his men; to Bury, Cromer and a dozen other towns. The Aslake gang met in a back room at the Bess of Bedlam. There was a meeting too at Intwood House.

In a dark alley running between two of the inns that lined Norwich marketplace, a band of men, dressed all of them in black and grey, shadow colours, huddled together outside a barber's shop, beneath an overhanging balcony. It was dusk. The dregs of the sunlight were too feeble to strike rays off the swords that a couple of the men had drawn; there was no other light in the alley. Most carried cudgels, held high in readiness in their hands.

A street away, the watch called out that it was ten o'clock. An hour for good men to be in bed. The streets were otherwise deserted, but the sounds of talk and laughter came loud from the inns.

A door banged; one of the men edged out to the centre of the alley, where he could see the pool of light flooding out from the left-hand inn.

'Now!' he hissed.

The men moved quickly, but silently, in leather shoes.

'I'll see you tomorrow in Upper Newport, John,' the man at the inn door was saying. 'At eleven, or shortly after.'

'George, mind!'

George turned, saw the approaching shadows, moved a step towards the inn door. It closed in his face. An instant afterwards the first of the gang reached him and the first blow landed on his shoulders.

In Rampant Horse Street a draper and his wife crouched in their nightgowns on the floor of the bedchamber over their shop. Their arms were wrapped around each other, but still they shivered as they heard each axe blow land, each splintering noise that announced the steady disintegration of their shop's shutters. There were voices below, loud, boisterous, menacing.

'Nearly there, lads.'

The draper reached for the stick that he always kept under his bed and tightened his fingers around the end. The axe blows stopped; there was heaving and creaking and panting below.

'Got it!' a voice shouted. 'In we go, lads.'

A few minutes past midnight. Down near Coslany Bridge, a boy in a grey tunic sauntered along the towpath, past the moored barges. He held a torch, a crude affair of pitch-soaked twigs, in his hand, its flames flickering in the light breeze. He brought his hand down sometimes, reaching out with the torch and straining to read the names painted on the bows of the barges. He stopped at one of them; glanced around him; then threw the torch into the barge and dashed off into the darkness before the flames took hold.

'The Bishop,' Sir Brian Stapleton said.

'Aye, and who else?'

'Serjeant Yelverton.'

'Yelverton accepted it?'

'That he did, William. Gloucester spoke to him himself, from what I hear, and made mention of the King's Bench.'

'That would concentrate Yelverton's mind wonderfully. He'd take on a dozen grim commissions rather than offend Gloucester before he secures his appointment. And who else?'

'Calthorp.'

'Calthorp! I'd never have backed him to take it on.'

Stapleton leaned forward, his cup of ale forgotten in his hand. 'Now this, William, is the most interesting thing of all. Lord Cromwell suggested Calthorp, they say, and because Calthorp himself put him up to do so.'

'He chose to sit on the commission? When every other man in Norfolk prayed he would not hear his own name?'

'And for a reason, it's whispered. They say Calthorp has a plan to end the troubles.'

'To end them? Why, you know and I know, Sir Brian, that there can be no end to these troubles. Even if Suffolk came out for Cambridge it would not end it now.' William paused; then frowned; then said, 'Was it whispered also what this plan might be?'

'Not a word. I had my ear pressed hard to the floorboards, William, but not a word.'

'Damn it, I'd give my good leg to know what Calthorp has in mind.'

'I, too. But they are to report to the King's Council this summer, William: within weeks, we both shall know.'

A summer morning, early. The sky was still hazy, but the day promised to be hot. William Paston sat in the solar of Princes Inn, on a plain oak chair drawn up by the window, with his bad leg stretched out and resting on a stool in front of him.

I shall know today, he thought. Unless he wants a thrashing, young John will make sure of that. He'll be back at two o'clock, perhaps, or three, bringing me the news himself, or better, bringing me Yelverton, or even Calthorp.

That was much to ask of John, for every thinking man in Norwich would wish to speak to the Bishop, to Serjeant Yelverton and to Will Calthorp, Esquire, after they rode through Berstrete Gate that afternoon. Other men would ride to meet them, to talk with them at the gate, at the Guildhall, at the Bishop's Palace or Calthorp

627

Inn. William had tried to mount Blazon the day before, to see if he too might ride out. But neither he nor Blazon had passed the test, so he was forced to sit in the solar, fretting and cursing, until John appeared.

Does John care? William wondered. Does he fret too, does he sit in the inns and argue what Calthorp's great solution might be? I wish it were so, but I'd swear he gives not a crooked farthing for any of it. Still, he is a dutiful son, whatever his failings. He knows how much it matters to me. He'll come home with the news this afternoon.

There was a good place for fishing at a bend of the river just to the east of Norwich Cathedral, in the shade of a decrepit tower called the Cow Tower. The muddy inner bank of the bend provided a copious supply of worms; the midstream would turn up bream, tench and the occasional old and aggressive pike. There were a regular band of fishermen there, boys and old men mainly, who fished for pleasure and did not trouble to take boats out of the city to the better spots.

John Paston knew them all by now; they all knew him. He nodded to them when he arrived, glanced across and nodded again whenever one of them made a good catch. He did not speak, and neither did they.

There had been arrangements to be made when he arrived back from Peterhouse, but those were settled now and never discussed. One of the old men kept his rod for him – he would not have dared to take it back to Princes Inn – and he gave this man the fish he caught. There were not often many. He would lose concentration sometimes and just sit, looking out at the forbidding expanse of Mousehold Heath on the opposite bank, watching the sails of the windmills creak round in the breeze.

Sometimes, as he sat, he thought of what he should tell his father. It was his task for the summer to keep the Judge informed. John did not learn the things his father wished to know while he sat on the river-bank. There he learned of bait and catches, sunshine and wind. Judge Paston did not care about those things. John had spoken of them once or twice, but his tales had been greeted first with impatience, then with contempt. Whispered negotiations in smoke-filled taverns; private encounters in dark alleys; public arguments in Council meetings: these were the things that brought the old light back to the Judge's eyes.

Still, this little problem had been easily solved. He could not bribe Edmund with fish, but he could pay for Edmund's news with his own promise of silence about Edmund's doings. He could not pay Secret Poursuivant at all; but Secret was a patient man, and he appeared to believe that one day his reward would come.

How fortunate it was, thought John, that his father never gleaned his news direct from Secret. Fortunate, too, that the Judge never seemed to speculate on what Edmund did while John was nominally haunting the taverns and the market stalls for gossip. Perhaps he imagined Edmund went fishing.

John glanced up at the sky. The sun was almost at its zenith. Soon it would be time to abandon his fishing; time to find Edmund and John Yelverton at the Adam and Eve, time to walk with them down towards Berstrete Gate. Time to ask Calthorp and Serjeant Yelverton what had been decided in London. That was not as interesting as fishing, thought John; but still, it would be worth discovering.

And then he and Edmund and John would walk, with the Serjeant, down Conesford Street to Yelverton Place. Jane Yelverton would feed them all. And they would walk on, he and Edmund and John and the Serjeant, to Princes Inn.

Father doubts still, he thought, whether we shall come. It terrifies him, the possibility that we shall not, and that he will be the last man in Norwich to learn the news. But he has no reason to fear. Father still has favours of his own to dispense: we will come to him, all of us, because we know that sooner or later we shall be repaid.

Afternoon: a hot afternoon. The shutters to the solar at Princes Inn had been flung open; just inside the window, a couple of bluebottles buzzed angrily.

On either side of the window and the bluebottles sat William Paston and William Yelverton. Between Paston's chair and Yelverton's stool, beneath the window-sill, a jar of ale and two cups had been set on a small table.

John Paston sat at his father's feet, on the sweet-smelling rushes that strewed the floor. His father had ordered him to stay and listen to what the Serjeant had to say. He knew it already, naturally: he had heard it at Yelverton Place, but he knew, too, that his father could not bear to acknowledge this self-evident truth.

Edmund and Elizabeth Paston had had no orders, and neither had John Yelverton; but being curious as to how the Judge would take the news, they were all lingering in a corner. From the window the occasional clatter of hooves and cartwheels, snatches of the conversation of passers-by, rose up from Elm Hill. Through the open door came the sound of Agnes Paston's voice as she scolded the housemaid, and the high yell of baby William, swaddled in his cot and hoping for a feed.

'Yes,' said William Yelverton. He took a long draught of beer and wiped a drip from the outside of the cup with the back of his hand. 'Yes, the Commission made a suggestion to the King's Council; and the King's Council accepted it and gave their verdict.'

'A good verdict?'

'Ah,' said Yelverton, embarking on a lawyerish speech, 'what is a good verdict? A correct verdict? There is no such thing, I suspect, in these circumstances. A thoughtful verdict? I think I can call it that. An informed verdict? Certainly, for the depositions went on for days. An acceptable verdict? It is acceptable to Stapleton, and Felbrigg, and a number of others who have heard of it.'

'Is it acceptable to the Earl of Suffolk?' John bravely asked.

'Now that is a most interesting question. Most unusually, Suffolk did not attend the King's Council when they discussed the matter. And if he has opinions on the verdict, they have not reached me.'

William leaned forward. 'A new election?'

'Not for the present, no.'

'So the city stays under Cambridge.'

'Oh no. Not that, either.' Yelverton smiled in enjoyment at the suspense he was creating. 'The King's Council accepted that John Cambridge is unable to govern the city, and that Thomas Wetherby is widely thought to be unfit to do so. So the government of Norwich will not go to an Alderman at all. Or rather, it will go to an Alderman of London.'

'Of London!' exclaimed Elizabeth, who had not known.

Her father did not exclaim anything at all. He met Yelverton's look, took in the younger lawyer's expression.

'Damn that grocer,' he said. 'I should have guessed it.'

John Welles arrived in Norwich on a blustery day in late summer. He was greeted in sullen state at the Berstrete Gate by two parties of Aldermen: Wetherby's adherents on one side, and his opponents, headed by John Cambridge, on the other. They rode with him through the city, past curious huddles of citizens and labourers, along Conesford Street where the great merchants had their houses, past Suffolk Inn, up past the Castle with its huge motte and ditches, through the markets, and to the Guildhall.

The sullenness did not discomfort Welles. He had expected them to be sullen. They did not relish the idea of a man who had not been to Norwich for forty years returning to milk the tolls and break up their little cabals. Welles was confident they would feel differently by the time he had fed them on Fastolf's sheep, poured them quantities of Fastolf's wine, and offered them all a few modest bribes. He was not unprepared, after all: he

631

had been planning this, or something very like it, for more than ten years. He smiled at all the onlookers and talked cheerily to the Aldermen. He ragged Thomas Wetherby about a deal they had struck over a ship at Yarmouth; he asked an Alderman in mason's livery about the houses he did not recognise, and a brewer about the best inns in the city. He marvelled over the churches in scaffolding on every street corner, and dismounted briefly in the marketplace to inspect the fish stalls, and to buy gingerbread for half a dozen urchins who were trailing behind him. He nodded with satisfaction at the sight of the chequerwork front of the fine new Guildhall and set the peacock feather in his cap a little straighter before handing his horse to a groom and leading the procession to the Mayor's parlour, where he was to be invested as Warden of the City of Norwich in the King's name.

From there he rode down, past Saint John Maddermarket, Saint Cross, Saint Andrew's and Saint Peter's, to Elm Hill. Past Princes Inn, where he glanced up to the solar window and waved at Judge Paston. Past the Maid's Head, and over the River Wensum into the part of the city called Norwich over the Water. He rode along the river bank behind the quays, past the mean little church of Saint Edmund and the splendid buildings of the Whitefriars. He stopped at a rambling mansion near the Pockthorpe Gate.

Two bowed windows stared blankly out at him. Between them, a series of statues faced into the cold west wind. Saint Margaret was there, John the Baptist in camelhair, the Virgin Mary, Saint Blaise holding a wool comb, and a pale and distressed looking Saint Catherine. John Welles inspected each of these cursorily and turned the corner to the north. This wall was adorned in more martial style, with ten extremely large effigies of famous warriors. Welles identified Samson, Hercules wielding a lumpen club and David facing up to Goliath. He turned back then towards the main door.

This time he knocked, and after a moment's delay the door opened in front of him. Secret Poursuivant, in his blue and gold tabard, stood in the entrance. He hesitated a moment, then reached to his little cap and swept it off with a flourish.

'Welcome,' he said softly, 'to Samson and Hercules House.'

Author's Note

All but one of the poems in French quoted in this book were written by Charles, Duke of Orleans, though some were probably written later than the dates at which they appear in the book. (The exception is the poem by William de la Pole, Earl of Suffolk, quoted in chapter 10.) The translations were very kindly done specially for this book by Professor Peter Ricketts of Westfield College, University of London.

Opinion varies as to the English poems, which appear to be rough translations of Orleans' French originals. Some scholars claim that they were translated by Orleans himself; others, that they are the work of Suffolk.

Jean de Waurin's Chronicles, or *Rerum Britannicarum Medii Aevi Scriptores* were written after de Waurin withdrew from Burgundy's army and include full accounts of the battles of Verneuil and Patay. I have slightly deviated from de Waurin's accounts, and have also used other sources for the descriptions in this book. Saint Rémy (Toison d'Or King of Arms) also wrote a chronicle from the Burgundian viewpoint. Some work thought to be by Christopher Hanson has survived to this day, but his and Basset's great works, if they were ever written, have all been lost.

Among the other surviving contemporary accounts of the events described in this book are Hugues de Lannoy's letters to the Duke of Burgundy (which include a description of his meetings with the Duke of Orleans and with the barber Cauvel) and Sir John Fastolf's recommendations to the King's Council following the Congress of Arras. The doggerel in chapter 26 is contemporary; that in chapter 3 is not.

The affairs of the Paston family are chronicled in depth in the Paston Letters, though only a few of the early letters cover this period. Will Calthorp figures in later letters, but only the outline of his life is known in this period. The Duke of Norfolk's barge accident is described by contemporary chronicles and by Fastolf's later employee, William Worcester.

The tangled events of these years in Norwich are outlined in the Records of the City of Norwich, and by Norfolk's great eighteenth-century historian, Francis Blomefield. Though I have simplified the background, they all occurred broadly as narrated here, including Alice, Countess of Suffolk's picnic in Lakenham woods.

My debts to other historians are too numerous to mention. I should also emphasise that this is a work of fiction, and that though it contains a backbone of historical truth, much of it is pure invention.

My particular thanks are due to Andrew Best and to Laura Longrigg, both of whom gave me invaluable advice and suggestions as the book was being written.

SUSAN CURRAN
Norfolk, 1988

Glamorous Powers
Susan Howatch

Jon Darrow, a man with psychic powers, is a man who has played many parts: shady faith-healer, naval chaplain, passionate husband, awkward father, Anglo-Catholic monk.

In 1940 Darrow returns to the world he once renounced, but faced with many unforeseen temptations he fails to control his psychic, most glamorous powers. Corruption lies in wait for him, and threatens not only his future as a priest but his happiness with Anne, the young woman he has come to love.

'*Glamorous Powers* is a brave and welcome new direction for Susan Howatch to take.'
Observer

'An intriguing and wholly involving story.'
New York Times Book Review

FONTANA PAPERBACKS

Reindeer Moon
Elizabeth Marshall Thomas

Yanan was born over twenty thousand years ago, in a lodge on the ice-swept tundra, in a land where death was always near. Her people were hunters, living in kinship with the tigers, and the wolves, struggling through the long winters when meat and wood were scarce . . . rejoicing in the brief, glorious summers.

In this land of great and terrible beauty, Yanan survived to womanhood – passionate and brave, richly sensuous and dangerously proud. From the perils of the hunt to the timeless wonders of love and marriage, birth and death, Yanan's life was a grand and thrilling adventure in a harsh, magnificent world . . .

'I lived and breathed this book . . . Yanan is fascinating, completely real . . . magnificent.'
Washington Post Book World

'Wonderful . . . a tour de force.'
John Updike *The New Yorker*

FONTANA PAPERBACKS

The Hearts and Lives of Men
Fay Weldon

Fay Weldon's stunning new novel is an adventure story in which, you will be glad to hear, love finally triumphs over lust, good will over satanic forces, and sheer kindness over piercing malevolence. The pace never falters; the language glitters. The wit is as ever razor sharp. Yet laughter, tears and a lump in the throat are never far away.

'The sixties background is impeccable and deftly evoked, the style is sharp and the jokes are acidly funny.' *Evening Standard*

'Every word of *The Hearts and Lives of Men* is a delight.' *Spectator*

'I spent a weekend reading *The Hearts and Lives of Men*, and a very good weekend it was too.' *Punch*

'It's unputdownable, of course.' *City Limits*

'Buy it you must.' *Company*

FONTANA PAPERBACKS

Fontana Paperbacks: Fiction

Fontana is a leading paperback publisher of fiction.
Below are some recent titles.

- ☐ CABAL Clive Barker £2.95
- ☐ DALLAS DOWN Richard Moran £2.95
- ☐ SHARPE'S RIFLES Bernard Cornwell £3.50
- ☐ A MAN RIDES THROUGH Stephen Donaldson £4.95
- ☐ HOLD MY HAND I'M DYING John Gordon Davis £3.95
- ☐ ROYAL FLASH George MacDonald Fraser £3.50
- ☐ FLASH FOR FREEDOM! George MacDonald Fraser £3.50
- ☐ THE HONEY ANT Duncan Kyle £2.95
- ☐ FAREWELL TO THE KING Pierre Schoendoerffer £2.95
- ☐ MONKEY SHINES Michael Stewart £2.95

You can buy Fontana paperbacks at your local bookshop or
newsagent. Or you can order them from Fontana Paperbacks,
Cash Sales Department, Box 29, Douglas, Isle of Man. Please
send a cheque, postal or money order (not currency) worth the
purchase price plus 22p per book for postage (maximum postage
required is £3.00 for orders within the UK).

NAME (Block letters) _____

ADDRESS _____

_____